KHANATE

OF THE

CRIMEA

Dnieper

Don

Tana
(Azov)

Astrakhan

Sea of
Azov

Caffa
(Genoese)

CIRCASSIA

Black Sea

Phasis (Rioni)

Batu

GEORGIA

Caspian Sea

Derbent

Sinope

Akhalziké

Tiflis
(Tblisi)

Amasra

Samsûn

Baku

Kerasous

Trebizond (Trabzon)

Kelkit

Tokat

Bayburt

Erzurum

ARMENIA

Sivas

Erzincan

Asterabad
(Astara)

Ankara
(Angora)

KURDISTAN

ANATOLIA

Diyabekr

Tabriz
(Taurus)

Lahidjan

Aleppo

Teheran

Tigris

PERSIA

CYPRUS

Euphrates

Damascus

Baghdad

SYRIA

Jerusalem

0   100   200 miles

Trebizond

Kerasous
(Giresun)

Sumela

Zigana Pass

Gulf of Persia

Gümüshane

Koyulhisar

Vavuk Pass

Red Sea

Sebinkarahisar

Siran

Kelkit

Peter McClure 1987

The Spring of
the Ram

The House of Niccolò
The Spring of the Ram

Dorothy Dunnett

ALFRED A. KNOPF   *New York*   1988

THIS IS A BORZOI BOOK
PUBLISHED BY ALFRED A. KNOPF, INC.

Copyright © 1987 by Dorothy Dunnett
All rights reserved under International and Pan-American Copyright Conventions.
Published in the United States by Alfred A. Knopf, Inc., New York.
Distributed by Random House, Inc., New York.
Originally published in Great Britain by Michael Joseph Ltd, London.

Library of Congress Cataloging-in-Publication Data
Dunnett, Dorothy.
The spring of the ram.
(The house of Niccolo; 2)
I. Title.   II. Series: Dunnett, Dorothy.
House of Niccolò; 2.
PR6054.U56S67   1988   823'.914   87-37847
ISBN 0-394-56437-5

Manufactured in the United States of America
First American Edition

Characters

(Those marked * are recorded in history)

Rulers
*France: Charles VII; Louis XI
*England: Henry VI; Edward IV
*Flanders: Duke Philip of Burgundy
*Pope: Pius II
*Milan: Duke Francesco Sforza
*Ottoman Empire: Sultan Mehmet II

Charetty company, Bruges, Louvain and Trebizond
Marian de Charetty, owner
Nicholas vander Poele (Niccolò), her husband and former apprentice
Mathilde (Tilde), her older daughter
Catherine, her second daughter
Julius, her notary
Tobias Beventini of Grado, her physician
Father Godscalc of Cologne, her chaplain
Gregorio of Asti, her lawyer
John le Grant, Scots engineer and shipmaster
Astorre (Syrus de Astariis), her mercenary leader
Loppe (Lopez), a former Guinea slave; bursar to Nicholas
Thibault, vicomte de Fleury of Dijon, husband of Marian de Charetty's late
    sister
Tasse of Geneva, maid to Marian de Charetty
Margot, mistress of Gregorio
Patou, assistant to Julius
Thomas, under-captain to Astorre

Medici company, Florence, Pisa, Bruges and Venice
*Cosimo di Giovanni de' Medici of Florence, head of the Medici Bank
*Giovanni de' Medici, his son
*Cosimino de' Medici, son of Giovanni
*Pierfrancesco de' Medici, nephew of Cosimo
*Laudomia Acciajuoli, wife of Pierfrancesco
*Angelo Tani, manager, Bruges
*Tommaso Portinari, under-manager, Bruges
*Antonio di Niccolò Martelli, sea-consul, Pisa
*Roberto di Niccolò Martelli, manager, Rome
*Alessandro di Niccolò Martelli, manager, Venice

The company of Strozzi, Florence and Bruges
*Alessandra Macinghi negli Strozzi of Florence, widow of Matteo Strozzi
*Lorenzo di Matteo Strozzi, Bruges, her exiled son

*Filippo di Matteo Strozzi, Naples, exiled elder brother of Lorenzo
*Caterina di Matteo, her daughter
*Marco di Giovanni da Parenti, silk merchant and husband of Caterina
*Jacopo di Leonardo Strozzi, manager, Bruges, and cousin of the late Matteo

Merchants and noblemen, Scotland and Flanders
Simon de St Pol of Kilmirren, landowner and merchant of Scotland
Jordan de St Pol, exiled vicomte de Ribérac, father of Simon
Katelina van Borselen, wife of Simon and niece of Henry van Borselen of Veere
Henry de St Pol, son of Katelina
Agnès, her servant
*Henry van Borselen of Veere, Knight of the Golden Fleece
*Franck van Borselen, Knight of the Golden Fleece
*Wolfaert van Borselen, son of Henry
*Mary, princess of Scotland, wife of Wolfaert
*Charles van Borselen, son of Wolfaert and Mary
*Alexander, Duke of Albany, Scottish royal nephew of Wolfaert and Mary
*Pierre Bladelin, Treasurer of the Golden Fleece and Controller to Duke
    Philip, founder of the Golden Fleece Order
*Louis de Gruuthuse of Bruges, Knight of the Golden Fleece, husband of
    Marguerite van Borselen

Genoa and Milan
*Anselm Adorne of the Hôtel Jerusalem, Bruges
Pagano Doria, sea adventurer
Michael Crack-bene, his sailing-master
Noah, his Negro page
*Jacques Doria, Genoese merchant, Bruges
*Prosper Adorno, Doge of Genoa and kin to Anselm Adorne
*Prosper Schiaffino de Camulio de' Medici, envoy of the Duke of Milan

Greeks and Byzantines
*David Comnenos, 21st Emperor of Trebizond
*Helen Cantacuzenes, his Empress
*Anna, their younger daughter
*George VIII, King of Georgia, their son-in-law
*Maria Gattilusi, Genoese widow of the Emperor's brother Alexander
*Alexios, son of Maria and Alexander
*George Amiroutzes of Trebizond, philosopher, Great Chancellor, Treasurer,
    Protovestarios to the Emperor
*Alexander and Basil, sons of George Amiroutzes
*Altamourios, Chief Secretary and half-Muslim cousin of the Emperor David
*Violante, daughter of Niccolò Crespo, Duke of Naxos, grand-daughter of
    Emperor John IV of Trebizond and great-niece of the Emperor David
*Bessarion (John) of Trebizond, Cardinal of Nicaea
*Paraskeuas, servant to the Cardinal's late mother
*Thomas, Despot of the Morea, brother of the late Constantine, last emperor of
    Constantinople
*Demetrius, brother of Thomas and joint Despot of the Morea

Persia (The Ak-Koyunlu, the White Sheep Tribe of Turcomans)

*Uzum Hasan, Muslim prince of Diyarbekr, lord of High Mesopotamia and of the White Sheep Tribe and grandson of a princess of Trebizond

*Sara Khatun of Syria, Christian mother of Uzum Hasan

*Sheikh Hüseyin, Muslim kinsman of Uzum Hasan's Kurdish wife

*Theodora, Christian wife of Uzum Hasan, aunt of Violante, and niece of the Emperor David

Diadochos, Archimandrite of the Greek Orthodox Church, chamberlain to Uzum Hasan's Christian household, and to Violante of Naxos

*Mahon Turcomannus, Uzum Hasan's envoy to the West under Ludovico da Bologna

Latin/Greeks, Modon, Constantinople (Pera) and Venice

*Giovanni Bembo, Venetian Bailie at Modon

*Piero Bembo, kinsman, merchant of Venice

*Nicholai Giorgio de' Acciajuoli, kinsman of the former Florentine dukes of Athens

*Bartolomeo Giorgio/Zorzi his brother, alum farmer and silk merchant in Pera

*Girolamo Michiel of Venice, partner of Bartolomeo

*Dietifeci of Florence, agent for Florence in Pera

*Bastiano da Foligno, partner of Dietifeci

*George Scholarius, Greek Patriarch of Constantinople

*Giovanni da Castro, godson of Pope Pius and former dyer, Constantinople

*Caterino Zeno, Venetian merchant, husband of Violante of Naxos

*Marco Corner, Venetian merchant, married to the sister of Violante of Naxos

*Doge Pasqual Malipiero of Venice

Eastern delegation to Europe

*Fra Ludovico de Severi da Bologna, Franciscan Observatine friar

*Michael Alighieri, Florentine envoy of Emperor David of Trebizond

Ottomans

*Sultan Mehmet II

*Grand Vizier Mahmud Pasha, renegade son of a mother from Trebizond

*Tursun Beg, Turkish secretary to Mahmud

*Thomas Katabolenu, Greek secretary to Mahmud

*Kasim Pasha, the Sultan's admiral

*Yakub, Kasim's deputy

*Jacopo of Gaeta, the Sultan's physician

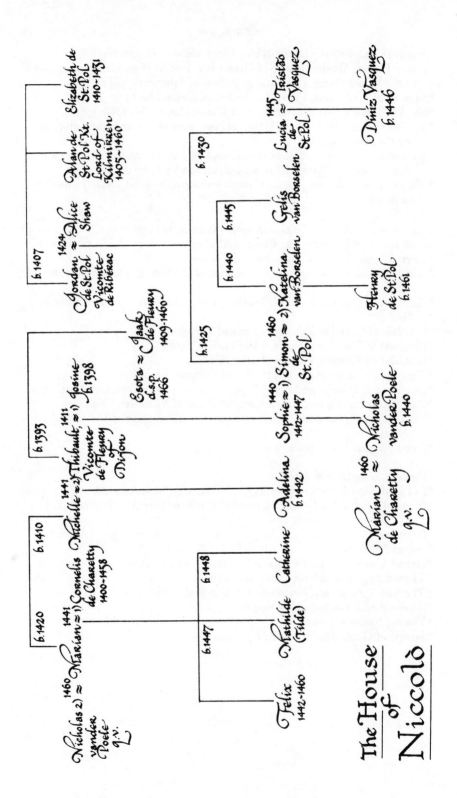

The House
of
Niccolò

The Spring of
the Ram

Overture

THE SPRING sign of the Ram is, of course, the earliest in the Zodiac; and Aries relates to the first House in the Wheel. You will have read the Divine Ptolemy on the subject. The Greeks considered the starfield of the Ram to represent the Golden Fleece sought by the heroic Jason; others called it the Ram of Ammon instead. You may now forget the whole issue. It is my business, not yours. Your business (and mine) is the star of Niccolò, whose foot I am required to set on the same quest as that of Jason.

Whether I can do it, I am not at all sure. He is nineteen years old, and clever. It is clever to begin life as a dyer's apprentice in Bruges and gain control of your employer's business by marrying her. A business in Flanders is worth something. Flanders is ruled by the Duke of Burgundy, one of the richest princes in the world, and feared even by the King of France, although Charles is supposed to be Duke Philip's overlord for the lands he possesses in France. Bruges in Flanders is a world centre of trade and finance, dealing across the narrow Channel with England and Scotland (although England is embroiled in its war between Yorkist and Lancastrian). Bruges houses merchants from the republics of Venice and Genoa and from the bits of Spain that are not under Saracen rule. It lodges a branch of the House of Medici, whose head, Cosimo de' Medici, is the power in my ancestral city of Florence. It deals with representatives of Pope Pius in Rome, and the war-worried Kingdom of Naples and the prosperous Duchy of Milan, whose Duke Francesco Sforza is so anxious to win Genoa from the French. It sends goods as far away as Constantinople and Asia Minor, because it likes the luxuries it imports in return, and has moreover a need for Asian alum, the powder which fixes dye into cloth. Aries is, of course, the sign of the wool merchant.

It is a pity that, intelligent as he is, Niccolò should have made so many mistakes while living in Bruges. The worst has threatened his wife and her business. He has antagonised a powerful Scottish nobleman, and must leave Bruges until the danger has lessened. But for me, he would have joined his wife's mercenary troop somewhere in Italy. It is I who have placed before him another prospect, brilliant as the Fleece, and in the same far-off country of legend.

Seven years ago, Constantinople fell before the Sultan Mehmet, and its Byzantine Emperor died. The other European lands of Byzantium were all in time overrun by these Ottoman Turks, my own Greek possessions included. There remained only one spangle of the exquisite culture which had survived for so long at the meeting-place of the West and the Orient, preserving the finest of both. This was the Empire of Trebizond, a garden on the southern coast of the Black Sea, no more than forty miles deep and the worth of three to four days journeying from one end to the other. There ruled the Emperor David of the Byzantine family of the Comneni, a dynasty of legendary beauty and wealth which had survived for two hundred years against the enemy tribes at its frontiers, sometimes through war; sometimes through diplomacy; sometimes through marriage.

The Emperor David of Trebizond, reports said, was sending a merchant to the West seeking Florentine trade, and offering to house a Florentine agency. I put it to Niccolò, whom the Flèmings call Nicholas: what had he to lose? He required to leave Bruges. He required to put his talents to use, otherwise his wife and her business would suffer. Where better than Trebizond? At least, he should take some companions and go to Florence and meet the Emperor's emissary.

He agreed. He has, I believe, no idea what is really going to happen. He may arrive in Florence and decide the longer journey is not worth the trouble. He may prove to be less exceptional than I think him to be. He may be more than I think him, and defeat me. But no. That is impossible.

Let us see, then – beginning with an event which appears to have very little to do with him at all. I shall not address you again, although I shall be present. I am still present, in the *Registrum Magni Sigilli Regum Scotorum*, The Register of the Great Seal of Scotland, where they call me Nicholai Georgei de Arcassoune, Grecus cum pede ligneo. My name is in fact Nicholai Giorgio de' Acciajuoli. I have a wooden leg. Niccolò broke it at our first meeting. He is making amends.

Chapter 1

CATHERINE DE CHARETTY, having chosen a lover just after the Feast of the Exaltation of the Holy Cross (a festival highly regarded in Bruges), was much put out to learn that, at nearly thirteen, she did not possess all the required qualifications. She began immediately praying for puberty. She prayed through her plans for elopement and, indeed, for a quite inconvenient period afterwards. The power of prayer, she had been taught, was invincible. By the time she and Messer Pagano Doria were beyond the reach of her mother, she would be (but surely) all woman.

Messer Pagano Doria thought she was one already. That had emerged at a critical stage of his courtship, and was one of the many things she liked him for. Another was his long eyelashes. Another was his regular teeth. Another was the expensive handkerchief he always tucked in the belt of his doublet, but never blew his nose on. She liked him for all these things even before he began calling on her aunt's house at Brussels, and then started asking her aunt and uncle and her cousins and herself out for supper, or to fish with him, or to join a party for fowling.

Sometimes he brought his own hounds and his own servants, all with the family crest on their livery. Sometimes he brought a little black page, who wore a turban and carried his falcon. Sometimes he came alone. At first, he hardly seemed to notice her there at his elbow, admiring his teeth and his tales about the Moorish princes in Spain who had three hundred ladies to sleep with; and the Genoese lords in the East who were much sought-after, too. Messer Pagano Doria was a sea prince of the best Genoese family there had ever been, and rich enough to be buying a round ship at Antwerp. Messer Pagano Doria had been everywhere.

Her aunt and uncle were flattered by the attentions of someone so well connected. They were not truly relations of hers: just business friends who had helped her mother through early widowhood, and had offered to take one of her daughters into their household to be

polished. Catherine de Charetty thought you could get polished quite
as well in a dyeshop in Bruges as in a wool merchant's mansion in
Brussels, but her mother thought not. Her mother would be much
against Catherine taking a lover, but her mother had a man in her bed.
Or had, before Nicholas left. On a long trip. On a matter of
commerce, everyone said.

Her mother wouldn't have let Messer Pagano Doria come so often,
because her mother always knew when Catherine had found a new
attachment. Catherine was conscious of the power of love. Her
confidence was not misplaced. In time, the lord Pagano Doria
rewarded her with some of his delightful attention. While speaking he
would smile at her and touch her cheek sometimes, so that her eyes
crossed as she looked at his rings. He had better rings than the Bruges
under-manager of the Medici company. Once he took her hand at a
difficult place in the marshes and once, laughing and talking to
everybody, he let her sit beside him in the cart going home.

They first began to become close at the jousting in the Grand Place
when the cousins who had set out with her somehow got lost. Instead
of joining the crowds, Messer Pagano and she walked about the streets
and the markets, the river bank and the wharves, and never stopped
talking. She heard all about London and Lisbon and Rome and
Sardinia and Ragusa and Chios and Damascus and Constantinople.
All the wonderful lands he had lived in. He talked about animals with
tails front and behind, and rubies bigger than racket balls, and flowers
whose one petal would scent a whole palace.

His clean, pink fingertips described things as he talked; or steered
her shoulder; or attracted her attention by tickling her palm. She ate
spicy pastries he bought from stalls for her, and consumed unknown
drinks, fibbing when she disliked them. When he took her home, she
wanted to embrace him from joy and from gratitude, and he smiled,
seeing it, and held out his arms for a hug. His warm arms and his big,
firm kiss reminded her of her father, except that Cornelis de Charetty
was old when he died, and didn't have skin like a rose-scented
cushion, or wear dark pleated satin that slid under your touch. The
lord Pagano's hair under his feathered cap was dark and satiny too,
but she daren't touch that.

That was how it began. There followed four days of unexplained
absence; days of mourning. Then he sent his black page to her aunt. It
proved to be nothing. He had to entertain some kinsman or other:
would the family help? Catherine wasn't mentioned at all. When the
evening came, he hardly addressed her. It was only at their return that,
dragging behind in the darkness, she became aware that he had held
back as well. Then he said, "But a tear, my sweet Caterinetta! No, no! I
cannot bear that!" And his arm came warmly round her waist and he
kissed the tear away, and then her mouth. Then her aunt called from
inside the house and he smiled, and turned away to his lodgings.

The next meeting she arranged herself, and the two after that, alone with him. Not completely alone. In a park, or by the canal, or down on the shore, with their hoods over their faces, since it was autumn. Each time, he scolded her and told her he ought to take her back to her aunt, but he didn't. The second time, he kissed her when they met as well as when they went away. The third time, he brought her a present. It was a little ring with a carbuncle in it, and a lace to string it on. She was to wear it tucked into her gown, in case her cousins were jealous. It had belonged to his mother, who would have thought of her as a little daughter had she lived. Catherine tied the ring in place herself although he offered to help. She knew, even then, that he believed her chest to be prettier than it was.

That day, he was tired from buying his ship, and they sat down almost at once under a tree in the orchards not far from Ste Gudule, and stayed there until nearly dusk. To keep her from cold, he wrapped half his splendid cloak round her shoulders, and kept her hands warm in his. She watched him all the time that he talked, and admired his buttons, and when she wanted to stroke the fur of his collar he let her provided, he said, she would allow him reciprocal privileges.

It was as exciting as he made it sound: he held her close with one hand and reached under her hood with the other to pull forward her long, hard-brushed hair, one swathe on each side of her neck. Then he combed it all smooth with his fingers, arranging it over her chest and forward down to her lap. She had nice hair: longer than Tilde's, although Tilde was older. She sat still and let him stroke it like that for a little. After a bit he said, "Caterinetta. You are a lovely woman. You are a woman, aren't you?"

She had been overwhelmed, and surprised. "Of course I am!"

He looked very serious.

She must have smiled out of nervousness, for his face suddenly changed. He heaved a sigh and, bending his head, dropped a little kiss on her throat through the modesty gauze. "I'm glad. I'm glad, Caterinetta; for a Doria lord . . . you know a Doria lord could never show his love to a child. It would be against the family honour."

Then it had come to her what he had meant. She dismissed it. She heard herself repeating, "*Love?*" Then she couldn't say anything else, because he lifted his mouth from her chest and put his lips on her lips and pressed them heavily, with his arm tight round her shoulders.

It was stifling, but she knew what it was. It was the kind of kissing that Nicholas and her mother did. She wanted him to stay like that till she got used to it. Instead, her mouth opened, spoiling everything. She tried to shut it again, but the weight was too much. She felt her teeth were exposed. She might even bite him. She drew off and so did he, quickly. He let his hands go. He said, "Of course it's too soon. It's wrong and too soon. Let me take you home."

She was too appalled even to cry. She said, "It wasn't my fault. It wasn't. You can do it again."

"Don't you think I want to?" he said. "Princess, I want more than that. But after next week, you won't see me. And by the time I come back, many years may have passed."

She was seized by a cramp in her stomach. She said, "You're sailing."

He nodded. "To Italy first, then who knows where? My greatest adventure, I think. And I have to make it alone."

"Take me with you," she said.

She could see the shock on his face, and an exquisite longing. Then he said, "No. No, how could I? There's no time for a betrothal, far less for a contract of marriage. Your aunt has no powers: I couldn't send to your mother in time. I can't take you, my loveliest girl, although I'd give a ransom to do it. I can't even see you again. I mustn't. I would go too far: I couldn't help it. And then you would hate me."

Madonna Caterina de Charetty negli Doria.

"You want to *marry* me?" Catherine said. She had to look down, for he was kneeling before her, his cap off, his warm, satiny head on her knee.

"I want you to be my lady wife. I want to show you the world. I want to spend Christmas at your side and show you to the princes of Florence," said Messer Pagano Doria in a whisper. "But how can it be?"

They were off in a week.

Her aunt and uncle wished them Godspeed, thinking he was escorting her homewards to Bruges. They went to Antwerp instead. There he paid off her woman, and he and she and his retinue rode round to the harbour and climbed aboard his new ship. His huge and wonderful ship called the *Doria*.

Fairly early in the voyage, she had to tell him she wasn't a woman, and she thought he was going to be angry, because he left her chamber without really discussing it. However, when he came back he just said that of course he didn't mind waiting for her or the wedding, and the papers wouldn't reach them till Genoa anyway.

She hadn't known that weddings needed papers, but evidently they did. After that, she got lovely food and more presents, although he didn't sleep in her bed as she thought he would. Still, he came quite a lot and played cards and told her more stories, and tickled and kissed her, which she liked very much. He had bought her a beautiful gown and he would walk up and down the ship with her, showing her off.

There were other women on board. Sometimes they winked at her but Catherine, brought up in a seaport, knew better than to respond. They were there, of course, to go to bed with the seamen. The master of the ship was decently cordial. The black page was polite, after Messer Pagano had taken him off for a few words, no doubt with a cane. It was all like a very good daydream, except for the old Flemish nurse he had bought her who kept boiling her baths in a bucket and producing purges to brighten her skin. Catherine took the baths and the powders. She intended to do him credit with the princes of Florence. And she had his assurance. Marriage as soon as was fitting. She would be a wife before Tilde. She would be married to a man older than Nicholas. Older and richer and better born than the man her mother had taken to bed.

So, as the ship sailed past the harbour for Bruges, round France and alongside Portugal and through the Pillars of Hercules to their landfall, Catherine de Charetty prayed her particular prayer. And praying, remembered, uneasily, the shrill voice and identical prayers of Felix her brother. And he had been sixteen that birthday.

At home in Bruges, Marian de Charetty, owner of the Charetty dyeshop, prepared with determination to give an excellent Christmas to Tilde her older daughter and all her servants and clerks; and tried not to mourn her only son Felix, who had indeed enjoyed manhood at last and had died of it; or her young husband Nicholas, forced by circumstance to take himself off to Florence; or her small daughter Catherine who was (as infrequent, rather indirect letters of vague content informed her) content in Brussels, and in no hurry to finish her polishing.

If Catherine de Charetty was happy, the lord Pagano Doria was also amazingly content. The voyage had been pleasant and profitable. The solitary misfortune would, please God, soon be remedied. And he had barely set foot in Italy before half his remaining problems were solved. He met Father Godscalc.

At the time, it didn't seem like good luck. It happened at Porto Pisano, the harbour for Pisa and Florence. They had only just anchored. He had his hands full with matters to do with harbour dues and customs and cargo, not to mention persuading his Catherine that it was not suitable, yet, for her to walk ashore in public. Not until they were married. Not until no one could part them.

It was the old Flemish bitch in the end who got her to see the sport of dressing up as a page: if he had a black one, why not a white one as well? Then he had dear Noah to console, whose little black heart he had broken already. It was a wonder that they were all on shore and ready to set out for Florence as soon as they were. Indeed, they were just mounting to ride when Catherine, in her pretty page outfit, brought her little horse close and said, "*Look!*"

He thought for a moment it was her aunt, or her mother. Instead, her finger pointed over the quayside crowd to where a boatload of pilgrims from Rome had newly landed. Among them was a priest: a tall, broad, youngish man in a stained hooded cloak of good quality, who was haggling with someone over the hire of a horse. Two servants stood quietly behind him, and a modest amount of salt-crusted baggage. The servants wore livery of a peculiar blue, but no blazon.

The lord Pagano caught his fiancée's hand and lowered it, smiling. Alas, they were not yet in need of a priest. In any case, he already knew which priest he wanted. He said, "What, my darling? It isn't someone you know?" While he spoke, he nodded to Crackbene his master, and drew her a little apart, while the others moved gently off. All the time she was speaking, he saw to it that her back was to the blue livery.

It seemed bad news, although it might have been worse. The man was a Charetty chaplain. The fellow had served a short time in Bruges, but most of his time had been spent with Marian de Charetty's cavalry company, now passing the winter in Italy. He would, she thought, be on his way home.

The lord Pagano rather thought not, but had no intention of saying so. The priest, of course, must not see her. She saw the importance of that. It was agreed, in the end, that she should return to the ship with the master, while he rode on to their lodging in Pisa. There, with the priest safely gone, she would join him.

It didn't strike her, he saw, that a man leaving on horseback for Flanders was bound to ride north, and not eastwards to Pisa and Florence. There were times when he loved Catherine just for her ignorance.

Chapter 2

I T TOOK AN HOUR to get Catherine de Charetty settled back on the ship with her servants, and longer for the lord Pagano to make a few essential enquiries, and then to get himself en route for Pisa again. The priest, of course, was ahead.

The lord Pagano Doria rode quickly, to the discomfort of his muleteers and servants, although he took the black page Noah up in his saddle once or twice. It was not in his nature however to be bad-tempered, although the towpath was dusty and busy. Until the winter floods came, the river road to Pisa and Florence was the quickest way from the coast, and there were plenty of travellers to talk to.

The lord Pagano Doria didn't linger, but he produced a joke or shared a piece of chaffing with most people as he passed, and men turned to look at him with pleasure, for he was a delightful man, although on the small side. They passed a donkey train carrying flour from the water-mill. A stocking-maker with his shears and his needles was happy to answer his greeting, and then two unemployed caulkers on their way to the ship sheds at Pisa. Then, taking the width of the road, a carter with jars of the new season's oil was attempting to pass somebody's factor just come from checking the vintage, and with a liverish stare and two willow jars at his saddle to prove it. When the factor scowled, the lord Doria lifted his brows at the carter, who laughed. A gentleman of the sea, Messer Pagano Doria; alert as a whippet; bright as the sun upon brass.

They were still jogging along, an assortment of travellers, when they were stopped in their tracks by a galley. All those on the towpath shouted abuse. Messer Pagano Doria, full of sudden optimism, merely thought how much his little Catherine would have enjoyed witnessing one hundred and thirty-eight feet of empty Florentine galley being tree-warped upriver to Pisa where, between the two bridges, she would be prepared for her next season's trip. Here, all around him and beyond, the road was a mess of dead leaves and mud. Where the road and river bent round ahead there was, as always, the group of

quarrelling unshaven men in canvas shirts and burst hose attempting
to solve some obscure problem of leverage and in no mood to stand
aside to let shoremen go by. Around Pagano Doria everyone (apart
from the caulkers) continued to shout as they covered the short final
space between themselves and the obstacle, where one or two
travellers had already halted. Among them was the employee of the
Charetty company called Father Godscalc.

He was standing on the bank of the Arno, looking down on the
galley, which was stranded. From the long shining structure, high in
the water and laden with arguing men, a mooring rope ran from the
stern up the bank to an elm tree, to which it was tied with a good
seaman's lashing. Another rope, thrown ahead from the bows,
secured the ship to an oak tree upriver. By reeling in the fore cable,
the crew would normally force the ship to move on, against the
contrary flow of the river.

The priest stood by the elm. At close quarters, he was seen to be
of unusual size, although his broad, large-nosed face with its heavy
black brows appeared tranquil. Now his hood was thrust back, the
hair stuffed under the rim of his cap showed thick and black as dyed
cotton. He had a throat like an elk's, and there was a new scar on the
fist at his hipbone. Behind him his two men stood at ease, holding
the horses. He himself contemplated the river where the Florentine
galley still reposed in all its elegant length while the thick yellow
water rushed past. It was stuck on a sandbank.

If you were in no hurry, the scene was entertaining enough. Below
the steep bank, bare-legged men swearing in every dialect from
Savona to Naples had been set to work with levers and shovels. The
crew were among them. On deck, supervising, paced a broad clean-
shaven official in a red pillbox hat and a black gown with gold
glinting about it. In the prow, two half-naked men toiled to wind in
the capstan: the distant oak tree was shaking. Other trees, scarred of
trunk and ankle-deep in the last of their leaves, had already suffered.
A thunderhead of crows towered above them. The lord Pagano
Doria dismounted, as the trunk beside the priest quivered. A nest
sprang into the air, touched water, and bobbed off behind on the
current.

The priest looked at the tree, and so did Doria. Dug deep into the
bark was (still) the noose of the galley's belaying cable. As they
watched, the noose slowly crawled tighter. There was a smell of
heated tow. The link rope, straight as a rule, was sensibly humming.
The lord Pagano spoke with some gravity. "They seem to be moored
at both ends."

The priest inclined his head, turning. He said, "I fear they will
hardly go far." He had a melodious voice, and spoke in Latinist's
Italian, learned somewhere in Germany. He said, "Will you apprise
them, monsignore, or shall I break the news?"

A fellow spirit. The lord Pagano Doria gave his charming, mischievous smile. "Allow me," he said. And, drawing his double-edged, gold-hilted sword, stepped in front of the priest to the cable.

"But – " said the chaplain very quickly. Pagano, smiling, paid no attention. Raising both fists, he chopped with his blade at the mooring.

The severed stay leaped like a whip, sending leaves, grass and gouts of sand spinning. On the foredeck of the galley the capstan, suddenly freed, tossed to the ground its two straining seamen. It then began to run backwards, unreeling the rope at the bow. Loosed, the galley swung immediately broadside to the flow of the river and, sliding backwards, remounted the sandbank. The supervisor fell down. The clamour that followed was the kind you might hear at a bull-baiting. Muffled below it was the circumspect laughter of the man with the donkeys and the oil-vendor. The vineyard factor, making intermittent use of a woodstack, was the picture of silent concern, but for other reasons entirely.

The two men by the elm tree faced each other: one, five-sixths of the height of the other. The lord Pagano Doria exclaimed, "Now, the Universal Creator protect me. Who could have foreseen such a thing? They will blame me, and rightly."

The priest appeared thoughtful. "You perhaps. Or perhaps the person who failed to untie the cable."

"Ah," said Pagano Doria. "You chide me, and rightly. It is not seemly that some poor man should take another one's blame. Even though, of course, it was his fault in the first place. Will you come and witness me making confession?"

The priest smiled. "If you wish. The officer on board may be hurt. You may need special rites if he assaults you."

"I?" said Pagano Doria. Perhaps because he was short, he knew well how to bring a little chill into his voice, a little coolness into his face, and then banish it, laughing. He said, "But we are not even known to each other. I am Pagano Doria, merchant, seaman and patron of a round ship just sailed in from Genoa. And you?"

"A famous name," said the priest. "As for me, I was born in Cologne, but serve in Italy as chaplain-notary to a small private army belonging to a dyer in Flanders. My name is Godscalc."

"And that, too, is not a name drawn from obscurity," said the lord Pagano with generosity. "We are well met, and I shall tell you a secret. The man on board has not recognised me yet, but his name is Antonio di Niccolò Martelli, and I knew him long before he was appointed sea consul. He will forgive me. I shall entertain him with news and with gossip, and he will relent. You will help me. Indeed, I shall tell him that you tried to prevent my small, stupid action. Come. Come and meet him. If you are going to Pisa, you cannot have too many friends."

"Friends?" said the priest with his slow smile. But when Doria sprang down through the grass to the water's edge, the black-haired priest followed quite readily.

Their reception was precisely what the lord Pagano had expected. There was an awkward ten minutes, but the Doria name and some evoked early friendship restored the sea consul slowly, first to acceptance and then to a show of resigned hospitality. It was sesto, time for the crew to stop working and eat. Perhaps Father Godscalc and Messer Pagano would remain and share his midday collation?

By then, they were aboard, Father Godscalc wading stoically out of the shallows, his skirts kilted up to his knees; and Messer Pagano more elegantly on the back of his horse, whose reins he gave to his servant. Then, in the warmth of his cabin, the Florentine sea consul Martelli handed out a good Rhenish wine while his serving-man unpacked a basket.

It held cold tortellini, a fowl, some eggs boiled in the shell and a pasty. There was plenty for three. The lord Doria talked, as he promised, and paid for his food with as much well-spiced news as the consul could have wished for. The priest, who had just come from Rome, was not too forward in comment, but supplied a few substantial anecdotes of his own which surprised the sea consul as much as Doria himself. Indeed, after the meal, Messer Martelli offered to show the priest himself through the galley, since Godscalc appeared to admire it.

Godscalc's worthy concern, Doria thought, was less to explore the galley itself than to see if his exploit had caused any damage. The sea consul, questioned directly, did not fail to chide Messer Pagano again, although in more lenient terms. There might have been a fatality. But no, there was no serious damage. A few strained timbers perhaps; a little rubbing. "She'll be checked. But it isn't of moment. She's an old lady, this one: served her term with the state, and coming up to be hired and refitted. Caveat hirer, eh, eh? He should know what he's in for, someone who wishes to rent a twelve-year-old ship at the end of the trading season. And the extra repair work is always good news for somebody."

A whistle blew. The mealtime was over. Together the priest and the sea prince walked with Martelli to the side of the galley, and prepared to go on their way. It was then that Messer Pagano Doria, calling his servant on shore, had unpacked and presented to the sea consul the lavish gift of six fine linen towels for his hatstand, and a piece of lace for his sweet lady wife, the Madonna. To make amends. To show his contrition. For the sake of old friendship.

He knew he was being generous. He was not surprised when the sea consul, deeply impressed, invited him (why had he not thought of it before!) to his house for supper that evening. Where was he staying in Pisa?

Swiftly forestalling an invitation he did not require, Messer Pagano mentioned that accommodation was already engaged in a tavern. He would ride there directly. The galley with Messer Martelli would, of course, take very much longer. When should he call at the sea consul's home?

"But go there directly!" said Messer Martelli. "Wait there! Repose yourself! My wife, my housekeeper, will attend to you. Take her your presents yourself. With – Do I understand Father Godscalc is of your party?"

Father Godscalc's disclaimer was unheard below the voice of Pagano Doria. Yes, said the delightful man, smiling. Of course Father Godscalc must continue to Pisa in his company. And might he also have the pleasure, the honour, of meeting the Madonna the sea consul's wife, of supping with Messer Martelli in his beautiful house? Magnificent! He was speechless with joy. He could not wait until they renewed their delightful friendship that evening.

They were on shore before the lord Pagano turned to his priestly companion and said, with mischief, "But perhaps I erred? I gave you no chance to decline. But indeed, the sea consul's wife keeps a good table, and he is an excellent man. Am I forgiven?"

"For arranging two lavish meals for a poor priest from Germany? My dear son," said Father Godscalc. "Even the crows would forgive you."

And so it fell out. Priest and sea prince completed their journey to Pisa, the latter conversing with grace, the former replying with modesty. Arriving within the stout walls, the priest, embarrassed no doubt by his fortune, sent his small suite and smaller luggage to the modest inn he had chosen. The Doria retinue – servants, hackneys, mules and African page – made their way, not unnoticed, to a larger one.

Pagano Doria, vivid, supple, amusing, led the way past the mills of the river to the docks where the Republic's galleys idled afloat, or stood stark on their blocks, being scraped and mended from their last trading voyage, the old citadel looming beside them. The sea consul's house, rented for his six months of duty, stood just beside it: a low, two-storeyed building with cellars below and a stair leading up from the courtyard.

A pretty woman stood at the top of the stair smiling at Pagano Doria, who kissed her lips in the city fashion and then laid his gifts, with care, in her arms. Then, with courtesy he drew back to present Father Godscalc to his hostess. This, of course, was the sea consul's lady.

Learning of her absent husband's enjoinder, the lady expressed herself delighted, and hurried to settle both guests in her parlour with a warming cupful of wine. For, as she said with a smile, it would take the galley three hours to drag through the river to Pisa, and they would sup all the more heartily when Messer Martelli her lord was safely come home.

Very soon after that, she began to talk of the carpet my lord Pagano had brought home for them from his last voyage to Chios, and volunteered to show him where it had been hung. The priest, half risen, was pressed back in his seat, with a fine missal from Mantua to engage his attention.

Certainly, it seemed to engross him, although he looked up and smiled every time the assiduous manservant came to replenish his wine and sometimes, it could be observed, he studied one page for longer than seemed strictly necessary. When at the end of half an hour he was still alone, he rose, perhaps feeling stiff, and made his way to an unshuttered window overlooking the quays. From there, without obvious haste, he made his way back through the parlour and down the stairs to the courtyard where he stood, book in hand, under an orange tree and turned a page with attention.

"Ah!" said the sea consul, walking in through the gates with his servant, two hours too early. "You found the house, Father Godscalc. And where is my lord Pagano?"

The large priest in the felt cap closed the missal and cradled it. He looked down. "I excused myself from the parlour in the hope of this very interview. I have something to tell you." Behind him, a shutter opened high in the house.

"Ah, yes?" said the sea consul neutrally. He led the way to a stone bench and they sat down together.

"It concerns the galley," the priest said surprisingly. "You noted, perhaps, my interest in the galley?"

"You have a lively mind, Father Godscalc," said the sea consul. For some reason, his face in the dim light looked younger.

"But I should have told you the source of my interest," the priest said. "The company which employs me belongs to Bruges. From a modest beginning, they have encompassed not only dyeing and broking, but the hiring of fighting soldiers. Such men need clerking, and spiritual comfort, and I have supplied both. I have this moment come from the company in its winter quarters near Rome. I am on my way to Florence where the seniors of my company are exploring a new opportunity to extend themselves. To proceed, they would require a great galley – this very ship, it may be; since she is free, and they are not easily come by. Hence, you understand, my anxiety over its condition."

The sea consul's interest was engaged. He said, "You spoke of a small company. But one which can raise capital to man and run a galley and can count on enough clients to fill it must be a large one. Who is its owner?"

"A widow, newly remarried," said the priest. "She is in Bruges.

Her husband is there in Florence ahead of me. He is to do business, I understand, with the Republic. With the Republic's senior citizen, Cosimo de' Medici."

"Indeed," said the sea consul. His gaze had become sharper. He said, "You know my name, Martelli? You know that we are galley conductors; that the Medici and the Martelli work together? Who is this man, the second husband of your employer, who proposes to requisition a galley?"

"That may not be his intention," said the priest. "It may not be within his capabilities. I am not sure. His name is Niccolò. He is nineteen."

"*Nineteen!*" said the sea consul, and smiled. "It sounds to me as if it will be of little moment whether the galley you mention will be seaworthy or not. You have not, I take it, been with the company long? The young man married the owner and no doubt her notary, her lawyer, her chaplain, her physician all found reasons to leave, and had to be replaced?"

The priest's eyes, of unblinking brown, remained fixed on him. The priest said, "No, they chose to stay. I was appointed because under young master Niccolò the business has expanded. He has a flair, I am told. Time will tell."

"You surprise me," said the consul. "I trust that whatever time tells, it will make pleasant hearing. But, you understand, I cannot help your company with the House of Medici. No one but Messer Cosimo and his sons arrange offers or decide on new dealings."

"Of course," said Godscalc, rising. "I merely wished to excuse my earlier reticence. I would not have you think later that I had deceived you. But one does not talk overmuch about a young master who has yet to prove himself. Ah . . . There is your lady, coming to scold me for detaining you."

The supper was good; the wine generous. Leaving late and together, the priest and the sea prince stood where their ways parted, in the yard of the sea prince's tavern. The priest expressed his thanks, as was due, to the author of his convivial evening. Only then did Pagano Doria look up into the calm, massive face and allow his smile to broaden to mischief. He said, "You owe me nothing. On the contrary. Madonna our hostess has passed me a gift for you, but as it is scented and silken I hesitate in case I offend. Unless you have a sister, a mother?"

"How else," said Godscalc, "could I properly interpret a kiss when I see it? I accept the kerchief, of course. I might advise you, as well, not to visit there often. Galleys are not, I notice, reliable time-keepers; nor are their officers."

"What, no homilies?" said Pagano Doria. "What a good fellow you are, and what a fright you gave me just now. What were you talking of, there in the courtyard? God or Mammon?"

"Of my two masters," said Godscalc. "We were discussing the

merchant called Niccolò in the Italian tongue. Nicholas vander Poele, of the Charetty company, Bruges, now staying in Florence."

"Never heard of him," said Pagano Doria.

Upstairs, in his room, he found Catherine de Charetty.

The lord Pagano Doria had had a long, if entertaining, day. It had reached a formidable, if exhausting, conclusion. He felt a little worn, but pleasantly gratified. And now here was this dear Flemish creature, who ought to be nine safe miles away on board the *Doria* and instead was in the same room as himself, in her wrinkled boy's tunic, in the very town where the Charetty chaplain was staying. Indeed, occupying the very room below which . . .

"Nicholas," said Catherine de Charetty. Her voice squealed like a saw. Her face was dirty. The bitch of a nurse wasn't here, then. "Nicholas is in Florence. That man said Nicholas was in Florence."

She had overheard. Pagano Doria closed the door and pulling his feathered cap off, crossed to the settle, and sat down beside the child. He hung his hat on her head, and then put one hand round the back of the settle and collected both of hers with the other. Her palms were dirty too. "I know," he said. "Or at least, I know now. But you're not worried, are you?"

She looked at him as if he had gone mad. Nicholas, aged nineteen, had lately married Catherine's mother. Nicholas was now the head of the Charetty business. Nicholas, made aware of this charming elopement, would stop it quicker than even her mother might. In his own interests, of course. Whoring apprentices who married ladies twenty years older than themselves had no time for young maidens' longings. Pagano Doria knew all about Nicholas. The girl was trembling.

It was tempting to gather her into his arms, but that was not the best way. He returned her look with affection and even the faintest amusement and said, "My darling, he'll never dream that you can be here. Father Godscalc has no notion either. I met him on the towpath, and made friends with him just to be sure. He's going to Florence. You'll stay in Pisa until they've both gone."

He realised his mistake, watching her face suffuse with red. She said, "You said we'd spend Christmas in Florence. You said I'd wear earrings. You said I'd meet princes. You said . . ."

"Of course it will happen!" he said. "They won't stay in Florence for Christmas! If they're going home, they'll have to cross the Alps soon. If they're sailing, why should they linger? You'll have your earrings, my love, and everything else that you wanted. Now, if you like. Except that I can't show you off until we are married. You do know that? You do remember? So your stepfather isn't really holding you up at all, is he? Only that small gift from God that you and I are waiting to share. And once that happens . . ."

She had calmed. She searched his face, her own brightening a little. She said, "Of course. When I'm a woman and married, Nicholas can see me as much as he likes. Can't he? Because he couldn't send me home then."

"It won't arise. He'll be gone before Christmas."

"I hope he isn't," said the child dreamily.

Despite the dirt, she was amazingly pretty, as perhaps her mother once was. The reddish brown hair flamed in the light of the brazier and her eyes were a very bright blue. He stayed quite still, except for the fingers stroking her hands.

She said, "I'd like to be a woman while Nicholas is still in Florence. I'd like to walk into a palace in earrings and gold brocade like the Duchess Bianca, and speak to Nicholas."

He said nothing.

She blushed. She said, "Tilde has little breasts."

Then he drew her to him, but carefully as always, and dislodged the cap, and put his other arm round her shoulders. He said, "Yours, my Venus, will be more wonderful than Tilde's, or any woman alive. I know it. I am waiting for you, Caterinetta."

She had relaxed. Her lashes lowered. She was tired: she had ridden a long way, with whatever escort she had forced to come with her. She was, he had found, an excellent horsewoman. And she was not without courage, the little thing. She said, her eyes lightly closed, "Who did you kiss?"

It took all his control to stop the shock travelling through both his arms. What had Godscalc said? Sisters, mothers.

Pagano smiled, his lips touching her brow. He said, "The priest and I supped with the sea consul, and his wife gave me the kiss of friendship on parting. A good woman, Caterinetta. My mother was very like that. My mother would have loved you. I love you."

"Earrings," she said; and fell asleep smiling.

Chapter 3

B Y THAT TIME, Nicholas vander Poele, juvenile leader of the Charetty company, had been in Florence for two or three days. With him were his notary and the company doctor. Other officers were expected, but not his wife, who was of course at home in Bruges with her older girl Tilde. The younger daughter Catherine had been sent off to Brussels before her stepfather had even left home. It had caused some talk.

By the time another three days had gone by, all the merchants in Florence knew that the Charetty company were here on the chance that they might get a great galley and set up a branch, fools that they were, in the East. No doubt they hoped the House of Medici would help them.

Since they could expect (everyone knew) a long wait, they had taken rooms in the Red Lion quarter. That they were not always to be found there had something to do with their preoccupations as merchants, and something to do with the temperament of their landlady. The day of 14 December was, however, an exception. Master Julius the company notary and Tobias Beventini the company physician were both in the parlour, for the purpose of improving their appearance.

Since not a great deal could be done for Tobie, their attention was centred on Julius, who possessed a certain kind of athletic good looks. With difficulty, Tobie was wielding the scissors. Julius was complaining.

"He's got a new plaything," Julius said. "Holy Virgin, that was my ear!"

"So I supposed," Tobie said. "If you don't want your hair cut, I'll be happy to get on with something else, and you can find a barber to look after your ear. *Who* has a new plaything?"

"Nicholas, who do you think?" Julius said. "He came back with shavings in his shoes and his doublet all covered with sawdust, and this ridiculous toy."

"Toy?" said Tobie. His mood lightened.

"Toy. Nicholas saw it at the Franciscans' and they let him make one for himself. He plays with it. He'll carry it to the Palazzo Medici unless we prevent him, and the lord Cosimo will give us alms for our halfwit and send us all back to Bruges. That was my *ear again*."

"Do it yourself then," said Tobie briskly. He tossed down his comb and the scissors, and went to pick up his cup of warmed wine from the windowsill. In a moment, as they both knew, he would go back and finish the job. Crossing the Alps interfered, as Tobie had observed, with a gentleman's grooming. Crammed into the modest house of their hostess with their servants sleeping in cart sheds, they hadn't expected the summons from God quite so soon. The appointment with the lord Cosimo de' Medici was for that afternoon, and Nicholas didn't know of it. Nicholas, oblivious, had gone out somewhere again. Perhaps to play with his toy.

"So what's normal about Nicholas?" Tobie said. "He likes to look like a halfwit. He has a genius for figures. The Medici bank, how amazing, have discovered it. They won't forget, will they? More. He is the kind of halfwit who seemed to like being a dyeshop apprentice. He married the Widow who promptly let him manage the business. He is managing the business. The fact that he killed five people in the process and ruined a sixth has made the Widow a little wary: one doesn't blame her. But the Widow still trusts in Nicholas her juvenile husband, and hopes that if he strays from the path of good Flemish practices we will correct him. Nicholas is bizarre. If he weren't, you and I wouldn't be here. We have discussed this before."

"Before Nicholas acquired a toy. I remember discussing it. I feel the need of talking it over again," Julius said.

Tobie was actually quite pleased. Although roughly the same age as Julius, he was older than Julius would ever be: his short acquaintance with Julius had confirmed it. He said, "Julius, everyone's got a toy. I like mine on my pillow. Captain Astorre likes to cook his and eat it. Godscalc hangs his on his girdle and counts it. The Widow prefers to accept hers in matrimony. When Nicholas gives up being weaned, I'll become anxious."

Julius brooded. He could see Julius despising the medical school of Pavia. Tobie said, "Nicholas managed the journey from Flanders all right. Deferred to you, joked discreetly with me, got on like a dyeworks on fire with the muleteers. And you know what the trip to the Franciscans was for. If it succeeded, he could put pressure on the Medici."

"He should have taken us with him. You know he should. That's what we're here for. To keep him out of trouble."

"Well, so far as I know he isn't in any yet," remarked Tobie. He picked up the scissors. "Let's get on with the other ear, or Monna Alessandra will personally send you her barber."

Alessandra Strozzi, high in Florentine society, low in means, owned the house they were staying in. Julius gave, unthinking, the smile that made people follow him, sometimes, in the street. He said, "Have you seen her glaring at Nicholas? She isn't going to be duped like her son and her daughter. Mother Strozzi is regretting that she offered to lodge us." He twitched the towel over his shoulders.

"Rubbish," said Tobie, snipping steadily. "She's getting free medical attention from me, and free legal attention from you, and we are the dear friends of her poor son Lorenzo in Bruges. It's only Nicholas she's regretting. Once a servant always a servant. Keep still, can't you? I'm only quoting. Has she asked you yet why you haven't married? She will. Florence needs babies."

"What's that to do with marriage?" Julius said. "My God, she shouldn't spurn Nicholas. The stud of Flanders. They'd have to build new city walls if Nicholas let himself go. Not but what . . ."

"Gossip, gossip," said Tobie reprovingly. "But I take your point. Since he married the head of the company he's led the life of a committed eunuch. But then, she's his livelihood."

"Unless he finds something better," said Julius. For two years as employee and tutor to the Charetty son, he had encouraged this cheerful lout Nicholas to better himself. Tobie could understand how Julius, more than almost anyone else, had been flummoxed by Nicholas's marriage.

Tobie said, "Who, for example?"

Julius turned his head and was nicked without even feeling it. He said, "Or someone worse. Could you do without girls at nineteen?"

Interested, Tobie considered. The topic was a new one for both of them. For all the months he had known Julius, Tobie had failed to catch Julius toying with anything. He said, "Maybe he prays."

Julius grunted, frowning. He said, not entirely obscurely, "I wish Godscalc would come."

"Perhaps he won't," Tobie said. "Perhaps he and the army have written a note excusing themselves from joining Nicholas. For Alexander the Great our leader is not. He was falling off his horse until yesterday."

"I thought – " began Julius. He yelped and restarted. "Do we expect Astorre's soldiers to fight? I thought we were taking them just to protect us."

"That depends," Tobie said, "on what the young man our master has found out at the Franciscans'. He should know by now if it's worth going on with the venture. Then all that matters is whether the magnificent Cosimo de' Medici will allow us to run it. That's surely Nicholas now."

Julius rose to his feet. The towel dropped, showering cut brown hair over Monna Alessandra's elegant tiles. His hair, finely tailored, clung to a thick-boned face with slanting eyes and a blunt profile which would have looked well on a coin. Tobie, who had almost no hair at all, gazed at him sadly. Julius peered through the segments of window glass coloured pink, green and yellow, and said, "Oh, Jesus Christ, yes. And he's got the toy with him. And his hose are mud up to the knee and his hair needs a cut. That's the spokesman of the Charetty business."

"Well, get the coffer out," said Tobie roundly. "You find his clean clothes and I'll cut his hair round his cap and wash his ears out. Then, when we get to the Palazzo Medici, you imitate his voice and I'll sit him on my knee and move his arms up and down. Where is the problem?"

"There in front of you," Julius said. "And I don't know if I want to solve it. I want to lead a quiet life witnessing wills and drawing up dowry engagements and counting the rings found on corpses. I think I'm leaving."

"Wait until Godscalc comes," Tobie said. "Then we can all leave together and Nicholas can repopulate Florence. I don't know. I might stay and help him."

"Do that," said Julius. "You know what Monna Alessandra will do? She'll geld you both."

"Personally?" Tobie said.

"No, she's no fool," said Julius. "She'll employ you to do it, and then dock your fee because you'll be too sick to handle the aftercare. Oh, my God."

The door opened. "You blaspheme?" said their hostess Alessandra Macinghi negli Strozzi, straight as a pair of book-boards. Her plucked brow, high as Tobie's, was finely printed by age in what could have been numbers. "It is time your priest came. You will make confession tomorrow, or leave this house of mine. Is that your fellow, this Niccolò?"

Julius, employee of widows, was readier than Tobie to answer. He said, "We've been waiting for him, Monna Alessandra. His Magnificence Messer Cosimo has sent for us."

"Hence the cutting of hair. I am glad that some circumstance brought the need to your attention. Do you propose to go to the Palazzo Medici with your Niccolò in his present condition?"

She finished the sentence, even though by that time Nicholas had entered the room. Studying him, Tobie tried to be objective, and succeeded. The head of the Charetty company of Bruges was a very large young man, and well-developed. His throat was stalwart; his face widely framed and most remarkable in repose for its eyes, which were large and misleadingly innocent. It was however seldom in repose, being expert in the business of imitating the faces of other people. A scar less than a year old marked it from eye to chin on one side. He had never explained it. Gossip had long since put it down to a belting by some ex-virgin's master or father, and if Nicholas was prepared to let the theory pass, then so were the few who knew better. His hair, the colour of dirt, had become wet during his walk, and was crimped like a spaniel's buttocks. In one hand he grasped a stained jacket, flung haphazard over one shoulder. In the other he held a small object. Monna Alessandra said, "Hah! And what is that?"

Nicholas looked at her fondly. He turned the same smiling gaze towards Julius and Tobie, lingering only on the bead of blood standing on one of Julius's ears. Julius's scalp moved in annoyance. Returning his gaze to his hostess, Nicholas held up to the object in question. It was very small, hardly two inches across, and shaped like two mushroom heads stuck together. "This?" he said. "It's a plaything. I made it. After my lord Cosimo has seen it, I'll show it to you."

Tobie and Julius gazed at him. Only Monna Alessandra took action. "You are stupid," she said. She walked forward, plucked the object from his hand and, crossing the room, thrust the toy into the brazier. It burst into flame. "Playthings are for children," she said. "You are an infant no longer. You are responsible. To your wife. To your company. To your colleagues. If they will not tell you, I shall. You will now clean yourself and your clothes and take the advice of your elders, or you will disgrace us all at the Palazzo. Do I wish the Republic to know that I have taken cretins into my home?"

Julius, mesmerised, gazed at the woman. Tobie preferred to watch Nicholas. He saw a single flicker of movement, then nothing more. Nicholas stood where he was, his gaze on the place where the little toy burned. It had, one supposed, taken some trouble to make. He had fashioned it, paring, shaping and buffing the wood, while holding that series of talks, as their representative, in the hilltop cloisters of the Franciscans. The Friars had not reproved him. He had joked, of course, about showing it to the Medici. In Bruges, he had liked to make playthings and puzzles.

Julius said, "Where have you been? The lord Cosimo has sent for us. You look disgusting."

"I know," said Nicholas. "But I've just found out I'm going to make a fortune. Say I'm beautiful."

Monna Alessandra stared at him, frowning.

"You're beautiful," said Tobie quickly.

"Ravishing," agreed Julius, staring also. "How?"

"By impressing the lord Cosimo de' Medici with our honesty, worth and acumen, which he is already inclined to credit us with, from the mere fact that we lodge with Monna Alessandra. Madonna, you are perfectly right. I shall dress. I shall be responsible. I shall listen to the wise heads around me. Has anyone cut Tobie's hair?"

"Find it," said Julius, "and I'll cut it. That extraordinary woman said we could make a fortune. So you believe her now?"

"What extraordinary woman?" said Monna Alessandra with some sharpness.

Julius, pulled up short, had the sense to answer carefully. "A lady from the Levant. Nicholas and his wife met her in Bruges. They valued her interest, of course, but we don't expect to see her again."

Tobie had forgotten the lady in Bruges. Optimism possessed him. Toys. Toys for the pillow. He turned his back on his hostess and lowered a lascivious gaze upon Julius. "Don't we? By God, don't we?" he said.

Attended by two servants in Charetty blue jackets, Julius and Tobie walked to the palace of the Medici, one on each side of Nicholas.

There was no need to ride. Florence was a town you could cross from side to side in twenty minutes, using the butchers' bridge over the Arno. Tobie, a native of northern Italy, was accustomed to Florentine fripperies and strode between stone and marble, bronze and ironwork, like a dog going home to his dinner. His attention, as in every city, was solely drawn to the skin, the limbs, the gums, the lids of the people he passed. Some, resenting his stare, spat in his wake, upon which he was quite likely to turn back and examine the sputum, which annoyed them even more.

Julius, trained in Bologna, looked about him with pangs of nostalgia. Throughout his time of rebellious exile he had tried to forget the things Italian money could do; the skills it could buy. But even in five years Florence had changed; become richer. Between the hill-mounting walls there were churches and towers and piazzas, gardens and loggias and galleries, doors like carpets and ribbons of arcaded windows. There were statues and shrines, fountains and cloisters. The market booths and their awnings were laid out like pigment on parchment. And through the city, the swift, yellow river. And about it, the pastures and the comfortable shapes of the hills.

Florence was smaller than Venice, although it was bigger than London. Venice (Julius had never been there) had long since lined its canals with the mansions of merchants made rich by carrying goods to the East.

Florence was rich as well, but from making and selling particular goods of its own – silk and fine woollen cloth and gilded leathers. And, of course, there was the income from banking. In the Old Market in summer, they said, you could count seventy-two bankers and bill-brokers seated behind their baize tables.

Somewhere in Florence was the branch bank of the Medici, just as there were branch banks of the Medici in Bruges and Milan and Venice, Geneva, London and Rome. They were managed by trusted families whose sons and nephews followed one another, selected by Cosimo de' Medici, the head of the company. Cosimo's home, where they were heading, in the Via Larga, was not a branch of anything: it was the centre of Florence, where all the real business of the Medici was done. In the large house lived Cosimo and his wife and his sons and his grandchildren. Pierfrancesco his nephew stayed in the next dwelling. And as well as his household staff Cosimo entertained all the famous who visited Florence: gave permanent beds to the representatives of the Pope or the Duke of Milan; kept his records and dictated his letters to the clerks of his chancery. For although he claimed to be a private citizen within an elected republic, Cosimo de' Medici was Florence.

Built straight on to the street, the Medici palace was monumentally square, with corbelled eaves wide enough to shelter the foot of its walls, where the servant benches were fitted. The two storeys were faced with rough-bevelled stone blocks painted in red, white and green, and the private apartments of the upper floor were lit by ten thin-pillared windows. Julius, looking up, said, "Five thousand florins. That's what they say it's been valued at. Five thousand florins for one house."

"Now there's a scandal," said a man sitting on one of the benches. Julius looked at him. He was wearing a good but stained cloak over the cap and gown of a priest, and his hair, too thick for his calling, wound all over his neck like black cotton. He got up, proving himself to be of powerful build and the same height as Nicholas, whom he addressed. He said, "The Charetty company offered me two and a half florins a month to save your souls no matter what thieving percentage lay on them; and pound for pound, that takes more effort than banking. I want improved terms. I want a lodging like this at the end of it."

Hearing, Master Tobie the doctor turned and exclaimed. Young Nicholas turned, and looked pleased. "Father Godscalc. But that's already written into your contract. In your master's house are many mansions, and one has your name on it, if you can make out the language it's written in. How did you know to be here?"

"I'll tell you later," said the chaplain called Godscalc. "I've just come from Pisa. I've news for you."

"The Tower has fallen?" said Tobie.

"The Pope has fallen?" Nicholas said.

"The army likes its winter quarters," said Julius, "and wouldn't want to sail to the East under Nicholas?"

"Oh, you'll get all the fighting men you'd have need of," said the priest comfortably. "Have you heard tell of a Pagano Doria?"

"Messer Niccolò!" said someone sharply.

"Dorias, yes. Paganos, never. Why?" said Nicholas.

"Messer Niccolò!" said the same voice, much nearer.

"His colours are murrey and plunket," said Godscalc. "Not one of the impotent poor. You don't know the man?"

He was thrust aside. A harsh voice said, "Messer Niccolò, you are awaited. His magnificence has almost lost patience."

The speaker, emerged from the nearest grand archway of the Palazzo Medici, was not a porter but a cleanshaven man dressed in a secretary's gown and a cap with black lappets like Julius's own. He was frowning at

Nicholas. Nicholas said, "This is my chaplain, Father Godscalc. He has some news for me."

"Then he can impart it within," said the secretary. "Have the goodness to follow me instantly."

Julius would not have cared to argue with him, and Nicholas didn't. In single file, the four passsed through the archway and into the Medici courtyard. Julius faltered.

"Judith displaying the dead head of Holofernes," said Nicholas helpfully, gazing at the fountain before them and the streaming sculpture within it. "*He* was a friend of Donatello's and *she* didn't like it. The sarcophagus over there was used for Messer Cosimo's great-great-great-great-grandfather's cousin."

"Is he still in it?" said Julius.

"They're possibly all still in it," said Nicholas. "Roman, Roman, Roman, Roman, Medici. Like a pie."

"If you will stop talking," said Tobie, "you will notice that we are being invited to climb to the salon."

In the salon was a fine carpet, an assortment of carved and gilded coffers, several stools, cushioned boxes and his magnificence Cosimo de' Medici, seated on a chair with carrying poles like the Pope's. Hesitating with his three companions in the double doorway, Julius scrutinised the wealthiest man in Florence, while their conductor went forward and spoke to him.

Seventy-two years of age and contorted with gout, Cosimo de' Medici commanded the room like another Judith seeking another Holofernes. Sallow, long-nosed and shrunken, he nursed his balding head beneath a swathed velvet hat, and dark glossy fur lined the robe he wore over his doublet. He listened to his official, his head bent to hear better. Then he lifted one hand and rapped on the wood of his chair arm. "Approach, then!" he said.

Julius looked to see if Nicholas had paled, or was trembling. Men in fear could shame themselves and their companions. Men puked in front of princes, and soiled themselves, and lost the bass of their voices.

A child, hitherto unnoticed, rose from the ground by the chair and pointing a stabbing finger at the controlling member of the Charetty company, said, "That's him! He did it!"

The child was a boy, aged between four and five and attractive enough, with fair hair curling under his cap and a pinafore of some fine material over his dress. He was glaring at Nicholas.

Nicholas said, "You got knots in it." The words made no sense, nor did he say them with respect, deference or even cajolery. Julius had heard him use the same tone of affectionate exasperation to Monna Alessandra's unfortunate water-boy.

The child said, "I didn't."

Julius stood very still, and so did Tobie beside him. The lord of

Florence stirred in his pontifical chair. He said, "My grandchild lies, Messer Niccolò. He got knots in it. You are here to correct him."

"Well, that's soon done," said Nicholas cheerfully. "Show me."

Beside him, Julius could see Tobie's feet, in their best boots, unmoving. He dared not look at his face. He stood still while Nicholas made his way towards the child and, reducing himself to a crouch, remained bouncing a little beside him. His hands hung inward over his knees and his round face, with its vast eyes, looked friendly. The child held out a hand. In it was a replica of the wooden toy Monna Alessandra had burned.

Tobie grunted. Nicholas, without turning, said, "I made two. Where's the cord?"

The voice of Cosimo de' Medici said from above him, "The child's tutor, a man of small faith, excised it."

Nicholas, fishing in his purse, had already produced another. The cord, no doubt, of the lost plaything. Julius studied the toy, cut like the first from fine wood, and with the shape of two solid mushrooms placed stem to stem. Nicholas took it from the child's hand, and then knotted and wound all the cord round the waist of the object, leaving free the last foot, and a loop. He hooked a finger into the loop, and let the object lie in his hand. "What did I say?" he said to the child. His eyes crinkled.

Unexpectedly, the child smiled in return. He said. "Do it smoothly."

"You remembered," said Nicholas. "Everyone gets it tangled up the first time. Shall I show you?"

The voice from the chair spoke. "Never mind showing him," said Cosimo de' Medici, "I wish you to show me. I am told that Euclid would weep from jealousy."

"I could make Euclid one of his own," Nicholas said.

Julius closed his eyes.

Nicholas said, "Meanwhile, there is no need for weeping, provided we all watch very carefully. For example . . ."

Julius opened his eyes.

The old man had lifted an eyebrow. Nicholas was getting up, his eyes on the child, and the child's face, uplifted, was shining. Nicholas stood. With dramatic slowness he curled the object up to his shoulder. With dramatic suddenness he unbent his arm and cast the object flying away. The cord, unreeling, hissed. The object described a miraculous loop and returned to him. He caught it. Still smiling at the child, he opened his hand to the floor. The object unreeled, and then rose to his hand and then dropped again. He kept it rising and falling. Then he threw it outwards again and, instead of catching it, flicked his wrist so that it made first one loop, then a series. He caught it. The child cried, "Make it walk!"

Julius risked a glance at Tobie. Tobie was wearing a look of contempt, which was reassuring. Cosimo de' Medici said, "Yes. Make it walk, Messer Niccolò. It cannot also speak?"

Nicholas, ending a sudden sharp movement, smiled without looking up. The object spun at the end of the cord. He lowered it bit by bit down to the floor where, of its own accord, it started to run off ahead of him. He followed it a little way, the child jumping around him, and arriving before the pole-chair allowed the thing to run up its cord to his hand. He said, "It is called a farmuk, my lord; and of course it speaks."

The child said, "It doesn't!"

The old man looked at him. "Ah, Cosimino, but it does. It speaks to grown men. One day it will tell you something. But first you must master it. Can you make it run smoothly?"

"I can! I can!" said the child.

"Then you must take it off and practise. Then, when this kind friend of yours has gone, you will bring it in and show me. Thank him for his trouble. That is good. And now go."

The child left, skipping, with the thing in his hands. His grandfather, turning, looked at Nicholas, and then at the two men standing still in the doorway. "Indeed, it speaks!" he said dryly. "And in Persian. I am right, I believe?"

"It is a Persian toy, monsignore," Nicholas said. "If I may present Messer Julius, notary to the Charetty company. And Messer Tobias Beventini da Grado, our physician. And Father Godscalc, our chaplain."

"I do not recall," said Cosimo de' Medici, "having invited them. But since they are here, there are stools for them. What do they want?"

Lean, lined and cynical, the sallow face surveyed them all. When the gout was severe, as at present, he had himself carried through the house, screaming in pain as he approached every door. It was said that when rebuked by Contessina his wife, he explained that to cry warning after the hurt would be useless. The stories about Cosimo and his lady were endless. Julius had seen her once. She was fat and placid and content to be excluded from office and conference while she ran the great house as easily as Nicholas's plaything.

Deceptive, like Nicholas. Nicholas, looking happy, was answering that awkward question without a trace of embarrassment. He said, "My companions came to save time. You know our company. We are brokers, dyers, commission agents. We have a cavalry troop. We are already extending from Flanders. We have served your agents as couriers. We have a mind to set up a branch in the Black Sea, in the remaining Greek Empire of Trebizond. We are here to suggest that the Charetty company might represent the merchants of Florence in that country. The Emperor of Trebizond will agree. We can offer him better terms than the Medici could."

"Then you have my congratulations," said Cosimo de' Medici. "You have indeed. For a man of your years to have amassed the means to undercut the Medici makes you, my dear sir, one of the prodigies of the world."

"Oh, our financial arrangement might well be the same as your own," said Nicholas easily. "Only, of course, we should supply them with soldiers."

There was a silence. Then the lord Cosimo de' Medici said, "There, perhaps, we have the theme of a discussion. Stay. I propose to send for some wine, and my son and my secretary. Then we shall talk."

He paused. "Like your plaything. It came, I judge, from the delegation from Persia and Trebizond now lodging at the Franciscan convent in Fiesole? With whom, of course, you have opened this matter."

"Of course," said Nicholas modestly.

Julius caught Tobie's eye, and peered circumspectly to see how the magnificent plan had struck Godscalc. Julius felt successful, and happy, and on the verge of becoming quite rich. The name of Pagano Doria did not even enter his mind.

Chapter 4

O NICHOLAS HIMSELF, the early summons to a meeting with
the lord Cosimo de' Medici was an advantage he had not
expected. Presenting himself, he felt precariously elated. He
was not, by now, straight from the dye vats and felt no
apprehension about the meeting itself. His plans were complex but
could be adapted. He had changed them once already, since coming to
Florence; since receiving the letters from Flanders. But he had told no
one about that.

He had begun to feel better ever since he found the little
delegation sitting there at the Franciscans' at Fiesole. They came,
as Messer Cosimo had said, from Persia; Trebizond; Georgia – the
lands Christian and Moslem which were under threat by the Turk.
Their purpose, led by a practised missionary of the Franciscan
Order, was to rouse the West to send an army to save them. They
had just come from Venice. They were to pass Christmas at Rome.
They were just about to see Cosimo de' Medici. And among them
was an envoy from the Empire of Trebizond who was far less
concerned for the Faith than he was to fix up a trading deal
between Florence and Trebizond.

Nicholas had enjoyed talking to him, all the time he learned how to
make his little toy. Since the envoy was Italian, it was simple. They
had reached a very good understanding, he and the merchant Michael
Alighieri from Trebizond.

It had been unfair of him, after that, to tease Julius and Tobie over
the toy, but sometimes he couldn't prevent himself. They were ten
years older than he was – one a pedagogue and a notary, the other a
highly trained doctor. Until they left Bruges, he had never been quite
sure whether they would come with him on a venture so personal. The
money behind him was that of the Charetty company, but he had
created it himself. If he lost it, the company would be no worse off
than it had been when he was an apprentice. If he increased it, the
profit he made would be his. If he ran into debt, his would be the

responsibility. He had a fund of his own, stored in Venice. Except for utter disaster, he ought to be safe.

It was the hunger for adventure in Julius that had brought him back to Italy, Nicholas thought. That and a spark of generosity and even pride, for Nicholas had been in some sort his acolyte. And also, of course, a dream of personal wealth. He could imagine how Julius saw it. Nicholas was taking the risk, but he had his elders to advise him. If he failed, Julius would argue, of course his wife would empty her long purse to save him. If matters fell out as they might, there could be gold and to spare there for everyone.

And Tobie? What had brought that sardonic doctor from the comforts of the company office in Flanders? Curiosity, he supposed. Curiosity of the intellect, which had brought him to tour Europe binding the wounds of its armies instead of pursuing a safe academic life like that of the famous physician his uncle. And curiosity about himself. The doctor's analytical eye that sometimes saw more than one wanted. Trebizond was his project; and he was Tobie's.

Sometimes, sitting designing something in his own room, Niccolò would let his mouth and cheeks and jaw fall into the semblance of Julius and Tobie and Captain Astorre or Godscalc and the lawyer Gregorio. Under his breath, he would recall, for his own entertainment, their favourite phrases and attitudes; the alarmed cadences of their voices. He liked them all: he meant no harm by it. As a boy he had done it all the time, openly. Now, since his marriage, he didn't. Nor ever made fun of the people close to him, now he was a burgess. And especially never of Marian, who had brought him up. Whom he had married. Whom he had in every way married.

He had heard from her since arriving in Florence. Her lawyer wrote every day, keeping him in touch with exchange rates and commodity demands and the letters arrived in two and threes, delivered by their own Milan couriers. Most he showed to the others; some he kept to himself. None of them, of course, was dated later than October. Marian inserted notes in her own hand: mostly practical adjustments to the lists he was carrying, or snippets of news likely to affect the market, such as the fighting in England to decide whether the Lancastrians or the Yorkists would end up with the throne. Until that was settled, it was unlikely that France or Flanders or England would send a soldier to fight for the Lord in the Levant. That left matters up to the Charetty company.

She said things like that, which made him smile; and mentioned friends sometimes. He was to buy a good rosary for the wife of Anselm Adorne. Lorenzo wished to send greetings to his mother Monna Alessandra, and to say that he had hopes that his father's cousin was failing at last. The lord Simon, who had caused all the trouble, had taken his wife back to Scotland. Tilde was well, and Catherine wrote that she didn't want to come home from Brussels.

All Marian's letters were signed *"your loving wife"*. He didn't need
any more personal message. When he sent the couriers home with his
answers he always included a note of his own. It would say something of
business, but more often include some absurd happening, some ridiculous anecdote that she could tell to Tilde and Gregorio, and then be
persuaded to repeat to her friends. Of love he did not speak either, but
ended each letter *"Thine, Nicholas"*. He knew, none better, how seals
were tampered with. What was private stayed private because it was not
committed to paper. Her restraint when they parted had been sufficient
burden to bear.

Waiting for the lord Cosimo to call in his son and his staff, Nicholas
saw nothing now in the way of capturing the Florentine agency for
Trebizond. He had at the tips of his fingers the privileges of toll, tax and
warehouse, compound, church and lodgings, food and wine and oil and
labour which the Emperor had been prepared to offer the Medici. He
had from Messer Alighieri, as full plenipotentiary, the extra privileges
the Charetty company could expect, in return for one hundred trained
soldiers. And that, passed on in moderation, would make it cheaper by
far for the Medici to employ him than compete with him. He had no fear
that they would offer armed help themselves. Milan had already tried
sending troops east. It had been a disaster.

He was not disappointed. When the Medici son did appear – a zestful
stout man of forty, followed by the men from the chancery with their
pens and their ledgers – the ensuing discussion was challenging, but did
nothing to weaken his case. On the question of troops, it was the old
man himself who interrogated him. Old Cosimo, the urbane head of a
tightly run empire of banking, who studied Plato and filled his house
with artists; who had once stopped a meeting in order to show Cosimino, interrupting, how to fashion his whistle, "and had he asked me, I
would have played on it too". Hearing that, anyone would have known
the farmuk couldn't fail.

Now Cosimo the grandfather said, "So the special terms depend on
the supply of an army. And what does the Emperor think is an army?
Ten? A thousand?"

"He would be content with a hundred, if bowmen."

"And you could take a hundred soldiers round the heel of Italy, up
the Aegean Sea, through the narrows at Constantinople and into the
Black Sea beyond without the Turks stopping you?"

"There are ways," Nicholas said. "Messer Alighieri is confident."
He met the old man's gaze with his own. The merry, shrewd eyes of
Giovanni the son had, he knew, never left him. Giovanni's hands, like
his father's, were twisted with gout. God, jealous of wealth, had visited
Cosimo and both his sons with this affliction. The oddest sight known
to man, so they said, was the spectacle of the three richest men in the
world lying side by side in the same gout-ridden bed, squealing with
anguish.

The lord Cosimo smiled, and his gaze, mildly ironic, shifted to Julius. "Youth and optimism. How fortunate you are in your young master. But let us look, we older people, on the less pleasant side. A company thrives on its reputation as much as on its actual profits. You may not contrive to smuggle your men into Trebizond. The Turk may attack Trebizond and ruin or kill you. The Turk may lay such a stranglehold on your trade that the tolls from the Black Sea will cripple you. If this venture fails, will it bring down your company?"

Nicholas supposed that, in one speech, he had hit on all Julius's own personal fears. But Julius, too, knew his business. "Not at all, monsignore," Julius said. "We are an old, well-funded business. We own our land and our buildings. The lady our owner is highly experienced, and has a good lawyer and excellent managers. The present venture comes from surplus capital and is expendable."

It was the truth, so far as it went. He didn't say what all of them knew, that only the initial funding had been supplied, from its surplus, by the Charetty company; and the risks now belonged to Nicholas personally. If he succeeded, the overall profit would be his. If he failed, he stood to lose what he had, on careful deposit in Venice. If he died – if he died, all he had in Venice or anywhere else would go to Marian. All he had of debts as well. He did not propose to die.

The old man was studying Julius, who gazed back with respectful sincerity. The old man turned to Tobie. "And you, Master Physician? You have no qualms about this heavy outlay?"

Tobie said, "The company's sound. We wouldn't be here if we didn't consider the expansion were possible. Nicholas wouldn't be here without his wife's confidence. What do you mean, a company's reputation?"

It wasn't a question anyone but Tobie would have asked. Messer Cosimo de' Medici smiled at him and said, "I place upon it the same meaning you do. You answered my question precisely." He turned again, and studied Nicholas. "So. Supported by an import tax of four in the hundred and an export tax of two, you will sell and buy goods of your own, and those of other companies for a commission. The Genoese do this already in Trebizond. So do the Venetians. You will not be popular."

"With a hundred soldiers?" said Nicholas. "We shall be popular every time the Sultan gets up from his prayer mat. We shall be popular all the time with the Emperor. He's tired of being exploited by Venice and Genoa. So Messer Alighieri maintains."

"I sometimes wonder," said the lord Cosimo, "if it is because Genoa is so sadly dominated by others at home that she behaves as she does in her outstations. It is a frequent quirk of the colonial. But let us proceed. Tell me. How will you transport all this to and from Trebizond?"

Nicholas produced his confidential voice. It was modelled on no one

Messer Cosimo knew. "I considered a round ship," he said. "But it seems a great galley is best. Fast, coastal, safer. Smaller, of course, but she'd carry a ton and a half of fine goods at higher rates than bulk cargoes could offer. Then, a round trip once a year to begin with; two later. In between, we'd ship wherever space offered. On the state Florentine galleys, at your rates. If you had a year-round flow of Caspian raw silk and dyes, you could level out and increase your production, and so could the spinners and growers."

He paused, to let the secretary catch up. Scribbling, the secretary said, "And your freight rates?"

"For cloth, one florin for each piece of cloth carried, or two per cent of its value. It's reasonable. It makes roughly five thousand florins per unloaded cargo excluding the company's own merchandise. We could manage on that."

"You have thought of everything," said Cosimo de' Medici. "And where would you acquire such a galley? You would buy one?"

"I hope you will sell me one, monsignore," Nicholas said. "If the Medici bank would lend me the money."

The secretary stopped writing and looked up. Giovanni de' Medici smiled. "Dear me," said the lord Cosimo. His face reflected a shadow of pity; a merest shade of impatience. He said, "You cannot pay for a ship? You cannot even contemplate hiring one?"

"I contemplated it," Nicholas said, "but it's cheaper to buy, and with borrowed money. I daresay I could raise a loan elsewhere, if it isn't convenient."

"Dear me," said the lord Cosimo again. He looked at his middle-aged son, who shook his head, visibly saddened. "Such a pity," said Messer Cosimo. "A gallant scheme, a young company. But the least of our galleys can cost five hundred florins."

Godscalc spoke. Nicholas turned his head. Godscalc said, "We are not asking for a state galley in prime condition, monsignore. We should be prepared to take the old galley now lying at Pisa, which suffered the accident on its journey upriver. Messer Martelli put its worth at three hundred florins."

Nicholas gazed at his chaplain, his face straight. In the chair, the old man sat still, in the way of one caught by surprise. Nicholas, obeying speechless direction, added, "And at, of course, a realistic rate of interest, in view of the short earning life of the vessel. Then we can replace it with a better one from profit, and with the slate between us wiped clean."

"Well?" said Cosimo sharply. He had turned to his son Giovanni, who shifted his bulk.

"It is possible," he said to his father.

Nicholas continued to look pleasant and businesslike. He said, "Provided also the ship came checked, guaranteed and fully equipped, to the satisfaction of your shipyard supervisor and my master. And, of course, Messer Martelli, if he would be so kind as to examine her. The rest, of course, falls to my charges."

He sustained, for what seemed a long time, the direct stare of the old man. The son murmured. The old man listened to him, and then to the secretary who bent over him for a moment, a sheet of paper held in one hand. Nicholas watched them with interest. Julius was shuffling. Tobie was wearing a mask of indifference, as if enduring some tedious lecture. Godscalc was smiling slightly, but the smile was more thoughtful than Nicholas liked. Pagano Doria? He'd never heard of him. There was a movement. The secretary withdrew, and Giovanni sat up. The old man started to speak.

He said, "You have convinced me that you are worth a short-term investment. If Messer Alighieri the Imperial envoy agrees, I am prepared to sanction your installation at Trebizond as agent for the Republic of Florence for the trial period of one year, from the time you arrive. I agree to your terms of operation, subject to their confirmation on paper, and their endorsement by Messer Alighieri. The price of the ship is too low. You may have a loan to buy it at three hundred and fifty florins, repayable within twelve months at an interest of twenty florins in the hundred against the security of the property and funds of your parent company. We would require prior confirmation of their credit standing, and their signed acknowledgement of obligation."

"I have powers to sign. And I can provide all the figures," said Nicholas.

"Then you accept?"

"Yes, monsignore. I thank you. I do." He could see the apprehension on the faces of his faint-hearted colleagues. It hurt to keep his face grave all the time the old man was concluding.

"Then Messer Alighieri will be invited to call, and the authority will be drawn up in a form agreeable to all parties, and presented for signing in due course. There will have to be a copy in Greek. Your notary is Messer Julius here? Perhaps he will remain. He may use my interpreter unless, of course, you object."

"No need," Nicholas said. "Master Julius studied Greek in Bologna. He was secretary to Cardinal Bessarion, who was born in Trebizond."

The lord Cosimo looked weary rather than thunderstruck. "Indeed! I find the combined accomplishments of your company, Messer Niccolò, somewhat daunting. Let us drink, then, to the successful outcome of a new contract. Wine, Giovanni."

"Vermin!" somebody said.

The voice came from the door. Although less than a shout, the remark was delivered with a certain snarling sonority that struck all competition into silence. The old man's nose drew towards his lips, like that of a goose. His son heaved to his feet. The secretary and two clerks were already hastening to the door, arms outstretched defensively. They staggered back, as the man who had spoken thrust past them and strode into the room. He came to a halt before Julius.

He was a monk: a man of middle height and some bulk, wearing the grey habit and tonsure of a preaching Franciscan – a Minorite friar of the harsh Observantine reform. A curiously untidy man, for all the simplicity of his garments, with a high-coloured face that seemed an explosion of pitted skin and black hair. Hair grew from the cavities of his stoutly boned nose and tufted his ears beneath the vigorous curls, and lay submerged in planes of threatening indigo below the curves of his jowl. His eyebrows sprouted hair, and the backs of his hands. There was hair on the nape of his neck. Naked among all this herbage were his underlids, pale and curved as the lip of a drinking-glass.

He pointed a finger at Julius. Something orange had stained it. He said, "Cosimo de' Medici, you do not know with whom you are dealing. Stop your congress. Destroy your agreement. Drive this man from your house and this company from your door. That man is Satan."

"Julius?" Nicholas said. He caught, successfully, a note of pleased interest.

No one smiled. Julius had gone ivory white, as if about to throw up in public. Tobie, after one glance at him and at Nicholas, had fixed the monk with a glare. The lord Cosimo's sallow face was without expression; his son looked angry. Father Godscalc got to his feet and, astonishingly, spoke to the interloper. He said, "Fra Ludovico, this is a meeting private to my lord Cosimo. He will hear you later, I'm sure."

Fra Ludovico. Attentively, Nicholas considered the name. He had heard it in Fiesole. The deputation from Georgia and Persia and Trebizond was led by a monk: a Ludovico da Severi who travelled the world for the Franciscans. He had been absent when Nicholas called. Good timber merchants, the da Severi, Alighieri had said. A son of that stable would have nothing against mixing crusades and business: a Charetty army in Trebizond was just what would best please their leader.

Well, if this was the same man, he had changed his mind. About the Charetty company and its officers. Julius, Julius: why won't you look at me?

Father Godscalc, having drawn the enemy gun, was suffering its bombardment.

"You would shut the mouth of the Lord's servant?" the monk was demanding of him. "You, a man of the Church! I will cry your sin as I cry theirs. You consort with thieves and fornicators: their torment will be your torment." He turned to the head of the Medici bank. A cloud of saliva lingered behind him. "Fling them from you! That man is a pollution!" He pointed at Julius again.

Everyone except Cosimo was now standing, but no one moved. They all looked at the tall old man in the chair.

Cosimo de' Medici addressed the monk. His voice was quite flat. "This gentleman is named Julius, a Bologna notary now employed by the Charetty dyers of Bruges. You have a complaint against him?"

"I know who he is," said the monk. "The convent-bred son of a student priest and an unmarried woman. The Church taught him his letters; the college of notaries showed him how to make money. Perhaps there are honest notaries: I have never met one. At any rate, this one was not. He stole the money entrusted to him and gambled with it. Church money, lost in sin and depravity. Then, when found out, he appealed to our saintly Bessarion of Nicaea, who made the loss good from his pocket. The man Julius was whipped from the city. I had thought him safely employed in some wicker hut in Geneva. But now I find him here, gulling your lordship!"

The blood rushed to Julius's face. He opened his mouth. Cosimo de' Medici said, "You will remain quiet, Master Julius. I am first concerned to question your colleagues. Is this known to you, Messer Tobias? Father Godscalc? Merchant Niccolò, are the owners of the Charetty company aware of this?"

Quicker than anyone, Julius got in his answer. "They don't know," he said.

Messer Cosimo probably reckoned it was true. Certainly, Father Godscalc, of no long acquaintance with the company, didn't contradict him. Tobie, his short lips in a bunch, stood surveying his feet and said nothing. It was left to Nicholas to move forward gently until he stood in the space beside Julius. He scratched his nose and said, "Well, yes, we knew. That is, the demoiselle de Charetty knew. The rest of us weren't supposed to. But" – he threw an apologetic grimace at Julius – "it was all round the yard that Master Julius couldn't afford a new tunic and hose until he'd finished paying his debts to the Widow . . . as they called the lady then. Afterwards she told me. Half his wage went to Rome, for Cardinal Bessarion. So whatever he did – and I don't know what it was – he atoned for it. And the Charetty company knew of it, and kept him. And all the time I've had a view of the ledgers, there's been nothing that a judge could take exception to. Or I shouldn't be here. Nor would he."

Fra Ludovico hardly waited for the last words. "He has admitted the theft. There is no proof that he restored the money: the Cardinal of Nicaea is in Germany. And whether he restored it or not, he is a confessed and unpunished rogue." He turned. "Is this, my lord Cosimo, to be your ambassador?"

"Let him speak himself," said the old man.

Owning up, Julius always stood straight. He had stood like this back in Bruges, when discovered in some fearsome escapade for which most of the blame belonged to Nicholas, his apprentice-servant; or else was truly the folly of Felix, Marian's son. Marian's late and only son.

Julius had never had to make an admission like this before. Julius said, "My birth is as you've heard. My parents died long ago. My father left what would pay for my education, but there was no understanding that I would remain with the Church. I think, had I been born of a normal marriage, I would have become a soldier. It isn't relevant."

"Go on," said Cosimo.

Julius said, "We were all wild at Bologna. We gambled, and other things. But once you qualify, it has to be different. Cardinal Bessarion was papal legate in Bologna then. He ran the city. I served in his chancery. He showed me that the quickest way to success was to become a cardinal's secretary. That was how the present Pope rose."

"You would call the Pope as your witness!" said the Minorite. "How can you listen to this?"

"In fairness," said the lord Cosimo. "Continue."

"Of course, I was silly," said Julius. "He was kind to me. He said he thought me the brightest of all his secretariat, but without the experience, yet, that I would have needed in Rome. The cardinal was beloved in Bologna: he could have stayed in the city for life. He promised me that in six months I should be his chief secretary, with all the salary that would go with it. I had been living well but economically. Now I thought that at last I could live as I deserved; have the pleasures I'd missed. I moved into a better house, and bought the clothes I needed, and hired servants . . . I drank good wine. I gave feasts for my friends. When I was asked to play dice with men I admired I didn't hesitate. And when my ready money ran out, I borrowed from the annates I had collected, because I could replace them from the first of my salary." He stopped.

"And then?" said Cosimo.

"And then the Pope died," said Julius simply. "And my lord Bessarion rushed off to Rome for the election. If he had been made Supreme Pastor, I suppose all my troubles would have been over. But they elected Calixtus, a Borgia. And the Pope sent his own nephew to Bologna in Bessarion's place."

He gave a sour grin. "I didn't know him, and he didn't know me. He brought his own clerks. All my bills of payment fell due, including the church funds, the annates; and I was ruined. Brother Ludovico knows, because his family came from Bologna, and he and the other Franciscans saw a lot of the Pope in those days. Constantinople had fallen two years before." He paused. "I knew of course about this deputation. I should have realised that the same man was leading it."

"And then you could have confessed to your employer. Perhaps," said Cosimo de' Medici. "Did you repay the money as Messer Niccolò claims?"

"Eventually," Julius said. "It was the cardinal who paid all my debts. I paid him back when I could."

"And who besides the cardinal can confirm this? You have heard he is in Germany."

"Marian de Charetty. Whom Nicholas married," Julius said. "You've heard. She entrusted me with all her business."

"But she is in Bruges. Who else employed you?"

"A man in Geneva," said Julius. He kept his face stiffly from Nicholas. "I never saved enough to repay more than a little. And besides, he is dead."

"Fra Ludovico?" said the old man.

The monk looked up at the chair. The eye nearest Nicholas resembled an egg on a spoon. He said, "Do I need to say more? The man is dishonest, the company heedless at best; at worst, as corrupt as himself. Send yourself to Trebizond. Do not try to satisfy God with a second-hand agent. Where the Church itself is in dreadful retreat, the unholy will never conquer the heathen."

Father Godscalc cleared his throat. "Your Persian envoy," he said, "is, I understand, of the Moslem faith?"

"What of it?" said the other man sharply. The top of his head, under the stubble, had turned a cochineal red. "I have spent my life abroad with the heathen. Do you think I cannot distinguish between the innocent pagan and the man born to the Cross who despises it, ignores it, treats it as would a limb of the Devil? The prince Uzum Hasan has not yet found the path to God, but he has a Christian wife, a mother raised in the Faith. His wife's confessor strives for him daily. That prince's envoy is living proof that Uzum Hasan seeks better things. Look at this Julius, with his smooth face and rich clothes and plausible manner. He was raised by the Church, and he consumed the goods of the Church in sinful riotous living. Which is worse?"

"He didn't invent the farmuk, either," Nicholas said. "My lord, the folly isn't disputed. But it was five years ago, and redress has followed. And the honesty of this company is unassailable. Your Bruges agents know in what ways we have served the Medici."

"I have that in mind," said Cosimo, with a certain small emphasis that Nicholas was glad to hear. "But my confidence is worth little if you lose the trust of the Church and the Emperor. Fra Ludovico: what if the notary Messer Julius were dismissed? Would the firm commend itself then?"

"He will not be dismissed," Nicholas said, without imitating anybody. He saw Tobie look round.

"Then the company had best go back to Bruges," said the Minorite, without moving his eyes. "There is work for its chaplain to do."

The suggestion, hurled against the monolithic form of Father Godscalc, brought a sigh from the priest. He said, "Well, brother, there is no doubt the world would be better if we all had your zeal in the Lord. I have a question, if Messer Cosimo will forgive me. Did I see you outside with a friend of mine?"

Across his folded arms, the friar inspected the priest. "I doubt it," he said.

"But I could hardly be wrong. Pagano Doria, newly landed from Porto Pisano? From his interest in me, I'm afraid, he became intrigued by the plans of the Charetty company. It occurred to me that perhaps we owed this visit of yours to something he suggested or told you?"

Silence.

Cosimo de' Medici said, "Well?"

The monk said, "The man is hardly a friend. An acquaintance. It was from him that I learned, yes, that the wealth of Florence was about to be placed in the hands of that miserable man. I chose to warn you. I have not looked for thanks."

"Giovanni?" said the old man. "We have heard, have we not, of Pagano Doria?"

Giovanni de' Medici gave an affectionate smile. "Of course, my father," he said. "He called here but this morning, to visit the Milanese envoy. He too leaves soon for Trebizond."

In the distance, Nicholas heard the old man say, "Indeed?" For a moment he lost track of the voices in the room. He thought of Marian, and all that might be happening in Bruges. He felt cold. His blood, warm and quick just five minutes ago, was crawling sluggish and chill through his veins. He found Giovanni the son was explaining something.

"But yes," he was saying, "Messer Doria's ship lies in Porto Pisano with its crew already spoken for, and its cargo beginning to mount in the warehouse. He sets sail after Christmas, I am told. In a round ship."

"I see," said the old man. He sighed. "Human nature. One can never be certain, Fra Ludovico. Here, it seems, is a man who gave you the most disinterested information which led you – with the best of intentions – to throw doubt on the honesty of the Charetty company. Your doubts may be justified. We have not been able to satisfy ourselves one way or the other. But what does appear evident is that this Pagano Doria was not disinterested. He hoped your warnings would dissuade us. He hoped the Charetty company would indeed be sent back to Bruges and that – surely? – he himself would be appointed as Florentine consul to the Emperor David."

"Is it possible?" said Tobie abruptly.

"It seems rather likely," said Nicholas.

"It is not so," said Cosimo's son Giovanni. "Not at all. I have said that Messer Pagano Doria sails for Trebizond. It is true. He proposes to settle and trade there. But he cannot represent Florence because he has already accepted another appointment. Pagano Doria, my father, is the new Black Sea consul for Genoa."

"*Genoa!*" Godscalc exclaimed.

Nicholas stood completely still, thinking. Then, aloud, he said what he thought. "It isn't so serious. We knew we'd have resentment to fight, and from the Genoese more than from Venice. Once in Trebizond, the common danger will draw us together. Till then, we shall have to be careful, that's all." He said to Godscalc, "You knew? Or suspected?"

"Suspected," the chaplain said. "Doria and I met at Pisa, perhaps not quite by accident. There was no word of a voyage to Trebizond. Afterwards, I made some enquiries. Fra Ludovico, I fear you've been used. It alters things. It might suggest to monsignore that the Charetty company could be trusted at least for so long as it would take to send to Cardinal Bessarion, wherever he is, and obtain his judgement on the matter of Master Julius?"

The Minorite made to speak. The old man held up his hand. "No," he said. "The decision is mine."

Nicholas waited, looking round at the silent gathering; wondering at the power of one clever man. At length, Cosimo de' Medici shifted in his chair. He said, "My conclusion is this. The Charetty company shall represent Florence, and papers will be drawn up to that effect. Messages will also be sent to my lord the Cardinal of Nicaea. In the event of an unfavourable reply, Florence will withdraw her support of the Charetty company. The Emperor will be informed. Florentine merchants will be told that they no longer need honour their contracts. If you have already departed, you may well arrive in Trebizond to find that you cannot recoup on your voyage. The risk is yours. Are you willing to incur it?"

"Yes, my lord," Nicholas said.

The old man held his eyes, it seemed to him, for a long time. Then he turned. "Fra Ludovico, what do you say?"

The monk's ruddy colour had cooled. "There are good Christians as well as bad in Genoa, my lord," he said. "I hope to learn what news the Cardinal sends. I bow, of course, to your lordship's judgement. But I would not lend gold, or send valuable cargo. You and your colleagues would lose it."

Nicholas spoke quickly. "We don't ask for gold; merely a ship on deferred purchase terms. Sequester the ship if you don't get the money. Call on my company if you can't obtain either."

"And the cargo?" said Cosimo de' Medici. "The good friar has a point."

Nicholas said, "I, not the merchant, would pay the insurance costs. I should expect him to refund it when satisfied."

Julius said, "Nicholas. It isn't fair. Our budget won't stand that." He had turned from pale to patchily livid.

The lord Cosimo said, "Indeed, that seems a little extreme. We are not talking of a group of blackguards, Father Ludovico; only of a past misdemeanour of one, now exposed to his masters." He turned to

Nicholas. "I will guarantee the insurance. I require you to sign the papers as well as your notary. That will satisfy me. I trust Fra Ludovico is equally satisfied."

"Thank you, my lord," Nicholas said. He looked at the friar. And after a moment the friar, too, bent his neck. He did not look submissive. But he had agreed.

"And *now*," said a voice.

A little slowly, Nicholas turned. The well-upholstered figure of Giovanni de' Medici stood before him. Giovanni de' Medici said, "I have business with you." He opened his palm. "Cosimino has rent the ears of his nurse and his mother because this thing has become tangled. This toy. This thing that walks. Who can restore it?"

Nicholas wrinkled his brow. "I suppose I can," he said. "But in return, of course, for certain business concessions."

Together, he and the lord Cosimo's son bent their heads over the toy, while Julius got out his penner and crossed to speak to the secretary. His hand was visibly shaking. Whereas Nicholas, fully himself, turned the farmuk in hands that were large and firm and warm as a mason's. The trial was over; and the lists cleared for the battle.

Chapter 5

OUTSIDE THE PALAZZO MEDICI unlikely things started to happen as soon as the Charetty company emerged into the late afternoon rain.

First, Nicholas dismissed the two servants. Then, ignoring questions, he walked down to the Arno, unlocked the door of a warehouse nobody knew he had rented, and invited his three companions to enter before him. Then he shut the door and confronted them.

Julius, who had continued to resist long after the chaplain and Tobie had fallen silent, was still repeating, ". . . do you think you are doing?" He stopped. His eye twitched.

"Calling you a fool to your face," Nicholas said. "Why in the name of the Ever-Virgin Mother of God did you not tell me what went wrong in Bologna?"

There was a pause. "You said everyone knew," Tobie said. He used the voice Julius mistrusted most.

"How should I know?" said Nicholas. "I was an apprentice." His expression was uniquely unpleasant.

Julius looked at him, confounded. From the time Nicholas was eighteen, squabbles, arguments had been the common history of their relationship. Since Nicholas had married the demoiselle de Charetty they had all, to their periodic annoyance, had to modify their behaviour in public. Nicholas *was* the Charetty company, and you didn't therefore take the back of your hand to him. When he had good ideas Julius, like everyone else, was ready enough to adopt them. But he wasn't ready – by God, he was not – to accept a full-blown tongue-lashing before his own senior colleagues. He said, "You silly young – "

He was interrupted by Father Godscalc, who addressed himself smoothly to Nicholas. "If you didn't know, you spoke most convincingly. About the repayments, for instance. But if, uh . . ."

"If Nicholas didn't guess right, and Julius didn't repay the money, Cardinal Bessarion is going to ruin the Charetty company. Well, well," said Tobie in the same voice as before.

"Of course I repaid it!" said Julius. "Do you think I'm a thief? Do you think I enjoyed standing there and telling the whole story?" Do you think, he drew breath to say, that I would bother telling all that to the most shiftless serving apprentice in Flanders? He didn't say it, since it was obvious.

Nicholas said, "Did you tell *nobody*?"

Up to that point, guilt had helped to moderate the notary's natural indignation, but there were limits. Julius snapped, "My God, who should I have told? The Eight on Security? The City Rackmaster?"

"Any member of this company who would bother to listen," Nicholas snapped in return. "We're here to raise funds on the strength of our name. Who'll trust us if we don't know the facts about one another? We'd have been spared all this nonsense if just one other person – Tobie, Gregorio – had been warned."

"And had informed you," Julius said. "You don't see it yet, do you? Who cares if a servant is born out of wedlock? You never did. Although you never brought yourself, did you, to tell us the truth about your quarrel with your famous Scottish lord Simon until it blew up in your face, and you had to leave Bruges? Bastardy isn't anyone's fault, but a professional man is judged by his reputation. Do you think Cornelis de Charetty would have taken me on if he'd known I was in trouble with the Church? Use your head."

"I need to, don't I," said Nicholas, "if you're not going to use yours? How's it going to help you keep afloat if you wreck your employer's business? It's also a trifle unfair to Godscalc and Tobie and Gregorio. They have reputations as well. If you see trouble coming, then tell them. I can assure you that they won't pass it on: they don't think I'm reliable. But they'll tell you if they think you've lost your wits or your senses or even your sense of what's funny. What do you say?"

"Go away," Julius said simply. He used different words, from his Bologna days.

"I'm going," Nicholas said, "to be agent for Florence in Trebizond. It's a question of where you are heading for."

"So you want me to leave. I'll leave," Julius said. "You couldn't keep me."

"Julius," Tobie said. It was his sweetest voice. "Think again, Julius. Nicholas stood up in there and told the Medici to tear up their contract because he wasn't going to dismiss you. Does that sound as if he wants you to leave?"

Julius felt himself flushing, but drew in breath, hard, through his nostrils. He said, "I'm going to ruin the company, am I not? So is Nicholas, but we always said we could control him. Or if we couldn't, we'd leave. I think he's more in control than I want him to be. I think I'm getting out."

The chaplain spoke. Whatever he said, irritatingly, his voice remained melodious. He said, "That would indeed ruin the company, I should think, just at this juncture. I am sure Nicholas will not make the point, so I will. We must appear undivided. Could you not see your way to . . . to deferring your departure for a week or so?"

"Until we're at sea," Tobie said. His voice sounded odd. "Far at sea, Julius. Then if you want to leave, we'll all help you."

Julius realised the sound he heard was Nicholas trying not to laugh. He looked at Father Godscalc and saw him suspiciously compressing his lips. Tobie suddenly let out a chirrup. Tobie exploding always sounded like one of his retorts on the boil. Tobie said, "Who was she, my boy? We loved the solemn confession. *A better house, a servant, some good wine . . . the mortal sin of the dice.* My son, you have sinned. Get thee to hell, eating black bread and yesterday's mince with the devils. But what *didn't* we hear? Go on. You owe us all something. Blow by blow, what did you spend all that money on?"

An austere man would have nursed his anger and held out. Julius, who was still, in his soul, half a student, stared at his colleagues and then unclosed his fists. "Oh well, you can imagine," he said. "There was this place where the cook had some dice. I told you about it. I didn't say it was me. It was incredible. It was truly incredible. We used to meet . . ."

They ended up rather drunk in a tavern. Gently maudlin, Julius allowed himself to be led back to Monna Alessandra's austere house and laid in his room by the chaplain and Tobie. On the way back to the parlour and Nicholas, Godscalc slowed down and halted the other man. "Before we go in. Who is Simon?"

"Who?" said Tobie.

Godscalc, who was merely mellow, repeated himself. "A kinsman of Nicholas?"

"Oh, that!" Tobie said. "Simon de St Pol. Landed. Wealthy. A merchant. Splits his time between Scotland and Bruges. Nicholas was brought up to think him his father. Instead, it turned out he was just the wife's bastard. My lord Simon disapproves deeply of Nicholas and threatened to ruin his business. That's why Nicholas is here, and not in Bruges nursing his marriage. Pity Ludo the Goodo hadn't found out about that. It wouldn't have mattered to anyone."

"Except Nicholas?" Godscalc said.

But instead of replying, the doctor merely pulled the cap from his head by one lappet and, entering the parlour, waved the object at Nicholas. Round his heated bald head, the fine, light hair was damp as a cat's. He said, "And which of my weaknesses, dear bastard apprentice, do you plan to turn to your purpose? I'm afraid Father Godscalc has none."

In tribute, Nicholas contorted the lower half of his face. "I'm sure I'll find something," he said. He was pulling notes out of his satchel and scattering them prodigally over a table. His face was pink.

"It won't last, the contrition, you know," Tobie said. "And Julius doesn't like being scolded by juniors. Even by senior juniors." He sat in the windowseat.

"So that's why you'll do it in future," Nicholas said. "You or whoever he goes to. Weren't you listening back there?"

"Am I your catshpaw?" said Tobie.

"Yesh," said Nicholas. He found what he was looking for, unfolded and smoothed it, and then held it out to the doctor. "And that's your reward in advance. Second column on the . . ."

". . . left; third down," said Tobie incomprehensibly. "You bastard. I couldn't get anyone to sell me one."

"What is it?" said Godscalc with interest. For a big man, he sat down like an athlete.

"Instructions on how to spend annates," said Nicholas. "Father, this afternoon you matriculated in clerical cunning. I hope it brought its own satisfaction, because I don't know how else to thank you."

"Godscalc and I find you fascinating," Tobie said. "So you think there will be fighting?"

"It's why we are being allowed to go east," Nicholas said. "If we survive, so much the better. If not, the Medici will be seen to have launched a token crusade. The Pope can't then dun them for anything."

"I'd worked that out," said Tobie. "What are my chances of coming back?"

"The same as mine," Nicholas said. "Better."

"I suppose so," said Tobie. "You're the Florentine consul and head of the first, tender offshoot of the Charetty company. Pick you off, and anyone with a grudge knows that the rest of us will pack and go home. That is, I certainly will. Julius might come over stubborn."

"And you, father?" said Nicholas.

Godscalc considered. "I suppose I'd have to stay so that Julius could confide in me. Does nobody want to know about Pagano Doria?"

"No," said Tobie. "World's full of Dorias."

Godscalc said, "This isn't one of the main branch."

Nicholas said, "How did you meet him?"

Godscalc watched Tobie's eyes close. "I saw his round ship in Porto Pisano," he said. "It had the new rig, which was interesting; and so was its cargo. Hides and French wine and Spanish wool. It had just made a short stop at Genoa, and was supposed to be planning a trip east at Candlemas. The ship's name was *Doria.*"

"And you remembered," said Nicholas, "that long ago a Doria was consul in Trebizond. Another of them refused the same job quite recently."

"I knew they had interests all over the Levant. I was curious. I walked round the harbour and discovered something else. There was talk about an old galley the Medici had ordered to be warped up to Pisa for refitting. They wondered what fools of merchants were buying it."

"Us," said Nicholas.

"Of course. My lord Cosimo's elaborate debate was just a performance. That is, the farmuk was brilliant, but you didn't need it. The bank had got the galley in readiness. They intended us to go to Trebizond from the beginning. The only person who could have stopped them was Fra Ludovico."

"With the help of the inventive Messer Pagano," Nicholas said. "Did he want to stop us, or delay us, or merely remind us of our lowly station? Did you talk to him?"

"At Pisa," said the priest. "It was he who caused the accident to the ship. Minor damage, but it could have been worse, and we got it cheap in the long run because of it. I don't know. I had the feeling that he knew who the galley was meant for. The wharfmen at Porto Pisano possibly told him some gossip. I even had the feeling he already knew who employed me, although I don't know how that came about. But his attitude was not . . . threatening."

"What, then?" said Nicholas. The large gaze, intent, was disconcerting.

Godscalc said, "He is a frivolous man. It's hard to tell what lies beneath it. Perhaps nothing. In which case he's all the more dangerous."

"He is Genoese consul," said Nicholas. "I would rather hear he was frivolous than think he had the weight of Genoese state policy behind him. Or the support of their merchants in Bruges."

"The Genoese merchants in Bruges? I thought Anselm Adorne was your friend."

Nicholas said, "He is also a friend of the Dorias. I wish I knew more. I will know more."

"How?" said Godscalc. Tobie had opened an eye.

"By asking Pagano Doria. He's in Florence. You know him. I'll call on him tomorrow."

Father Godscalc, whose study was mankind in undress, was extremely content, the following morning, to set out with his precocious master to visit the amiable, amorous sea prince of his Pisa encounter. They left Julius in bed. Tobie, who had exhibited a strongly casual interest, had been dissuaded from coming. The degree of Tobie's fascination with Nicholas sometimes grated on Godscalc.

On the walk through the town, Godscalc imparted what he knew of those fertile Genoese the Doria who were able, two centuries since, to field two hundred and fifty kinsfolk in any one battle. The family owned prodigious property, had interests in banking; had produced great seamen, admirals, army commanders.

Godscalc said, "This particular Doria we are visiting is not responsible to any of the known Doria companies. He has been in the Levant, and in Sardinia, and has had an interest in many different concerns, not all of which have prospered. But at present, it seems, he is well enough placed. His clothes are rich, his attendants sufficient. His manner would be acceptable in the highest circles. And if the round ship is his, he must have good dividends, or the confidence of a well-funded banker."

"Then he is an adventurer?" Nicholas said. All the time he was talking, Godscalc saw, his eyes were moving, from face to face, from building to building. Sometimes an adult would return a slight bow. Twice, a child shouted a greeting. In two days, he seemed to have met a lot of people. They were now in the Orsanmichele quarter, and passing the silk merchants' counting-houses. Soon they would come to the Via Por Santa Maria, where the Bianchi silk offices were. In their wide sheds and basements, the manufacturers received the sticky raw silk and sent out their scurrying messengers to low, dark homes all over the city where the spinners, the weavers, the throwsters, the warpers, the dyers each did their work, until the bales lay ready for export: the deep, glossy silks and profound, jewel-bright velvets for which Florence was known.

Soon, Nicholas or Tobie or Julius would be calling on all these men – the Bianchi, the Parenti, the manager of the Medici silk workshop – to contract for silk to sell in Trebizond, and obtain orders for rare dyes and raw silk to bring back again. Pagano Doria was to sail east after Christmas. February was the earliest any round ship could normally leave, and as early as Nicholas, too, would be able to cross the seas safely. The two might well set out for the Black Sea together, the round ship depending on wind, and the galley depending on oars.

Normally, there would be no competition, for different ships carried different cargoes. Nevertheless, thought Father Godscalc, it would be interesting to find out what Genoa was sending to Trebizond. If they discovered. He knew, from his encounter with Pagano Doria, that there was about the Genoese sea prince a polish, a subtlety, that no apprentice, however gifted, had the means to acquire. He didn't wish ill to the youth now walking beside him but, like Tobie, he felt he had been made party to a piece of arbitrary management and, lacking Tobie's clinical detachment, he could not find it in him to approve, no matter how clearly he understood it. Embarking on his first major project surrounded by older, capable men, Nicholas had to seize what chance he could of ascendancy. But he was of obscure birth, and just nineteen years old. And Pagano Doria was not Julius.

The sea prince's house, when they reached it, was not large but exceptionally elegant. Something about the lanterns, the courtyard, the greenery spoke of the feminine, and the chaplain felt no surprise when, on being ushered up the wide steps to the salon, the first impression he had was one of a thick, citrous scent not unlike incense. It had no obvious source, but resided in the carpets, the heavy fringed cloth of the table cover, the pierced container from which warmth drifted into the room. It seemed to say that the owner of the house was not Pagano Doria, and that she was not far away. He looked at Nicholas. "Au revoir," Nicholas said, walking forward. "As the foxes say at the furrier's." Godscalc chuckled.

Doria entered almost as soon as his manservant departed to summon him. He came in on his toes, like a swordsman or a dancing-master, as if in mockery of the two tall, stolid men standing before him. But there was nothing malicious in his expression (if nothing contrite either). He said, "My dear friend Father Godscalc, how happy I am to see you again, even if you have come to chastise me. And this is your genius, the gifted fellow all Florence is talking of. Messer Niccolò vander Poele, is it not?"

Nicholas took a step forward. Beside tawny velvet, his cloth pourpoint and jacket looked undoubtedly workmanlike. In the scarred and unscarred sides of his face, the dimples made pits of coyness: his open eyes were as clear as an infant's. Godscalc thought again what a handsome head the Genoese had, well set on his powerful shoulders. His legs, too, swelled and tapered to his heeled silken slippers, all to scale, so that his lack of height was hardly noticed unless you stood close, as Nicholas did. Nicholas said, smiling down, "It takes one genius to know another, my lord. Why should Father Godscalc chastise you?"

"Sit!" said Pagano Doria. "There and there, and be comfortable. And you will take malmsey and ginger? It is freshly drawn from the keg; the ginger, pure. You have your own famous doctor – what need you fear? For of course you do not know me: you wonder if I am malicious. Am I right?"

Swiftly, they were all seated and the difference in height had been banished. Wine was poured and offered and courteously drunk. To Godscalc it tasted as normal. Godscalc said, "You must know I have been told of your appointment."

Doria smiled. "And I of Messer Niccolò's. I salute him."

Nicholas smiled again. "Thank you, my lord. It would seem to explain the damaged galley and the information laid against Master Julius. At any rate, the Milanese ambassador has agreed to see me this afternoon, and he will no doubt wish to send north, to discover whether these acts of subversion are supported by official Genoese policy. Florence, naturally, would be unhappy to think so. And obstructing a Christian army will not commend any kingdom or state to the Pope."

Godscalc blinked. The sea prince also checked for a moment. Then Doria sprang to his feet and, placing his cup carefully down, laid a light hand on one of Nicholas's shoulders. He knelt, without removing his hand. Unbidden, Godscalc thought of Tobie when quizzing an imbecile. The Genoese said, "But what is this? My appointment wasn't confirmed until I came to Florence – I had no reason to damage your ship; I was chaffing your good priest about it. How could I have known it was yours? It belonged to the State. And as for your notary . . ." He removed his hand and rocked back on his heels, drawing a stool and collecting his wine as he sat on it. Hands clasped round the cup, he shook his head, smiling faintly.

"Did it seem suspicious? I merely met Fra Ludovico in the street, and answered his questions about all my doings. I had been most struck by all I had heard of you, and your company. You do not know how impressed these Florentines are. And he, anxious to know who goes to Trebizond, asked for the names of these eminent men. I fear it was no fault of mine that he recognised that of Master Julius. He had met him before in unhappier times. When I realised it, I was sorry, but there was nothing I could do. Either the man would be vindicated, or a weak link in your great company would be cut away. I could not see great harm being done."

"But you were not surprised by our visit," said Nicholas.

"No," said Pagano Doria. "Wise men make due enquiries before they reach conclusions. I thought you might come. But Father Godscalc I knew for a good man, who treats his fellow-men generously. I should say to him, by the way – Father: keep no secrets on my behalf. I have taken my leave of the lady, who has confessed to her husband. Tell Messer Niccolò what you wish. A man like Messer Niccolò is no stranger to the lovely dilemma, when beauty swears she will die unless you give her your favours."

The wine was pure, but it was extremely strong. Through a faint haze, Father Godscalc saw Pagano Doria smile at the younger man, and heard Nicholas say, "I must not, of course, contradict what you say under your roof. As a man happily married, however, my only concern must be my wife's present and future well-being. The ambassador will find you here if he wishes to question you?"

Again, the threat. And now the priest was sure that the sea prince was disturbed by it. But why? The Milanese envoy lodged with the Medici, but that was simply a mark of the unspoken alliance between the old man Cosimo and the Duke of Milan. And Milan itself had an interest in neighbouring Genoa, whose turbulent citizens rebelled like the storms of the sea, unseating doge after doge.

And there, of course, was the nub of the case. Milan disliked the present French interference with Genoa. Milan disliked the French, and was as determined as Florence and Naples to keep them from power in Italy. So Milan would not care to see a French puppet (as they might see Pagano) ousting a Medici-backed Charetty company. Milan might see to it, quite simply, that the Genoese round ship never left Porto Pisano.

Pagano Doria lifted his arm and swallowed his wine with a flourish. "Ah, my dear Messer Niccolò, if you must know," he said, "I have received no instructions from Genoa. I shall, of course, do my best to make them a fitting consul, but that is their only concern. There are no deep-laid plots here against Florence. Merely . . . I have a living to make. And a talent for amusing myself, and sometimes others. Men of genius, serious men, must despise me. I doubt if you need be afraid of me, though. You, with your soldiers, your staff men like the doctor, the lawyer, the chaplain here. If I tried to cause mischief, I abjectly failed. You are Florentine consul, and you are leaving in due course for Trebizond. What can I do to harm you, and why?"

"Sink my ship. Steal my markets. Serve double-strength wine," Nicholas said.

"Shall I water it?" said Doria. The eyes, bright as a pheasant's, were for a second derisive.

"Only if it discommodes you," said Nicholas. "After all, we shall shortly have something to celebrate. What will you take for your ship and its contents?"

Doria's back slowly straightened. His lips, shapely and red, parted in a smile of delight. He said, "A munificent gesture. My dear Messer Niccolò! You will cripple the Medici family! I am sorely tempted."

"Then accept," Nicholas said. "No unpleasant voyage in February; no threat of war with the Turk, or with me." His voice was perfectly pleasant, but Godscalc saw that his gaze and that of the Genoese were locked together. Then, with a sound like a small sigh, the Genoese sea prince looked away. "Alas!" he said. "Even if you could borrow so large a sum – "

"I can," Nicholas said.

Godscalc looked at him.

So did Pagano Doria. "I think I believe you," he said. "But even so, the fortune I shall make in Trebizond, Messer Niccolò, will be much larger. Without, of course, detracting from yours. There is plenty for all. The land of the Golden Fleece. The land of Colchis, where the flying ram made its way, the gift of Hermes. Whither Jason was sent on his impossible mission; sailed on *Argo* advised by his wooden oracle; reaped the fields full of soldiers; drugged the dragon with Medea's assistance."

He laughed. "In Burgundy, they've created an order named after it, haven't they? Supposed to summon men to free Constantinople. To rouse the Christian world, as that fool Fra Ludovico thinks he's doing. But you can't govern a state with paternosters – who said that? And the great Order of the Golden Fleece was really invented, so they say, by Duke Philip in honour of the fleece at his mistress's thighs. Have you heard that?"

"Everyone's heard that," said Nicholas. "Which do you want to be? Jason, the ram or the dragon?"

"I am quite happy," said the Genoese, "being Pagano Doria, unambitious though it may appear. I intend to go to Trebizond. We shall compete in some things. I shall not promise to be an easy opponent, but you are free to deal likewise with me. If you are afraid, or do not believe me, of course you will inform Milan and have me stopped. But I see a courage in you, a liking for risk and adventure that does not stoop to old men's expediencies. But it is for you to say."

Godscalc glanced at Nicholas. He appeared sober still, except that his colour was a little high, and his eyes very bright. He was looking directly at the other man. A long moment went by. Then he said, "Yes. If it must be."

Pure delight informed the sea prince's face. It was, you now saw, a self-seeking face; an artful face. But its expression was not one solely of triumph in the wake of an interview that might well have ruined him. It was one of outright rank happiness, as of a man stepping into an arena which he knew would lead, through whatever teasing and testing and trickery, to a reward of undreamed-of riches.

Nicholas rose, his gaze on the other, and Godscalc could make nothing of the look on his face. Then he put down his cup and without thanks, or farewell, or courtesy, turned and walked out of the door.

On the way from the courtyard he passed, with hardly a glance, the figure of a short, well-dressed woman wearing a face-veil and large coloured earrings. Father Godscalc, following quickly, did not see her at all.

Chapter 6

BECAUSE SHE WAS in the courtyard that day against orders, Catherine de Charetty had her first little tiff with her fiancé. She enjoyed it. She was far from tired of being fondled, but it made a change to be scolded a little. She remembered her father scolding her, and the extravagant presents he brought to her afterwards.

She had come to Florence against orders as well. That is, she had announced she was leaving Pisa, and so he had been forced to bring her. She had come to realise how disappointed he was that she was still too young to marry, and sometimes it made him restless, so that he went out without her to find company. She knew from her mother's friends that men, unlike women, got into trouble when they left home. They drank too much, and gambled their money away. It made her weep, now and then, to think about it. Pagano noticed it, and after that he stayed at home more. To begin with, when she and her Flemish nurse went out shopping, she suspected that Pagano was having a visitor. But when, once, she remarked on the smell, he merely produced with a flourish the source of it, and she had been ashamed as well as delighted. The scent had been mixed specially for her, and the apothecary had come that very day to deliver it. There was no one in the world like Pagano, even if he still could take her nowhere unless she was heavily veiled; and if there were princes in Florence, she hadn't met them yet.

Of course, she hadn't met her stepfather Nicholas either, even though he didn't leave Florence right away, as Pagano thought he would. By asking frequently, she learned that not only Godscalc, but her mother's doctor and notary were in Florence with him. She understood very well, of course, that she would be sent home immediately if any one of them saw her before she was married. But she was hurt that Pagano would not trust her even with the name of the place they were staying at. Then, coming back from some trip, she had seen Nicholas coming down the steps into her very own courtyard, and the priest Godscalc striding down after.

Nicholas was terribly different. She had forgotten how plainly and cheaply other men dressed compared with Pagano. The scar showed more distinctly than she remembered and he seemed preoccupied and solemn and unattractively powerful. A tear ran down the back of her throat and she sniffed, because he was part of her home, and she hadn't been home for a long time. But he looked, as Pagano had said, like a man who would send her back in a hair shirt and a chastity belt. It didn't sound at all comfortable. The old, funny Nicholas with the dimples would have joined in the game of deceiving her mother. But this Nicholas was her mother's husband. And slept in her bed.

She had watched him leave with the priest, and had climbed the steps and entered her house in resentful mood. Then, when Pagano had shown his annoyance, she had enjoyed making him piqued in return. For what was he doing, talking to Nicholas?

The answer was dull enough. Nicholas had called unexpectedly to buy some of Pagano's cargo. Nicholas might, it turned out, be staying in Florence through Christmas, but that would be nothing to them. She and Pagano would hold a festival of their own, with Pagano's particular friends. And so long as she wore her veil, he would take her out visiting. He had other friends who would be happy to see her. There would be music and miming. There would be pageants and balls. So long as she went only with him, and never where she might meet Nicholas.

That evening he brought her a bracelet, and marzipan, and a dog, and a dress she was to wear only for him, once she had charming little breasts there and there. She didn't mind now, when he showed her how he would caress them. Before going to bed she had another hot bath, and the new medicines that had come with the scent. By now she guessed what they were for and never objected. Sometimes, after the Flemish woman had gone, she got up through the night and took more.

By that time, the presence of a veiled midget (with dog) in Pagano Doria's house was known to Nicholas, for the simple reason that he had the house watched. The woman didn't interest him in the least. The plans of Pagano Doria towards the Charetty company were another matter. He was watchful in other ways too. The round ship was already manned, and its cargo was different from his. There was no rivalry there. But when he came to choose his own command and his crew, he tried to ensure that Doria was connected with none of them. And he took the best advisers – the Martelli, the Neroni, the Corbinelli – to help him find the men he wanted, down to the caulkers and carpenters.

The threat of mischief, however slight, however whimsical, helped him a little by drawing his own group together. It also disguised the real problems. One of them had been, of course, defined already by Julius. Nicholas's position as leader was so far purely formal. He had the nominal power. He was married to Marian. He had ideas they respected and welcomed. But all he possessed, so far as anyone knew, was a freakish ability for intricate planning, and numbers. It had got him into chilling trouble already, and not even Marian believed him perfectly capable of controlling it. He knew very well that this was why Tobie and Julius were haunting his steps. They were the watchdogs. Whatever he did with his numbers, he was not to use them to kill people he knew. A fair bargain.

So, he had to show what he could do, both in his measures against Pagano Doria, and in the whole elephantine problem of equipping and launching a maritime trading expedition: a matter about which he knew precisely nothing. The miraculous thing was that, as soon as he started, he became so carried away that he forgot about impressing anybody. And did not know that, of all things, it was his rocketing high spirits that swept the other men with him.

He bought experts, and stripped them bare with his questions. But he also sought to learn at first hand himself. People enjoyed teaching him. He took advice from everybody. He spent a day in the dry dock at Pisa, talking to carpenters. He inspected the mature wood stocks in the citadel, and watched the new-felled timber floating down on the Arno (the storms were coming at last), and tried his hand at the planes and the saws. He examined canvas.

He peered into ovens and had long talks with bakers and soap-boilers. He had dusty conversations with masons. He spoke to old men with warped hands and learned how to ram cargo. He found the wine-shops that seamen favoured, and sat and drank and ate liver-sausage and talked about weather and currents and landing-places, gaming-houses and brothels. He learned who took bribes in what harbours. He found out about the universal war between oarsmen and mariners, and useful tips about useful accidents, such as how to throw a man overboard in the night.

He had himself invited to supper with men who had farms in the country, and helped with the wine-making. He did a lot of comradely sampling before he chose the kegs he would carry to sell, and the kegs for his crew, and the special barrels for presents and bribery, and arranged for the pigs and hens and cattle and sheep he'd need for the first few days of the journey. He found a cook at a party after a cockfight, and a trumpeter at a wedding. He talked to Monna Alessandra about silk.

He began, of course, with other things. He learned that Monna Alessandra had been less than thirty when Matteo Strozzi her husband died in exile, leaving her with her five little children, of whom her two living sons were exiled still. To foster the careers of her sons, she had sold piece by piece all Matteo's farms and houses and vineyards, leaving her with this pitiful home of fewer than ten little chambers. Her oldest son, a very genius, worked for his father's cousin in

Naples. Lorenzo, poor boy, was unhappy in Bruges. The demoiselle de Charetty, she knew, had been kind to him.

Nicholas murmured. He remembered poor Lorenzo. He remembered, he said, Caterina her daughter, married to Marco di Giovanni da Parenti the silk merchant.

Ah, said Monna Alessandra. That was so. Parenti. A Latinist; a so-called philosopher and, of course, rich. His grandfather had made a fortune from armour. But gente nuova, of the medium rank only. With a larger dowry, Caterina could have married a nobleman. But where was the money? To think of the farm, the very palace she had sold to that boor Niccolini. The provender one then took for granted. The oil, the wine, the corn. A little barley, some walnuts, a pound or two of good pork. Sometimes, when he remembered, the boor Otto would send her a pack of such things and she would be expected to value the favour. Otto, who had done nothing to help her sons back from exile. Every day, at Puzzolatico, she would tend the mulberry bushes with her own hands and buy the seed, the silkworm eggs in the spring.

"Tell me about the mulberry bushes," Nicholas would say gently. He learned a lot about silk before he did anything about collecting his cargo. And Monna Alessandra, who also knew what she was doing, deduced a number of things about this fellow Nicholas, and made up her mind to learn a few more.

It was one of the six Martelli brothers who talked to Nicholas about possible sailing-masters. Watch out, they said, for the German Johannes le Grant. Red Johannes. He's your man, if you're sailing about Constantinople. He watched out; but if Johannes le Grant was in Florence, he didn't make himself known. Meantime, on Martelli advice, Nicholas found his navigator and helmsman and, soon after that, they set up their tables before the sea consul's palace to recruit the seamen they needed. Julius helped.

By this time, Tobie, Julius and Godscalc were all experiencing the uncertain euphoria of men caught in a whirlwind of fresh fish. They rushed behind Nicholas, arms outstretched to seize the largesse that showered upon them, and spent lamplit nights cramped over vellum, reducing it all to some sort of order. The formal visits, the contracts, the solemn conclaves with bankers, the heavy chests obtained from the Mint, the lists, the registers, the ledgers, multiplied to keep pace with his momentum. Christmas came, and the momentum failed to slacken, since Nicholas had by then found himself allotted a minor but tangible place in the hierarchy of the Medici. He met, in time, most of the family. Cosimo's sons Giovanni and Piero interviewed him separately, and he became familiar with the house of Cosimo's nephew Pierfrancesco and his wife Laudomia Acciajuoli. It was Monna Laudomia who found him a Greek tutor when he decided that he wanted to know more than Julius could teach him. Julius agreed to sit in on the lessons in case the man got it wrong. Privately, he was relieved. Five years had passed since his studies in Bologna, and the subsequent spells at Louvain as poor Felix's tutor had barely freshened his memory. Nicholas, as Felix's servant, had actually learned more than he had.

Bologna. All that seemed now to have been forgotten. The unpleasant Fra Ludovico had gone to Rome to proposition the Pope, it was known. His assorted group of Eastern companions would (he asserted) muster an army of 120,000 against the Sultan, provided the Western world raised the equivalent. The Pope quickly suggested that the party should slip over the Alps and put the matter to France and Burgundy, without whom a worthwhile crusade was impossible. The envoys agreed, while holding out for their travelling expenses. When they got those, it turned out that Fra Ludovico would rather like to be Latin Patriarch of Antioch. The Pope appeared willing, but deferred the actual appointment, unlike the travelling expenses, until the friar should come back from his mission. And the best of luck to him, concluded Julius. Antioch needed such men.

During all this period the work didn't lessen, but allowed some time for leisure. They had become used to their lodging. The repopulation of Florence had ceased to form part of Monna Alessandra's conversation. Tobie, who was playing his own small part in that quarter, seldom came to the house in his free time. Monna Alessandra had warned her paying guests about the loose women of Florence who were required to wear gloves, high-heeled slippers and bells, to warn the eye and the ear of the godly.

Tobie took the lesson to heart. Julius, who slept in the same bed, swore that if a bird struck a bell with its beak, Tobie would be half into its cage with his eyes shut. Julius preferred bruising sports like the calcio and palloni. Quite often, attending, he caught sight of Pagano Doria. The little rat usually had two or three men at his side; and once the petite veiled woman. The sincere smile appeared everywhere, twinkling under broad, rakish hats with conspicuous jewels in them. Julius noticed that he had regular, unbroken teeth to the back of his jaw on each side. He stopped and spoke to Nicholas now and then, recommending a tailor, a tavern, a merchant who sold decent mattresses or practical tableware or stout travelling boxes. The twinkle, to the jaundiced eye of Julius, was meant to convey that Pagano Doria could consume the Charetty company any day between dinner and supper, but preferred biding his time until he left Florence. Nicholas gave no sign that he minded, but it made Julius uneasy. He spoke to the others about it. For example, January had begun, and with less than five weeks in hand they still had no sailing-master.

The Feast of Epiphany approached, a celebration dear to the Medici and regularly marked by a play presented by the famous company of the Magi, and an elaborate procession up the Via Larga itself to end at the crib in the friary of San Marco. Friends, clients, supporters, dependants of the Medici, obeyed the President's summons to ride, pose or even perform on such occasions. When Cosimo de' Medici was the president no one refused; certainly no one from the Charetty company. Already, their room at Monna Alessandra's was littered with costumes for their share in the pageant, and above the window a humorist had tacked a pair of crowns and a single frayed wing. Nicholas was sitting alone in the muddle, adding figures, when Godscalc of Cologne opened the door and walked in.

"No," said Nicholas.

"Well now," said Father Godscalc. "As it happens, I wasn't going to assault either your virtue or your vices. I had in mind an enquiry." He spoke with perfect placidity. Chaplain, apothecary and meticulous penman, he had worked as hard as any since Pisa and, drawn into his company's vortex, had continued to weigh up its members. The complex simplicities of Julius and the absent Astorre he knew well already. Tobie, with his acid doctor's brain and inquisitive nature, was more apt to resist him: he didn't fully understand Tobie yet. Nicholas who, after all, had advised his appointment, had shown a preference for evading his pastoral attentions, but had otherwise appeared free and open with him from the beginning.

Godscalc observed that this candour had limits, both on the part of Nicholas and on the part of the others, discussing him. Born to gossip, neither Tobie nor Julius ever talked to him about Nicholas, which was odd in two grown men set under another much younger. Godscalc had expected flashes of resentment and pique, and sometimes heard them, disguised as impatience. But even such moments were overlaid by something else he couldn't quite fathom. They never joked about his curious marriage, even in private. He gathered they respected Marian de Charetty. They also respected, he saw, the presence of a peculiar talent and, perhaps to protect that talent, had closed ranks about it. But for Tobie's wine-loosened tongue, Godscalc would never have learned, he supposed, of the inadmissible connection between Nicholas and the house of St Pol. And yet both Tobie and Julius were uneasy prefects; like beings of one species set to guard another of unknown capacity. It seemed to Godscalc that, whether they knew it or not, the men who worked with Nicholas were afraid of him. And since they were human, that made them unpredictable.

Now, as was his duty, Godscalc had come to discharge a small errand. Waiting for him to continue, Nicholas sat at ease, pen in hand, without rushing to shorten the silence. Godscalc cleared a space from a chest-top and perched his bulk on it. He said, "You have no ship-master yet."

Nicholas swung his head back like a joy bell and lowered it, beaming. He laid his pen carefully down. He said, "You want to talk German. You've been talking German. You've found Johannes le Grant?"

Without blinking, Godscalc discarded five minutes of careful preliminaries. He said, "Yes. He's good. He's not sure if he wants the job, and would prefer time on his own to consider. I'm not to tell you how to get hold of him."

There was a persuasive silence, which he resisted agreeably.

Nicholas said, "It's very disconcerting. Tobie and Julius break promises all the time. He must be very good."

"He is," said Godscalc.

"But I have to wait for him. And you're not going to tell me what will attract him. He's German; and an engineer; and selective."

"He's an engineer," Godscalc said. "A pioneer, also. He dug countermines in Constantinople and nearly got rid of the Turks by flooding their mines and burning their props and forcing smoke and obnoxious smells down the tunnels. Very obnoxious smells. That's all I can tell you. I'm not wearing one of those things."

Nicholas picked up, between finger and thumb, an Epiphany costume of Judas-pink satin. "No. That's for Tobie," he said. "You don't want to go on his cart, you'd be blinded. And the one in front of it's taking a leopard. That's your dress over there."

"Where?" said Godscalc. He saw a breech clout and a mound of wool and two sandals. The mound of wool was a beard.

The door opened. "Have you told him?" said Julius, strolling in. "A holy hermit, they want you for, father. The third best float in the procession. Palm trees. Caverns. A pillar to sit on. They'll cheer you all through the city. I begged and begged, but they said it had to be a man in Holy Orders. They said they'd try to hide a brazier somewhere if the horses didn't mind. Nicholas will be with you."

"Fully dressed?" Godscalc said.

"You have your Faith to warm you," Nicholas said. The rebuke hit, to a nicety, the voice of a priest they both knew.

Godscalc said, "Then I must assume you will be more than fully dressed. As whom?"

"I'm the lion," said Nicholas. "Cosimino wanted a real one, but they said it would fight with the leopard."

"And the horses wouldn't like it," said Godscalc flatly. Of course he saw why they protected Nicholas. And he, too, for a moment felt a pang, for them and for him.

On the day of the procession, fear was not in Godscalc's mind as the four senior officials of the Charetty company pressed their way through the packed streets to the Piazza della Signoria where, the night before, the decorated tableaux carts had been assembled. The draw-horses and oxen had passed through before them: fresh dung curled round his toe-thongs. His colleagues had not lied, although their respect for the truth had been sparing. He was to appear, in holy garb, on one of the chariots; but a long and thick cloak was fortunately part of the costume. Julius, beside him, was a magnificent Roman. There were petals all over his armour where groups of girls had sought (and failed) to attract his attention from upper windows lined with Epiphany dolls. Nicholas padded behind, his head under his arm, talking to a Judas-pink Tobie.

And that, of course, was quite ludicrous. All around them, in silks and furs, jewels and feathers, were other Medici men, heading for gilded chariots where they would arrange themselves, retinues of the glittering Kings. Tobie, in cerise silk and ostrich plumes, was meant to be of their number. It was out of the question that the Medici, experts in protocol, had intended Tobie's master to come as a lion.

Monna Alessandra, surveying Nicholas in her doorway, had emitted a sigh that would have felled a small tree. Before leaving the house, Godscalc himself had at least cornered the lion and tried to make him see reason. Nicholas had listened politely, fastening the fur up to his throat and placing his tail carefully over his arm like a pallium, before lifting his head from the table. He buffed both his eyes with his cuff. "You think I'll offend the Medici?"

Godscalc said, "They must have sent you a costume."

"I took it back," Nicholas said. "My lord is Cosimino, you see. Not his grandfather."

Godscalc had said nothing more. Shrewd; shrewd as the cleverest merchant among them. So sharp he'd cut himself; one of these days.

When they reached the Piazza della Signoria, the horses were still in their lines and the carts, which had been standing all night, had hardly got their covers off. It was starting to rain. Above the roar of the encircling crowd and the high Tuscan voices of the performers, the orders, the warnings, the appeals of the organisers rose from four or five different places, hoarse and tetchy as ravens. Tobie disappeared, hustled off by a fellow in Medici livery. Julius followed him. Nicholas said, "That must be us."

The float stood, last of four, between the yellow bulk of the Republic's Palazzo and the arches of the loggia with which it made a right angle. Prison, fortress, council chamber, the Palazzo filled the grey sky. Its corbelled battlements thrust over their heads, and the tower above dissolved into the clouds, from which a bell had begun tolling. The noise slackened below, and then began to climb as if fit for eruption. Arriving at the designated contrivance, which contained a lot of sand, a painted cave and a palm tree, Godscalc found a pair of steps and began to climb into it. He said, "Excuse me." It was dry in the cavern, and there were two hermits there already. He bent and crawled in beside them. Someone said, "Where's the lion?" He crawled out again.

The lion was leaning against the next float, its tail hanging negligently over its arm. The cart contained a large sheeted object and several excitable workmen, to whom Nicholas appeared to be offering comments. The rain, increasing, beat down on his face. Still talking, he put his head on. His voice emerged from its jaws. On the float, a man in an ancient black cap dropped his arms and strode to the edge of the cart. Two other men promptly hauled the sheet down, exposing a large terracotta statue of St Anne on a rock, with accommodation here and there for performers. A fourth man, leaning over her lap, began attempting to pull the sheet up again. The man in the black cap stood glaring down and Nicholas, looking up, examined him amiably. The man said angrily, "My Marzocco!"

He was addressing Nicholas, who courteously took his head off. The eyes of the man on the float followed the sweep of wet fur and whiskers, and the eyes of the lion peered back from the arm of its owner. The speaker, it could now be seen, was as elderly as his hat, with a dry yellow face rusticated like the stones of the Palazzo, and a set of grey whiskers singed brown at one edge. Nicholas said, "Monsignore?"

"Who made your head?" said the man. "You have no right to it."

"Why?" said Nicholas.

"It is mine," said the elderly man.

Nicholas hefted the lion's head in two capable hands and held it up to the man on the float. "Allow me to return it," he said. The elderly man made no move to take it. The man on the lap of St Anne abruptly gave up the battle to shroud her and leaping nimbly down began to come over. The other two bundled the sheets off the float and left with an air of efficiency. There was a pause.

On the other side of the square, the first chariots had been harnessed and horses were being pulled through towards them. A negro boy leading a leopard hesitated beside Godscalc's cart and the leopard lowered and fluttered its hindquarters. A pool of liquid formed by the wheel and ran out across the brick paving. The boy, tugging, drew the leopard forward. The leading float of the four was packed with persons of consequence, among whom was an Oriental whose back seemed familiar. The leopard jumped in amongst them and they all leaned over backwards.

By the float of St Anne, Nicholas was gazing, neck twisted, at Godscalc's glistening wheel. He said, "That's a pity. It'll simply attract other leopards." Above one ear, with the patience of Salome displaying the platter to the Tetrarch of Galilee, he was still sustaining his head. No one took it; but the younger artisan, who had joined the first, leaned over and looked at the lion, and Nicholas. The newcomer's face, which was dirty, was encircled by a wool vizored helmet, and his arms, wet with rain, were corded and hard as the legs of a whippet. He said, "No, no, no. Keep the head. It's copied from his Marzocco, that's what he's saying. The Marzocco; the lion: the civic symbol of Florence in the Santa Maria Novella. His. That's his sculpture."

The old man said, "I have told him. It is my design. Mine. I require to be paid."

Nicholas lowered his arms. "Monsignore is a sculptor!" he said.

The younger man said, "Maestro, the procession must move. We can't keep her dry any longer." He and the older man both turned and looked at the St Anne, down whose gilded bosom the rain was now flowing.

Nicholas said, "Maestro! The Marzocco lion! I should have known!"

"No matter," said the sculptor over his shoulder. He frowned at the St Anne.

"Your doors," said Nicholas wistfully. "The gates to Paradise, someone said."

"That was Ghiberti," said the younger man, frowning at Nicholas.

"Your dome!" said Nicholas quickly. "An unsupported miracle of miraculous structure!"

"You speak of Brunelleschi," said the younger man. He glanced, with apology, at the sculptor's back.

Nicholas looked at the statue. He lowered his voice. "Not that?" he said.

"That is the master's," said the man in the helmet.

"But," said Nicholas.

The bearded man turned. "But what, born of a pig?"

"The head," said Nicholas. His voice was humble. "The head? The torso? And the length from the knee to the ankle . . ."

"What of it?" said the sculptor. "Damianus. Vitruvius. You have never heard of them."

"But look at the geometry," Nicholas said. "If you went by Damianus and the *Optics* alone, you needed a base one foot ten inches shorter."

Godscalc lifted his head from his hands and looked across at the profile – agreeable, innocent, friendly – of his unassuming friend Nicholas. No one spoke. Then the younger man in the grey helmet said softly, "Given the dimensions of the Via Larga perhaps. But not in the Piazza San Marco."

"Forgive me," said Nicholas. "But the Medici are your patrons. They will be riding alongside."

"On tall horses," said the sculptor. He was looking at Nicholas.

"No. On palfreys, because of the gout. An angle of twenty to twenty-five degrees, I should say, whereas you've compensated for sixty. When you make a fountain – "

"Judith and Holofernes," said the old man. He was still looking at Nicholas.

" – when you made that, you allowed for no distortion at all because the spray keeps spectators at the distance you want. But what if they narrowed the bore of the waterpipes? You can't think of everything.

You can't allow for optical corrections in terms of alternative angles. At least – " He stopped, his eyes unfocused.

"What?" said the helmeted man. He put up a hand and slowly pulled off his cap. Underneath was a shock of carroty hair.

"Alternative angles. Of course, you *can* allow for alternative angles. And you could do it with colour," said Nicholas. He shoved his head under his arm and picked up his tail, which was trailing. His hair had frizzed in the wet and his face was fresh as an apple with a split down the side. He said, "I think you could do it with colour. Nice to have met you."

"God damn it," said the red-headed man. Nicholas smiled. The square had started to empty, and so had the horse lines. A little ahead, the chariot bearing the host of noblemen and the leopard had already drawn off, followed by the float from which peered Tobie's dissatisfied face. A nun came pushing towards them, shepherding a group of sober young ladies with wings. The red-headed man said, "The singers. We'll have to get off the float. Maestro?"

The black hat turned. The sculptor looked down his aged nose at Nicholas, the rain soaking his smock. The artist's experienced gaze examined the large-eyed face, the athletic shoulders, the narrow flanks, the long legs. "Oh, bring him," he said. "He knows what he's talking about."

The red-headed man spoke to Nicholas. "You would miss the procession. We're leaving the float and going back to the Maestro's workshop."

"I'm not here for the procession," said Nicholas. "I thought you were German."

The nun had arrived and was standing exclaiming at the foot of the steps. She expressed rapture at the St Anne, and at the sculptor of the St Anne, who carefully descended from the cart, bowed, and began to make his way, with difficulty, through a large number of admiring citizens. Nicholas laid down his head and handed a number of flushed young women up the steps into the cart, where they disposed of themselves prettily. The red-headed man vaulted down and a man came up leading horses. "No, I'm not German," said the red-headed man. "I worked in Germany for a while. John le Grant is my name. And young King James is my lord, if I have one." He stopped, finding himself alone, and turned round. "You don't like Scotsmen?"

"Lions aren't particular," Nicholas said. "I like them, as you might say, but they don't like me. My name is Nicholas. I have with me a most discreet hermit. Did you hatch this between you?"

Godscalc rose and left his float, with some dignity. "No, we didn't," he said. "I assumed one mathematician would smell out another. And the Maestro, of course, has been working on the Martelli chapel in San Lorenzo. Nicholas, that was Doria's page who came with the leopard."

"Doria?" said John le Grant.

"Pagano Doria," said Nicholas. "He sent a man last night to tamper with the lynchpin of Godscalc's float. The page came to check that it was still tampered with, which it wasn't. It's quite safe, Father Godscalc, if you want to go back to your cave."

The red-headed man said, "What's the point of that? I invited you. I'm inviting him. The workshop's not much, but we can rise to mulled wine."

"I need a sailing-master," said Nicholas.

"Don't rush it," said John le Grant. "You've got your foot in the door for mulled wine. From an Aberdeen man, that's enough to be going on with."

Chapter 7

THE COMPLEX OF dwellings, garden and workshop to which Nicholas and Godscalc were taken belonged to the Cathedral, and stood on a corner behind it. Even on foot, they reached it in minutes. Disregarding the house, which had the appearance of a classical quarry, the Maestro led the way along a well-trodden path to his bottega, holding Nicholas firmly by the arm. John le Grant and Godscalc followed, talking English. Once within, the master sat himself on a box covered with a burst satin cushion, heavily stained. Godscalc disposed his damp cloak about him and found a place on a bench, while John le Grant went and poked in an oven and began to busy himself with heating some wine. Nicholas climbed out of his skin and hung it beside two nightcaps, a hat and a towel, on a stand whose arms ended in fingers. He began wandering about rather silently, looking.

The mulled wine, when it came, was exceedingly strong. Afterwards, Godscalc remembered a number of things about the bottega: the smell of oil and earth and mineral and insect colours familiar to him from his cell; the glisten of marble dust that covered the stools, the bench he was sitting on, and whitened the cloth full of rasps, files and chisels that lay near the yard door. He remembered the covered work-tubs, breathing chill odours of coarse wax and glue. He remembered Nicholas, pausing beside the open crate full of exotic cloth; staring at the laced bundle of drawings; the jar of pens; the crock of brushes; the wall hung with shears and ball-peen hammers and saws and the one stacked with ladders, easels, scaffolding, and upright sheaves of primed panels. There were shelves of marble busts and clay models, bronze figurines and partly made limbs, and in the depths of the room a mirror doubled the light. The place was empty because of the holiday, but someone had left exposed on a table a pad of parchment glued on a board, with a straight edge and some lead lying on it. Someone else had overturned a basket of charcoal sticks, and the black and tender willow turned to powder under le Grant's feet until Nicholas knelt in his shirtsleeves and slowly began to gather them up. The sculptor said, "Stay there." Nicholas paused and looked up.

"The Maestro's fee for use of his head," said John le Grant. "He wants to draw you. While he does, we can talk. Can he drink?"

"No!" said the sculptor. "On one knee, with the hand raised. Just so. John, the chalk. Ghiberti! Brunelleschi! No. He will not move, nor will he drink until I have done. And take his shirt off. Have I said something amusing?"

"Yes," said Father Godscalc. "We had a disagreement, the other day, over costume."

He pulled off the new model's shirt and hung it over the lionskin. Nicholas looked resigned, but not especially embarrassed. His premarital prowess in Bruges meant, one assumed, that he was well aware of his own physical presence.

Godscalc sat down, and accepted the steaming cup that le Grant handed him. Le Grant said, "Pay no attention to the Maestro. He and Brunelleschi and Ghiberti all worked on the siege plans for Lucca together. They understand one another. Michelozzo as well. They were planning to divert a river and flood the place. From, of course, quite the wrong angle."

"What!" said the sculptor. He stopped drawing. "Herring! Farting underground animal!"

"Don't stop. Tell me where the plan is, and I'll put it on the floor and see if Nicholas can sort out the error."

In what followed, Godscalc took no part. The argument moved from siege fortifications to gunnery, and from there to ships. John le Grant refilled the cups. The master drew. They discussed the weaknesses of the lateen rudder system and the rigging of triremes. Outside, the rain stopped, and began again. The sculptor held his pad at arm's length and said, "That's all right."

"You can move," said John le Grant.

"No, I can't," Nicholas said. "If you have a hook on the wall, you could hang me on it. When did you leave Aberdeen?"

"A long time ago," said the engineer. He found a beaker and filled it, while Nicholas was rubbing his back. "I used to import salt, and sail fish to Sluys, and one thing led to another. You're going to Trebizond? Why?"

Nicholas took the beaker and, sitting, drained it rhythmically. He said, "It seems a good idea. To set up a branch – "

"I know about that," said John le Grant. "Personally, why?"

"Personally to set up a branch," Nicholas said.

The sculptor snorted. "With John, you'll have to do better than that. Scotsmen like to know where they are. Sheep excrement. Players on bladders."

Godscalc saw Nicholas pause, and tried to guess what he would do.

Ever since John le Grant had been mentioned, he supposed that Nicholas had been watching out for the engineer. At the float, he must have recognised the sculptor at once and, remembering the Martelli connection, had thought le Grant might be there. And, with diabolical art, had coaxed him out of cover and set himself to attract him.

He had succeeded. He would get his sailing-master – there was little doubt about that. Unless, of course, he gave the wrong answer now. John le Grant had fixed Nicholas with a stare. He had pale eyes and red brows and freckles, and dry, youngish skin bitten in lines. He said, "If I'm to work with a bairn, I want to know the strength of his will to succeed. And I want to know what he'll do if he botches it. You got too big for Bruges?"

Nicholas said, "No. I expect to go back."

"So," said the engineer, "what's the carrot leading you on? You want to make a name for yourself? You want to fight for Christ against the Turk? You want wealth? You want power? You want freedom and licence? You want risk and adventure? You don't want anything, but are obeying other folks' orders? Which?"

"All the venal reasons," said Nicholas. "And another one. Like you, I enjoy solving puzzles. Someone is trying to get in."

The hammering on the workshop door had begun as he was speaking. The sculptor, muttering, rose and flung it open. A Roman soldier stood there. He caught sight of Godscalc and Nicholas and said, "Oh, there you are."

It was Julius. Nicholas said, "Maestro, forgive me. It's one of our company. Has something happened?"

"You missed it!" said Julius. He bowed to the sculptor, looked at le Grant and returned his gaze to Nicholas. He said, "In the middle of the Via Larga, in front of the Palazzo Medici! This great float with the leopard on it, and the Negro, and Pagano Doria – Doria! – and his friends, all done up in yellow velvet. And then the cart suddenly jams, and the one behind collides with it, and the horses break from the harness and get through into the courtyard of the Palazzo and start to kick all the Medici's best carving, with Doria yelling and the people screaming, and the leopard . . ."

"It attacked?" said Godscalc, rising.

"No. It just piddled," said Julius. "Gallons. People ran, just the same."

"That cart was made by the company's own excellent carpenters. How could it have broken down?" the sculptor said. "It might have been ours!"

"It might have been ours," Nicholas said. "Who knows? Maybe someone tampered last night with the lynchpin."

Godscalc said, "Nicholas."

"And speaking of Trebizond," Nicholas said, "that's another reason, while I remember. I'd quite like to get there to spite Pagano Doria."

when at any moment his ships may be commandeered by one king or another, his loans dishonoured? The Pope and the Duke of Milan send to make peace between these English claimants, and do you know why? So that once England is settled, she will agree to attack King Charles of France. And will they rest in peace even then? No! Because the Pope will send them on this crusade to save the Levant from the Turk. Ruinous!"

"Perhaps," said Nicholas, "Brother Ludovico of Bologna will induce the Duke of Burgundy to launch a crusade whether France is invaded or not. He seems persuasive."

"That man?" said Monna Alessandra. "He is the son of a timber merchant! He spent his youth tying knots – ha! – in the woods; arching saplings for shipyards. But the Duke of Burgundy is not a man to be bent by another."

Nicholas pursed his lips. "According to Gregorio, he is calling a Chapter of the Golden Fleece in the spring."

"Where the well-born of Burgundy will dress in matched velvet, and feast and parade, but will do nothing. It is a club for men children, like all societies. Why do you speak of it? You don't imagine some Burgundian army will arrive on your heels? Twenty years ago the late Emperor of Constantinople visited Florence. He appealed for help; he was the guest of your friend Cosimo de' Medici himself; but Constantinople still fell. When he speaks to you, does the lord Cosimo mention God?"

"Sometimes," said Nicholas.

"You smile. As a matter of form, you imply. But all his other talk, I am sure, was of trade and of money."

"That is why I am here," Nicholas said.

"Yes," she said. "Yes, of course. He would talk of what you understand. What does a rustic know of Aristotle, of Plato, of the great thinkers whose writings occupy the minds of men like my Matteo? He would talk of trivial things."

"Of trade," Nicholas said. "It enables thinkers to eat, write and sell books. I can bring you no news of exalted discussion, or politics, or the prospects for Lorenzo and Filippo. In my position, to pretend erudition would be foolish."

"Many would not agree with you," said Monna Alessandra. "If you called it aspiration, for example. But you are probably right. The victim in such cases is often the marriage. So. You plan a long absence, but you have no mission, that I can see. You are not a second Jason. Your mind is merely on gold and power and the delights of the flesh. I know this kind. Have you been to Mass more than thrice since you came here?"

"I don't think Jason went to Mass either," Nicholas said. "But yes. I have no mission to fleece the Orthodox Church or the Sultan. The lady my wife has a business. I would like to see it prosper. That is all."

"For her sake?" said Lorenzo's mother.

Nicholas paused. Then he said, "You know my kind: you must judge. Perhaps Lorenzo has an opinion."

"Many people have. I know the gossip," said Monna Alessandra. "If I were the Medici, I should want instead to know the facts. A good marriage is worth five per cent in the pound in the money markets. A bad one can be worse than tin money."

"The facts?" said Nicholas. "It is a legal marriage, but only for business purposes. I inherit nothing beyond an agreed salary. The demoiselle's heirs are her daughters."

"Only for business purposes?" said Monna Alessandra. "You are a vigorous man. I heard differently."

He stayed where he was. "I will talk about what will affect money markets," he said.

Her pencilled brows rose, in the same Florentine irony he had seen in Cosimo. "A silly woman may affect money markets," she said. "Your wife is old. She needed a man and a manager. They did not need to be the same person. So she had her reasons. Perhaps she was afraid you would leave. Perhaps she was afraid you would bed and marry one of her daughters. Perhaps she was afraid you would do away with her son . . . who indeed died abroad in your arms, so they tell me. Or perhaps she simply conceived an old woman's craze for a boy. May and December. It is a cogent question, you see. Without an answer, the market cannot read your intentions or hers, or forecast the future of the Charetty company."

"Why not open a book?" Nicholas said. "I didn't know how lucky we were, that Monsignore Cosimo signed us with no further questions. I am a guest at your table, and should enjoy hearing your views on another subject."

"Well enough done," said Monna Alessandra. "But if you do not discuss her, you do not defend her. Myself, I would ask: is it fair to demand of a lusty man in the flower of his youth that he should be married, and chaste? Nature will speak in the end, and she will hear of it."

"No," said Nicholas. For years, he had never really known – had refused to know – what anger was. Now, more and more, he found he had to contend with it. He sat very still.

"No?" She was amused. "Did I not hear of one the other day? The *splendid woman*. The splendid woman, passing through Bruges, who said you would make a fortune. Is she in Florence?"

"No," said Nicholas. He debated for a moment, his eyes on his platter. His voice, when he spoke, sounded laconic. "There are all kinds of commitments. The vows of an apprentice when he marries his mistress are tolerably binding."

"In his own interests," said Monna Alessandra. "But when a richer, younger mistress appears?"

He found he had his knife in his hand. He laid it down with a rap.

He said, "I know, madonna, the lady my colleagues referred to. Her name is Violante of Naxos. My wife and I met her in Bruges. She is married. She is at present in Venice. And she has no more interest in me than I have in her. May we now change the subject, Monna Alessandra? Or I regret I must go."

She changed the subject, having learned, no doubt, much of what she wanted to know. He spoke automatically, while his mind referred him to all that had been said. He felt bruised. On the other hand, all he had said had been true. Or was true by now. The scent in Pagano Doria's Florentine house would have vanished long since.

Just before they embarked, Cosimo de' Medici summoned the company to his presence. It was one of his better days. He rose to receive them with his heavy-lidded sardonic gaze, the embodiment of the old Maestro's droop-nosed St Cosmas with his coarse hair and lined cheeks. Tobie wondered if, surveying them, the chief citizen of Florence observed a difference in the Charetty company: an air of assurance which had been missing in December. Since then, like a new galley put through its trials by a master, Nicholas had been tested in public in a field of the greatest complexity which was new to him. Now he had completed the course, and few could complain of the outcome. Of course, he had needed his officers, and had used them. They knew where, but for them, he would have made an ill-informed decision, or would have failed, through inexperience, to identify a lack, a trend, a danger. But equally each man had to admit – even Julius – that none of them could have equalled the outpouring of energy, intellectual and physical, that Nicholas brought to the endeavour. Because of his gifts, Julius and Tobie, Godscalc and Astorre had come prepared to tolerate him as nominal leader. John le Grant had made his own assessment, and accepted him. It was unlikely they would ever cease watching him. It was unlikely they would ever be less than critical. But he had proved himself again to be able; and youth, strength and good humour had further sweetened the pill. They were, for the moment, a unit.

Cosimo de' Medici said, "You go to trade. You represent the Republic of Florence, and I know that I can rely on you all to remember the trust we place in you. You also represent something wider. Since the pagans descended on Rome, the Greek and Latin worlds have been the poorer for the growing gulf between them: the contempt the ignorant on each side have had for the other. The need to heal the breach has never been stronger, now that Constantinople itself is in Turkish hands, and the heathens cast envious eyes on the Christian lands at their frontiers.

"Unlike Venice and Genoa, Florence has no colonies in the East. We have never striven to seize land there; we are not disliked. We wish to sell and buy in these cities, but the loss if we did not would not destroy us, as it might destroy them. We are not therefore sending you to hold back the hordes single-handed. We are sending you in the hope that, where you find Florentine traders, you will assist and protect them; and that in serving the Grand Comnenos of Trebizond, the Emperor David, you will at the same time do God's work in making our two churches and our two purposes one. May He protect you and bring you back safely."

Outside, Julius said, "What do you think he was saying?"

Astorre had disappeared, to plant a fifth crop of candles in a church that had caught his fancy. Father Godscalc, after some hesitation, had gone in after him.

Tobie said, "Wasn't it obvious? Don't kill yourselves for Venice or Genoa, but keep the Emperor happy."

Julius said, "You should have talked to captain Vettori of the Florentine galleys. Stout fellow. Went to Constantinople in May, and threw a feast on his ship for the Sultan. I'm glad," volunteered Julius, "that we're not to hold back the hordes single-handed. I'd rather offer them banquets."

"You wouldn't enjoy it," said Tobie. "They're forbidden strong drink, and they prefer handsome young lawyers to women. Holding off the hordes is what you'd be doing." He paused. "Look. Get it straight, for God's sake. The Sultan rules Constantinople, but Pera is still full of Florentine traders. And Venetians. And Genoese. Trade has to go on, even if the Pope doesn't like it. The lord Cosimo makes a fortune in banking but builds altars and churches to redress the balance in Heaven. He gives feasts for the Sultan of Turkey, and sends us and our army to Trebizond. We're the appendix; the special Redemption clause. Now where are you off to?"

"Into the church after Astorre," Julius said. "To see if he's lit enough candles. And what about the new consul for Genoa, may God crown him with fire? He's on his way to Trebizond now."

"What?" said Tobie. "How do you know?"

"The man watching his house. The servants behaved just as usual, but he found out just now that Doria's whole party left for Porto Pisano last week. And the round ship was told to be ready to sail when they got there."

Tobie engaged in a long, thoughtful curse. Then he said, "What's the wind?"

"Perfect," said Julius. "He'll sail out on the tide. Constantinople and Pera by March. Trebizond maybe by April."

Tobie walked. "He may never get there," he said. He walked again, slower. "On the other hand, he may. If that's the church, I'll come with you."

Chapter 8

THE ROUND SHIP *Doria* had indeed sailed, and in triumph. For the little gift of God for which Pagano Doria and his young fiancée were waiting so anxiously had made its appearance at last.

From Christmas onwards, the sea prince had been watching the weather. The Charetty galley would leave in February. Compared to his, its route would be coastal. Its crew, however, was bigger and in variable winds it was faster. To reach Trebizond first, or even neck and neck with the Florentine, he would have to sail soon. It would suit him to be first into Sicily, Modon and Pera, leaving what small inconveniences he could for his underprivileged friend. But especially, he did not wish to come last and find the boy and his galley already occupying prime berths and depôts and the Emperor's favour. The Genoese colony had no idea they were about to acquire a new consul. He did not even know if they still kept their traditional suburb, their church and their castle. That was why he was supposed to be going: to confirm and, if necessary, restore the standing of Genoa in the Emperor's eyes. He proposed to do so, with a flourish.

He believed he could set sail in January. The only problem was his little Catherine, who thought of nothing but marriage, and who might feel alarm at the prospect of fresh travels without it. That he was highly regarded by the Genoese signoria she did of course know: she expected it. Of Trebizond she knew nothing. That he meant to sail to the East, and remain there, was something he had hoped to break to her after their marriage.

He would have to do it now. Indeed, some diversion was needed. Secure in his arms, as he had thought she would be, the child would hardly have cared where they were. As it was, romantic love kept her happy enough, but he knew that she was growing tired of the little of Florence she knew, and the limited company that she moved in. She chafed at the veils, and wanted to display her new charms and possessions. When upsets occurred, because of an absence of his, or an overindulgence in sweetmeats, it required all his patience and arts to restore her to the loving child she could be. It took all his resolve to be kind when, a week after Epiphany, he found her weeping in bed and declaring that she wanted him to take her back home.

It was not as bad as it sounded. She wanted to marry him. But when she felt less than well, and her stomach ached, and her skin became inflamed and tender and sore, she wanted her mother. Of course he was her chosen lover. He was the most wonderful man in the world. But now it was time to marry, and go off back home.

He had tried to explain, back in Brussels, what a long trip he was about to embark on. It was the thought of losing him for many months that had persuaded her into coming. Now, in her discontent, she considered that many months had passed. He had surely completed his business. He could sail the ship home, and buy her a house, and she would be a married lady in Bruges, with a bracelet and earrings and a terrier. Nor did talk of honour this time convince her. Who was to know if she was a woman or not? And he had the papers, and his friends to be witness and (he had said) a nice priest. Didn't he want to marry her? The weeping, gaining in volume, had turned into frenzy.

He had dealt with such fits of emotion before, but had the wisdom now to get the Flemish woman instead of himself to restore the child to her senses. When he returned, she was lying huddled in blankets with a hot swaddled brick in her arms and steaming flannel over her stomach. He crossed softly and sat on the bed. The terrier squealed, and he rose and sat again. He said, "Caterina. Would you like rubies, and more dresses of silk than the Duchess has?"

She peered at him over the brick. She had circles under her eyes. He touched her cheek.

"Do you know what has happened? The Emperor has sent for you."

She was not excited. "In *Germany*?"

"Where would be the fun in going to Germany? No, my sweeting. Another emperor. The richest, noblest man in the world, who has invited your Pagano to his court, and wishes to see his Caterinetta."

She had never failed to believe him before but at present, he saw, her imagination could not deal with the matter of emperors. She said, "Who?" Her voice verged on the querulous.

He wondered what she had been taught. He doubted if, outside his stories, she had any idea of the world outside Florence and Bruges. He said, "We have been invited to the court of the Byzantine Emperor. The Emperor David of Trebizond. He has rubies and silk dresses for you, and chests of silver for me. But unless you come I shan't go. You mean more to me than any emperor."

She stared at him. "It hurts," she said.

He hesitated, then bent slowly and kissed her. "We shall make it better. Don't think of it now. But when you feel well, come and ask me about it. Trebizond, Caterinetta. Where they make lovely girls into princesses."

He left the child after that to her nurse. The upset continued next day: instead of speaking to him, Catherine hugged herself whimpering; and when the dog tried to lick her, she slapped it. Pagano Doria looked at the sky, and tested the wind and then sought out the stout nurse and questioned her.

The woman was useless. All that could be done was being done. Who knew what the girl had eaten? Something from the dog's dish, like as not. Certainly she could not travel as she now was. Messer Pagano would have to be patient. Or if he doubted her, call in a doctor.

Pagano Doria preferred not to call in a doctor. On the other hand, if the illness developed, he could not avoid it. If the illness developed, he could not sail with her anyway. He conferred with Crackbene his master, and sat at his papers, interviewing people, dealing with all the last-minute details of sailing. Now and then he could hear the girl crying in a lonely, dispirited moan. Touched, he had tried to cheer her at first. Now he sent in little presents: a pot of herbs, a lotion, a phial of red for her lips. That night he went to bed thinking he had lost his game against Fate. He could never sail at the right time. The girl was dying; or was at best an invalid.

He woke to the sound of a scream, and the bang of a door, and running footsteps. Fumbling to find tinder and candle he heard a second door open. The nurse spoke, and was answered by the girl's voice, thin and shaking.

By the time he got to the door, it had closed again. He rapped, and nothing happened. Then he heard the nurse's footsteps again. The door opened and she appeared, her face shapeless and red in the light of his candle. She held the girl's door shut behind her. "You heard it?" she said. "Such a fuss. But you've no need to worry, my lord. Come back in the morning and the little lady will be ready to see you, and as proud as a queen."

"What?" he said.

"What do you think?" said the nurse. "The Holy Mother knows I've worked hard enough for it. I never guess; it's unlucky; but I thought this might be the moment. They get frightened. You'll hear her crying, but never worry. Turn over and get you a good night's sleep, my lord Pagano. Make the most of your sleep. Because if I know that little lady she will keep you busy in more ways than one. The bigger the pain, the bigger the hunger. That's the truth about virgins, Messer Pagano."

He let her go back to the room, and returning, stood by his window, enjoying the night. Then he went back to bed and slept soundly till sunrise.

Catherine received him next morning. Sitting erect with her russet hair combed and a silken shawl wrapped round her shoulders, she was a different girl from the creature of yesterday, although her cheeks were white still and her eyes circled and brighter than normal. They held, as she watched him, a timid and rather charming appeal. But mixed with the traces of strain and alarm was pride, as the nurse had expected, and the edge of a tremulous happiness.

He dispelled all her doubts by flinging himself at the side of her bed and covering her with the lightest of kisses. Then he gave her the ring he had kept for this moment. Tears came into her eyes. But when he pressed her lips hard with his own, her arms came round his neck as if she would absorb him.

They were married one evening in Florence, just before they achieved the secret retreat from their lodgings. She had fought tooth and nail for an open ceremony, a public Mass, a flaunting of her new state before Nicholas, and he had to explain his reasons for secrecy. Once Nicholas knew where the round ship was sailing, his jealousy would be boundless. He would envy Pagano his beautiful bride. He would envy them both their golden future in Trebizond. He might even, Pagano told her, take ship and set out to stop them.

"He wouldn't *follow* us?" she had asked. She was white still, and moved about cautiously, content enough to be married in name. When she was ready, he had to lead her to the next barrier. He had promised her a wedding mass at Messina. And after that, he had let her understand lovingly, he would make her really his wife.

She hardly heard him, he thought; there was so much else happening. And now that she was a woman, all thought of returning to Flanders had gone. He had offered to write a long letter to her mother explaining it all, and she saw it go off, with his seal on it. Otherwise her mother would never believe it. She was going to Trebizond to learn how princesses lived, and dress in silk gowns and bracelets and rubies.

He thought she might even get them, if they were lucky.

Nicholas sailed two weeks later. It was a pity, and perhaps even a danger, that Doria had stolen a march on him, but a round ship could go where a galley could not, and it would have been folly to risk his ship earlier. Also, he had an instinct about Doria that he trusted more than the weather.

The last letter from Marian his wife came just before the *Ciaretti* left port. It said a little more than he was accustomed to hearing, because it was written at Christmastime; the first that had passed since they became man and wife; and they could not share it. As boy and mistress, they had never spent Christmas apart since he came to her dyeshop at ten, although the relationship had been shaped, for most of that time, by the berating edge of her voice and the frequent whack of the dyemaster's stick.

Even though he remembered, he did not smile, reading. Tilde was turning out a fine girl although it worried Marian that she hardly went out with her friends, but lingered about the office or dyeshop instead.

With young Catherine in Brussels, now her mother could do what she wanted; everything had become less troublesome, in a way. But that should not be so, because Catherine was a member of the family too, and it was wrong that she should come to think of her uncle and aunt as her parents, and Brussels as her home. Marian thought that in a short while she would send Gregorio to Brussels to talk with her. Cool and sensible, Gregorio would weigh matters up and would bring back a report she could trust. She prayed for Nicholas. She had made him a scarf. It was not in the Charetty colours. It was for him, himself. She had put her thoughts, she said, in the stitches.

When he unfolded it, he saw how fine it was, and guessed, since her days were so full, that she had worked every night to complete it. Every night, probably, since he went away.

He had sent her something too. A little music-box which uncoiled like baled cloth, and had perfect small teasels for hammers. He had made it himself, and got someone to cast it in silver. Her name was engraved on the side.

He had told Gregorio, but not Marian, the developing story of the *Doria*. He would be careful, of course. But his brief acquaintance with Pagano Doria had indicated a light-hearted man, amused by small devices. Godscalc thought the same. "That is a man," said the priest, "who sees the world as a mirror for his own excellent person. He toyed with me. He will toy with you. He does not seek to destroy us because we illuminate him."

Often, Nicholas found himself disconcerted by Godscalc. He said, "I thought perhaps I imagined it. I've felt, all these weeks, that Doria could have stopped this voyage of ours, if he'd wanted."

"And now he wants you to chase him," the priest said. "I am glad you've decided against it. Is chastity difficult?"

This time, it was not asked by a woman intent on dissecting another woman. Nor, it seemed, did the question hold any special pastoral emphasis. Nicholas said, "Why do you ask?"

"I'm not sure," said the priest. He wrinkled his brow so that the mess of black hair tangled into his eyebrows. He said, "He will look for a weak spot." His brown gaze, though direct, remained civil.

Nicholas said, "We'll dress Tobie up in my clothes. You liked Doria?"

"No," said Father Godscalc. "I think I was sorry for him."

"For *him*?" Nicholas said.

Shortly after, they sailed; precisely on time, thanks to the north winds of February. The mainsail was not painted; but in place of the lilies of Florence there flew from its mast a large silken flag in a peculiar blue which had cost Julius, in professional pain, three-fourths of the price of a weaving-loom. Below the mast lay one hundred and thirty-eight feet of floating debt called the *Ciaretti*.

The trumpets blew as she rowed out of Porto Pisano. The flourish

sang through the boisterous wind and drowned the imprecations of
fifty good seamen and a hundred highly paid members of the Charetty
army, seated three to a bench and attempting to keep time with each
other. They had been forbidden to sing leaving harbour, on account of
their unlikely repertoire.

Every other man stood on deck and watched the land recede, their
hair and cloaks snapped by the wind, and their blood hot for
adventure. Nicholas turned and looked at them all: the marine
bowmen already in place on the fighting-stage of the prow, or by the
mast, or on either side of the long central gangway. The mates, the
caulkers, the carpenters, the rowing-master and trumpets; the rest of
his team of eight helmsmen. Then, in the stern with the pilot and
steersman, his friends the officers of the ship and the company.
Godscalc its reserved and powerful chaplain. Tobie, bald and acid, its
barber-surgeon. Julius, former master and ally, its notary-purser,
with beside him the black face of Loppe, and their servants. The
bearded, complacent face of captain Astorre with Thomas his deputy.
John le Grant, seaman and engineer, with his eye on the wind and the
helmsman and a hand already half raised for the vital order, when the
oars would cease their massive drive and the ship would shake and
thunder and chime like a battlefield as, one by one, the sails would be
brought to break out and belly. He flung his arm up and, as they had
practised, it happened.

And so they were sailing, with the oars shipped and the cables
formed in their whorls, and men, excited and bright-faced, jostling,
talking together. His men. His ship. His risk. His success, or his
failure. No, Marian's.

He knew, better than anyone there, the size of the task he had
chosen. He knew he had to make the crew his, before Trebizond. Or
at least give them a pride in themselves, and their owner. He believed
he could do it. But deep-sea sailing was new, although he had spent
half his life at a seaport. He emerged from his winter congested with
study. He went to sea: the earth fell away and instead there was space,
into which he sprang vividly whole.

Julius watched, like the rest, as Nicholas overran the ship like a
wave, making it his own from the hold to the mast-basket. Passing
Tobie his bucket, he said, "He's taken to it." Tobie groaned. He had
taken to it; but in many ways he was isolated still by his ignorance.
The mechanics of sailing were simple – a matter of opposing forces, of
stress, of angles, of pure mathematics. The weather was not simple at
all, nor the pattern of human effort he had – through John le Grant –
to control and depend on. At sea, even material things – wood, rope
and canvas – changed their character; and had to be studied afresh. He
could not judge, as yet, either his boat or his men. When, suddenly,
the sea ahead turned rough and dark and the sky blackened, it was
John le Grant and his seamen who tested the strength of the coming

squall and saved time and effort by risking staying at sea instead of rushing for shelter. Already, le Grant had the respect of Astorre and the crew. On such occasions as these, Nicholas was a silent observer, with nothing to contribute.

There remained another unconquered dimension. Driving past Elba and Corsica, witnessing unreel on his left the coastline of Italy, Nicholas became aware of a limitation. He knew the political divisions of Italy: without that much, you could hardly organise trade, or a courier service, or plan to contract out an army. He knew where the lands of the Republic of Florence gave way to the lands of the city state of Siena; and where that in turn met the Papal States. Putting in to the harbour of Civita Vecchia, he pulled Tobie unwillingly to his feet to show him the hills on the horizon where, the year before, Tobie had confirmed the discovery which had made this venture possible. There, under the scrub and the turf, was the superb deposit of alum which Venice was paying the Charetty company to say nothing about. Sooner or later, of course, someone else would make all the deductions and find it. But by then . . . perhaps he would have found compensations.

That, so far, had been the extent of his interest and knowledge. It was the same when Rome had been passed, and the southern boundary of the Pope gave way to the frontier of the disputed Kingdom of Naples, where last year Astorre and the army had fought for King Ferrante against the French-supported John of Calabria. He thought he knew all about the Italian coast, although he had never seen it before. Then he caught snatches of conversation between Pavia-educated Tobie and Godscalc the priest, his sick-visitor.

Serving Julius and Felix in Louvain, Nicholas had learned to understand Latin. To a mind that absorbed and retained, its grammar was easy. But Godscalc and Tobie were quoting poems; recalling legends; speaking of great civilisations as if they mattered today. It had not occurred to Nicholas to wonder who had possessed these lands before, or what mistakes they had made, or what successes they had had. The world today held enough of wonder and challenge for him.

He did not dismiss what he heard, because, if nothing else, he was intelligent. He placed it in his memory, to be thought about.

Outside Naples, they armed. Later, they might expect roving pirates, although they were less common in winter. All the time, there were Genoese vessels lying in wait in these waters, to board and rob and kill as the French masters of Genoa directed.

The *Ciaretti* passed through them unscathed. Pagano Doria had been speaking the truth. Whatever he held against the Charetty company, it was personal. No orders had come from Genoa to hinder their voyage.

Many of the harbours they used had seen the *Doria*. In Sicily, they learned they were only ten days behind. The round ship had paused at Messina, picking up grain; unloading Catalonian sugar and all those strings of fat cheeses. They had done more, as Julius returned on board, flushed, to complain. There was no water to spare at the wharf. Nor were there any hens to be had, or beef – live or salted – or biscuit, or fish in the keg. Another purser, well provided with florins, had cleared out all they had.

It was raining. Nicholas, wearing his boat cloak over a fuzzy felt cap, said, "Where's the list?"

Julius said, "They want three times the usual prices. And we have to wait."

"What do you wager?" said Nicholas.

He came back in three hours, followed by a train of porters carrying everything. The prices were half what was normal. Julius was surprised and resentful.

"Well, you did it yourself," Nicholas said. Sicily was full of the new season's vintage, and he had deployed it like Bacchus.

"What?" said Julius.

"Fought for Ferrante in Naples. The viceroy in Palermo knows all about the Charetty company, and so does his agent in Messina. Water, cattle and chickens."

Julius went red. He said, "How did they know?"

Nicholas grinned. "Letters from Monna Alessandra. Don't you remember? Lorenzo's brother trained in Palermo."

"She wrote letters of recommendation for you?" Tobie sounded disbelieving.

"Well, she wouldn't write them for you," Nicholas said. "And we've got all Doria's cheeses."

"Cheeses?" said Julius.

"Yes. He sold them to his agent in Messina, and the agent's had to sell them to us. By the viceroy's special order. At half-price. They're good cheeses, too," said Nicholas. "I think Messina's been bad luck for Doria. Did you hear that he married while he was here?"

"That was sudden," said Tobie.

"No; a girl with a dog. She was on the galley already."

"The veiled midget?" said Julius.

"She isn't veiled now. And she isn't a midget. She's a child: twelve or thirteen years old, says the agent."

Godscalc said, "I don't like the sound of that very much."

"At least they're married," said Julius.

"Even so," said the priest. He looked at Julius and then at Nicholas who shook his head, and then smiled, and then heaved up the wine flask.

"And what about the rest of the journey?" Julius said. "Have you got letters for every provision merchant? They may not know Lorenzo Strozzi's brother, whereas the Doria have served them for centuries. No water; no food. We'll be living on biscuits."

"Well, biscuits and cheese," Nicholas said.

At times during the sail from Messina across the flat Ionian Sea, Julius returned to the question, but with lessening conviction. The crew had settled into a team. The cook had learned how to create dishes for Astorre's satisfaction. The soldiers, natural athletes, had succeeded with small trouble in mastering their work at the oars, and more besides. They knew, too, enough jargon to converse with the seamen, and were learning more every day. At meals, the leaders of the Charetty company spoke Greek together while, at odd times and in odd corners, Nicholas made the African Loppe repeat all he had ever learned of Arabic. With the aid of Loppe, also, he taught himself the art of swimming with credit. When, over supper, his officers raised, again, the question of the *Doria*, he answered calmly, "I doubt if the *Doria* can spare the time to stop where we're stopping. We'll only cross tracks at the big ports. Modon next, for example. He's got to unload there."

"Then let's pass it," said Tobie. "Take on supplies somewhere else, and go straight on to Gallipoli."

"Well, we can't," Nicholas said. "We've got to pick up our passenger."

They had assumed they were now in his confidence. He had said nothing at all of a passenger. Julius looked exasperated. "Didn't I tell you?" Nicholas said. "The Greek with the wooden leg. Nicholai Giorgio de' Acciajuoli. John doesn't know him." He explained amiably to John le Grant, ignoring the others, "We call him Greek, but he's from the Florentine race who used to rule Athens. He came to Bruges, raising money to ransom his brother. Without him, we might not have thought of this voyage."

"What's he doing in Modon?" said the engineer.

"Trading. Bartolomeo his brother is free now, and sells silk in Constantinople. Well: Pera, over the water. With the help of Acciajuoli, we'll do business with him."

"You're talking of Bartolomeo Zorzi? I saw him captured. Silk, yes. And more. That's the man that runs the Venetian alum monopoly. Did ye know that?"

Nicholas grinned and waited.

"Yes. We knew that," said Tobie. "Well, are we going to stand here all day? I'm freezing."

They moved away, all but Nicholas and John le Grant. "So it's a matter of alum," said the engineer. "And you with a dyeshop: of course, you and your guild'll need fixatives. Well, a friend with a pinty leg'll do ye nae harm. The tax the Turks put on alum is shocking."

"Shocking," said Nicholas. "We need all the friends we can get."

"Well?" said the red-haired man at length, "are ye going to tell me what you're up to, or have I got to get your notary drunk?"

During the last days at sea, Nicholas had made up his mind about John le Grant. It always pleased him to talk about Tolfa. Nor did he see why Julius should have all the fun. He collected some wine, and took John le Grant off to the stern castle.

Later, Tobie saw them emerge. The engineer was looking thoughtful. Nicholas, on the other hand, was dimpled in the private, conspiratorial manner of a hot pool on the verge of explosion. He did not look like a man who was giving due thought to Pagano Doria.

Which was a pity. Because the first thing they saw in the harbour at Modon, within the Venetian seawalls and under the flag of St Mark, was the immense, castled bulk of the round ship *Doria*.

Chapter 9

THE FORTRESS OF MODON, or Methoni, was Venetian. Its harbour was good, and its position was even better: at the south-
western point of the old Greek Morea peninsula, halfway
between the heel of civilised Italy and the pagan Ottoman
lands to the east. It was the Serenissima's chief naval base in eastern
waters, and their main port of call for the Holy Land. Ships from
Venice made their way thence to Crete or Cyprus or Alexandria, or up
the Aegean Sea to Negroponte and Gallipoli and Constantinople. Men
called Modon the eye of Venice, as Corfu was its door, and two
thousand people lived and worked there.

The round ship called *Doria* lay now in the mole, below the long,
turreted seawall with its double gate and regular towers. Tilted on the
hillside above Modon the wall continued, embracing the town, with its
houses, churches, workshops, hostels, barracks, taverns, brothels,
store-sheds and markets; the Bailie's handsome residence, and the
citadel, interspersed with the red of turned earth and the beige of winter
grass and the bare branches of fruit trees between. On the left, the
church of St John had its own landing stage. And at intervals all round
the walls the battle-towers kept watch, and the arms of the windmills
wheeled against the wet skies of a Grecian winter, watched by Monna
Caterina de Charetty negli Doria.

For Catherine, the distance between Messina and Modon could not
be measured in sea miles. In Messina, she had completed her wedding
rites in the eyes of the Church. On shipboard after the wedding mass
she had refused the attentions of her wonderful husband, sobbing and
whimpering. It was Pagano himself who had coaxed her to tell him the
terrible things she had heard, and then to point out the shipwomen who
had described them to her. She heard they were thrashed. Certainly,
they were ashore in a trice, and if others came in their place, they didn't
come near her. And Pagano, who understood everything, said that real
love was nothing like that but, until she could trust him, they would
make love with their hands. He would show her.

She was nervous at first, and pulled away often. Then she grew accustomed to his light caresses and, from agreeable, they became delightful enough to make her head turn and send small convulsions through her body and limbs. When the first large convulsion arrived, she thought something was wrong, and had to be taught how to enjoy it. For a while there was nothing else she could imagine that would give her more happiness, and then she realised that something was lacking still. Her husband's share, that the women had told her of.

The time had come, she well knew, to think about that. She denied him her bed while she did so, because she was no longer sure any more what she wanted. When a second night passed and she was still unwilling to let him coax her into pleasure, he had drawn back himself and said, "Catherine, Catherine. Do you think I would ever hurry you? Let's stay friends until you are ready. It's only . . ."

"You would like it," she supplied. She liked to think that he would.

He smiled. "You don't know, do you, what it means to me? There's no reason why you should. But no. I can wait. Only Nicholas won't."

"*Nicholas?*" The name, from the past, seemed an idiocy. She stared at him.

He said, "I didn't mean to tell you. I don't want you frightened. But he is following."

"*Our* Nicholas?" Catherine said. For the first time since Messina, she thought of Nicholas and her mother together. She felt herself turning red, and tears came into her eyes.

Pagano said, in his nicest voice, "You're quite fond of him really."

Her breath caught like the clap of a bellows. "I hate him!" she said. "How could he . . . ?"

He stroked her hair while she gulped. He said, "It's the most extraordinary bad luck. You see, he doesn't even know you are here. He's going to Trebizond as I am, on business. They say he's to be Florentine consul. That means he'll be there while you and I are at court. Of course, he won't disturb you; I'll see to that. He'll hardly know you, with your gowns and your jewels. And he'll have to work very hard, I can tell you, to get any business because I mean to take it all. In fact, he won't like it in the least. Perhaps I should see him at Modon and tell him I've married his stepdaughter. Then he'll be bound to go home to your mother."

Nicholas and her mother. She said, "No."

And then he dropped his hands and said, "No. Because he'd try to take you with him and get our marriage annulled. Since we're not man and wife, you see, Catherine. That is, only on paper."

She said, "I wouldn't mind him in Trebizond. He's only an apprentice."

"You wouldn't?" Pagano said. "But you hate hiding. And at Modon, you'd have to stay out of sight. I think I should tell him. Then he'll go home to Flanders. After all, everyone thinks we are lovers. So will he."

She laid her cheek on his chest. She said, "I couldn't wear a veil all the time. Not in Trebizond."

"You wouldn't need to," he said. "Once Nicholas has got his cargo that far, he will have to stay until he's finished his business. And by then he'll have found out how happy we are. He'll be in no haste to get back . . . Catherine, do you really not mind if he sails to Trebizond too?"

"No," she said. "But I want to be in Trebizond first."

He laughed. He had wonderful teeth. He said, "And so rather do I. Let's think how to do it. Shall we? You and I? A little mishap at Modon; a little deterrent at Constantinople. But my Caterinetta must stay out of sight meanwhile. Agreed?"

"Agreed!" she exclaimed.

They played a card game, and then another; and then a tumbling game he had taught her, in which she found herself, as nearly always, in his arms. Then she thought of Nicholas and heard herself saying, "Really, I ought to know. I'm married. I ought to know."

And he laughed, in a way that wasn't quite right because he was so surprised, and said, "But you do know, my precious. All except the last and sweetest iota. Blow the light out, my little princess, and let me give you your crown."

It was something of a shock, but rather less than she had feared. The second time, she recognised that this was fulfilment, and no artifice could ever compare with it. She also knew, a discovery she would not forget, that for the duration of her hospitality the lord Pagano Doria lost his sovereignty: art and artifice vanished in stress. As often as she chose to become queen, she caused him to become less than princely.

Next day she walked on deck, to and fro, calm and smiling and silent. She hardly spoke, all that voyage to Modon. But every dusk she made her way to their cabin, and he joined her. What was common practice, she had no way of telling. He was as witty as ever; as considerate and as charming. She made deductions, from what he appeared to think proper. Marriage, it seemed, resembled a tournament, where some submitted to organised bouts, and some fought at will, expending senses and strength in their vehemence. Catherine, held in high pleasure, had no reservations, while recognising at once which was natural to him. She pleased herself, fostering it. And made herself his most adoring audience, when he spoke of plans for hampering Nicholas.

By the time the Florentine galley arrived at Modon, the *Doria* had been there several days, and (for a Genoese) its commander had become quite an acceptable visitor at the Venetian Bailie's house.

These days, Modon was crammed. Always a well-used maritime junction, serving Venetian ships coming in from Constantinople, Cyprus, Syria; storing raisins, ashes, cotton and silk for the next fleet; offering repairs and provisions and hospitality to the travellers who poured through its gates, it was now one of the few Venetian colonies in the Turkish-occupied peninsula, and full of refugees. It was also a fortress. Over all ruled the lord Giovanni Bembo the Bailie, a patrician and capable: a man who could entertain kings on their way to Jerusalem and spies who had news of the Turks. For him, Pagano Doria represented light relief. And besides, it was the quiet season for shipping, for more reasons than one. Pagano Doria told him everything he wanted to know: some of it almost true. He unloaded and loaded his cargo; exchanged visits; entertained and was entertained. At no point was he accompanied by a woman.

When, with a swirl of trumpets and a couple of bangs from her cannon, the *Ciaretti* swept into the bay of Sapienza, the Bailie had already heard a good deal of the galley. She looked better than he expected, slipping past under oar to her berth. She and the round ship saluted each other impeccably. As soon as they were settled, he received their messenger, with the formal letters endorsed by the Medici. In return, he sent his chamberlain on board with a gift of strong rumney wine and an invitation to sup at his house the next evening. Unavoidable, naturally. He thought he might get the man Doria to help with the honours. One wondered what had come over the Medici, to give a peasant a consulate, even if he had a shrewd eye for a bargain. Battle fodder, poor lad. Intent on making his name and his fortune.

On board the *Ciaretti*, the sharp eyes of Julius had scanned the round ship as they passed. The little devil Doria was there. He saw the fronds of his feathered cap above a cloak thick with gold, and glimpsed his face, glowing with pleasure. Doria bowed, but Nicholas didn't. Nicholas said, "I hope the bastard blows himself up."

"Well, we've caught him," Julius said. "We've caught him, and le Grant says we could pass him, if we get out quickly. I don't know. I'd rather like to meet him on shore and have a little talk about those stores at Messina." One of his grievances in Florence had been the cowardly attitude of his fellows. Because Doria was Genoese consul, it would be undiplomatic to knock him down in the street. Julius had chafed. But for Doria, that fiend of a priest would never have shamed him before the Medici.

Now Nicholas said, "If we meet him on shore, we expect you to shame him with courtesy. Don't get into a brawl; it would suit him. In fact, I'd like to know what little snare he's prepared for us here. I'd like to know why he waited here. Look. There's a galley from Rhodes at the steps. We'll get news."

"We'll get it from Acciajuoli," Julius said. "Your privately contracted passenger with the wooden leg. Your oracle, as it were. Wood, you know. Why not a log of this trip for the Golden Fleece? You might get a knighthood. No, I'd suit it better. You're the Ram and I'm Jason. We need a Medea."

"Tobie," said Nicholas. "Give him a wig and he'll cook up some poison. We'll send it to the *Doria*." Julius was reassured.

It was their eighth landfall. They knew all the formalities. They received the Bailie's invitation and enjoyed his rumney and were informed that their wooden-legged oracle Acciajuoli had been detained in Patras, but should be ready to join them by sailing time. Only Nicholas seemed to find that exasperating. They fell, rather quickly, into their routine for repair and provisioning and added an extra precaution. From the moment of berthing, the *Ciaretti* was guarded. And her crew were not allowed on shore; only her officers.

The precaution, though wise, seemed unneeded. If Doria intended some mischief, it had not so far become apparent, although the town was full of his men. In the course of the day's business Julius glimpsed and nodded to Crackbene, the *Doria* captain. The other man responded without rancour. Later, Nicholas came face to face with Doria himself, getting into his skiff.

He had expected it, but was still chilled with some sense of foreboding. It was stupid to take Doria seriously. Whatever it turned into at Trebizond, their rivalry so far was no more than a boys' competition. Once, he would have delighted in it, and the chance to use all his ingenuity. Now he was not so sure. He had counted on Acciajuoli to prime the Venetian Bailie with all he ought to know about the Charetty company. Instead, Acciajuoli had not yet arrived, and all the Bailie knew had been imparted by Pagano Doria. Chance had given Doria a new weapon: he needed no other. And he had had time, too, to protect himself against anything the *Ciaretti* might do. Le Grant, pestered by Julius, had produced a number of ingenious ways of blighting the *Doria*, such as feeding rats by the score up the anchor-chain. Nicholas had put a stop to it. Julius had returned to his depression. Well, Julius would have to wait.

Now Doria looked up from the skiff, his feathers blowing, and said, "The greyhound of the seas, my dear man. If I hadn't been held up in Corfu, you wouldn't have glimpsed me until the Black Sea. But never mind. I hear we shall see you at supper tonight?"

It was news, but it needn't appear so. "Unless we sail first," said Nicholas. "How are you for cheese? We have more than we need. I'll send a box over."

"But how kind!" said Doria. "What can we give you, that you would appreciate?"

"I shall try to think of something," Nicholas said.

On board, Nicholas saw Godscalc was watching him. Godscalc said, "This supper party. You're worried?"

The question was what he needed. It was all ridiculous: he saw it, and laughed. "Not really. With Tobie's Latin and Julius's Greek and John's guns and your God, our total resources will blind a mere Bailie."

"You have come so far on your wits," said Godscalc in his dulcet German-tinged Flemish. "You have no need to doubt them."

"I don't," said Nicholas. "A pack of cards and a song, and they'll love me." He added, in case of misunderstanding, "It's all right. But I know what I'd do, if I were Pagano Doria."

The evening unfolded, and he watched himself being proved right. The Bailie's seamen, who fetched them, provided their escort to the gates of his palace. It was impressive, as Venice intended. It was more old-fashioned than, say, the new Medici house in Milan, but reminded him of it in its profusion of marble floors, its gilding, its painted ceilings and walls. The room in which they were entertained was large and well warmed and blazed with a display of the Bailie's family silver. The candelabra were distinguished; the table linen exquisite; some of the platters antique and quite precious, although clearly the best had not been put on show. The gathering, too, was fairly modest. The five from the Charetty, the Bailie and his chaplain, secretary and captain of galleys; and Pagano Doria. They seated themselves, and wine was poured, and well-sauced food was lined up before them. On orders, Tobie sat beside Julius, restraining him.

It was the Bailie's intention, as well, that the evening should pass as smoothly as might be. A practised host, he preferred light conversation while eating, trusting to the free-flowing wine to produce confidences later. To soften the blow, too, of the news he had to deliver. Meanwhile, he did not probe, as might be unmannerly, into the reasons behind the Medicis' apparent decision to expand in the East, or enquire whether the Head of St Andrew was likely to convince the Pope to send a fleet to rescue the Morea. In any case, he had already discussed these matters in his many talks with the lord Pagano Doria.

There were topics, of course, which he would not broach with a Genoese, anyway. When talking of Trebizond, one did not naturally refer to the friction between the Genoese bank of St George and the Emperor. Both sides, of course, erred. The Emperor extracted illicit duties and harboured Genoese rebels. Once, a slap on the face at a chess game had set the Genoese raiding his empire for prisoners. When they captured them, they had sent him a jarful of salt ears and noses. In its time, the Genoese colony at Trebizond had been put to the sword for its arrogance, and later avenged by its fellows in fire. And, of course, his own countrymen suffered. Venetian galleys had been forced to burn Genoese shipping at Trebizond. When the Genoese took the best sites, the Venetians had to complain. They had to complain, too, when the Emperor failed to build or repair as he promised.

The Emperor David of Trebizond was extremely loath to part with his money. The Bailie had heard that he owed the bank of St George thousands of lire. At one point, the Mother Republic had told all her merchants to leave. But they needed the trade, and the Emperor needed them, and Genoa required support for her other, bigger headquarters, so the colony was still there, even though consuls were hard to find. Until now. The Bailie had no objection to Doria, a civilised man. He had no fears, either, for his own very able counterpart in the city of Trebizond.

Having reviewed what he could not discuss and what he had already exhausted, the Bailie, a diplomat of long standing, resorted this evening to polite trivialities. He began with the sea and the weather, asked for news of the voyage and then showed his personal interest in each of his guests. He was discussing lading matters with the notary Julius when the word Bologna was mentioned. He was at once reminded of Bessarion, that great churchman of Trebizond whose mother still lived in that city, and whose library had been left in this very town, Modon. He was speaking with, he thought, modest acceptance when Messer Pagano dropped his knife with a clatter, and began talking with animation of nothing until the Bailie, taking the hint, changed the subject.

He tried to engage in conversation the very young man with the scar. He found it hard to think of him as a consul. He had hardly begun when Messer Doria, seeking to help, asked the youth civilly if he yet had a son or a daughter. The young man's answer was unenlightening enough, but from what Doria let fall in confusion it seemed that the youth's wife was forty, and he and she had been together since he was ten. The Bailie switched the conversation again.

It was Doria, in the end, who came to the rescue. He gave up, like the Bailie, the effort to find common ground and reverted to chatting instead of acquaintances known to himself and the Venetian; of spicy intrigues and amusing vendettas and scandals. The Duchess of Athens. The scholar Filelfo and his mother-in-law. The home life, God help them, of these crazy Byzantines. The Emperor David's late brother who tried to kill both their parents. His mother who slept with her treasurer. His sister the Empress who had been caught in the marital position with her brother. A different one. And this, which the princess had told him . . .

Seduced from his difficult duties, the Bailie gave the Genoese his cordial attention. It left Nicholas stranded, Godscalc saw. The talk had turned to high social tattle, and Nicholas had no social experience.

Lesser officers could chat to each other, and the men from the *Doria* fell into conversation soon enough with their opposite numbers. Godscalc watched; wondering if Nicholas would give up and join them. Doria was saying, "All the Sultan does, we are told, is favour his own sex, which could be a tactical advantage. Does the Emperor realise it? Are his envoys too plain?" He broke off. "Alas! I think I have shocked Messer Niccolò! Would you be wise to turn back? My dear fellow: one glance at your handsome notary, and Mehmet will go mad."

Julius opened his mouth. "That's why I brought him," said Nicholas. "My lord Bailie, forgive me. You and Messer Pagano must be weary of discussing the Sultan. But I see a ship from Rhodes in the harbour. I wondered if you had anything recent to tell us?"

Wrenched from his pleasant diversion, the Bailie thought, on reflection, that he might as well pass on his news. If it brought the evening to a premature end, his guest had no one to blame but himself. He said, "Of course. I had thought to leave serious matters till later but . . . By all means, let it be now, if you wish. The ship you saw did bring news. It seems to be true. It affects us all. It is better, I fear, for me than for you. My lord Pagano, this is new to you also."

Doria turned his head sharply.

"About the Turk?" Nicholas said.

The Bailie looked at him. He was not an unfeeling man. He said carefully, "You know about this young Sultan. He builds an empire. Today he is concerned to drive the Greeks and the Serbs from the northern part of his lands. Tomorrow he will look to the south, to Asia Minor, where his lands are at present surrounded. Part is occupied by the Empire of Trebizond, which pays him tribute already. In the rest, he is baulked by powerful tribes. The rival Turcomans of the Black and White Hordes and their princes. The Sultan of Karamania. The emir of Sinope. The Christian princes of Georgia, Mingrelia. Many of these are uniting against him. Many are allied in marriage. Some of them have envoys in Europe, with Fra Ludovico da Bologna. You have met him."

Pagano Doria said, "And, my lord, you think the Turk is about to cross into Asia?"

"I ought to rejoice," the Bailie said. "What has occurred will divert his attention from the Morea. But it is nevertheless a tragedy created only by laziness, vanity, ignorance."

"What happened?" said Nicholas.

The Bailie placed his fingers together. He said, "Perhaps the Emperor of Trebizond expected too much from his alliances; his appeals to the West. He had sent to the Pope. He had sent to Philip of Burgundy, promising to make him King of Jerusalem. There has been no time, of course, for any response. But the Emperor thought enough of his prospects, it seems, to withhold his annual tribute to the Sultan. Instead of paying his three thousand pieces of gold, he sent to Constantinople demanding remission. Unwisely, he entrusted the message to men who were already armed with a demand of their own. Not a demand: a deliberate insult. He used the envoys of his niece's husband, the Persian prince Uzum Hasan."

"A powerful man," Nicholas said. The priest looked at him.

"His envoys think so," said the Bailie. "The envoys of Uzum Hasan went to Constantinople and committed their madness. They announced that the Emperor of Trebizond wished to pay no more tax. I doubt if they were tactful. Then they told Sultan Mehmet that their own prince Uzum Hasan desired an account to be settled. The Sultan's grandfather had promised an annual gift to the grandfather of Uzum Hasan. For sixty years, it had never been paid."

Doria's eyes shone. "They demanded all the arrears?"

"They demanded all the arrears," said the Bailie. "Equipment for one thousand horses, added to one thousand prayer rugs and one thousand measures of corn. Multiplied sixty-fold."

"Imbeciles," Tobie said.

"The King of Kings didn't pay it?" Doria suggested.

The Bailie said, "He didn't keep the envoys, or kill them. He told them to go in peace, for soon he would bring these things with him, and pay what debt he might owe. He keeps his promises, Sultan Mehmet. He means war. Against, one assumes, Uzum Hasan. Against, very likely, more than Uzum Hasan. They say he is building a fleet there in Constantinople, the like of which has never been seen."

The Bailie paused. The Bailie said, "You, my lord consul of Florence, my lord consul of Genoa, knew the danger, I should suppose, before you left Italy. In sailing east, you have already committed yourselves to more than the business of trade. You are brave men. I shall not ask what you carry, or what you propose to do: we here in Modon are trading ourselves under sufferance. But I salute you."

"Capers, mainly," said Nicholas cheerfully. The high spirits were genuine, Godscalc noticed. He supposed he ought to find that reassuring. Nevertheless he was relieved when the visit ended quite soon. After such news, there could be little to say. What there was, he hardly heard anyway.

Rather more important than capers, the *Ciaretti* was bringing a hundred armed soldiers to stiffen Trebizond. If the Turk ever suspected, they'd never win past Constantinople. And if the prankish Pagano Doria ever found out, it could be equally dangerous. Meanwhile, what they had heard merely attached names and dates to risks they already knew. Before, there had been a chance that the Medici trial year would elapse and the Turk would do nothing in Asia. Now, the summer might see an attack. But not necessarily on Trebizond. Remote, mountain-girt Trebizond from which the Sultan was already milking off tribute. *That secluded Paradise*, Bessarion had written, *rich with all the treasures of the earth*.

The doctor Tobie, who spoke a different language from Bessarion, had put it at once in a nutshell. "You want to know about our business venture in Trebizond? If the Turk doesn't attack, or attacks someone else, we're in clover. If the Turk attacks and we win, we're in roses. If the Turk attacks and we fall, then you and I get a stake up the arse, Julius gets cut for a eunuch and Nicholas gets to wind up a dye business as well as a farmuk. It'll make a real mess of his ledgers."

"He'll adapt," Godscalc had said. He half meant it. It was his reading of Nicholas, then.

After the animation of leave-taking, the Bailie's guests were on the whole a subdued party, walking downhill to the sea gates. Of the Charetty company, Julius had his mind on arrows for crossbows. Both Tobie and Godscalc were thoughtful. John le Grant, who said very little, had long ago lapsed into silence. Only Messer Pagano, leaving his officers, had linked his arm through that of Nicholas and now fell into step with him, talking. On each side of them came the Bailie's guard with their torches, and behind, their own servants had joined them. Among them was Loppe, taking care to keep clear of black Noah.

Doria seemed in good humour, and in no want of a more friendly companion. He produced a stream of good stories, some (in a murmur) at the expense of their recent and well-meaning host. Julius distrusted Pagano's style of humour. Nicholas evidently did so as well. He smiled now and then, but without undue resort to his dimples. It was the first time Julius had observed this phenomenon.

Pagano Doria knew Modon. Instead of making direct for the shore, he got their escort to take them nearer the fringe of the town, where the solid houses were fewer and reed-thatched cabins clustered instead; the homes of the smiths. This was not the Arsenal. This was the quarter for native craftsmen. Here they worked out of doors, red-eyed tailors of iron, seated crosslegged each in an apron of light from his window. A boy or woman knelt tending every fire. The bladders swelled and sank to their thrust, half-buried like burrowing piglets. Behind the chimes of the anvils, their eager confusion of panting recalled the hunt, and the kill. Yet nothing could have been more still, or more peaceful.

That is, until Doria's party approached. Then heads turned, and children jumped to their feet, and the wayward chords became spaced and irregular, and were replaced by the drumming of bare feet on dirt, and the sound of harsh voices. Lean bodies fenced out the light, and hands poked and jabbed, clutching objects of leather and metal. "Buy! Buy!" they were calling.

The Bailie's escort closed politely about them. But Julius put one hand on his purse and one on the hilt of his dagger, and wondered why they were here.

Pagano, the firelight ruddy on his straight nose and well-spaced cheeks and mathematical chin, was quick to tell them. "Messer Niccolò! We represent the Western world: the Bailie said so. We are fellow-voyagers, friends on this Argosy. Against the dragon, the Turk, I will defend you, as you, I am sure, will defend me. But in trade, in the matter of bringing back gold, we are rivals."

"Isn't there enough for us all?" Nicholas said. His voice had altered.

Pagano Doria laughed, and the firelight illumined the amphitheatre of his teeth. He said, "Not for me. I shall be satisfied by nothing less than the whole Fleece. But in chivalry it is usual for knights to face each other equally armed."

"Knights?" Nicholas said.

Doria glanced at his neighbours and smiled. "Gentlemen, then," he made amend.

"Gentlemen?" Nicholas said.

The smile lessened, but did not vanish. "But of course," the Genoese said. "A consul can be nothing else."

"No matter what he does?"

Pagano Doria, with four men and his servants behind him, looked across the dark space between himself and Nicholas, standing taller than any man there save the chaplain. Around them the voices of vendors still chattered and shouted, but the escort were silent. Loppe had moved nearer Julius. Beside the black page, a white page had arrived by the Genoese party. "But of course," said Doria. "You are Florence; I am Genoa. We make our own laws."

"But you think we should be armed," Nicholas said.

The light of the fires, playing through the crowds, struck starry colours from Doria's wide hat with its jewels and streamers, and two sparks from the caves of his eyes. He threw out a gloved hand. "Look there, on that stall. I have had two daggers fashioned. They are identical, except that your name is on one, and mine on the other. The price is fair. Unless you object, I propose that we each present one to the other. A symbol, you might say. Whatever is to occur, we set out as equals."

The weapons were there, laid on a table by one of the anvils. Men drew back, and Doria walked past and fingered them. He said, "Or perhaps the price is inconvenient. Let me present you with one."

Nicholas had stopped sounding like someone else. The laugh he gave was Claes's laugh, uninhibited, all the way from boyhood and Bruges. "Not at all. I'll take them both," he said. "And present you with one later on."

The pause before Doria also laughed was very small. He said, "You don't like my fancy. Leave it. The smith will not mind."

But as he was speaking, Nicholas opened his purse and put coins on the table. It was more, Julius saw, than the weapons were worth, although they were good ones. Then he picked up one of the daggers. Before he could pick up the other, Doria laid a coin down himself and took the other blade neatly. He said, "I prefer to pay my way now."

"Like a gentleman," Nicholas said. He reflected, and then removed his extra coin. The smith's hand, stealing out, recovered in silence the price of the two. Pagano Doria tilted his blade so that the firelight exposed the inscription. Then he held out his hand.

"Messer Niccolò: your mistake. You have the weapon with my name."

"And you have the other with mine. What mistake?" Nicholas said.

This time, the silence was longer. The red light flashed from the steel into their eyes. The bodies and heads, pressing about, seemed suffused by it. The jewel in Pagano's hat flashed and flashed again.

It was not, Julius saw, being lit by the fire or the knife blade. It was catching the light from the harbour. From, no doubt, the basket-light on its post at the mole.

It was not catching the light from the mole. It was throwing back fire from a fire on the water itself. From a ship on the water. From a great galley at anchor. From the *Ciaretti*, enfolded in crimson-shot smoke.

Their ship was in flames.

Chapter 10

B Y THE TIME Julius drew breath, others had shouted, and men were turning, alarmed, towards the glare in the harbour. At first, no one seemed to move. Julius struggled, hammering with his fists on the shoulders of others until suddenly he was loosened as men started forward. The rest of the town had already roused. Fire was serious. Modon had seen fire often before. Trumpets blew from the walls. Men and women emerged from their houses. The ways down to the gates and the shore carried a growing concourse of people. Only Nicholas didn't run. He stood, a boulder in a stampede, and stared over and beyond the moving heads of the crowd to a small figure just at its edge.

Julius saw him. Nicholas was staring at Doria's page. At the black servant Noah. Or perhaps at the white who, Julius saw, broke away presently, grinning. The next moment, both pages had turned and, racing away from the crowd edge, had vanished. Then Nicholas started to run, but not to the shore. Head lowered, blunt as a ram, he drove across the thrust of the crowd, in the direction the pages had taken. It was, of course, senseless: a belabouring progress against close-packed, hurrying people that made no speed at all. Julius, making use of his wake, overtook him. He seized an elbow and roared. *"Look! The* Ciaretti's *on fire!"*

Nicholas paid no attention. His eyes, fixed ahead, were searching the further side of the crowd. Julius struck him and Nicholas wheeled. Julius dropped his arms. Then, saying nothing, Nicholas turned and continued his incongruous charge in the same direction as before. Julius stood in the torchlight and stared after him, rocking under the impact of other men's bodies. Tobie crashed into him, grabbed him and said, "I saw that."

Julius said, "Saw him ready to kill me?"

Tobie got his hand up and, declaration of war, hauled off his cap. His hairless scalp glistened. "You go," he said. "Leave him to the company doctor."

A second passed, and then Julius said, "Yes," and set off. Over his shoulder he saw Tobie begin, in his turn, to force his way after Nicholas. Who had lost his wits, or suffered a fit. Who had received notification, you might say, that hell existed and he was to prove it. Rarely fanciful, Julius didn't like what he had seen in Nicholas's face.

When Tobie caught him, Nicholas had struck beyond the last, busy pathway and was casting through alleys in the flickering darkness. The glare from the burning *Ciaretti* distorted everything. Leaping from one inky shadow to the next were goats which ought to be people; cats which were possibly children; men and women who showed their fear and resentment when a foreign giant dashed headlong between them and ran on in silence, followed by a smaller man without the price of a hat. When Nicholas began to slow, Tobie slowed also, hoping that matters were returning to normal. Against that, Nicholas had thrown not a glance towards the distant seawall, and the crawling column of red that disfigured the night sky beyond it.

Nicholas stopped. Breathing hard, Tobie advanced. He said, "What did you see?"

A man winded by effort will pant. Instead, Nicholas stood taking in air in erratic and terror-filled spasms, as if escaping from something rather than running towards it. He was also shaking.

Tobie walked round and stood firmly in front of him, scanning his face. He said, "Is it more important than the ship?" He saw what had shocked Julius.

Nicholas looked at him. There were people standing in doorways and watching them. Women and grandfathers, mostly. All the able men were down by the shore. All except the owner of one hundred and thirty-eight feet of floating debt, now consolidating itself into cinders.

Nicholas said, "You wouldn't remember her."

"Who?" He thought he knew.

"Catherine," Nicholas said, proving he didn't. "The little one. Marian's . . . He'll have her back on board. A boat. I need a boat."

Catherine. "*Catherine de Charetty?*" Tobie said. He didn't show disbelief. He said, "How? Where?"

"With Doria," said Nicholas. "The white page. With the black one." He looked at Tobie, and the red light striped his cheek, over the scar. He said, "Don't you remember? He married in Sicily. She was on board. Veiled. Twelve or thirteen, they said. She was even in Florence. She was in Florence, and I didn't do anything." He looked at Tobie with recognition and almost with a recognisable manner. He said, "Go to the *Ciaretti* and do what you can. I have to board Doria's ship."

"Why?" said Tobie. He had had time to think quickly. "Kill him; take her away? She's been his wife ever since Sicily. Tonight, he has fifty men on that ship, and he'll laugh at you. Your galley is burning.

He'll laugh at that as well. You have to see to that first, or give the family another disaster to deal with. What will a few hours do to the girl that hasn't been done already?"

He conveyed brisk impatience. He had no idea whether the man had had a nightmare or whether there was an atom of truth in what he was saying, nor did it matter. He thought he could get him back to his ship. The question was whether, once there, he had any stamina left to do any good. But even that mattered less than getting there.

Tobie said, "You really can't desert your own crew. Tomorrow, let's try something that has a chance of succeeding."

You could hear the roar of people, far away, behind the nearer sounds of shuffling feet and people talking. After an agonising space, Nicholas said, "Yes."

On the way downhill, Tobie quickened his pace and then broke into a run. Nicholas did the same, after a moment. The wetness had dried on his face: he had been unaware of it. On the shore, the waves slapped at the quays in scarlet peaks and black shadows. Between the sea and the shore, the crowds of would-be helpers were in disarray and, dismayingly, Julius and the rest were still among them. Where skiffs and ships' boats had claimed every stanchion by daylight, now the places were empty. Ranging fast round the beach, someone had found a shallop, but it was holed. By the time a shed had been unlocked and a boat launched, the smoke, pumice-grey, was pouring towards them and turning the water to lava.

Godscalc, Julius and le Grant were scrambling in just as Tobie pounded towards them, Nicholas following. Tobie sprang into the boat, his fingers dug in the notary's shoulder. Julius, who had opened his mouth, slowly shut it. Nicholas stepped into the boat as if it were empty and sitting, got hold of his oars and settled them, too, as if they belonged to somebody else. When le Grant barked, he leaned forward and pulled with the rest. They were well into the harbour when Tobie saw his eyes become aware and his lips part. He inhaled: a vast breath, which went on to include all the air in the Morea. Then, with visible purpose, he turned his head on his shoulder and began to study the fire on his galley.

First, Astorre and the crew were still on board, and active. So much could be glimpsed as the smoke wavered and curdled. In the same uncertain moments of vision, you could see that the ships at anchor were supplying help also, sending skiffs or moving up cautiously. Two of the boats from the *Doria* were prominent among them. When, coughing furiously, the Charetty rowers swung their way through the murk and came at last near the flames at its centre they could hear the shouting from the far side of the galley, and the splashing and hissing of water. Although her leaders were absent, the *Ciaretti* was not being abandoned.

They shipped oars almost under her side, with the heat radiating down on them. Gasping, they twisted to look at her. The length of the hull on this side was intact, although above their heads, the parapet of the outrigger frame and the frame itself were gapped and blackened and smoking in places. The port divots for the ship's boat hung empty, but were not warped. They had either cut the boat loose, burning, or had launched it. The *Ciaretti* carried gunpowder, Tobie remembered. If there had been time, Astorre would have dragged it out and sent it to sea.

The force of the fire, it now seemed, was in the middle or on the opposite side, because none of the helping boats were now visible. Not that anything was especially visible, except in glimpses. High against the black of the smoke, the rigging glowed red as a joy-frame for fireworks, already melting to nothing. The mizzen mast wasn't there: they could see the scars of its falling. No doubt it floated somewhere beside them, with its yard and its tangle of cordage. The sail, thank God, had not been stepped. The smoke thickened and swirled. Mixed with it were burning fragments. Overhead, a blazing stanchion slackened and dropped, to strike the sea hissing beside them. They were on the lee side of the wind, and the water was littered with debris.

Someone said harshly, "Right. The other side," and he saw that it was Nicholas, and that he and le Grant were now working together. They pulled round the stern, looking upwards. The rudderpost was undamaged. The stern-castle had lost canvas and curtain and its woodwork was blackened and charred, but the structure still held. While looking, they found their oars striking wood. They had come across the first of the flotilla of helpers and had to pick their way half-blind between them. There was shouting, some of which they made out, and some of which was drowned in the groaning and cracking of timbers and the blustering sound of the fire and the hiss and smack of the boisterous water. Within the ship, too, the noise of men's voices was urgent and continuous but also oddly diffuse, like an argument heard in a steam bath. As they passed other boats, gleams of red picked out faces and arms, and once a cargo of sandbags. The *Ciaretti*, Tobie remembered, carried sand as ballast as well. If they could reach it that, too, would help. They cleared the high stern at last, and the smoke swirled and let them see what the others were telling them.

It was not the half-ship they had expected to find. The companionway was not only unburned but let down, and a chain of buckets moved up and down it. Above, there hung for a moment the manic face of the bearded Astorre, red as the axe in his hand. He croaked, "Clods! Were ye sleeping?"

Nicholas stood up in the boat. "How bad?"

"From the hold up. The smoke's holding us back. She's still watertight and I think we'll keep her that way. We're getting on top of it."

He went on yelling hoarsely as they clambered aboard. "Two missing; two hurt when we got the mast down. Is that fool of a physician sober?"

He had sent someone already, Tobie found, to secure his medical bag in a safe place. A man who could command a mercenary troop could handle emergencies. But he was better pleased than he would admit, Tobie guessed, to have Nicholas there. To take the burden. To report to the owner his wife. And Nicholas, responding, had without doubt accepted his duty. First, the ship. Then, hallucination or not, the other matter.

If you were used to a battlefield, or a hospital, you knew what it meant, working through the worst of a crisis. In an hour of unthinking, automatic outpouring of ideas and energy, they stopped the spread of the fire. By the time another hour had gone by, they had it mostly smothered and safe. One by one, the ministering boats came to report and drew off, each crew with a jar of strong wine to reward them.

Once from the sea, and once by hailer from his own deck, Pagano Doria himself had expressed his regrets and asked if more help were needed. The Bailie had sent similar messages, with promise of shipwrights and timber. The last assault on the fire was at that time at its worst, and it was John le Grant who each time received and answered the greeting. Nicholas, below in the hold, had from his arrival not so much directed the attack as embodied it. There were patches of glistening red on his skin, and he carried the reek of burned hair. Godscalc, remonstrating, had been brushed aside. Julius sympathised. "Nicholas thinks he's an expert. The dyeshop burned down last year."

"And he ran into the heart of the fire?" Godscalc said.

Tobie overheard, heaving water. His scalp glistened. "The dyeshop was paid for," he said.

"Indeed," said Godscalc. "Well, I may be wrong, but I think that something else is being paid for just now. Perhaps you should restrain him."

"*Twice?*" said Tobie; before he realised that Godscalc knew nothing. He didn't try to explain. Time enough to consider that later.

The second hour passed. As the upper fires died, darkness reclaimed the harbour except for the rolling grey smoke from the galley. On board, they worked now by lamplight, picking their way through a wintry landscape of rubble and charcoal. They moved debris, and cut down and lashed what was dangerous and began for the first time to search out and assess the real damage. During this, the missing crew member was found: a lump of rags, flesh, hair and bones among the tufts of Charetty wool, the warped frame of a lamp at his side. The wool was a pile of black scales and glitter: the sweetened smoke hung like a fog.

Soon after that, Nicholas had whistles blown for a rest. In the glimmer of tallow, the men straightening from their work might have been cut from black paper and mist: their eyes red, their throats raw with the stink of charred wood. Broth was heated and thrown into cups. Burns were wrapped, and a sleep rota agreed on. The tattered canopies were replaced with old canvas, and blankets and coverings searched out to keep resting men from the cold of the night.

In the patron's cabin the fine wood was cloudy and black but had not caught, though the fire had reached through the door and set alight the carpet, the table, the curtain. Their fragments lay still on the deck where they had been dragged away. The cuirasses and weapons still hung on their hooks on the wall and were sooty and warm to the touch. Summoned, the senior men of the Charetty company followed Nicholas there and sprawled on the congealed tar of the boards and swallowed the soup and the bread and the smutty wine that was all that Loppe could find.

Tobie, last to enter with his bag and his clean hands and his unsavoury shirt, looked around at a circle of striped clowns and grunted. Smeared, singed and hollow-eyed, but none of them injured beyond the burns that everyone showed. The human losses had been as Astorre said. Two soldiers caught under the falling mast and for whom he could do nothing. A marine presumably knocked overboard and still missing. And a sailor who had, it seemed, taken a thirst and a lamp to the warmest part of the hold, and there drunk himself into the stupor from which the fire had resulted.

Of course it was bad, but nowhere so bad as it might have been. Because of the sand in her ballast, the slow-burning nature of wool and a number of more unusual factors, the greater part of the ship was intact. She was afloat, and she was not taking in water. How much of the cargo was safe was not yet established, nor what equipment had gone; nor what precisely was needed to repair and replace what was damaged. Between now and dawn there was still heavy work to be done.

Aware of it, no one spoke very much. The single lamp flickered. Nicholas, in the shadows, had a cup of broth in one hand and a stylus in the other, with which he made notes, from time to time, on a tablet propped on one knee. Tobie wondered where the tablet had come from, and if the company books had survived. He saw Julius was watching as well, but had no intention of speaking to Julius. Then le Grant stretched and shifted and said aloud what they were all thinking. "Well: it might have been worse. A week, and we might be at sea again."

Astorre grunted. His face, without eyebrows, looked naked. He said, "You tell a soldier to stay on board and he stays. Tell a sailor he can't go ashore and he drowns his sorrows and tips over his lantern. Cheaper to let them ashore."

No one answered. Tobie looked over to Nicholas. As if he had just heard le Grant speak, he looked up. "A week? No. We have to be able to sail in a day."

Tobie saw the rest exchange glances. "We can't," said le Grant flatly.

Nicholas remained looking up. "Why not? We have unlimited help. We can buy what we want from the arsenal. We refit what we can. We buy ready-made what we can. And at the end of the day, we collect what we haven't managed to finish, load it on board with the workmen, and sail with it. This isn't a round ship, it's a galley. All we need is a seaworthy hull, the right number of oars and enough benches. If you can't get those in time, then I can."

John le Grant looked at him. "Aye," he said. "Ye need even less for a raft. What about that?"

He and Nicholas stared at one another without noticeable animosity. Nicholas said, "All right, I've understated it. But not by much."

"That's your opinion," said the red-haired engineer. "As, of course, a seagoing man. Allow me to advise you. I can get this ship seaworthy in twenty-four hours for rowing right round this harbour, and she won't take in a drop. But the Aegean in March? That's for dummies."

"I'm in a hurry," said Nicholas. He held the lamp out of the way and threw the tablet over the deck. "Twenty-four hours."

"Why?" said the engineer. He picked the tablet up, but didn't look at it.

Tobias Beventini didn't look at it either, because the light had shown him Nicholas's face. He wondered if the others saw what now existed, fixed, beneath the dirt and the burns. He had been wrong, and twice over; and Godscalc had been right, with nothing to go on but guesswork. Despite the disorientation on shore, Nicholas had possessed, after all, the reserves to deal with the fire. Such things normally brought their own mercy. Now Tobias Beventini looked at Nicholas and recognised that not for a moment had Nicholas let the matter slip from his mind. It still occupied all his real thoughts as he sat there. And as awareness reached him, he heard Nicholas repeating the engineer's question. "Why the hurry? I have something to raise with Pagano Doria. He won't like it. He may dislike it so much he lifts anchor. And if he tries to leave, I want to outsail him."

"I". Not the company "we". Not either the disarming tone they were familiar with. The face of le Grant showed he could make nothing of it. Tobie, half-prepared to be called on as an ally, wondered if Nicholas even remembered his existence. It was Loppe's voice which broke in before them.

"Messer Niccolò?" Alone of them all, he gave Nicholas the title, and his Italian name. Nicholas rose to his feet.

Loppe said, "The smoke has cleared. The *Doria* is not in the harbour."

The cold of the night swirled through the masked door as Nicholas left. The others, scrambling, followed. At Tobie's side, Julius said, "That business on shore?"

"Yes," said Tobie. With the rest, he got to the side.

It was true. Where the round ship had lain was pooled water, reflecting the light on the mole, and the bow lights of the small ships at anchor, masked by the last drifting smoke from their fires. The fires which the *Doria* had helped to extinguish. And then, politely withdrawing her skiffs, she had made herself ready for sea and, in the smoke and the darkness, had vanished.

Godscalc came up. He said, "She must have been provisioned already. He meant to go."

"I should have known. Of course he meant to go," Nicholas said. "He started the fire."

There was a second's pause. "Rubbish," said Astorre.

"You think so?" said Nicholas. When he turned suddenly, Astorre had to look up to him. Crewmen, taking notice, were listening. Nicholas didn't look at them, but his voice was pitched louder than usual. He said, "It wasn't an accident. I lifted the head of the man who was burned. His skull was caved in. If Tobie looks, he will tell you. He lay on the Charetty bales – the only uninsured part of the cargo. The silk escaped. The structure of the ship escaped – the *Doria* boats helped us themselves. He didn't want the ship lost. He did want to delay us. He did want to get his people aboard to see what we carried; what we were protective about. I suppose there is no doubt at all that Pagano Doria now knows we have soldiers aboard, and how many. Captain Astorre?"

In the half-naked face, the unimpaired eye glittered and the scarred one folded into a scowl. Astorre said, "D'you think we gave them an inventory?"

"No. But he'd see some of you worked as a team, and hear your language, and learn, of course, that you were their commander. Not just Doria's men, but all the crews who came aboard will have seen that. How on earth could you have helped it? Your job was to save the ship, and you did. But only Doria has a vested interest in telling the Turks."

In the uncertain light, the face of Julius showed a bemused fascination. He said, "But Doria couldn't have started the fire. He was with us." He paused, and his face changed again. "The daggers? Was the detour to the smiths' quarter to delay us?"

"I should think so," said Nicholas. "He needed time for his men. And he likes his sport too. He enjoyed the idea of a challenge." He stopped, and Tobie saw how shallowly he was breathing. Then he said, in the same, very clear voice, "As for who started the fire . . . there is one man missing still. A marine, whom no one knew very well. We may find his body. But I rather think he's now safe and well on the *Doria*."

He had half the crew listening now, and throaty murmurs answering him. It was Julius, surprisingly, who said, "I don't see it. You think he'll betray Astorre and the rest to the Turks, and get the galley himself as a prize? But you heard him. You may be rivals in trade, but your soldiers will keep all the trading colonies in Trebizond safe. It's in his interest, too, to get your men past Constantinople."

"You'd think so," said Nicholas thoughtfully. "You'd really think so. But what his true interests are, we really don't know, do we? That was one of the reasons for the little talk I expected to have with him. And it's really quite an incentive to stop whining and get this galley out to sea after her. For one of the things I fancy least is having Pagano Doria board my ship and kill my men and burn my cargo and sail into Constantinople ahead of me."

He turned, a youth with a scarred, dirty face, and stared at the crew crammed all about him. "Can we catch her?"

"*Yes!*" they roared.

John le Grant paid no attention. He said, "You want us to prepare for a race with a round ship? And what after that? Your wool's gone. You face the cost of repairs. And even if you reach Constantinople before him, the rumour of Astorre and his men may have got there. Why not cut your losses and turn back from Modon?"

"Award a triumph to Messer Pagano?" Nicholas said. The men were shouting still. "*They* don't want it. I can't believe you want it either. And I – I've still got this knife with his name on it."

Chapter 11

W HAT NICHOLAS HAD given was a performance. Well, he was used to that. The accounts of the feats of mimicry, the practical jokes perpetrated in his juvenile past, had always seemed uniquely repellant to Tobie. At the same time he had seldom heard something like this carried off quite as neatly.

At the time he said nothing, but accepted the orders that poured upon him from above and refused to engage in controversy with anybody. He did, upon demand, examine the corpse of the man in the hold and he was able, with every justification, to confirm officially that the man had been done to death before being incinerated. After that, he did what he was told for a number of hours until, according to rota, the time had come for him to sleep. Then, instead of finding his blankets, he watched for Nicholas.

He found him coming up from the main hatch, his face grey and black in the cold dawn. He put himself in his way.

Physical punishment, Julius said, never overwhelmed Nicholas. With one singular exception, all Tobie had seen agreed with that. Even-tempered, strong as a bullock, he took what life chose to give, and was either resigned or contented. Now, he was weary but not truly exhausted, and any distress was contained, as the fires had been. He said, "I thought you would come."

The big stern cabin was littered with sleeping men. Tobie collected his gear and accompanied Nicholas to the prow, where the little chamber for ropes and sails was untouched and, for the time being, empty of sleepers. Tobie entered. A nest of sailcloth invited, and a moment later Nicholas, lingering to ask some question outside, came in and dropped down beside him. Someone had left a small makeshift brazier: the floor had dried, and the air was gratefully warm. Nicholas sat hugging his knees, and apparently waiting.

Tobie bestirred himself and sat fully up. He said, "Catherine de Charetty."

"Yes?" said Nicholas.

"Yes what?" said Tobie. "You haven't mentioned her. The crew needn't know, but the rest very positively must. What are you playing at?"

Nicholas said, "You didn't tell Julius, or Godscalc. No. Or they would have spoken."

"Maybe you've gone off your head," Tobie said. "Maybe you've mistaken the girl. Or maybe you're indisputably right, and she's Doria's wife, and you are risking your ship and your men for a twelve-year-old. I'm not saying you shouldn't. But the rest of us, wouldn't you say, have at least the right to know, and to choose?"

"You think – I hadn't thought of that," Nicholas said. He sounded surprised. After a moment he said, "You saw that man's skull. But you think I invented Doria's part in the fire?"

"Didn't you?" Tobie said. Normally, he enjoyed a chance to test Nicholas. Normally, he found it amusing.

Nicholas said, "No. If we catch him, I'll prove it."

Tobie said, "Look. I know you think you saw Catherine. I know what it means. Whatever the risk, Julius and Godscalc and Astorre and I would take it, to find the child and discover what's happened. Half Astorre's men know her too. So if you're sure, why didn't you tell them back there?"

There was a long silence. Then Nicholas said, "Back there, I thought the *Doria* was still in harbour. There was a chance of seeing the girl, of keeping everything quiet, of handling the whole thing in private."

"And later?" said Tobie. "You'd rather the crew didn't know. I see that."

"There hasn't been much of a 'later'," Nicholas said. "But the other reason is much as you say. He's a great man for sport, Pagano Doria. I saw her in page's dress, in the dark, for a moment. He must have meant me to see her. What if he meant to deceive me? A little girl with the same eyes . . . hair . . . I'd virtually ruin the real girl by proxy, chasing him all over the East with accusations. He would like that very much."

"Then you're not sure?" said Tobie. "All of this is . . . just in case?"

"He caused the fire," Nicholas said. "And when you saw me, I was sure. And whether you all come or not, I shan't leave him alone until I make sure, if I have to walk or swim or crawl to catch up with the *Doria*."

Tobie watched him. "Tell me about her," he said. "The little girl. They sent her to Brussels?"

"They think she's still there," Nicholas said. "She kept writing to say she was staying. Over Christmas, even. Marian . . . The demoiselle was concerned. She said in the last . . . Gregorio was going to Brussels to see her. If he did, they'll know by now." His eyes were on his hands. The backs were raw, with no fluff left anywhere on them. Tobie knew what the palms were like: his own were the same.

Tobie said, "What sort of child was she? Pretty, I thought. A bit silly. But I hardly saw her."

Nicholas looked up. "I was pretty silly at twelve. Weren't you?" He made to clasp his hands, and then left them open, dropping his gaze again. He said, "The girls were born years after Felix. He was nine when I first went to work for them, and was being cruel to Tilde, out of jealousy. Catherine was the little one, three. She was slow, coming down stairs. I used to carry her."

Tobie reclined, propped by the sails, and considered Claes, the former apprentice. Then aged ten, he supposed, and newly come from the less-than-merciful hands of his uncle Jaak in Geneva, but still smiling, still helpful, still happy. With a three-year-old perched on his shoulders.

Nicholas stirred. "After that, I suppose she grew the way you would expect. She didn't want to be treated like Tilde. Felix always ignored Tilde, or baited her. And Cornelis . . . Their father had a kind heart, but was strict, and a little unthinking. Catherine learned to cajole, and avoid trouble, and make people love her. She wanted the reassurance of love."

"Who doesn't?" said Tobie; and was led into a thought of his own. Toys for the pillow. But Claes, grown up, had turned to the farmuk, to puzzles. And a record, once, of simple, physical wenching. He said, "But what you mean is that she would be ready to fall, if a determined man courted her?"

"I had married her mother," said Nicholas baldly. "Also . . ." The painful tone sank, unexpectedly, into one of parental defensiveness. "Also we'd refused her a lapdog. It was impossible. Marian told her."

It was, in view of everything, perhaps the most ludicrous thing he could have said. And the most convincing, thought Tobie later. At the time, it moved him to a conclusion. "Well, for what it's worth," Tobie said, "I think there's no doubt we have to follow that ship. I'll tell our own people why. You'll get the best out of the crew – they want revenge for the fire. And you'll have no complaints from the rest of us." He paused. "You were surely going to tell Astorre and Julius?"

"I suppose so," said Nicholas. After a moment he said, "I *saw* her in Florence. Outside Doria's house." His hands glistened, one gripped in the other.

"Then she must have seen you," said Tobie sharply. "She can't be unhappy, or she would have come to you. I know it's terrible, but he may be a man who makes women happy. And he married her. We know that."

"In a way," Nicholas said, "it's the worst thing we know." At the time, Tobie thought he saw the logic of that. Again, later, he wondered.

They fell very soon into silence, during which Tobie's eyes closed. He opened them when Nicholas got up silently and went out: either he had already rested, or felt little need of it. Tobie lay in the warmth, and the problem dissolved before he knew it into oblivion. It was full daylight when he woke, and scrambled out, and found the cook and John le Grant together, and received, eating and complaining from habit, his Herculean orders for the day.

A methodical man with certain rules of his own, Tobias Beventini shirked none of his duties. At the same time he made it his priority to seek out Godscalc and Astorre and Julius and relate to each, on his own, what he had already told John le Grant, who had never heard of Catherine de Charetty, but ought to know, too, what he was probably going to be killed for.

He did wonder, lastly, whether or not to tell Loppe. He finally did, but found that Loppe already knew.

Under the same cold and fruitless skies of February, the news of the loss of Catherine de Charetty reached her mother in Bruges.

Returning from his errand in Brussels, the lawyer Gregorio of Asti had never in his cool and crowded career climbed the stairs to his mistress's room more reluctantly, nor asked for admittance. He thought, as her voice invited him in, that she sounded almost prepared to hear what he had to tell her. He opened the door.

Although not prone to marriage, Messer Gregorio had long been the companion of a handsome and intelligent woman, and could appreciate good looks and courage, even in a woman ten years older than himself who owned and managed a business. He had only been with her a year. He himself was a Lombard and, fresh from Padua law school, had obtained his first post as a junior clerk to the Senate in Venice: an excellent training for a man with ambition. Approaching the end of his twenties, he had thought it time to move on, and had been attracted by what he had heard of the Charetty company. He knew of it already – his father, now a broker near Ghent, had known the man whose widowed daughter currently owned it. A business run by a woman of forty seemed to offer a chance worth looking into. One day, perhaps soon, she might wish to retire, or sell.

When he had found, installed at the widow's right hand, a teenage apprentice she was planning to marry, his impulse had been to walk out immediately. He had not left. Mesmerised, he had discovered his first interpretation of the situation to be at fault. Nicholas was unlike anyone he had met. The widow, far from being an object of contempt, won his compassion. Inviting ridicule, she had persevered with this unsuitable marriage. Sooner than most people, Gregorio had begun to understand why.

Given his choice, he would have gone with Nicholas to the Levant; but that would not have been wise. The business needed what he could give it of skill and of industry. He remained to nurture it, not now with an eye to his own advancement, but for the demoiselle's sake, and from interest, and from the hope of a stimulating future as Nicholas grew and developed as he thought he might. Of the dark side of Nicholas which Tobie had once discussed with him, he had seen nothing more. Nicholas had made his mistakes, and they had been deadly ones. With Tobie at his side, and Julius, he could surely wreak no more harm.

But now, his mind was on the woman whom Nicholas had married and left behind. Since the departure for Italy, Gregorio had watched Marian de Charetty try to create, after marriage, widowhood, marriage, a fourth identity in her adult life: one of the wife and manager who has opened the door and allowed a young husband to taste unfettered the sweets of the world.

The five months without Nicholas had been less difficult than many she must have experienced. She no longer had young children to care for as well as her business. The business itself, well managed by himself and others chosen by Nicholas, was thriving along the lines they had planned. The death of Felix her son was receding; the absence of Catherine her youngest daughter was in many ways a relief. She had time for leisure, and friends, and to find herself.

The mortal loss, it was apparent, had been that of Claes himself. Of Nicholas, the child she had found and fostered and given a place at her side, and eventually a marriage partnership to. Until, one day, the partnership was no longer one of business alone.

Then, in admiration and in pity, he had watched her bloom: discard her heavy widow's headgear for dressings that flattered her dense, red-brown hair; and find jewels and gowns that did justice to her high colour and blue eyes and pretty, plump flesh.

She kept them after Nicholas had gone. Indeed, as the weeks went by, Gregorio thought that the robes, the chemises, the overgowns, the long sleeves, became lighter and younger still, as if waiting for Nicholas she used the time to become a more fitting bride for him. Or as if, left to a life so nearly that of the rigid widowhood she had left, she needed to affirm to herself and her circle how much things had changed.

They had both known, she and Nicholas, that the parting would be a long one. His reluctance to go had been genuine, or so Gregorio believed. The reasons behind the decision had been as complex as the reasons for the demoiselle's in urging it upon him. Nominally, it had been to remove him from danger: from the Scottish lord and his father whose enmity he had incurred – had even, sometimes it seemed, set out to achieve. In fact, Gregorio thought, it was instead the act of a generous woman who had opened the cage door rather than deny the skies to a loved companion, but who longed, hour by hour, for the time when the companion would return.

Wiser in some ways than Marian de Charetty, Gregorio her lawyer did nothing to disturb what peace of mind she could find. In obeying her wish to have news of her Catherine in Brussels, he anticipated nothing more than an interview with a sweet but spoiled child, and the trouble of reconciling her to returning soon to her home. What he had found had first shocked and then sickened him. The demoiselle had to be told. But what he had to tell her would be a fraction of what he knew. Lawyers gossiped to lawyers. Lawyers did business with harbour officials. Over the weeks, he had learned a great deal that he had kept from her. But not, until now, about Catherine.

So, entering his mistress's office, he saw her seated, as ever, behind the great desk with its scales and its inkpot, its ledgers and showcard, decorated with small tufted wools, bright with the dyes of the East. And, now, a small silver box with her name engraved on the side which contained a coil of carved wool and a row of small hammers like teasels.

She wore pearls and double-cut velvet, folded into a high jewelled girdle that flattered her breasts. Her face was patched with past weeping. He said, "Demoiselle. What have you heard?"

Her eyes were half-closed by her lids. She said, "You look tired, Goro. You know where the wine is. Pour some for me too. I think we both need it."

And when he had done that, and seated himself, and repeated his question, she said, "The same as you, I expect. Tell me first."

She listened while he told the sorry story. All the letters, the reassuring, grubby letters which had come so haphazardly from her little daughter since early autumn had been fiction, written all in a day by the same little daughter and consigned to a middleman to send off at intervals. Catherine had stayed in Brussels only a matter of weeks, and had then left from Antwerp by ship, deceiving her host and hostess into thinking she was on her way home. She had left with a Genoese, a man who called himself Pagano Doria. And the ship had been sailing for Florence.

He laid on her desk the letters of distraught complaint and apology which had been pressed on him by the silly merchant and his wife who were supposed to be housing her child, and training and teaching her. And who had not been able to prevent her meeting a plausible and personable man who had found it simple to lure her away.

The letters said, in self-defence, something about Catherine's fickle character which might have been more gracefully left unsaid. The letter ended with an offer, stiffly written, to help underwrite the payment of any financial demands that the rogue might now make. Although, as the demoiselle de Charetty well knew, their own resources were not without limits; otherwise they would never have incurred the anxiety of taking a child of unformed character into their home.

He watched her read to the end. He said, "I told them there had been no ransom demands."

"No," she said. She laid the last paper down. "No. He has married her."

There was a breath of a pause. "Who?" he said.

Her eyes opened on him, and remained there. "Pagano Doria," she said. "He has written from Florence. The marriage was contracted and witnessed in the city. He asks for nothing. He merely wishes me to know it has taken place."

His mouth was dry. He said, "Without you, it can't."

She remained looking at him. "He says he has taken advice, and it is legal. He sent the papers beforehand to her godfather, Thibault de Fleury, in Dijon. My late sister's husband. One of the many . . . Nicholas ruined. Thibault, or someone holding his hand, would be happy to sign them."

Wine forgotten, he stared at her. He said, "It isn't legal. She is under the age of puberty."

The letter from Florence was there, too, on her desk. She lifted it in her sturdy fingers and held it, a little at arm's length, to find the passage she wanted. Then she read aloud:

> *You may imagine my sorrow and hers at forgoing a mother's blessing. I wished her to return to you a child, until she could come as a woman and join me. You do not need me to tell you of our Catherine's impetuous nature. Where I would have wished for an absence, she insisted that we should not be parted. I need not tell you, I hope, that for as long as your daughter was a child, she remained an innocent, guarded from all that might corrupt. In Florence my patience has been rewarded. She is a woman, and wished the privilege of a woman, to marry where she loved. Because of that, I trust you will forgive her and me, and when, one day, I have the happiness to bring her home, that you will receive her as your ever-loved daughter, and me as your ever-loving son.*

At that point, Gregorio of Asti said, "Demoiselle. Forgive me." And left the room quickly and in time not to vomit before her.

He knew he would do her no service by going back before he was ready. When he returned, he knew what to say and to do, and knew from her face that she was arrested by what had clearly happened, and thought differently of him because of it. He said, "After the morning you have had, such a lapse was an impertinence. Forgive me. But let me make you a promise. This is the last weakness that you or I will show in this matter." He paused. "It is, I assume, Catherine's half-inheritance he is after?"

"I should think so," she said. "Nicholas, as you know, falls heir to nothing."

He frowned. "But even Catherine's share will only fall to him after you have gone. And Nicholas may still be there to manage it." He looked up. "Nicholas was in Florence over the winter. If Doria didn't know that, or was careless . . . Your next letter could be from Nicholas, to say he has her safe."

She shook her head wearily. "No. Read the letter yourself. It is the work of a silly, cruel man. He knew Nicholas would be in Florence. He hid Catherine from him. By the time he wrote this letter to me, she was married and they had left Florence. He has promised her, he says, a *messa del congiunto* in Sicily."

Gregorio took the letter and held it. "Why is he going to Sicily?"

"Oh, read, and you will see," said Marian de Charetty. "It is only a trading stop. His real destination is Trebizond. He has been made Genoese consul. He wants to get there before Nicholas, and give him, he says, a stepson's embrace."

They looked at one another, and this time nothing was said. Then Gregorio said, "I shall go there."

She shifted a little in her tall chair. "Perhaps," said the demoiselle. "Later. Just now, I need you to look after the business. I have sent off a message already to tell Nicholas what has happened. It may never reach him. At best it will take months. You could be no quicker. Meantime, the harm has been done; the marriage has taken place; they have consummated it. And at least in Trebizond he cannot hide her as he did in Florence. Sooner or later Nicholas will find out what has happened, and will do what he can."

"So? But you are going away?" said the lawyer.

"Quite a long way. To search out the marriage," she said. "It took place in Florence. I shall go to Florence. And Thibault de Fleury signed the documents. I shall go by way of Dijon, and see him, and get copies of all the papers I can. Don't you think that would be wise?"

"Yes, I do," he said. It was probably wise. If she could prove to the world that Doria's marriage was false, then he would probably abandon Catherine. He would certainly have lost hope of her fortune. But neither of those things would help Catherine now. Indeed, they might do the opposite.

Then he saw why she was doing it; and perhaps the only reason she was doing it. With his marriage invalid and Catherine freed, Pagano Doria would have no reason to tamper with Catherine's protectors. She feared for Catherine. She feared as much, because she knew him, for Nicholas.

She said, "I shall go as soon as I can, and I shall write you from Florence. Wait a reasonable time. You have a good staff, but they need a little more training. But if you fail to hear, or feel you must stand where you may be needed, you have carte blanche to go where you wish. In Venice, we have funds, and there news will come to you fast. Take lodgings, an office. It was what he meant to do anyway. And if you have to go to Trebizond, go."

He said, "The office can manage without me. Take me with you to Dijon."

She smiled, almost as she had done when Nicholas was there. She said, "I am so lucky to have you all. But you said it yourself. This, today, was the last time we can afford to show weakness. If I were ever to forget, I have only to look at that letter."

Later, she said, "Anselm Adorne. I keep few secrets from that family, but they are friends of the Doria."

"I shan't tell them," he said.

She frowned. "And Lorenzo Strozzi? Nicholas stayed with his mother in Florence."

He said, "But Nicholas knew nothing of Catherine. The Strozzi can know nothing either."

All he had told her was true; but he still felt a traitor. He left as soon after that as he could, and plunged into long thought. Then he took paper and pen and continued, as usual, to make four copies for four different couriers of a long coded letter to Nicholas.

The morning after the fire, Messer Nicholai de' Acciajuoli of the wooden leg returned to Modon from Patras, missing the plague by a day. Arrived in Modon, he took one look at the hulk in the harbour and, after closely questioning the Bailie, sent polite word to the young Niccolò vander Poele, patron of the galley *Ciaretti*, that he no longer felt able to sail with him. He would be pleased, however, if the same young man would call at his rooms near the waterfront.

The message reached Nicholas, but he did not respond until evening. By then, he had worked for twenty-four hours and knew that what John le Grant had said was correct. They could, after a fashion, row out of Modon tomorrow. But to do what ought to be done would take days. He couldn't catch the *Doria*. It seemed to him uncommonly likely, however, that the *Doria* would take the trouble to wait for him; if only to witness his downfall.

In one way, the new plan was unpopular. The morning of his wretched sessions with Tobie he perceived, by the galvanised work of his fellows, that the affair of the child was now known to them.

Le Grant, the newcomer, sensibly ventured no comment. The priest, finding himself near at one point, volunteered information. "I have to say I am sorry. I saw the child, I think, in Porto Pisano. A pretty thing, with brown hair, in a page's dress. Spirited; not unhappy; not under duress."

And he, not knowing what to say, had merely said, "Thank you."

To which the priest had added, "Not, of course, that any excuse exists for such conduct."

So much for Godscalc. Astorre, probably just after he heard, came thrusting into the conference he was holding with a pulley-maker and took a handful of his shirt at the shoulder and said, "I'll kill him. Lead me to him. I'll slit his loins and feed a dog up his belly. I'll . . ."

For the sake of the pulley-maker, he had fobbed off the captain in some fashion. His own language had been quite picturesque too.

But the most excitable exchange, of course, had been with Julius, who seemed to want to fight him for concealing the discovery. With justice, in a way. Julius had on occasion bear-led Marian's two little girls, just as he had tutored Marian's son and beaten Marian's apprentice. It was Julius who, after a series of furious questions, had suddenly taken it upon himself to plan, accelerate and execute the whole complex operation in order that they should put to sea, not in twenty-four hours but before dinner. It had taken le Grant and Tobie to explain and quieten him. At first, the crew, too, were dashed by the change of plan. But only at first.

His mind full of rope, Nicholas finally rapped on the door of the Greek's lodgings and was led to his parlour. He was between trips to the pitch-maker, the ironsmith's and the cooper's yard; he hadn't eaten since midday, or done much to better his clothing. The one-legged Athenian, who was in fact of Florentine descent and connection, rose in his perfect gown and swathed hat, and greeted him with a pleasantry.

"It's the new Charetty colours," Nicholas said. "Ship and doublet to match. Forgive me, monsignore. I have had no time for grooming. I am sorry, too, that we are to be deprived of your company to Constantinople."

"Stamboul," said the Greek. "You must revise your term, now the Turk has possessed it. And Pera, over the water. You will meet my brother there, whom your Scottish king helped to ransom. Or no, it was not *your* Scottish king, but my lord Simon's. You enjoyed your first voyage at sea? Until, of course, this sad occurrence."

"I enjoy most things," said Nicholas. "We sailed past Tolfa. The Roman alum is still undiscovered, I hear."

The Athenian smiled. His face, dark and bearded, was not young, but remained handsome and suave as the day Nicholas had seen it first on the quayside at Damme, eighteen months ago. And last, in September, on board a Venetian galley at Sluys, when he had met Violante of Naxos, and the trip to Trebizond had been mooted.

There was gold belonging to Nicholas lodged in Venice. There was also a respectable deposit in the name of the Charetty company. They did not talk about that; for much of it came from their private and continuing fee for locating alum near Rome, and then keeping silence about it. Venice valued her Turkish alum monopoly. Now Nicholai de' Acciajuoli said, "Of course, someone will find Tolfa one day, as you and your physician did by deduction. The Pope's godson da Castro is seeking it. Should he find it, the Pope will seize and exploit the alum. But every day that passes meantime makes my brother happy, and equally, surely, the Charetty company. So you go to Trebizond, despite your small mishap?"

"It is what we set out to do," Nicholas said.

"And you will cherish, as well as you may, those generous colleagues of yours and mine, the Venetians?"

"In so far as I can," Nicholas said. "The Genoese consul Doria is going to be troublesome. We suspect him of causing the fire."

"You do!" said the Greek. "Then I share your concern. He sails ahead of you?"

"Into Constantinople. Stamboul. We don't know his influence there."

"He knows the Greeks," said the Athenian calmly. "All the Doria family do. He will have friends among the families the Sultan has induced to resettle. As for the foreign colony over the water . . . my brother will tell you what goes on in Pera. The Genoese are disliked there in general, and the Venetian Bailie is the Turks' preferred spokesman. Did the silk survive?"

"Yes," said Nicholas. "The fire was very selective. You were going to tell me about alum."

The other man looked surprised. "I thought I had."

"We talked in Flanders, on the galley. You spoke of alum near Kerasous."

"Dear me, did I?" said the Greek. "But that is a little way along the Black Sea from Trebizond. And the mine is not on the coast, but in the hills some way to the south. And the loads that can be brought into Kerasous are subject to quite terrible taxation as they pass through the straits of the Turks. It is complicated."

"I can see that," said Nicholas.

"Hardly worth pursuing at present," the Athenian said.

"I can see that, too," said Nicholas. "But your brother the lord Bartolomeo could, I'm sure, advise me. Will he come with me to Trebizond?"

"With you?" said the Greek. "Ah no. His business is in Pera. Alum, silk. Much like your own. There may be a passenger or two he could put your way. The Emperor sends merchants, courtiers. The Emperor likes buying silk, collecting news. You may find yourself with some such aboard."

"With horse trappings?" Nicholas said.

The Athenian looked at him and laughed. "You have heard. The Persians breed pretty horses, but their envoys have their brains in their hooves. If it is true that the Sultan is assembling a fleet, you will be able to confirm it. What he has will be in Gallipoli, which you will pass. You will hear rumours about whom he will use it against. Some say it is purely defensive, in case our mad Ludovico of Bologna stirs up some crazy duchy against him."

"So you don't advise me to stay clear of Trebizond?" Nicholas said.

The Athenian examined him. "No. And, my cynical friend, I say so as much for your own good as any it may do Venice or Florence. I did not deceive you in Flanders."

"No," Nicholas said. "Why should you, when there are so many others?"

He was given something to drink, and they talked, to some point. Then he left, to tackle his next six engagements.

At the end of five days, he was able to sail out of Modon. His mood was not one of happiness but more of dark and positive determination.

He was aware of the fact that only one stage now lay between him and the Fleece. And that unlike Jason's, his wooden oracle had preferred not to embark.

Chapter 12

MESSER PAGANO DORIA'S patience with his young lady wife during the passage from Modon to Constantinople, City of the Thrice-Blessed Virgin, ex-Tabernacle on Earth of the Bride of the Lord, was regarded as something amazing by everyone on board the *Doria*, from Michael Crackbene his captain right down to Noah, his eager black page. There were those who put it down to infatuation, and those who remarked, and rightly, that my lord Pagano Doria was an unusually equable man. There were still others who thought of another possibility.

A man of experience, Doria could see for himself that the incidents at Modon had quickly lost their diversionary value, so that he had to rely on the marriage bed. It was not a penance. Her attraction for him was considerable. She was one of his most promising pupils and, when he could, he devoted himself to her, forgiving the stray acts of wilfulness. Someone else, eventually, could train her out of those. So single-minded did he make himself that, when he turned off the terrible nurse (with his wife's eager approval) in the last days at Modon, he had selflessly replaced the bitch with two of the plainest servingwomen he could find. It had not entirely pleased Catherine. Incomparable women had pretty maids: only the plain chose the ugly. He apologised, charmingly.

As for Catherine herself, it was quite painful at times to deny his embraces, but she felt it was good for him. She had tamed Felix her brother by refusing approval and companionship, and Felix had liked her better than Tilde. The escapade at Modon had proved an un-planned test of her power over Pagano. It began as a kind of joke. Unknown to him, she would dress in her page's costume, attach herself to his suite and, unnoticed in the darkness, observe her mother's husband. Since her ultimate lesson in carnal knowledge, she found it less disturbing to think of her mother and Nicholas. She could under-stand an old woman's temptation. She found it less easy to understand Nicholas, who presumably had no idea what he was missing.

Standing there in her pretty costume, she found herself speculating on what Nicholas would say if he saw her. Then he looked straight at her. She was sure, even then, that in this dress and setting she was unrecognisable. And then she had seen his face alter. Become strange and alter, and all because of her! She realised she ought to run for Pagano's sake, but was laughing with excitement so much that it brought on the hiccoughs and someone had to half drag her along. Noah, the little black bastard (as her late nurse frequently called him); who went and told Pagano as soon as he arrived on the round ship.

But by then she was standing, showered in soot at the ship's rail, lost in the spectacle of the Florentine galley on fire, and when Pagano walked over, looking hot, she was thinking of nothing else. She had rushed to him and said, "Did you do it? You did it, didn't you?" in sheer delight, because although they had talked of ways of keeping Nicholas and his ship in harbour, fire had never been mentioned.

Immediately, he had looked a little less rigid. He had said, "How could I have had anything to do with it? I've been ashore all evening."

"Is it bad?" she had said.

And he had put his arm round her and said, "It's not as bad as it looks. Nicholas is quite safe, but of course he can't sail for a while. Caterinetta, I have to scold you, but I have a lot to do first. This smoke is bad: I think you should go below and get the girls to make your boxes secure. If I see a chance, I might set sail this evening. Then poor Nicholas will have no hope of reaching the Black Sea before us."

She was so pleased that she relented. She put her arms round his neck, coughing a little, and said, "I didn't mean to upset you. I didn't think he would see me. And you were away the whole evening."

He had rested his hands at her girdle. When he rearranged them she recognised, with complacency, that she had won. "Well," he said; and he was smiling. "I shall be away for a little more of the evening, until we are ready to leave. But after that, there will be the whole night, and tomorrow, and many days and nights after that to make up for it. And then I shall show you Constantinople, Queen of Cities."

They smiled. He joined her below decks, and they mined pleasure out of each other, warm and blind and enclosed, as long as the seam yielded gold. He fell asleep with the last gleaning half reached for. She didn't hold it against him, but lay stroking his hair between her two, new, blue-veined breasts, round and swollen as Tilde's.

Her mind wandered to Nicholas, and the way he had looked when she had surprised him on shore. She had the impression that Pagano didn't mind so much, now, if Nicholas followed them. She was glad. She wanted Nicholas to see her being received, properly dressed, at the Imperial Byzantine court at Trebizond. She wished he could see her now, being kind to Pagano. Then he could go home and think about it, in Bruges with her mother.

Far from launching an idyll, that night was the last she and Pagano were to share for some considerable time. First, bad weather struck. Then, the small gift of God, once so longed-for, made its second appearance: an inevitability which no one had reminded her of. Her new and plain women were less practical than the old nurse, and also less shrewd. They called her affliction the Curse, without reverence; and smiled behind their hands at her angry resentment. (This – this! – was a bodily insult she must now expect to contend with for most of her life.) Of course, they slyly remarked, Madonna might get her husband to remedy it. She learned what her husband had to do with it, and became very thoughtful, hugging her hot brick as she clung first to one side of the mattress and then the other, while her head and feet changed heights continually.

When she did come on deck, Pagano said they were in the Aegean Sea, and if the clouds cleared they could look behind and see the clouds on Mount Athos. He quite often produced names of places as if she had been here before, and ought to know them. Mount Olympus. He had been boring about Mount Olympus, and he was even boring when he talked about Jason and the Golden Fleece. When she told him so, he switched to Helen of Troy, which was better.

The Charetty household had not been a great place for stories, and Felix's tutor had never tried to teach geography at the same time. She had also seen plenty of seagulls at Bruges, and fish, for that matter. The sea was full of islands and rocks, and the coast was just cliffs and rocks too, with fishing huts no bigger than pebbles. During the day there were plenty of boats about, moving from island to island, and Pagano thought she might want to look for their flags, but she didn't. None was as big as their own although she saw two smaller cogs sailing ahead, on the same route as themselves. They passed flocks of fishing boats every night, with their flickering torches and the men in the bows with their tridents. The boats, when you saw them in daylight, were loaded with wriggling objects like cockroaches. Pagano asked if she preferred squid or octopus. She was meant to know he was joking. If they were selling fish, she thought they must be in a poor way of business to have to rely on passing ships for their market. Pagano, when she opened the subject, wasn't interested. Pagano liked the sort of business you did over a pitcher of wine, with gold changing hands, and other men handling the cargo. For a sea prince that was, of course, as it should be.

In fact, the *Doria* didn't stop anywhere until they reached Gallipoli and even then it was only to satisfy the Turkish governor, who was also an admiral. The harbour and shipyards were full and they were not allowed on shore. When she complained, Pagano said they were in a hurry, because the north winds started in March. She didn't see that they could be any worse than the winds that were blowing already. A round ship was supposed to be comfortable compared with a shallow galley that took in seawater all the time. But the draught from the sails was bone-chilling, and the cold and the damp got in everywhere. There was mould on her new velvet dress.

The noise, too, was frightful. The wood squealed and creaked and the stays throbbed and whined and everything banged and rattled all through the night. On top of that, the crew talked all the time, shouting because of the wind, or sang, or barked responses to orders. They hailed other ships, exchanging news about events, and the weather. At the slightest change of sail, the thud of their feet on deck was like a landslide. And, like everybody else, they stank worse than the cattle below. They didn't shout greetings to her, because of Pagano, but they eyed her, and some of their chants made her uneasy. So she stayed mostly below, not enjoying her food, especially when the joggling started. That, Pagano said, was because they were in the Hellespont, and it was like going up a wide river with the current against you. The river led to the Sea of Marmara, which the Greeks called the Propontis, and which would be smoother unless it was squally. And after that, the channel narrowed again, to take them to Constantinople. Their final call before the Black Sea.

Catherine retired to bed, and asked to be called when they got to Constantinople.

A lint field, they say, is a troublesome crop; but a maidenhead can be worse, for less profit. Pagano Doria did not, after all, wake his bride as the cog entered the Bosphorus, the stream that washed Europe and Asia. On his left was the base of the triangle that formed Constantinople. It was marked by a wall: a long, towered wall set on sea rocks and broken by tall crested gates and the slipways and moles of old palaces. Behind it, thrust upwards by steep, hilly ground and the debris of two thousand years were the scattered houses and pillars, cisterns, amphitheatres and basilicas of the half-empty city which had once been the capital of the world, and was now the Sublime Porte of the Ottoman.

Doria studied it, to see what might be useful. The stories he had tried to tell Catherine were only pastimes: he knew how to talk of the past, but found it of limited interest. The changed city over the wall struck from him no pity, no anguish, no nostalgia. He had been here a long time ago, and had made some money, he couldn't remember quite how; and had made acquaintance with a new form of luxury, he remembered very well how. Thinking, he smiled at young Noah who, in a new turban and glistening gold buttons, smiled joyfully back.

Refinement of sensual pleasure was what many people had sought and found in Byzantium, once a little Greek trading colony. A thousand years after that, as part of the Roman province of Asia, it had become the Constantinople whose temples for both worship and pleasure were there, in ruins, over the wall. Then the Western crusaders had arrived; the Byzantines had fled elsewhere; had returned; had given way to the Turks. And throughout, of course, the hedonists had needed decent traders to serve them. His own Genoese had built their merchant station at Pera, across the Golden Horn inlet, to look after that.

They had, of course, dug their own graves. They had been arrogant and then rash, both before and during and after the Turks' conquest of Constantinople. When the smoke cleared away, it was the Venetians who were allowed to replace their Bailie in Pera; the Venetians who had the franchise of the Phocoea alum mines and the privileges, while the Genoese were allowed a low-rank Elder to look after their diminished affairs. The Sultan, like the Emperor, had lost patience with Genoa.

It would be amusing, therefore, to see what the Doria charm and the Doria wits could do for him against those sort of odds. His ship turned, sails bellying, into the Golden Horn and, rounding the point of the triangle, dropped anchor in the roadstead. Her guns boomed in salute: her trumpets sounded. Tapestries hung at her sides: he himself was dressed in furred robe and doublet, with chains and jewels plainly displayed to those who were watching from the shores and the walls and the water. He had avoided, with care, flying the official consular flag of the Bank of St George. However exalted his state in Trebizond, here he was merely Pagano Doria, a private Genoese trader, who hoped the Conqueror Mehmet would permit him to unload at Pera; to sell and buy some of his goods; to restock and provision, and to sail without hindrance the eighteen watery miles that lay between him and the Black Sea. In exchange for which favours, he had information to impart, and a gift of some value.

He waited, with confidence, his boarding by the Sultan's officials; and hoped the pretty child, his creation, his creature tutored for nothing but love and able for nothing but love (apart from stirring up trouble) would sleep late, and wake in good looks, as was necessary.

At Gallipoli, Father Godscalc and Nicholas had a difference of opinion. Naturally, this had happened before, and not only with Godscalc, since more and more Nicholas had become inclined to speak his mind about what they should do. Up till recently, he had employed a deprecating manner in council accompanied, Godscalc had noticed, by a persistent use of hard reasoning. He usually got his own way.

He got his own way now, but had dropped the humility. That was since his trimming at Modon: the Bailie's table, the girl, and lastly the nicely judged exercise of the fire. *For one of the things I fancy least, is having Pagano Doria board my ship, and kill my men and burn my cargo, and sail into Constantinople ahead of me.* He had meant it at the time, although events had caused him to reverse his plan. It had been the view of Tobie, and Julius, that his distress about Catherine had been genuine. He hadn't stinted in fighting the fire; and had shown himself able to organise. His crew, hitherto cautious, had been captivated by those rousing speeches. Nicholas could get them to laugh when he wanted to; and he could get them to work.

To his colleagues he had displayed his rage over his abducted stepdaughter; and his determination. So, too, they had accepted the harder edge he now used in his dealings with them. Perhaps it would have come anyway, as a result of his failures at Modon. Adversity, in Godscalc's experience, made a very good teacher. The greatest problem Nicholas had was his youth. Two problems. Nicholas was now in his twenty-first year: an age at which other men not only led armies but could satisfy a harem. Were the functions interdependent? As a man vowed to celibacy, Father Godscalc sometimes wondered.

By Gallipoli, the tension on board the *Ciaretti* could be felt. They had lost a day in the Aegean because the *Doria*'s sailspread was bigger and open seas suited her better. It would be offset in the Hellespont and the other narrows ahead, where the Florentine's oars would pull her close to the wind, and tease out the north-running currents. Le Grant reckoned they would make up two days, but they would still arrive in the Sublime Porte four days after Doria. Unless she waited, they were going to miss her.

There was no need to underline the irony of it all. With what he now knew, Doria could have them stopped at Constantinople. And yet, against their own interests, they were striving to catch him, because Catherine de Charetty was thought to be on his ship. Thinking about it, Father Godscalc reached a conclusion. At Gallipoli, he put it to Nicholas. "Let me disembark and try to get to the Sublime Porte ahead of you. I might just catch Doria. Or, better still, get the girl on her own. If I brought her back, you needn't – "

"Call at Constantinople? Of course I should. At best, I've got business there. At worst, they'd put a ball through my hull if I didn't. And how could you bring her aboard? Doria would simply have the Turks search us."

Godscalc kept his voice even. "All right. Perhaps I couldn't bring her away. But I could make sure she *is* Catherine de Charetty. I could speak to her, even."

"No. It's too risky," said Nicholas.

"Riskier than staying on board?" said the priest.

Nicholas said, "We want Doria detained, not the Latin Church. You'd never get out of the harbour. Anyway, if anyone boards the *Doria*, it's going to be me. I think she'll still be there when we arrive."

"Because he'll have told the Sultan about Astorre's army?" said the priest.

"He might have," Nicholas said. "He'll do one of three things. Keep quiet and let us sail through to Trebizond, because he wants Astorre's protection almost as much as we do. Or keep quiet and threaten to tell if we make a nuisance of ourselves over the girl. Or betray us and Astorre, and get rid of us without going further."

"Or just leave," Godscalc said.

"No. He'll wait."

"Because he wants to be there at the slaughter?" Facing such impervious calm, Godscalc heard his voice roughen. He was frowning at Nicholas.

One dimple appeared and disappeared. It was a sign of impatience. "Because I sent messages by a dozen different fast boats from Modon announcing a state visit to Constantinople by the lord prince Pagano Doria, Genoese commissar of the bank of St George. If they don't shoot him out of the water, they'll kill him with welcoming parties while privately racking his servants for secrets. I wrote the Venetian Bailie as well."

"About the girl?" Godscalc said, after a moment. He began to understand the look he sometimes saw on Tobie's face.

Nicholas still looked, if anything, impatient. "Well, of course. I told the Bailie I believed Doria's wife was a kinswoman, and I should be glad if he'd call and ask her to wait for me. Of course, Doria can refuse to let her be seen. But that itself would tell us something."

You couldn't tell, Godscalc thought, if it was true self-assurance or another aspect of the veneer he had assumed ever since Modon. Godscalc said, "You really think the *Doria* will be there?"

"Yes," said Nicholas. "I consulted an oracle."

"Well, now kindly consult me," Godscalc said. "Once you arrive in Constantinople, you won't be able to move anywhere without being seen. But someone could land before then. There is a house of Franciscans just inside the Marmara wall. We will pass it."

Nicholas looked at him. "Would it harm them to help us?"

"I don't see why it should," Godscalc said. "I disembark there while you continue to sail round the city, taking your time about arriving. The Franciscans take me the quick way on foot through the city, and ferry me across to where Doria is staying in Pera. Then I join you. Bring her back with me, indeed, if I can."

"All right," Nicholas said. "You go. And I'll come with you."

The Universal Creator, tired of Catherine de Charetty's complaints, decreed that the ancient capital of the world should receive her with a welcome that, at last, managed to exceed her expectations.

It began with the sound of trumpets and cymbals; and continued with the approach of a fleet of caiques hung with streamers and silks and manned by crews of picked oarsmen in livery. Then people started coming aboard: thundering up the companionway in furs and jewels with scented gloves in their hands; and followed by servants carrying boxes and vases and bales, all containing gifts for Pagano.

It seemed they thought he was a representative of the bank of St George and the Republic. Even when that was corrected, they seemed to esteem him none the less. For he was, indeed, Genoese ambassador to the Empire of Trebizond, and deserved to be fêted. The envoy of the Venetian Bailie, especially, made a point of it.

At first, she thought Pagano was a little bewildered by the extent of it all. In the middle of some of the earlier speeches she saw his mind was clearly elsewhere. But soon he returned to himself, replying to each verbose compliment with wit and vitality; dispensing wine and sweet-meats with a princely and prodigal hand. And for the first time she took her place unveiled at his side, and received the open admiration of well-dressed men who were not Pagano's gaming friends but the kind she had watched, veiled, in Florence. Then the Genoese elder, a thin man of flustered appearance, was inviting them to disembark when they could, and occupy his poor house for the length of their stay.

Pagano, of course, had tried to explain that they were leaving immediately, but had been overruled. He had begun to insist, when the elder leaned over and murmured something in Pagano's ear, and Pagano nodded and then, smiling, changed the subject.

Afterwards, when she asked him, he said that after all they might have to stay for a day or two, since the merchants, it appeared, had gone to a great deal of trouble to prepare feasts and entertainments for them both. Also, as a matter of courtesy, he was to be invited to visit the Sublime Porte itself: Constantinople, which the Turks called Stamboul.

Catherine didn't care what they called it, but was wondering what gown to wear for the Sultan. When Pagano said that the Sultan was not in the city, and in any case did not receive women, she suspected him of deceiving her. Then the thought was swept aside by the excitement of disembarkation, and the journey, with music, to the elder's little house with its courtyard and gallery; and then the feast at the Bailie's that night.

She wore her velvet gown, with pearls embroidered over the mildew, and led her dog. The Bailie was especially taken with it, even when it worried his gown-end. The Bailie, a sallow Venetian with an affable manner, spoke to Pagano as if really concerned about the course of their journey, even though Venice and Genoa were rivals. He then enquired about the Florentine ship, the *Ciaretti*. "Owned, I understand, by Madonna's own kinsman, this Messer Niccolò. I look forward, as you must, to his arrival. A delightful man, I am sure. You will permit us to give him a reception."

She was speechless. For a moment, Pagano too looked taken aback. Then his face slowly smoothed out and cleared and became attractively pink. It was a look of relief and success, and she had seen it before, when he had been short of time, and dependent on finding her willing. She could see no connection with Nicholas.

Now Pagano said light-heartedly, "You have news of Niccolò? Monsignore, I am glad. He fell into some trouble at Modon, and we had to leave him behind, as I fear must happen here. But we shall meet him in Trebizond. We count on it."

The Bailie had turned to her, gallantly chiding. "He hoped very much you would wait for him, madonna. What does a day or two matter? Indeed, you will meet, I am sure. None of us is likely to permit such a charming pair to leave Pera lightly."

In their chamber that night she found Pagano briskly attentive but disinclined to waste breath on chatter. He said he supposed some fishing boat had brought news of Nicholas's coming. What did it matter? He must be a week behind them at least. Perhaps they would see him; perhaps not. It depended on the Sultan's viziers as much as on their good friends in Pera. He did not want to offend the Bailie. He must not offend the Sultan. She would understand that.

She understood that, more or less. They spent the whole of the next day visiting the other residences of the colony, taking wine and being entertained. She received a great deal of praise, although the men were inclined to stand in corners and speak in low voices together. One woman commended her courage in going to Trebizond but, before she could reply, another broke in to ask why a new bride should care for such things? It could be war in Bosnia, Belgrade, Albania. If one hesitated every time there was a rumour, one would never go anywhere.

They were talking, she knew, about the Turks, but she had no fears. Pagano had said there was no possible danger and if there were, did she not trust him to protect her? And meanwhile they would receive, undiluted, all the court had to offer.

Her only concern, then, was her wardrobe. She found the matter solved by the Venetian Bailie who, tireless in service, sent her presents of velvet and silk and asked merchants to call on her with precious things he thought she might like. Their chamber began to look like a store. She thought, if Pagano agreed, she might sell some of the velvet at Trebizond, and use the money for something she wanted. Now she saw other rings, she was a little displeased with her carbuncle. She could sell that as well, for a real ring. Pagano, she understood, had to keep his money at present for trading. Of course, he was right.

The following day, they became hosts in their turn. Pagano had a banquet laid out on his ship and all the colony came. He was especially kind to an old man of fifty whom he called Master George Amiroutzes and who spoke terrible Italian with a heavy Greek accent. His eyes were light, and ringed as if by a crayon with lash-bristle. He had a big nose and a supple, talkative mouth, and a striped beard and curling brown ringlets. Catherine thought him probably some sort of teacher, and was not impressed by his long, plain black gown or his supposed acquaintance with Florence. He also claimed to know Genoa which

Pagano, the soul of courtesy, of course allowed to pass uncontradicted. He and Pagano spoke Greek together, and the man redeemed himself on leaving by kissing Catherine's hand and comparing her to Helen of Troy, with whom of course she was familiar. Pagano had escorted him to the door, and returning had touched her cheek fondly. "What a delightful hostess you are! Who else could so have impressed the Great Chancellor of Trebizond, the Count Palatine Amiroutzes?"

Of course he should have warned her. In Trebizond men wore tunics, or long jewelled robes, and gorgeous cloaks, and Asiatic boots with long toes. She had asked. Now, when she complained, her husband embraced her. "Why, what more would you have said to him if you had known? He's a lay philosopher; he has travelled the world. But he's a man who can talk also of ordinary things. You will get to know him much better. I've asked him if he would care to sail with us to Trebizond."

"You didn't ask me!" Catherine said; and was glad to see him abashed.

"Nor did I, my princess. Then if you don't wish it, of course he won't come." She was comforted.

She was still sleeping next morning when the summons came for Pagano to travel over the water to present himself to the lord Mahmud Pasha. The Grand Vizier had sent his Greek secretary. Catherine's maidservant woke her when Pagano was ready, and he came to the bedchamber to see her. Taking his leave, he was amusing and playful as ever, but a shade inconsequential. The Grand Vizier was, of course, the Sultan's right hand; but Pagano could make anyone living admire him.

She waved her final farewell from the balcony. Looking down, wrapped in her cloak, she saw that it was a real cavalcade, with an escort and all Pagano's bodyservants in cerise velvet and silver, two of them drawing the cart with the presents. Noah had a ruby clasp in his turban and that look of adoration that he wore when close to Pagano. She had no time for Noah. Pagano himself wore cloth of silver and was mounted on a white Arab horse their host had kept for this day. Her husband, who doted on her.

The secretary, also mounted, had a clear olive skin and a little beard trimmed like fine silk. He wore a tunic and leggings, and his hat had a jewelled cockade in the front. He smiled and bowed his neck, when she waved to Pagano. He was really quite young. She went back to bed.

She woke the second time warm and confused, and thought she was in bed on the *Doria* with Pagano asleep on her breasts. His weight pleased her.

Someone said kindly, "Is it?"

Someone replied, in a voice she had never heard before, "Yes."

Then Catherine opened her eyes. Nicholas was installed on her bedcover, watching her.

Chapter 13

NICHOLAS, HER MOTHER'S apprentice, was in her room. Her mother's husband.

His face was in shadow, but Catherine knew who it was. And even then, in the midst of her shock, her imagination leaped to see herself through his eyes. How the red-brown hair on her pillow would seem the identical shade of her mother's. How her eyes were the same blue. How her face was young, and fresh and unblurred, as her mother's was not. Then, and only then, did she cast wildly about her to cover her bareness. She found her modesty unimpaired. The sheet was up to her chin and her cloak, for good measure, laid over it. The cloak lay on her breast, not Pagano.

"Catherine?" Nicholas said. He sat as still as a cat at a mousehole. "Don't be afraid. Your woman is here, and Father Godscalc. I should have waited, but I have to go soon, and I had to see you. Tell me what's happened."

One of her women *was* there, looking frightened and even plainer than usual. *Godscalc?* That was the chaplain her mother had hired, to join the army somewhere in Italy. She saw a big man with a tonsure and black, untidy hair, but hardly remembered him. She heeled her way up the mattress and sat with the sheet wrapped like gloves round her collarbones. She could hear her own shortened breathing. She stared in exasperation at Nicholas. Claes.

A gentleman would have called, by arrangement, with bridal gifts. Or contrived (dazzled) to see her at some superior function. Or challenged Pagano to fight him. Or climbed a rope and attempted to abduct her. Nicholas sat planked on her bed in his old clothes, like a busy cook who had run down a kitchenmaid. And had brought the family priest with him.

Catherine said, "I remember Father Godscalc. He was in Italy when you killed my brother Felix."

He had his back to the light, and didn't stir. He said, "We heard you had married."

"Did you?" she said. "Well, you heard right. You can't break it, either. Pagano got all the papers. Twice. We married in Florence, and then in Messina. Not some hole-in-the-corner affair in a borrowed chapel."

"But not with the blessing of your family, either." It was the priest's voice. He was not even Flemish. He had nothing to do with it. She stared at him. She said, "The family signed the papers. You don't know them."

"Who?" said Nicholas.

"My godfather. My uncle. Thibault de Fleury. You saw his brother dead, too," Catherine said.

The maid suddenly whined and Catherine turned on her. "Do you think he's going to kill you? Don't be afraid. He gets other people to do it. He couldn't even ravish you unless you were old." She turned back. "I expect my lord Pagano at any moment. He fights men who insult his wife."

Nicholas made no comment on that at all. He said, "Does your mother know?"

Naturally, it would be all he could think of. She said, "Now she will. Pagano wrote her from Florence."

He said, "Pagano did?" but she saw no point in repeating herself. He said, "You left no word for your mother before Florence?"

She made her tone insolent. "No. She would have stopped me, wouldn't she?"

"Yes," said Nicholas. The flow of questions had stuck. He sat bent like a man with the stomach ache, his arms folded, his eyes on the floor. Then he took a quick breath and looked at her afresh, with no sign of annoyance or anger. He said, "Look. Never mind all that, it doesn't matter now. We're here just to be sure of one thing. That you're with Doria by your own wish and of your own free will, and that you're happy. Will you tell us that, Catherine?"

She recognised, with pleasure, the opportunity he had given her. She dropped one hand on her lap, and gave him a disdainful smile. The sheet, gracefully maintained at her breast, exposed one naked shoulder and a fall of fine russet hair. She said, "How could you imagine my happiness? My marriage is perfect. My husband is better born than anyone you have even met. And don't think you can spoil it, for he thought of everything. He waited till I was a woman. He gave me a dog."

Nicholas looked at her. It was his stupid look, straight from a fight in the dyeyard. He said, "I knew that was the mistake."

The priest said, "Take it steadily."

Nicholas acknowledged it, if at all, with an unhurried fall of his eyelids. Then he began again in his most ordinary voice. "I'd like to talk to your husband. I shall wait as long as I can. But whether I do or not, I shall be writing home, Catherine. What shall I say to your mother?"

"What do you usually say to my mother?" she said. "Ask her if she would like me to send her something from Trebizond. Pagano will see to it."

"When will you come home to Bruges?" Nicholas said. His voice throughout had been easy and level, only changing in the amount of breath he brought to it. Normally, Nicholas had more voices than anyone she knew. But then, he had nothing else.

She said, "I don't really know. These days, I find the idea of Bruges a little revolting. I suppose Tilde doesn't mind, but my husband isn't used to such things in his family. I suppose we might buy a town house in Brussels."

"Not Genoa?" Nicholas said.

It seemed an odd idea, but she lifted her brows. "Or Genoa," she said.

"When, Catherine?"

She was becoming bored. "When he's finished in Trebizond. I don't know when. Ask my husband," she said.

He rose off the quilt then, and stood as if at a loss by the bedpost. Godscalc drew a breath and Nicholas looked at him and said, "No. What good will it do?"

Godscalc said, "Very well. But there is almost no time. You can't leave them to face it alone." He hesitated and then said, "If you like, I will stay."

"No. You mustn't," said Nicholas.

Anger rose in her. They were talking over her head. They were discussing, apparently, how long it would suit them to coerce her. Catherine drew a long breath, and emitted a single, deliberate scream, followed by the names of her page and her manservant.

The manservant came in immediately but looked at Godscalc, who said, "It's all right. We're leaving. The Madonna is over-excited. Stay with her." All the time he was speaking he was looking over his shoulder at someone else who had come to the door.

It was a man, cloaked and hooded, she didn't know, although she thought she smelled incense. Nicholas knew him. He went and spoke to him in a low voice and then turned back to them all. He looked first at her, and then at Godscalc. Godscalc said, "What?" and without waiting for a reply pulled open a shutter. Then he said, "She's in, and dropped anchor. Let's go."

Nicholas said, "It's too late. She'll have been boarded already."

"And?" Godscalc said. He had a large face, like a pudding.

Nicholas said, "Someone has told the Grand Vizier that we have Julius and le Grant on board. A troop of Janissaries is on its way to arrest them."

She heard it. "Master Julius?" said Catherine de Charetty, with all the authority of her mother. "Master Julius? What for?"

Nicholas turned to her. "He knows the wrong people," he said. "He was a favourite of Cardinal Bessarion. In these parts, Bessarion is regarded as a traitor to the Greek Church and an enemy of the Turks."

"And John? Why John?" Godscalc said; and Nicholas gave a wry smile.

"Didn't you know? He nearly saved Constantinople. It was his countermining that defeated the Turkish sappers over and over. He came to serve under Giustiniani Longo. Longo, the Genoese leader. A Doria man."

"A friend of the *Doria?*" Godscalc said.

"Related to them, just like Catherine's husband. So John is twice damned, as a sapper and a Genoese-lover, and not likely to be spared by the Sultan. My lord Pagano, though, has nothing to fear. Not after his acceptable trip to the Vizier this morning."

Master Julius. Her mother's notary. Well, he had chosen to go with Nicholas. Catherine said, "My husband took gifts. Everyone has to." She said it sharply.

"I know," Nicholas said. "I've been afraid of what he might give. But he chose to take the black page, not the white one."

"*Nicholas,*" Godscalc said. But this time he received no acknowledgement.

Catherine de Charetty said nothing as her mother's husband came forward into the light, and hesitated, and then knelt at her side. He said, "So long as you're happy, none of us will interfere. But if anything should ever go wrong, you have only to call. I shall be at Trebizond. There is a ship, and you have many friends, and people closer than friends. We are always there for you."

"I don't want you," she said.

They spoke very little on their way to the ferry that would take them over the Golden Horn to where the *Ciaretti* lay off the point, surrounded by guard boats from which, even at such a distance, they could see the glitter of steel. The monk from the Franciscans' had been right, in the message he'd brought them. The Turks had sent an armed detachment to halt the galley and board her. The excuse, it seemed, was to take John and Julius. On the *Ciaretti*, they had been prepared, of course, for boarding by customs officials; by delegates from the Porte. They had all been carefully primed what to do; what to say. But being overrun by a troop of enemy soldiers was another matter. Of course Nicholas had planned for it: he had planned for everything. Except, of course, that the lives of two of his men might now be forfeit, or at the very least, hostage. But one didn't know, yet, how much that meant.

It's too late, Nicholas had said, back there in Pera; and for a shocking moment Godscalc had thought he meant to leave the ship to her fate, as had nearly happened at Modon. But this time Nicholas had set off downhill at once to the shore; although what lay before him, Godscalc saw, was a fiendish replica of the earlier occasion. Whatever his concern for the girl, Nicholas had to abandon her for his men and his galley, now exposed to something at least as dangerous as the fire, thanks again to Pagano Doria. No one else could have told the Turks that le Grant and Julius were on board; reminded them of le Grant's war record; exposed the link between Julius and Bessarion. Unnoticed by anyone – unnoticed by himself as well as the young, the immature Nicholas – Doria had always held the fate of these two men in his hands. Julius, who had shared some at least of Nicholas's boyhood. Red-headed le Grant, who had so readily joined them after that ingenious masquerading in Florence. Who had once fought, it seemed, for a Genoese leader. Well, there was little room now to doubt where poor le Grant's loyalties lay.

At the water's edge, Nicholas stopped, on the point of jumping down to the skiff. He said, "Wait. You should stay. If anything happens, there must be someone to look after the girl."

Godscalc looked at him. He said, "I have a shipload of souls to look after. She has Pagano Doria." Nicholas said nothing more.

It was cold on the water. As soon as the oarsmen started to pull, Nicholas got a flask from his pouch, took a long swallow and, wiping its mouth, held it out. Godscalc hesitated, and then, accepting it, did the same. The strength of the spirit surprised him into coughing. He passed the flask back, but although Nicholas drank from it twice more in short, savage snatches, he didn't share it again. Nor did he appear to be watching his ship. Instead, all the time he kept his eyes on the long seawall of Stamboul as it began to come nearer. Behind it stood the dome of the Holy Wisdom, once the greatest church in the world. Nicholas said, "What does it tell you, this place?"

Godscalc looked at him. The flask, tilted a little, had made a spreading stain on the man's dark felt cloak. Godscalc said, "You want a sermon on human weakness, greed, courage? A history lesson? It tells me what all cities have to tell."

"All cities?" said Nicholas. "I thought this was the New Rome, the new Jerusalem; the second Mecca?" He lifted the flask again and checked, meeting Godscalc's brown eyes.

They were getting near. Godscalc said, "Must we? Well then, yes, you are right, it is a special case. Zeus and Jupiter. The Latin God, the Greek God, the Muslim God. A spiritual stew. The reek is one I am used to; I need a smell to diagnose illness, as Tobie does. Why, does it worry you?" It was, under the circumstances, an extraordinary conversation.

Nicholas turned. "I don't know," he said. "I only feel an abomination somehow in the air."

They were among the guard ships, and turbanned men were baying at them. Godscalc said, "Because of the Turks? Doria?" He saw

Nicholas express a convulsive and irritable negative. It seemed to restore him, like a sneeze. The reek, not of spiritual decadence but of alcohol rose from his person. They were being urged to their feet and prodded by maces towards their own companionway.

Godscalc went first. Behind him, Nicholas said in a voice thickened but perfectly sane, "After winning, the Sultan made a gift of four hundred Greek children to the rulers of Egypt and Tunis and Granada. I thought I saw a dead child. I felt as if a wave of doom were waiting to fall on me."

"Well, it is," Godscalc said. "But we all expect you to deal with it. So get on board that galley, and act."

Bound and bleeding in the cooking quarter of the *Ciaretti*, Julius heard Godscalc's voice through the Turkish babble from the flotilla outside. He was speaking in Flemish, and Julius, with what he could muster of viciousness, hoped that the person he spoke to was Nicholas.

At present, what remained of his mind was equally divided in hatred between Pagano Doria his tormentor, and Nicholas, the conceited clown who had allowed this to happen.

As instructed, the *Ciaretti* had taken its time about rowing the last miles to the Horn. It had not been difficult. As instructed, they had not resisted hailing and boarding, even though it had occurred before they had even dropped anchor. Instead of customs searchers and harbour officials, they had been boarded by Janissaries: silent, muscular men with white felt hats and an armoury of weapons, sharp and blunt, which they used. With them was a soft-spoken man called Tursun Beg, in a fur cloak over a long buttoned robe and a cap with a turban wound round it.

The ill-treatment had begun immediately, when they found the priest and patron were missing. They knew the name Niccolò. John le Grant had been slammed out of his senses for failing to follow the dragoman's distorted Italian and had yet to come to himself. Julius, although he hastened to answer, had received two blows to the face and, when he resisted, a kicking that had ended when they dropped him here, his arms and legs bound. Behind him, scorching his back, was the oven. And beyond that was the cooking fire, with a pair of tongs in it. They were used to getting co-operation.

Above him on the deck of the poop, all the senior officers of the ship had been collected together and made to stand in the open, encircled by men with axes, maces, daggers and pikes. Among them was Tobie. The rest were the Florentine complement. Other armed men occupied the length of the gangway, back to back and facing the uneasy oarsmen, who still sat, one or two on each bench, as when they rowed in. One or two, instead of three. This was a trireme. From below came the hollow sound of voices and footsteps, as the rest of the boarding party worked their way through the stores in the hold.

Tursun Beg looked like a man who could count. Lying burning and freezing, his hair in the dung from the beasts in the stable beside him, Julius peered up at the Turk and his dragoman and answered everything that they asked. He told them that Messer Nicholas the patron and his holy man would be returning. They had merely hired a ferry across to Pera, where the patron had a married kinswoman. He gave the name of the kinswoman's husband, the Genoese Pagano Doria, but it effected no change in the dark disinterested face with its neat black moustache.

The next question should have been about the number and origin of his oarsmen. Instead it was an order to summon before Tursun Beg the notary Julius, and the engineer-captain John le Grant.

Amazed, he had gazed up through swollen eyes at his questioner. The mace had already sunk into his ribs when he saw Loppe moving weightily forward and heard his voice, in sonorous Arabic, launching into a reply in his place.

Seen from below, Loppe was the size and width of the mainmast. He was also, unusually, stripped to the waist. Above the white drawers, his muscles were shapely as unbarrelled pitch. He turned and, talking still, stabbed a finger first towards Julius and then towards the unconscious form of le Grant.

Breathing was painful, but ignorance was much worse. Julius scraped up some breath and croaked, "What is it?"

Loppe looked at the robed Turk, who nodded. Loppe said, in Italian, "They've given me my freedom, Master Julius. Imagine that!"

Nicholas had given Loppe his freedom the previous year. Loppe spoke the languages of all his previous owners and was probably working hard on Hungarian. Julius said, "What do they want?"

Loppe smiled. "To put you in prison, Master Julius. And Master le Grant. He'll be executed for fighting the Sultan."

"I haven't fought the Sultan," said Julius.

Loppe said, "Well, maybe not. But this letter came from Cardinal Bessarion, addressed to you in the care of Master Nicholas. The Turks have got it."

Bessarion. From the recesses of his aching head, Julius remembered as if from another world his misdeeds at Bologna, and the need to get Bessarion to vouch for him. He said, "What did it say?"

Loppe said, "It was a friendly letter, Master Julius, so I suppose it was the good news you were waiting for. It talked of telling my lord Cosimo de' Medici what a fine man you were, and that they could rely on you, wherever you went in the East, to see to it that all men should be encouraged to return into the unity of the Catholic and Universal Church, and spurn the Eastern errors of worship. They think you're a Latinist spy sent to subvert the Greeks and get them to join a Papal Crusade. They're going to execute you as well, Master Julius."

He could never have learned all that in the exchange he had just had. He was giving, Julius realised, the news he had already gleaned from others. He might have more.

"How did they get the letter?" Julius asked.

"It came to the Greek Patriarchate, Messer Julius," said Loppe. "As you know, they depend on the goodwill of the Sultan. And in any case, the Grand Vizier had heard about you and the Cardinal Bessarion. Tursun Beg is his secretary. He says Pagano Doria had an audience with his master this morning."

Pagano Doria. And he couldn't even draw a decent breath to hate him with. Above him, Tobie's round, light eyes held a warning. He had taken off the fur hat he had put on that morning and his face was a cold-looking lavender. Julius closed his eyes, releasing Loppe from risky conversation and making it easy for the Janissaries to lay hands on him. Nicholas, you bastard. And there was no point in struggling, even if it were possible. He'd only involve the whole crew.

That was when he heard Godscalc's voice from the water, and opened his eyes. Tobie, who had a better view, was already striving to see over the side. Then he said in Flemish, "They're both there. Not the girl."

So he hadn't even got Catherine. It had been his, Julius's, place to take the girl back for her mother. They had had bitter words about it. But Nicholas had gone off just the same, and left them to get into this mess, and had done no good in Pera either. Nicholas thought he'd guessed what trick Doria had up his sleeve. But he hadn't. Above him, Tobie shifted a little.

The Turkish official, also disturbed by the noise, had turned from his prisoners. Stooped to lift them, the Janissaries straightened. After a moment Tursun Beg walked himself to the head of the companionway, and gave an impatient sign for Loppe to join him. Beside Julius, John le Grant opened his eyes, winced, and said, "What?"

Julius said in Flemish, "It's all gone wrong. They know who you are. They think I'm a dangerous disciple of Bessarion's. They've hardly looked at the ship. They'll probably impound it, when they've executed us."

The engineer looked at him blearily. Then he said, "I've pissed mysel', God damn it. Where's Nicholas?"

"Just coming on board," said Julius with painful bitterness. "What can he do?"

"Jesus Son of David," said Tobie suddenly from above. His eyes were on the companionway. Twisting a shoulder, Julius tried to lift himself and see what was happening. As he watched, Godscalc stepped up on deck. His cloak was creased, and his hood, fallen back, showed the bristled black tonsure which the church permitted at sea. His attention seemed equally divided between Tursun Beg, to whom Loppe was trying to make him known, and a commotion from the

ladder behind him. Julius saw Loppe step to the side, and then
Tursun Beg. There was a splash, and a lot of shouting. Julius looked
up at Tobie.

"Nicholas," Tobie said. He spoke in a clipped voice.

"Escaping?" said John le Grant. He sounded surprised. Below, the
shouting increased. They could see the top of the companionway
sway. The head of Nicholas came into view, its toneless brown hair
frizzed like a ball of brown wool with the damp. His hat was missing,
and his cloak had half fallen off. From his belt to his boots, he was
soaked in dirty seawater. His face was rosy with pleasure, and he was
talking with large and positive gestures in incomprehensible Flemish.

In taverns in Bruges and Louvain, Julius had tracked them both
down, Felix and Claes, by that joyous voice and uninhibited laugh.
Paid their bills, led them out, held their heads while they retched.
"Escaping," he said.

Chapter 14

IF NICHOLAS HAD ESCAPED, it was only, of course, in a figurative sense. Like everyone else, he was still surrounded by Janissaries on board the impounded *Ciaretti*, whose sailing-master and notary had been beaten, bound, and were about to be removed to suffer the ultimate penalty, while the rest of her complement (her sober complement) awaited, sickened, the end which fate was preparing for them.

Tobie, herded with the rest on the prow, tried to imagine, bleakly, why Nicholas, just at this juncture, should have resorted to wine; and concluded that the girl was the cause. For all he knew, the same might have happened in Modon, had not the fire claimed all their energy. He tried to read Godscalc's face, but it was void of expression. Julius, who must have been in considerable pain, was incandescent with anger. Le Grant, also under sentence of death, merely lay, looking puzzled. Loppe, whom one might have expected to show more distress than any one of them, merely looked vaguely content. Hesitantly, hope revived in Tobie's sharp, Pavia-trained brain. He looked hard at Nicholas.

Like Loppe, Nicholas also looked vaguely complacent. His lower half still trickled with water from his mishap on the steps. His elbows, twined in the arms of two Janissaries, were knobbed like the wings of a pullet, and you could have put a caterpillar as soon as a crust between his smiling, generous lips. They made to hold him in front of the Bey, but his legs buckled a little, and his feet, unexpectedly straying, carried him out of his captors' surprised grasp and ambitiously onwards. He arrived before they knew it at the roped-off square of the kitchen and stood staring down at his red-headed acquisition from Aberdeen. He sucked his breath in reprovingly. "You've pissed yourself," Nicholas said. He spoke in Tuscan.

The red head jerked. "Well, by God, you've filled your boots as well as your drawers, and they didn't give you the blunt end of an axe on your skull. They're going to hang us," said John le Grant in the same language. Tobie heard him.

"No, they're not," Nicholas said with confidence. His gaze, straying, found Julius tied up, and he transferred the smile to him, widened. "Impale you, they might. Bury you up to the neck. Tie you in a sack with a dog and then whack it. Fire you off from a cannon. Canon law, Julius. Couldn't fire John, he's too wet."

"They know . . ." Julius began. He used Flemish.

"And you rowed very well," Nicholas said, still in Italian. "Won your wager." He turned his attention to Loppe at his side, and the Bey. He said to Loppe, "Tell your new chief he owes Julius three girls and some ale. Debt of honour. No, not ale; the skin-clippers think that it's wicked."

The men on the poop, frozen till now, were looking at one another uneasily. Tobie stared hard at Loppe. The Janissaries by the kitchen stood prepared, their eyes on Tursun Beg, who had given them no signal yet. The Turk spoke curtly to Loppe, who replied. Nicholas, evidently noticing, leaned and poked Loppe in the side. The negro turned.

Water from Nicholas's cloak streamed over his boots and formed a pool which spread to where Julius was lying. Goat manure stirred, rose and floated into his ears. Le Grant suddenly choked and Tobie, watching, cursed him under his breath. Nicholas said to Loppe in playful Italian, "You're a eunuch."

Loppe, glancing nervously at him, returned his attention to Tursun Beg who was asking a question. Nicholas prodded the negro again. "Aren't you? What's *big black eunuch* in Turkish? Want to help row us to Trebizond? Give you three boys."

"Messer Niccolò," said Loppe, turning fully. What Tobie could see of his face looked mildly desperate. He said, "My lord Tursun Beg asks where the rowers are. The benches are half empty."

Nicholas stared at him. The necessity for keeping his weight on both feet evidently escaped him and he sat down, delayed by his cloak, in the water. It ran under le Grant and stopped him choking. Nicholas embraced his knees with one hand and waved the other. "Well, tell him! All the officers had to row, and we had a wager."

He sang to himself while Loppe translated, and answered questions, and the damp, cold wind stirred his hair and his clothes and made Tobie, watching, suddenly shiver. Then there was silence.

Tursun Beg had turned from the Negro. For a moment, his black eyes considered Nicholas. Then he gave an order. Two men, reaching, jerked Nicholas viciously to his feet and held him, painfully. Nicholas stopped singing. Then Tursun spoke; and this time the dragoman translated. The dragoman said, "You are to answer. Half your rowers are missing."

"That's right," Nicholas said. "Three girls and a . . . You didn't row." He looked indignant.

"Where are the rowers?" said the dragoman.

Nicholas looked surprised. "Well. All over the Aegean and Marmara. With their families. In Paradise. We did take on others, but they kept deserting."

"Paradise?" said the dragoman.

"Giving them the benefit of the doubt," said Nicholas generously.

"The honoured Tursun Beg means, messer padrone, do you say that some oarsmen died? How did they die?"

"They made a good death," said Nicholas. "Ask the chaplain over there. Repented, all of them, to a man. We buried some overboard. Look, I'm wet."

"*Of what did they die?*" said the dragoman. His voice, in its urgency, was nearly as peremptory as that of Tursun Beg.

"I don't know," said Nicholas. "I'm going to change. Didn't you look in the ballast? We sanded up two of them there, to last until we get to Trebizond. That's where they came from, and that's where they wished to be buried. We didn't have any Turks. I know how to bury a Turk. I've seen it. Under a hat on a gravestone. Maestro Cappello, Madonna Cappello, Bambino Cappellino. Funeral musica di cappella. Mourning wisps of capello. Cap – cap – cap that, my caprone," said Nicholas. Tobie stopped trembling and stood, suddenly, very still. He felt himself flushing.

Tursun Beg, on the contrary, was sallow. He jerked his head and Nicholas was pushed, talking, towards his own cabin. Two of the Turk's companions lifted the hatch and climbed for the second time down below. They came back very quickly: so quickly that their faces were white. And they called their news, in Turkish, from the hatch. News that struck, like a blow, everyone within hearing. News that transformed the whole ship.

Like tacks to a magnet, the living pattern of men filling the end-decks and gangway and benches of the great galley *Ciaretti* rearranged itself. Those who belonged to the ship stood where they were, looking about them. Those who did not, began to move with the first words of the announcement, springing away from both captives and oarsmen; leaving clear the tight groups of officials at poop and at stern. Nicholas, in a dry doublet, had come out of the stern castle with both hose in his hands and was trying to stand on one foot while he assumed them. Tursun Beg saw him and turned. He shouted.

The dragoman swallowed. He said, "My master says, do you not know that you carry the plague?" The rumble of horrified voices rose and fell all about him.

"The plague?" Nicholas said. "It's the goats. Well, it's Messer Julius now as well. There's no smell from the ballast. Two good dry corpses, ready for home."

"They have the plague," said the dragoman. "My master's barber knows the signs well. You cannot stay here."

"Can't I?" Nicholas said. He hopped, and pulled one stocking up to his ankles with its laces in knots. "All right," he said. "But you'll have to find me a lodging. I suppose I'd better meet the Grand Vizier and sort out this business of le Grant and my notary. What prison . . . My boots. Wait until I put on my boots. What prison are you putting them in?" His speech, though happily slurred, was quite easy to follow.

"They are to stay aboard," said the dragoman rapidly. "You are all to stay aboard. You are to sail without going ashore. Water and supplies will be brought to you, but no one else will set foot on this ship."

Nicholas rested his toes on the deck. "We were expecting the Bailie!" he said. He sounded more surprised than aggrieved. "And the Florentine agent. And Messer Bartolomeo Zorzi and his partner."

"None of them," said the dragoman.

Nicholas looked bemused. He said, "Well, of course. If you say so. You don't have any laws about where I've got to sail?"

"Where were you going?" said Tursun Beg softly. The dragoman translated.

"To Trebizond," Nicholas said. "I thought you knew that. We're to stay there, to represent Florence."

"Then," said Tursun Beg, "I think, Messer Niccolò, you should pursue your excellent plan. I think you should take aboard what you need, and set sail directly for Trebizond."

It was the last pronouncement he made. He said something aside. A whistle shrilled, and voices shouted from one end of the ship to another. There was an urgent shuffling of feet. With dignity, Tursun Beg and his entourage turned and descended the companionway followed, with fearful alacrity, by the host of their Janissaries, their hatchets glistening, their plumes jerked by the wind. As their rowboats cast off, Tobie ran down the steps from the poop and crossed to where Nicholas stood surveying the general departure with the greatest good will, waving frequently from the outrigging while he attempted to get the other leg covered. When the sea round them was empty but for the far-distant unhappy circle of guard boats, he finally put both feet down and looked about him. Every man left on board seemed to be crowded about him. "Three cheers," said Tobie with careful sarcasm. They gave them, in a whisper.

Nicholas failed to look embarrassed. "Well, I should think so," he said. "Look: for Christ's sake, get down and start sawing the woodwork. Astorre and the rest'll be dead. Loppe, I insulted you. You are reckoned a three-ball man from this day for services rendered. St Nicholas, patron of pawnbrokers. Tobie . . . ?"

All but a touch, the thickened speech had vanished. Nicholas was sober. He had always been sober. "John's all right. You've got a fine, battered notary, though," Tobie said. In a mess of cut ropes, John le Grant sat up rubbing his arms and seeking tenderly the lump where the Turk's mace had caught him. Someone had dumped straw all round Julius and Tobie had slit his shirt and was strapping him up prior to moving him. Julius, in between being stoical, was gasping and swearing under his breath, largely at Nicholas.

"Now, now," Tobie said. He felt silly with elation. "We thought Doria was going to report our hundred soldiers, and planned accordingly. And it worked. All those beautiful fitments they made at Modon, and boxes, and barrels. They'll have cramp and arthritis for weeks, but it saved them. Not to mention my convincing plague paintwork."

"You mean it was lucky we had the two dead men," said John le Grant. "I think I know what Julius is complaining about. But Doria outplayed us all. It was clever." He paused. "What was that about a letter from Bessarion?"

Tobie said, "The Medici bank promised to back us provided we received a clean bill of health from the cardinal. The clean bill of health seems to have come, if at an inconvenient moment. We'll get copies from Florence. Right; let's lift him now."

Nicholas and two of the seamen helped carry Julius to the cabin. The senior helmsman said in Nicholas's ear, "Christ, Messer Niccolò, that was funny. It was all I could do to keep quiet."

Nicholas grinned. Behind them, small drifts of laughter were beginning to pass from one side of the ship to the other. The cook's fire flared. Men were gathered in groups round the main hatch. Nicholas said, "Well. We all want to relax, but I suppose we mustn't look like a happy ship. And whatever else, Captain Astorre and his men must stay below until dark. What about getting the canopy up, and some wine broached? Don't bother Messer le Grant: you can do it amongst yourselves. But quietly, yes?"

He stayed with Tobie and Godscalc until Julius was bandaged and settled. Tobie said he had seen worse from a hunting fall, but it was still a matter of broken ribs and a collarbone and some cuts and heavy bruising. Godscalc went off and came back with something hot, with a powder in it. Sipping it one-handed, Julius was reminded for the first time, drowsily, of his other grievances. He said, "That poor little brat. What went wrong?"

Godscalc said, "She wouldn't come, Julius. She is actually married, and he is being a good husband. She is happy, and clearly adores him. He has written, she says, and told her mother."

Julius said, "You believed her?"

Godscalc said, "She had no reason to lie. Doria wasn't there." Tobie, methodically repacking his bag, wondered why Nicholas was not being allowed to speak. Reclining on the next pallet, the inebriated Florentine consul had helped himself to a cup of the very good wine someone had brought and was this time authentically draining it. He then poured another.

Julius said, "But Trebizond, if there's war? She shouldn't go there. And he won't stay a good husband. It's only her money he wants. I say we abduct her regardless."

Tobie said gravely, "We could. We have to pick up passengers at Pera."

Godscalc said, "Have we? I didn't know that."

Nicholas said, "People going to Trebizond. Tobie got word from the Greek's brother Zorzi. It'll have to be done at dark, on the Bosphorus side, since we're supposed to be a ship with the plague. Julius, we can't force her away: she'd just run back to him. And anyway, where should we take her? We're going to Trebizond ourselves." He paused, and then said, "If turning back would help Catherine, I would do it."

"It wouldn't," said Godscalc. "If you had been with us, Julius, you would agree."

Julius gazed at him for a while, with a puzzled look, until quite suddenly the opiate sent him to sleep.

Watching him, Tobie asked a soft question. "Will the war involve Trebizond? What did the Franciscans tell you?"

Godscalc said, "You saw the fleet at Gallipoli. They say there are three hundred Turkish ships gathering there. The Sultan is not in Adrianople, but has installed his second Vizier there, as if against a long absence. Meanwhile Mahmud Pasha the Grand Vizier is here in Stamboul, with all his household. He's a successful general: he quelled Serbia, where his father came from, three years ago. If the Sultan takes his army to war, Mahmud will probably lead it." He halted.

Nicholas, Tobie noticed, was watching them all, but not really listening. He had heard it before. The chaplain said, "The strongest rumour agrees with what the Bailie told us in Modon. The Sultan has his eye, of course, on all the Black Sea ports, including Trebizond. But his first quarrel is with Uzum Beg, who insulted him. And he may want to act quickly, just in case the West listen to Fra Ludovico da Bologna and send a rescue fleet over this summer."

"First Uzum Hasan. And then Trebizond?" Tobie said.

For the first time, Nicholas spoke. "It's anyone's guess. But remember. The Empire of Trebizond is just a two-hundred-mile strip along the Black Sea coast, about forty miles deep. Between that and the rest of Asia Minor are those mountains. They're why Trebizond has remained protected so long, and they may still protect it. The campaigning season is short. At the end of a long expedition against Uzum Hasan, the Sultan is unlikely to tackle the Pontic Chain."

"What if he beats Uzum Hasan quickly?" said Tobie.

"Then Trebizond might suffer a brief siege, which Astorre says it can stand very well. On the other hand, the Sultan might lose. Uzum Hasan can call on a lot of help. Otherwise, why that ridiculous levy of horse-harness?"

"You mean the Pope and the Duke of Burgundy are going to send a crusade?" Tobie said.

"I mean I think Uzum Hasan and the Emperor of Trebizond hope that the Sultan thinks the West is going to send a fleet to attack him," Nicholas said.

"In fact," said Tobie, "we need an astrologer. What happened to your ominous Greek? I thought he was going to read the entrails for you."

Nicholas said, "I don't know if I'd believe him if he did. The truth is that no one knows what will happen, or will know for a month, because land campaigning can't start until then. By that time, we'll be with the Emperor in Trebizond, and committed. I'm willing to take the risk and go on, but if anyone else isn't, now is the last chance to say so. We can't stay in Pera. We can only turn back, or go and accept whatever is going to happen."

Tobie said, "You're a bit late, aren't you, with the offer? Julius is asleep, and le Grant is getting the ship ready to leave."

"Le Grant knows the position, and all the senior officers," Nicholas said. "And you heard Julius. He wouldn't abandon the girl. He knows there may be war. We've always known this."

"Well, that's true," said Tobie. "It only worries me when I hear it translated into dates and numbers and long Turkish titles. Then it's Trebizond, come what may, with our arthritic hundred?"

"Why not?" said Nicholas. "Jason went. If he and Pagano Doria can manage it, I don't see why we should be frightened and poor instead of frightened and rich. So we go?"

"Well, of course," said Godscalc mildly. "What is all this about? Did you think we were going to swim back to Bruges?"

Nicholas smiled at him. "It's not about anything but Tobie's liking for taking plumb readings. Like you. I don't mind. A pledge. To Trebizond, and a pox on Pagano. Which reminds me – "

"Yes," said Father Godscalc smoothly. "I thought of that. And so did you, of course, when you entered that house. The *Doria* and her commander will have to leave Pera too."

As the Ottoman troops had departed, so with speed did the provisioning craft make their appearance, take their orders, and return with the water and food the galley demanded. No one set foot on board. The casks and boxes were winched up with a boom for crane and settled below, where unscrewed panels and gaping barrels and chests showed where the craftsmen of Modon had concealed ninety-eight soldiers and Astorre.

To the watching boats as dusk fell the Florentine galley might have seemed to lie dark on the water, sober now and aware of her fate. Instead, behind the drawn curtains and heavy shutters, there was taking place a celebration of muted exuberance. When sleep came, it claimed contented men.

Through it all, Nicholas fizzed and exploded among them, with a cup never far from his hand. Godscalc made no effort to check him, then or later, when he took the mattress next to him for what was to be left of the night. Rising from his knees, he looked across once, before he rolled into his pallet, but Nicholas was quite still.

Halfway through the short night Godscalc spoke in a low voice, "Are you not asleep yet?" He heard a short exhalation, possibly of amusement.

Nicholas said, "In spite of all I've drunk?"

It was still too dark to see outlines. The cabin was full of the sound of other men's breathing. Godscalc leaned his weight on one elbow and addressed the darkness, clasping his hands. He said, "There wasn't a dead child. There is a perfectly happy living child who may never need help. But if she does, there is no better person she could wish to have near her. It is not your fault, what has happened. You could have done nothing else."

"You don't know. It is my fault," said Nicholas.

Beyond, Tobie, himself long awake, heard the exchange, which ended there. Once he, too, had been tempted to interfere, but had been wiser. His was not the voice Nicholas needed, nor Godscalc's. As he had seen long ago, the voice Nicholas needed didn't exist.

Long before that, the sea prince Pagano Doria returned to his loved one in Pera, leaving behind him a critical and not unsatisfactory interview with the Grand Vizier Mahmud in the New Palace, and a short, humble one in the painted paraclesion of the church of the Pammakaristos, the home of the head of the Greek Orthodox Church in the Ottoman Empire.

Clearly, the Ottoman Empire needed the skills of the Greeks, and the Greeks needed some sort of local controller. Hence, with his usual clemency, Mehmet the Conqueror had spared the required number of churches in Stamboul and had appointed as Patriarch the man George Scholarius, of all Greek theologians the one least likely to support or promote union with the Church of the West. Once, at the Pope's famous council in Florence, Scholarius had spoken and voted for union like Amiroutzes and Bessarion. But there is no man firmer in his opinion than the man who has changed it. The Sultan gave the Patriarch a new jewelled cross and allowed him to instruct him in the Christian Faith. Know thy enemy.

Recrossing the Horn, Doria saw that the *Ciaretti* was no longer delightfully jostled by guard boats and deduced that le Grant and the poor fellow Julius must have been removed already in chains, with Master Niccolò presumably running after wringing his hands. Because of the Florentine connection, Mahmud would probably leave the ship and the young man alone. Doria suspected, also, that the Venetians were keeping an eye on the Charetty company. The actual fate of the two accused men hardly troubled him. The case would keep the galley hanging about for a very long time. That was all he cared about. That and giving another tap on the chin to this poor bemused youth who had thought to best a Doria. It remained to be seen, of course, if it had been a tap and not a blow that could kill. He hoped not. One should conduct such matters with artistry.

He rode with his immaculate retinue into the elder's courtyard, dismounted, and was immediately accosted by his captain, who had apparently been waiting for him. Running down the steps behind Crackbene was the manservant he had left to serve Catherine. And at the top of the steps, her hair unbecomingly loose, stood his wife Catherine herself, looking agitated.

Pagano Doria said to Crackbene, "Quickly."

He was an experienced captain who ran the ship, and did what he was paid to do, without comment. He said, "The *Ciaretti* was boarded, but they didn't take off the prisoners. They say they have the plague on board."

"They haven't," said Doria.

Crackbene said, "It's possible. There is an outbreak at Patras."

Catherine's servant had arrived. "My lord! He came. As you thought he might. Messer Niccolò of the Charetty, to see the Madonna. I allowed him to – "

"Be quiet, fool," said Doria. He said to Crackbene, "So, you see, there is no plague."

"They showed them bodies."

"They searched, then? What did they find?"

"Only two bodies," said Crackbene. "Half the crew were missing, deserted or dead. They had taken some fishermen to help them through the narrows. The rest were all the original seamen, and the officers."

"Then they've given up," Doria said. "They let the soldiers go while they were still in Venetian territory. Unless he hid them somehow on board. Is it possible?"

"Hardly," said Crackbene. "In any case, I looked at the load line. They hadn't discharged cargo since Modon, but the ship was riding much higher."

Doria gazed at him. He said, "So we frightened him. He dismissed the soldiers, and he's going to Trebizond with nothing." He swore to himself, and then again, as his eyes were drawn to Catherine. Doria said, "If he's even going to Trebizond now. Wait here."

"I shall, of course, monseigneur," said the captain civilly. "But I shall have to see to matters soon. Since the patron of the plague ship visited the madonna, we too have been ordered out of Pera. We have until tomorrow to leave."

It was, of course, what Pagano Doria had once wanted most: to be allowed to leave Pera quickly. But this deprived him of the time he had hoped to use in pursuing his new contacts in Stamboul. In discovering what had become of those vanished Charetty soldiers. And even, perhaps, of persuading the Grand Vizier and his officials that there was no plague on the *Ciaretti*.

On reflection, he saw that no man, fearing plague, would risk his life on the word of a Genoese; even a Genoese already commended for the delicacy of his presents. Even the presents, as it turned out, had been useless. In the delightful game he and this young man were playing, it seemed that he had lost the skirmish of Constantinople. He only hoped, as he made for the stairs, that the foolish child had not ruined the end-game.

To Catherine, shivering with cold and fear and excitement at the top of the steps, this final delay was inexcusable. Pagano, having seen her, chose to stay talking below. She saw her manservant there, spoiling her news. Telling the wrong story, even. She called his name, high and sharp as a whistle, before she saw he had stopped speaking and was moving quickly towards her. He looked anxious, and she began to relent. When she felt the desperation of his embrace, she even forgave him. He held her off and looked at her. "Not here, but tell me inside. Are you all right? Did he harm you? If only I had been here! And those fools let him in?"

She told it all in her chamber, in the comfort of his arms, while he stroked her hair gently. At the end, he said, "What a husband am I, to expose you to that. What if he had tried to abduct you? He might do it still!" His arm tightened.

"Not now," said Catherine. "He was ashamed, when I told him what our marriage was like. He said he hoped I was happy, and left."

"The insolence!" said Pagano. "As if it were any business of his! And to force his way to your bedroom while your husband was gone. He was afraid to meet me."

Catherine pondered. "He said he couldn't stay long, because the ship had just come in. He said he wanted to meet you; but then someone brought a message and they both left. Pagano?"

"Yes, sweeting," he said. He smelt of salt, and the perfume he used for important audiences. She had forgotten to ask him about the Grand Vizier. She said, "It isn't true that Master Julius is going to be killed? They said you had something to do with it, but of course I told them you hadn't."

Pagano smiled into her hair. "Your mother's notary? Is it likely, my darling? No, of course no one on board the *Ciaretti* is going to be killed. It was only some sort of trick. He is an amusing young man, your mother's husband, when he isn't frightening my Caterinetta. But perhaps he will take your word for it now. You are happy and safe and protected, and he can go back to Bruges."

Until Nicholas himself had said otherwise, she, too, had thought she was going to lose him. It would have displeased her. She had nothing to fear, now, from Nicholas. She wished very much to hear what her husband would say to Nicholas the next time they met. She said, "Oh, he's still going to Trebizond. He has his mind bent on trade and making money, you know. He doesn't know any better." She caught her husband's hand in both her own. "I'm a trouble to you, Pagano. Bringing Nicholas after me. And now he's caught up, and you won't get to the Black Sea much before him."

"Wait and see," said Pagano, and kissed her. When he excused himself a little later, she let him go, because she could see they had to sail soon, and she and her women had the hateful packing to see to.

He came to bed late and tired, but still able to please her for a little. They were to sail the next day after noon. She lay awake long after he had fallen asleep, thinking of all that had happened. Then she slept very soundly, and was wakened by the dawn light and a short, quiet sound which (rarely heard) was Pagano swearing.

He was standing, handsome and naked, in the cold of the open window. She lay in drowsy felicity and contemplated him. To make him turn, she said softly, "What is it?"

In the faint light, she couldn't make out his expression. Then he said, "It's nothing. The *Ciaretti* has sailed. We shall catch him up in no time. Go back to sleep."

But she was still awake when he moved from the window and, instead of returning, began to put on his clothes. They had not been laid out as they usually were, and she was reminded of something. She said, "Pagano. Yesterday, I had to walk Willequin alone in the rain."

He went on assembling his garments with what, in anyone else, would have been a fit of suppressed annoyance. But his voice to her was unchanged. "My little lady, you should ask someone to take your dog for you."

"Well, Noah does it," she said. "But he wasn't there."

He reached for his cloak and came to kiss her. "No. He found a relative in Constantinople, and wanted to stay there. I must go down to the wharf. I'll send the carts for the baggage."

"A relative of *Noah's*!" she said. "In *Constantinople*?"

His hand on the door-latch, he glanced back at her. "The Black Sea is the biggest known market for slaves, you know that. And others are captured at sea with their masters. Noah was hardly surprised to see a favourite cousin, and will be very happy to stay. You don't miss him?"

She thought how selfless he was. She didn't miss Noah; not at all; except when she needed someone to take out her dog.

In the dark just before dawn, Nicholas had his ship rowed out of harbour, led by a pilot boat which left him at Tophane. For the rest of the narrows, they had a very good rutter and John le Grant and the Ragusan, who knew every rock.

Just past Tophane, a fishing-boat hailed them quietly and passed up some baskets of sprats and a large number of unwieldy parcels and boxes, followed by several people. It then fell back and waited.

The business of getting Astorre's men out from the hold and back on their benches had begun, and Nicholas was below. It was Julius, his sling glimmering white in the dark, who welcomed the group of passengers and showed them, with their possessions, to the lower cabin. He then took to the master cabin the four men who had brought both the books and the passengers, while the bales that accompanied them were carried down to the hold. There Nicholas, Tobie and Godscalc presently joined them.

The four were all dealers in silk, and two of them were also dealers in alum. Julius, formal in black, introduced them. Messer Bartolomeo Giorgio or Zorzi, brother of the one-legged Greek. Also Girolamo Michiel of Venice, Messer Bartolomeo's business partner. And, of course, Messer Dietifeci of Florence, the agent for Florence at Pera. And with him, his Florentine partner, Messer Bastiano da Foligno. Julius reeled it all off in his splendid Bolognese accent, a confident man despite the pain in his chest; because his name had been cleared and his conduct forgiven and if anyone could conduct a business meeting with proper decorum it was an experienced Bologna-trained lawyer.

Then Nicholas settled down to ask questions, and all the trading matters they had come to Pera to negotiate were picked out and examined and fitted into their programme, one after the other, like beans being pushed in a drill.

At the end, Bartolomeo said, "You don't waste much time, my friend Niccolò."

Like Nicholai Giorgio de' Acciajuoli, his brother was dark and bearded, but built on a shorter and stockier frame, with a nose wide at the roots and square, practical hands. Nicholas said, "It is as well to settle these things. The market is big enough. I don't see why Bursa should have more than its share. At any rate, I'm glad to have met you, if briefly."

Zorzi smiled. "In lieu of myself, I allot you my patron your passenger. The fee will be well worth your while. There are two servants and a priest, whose passage and keep will also be paid for. They have all been assured, needless to say, that you are free of the plague. I have to congratulate you on the ruse."

"I had help at Modon," Nicholas said. "As you know. I have to thank you, too, for what you brought. But we mustn't keep you. It will be getting light soon."

They rose. Bartolomeo said, "You said you had letters for Bruges? The Venetian galleys should leave in a fortnight, and if you address them to Messer Martelli in Venice, he will see them passed on. Dietifeci?"

The Florentine agent nodded. "Yes. I have dispatches myself for the Medici. Da Castro is sailing, and will carry them."

"Da Castro?" Nicholas said. He was looking at Tobie.

"The Pope's godson. He had a dyeing business in Constantinople at one time. Now he works in the Apostolic Chamber, but spends all his spare time prospecting for minerals. Do you know him?"

"Yes, of course," Nicholas said. "I met him at your cousin's house at Milan. So did Messer Tobias. And he's going home? I'm sorry to miss him."

"I'm not," said Tobie, as they stood at the rail, watching the four men depart. "Not if you remember what mineral that man Giovanni da Castro wanted funds to prospect for."

Nicholas grinned. "He won't find it. Anyway, you can't protect Tolfa from here. My God, Tobie: mention alum and you'd think someone was trying to rape you. What's so sacred about a monopoly?"

He could feel Tobie scowling. Then Julius, coming up, said, "Well, aren't you going to pay your respects down below to your passengers? You're taking their money, so you might as well offer some courtesy."

The tone of voice was not one he associated with Julius; but then, since the Janissaries, Julius's moods had been variable. Tobie said, "I'll go with you, if you like." The voice was his usual, inquisitive one.

Julius said, "Let him try on his own. The idiot's got to learn some time."

Nicholas beamed at Julius, which always annoyed him, and went off to the stern. In the event Tobie, perhaps held down by Julius, failed to follow him.

He thought he knew whom Bartolomeo Zorzi, brother of the Greek with the wooden leg, would have placed in his care, with a priest and two palatine servants, to be taken back to his office in Trebizond. Spiritual stews. He wondered how Godscalc would take it. Instead of Nicholai de' Acciajuoli he was, after all, to have some sort of oracle.

He thought so all the way down the steps, and up to the curtain over the door, and even when he rapped on the timber, and the hanging was drawn aside by a man in Greek robes, with the forked white beard and black hat of a confessor.

Then he smelled the perfume: harsh, expensive, disturbing; and knew what had been put in his way; and by whom; and why.

Chapter 15

"THE PRINCESSES OF Trebizond are famed for their beauty." So his one-legged daemon had said to him last autumn in Bruges, introducing this woman. "We need a Medea," Julius had declared just the other day. Now, Nicholas thought, gazing at the presence enthroned before him, they probably had one.

Violante of Naxos, princess of Trebizond, was then, and long to remain, in the full bloom of her looks. In Bruges, she had been gowned in the rich and dashing Venetian style, as was proper to a lady whose husband had purchased the Charetty company's silence over Tolfa. In Bruges, her husband had talked of alum, and she had been silent. But Nicholas remembered the gaze of Marian de Charetty his wife resting on her.

Not in envy of her spacious Byzantine eyes, underscored with amusement; or the severe nose with its brief dimpled apron; or the mouth made like grapes on the vine. Not even because of her body, boneless and lithe as a fish. Nicholas, who had long fathomed his wife saw the pain, and understood it owed nothing to simple jealousy. He thought perhaps it sprang from fear, and that there might be cause for it.

He thought so now, standing inside the doorway of the guest-cabin whose damaged wood was already half hung with damask. Behind a wall of silk tapestry a bed was being unpacked: he caught glimpses of two servants, a massive, clean-shaven man and an elderly woman. At his back, the Greek Archimandrite remained standing, black as a keyhole from his stiff veiled hat to his wide-sleeved black rhazon. Round his neck hung an old copper pectoral, lettered in blurred white enamel. He said in Greek, "Lady. The Fleming."

The chair they had brought for her to sit on was heavy, and gold like a throne. Above her swung a lamp made of some thin greenish glass worked in silver. The oil it burned was scented, and its light fell, in the main, on himself. Today, she wore a high-necked, narrow gown that could have been either Venetian or Trapezuntine. Its cuffs, thick with fur, half covered her folded hands, corded with rings. Where before her hair had been covered, she now wore it folded beneath a little crown-veil stitched to a narrow jewelled headband. Below it, silver earrings flashed with points of red, each brushed by the hair that spiralled, loose as gold wire, from her temples. The hair showed, too, bright as foil for an inch under the band. Between her legs, he thought, it must be the same. Duke Philip, I salute you and your Order.

It had been a long time, and for a moment, he was stifled.

She said in Italian, "We have met. Do you know who I am?"

"Indeed, madonna," Nicholas said.

"Highness," the monk's voice corrected him. Outside, the stamp of feet and shouting reached a crescendo. Nicholas braced himself as the ship gave its lurch on the sail breaking out. The heavy chair before him didn't move, but without compunction he heard the monk sidestep and recover himself. Take note. I am not to be patronised.

Nicholas said, "Highness, your name is the lady Violante. Your father rules Naxos. Your mother is niece to the Emperor David of Trebizond and you, and each of the ladies your sisters, are married to lords of the Republic of Venice. I came to wish you welcome on board the *Ciaretti*. And your chamberlain."

"Diadochos," she said. The monk inclined his head. She said, "We accept your greeting, and thank you. You will discuss with Diadochos practical matters to do with the journey. I should like, first, to command ten minutes of your time. Is this possible?"

She spoke as Marian might, at a business meeting. But no. With no remotest expectation of being refused. Before he had even agreed, the big servant had parted the tapestry and, advancing, set a stool for himself and the monk. They were not from his stock. He began to wonder how much baggage they had brought on board and what it would do to his load-line. As he sat, she said, "And so. You have brought the soldiers?"

His pause had already given him away, so he threw a glance towards her attendants.

She said, "They will not repeat what they hear. You have brought the soldiers and you have not changed your intention of staying in Trebizond?"

"The Emperor will have the soldiers," he said. "And I couldn't recoup my voyage, as you know, unless I stay through the trading season."

"You didn't, then, ask Zorzi to accommodate you," she said. "Certainly your profit from Trebizond will be many times greater."

He said, "Trebizond is where my post is. Although I hope Messer Zorzi and I will be able to put business in each other's way. Much depends on the possibility of war between the Sultan and my lord

Uzum Hasan. It would help to know the intentions of my lord of Persia."

The heavy domed eyes turned to the monk. She said, "Ask Diadochos. Diadochos serves the wife of my lord Uzum Hasan, and sometimes his mother."

"His mother?" said Nicholas.

"A Syrian lady," said the monk. "She shares the women's household with Hasan Bey's wife, and her children. The *Christian* women's household."

Nicholas looked round. On the throne, the young woman regarded him calmly. She said, "The lady my aunt is Hasan Bey's premier wife. It is unusual in a harem for a Christian to hold this position. He has, of course, several others."

"I see," said Nicholas. "And he is preparing for war?" He returned to the monk.

The bearded face held no more expression than the woman's. He said, "My lord Uzum Hasan has many battles behind him. He hopes for peace, I am sure. But if the Sultan threatens his lands, his passes, his safety, he has strong allies who will help him fight. Georgia. Sinope. You have met their envoys in Europe."

"And that is why he challenged the Sultan?" Nicholas said. "He and the Emperor?"

"Challenged?" said the woman. The lines of amusement creased fractionally under her eyes. "Ah. The matter of unpaid tribute. I do not know, and neither does Diadochos. But I imagine it is a gesture. My lord Hasan Bey feels himself strong. The Emperor David as well. Both have received slights in the past and would like to repay them. Their people applaud. And the Sultan, with other cares of his own, will threaten but do nothing else."

"So they hope," Nicholas said.

"So do we all," said Violante of Naxos. "Let us assume, then, that Trebizond is in no danger of war. You will arrive with your cargo. You will commend yourself to the Emperor with the greatest gift he could conceive: the presence of a hundred trained soldiers to add to his consequence and his sense of security."

"Ninety-eight," Nicholas said. "We lost two. But yes?"

She waited until he had finished, and longer. Then she resumed. "Your company has much to commend it. It has, however, disadvantages also. You yourself are the greatest of these."

In the game they appeared to be playing, that had always been one of her possible lines of attack. Nicholas said, "It's a pity. But unavoidable, I'm afraid. My wife owns the company."

"But you need not appear to lead it," she said.

"No," he said. "But I shall."

She said, "Your wife wishes it? She is loyal, I am sure, and you are happily married, I can see. But others might think that the emissary to an Emperor should be a notary, or a clerk perhaps in orders . . . ?"

"Master Beventini is very able as well," Nicholas said. "It is their choice that I should lead. They'll make more money." She looked her question, and he found himself suddenly smiling. He said, "I have few gifts, highness, but those I do have, I put to good use. I mean to make the Charetty company one of the wealthiest in the Levant."

The monk moved, but the lady did not. She said, "I have heard of you."

"Then you knew that," he said.

"Yes." She lifted her hand and snapped her fingers without turning. "If it is unpacked, we can offer you a new sort of wine. You don't take offence?"

"Frequently," Nicholas said. "I seldom show it. My company works as a team, and my men trust me. Is that what you wanted to know?"

"And you are ambitious. And you are prepared to fight to protect your trade. But pleasant, of course, though your natural attributes are, you will negate all these things unless you learn how to retain the Emperor's interest."

Her Italian had a heavy Greek accent which was not the Greek he had heard in the voice of Acciajuoli, for example. He wondered if Trebizond had its own vernacular. He had forgotten to ask. If so, he ought to learn it. He said, since this was where, clearly, she was leading, "But where, highness, could I learn such a thing? Unless you yourself were prepared to waste time teaching me?" He remembered three things he had forgotten to tell le Grant, and wondered what speed they were making, and what the others were doing. He realised he knew what the others were doing. He wished they were right.

"I?" she was saying. Her eyebrows, thin as the thread of a spider, were pencilled together. They rose, blown by the faintest impatience. She said, "I can hardly imagine who else could teach you. Take your wine. You can learn much by observing, of course. But we are not talking of dress or of etiquette, although these, too, are important. The Emperor's is a high-bred court which values erudite pleasures. What have I said?"

What does a rustic know of Aristotle, of Plato? He stopped smiling and said, "Forgive me. But my want of erudition seems to have struck a number of people of late."

"But you can read?" she said. "If you are shown something, you can guess at its contents. As for the rest, I do not pretend that Diadochos or I can turn you into a Ficino in three weeks of, no doubt, squally weather. But we can teach you to recognise names, and the themes of current works that might engage the Emperor's attention. It is unfortunately true that learning is not hard, in some circles, to simulate. When we reach Trebizond, we can offer you perhaps one or two manuscripts with which to familiarise yourself. In these, the Palace is well provided."

"No," Nicholas said.

The lips curled. "You are afraid? Trust your capabilities, Messer Niccolò. Making money demands several skills. You have these. You should be more afraid, I would have thought, of appearing a fool."

"I've had practice at that," Nicholas said. "And it's carried me far enough. Pretending to wisdom I don't have is another thing. Manners and etiquette I shall learn about willingly."

The painted eyes looked at him curiously. "You have no yearning to know more? To enter the world of ideas; consider the fruits of other men's minds; add to the quality of your own? So what have you to offer the Emperor?"

"Trade. Money. Soldiers," said Nicholas.

"And, surely, something more," she said thoughtfully. "You are not uncomely. You can entertain, I am told. What could you do for an Emperor which his circle of wits, philosophers, preachers cannot already provide?"

Nicholas thought. He said, "I could make him a clock?"

He knew, from the sound of her laughter, that she had learned more about him than he thought; and was sure of it when she consented to let him explain. He enjoyed lecturing her. He could feel the antagonism of the Archimandrite behind him.

She made no effort, after that, to force upon him any programme of arcane instruction. She did dictate, with his consent, the time and place for a number of lessons on the court of Trebizond and its requirements. She was concerned, she said, that he should uphold the credit of Venice as well as the credit of Florence. And that above all he should please the Emperor.

He wondered that, through it all, she had never mentioned Louvain University, and then realised it meant nothing to her. It had meant nothing either to Julius, who had always fumed because Felix, son of a dyer and broker, had been forced to go to Louvain. Nicholas knew what the reason was. Towards the end, apprentice to mistress, he had tried to persuade Marian to allow Felix to leave. She had been hard to convince. *I felt Louvain was important*, she had said. He remembered, too, what he had answered. *The demoiselle would find, I think, that it has served its purpose.*

Had it? Perhaps. It had taught him real humility, not the humility of the deprived. It had taught him enough to eschew it, when the need came. When Violante of Naxos said, for example, "To sell silk, you must wear it."

"It depends on the price," he had replied.

Towards the end, the lady of Naxos had frowned. She said, "You understand what I have said? You are agreeable?"

"Have I anything to lose, highness?" Nicholas said. "Provided, that is, that I keep my head. Sudden adoption might turn it."

There was no one here who would rush, like his friends, to proclaim what undoubtedly was going to become of his head: capo; capo; cappello; *decapitato*. The lady said curtly, "We shall begin then, tomorrow."

He was not quite as ready as she was to end the discussion. He managed, delaying discreetly, to pose one or two real questions and obtained, to his gratification, one or two real answers. He did not try her patience by talking too long, and drew the conversation, when the time came, to a seemly conclusion. He even managed, on leaving, to kiss the lady's hand as one born to the purple. He was a very good mimic.

Upstairs, he faced all his masters, all his senior colleagues in the master cabin. "Well?" said Julius. Flushed with fever and prurience, he sat up like a wounded Apollo. It came to Nicholas that Julius had not seen the lady Violante uncloaked, although the lady Violante had undoubtedly seen him. It decided him, reluctantly, on the course he must now take. He looked round at them all, sprawling at supper, and gave them a vague and affectionate smile.

"Fine," said Nicholas. "She wants lessons in Flemish."

"I'm free," Julius said.

"Your arm's too sore," Nicholas said. "Anyway, she wants lessons on the farmuk as well."

"That for a tale," said John le Grant. "Anyone with an aunt married to Uzum Hasan has a good idea how to play with a farmuk. And more."

"I know," said Nicholas. "I've got the cord round my middle, and running. Round my middle's all right. I got her to talk about alum."

"It doesn't sound very likely," said Tobie. "On the other hand, now I look at you, perhaps it does. What about it? Zorzi said a ship was just leaving for Flanders. I remember, because I worked out the profit would buy a few buttons."

The profit, if the ship left and if it arrived safely, would pay for the *Ciaretti*. He was trying not to count on it. Nicholas said, "That was Phocoean alum, and the last of it meantime until they quarry some more. But the lady says there are still stocks at Sebinkarahisar."

"Where?" said Captain Astorre angrily. Business was no concern of his, but topography was.

"Koloneia is its old name. To the south-west of Trebizond, and just outside the Empire, but worked by Greek miners. Then it's brought up by packhorse to Giresun, pays its tolls and gets shipped off to Europe."

John le Grant said, "Giresun is its Muslim name, Nicholas. The Greeks of classical times called the port Cerasus. Kerasous. Cérasonte. Cherries and Amazons."

"What?" said Astorre.

"Lucullus the Epicure, that's what," Tobie said. "All the cherries you've ever eaten take their name and stock, my friend, from Kerasous. Lucullus found them here in Roman times and sent them to Italy. Eighteen hundred years ago, Xenophon's Ten Thousand passed through Kerasous, bickering. Pits and gallows. And now Nicholas's alum miners and us. It's next door to Trebizond."

Julius said, "Well, go on. Amazons?"

Tobie's formless pink face with its neat curling nostrils and hairless scalp shone in the lamplight. He said, "Call yourself Argonauts? This is the original home of the Amazons. Female warriors, like the lady Violante and Alessandra Termagant Strozzi. Tits and gallows. Two of them built a temple to Mars at Kerasous and there are still funny ceremonies on Kerasous island."

"There's a monastery there," Nicholas said. The lady Violante had told him that. She had talked also of cherries and Europe, her eyes fixed on his face. He remembered something else. He said, "John. How did Constantinople finally fall?"

"John stopped talking," said Julius.

Le Grant said, "Lots of reasons. The Turks dragged their fleet over the hill and got into the Horn. That was the ultimate one. Why? They couldn't even get guns over the mountains round here."

"Couldn't they?" said Nicholas. "So anyone using cannon on Trebizond would have to do it from the sea?"

Astorre's sewn eye glittered. "How often do you need to be told? Anyone can land and burn the suburbs, but the fortress's impregnable. Same in Kerasous. Same in Sinope. And none of them can be surrounded, unless someone can persuade an army to cross Anatolia and climb the mountain range at its back. So are we landing at Kerasous?"

"Not on this trip," Nicholas said.

"He's planning a private expedition," Tobie said.

Sometimes, like this, they forgot he was married. He didn't remind them.

"All right," Julius said. "You take the Amazons and leave us Violante. What's she like, Nicholas?"

"He doesna know," John le Grant said. "Too busy talking of alum."

Nicholas said, "Think of your favourite woman, then double it. I have to tell you something about her." He had flattened his voice, and saw them sober, responding. John le Grant said, "What?" Under the red brows his eyes were sharp as needles.

Nicholas said, "She is a friend of Pagano Doria's. She had an interview with him in Florence. I knew, because I had the house watched, but she doesn't know that. So be careful."

Julius said, "You didn't tell us. You mean she knows about Catherine?"

"She may. But Catherine, I'm sure, doesn't know about Pagano and the lady. The idyll is unmarred."

"But you still didn't tell us," said Julius.

"I didn't expect to meet her again. I'm telling you now," Nicholas said.

Tobie said, "Well, never mind that. What's behind it? An affair on the side? It would have to be limited, with Catherine there every moment. So what? He's Genoese consul, and she's the wife of a Venetian merchant. It could be a league against us. It could be that she's after his secrets?"

"Or vice versa," said Julius. He had gone rather pale. He said, "The alum, Nicholas. She could tell him there's alum at Tolfa. I know it's in the Genoese interest, too, to keep the discovery quiet, but Doria won't worry about that, if he can spite you . . . And my God, you talked to her about this other quarry in Asia?"

"Sebinkarahisar? That's common knowledge," said Nicholas. "As for Tolfa, you forget. Violante of Naxos is married to the rich and noble Caterino Zeno of Venice, who bought our silence to preserve the Venetian alum monopoly. Is she going to tell Doria about the new mine, and defy both her husband and the Serenissima? Surely not. Lovers I expect Zeno would manage to forgive. But if he ever learned that she'd divulged a Venetian stratagem to a Genoese consul . . . She's too clever to risk it. Not for the sake of Pagano Doria."

"He charmed Catherine de Charetty," Julius said.

"Catherine is thirteen years old," said Nicholas. "This woman is between twenty-five and two thousand. She also knows, by the way, about Astorre's men. She was bound to find out, and I don't see it can do any harm now. Anyway, I thought we'd continue to let her think we know nothing of her affair with Doria. If she has to be tackled, I'll do it."

"I'm sure," said Tobie. "And tell us, of course, all that happens. We shouldn't like it to slip your poor silly mind again."

He tried not to be angry. For various reasons, it was quite hard. Of course, they had the right to question him. It was partly why they were here. Julius complained out of vanity and Godscalc – you had to suppose – because of his cloth. Only Tobie, when he attacked, applied the casual skill of a man dissecting a carcase. Yet, of them all, Tobie could sometimes come close to the bone. Of them all, too, he enjoyed girls with a natural and well-disposed liberality once shared by Nicholas. But of course their ways in that matter had parted. And now, banishing anger, Nicholas was left addressing the doctor with a somewhat inappropriate vehemence. He said, "Look. I had Monna Alessandra breathing down my neck. I wasn't going to set off a rumour that might get back to Bruges about Violante of Naxos having secret assignations with lovers in Florence. Have a heart. Mine, if you remember, had my instructions nailed on it in Bruges. I'm to tell you everything. What I eat, where I go, when I shit . . ."

"I hope you are," Tobie said. "Telling us." He looked unfriendly. Not threatening, but unfriendly, and even impatient.

"Of course," said Nicholas who, for the moment, felt unfriendly too. "Word of St Nicholas, patron of sailors, pawnbrokers . . ."

". . . virgins, and children," said Tobie.

You could always rely on Tobie to finish your thought for you.

Chapter 16

IN BRUGES, IN the same month of March, the skies fell on the lawyer Gregorio of Asti. He should have been prepared. Ever since the letter from Pagano Doria in Florence, the house at Spangnaerts Street had felt like a smothered volcano.

Against all his advice, Marian de Charetty had told neither her friends nor her household about her daughter Catherine's elopement and marriage. Through all her preparations during the last weeks of February and the beginning of March, she remained adamant. Until she returned with the facts, no one else was to know of it – not even Tilde. Catherine de Charetty, the world was led to understand, had been sent from Brussels to Florence to complete her education. And there her mother was planning to visit her.

Once before she had made this mistake, and failed to take a son into her confidence. Being only her lawyer, Gregorio could not persuade her that she must, at the very least, break the news to her remaining child, Tilde. She remained as strong in her obstinacy as in everything else: as if to give way in one thing would allow all the rest to crumble. And she seemed hardly to see the embarrassments. The natural questions of Lorenzo di Matteo Strozzi, whose mother resided in Florence. The stir among her fellow brokers and dyers, that the demoiselle should feel free to travel for pleasure, with half her company already absent. And, most predictable of all, you would think: the surprise and resentment of Tilde who, though the elder, had never been offered such an adventure. And believed, of course, her mother was going to Nicholas.

At least, Gregorio thought, he had been able to disabuse her of that idea. Long before her mother reached Florence, Nicholas would have gone. Either forward, or back.

Apart from the practical, there was little enough he could do for Marian de Charetty. February had been a month, he could imagine, of empty anniversaries. Last year, he had not been here for the Shrove Tuesday carnival; but he supposed it had meant something to

Nicholas, and to the demoiselle also. Their marriage had followed in five weeks.

It was the time of year, too, when young girls like Catherine and Tilde, guided by parents, sometimes found husbands through the traditional intermediary of the carnival. Last year, both the demoiselle's daughters had been under age. This year Tilde, at fourteen, had looked forward to the delights of attending, properly gowned, unhampered by Catherine.

Instead, Marian de Charetty, explaining nothing, had locked herself and her daughter into the house all that day, and had turned away all who called, pleading sickness. Gentle Tilde, roused to weeping rebellion, had been rescued at last by the coaxing of Anselm Adorne's wife who called and, with the obstinacy of a good lady accustomed to public life, had refused to leave without Tilde and her mother.

After that, the little distance between the demoiselle and her daughter remained, and widened as the plans for the mother's journey filled all her days. Stress made her over-meticulous. Gregorio was primed again and again on his duties, as were all the others in the good team that Nicholas had left: Cristoffels and Bellobras, Henninc and Lippin. The demoiselle would take with her Tasse, the maidservant from Geneva who had sought her out when her master's business collapsed. For the rest, she would hire men at arms to escort her. Florence might be her ultimate destination. But only Gregorio knew that she was travelling first and foremost to Dijon in Burgundy, to wrench the truth from her brother-in-law Thibault de Fleury, who was seventy and senile but had still, according to Pagano, signed the marriage papers of his god-daughter Catherine.

It would not be a pleasant visit. Thibault de Fleury was also the grandfather of the bastard Nicholas, and had been ruined by him. Thibault de Fleury's first wife had borne the mother of Nicholas. The sad, dead, profligate mother, who had been rejected by her cuckolded husband – the cuckolded husband to whom Nicholas, grown, had become anathema. It was, of course, why Nicholas had been sent from Bruges. While his mother's husband still divided his time between Flanders and Scotland, neither Nicholas nor the Charetty company could feel safe from his hostility.

Meanwhile, it was to no one's advantage to publish the connection between Nicholas and the Scottish lord Simon. Certainly Simon and his second well-born young wife would never contemplate doing so. In the Charetty company, the secret belonged only to Gregorio, Tobie and Julius, who had received the confidence of the demoiselle after last year's disasters.

Gregorio had told no one else; not even Margot, his discreet and sensible mistress of many years. But sometimes when she wondered aloud, as they all did, about the nature of the marriage between the

Widow and the young man who had been her apprentice, Gregorio would say, "Don't grudge him comfort, for I think it brings him that. His own family have had none to give him."

That year, Marian de Charetty had taken the trouble to ask to meet Margot, and had approved of her. When, in March, he completed his first twelve months with the Charetty company, the demoiselle had invited them both to a gathering of all those who served her in Spangnaerts Street, and had thanked him publicly for all he had done. Her father and his had, long ago, been friends. When privately, later, she asked him why he had not married, he had felt he owed her the truth: that Margot was already tied in marriage, and could not be released.

But for that, he thought she might have even confided Tilde to their care, for a home had to be found for the girl in her absence. The shortest trip, to Dijon and back, would keep the demoiselle from Bruges for six weeks. A return journey to Florence would take twice as long. If she had to stay to start legal proceedings over the marriage, the demoiselle might not see her business or her elder daughter much before the Flanders galleys arrived in the autumn. If she did go to law, Gregorio proposed to join her in Florence, whether she wished it or not.

So matters stood when the two letters from Nicholas came. Marian de Charetty had been absent on business all that day. At dusk, Gregorio had dismissed the clerks from his office but stayed at his own desk for an hour, studying papers and checking over the day book by the light of the good wax candles his employer allowed him. When the bell rang at the gate, he heard the porter go out, and soon afterwards someone knocked at his own door. It was one of the Charetty couriers, still spurred and cloaked and unfastening a satchel of letters among which was one for him, and one for the demoiselle, both from Florence and both sealed by Nicholas.

It was an occasion, a budget of news from young Claes. That is, from Nicholas, the demoiselle's husband. There was no getting rid of the courier, who knew no more than the last stage of its transport from Geneva to Bruges. Gregorio sent for mulled wine and told the fellow to sit and got some of the news of the journey while he took the letter up to his desk and unfolded the wax paper and severed the threads.

He knew the code so well by now that he got the gist at the first scanning. Then he picked out the items written in clear and entertained the courier – and the man who came agog with the wine – to a crisp resumé.

"It's their last letter from Florence. They've acquired a fine galley from the Medici, and were expecting to sail right away. They've got their cargo of silk, and a good many other commissions and a full crew, he says, of experienced men. Their captain's John le Grant, the engineer from Constantinople. And best of all, they've been given authority. The Medici and the Emperor's envoy have appointed the Charetty company to represent the Republic of Florence in Trebizond." The ring in his voice was hardly forced. Nicholas, by God. He had done it.

The courier, sprawled on a bench, rested his heels on his spurs and raised an arm in a burst of euphoria. "Here's luck to you, Claes, you young bastard."

"Gregorio?" said a curt voice behind him.

The courier got up quickly, stumbling. The manservant jumped to one side. Gregorio, his black skirts hitched on his desk, put his own hot wine rapidly down and stood, the letter still in his hand. He said, "Demoiselle."

Marian de Charetty came into the room as she was, her cloak still fastened, her hood fallen back from her headgear. She walked to Gregorio and then turned to the other two men. She said, "You may go."

The manservant had already slipped through the door. The courier, uncertain, gave her a bob and, still holding his cup, bent and hauled up the satchel and made hurriedly for the door. On the way, he turned and threw a comical glance at the lawyer. Gregorio knew better than to give any sign in reply.

Once or twice since Nicholas went, he had seen her angry like this. She never quite lost her high colour, but it settled on the rim of her cheeks, and brought out the brilliant blue of her eyes. As a girl, it must have suited her. Tonight, with her face sharpened with worry, it distressed him. Surely, now, a casual reference to Nicholas should not upset her so much?

Then he saw, from her fixed gaze, that she had not even heard, very likely, what the courier said. Her anger was all for himself.

She said, "Sit down. Is that a letter from Nicholas?" She wrenched apart the clasp of her cloak. He heard it tear. But when he moved to help her she moved away and, labouring with the weight of the cloth, flung the garment on a stool. Then she walked to the high chair and sat on it. "Well?" she said. "Read it."

"There is one for you," said Gregorio.

It lay on the table beside her. He saw her look at it, with the first hesitation she had shown. Then she picked it up and, taking a knife, opened it with precision. He guessed that the reading of her husband's letters had been, until now, a private ceremony with its own place and hour, silently cherished. Tonight, the moment thrown away, she was reading. And he saw, in the remorseless light of the good white wax candles, that she looked haggard.

At the end she said, "Yes. And now, show me yours."

She had never asked to see one of his letters from Nicholas before. He said, "It will be the same. This business of Julius and Cardinal Bessarion. Did he steal the money? Did you make him repay it?"

"I have never heard of the transaction before. Does it matter? If Julius took something, he will have restored it. He has not the boldness to cheat in great matters. I am merely being informed so that, if required, I can support the claim Nicholas appears to have made. Cardinal Bessarion will, I am sure, bear witness for Julius. The lord Cosimo will accept his endorsement. His commitment to us will be uninterrupted. Give me your letter, please."

He said, "It is the same. It's only got some market prices in cipher, which I can't make out until I work out the code. What matters is that Nicholas has seen nothing, clearly, of Catherine, but is sailing on the same route. He's bound to find her. And what's more, according to this, he has met Doria, and knows at least that he's a troublemaker. He helped denounce Julius. He's going to Trebizond as the Genoese consul."

It had appalled him, that news. She looked as if nothing more could appal her. He paused, trying quickly to choose the best argument. He said, "Demoiselle, if Catherine is unhappy, Nicholas will have found her by now. Perhaps he is already on the way home. None of us will grudge it if the venture fails because of that."

She said, "If you do not give me your letter, I will send for men who will take it from you."

He gave it to her, because her eyes were shining with tears, and he knew that it was lost, the secret he and Nicholas had tried so hard to keep. After a while she said, "I am sure you know the cipher by heart. Tell me what these passages say."

Then he said, "You know, I think. Demoiselle, we tried to spare you, that was all." After a moment he said, "Give me the letter, and I will read it for you." Even then, he did not look down at it; but found himself saying, "How did you find out?"

"Did you think," she said, "that I would leave anything undone to find the nature, the business, the past, the prospects of the man who abducted my daughter? You discovered so little, didn't you? The men I sent found out more."

He said, "What have they told you?"

Her eyes had dried. She said, "That Pagano Doria did not own the round ship he sailed on. He was merely hired to crew and equip it, and sail it first to Genoa, where he was meant to establish a trading base. After that, he was to take it to Trebizond and set up an agency in the name of his master." She looked at him bleakly. "It was not hard to find these things out. The ship had been impounded in Antwerp since the arraignment of its owner for treason. Now it's called the *Doria*. Then it bore the name of its first owner. The *Ribérac*."

He was silent.

She said, "You recognise the name, of course. Jordan de Ribérac was accused by the French king last year of treason. He would have suffered death, but he escaped to the family lands he still held in

Scotland. The French took his French money, his French lands and his ships, but missed the trading cog he had just sent to Antwerp. Full, as it happened, of arms and armour."

Gregorio said flatly, "From Gruuthuse."

"Yes. Like everyone, he traded with Louis de Gruuthuse. So. I have no need to tell you, I see, who the vicomte de Ribérac is. Or that he has an estranged son who is my husband's bitterest enemy. My lord Simon found the round ship in Antwerp. He realised it belonged to his father, and claimed it as such. Then, knowing Pagano Doria, one supposes, for a seaman and an unscrupulous rogue, he empowered him to pursue and, I expect, destroy Nicholas, taking my daughter as lure. You knew that. You knew Simon of Kilmirren was behind all Doria was doing. And you did not tell me."

"No," he said.

"But Nicholas knows?"

"Of course. I sent word. I half-killed a courier . . ." He broke off, and said quietly, "He has known about Simon from the moment he set foot in Florence. But not, of course, about Catherine."

"So you had discovered this long before I sent you to Brussels; and said nothing. You could have saved Catherine."

"Do you imagine I haven't thought of that?" he said. "But the ship had left by that time. I had no idea she was on board. I wasn't in Antwerp myself. There was nothing then to link Doria with Catherine. Her letters to you were still arriving."

But already she was throwing him, numbly, another challenge. "You told Nicholas, and yet he has sailed. Why? Why did he go on? The whole purpose of his leaving Bruges was to remove him from Simon."

Gregorio said, "The galley is only on loan. He has made other investments. He had to go on, or the company would have suffered."

She said, "One load of alum from Phocoea would cancel all of his debts. Against that is his safety."

Gregorio did what he could. He said, "Would it have been safer for him in Europe, with Simon still close? At least, chance has taken Nicholas to where Catherine needs him. He may bring her home."

The blue eyes were fixed on him now. She said, "He left Florence knowing nothing about her. Perhaps he will find and rescue her. But what good will that do, if Doria has orders to get rid of him?"

Gregorio said, "Nicholas himself doesn't believe that. He has said so, in my letter. He describes Doria as a dangerous, competitive child, but not an assassin."

"What does Nicholas know? The man has abducted a twelve-year-old child. He is working for Simon. Don't you understand yet," said Marian de Charetty, "that Nicholas cannot understand evil? Has learned nothing? Cannot conceive it exists? More. Nicholas, through beating and injury, will not think evil of Simon. You know that. When he finds out the truth about Catherine, he will be bewildered: he will not know what to believe. He may be able to hold off Doria, although it is likely, to my mind, that Doria is biding his time until there is a prize worth falling heir to at Trebizond. But Doria hardly matters. It is the wound of Simon's enmity that harms Nicholas most, and could disarm him."

There was a little silence. Then Gregorio said, "I have been trying to find Simon, to confront him. He has been in Scotland for weeks. But they say he may come for the Golden Fleece. The Duke is holding a Chapter."

"You would speak to him?" she said. "About this? About Doria and Catherine? But I told you. The connection between Simon and Nicholas is not to be made known."

"Of course," said Gregorio. "We all respect that. But the feud is public knowledge; indeed, is in the realm of entertainment by now. The lord Simon and the young comedian Nicholas provoke one another; that is universally known. Hence – everyone knows – Simon and his wife think him intolerable. But a deliberate attack on his life would be thought quite uncalled-for, and Simon will never admit quite to that."

"So what would you gain," she said, "by meeting him?"

"Information," Gregorio said. "Because he is vain. He has been mocked. He wouldn't be human if he didn't want us to know a little, at least, of what he has planned to ruin or ridicule Nicholas. He may say little enough, but we should know at least something of what to expect."

"But we could do nothing about it," said Marian de Charetty. "A letter from you to Nicholas would take four months to reach Trebizond."

"It would help me to punish him," Gregorio said. "Through the law. Or my sword."

She was bleached with fatigue, but that touched her. Her anger, three-quarters rooted in fear, had long since drained away. She said, "That is more than I or the company would ever ask. I have been – forgive me, I have been hard on you. I know you understand. But whatever happens, you mustn't forget what I have to remember, through everything. In his own eyes, if not the eyes of the world, Nicholas is Simon's son."

"Tobie knows it. And Julius," Gregorio said. "They will help him."

He spoke firmly. He would not have her guess what in his mind was painfully certain. That Nicholas, despite every promise, would have said nothing to Julius or Tobie or anyone else about the man behind Pagano Doria.

She left, with her escort, in a week. Before that, Gregorio was much in her company. She was making a long journey and there were dispositions to make, and papers to put into his care. Now, too, she admitted him further into her personal affairs than ever before. Harmony had returned to their relationship and, indeed, the relationship itself had subtly altered. It was due, he was aware, to his assumption of a duty he had taken for granted: his resolve to question Simon of Scotland as soon as he could find him. Question and caution him. The Charetty company was not without men.

He knew now when to expect the encounter. Duke Philip did indeed plan to hold a Chapter of the Golden Fleece Order in Flanders, and among the knights to attend would be Franck and Henry van Borselen, kinsmen of Katelina, my lord Simon's wife. It would be a historic occasion. The lady Katelina would come from Scotland. And Simon, her husband.

Even the limited amount he had told her about that had made the demoiselle uneasy. "Goro? You will be careful? And you will write and tell me what happens?"

"Lawyers are always careful," he said. "I wish I could come with you to Dijon."

"No. We talked of that. I shall write to you. You may do better, in the end, to travel to Venice and use the money there to take lodgings and see what word you can get from the East. If I need you in Florence, you could reach me from there in a week. And if I come home, you would be halfway between Bruges and Trebizond."

It sounded sensible enough, but too casual. And she had suggested it twice. He said, "You *want* me in Venice?"

She was pale, again, for a high-coloured woman. The afternoon had been spent at the Hôtel Jerusalem, making arrangements for Tilde. Of all those who had offered to shelter her daughter, Adorne and his wife had been most pressing and, finally, the demoiselle had agreed. It was the arrangement, Gregorio thought, that probably Tilde would like best. He had not tried to change it.

But now, although she was tired, something in her mild insistence disturbed him. When she did not answer at once, he put his question again, worded differently, "Are there other reasons why you want me in Venice? To keep a balance against Doria and Genoa?"

"It would be sensible," she said. Then she said, "No. I want you there, watching. I'm afraid of the Venetians."

"Afraid?" Gregorio said. "But it was Venice who launched this whole scheme. Who suggested the alum contract. Who told you that Florence wanted an agency. Nicholas saw no danger in it. He lodged his money there."

"I may be wrong," said Marian de Charetty, "but they pushed us, it seems to me, from the beginning. The one-legged Greek. Zeno. The . . . others. Of course, they wanted Astorre and his soldiers. That would add to their safety in Trebizond. They wanted someone to share the shipping risks, and bring their raw silk, and consolidate trade with the Emperor, who was falling out with both Venice and

Genoa. They might even have wanted to . . . seduce the Charetty
company to the side of the Serenissima and away from our equal
friendship with Genoa. The friendship we had before this business of
Pagano Doria."

"He is only one man," Gregorio said. "We have no reason yet to
distrust all of Genoa. Nor can I see Venice as a danger. She needs
us."

"That is why she *is* a danger," said Marian de Charetty. "She needs
us in Trebizond. She is pushing us there. She is pushing Nicholas all
the time, the way the Greek has done ever since he saw him at
Damme. I don't think we shall see Catherine home, because no one
wants Nicholas to turn back, perhaps not even Simon." Her voice
suddenly split. "Is it even possible that Venice is *using Simon*?" she
said.

"No. You are imagining it," said Gregorio. "Sit, demoiselle. I am
going to give you some wine. Demoiselle . . ."

She said, "I am sorry. It is just that I am tired." She paused and
then said, "I have longed only that he should be happy. As he used to
be, always."

"Men who have such a blessing rarely lose it," Gregorio said. "He
needed a bigger arena, whether Venice opened the door or anyone
else. And whatever happens, he will deal with it, and come home to
you safely." He didn't know if she believed him, but she gave the
appearance of doing so. Calmer, she accepted the wine and sipped it
presently, talking of trifles. Then she picked up her cloak and her
letter, and carried them both to her room.

After that, they were never in private. The day she left, all the
arrangements perfected, he and the other officers of the company
rode with her retinue as far as the city gate, and the senior guild
members and fellow merchants came, cloaked and hooded and hatted,
to wish her Godspeed.

She had taken Tilde on her horse as far as the gate. The girl and the
handsome small woman made a single shape of wrapped fur and
velvet, with the woman's rich glove on the reins and the girl's fine,
shining hair falling over her shoulder. At the gate they clung, and
parted, and Adorne lifted the girl to his saddle.

Tani, of the Medici company, had black ribbon pinned to his
cloak. Taking leave of him, Marian sought out the reason.

"Madonna, I thank you. The death is not in my family, but in the
house of my master in Florence. A child, barely six, but bitterly
mourned. Cosimino, the little grandchild of my lord of Medici."

She said what was right, and rode on; but her heart was with a child
of thirteen who had lost not her life but her childhood in Florence.
And a happy innocent – surely happy, surely innocent – who, through
none of his doing, might by now have sacrificed both.

Chapter 17

THREE THOUSAND MILES east of Bruges, the child Catherine and the youth Nicholas were close to their destination, and almost within sight of each other. As with most young when parted from their agonised elders, each was confronting known dangers with inherent hardihood. Which was not to say that Marian de Charetty was wrong in her fears for them.

The Black Sea, although salt, was more like a great inland lake, joined to the Middle Sea by one channel. From Constantinople to the Caucasus Mountains at its far end, it stretched for seven hundred miles. Its northern, black-bouldered shores gave on to the Khanate of the Crim Tartars, with the fur lands of Muscovy to the north of it. The Genoese, wily traders, had fixed on the Crimean coast their station called Caffa, big as Seville, and bursting free, at this moment, from the long winter's ice.

On the south coast of the Black Sea rose the mountains of Asia Minor: thickly forested where they plunged to the dark iron sands of the sea, with stout forts on the headlands and ancient Greek towns built half on the mild, fertile shores and half fitted into the mountains behind them. Beyond the mountains lay the rocks and plains of Anatolia, Persia, Syria, and the caravan routes to Baghdad and the East. It was its position at the end of the Silk Road that had made Trebizond the emporium of Asia, older than Rome or Byzantium. Now it stood, the solitary gem in the empty Imperial crown: the last unconquered outpost of the Byzantine Greeks.

Towards it sailed the *Doria* (once the *Ribérac*) and the *Ciaretti*, sometimes abreast; sometimes overtaking or passing each other. The winds, always freakish in March, blew one way in the morning and another when the sun passed its height, sometimes favouring the round ship and sometimes the galley. Of the two, the galley made, perhaps, the more memorable voyage. For one thing, she was still in the hands of her workmen, as the smiths and carpenters began to strip out the false compartments below. The morning after Tophane, the noise of saw and mallet halted only for Godscalc, who called for a blessing on this their voyage amid a deep and reverent silence.

Absent from the ceremony was their Imperial passenger, her priest and her servants. A separate droning issuing from somewhere under the poop confirmed the crew's suspicions. The robed and bearded figure with the lady Violante was indeed a Greek priest, and liable to pray in the Greek manner. Later, the repressive figure of the female servant issued, wrung the neck of a hen, plucked, gutted and cooked it on a small personal stove, and then vanished again.

There was no question, it appeared, of the lady her mistress joining the ship's officers for entertainment or refreshment of any sort. She remained in her quarters as the galley sailed on through dusk and nightfall. In due course the priest emerged, made his way to the common cabin, bowed and, saying nothing, unfolded a mattress and, lying down, went at once to sleep. Shortly afterwards, the eunuch emerged from the curtain of his mistress's quarters and took up his position cross-legged before it. From inside the cabin could be heard snatches of the lady's voice talking in silvery Greek, punctuated by someone playing the flute in a way that could only be regarded as melancholy.

Halfway through the night, which was spent sailing, the wind rose and extra seamen were roused from their sleeping-benches to see to the sheets. The flute had long been silent. The scream, when it rose above the roar of the elements, was therefore all the more startling. Nicholas, who had been in the bows, dodged the length of the gangway and was brought up by John le Grant, his voice stoical. "The doctor's got it in hand. Nothing fatal."

"Oh, good," said Nicholas, his arms hanging loose.

John le Grant's white-lashed eyes glinted. "The serving-woman came out with a slop-pail, and one of Astorre's men went at her with his breech clout undone. You mind. No shore leave at Modon."

"Which of them yelled?" Nicholas said.

"Oh, he did. She knifed him. Nothing serious. Nothing too serious. Astorre says the gomeril's got thirty-five children already to his absolute knowledge."

"And Tobie's got it in hand," Nicholas said. "Well, that leaves us with ninety-seven entire soldiers. Who needs perfection?"

"Perfection would spoil you," said John le Grant. "The passengers knifing the crew, half the galley in holes, two priests and a whistle on board and the Turkish army ahead. It's not a ship. It's a nervous wreck, laddie."

Perfection did spoil him. Recalling his duty as patron, Nicholas straightened his face and made his way along the plunging, wind-buffeted gangway to drop down to Tobie's quarters and inspect the suffering injured. The doctor was not so much reassuring as resigned. "He'll do. I've never heard language like that since I was with Lionetto. I learned fourteen new words. Did you see the woman?"

"No. He didn't hurt her?" said Nicholas. He got up from speaking to the would-be assailant, whose complaints had reduced themselves to heart-rending groans.

"That one?" said Tobie. "She wiped her knife like a butcher and marched straight back to her mistress's cabin. I thought she'd come back for his kidneys. Are you going to apologise for this fool? Or I'll do it."

"You're tired," said Nicholas. "Learning all those new curses. Leave me to deal with the lady Violante."

John le Grant, who had followed him, clapped his shoulder. "You do that," he said. "She'll set you to rights. There's a pair of sure hands on that lady. She'll clip you, stamp you, take the ticks out your ears, and you'll come out that door without touching the ground with your trotters. I'll have a drink waiting."

After that, it would have seemed like cowardice to put it off until morning. Nicholas vaulted down the poop steps and knocked on the princess's door-frame. Afterwards, he was sure he had knocked, although of course the Archimandrite was not there to hear, and the eunuch had deserted his post on the threshold. So, hearing a voice upraised within, Nicholas set his hand to the curtain and, lifting it back, stepped inside.

The glass lamp was extinguished. All the light came from the bed, where scented oil flamed in a low, burnished container. The illumination fell on crushed pillows and disturbed silken sheets, and on the bent golden crown of the princess of Trebizond, standing beside them. Her face, shadowed, was turned to where, at the back of the chamber, her elderly maidservant was moving about, talking as she set things to rights. At first all Nicholas could hear was the old woman's querulous voice, and all he could see was the lady's brilliant hair, caught back in a single fat plait like a lion's tail; and the thick embossed silk of her robe, and one small unjewelled ear, masked by wisps of gilt hair.

Then the curtain fell closed behind him and, at the sound, the princess of Trebizond turned. Her nightrobe, swung by the movement, warmed the air with the scent of her body, and for a second time in that place his breath shortened. The delicacy of her face was cause for wonder. Her features were built on the thighbones of mice; her eyes lay fronded in fish pools, their lids upper and lower like molluscs. Her lower lip was a button of coral; her chin round as a shell. Below her throat were two pearl-white globes, and below those, a dimpled crevice, and below that, there was no golden bouquet such as he had fleetingly imagined, but the tender swell of a smooth naked mount with a cleft whose place, barely seen, was discreetly tinted with rose. On either side of her body, the silk of her bedgown fell straight to the ground. His eyes, slowly travelling, followed it.

Then the woman saw him, and squawked. But Violante of Naxos stood quite still and composed, and said, "Am I the wife of a tradesman, who has to cover herself before servants?"

"Before no one, lady," said Nicholas. The heavy pulse beat in his neck, and he could feel it shaking his body.

"Or," said the lady Violante, "would you thank me if I set you no higher than the animals who are your soldiers, to be stirred by a woman beyond civil constraint?"

"I have come to beg your pardon and your servant's for that," Nicholas said. Her breasts were perfect, and their tips developed by marriage, soft as small feeding birds. He felt his face growing white and called, violently, on his intellect. Then he realised that she knew what had happened on deck; had heard the commotion; must have known he or someone would come. Had, probably, recognised even his steps. The anger he felt against his own body died as he analysed that. He said, "Shall I ask your priest to come in?"

"Why?" she said. "Unless your man is dead, and Phryne requires to be shriven. But she is not, as a rule, careless."

"Nor was she this time," Nicholas said. "I wondered if she or you required comfort, that's all. Let me apologise once more for the man's importunities, and leave you to resume your night's rest. I'm sorry if I disturbed you."

She smiled. "Rest assured," she remarked. "You have not disturbed me, nor could."

He withdrew politely, and found a place to wait in the darkness, until he could smile. Then he went back to the others. When, next day, he saw her again, neither mentioned the incident.

The round ship, with its marriage bed imposed no such restraint on its principle. Well provisioned, their vessel put in seldom to port and, being less able for battle at sea, took some pains to avoid other traffic. Once, the Euxine was notorious for its pirates because the pickings were rich – ships laden with slaves and honey and furs coming from Caffa; the archons' tax ships with their boxes of silver; the Venetian galleys with their smell of Bactrian camel enwrapping the silk and the spices and indigo.

But Venice had not risked her galleys so far this year; and although Doria took his precautions, there was an unusual emptiness about the Black Sea this month. The undersized dolphins wheeled in free water. The fishermen gathered busily, dragging their nets. The smaller cogs coalesced as if for reassurance, and were conned by news-gathering balingers, swift as insects, visiting group after group. But where, normally, the release of the ice brought the big ships into the sea with their freights for the West, now men were holding back. Before war, trade folded its hands and gave way. You did not send out your ships when heaven knew whether you might not need them tomorrow to fight them, or (God forfend) to escape in. The *Doria* and the *Ciaretti*, manned by men who were prepared both for trade and for war, were alone among great ships in entering the Euxine this season.

They were not always welcome. At Sinope, the emir refused them harbour, professing to believe that they had sickness on board. The excuse hardly rang true. The coast, swift to hear every rumour, knew by now that the great galley had been joined by the Emperor's great-niece, and the round ship by Amiroutzes, his treasurer. So they were plague-free, while Stamboul thought otherwise. To a wise man like the emir, with a foot in both camps, it was reason enough to be cautious.

The presence of Amiroutzes (through a misunderstanding) was a source of constant affront to young Catherine. He occupied Pagano's attention. He gave her lessons she had little wish for. Like the *Ciaretti*, Doria's ship had turned into a schoolroom. Looking down on his Jasons, Zeus lord of the sacrificed Ram might have wondered what they were thinking of. What, to Hercules, was protocol? Or to the dragon?

At Sinope, the galley was ahead. The round ship passed it three days later, and called into Samsûn to warn the harbour officials that a ship with the plague was behind them. Lying waiting for the return of his messenger, Pagano Doria was unsettled by the sight of the *Ciaretti* approaching him under oar at the speed of a fully manned war galley. He saw as she passed that she *was* fully manned, and by faces he remembered from Modon. Also that the load line was exactly the same as when she had been supposedly stripped of her soldiers. Michael Crackbene his captain seemed to know how it might have been done. He seemed also to think it amusing. The galley did not even attempt to turn into Samsûn.

They were then within five days of Trebizond, and March was ending. On both ships, the men of God had looked at the calendar and taken their masters aside. Barring shipwreck, they would arrive at the Imperial court during Easter Week. Did they want this? Lodgings crowded, other merchants preoccupied, the Emperor and his lords deeply involved in high ceremonial? The arrival of the new Genoese consul, the new Florentine agent, would hardly be noticed. And how, after three weeks at sea, could they approach the magnificence which would be required of them?

Nicholas said, "The Flanders galleys used to do it every year, coming to Sluys. You clean up the day before and sail in like a circus. Come on. You're getting lazy." Being now a unit of two hundred and fifty men with a common repository of extremely lewd songs composed for them by their patron, they made the motion of throwing things at him, including abuse, but submitted with resignation to the plans he outlined.

Later, sharing food in the cabin, le Grant said, "Doria will arrive first, if we pause. And they'll look spruce as well. They have the space to clean up as they sail."

"I thought Trebizond had a Roman harbour of sorts?" Nicholas said. "He'll have to row into it, surely. Fifty oars?"

"He'll still look smart," le Grant said.

"Xenophon," Nicholas said incomprehensibly. He looked at them all severely. He said, "I won't say I admire him, but after three weeks of Diadochos, I can claim to know him like a brother. Just when Xenophon and his Hellenes were marching this way, they all got vomiting drunk on the local honey."

"Two thousand years ago," remarked Tobie.

"That's Greek bees for you," said Captain Astorre. He gave a long cackle. The nearer Astorre got to fighting, the cheerier he became. The prize spectacle of the lady Violante's training had been Astorre's accomplished prostration which, done on his belly like the fieldsman he was, was going to take him across the Emperor's carpet, hardly stirring the grasses. (The other spectacle, not directly spoken of, was that of Master Julius caught within range of the lady Violante.)

Collecting himself, Astorre addressed Nicholas: "So what's come into your head? There's no honey in March."

Tobie was also staring at Nicholas, but with a different expression. He said, "Wait a moment. You've done it, haven't you? Whatever it is, you've damned well done it without consulting us?"

Nicholas turned his mouth down like a gargoyle. He said, "I've made a little arrangement, that's all. The last night of the trip, a gift of the local black wine will be rowed out to the *Doria* from the Genoese settlers in Kerasous. Well, apparently from the Genoese settlers. I'm told it's not too hard to present the patron with one thing and see that the sailors get their share of the rest in his absence. It'll blow their heads off."

Captain Astorre threw back his head in a fit of collected laughter. Then he got up and made his way to the door, clapping Nicholas on the shoulder as he went. "Good lad," he said. "Good lad. I like that. And once get us on shore, and we'll lift the little lady out of that fellow's clutches and kill him." He gave a black-toothed grin round them all and strolled out.

"Well," said Julius, "that's silenced the great Nicholas, hasn't it? I wonder why? Can it possibly be that you've forgotten, in all your amusing plans, that young Catherine's still with that bastard Doria? By God, you're planning to get your own back, aren't you? The *Doria*'s oarsmen will row her in drunk. That'll show him. He steals the demoiselle's daughter. He spreads lies about me and Bessarion. He fires your ship, he kills men at Modon. John and I all but lose our lives at Constantinople. And is this all you're planning to do?"

Where Astorre had addressed (as he often did) a precocious boy, Julius was speaking adult to adult to Nicholas. Nicholas, his face blank, drew breath, but Julius went on before he could utter. He said, "Since that woman came on board, Catherine and the rest of us could go hang. I wouldn't mind, except that you're supposed to be leading us."

Fortunately, they were where they would not be overheard. Fractiousness from Julius was not new, these days. Nicholas, suddenly running short of soft answers, said, "She's my stepdaughter. Of course I've forgotten her."

Before the silence could develop, Father Godscalc said, "The child's well-being may well depend on cultivating the lady Violante, Julius. Once Doria has vanished into the Genoese compound, she may be the only ambassadress we shall have. I doubt, from what I have seen of the gentleman, that he will bring his little lady much to court, if at all."

Nicholas said, with some brevity, "They don't have wives with them, the merchants. They didn't in Pera, with very few exceptions. They live with local girls, or their permanent mistresses. Catherine wouldn't know the difference, so long as she saw some apparent high life. I don't know which side the lady Violante is on, Julius. But it would be unwise to warn or offend her."

"That's your opinion. I'm going to ask her," said Julius. "If she's Doria's whore, and a spy, we ought to know. If she's merely his whore, she should be as glad as we are to get Catherine away from him."

"Don't be an idiot," Tobie said. "If Nicholas can't tell what she's up to after three weeks of platonic instruction, she's damned likely to open her mouth when you walk in and jump on her. That's what you're planning, I take it?"

"*Platonic instruction?*" said Julius.

"Well, Aristotelian and Homeric as well, with a touch of the Livys," said Nicholas quickly. "When I tell you that the Archimandrite is there for every session, you can imagine the complexity. Or if not, I can draw diagrams for you. Julius, if she's on Doria's side it's best she doesn't think we suspect her. Don't you think so?"

Julius, who had also tasted the black Trapezuntine wine, said, "If you say so. I've lists to see to," and got up and went.

Godscalc said, "I think – "

"I know," said Tobie grimly. "If we don't watch Master Julius he's going to do something awkward in Trebizond. Such as walk into the Genoese castle with the good Captain Astorre and try to remove that child bodily. Or involve the Emperor." He thought. "Perhaps that's what Doria is hoping for. We'd look fools. He's in the right. It's a marriage. And you say the girl is besotted."

Godscalc said, "When Julius has calmed down, I'll speak to him. It's true that the girl is fond of her husband, and he seems to be treating her well. We know he is an adventurer and a charlatan, but would she be the better or worse off for knowing it? And meanwhile she wouldn't believe it. Nicholas is quite correct. You can't do anything about the young lady until she herself asks you. Keep open what channels you have – and the princess Violante is one of them. I should like, however, to ask: Nicholas, what do you think Pagano Doria will do? He owes you something already, after the plague. The black wine will demand a riposte."

"You still think it's a game?" Tobie said.

"I still think everything he does is a game," Godscalc said. "Including murder."

"You said you were sorry for him," Nicholas said. He had gathered his nose and upper lip in a long, thoughtful pinch. Now he pulled his hand away. "No. A little polite persecution here and there, but nothing serious yet, unless I'm quite wrong. He didn't burn the ship to destruction. He didn't betray Astorre's men, although he was willing to get rid of you, John and Julius. He didn't kill me in Modon."

"You sound as if you regret it," said Godscalc.

"Well, no," Nicholas said. "Except for all the time I wasted working out possible traps and ways of eluding them. Some of it would have been rather fun. But he didn't do anything at all that would stop us. He wanted us with our ship in Trebizond because, after all, he's heir to half the business through Catherine. He can't touch the business at Bruges while Catherine's mother is there, but he could take control here without being stopped for a long time. So my guess is that we'll be allowed to establish our agency and make our profit and stock our warehouse before he does anything. And even then, he won't do anything that discredits the company or the merchandise."

Tobie said, "Well, that's obvious. You're the one he's playing against. You're the one he needs to show up for a dangerous fool."

"Or cause to have an accident," said Father Godscalc.

"Maybe," Nicholas said. "But he'll discredit me first."

Tobie's eyes gleamed, and Nicholas grinned at him. "Go on. How would you set about it?"

Tobie's pupils became points of conjecture, and his small pink mouth curled. "Exactly what has the lady Violante been teaching you?" he said. His tone was one of the most dulcet enquiry.

"I thought of that," Nicholas said. "It was when she said I had to crawl away from the throne with my drawers down that I began to suspect her." He had recovered his placidity. He said, "I'll check over all I've been told with the Florentines, but I'll be surprised if there's anything in the least misleading. And from beginning to end she's been chaperoned. A good sign, on the whole."

Godscalc said, "Yes. I'd have seen to that, if I were Doria."

"He may still do. Circassian slaves in my bedroom. Yours, too."

Tobie's expression lightened. "We'll all be corrupted? Proofs of inconceivable depravity? Girls and buggery? Drink and hashish and opium?"

"That's right. Try it all, but don't sign anything," Nicholas said. "Father, your services are held in the Latin style. Could he cause mischief there?"

"If he wants to. We have leave to follow our own practices in the church of our compound. So have Doria and the Venetians. But not elsewhere. We should not discuss or dispute or invite to attend any member of the native Orthodox Church. Of course, if we hold no service at all, we are godless." He saw Tobie's eyes were fixed on him. Tobie wanted to know whether Nicholas had ever used the chaplain to make his confession. Once, he had asked him outright. Godscalc had not thought it was his place to answer him.

Nicholas himself was still conning the possible dangers; presumably not for the first time. This exercise, one understood, was for the sake of his colleagues. What he himself was going to do, about Doria and about Catherine, was very likely, Godscalc reflected, already clear and set in his mind. Nicholas said, "And of course, our book-keeping. Our figures must be impeccable, the receipts beyond dispute. The goods in our safe-keeping must be secure. Our servants must be well treated and paid. Even behind our own walls, we must speak only with admiration and respect of the Emperor and all his household. What else?"

Tobie said, "That's already more than any human being can guarantee. If he thinks like you do, he's going to catch us out in something. Collapse of the Charetty leadership; and Pagano Doria takes over the goods, the credit, the contacts, the staff, the goodwill of the Emperor and the Medici. I don't think you want to get that girl away. So long as she's there, she might help protect us."

He was watching Nicholas once again. Nicholas stirred. He said, "She has no idea what he's up to. And of course he's not going to ruin us. We're going to ruin him. Father . . ."

He was frowning. Godscalc said, "Yes?"

Nicholas said, "Catherine doesn't know, you said, that he's a charlatan. And might be better not knowing."

Godscalc said, "Well, you saw that for yourself. And he can't afford, remember, to disillusion her. All his claims derive from his marriage. What were you planning to do? Put Circassian slaves into *his* bed? Beat his seamen until they confess that he committed murder and arson at Modon? Ask the lady Violante to boast of her conquest? Persuade the girl herself that your life depends on her giving up her husband and lover?"

He was looking at Nicholas as if, Tobie thought, there was no one else in the cabin. John le Grant, present throughout, had not spoken. Nicholas said, "You mean he is the sort who can stay true to his wife, and will honestly manage the demoiselle's business, or indeed any other? Report says he has never shown such integrity before in his life. He has always run through the money, and left. Do we have to wait until then to part them?"

Godscalc said, "You know what I am saying. Give him a chance. And the child. If, despite all he hopes to gain, he deceives her, then give her your help. But to encourage him to be false to her would be ignoble."

"No Circassians in his bed," Nicholas said. He spoke a little blankly.

"Nor those other ruses which can remove a man from his pedestal. I'm sure you follow me."

Nicholas said, "You're tying my hands."

The priest gazed at him calmly. "His also are tied. He cannot, remember, spoil your goods or your credit. He wishes to inherit a flourishing company. On the other hand, you are free to interfere with his trade. The girl will not suffer from that."

Nicholas was staring into space. He said, "I need a friend in the Genoese castle. But we can't get in."

"We don't need to," said Godscalc. "They'll all come out. Merchants, servants and everybody, for the Easter processions. Captain Astorre might see a soldier he knows, or John a Genoese who might be bribed. You'll like the Easter music. It's all done in acrostics."

That there was a duel of some sort going on was quite clear to Tobie, but he could not make out what the grounds for it were. After a moment, Nicholas removed his eyes from the chaplain and said, "Well. It shouldn't be beyond us to solve them. Our tongues aren't tied, except in the presence of godliness."

"That wasn't godliness. That was just common sense," said the priest in a friendly way. You remembered that he was used to armies, and had been the first to make the acquaintance of Pagano Doria. Recognising as much perhaps, Nicholas made no response, other than a wry tilt of the head and the production, highly suspect, of one dimple.

A percipient fellow, for a clergyman, and able to manage Nicholas to some small extent. On the other hand, the chaplain had been in the Italian wars virtually through all his association with the Charetty. He barely knew the demoiselle his employer, to whom, exactly one year before, Nicholas had been formally married. More important than that, he didn't know what Tobie and Julius and Gregorio knew about Nicholas. Or he might have realised, Tobie thought with some irritation, that he was probably wasting his breath.

The night before they entered the harbour of Trebizond, Nicholas asked to be received by the lady Violante.

They were at anchor, so he had used his razor again, to remove the fair bristling growth of the sailing nights. All over the ship, men sported the harbour-badge of fresh cuts as they turned barber for one another, and decent clothing was shaken from boxes and pennants and

hangings unwrapped. The ship reeked of paint and tar and damp wood
and jangled with the noise of sawing and hammer blows, clanking
buckets and stampeding feet, and the calls and conversation of men
disagreeably employed who yet saw at the end of it a prospect of warmth
and fresh food and an unmoving bed and dry clothes and women.

As ever, the Archimandrite was in the cabin, his black robes over-
whelming his sitting stool. In all that time, he had been absent only
once, on the night of the stabbing, when, of course, nothing had
happened. Instead, Violante of Naxos had made sure that he understood her contempt for him. It had been a cruel demonstration, as well
as a needless one. He knew his own deficiencies better than she did.

Since that night a routine had been established, which he now
followed precisely. After greeting the lady in Greek, Nicholas moved to
her other side and, invited, dropped to sit, straight-backed and motionless, on a second stool. He was wearing his shore-going doublet and
shirt for tomorrow, although not the short robe which would naturally
cover it. The cloth was good enough, and reasonably cut. What was
wrong with it he already knew from his tutor. And she, in turn, now sat
and considered him.

Violante of Naxos, between birth and young womanhood, had
initiated many people into many mysteries. She had been trained
herself in the dance, and in the arts of music and painting. The practice
of high manners had from childhood been as natural to her as breathing.
She required it in others, and discounted those who thought it
unnecessary. She had been taught how to read and to write, and knew
her poets and a wide enough range of other writings. More important,
she knew what should be known by a man of high rank holding
conversation with his peers. Where her own learning ceased, that of
Diadochos meantime served. In the case of this Flemish youth who had
everything to learn, one could only do so much in three weeks. Set the
door a fraction ajar. Judge, if one could, how much or how little lay
behind it. And of course, she could make no test of his higher intellect.
Formal learning, she saw, he preferred to avoid. Such misgivings, she
well knew, were common.

She had thought to shock him, at the beginning, into a state she could
handle. To appear disrobed before him was a small thing, misunder-
stood only by men of the Church and those little acquainted with life. It
was not the first time she had used such means to achieve a quick
ascendancy. And he had responded – there had been no mistake about
that. Only she had been disconcerted by the speed of his recovery. By
the end of the first twenty-four hours, then, she knew she had a
competent actor. It had taken her a week to discover what she really
had.

And, of course, he knew that she had been able to reach some
conclusions. He had been under scrutiny more than once, she deduced,
by those who found themselves suddenly doubting his simplicity. If

naïveté had once been his cloak, it could never be so again. He had to find other protection, and was doing so. It would not be a quick transformation, or a simple one. But one day his mask would be in place, and impenetrable.

He had already realised that he needed her in his strategy. He also needed her for what she could teach. In three weeks, he had trawled knowledge from her until she felt exhausted. Last of all, she had told him what to expect on arrival. The merchants lived outside the walls of the City of Trebizond, and near to the harbour. The Florentine quarter was small, but Michael Alighieri had built a fondaco there, an assemblage of living quarters and storehouse and stables which would serve as a temporary home for himself and his officers until a better could be built. He knew who would come on board when first he sailed in, and which members of the Imperial household would escort her on shore to the Palace. At that point, he would receive his message of welcome from the Emperor and, some days later, a summons. Meanwhile, he would be offered gifts and provisions and lodging for his soldiers and seamen. He had memorised it, to the last detail.

Now he said, "Highness, we are concerned, as you know, about the Genoese consul who will expect similar treatment. He has on board the Emperor's highest official."

He had not asked before about George Amiroutzes. He was clever enough, she thought, to have extracted all she could teach him before he risked dangerous ground. She said, "I don't think you may expect the Emperor's Great Chancellor to malign you at court, any more than his great-niece need praise you. One makes use of a vessel. One does not take on the stink of its timbers."

She saw him discard something other than a sober reply. He said, "The Treasury and the Wardrobe are often the same. If his excellency buys for the Palace, it would be useful to know if he shares the Emperor's tastes."

The Emperor's tastes were something that would shock even this agile deceiver. Amiroutzes liked experienced women. The lady Violante said, "His excellency prefers books and wise discourse to luxury. He is a learned man, born in Trebizond but fluent in Latin. He represented the Emperor twenty years since at the great Church Council in Florence: impressed the Pope; dined with Cosimo de' Medici."

Nicholas said, "So he knows monseigneur the Cardinal Bessarion."

She said, "Extremely well. The lord Amiroutzes approved of union between the Greek and Latin Churches, as Bessarion did – and, indeed, the present Patriarch, before his reconversion. My lord Amiroutzes has also acted as envoy to Genoa. A discreet and subtle negotiator. It is, of course, in the blood. His lady mother and the mother of the Sultan's Grand Vizier Mahmud were both ladies from Trebizond. Indeed, cousins."

She broke off, to observe. Her listener's eyes were alight with what could have been genuine pleasure: the dimples arrived and were packed off, as if into some basket of stage gear. She found Diadochos watching her. She had long found the Greek monk a nuisance.

The young man said, "But how sad for such lords! Related, and yet on opposite sides!"

"It often happens," she said. "A princess of Trebizond marries abroad, and one of her ladies becomes wife to a prince of that country. The Sultan conquers the country, and a son or two of the lady changes faith and joins the side of the conqueror. Sultan Mehmet makes good use of such men. So with the Emperor. He does not penalise my lord Amiroutzes for a relationship he cannot help. So should all kinsmen learn to practise forbearance. You agree, my Flemish apprentice?"

His artless smile widened without changing in quality. It told her nothing. He asked, mildly, one further question about Amiroutzes, and then left the subject for another of no great importance. At length, in his own time, he took his departure. She had done nothing either to detain or to dismiss him. Nor, although he might have hoped for it, had she told him anything else. Only, when he had gone, she sat thinking of Venice; and reviewing, one by one, all the intricate plans she and others had skilfully laid there. Some would have to be changed.

Caterino my husband, it is not as we thought. It is not as I thought. Something has to be done about this person Niccolò.

Chapter 18

S O THERE CAME TO the poisonous honey of Trebizond the two vessels from barbarian Europe, the four months of their travelling over, and winter turned into spring. One after the other, they crossed the wide, irregular bay towards the green amphitheatre which lined it. In its midst, the classical City gleamed on its tableland, alight with marble and gold against the dark mountain forests behind. There stood the fabled City, treasure-house of the East. There were the groves that had once known the Argonauts, haunted by legends of sacrifice and redemption: of the tree and the scaffold, of the ram and the lamb each impaled there. There was the frontier of Islam.

On both ships men prayed, or were silent, or uttered reassuring jokes and obscenities. On each, the leader, smiling, ordered wine to be broached for the company; and the eagerness on the face of Doria and on the face of Nicholas vander Poele was the same.

The legend caught Catherine de Charetty in its grasp, and kept her there till she landed, and after. The barge which came to fetch Treasurer Amiroutzes was covered with gold and flew the Comnenos eagle of the Imperial dynasty. A handsome Genoese boat took herself and Pagano to shore because, for some reason, their own seamen were not fit to row them. At the little harbour called Daphnous, the steps of the wharf were of white marble, and its walls had reliefs on them, and the names and titles of Byzantine emperors; and carved and painted creatures stood on either side of its gates. By then, the Genoese community had come there to greet them, in gowns and coats and caps of their own familiar Italian fashion. But the boys who scampered to take the mooring ropes and the men who came to shoulder their baggage were quite different. They were bare-legged and bare-headed, and wore cotton shirts and coarse overtunics and their skins were of every colour: blond and olive and walnut and ebony. Free men, perhaps, Pagano said; but more likely slaves. Trebizond and Caffa, over the water, sold Tartar and Circassian slaves to the world.

Landed, she had gazed at the high ground backing the harbour, and the big houses there, set among vines and pastel bouquets of fruit trees. She glimpsed tall doors, and window grilles; and a loggia. She said, "It looks Italian."

Beside her, Pagano glanced round at the others and smiled. He said, "Indeed, sweeting. These are the suburbs, where the merchants live, and the richer burghers and some kinds of artisans. The City is high over there, behind the long walls. The Palace, the court, the Citadel, the churches, the people who serve the Basileus. We shall be invited there soon."

"The Basileus?" she had said.

"Another name for the Emperor. His ancestors have been living there since the Fourth Crusade sacked Constantinople. Behind those walls, it is not Italian," said Pagano. He held her arm, because no one brought horses and the ground for some reason was rocking.

No one had brought horses because the home of the Genoese colony was here, on the headland between this harbour and the next. Until invited, they were not to climb to the City with its golden domes and its palaces; and for a moment she felt disappointment. But there were old men all about her studying her, and asking dull, polite questions. So she walked in as stately a manner as her sealegs would allow and showed absolutely no surprise to find that she and Pagano were to share a great fortified building within a walled and moated enclosure high on a ridge, and provided with yards and warehouses, wells and bakehouse, stables and mews, smiths' and carpenters' shops and other buildings whose use she couldn't imagine. The fondaco was called Leoncastello, or Lions' Castle, and had two lions, eaten by salt, on its gateposts. Overhead flew the flag of St George, and within the gates had gathered a large number of uneasy, vaguely welcoming people, few of whom were women.

They had not been expected, and so the consul's rooms were not prepared. It didn't seem greatly to matter. After shipboard, here were solid walls and a roof, and the ground was ceasing to move. After such confinement, it was enough to perambulate, thought suspended, while servants came and the place was hastily brushed down and sluiced. It didn't occur to her to question what was being done or to take charge of it. Her women, after hovering, had gone off to unpack their own things and hers. Sometimes Pagano came to find how she did, and seemed pleased to find her contented. Away from seamen's society, Pagano's language, she observed, had recovered its Genoese purity, and all his beguiling ways had returned. Already the anxious faces about him were changing and warming. From one of her windows she could see him sometimes below in the yard. She could hear his compatriots laugh as he made some easy joke, or chaffed a servant or two. Pagano her husband, in his beautiful doublet, smiling with his fine teeth in Trebizond.

She returned often that day to her windows. Beyond the yard she could see the expanse of the gulf to its furthest blue arm from which they had come. Below the acropolis lay the arms of another small harbour. Elsewhere, the gritty dark shore was uninterrupted save for rare jetties packed with skerries and fishing boats. The few great ships like their own stood off in deep water, stoutly anchored. If the Emperor of Trebizond had a fleet of thirty war galleys, as Pagano had assured her, they were not visible here.

Where the hilly ground met the shore were dozens of fisher shacks, untidy with creels and nets and children and goats and ragged cloths drying. Behind and above lay the handsome suburbs she had seen when they landed. From there, the wind brought her woodsmoke. Now and then something else crept through the small landward windows, obsequious as a Colchian serpent. It was a scent not yet familiar: the compound of fruit, musk and incense that was the essence of Trebizond.

But here, she was in Italy; or very near it. In those villas were other merchants. Over there, on a promontory a little less steep than their own, stood another trading enclosure, with towers and rooftops which flew the Venetian Lion instead of the Cross of St George. There lived Pagano's compatriots, rivals, enemies: the merchants and Bailie of the Republic of Venice. She was studying it when she saw the Florentine galley arrive, and heard, at a distance, its trumpets and guns.

Nicholas. Soon her mother's servants would all come ashore. Master Julius. Master Tobias. Captain Astorre. Godscalc, the foreign chaplain who had helped Nicholas enter her room. Loppe, her late brother's negro, and the thin shipmaster who was new, with red hair. Not making, of course, for this castle or the Venetian palace but for some cheap hired fondaco over there in the suburb. Nicholas in his artisan's clothes who was going to meet Pagano at last, and be abashed before him. And humbled. And jealous.

She turned aside then, and went to find Pagano and see how her gowns had survived the unpacking.

The Charetty company, settling in turn in the Florentine fondaco, responded in its various ways to the new situation.

Julius became disagreeable. Tobie, amused, put it down partly to the change from maritime life which took some men oddly, like a return to home life from a war. It had other causes. Although Julius knew that the City was meanwhile forbidden, he longed like Catherine to go there; to see the marvels, to affirm the success of the voyage. Instead, he was working to plan as they all were: landing and storing their stock; furnishing the house and arranging services and provisions; interviewing Alighieri's caretaking staff and appointing others to help them.

Regularly, eating together, they turned over their problems with Nicholas. Most of the nuisances had been foreseen: the clamour of would-be vendors at their gates; the attempts to set extortionate prices; the caution of the Greeks around them towards the new foreigners; the small resentments among their own men over precautionary restrictions. From his own days in the army, Julius knew how to deal with that; as he knew how to set up a bureau and prepare the accounts and the ledgers for business. He helped receive the unofficial, swift courtesy calls from other established Latin merchants, including the secretary of the Venetian Bailie, and was inclined to talk when he should have been listening. He had, indeed, strong views on many things, which he freely expressed to his colleagues in private and on which, Tobie noticed, Nicholas seldom commented. It was left to Godscalc, or Astorre or himself to point out the weakness in his argument, if there was one. Only if the idea was good would Nicholas at once endorse it.

He was their nominal leader, but with Julius he was still being careful. For Julius, alone of them all, had once been considered fit to lead the first Charetty expedition on his own, although he'd never known it. Once, on a hot night in a war camp in the Abruzzi, Nicholas and Tobie had talked of opening an overseas agency under Julius with the young Charetty boy, Felix, to help him. But now Felix was dead, and Nicholas self-banished from Bruges. More than that, the promising franchise they had expected had turned into a project much more perilous.

Nicholas had never said so, but it seemed to Tobie that Julius would have found the management of this venture beyond him. And yet, of them all, Julius alone owned to some ambition to lead. The innermost part of Tobie's life, although he would never admit it, seemed to belong, as Godscalc's did, to the strange, deep exigencies of his profession. Pushed further, he would have conceded his interest in Nicholas. But for Nicholas, he would never have renewed his contract with Marian de Charetty, or followed her husband into this risky personal venture. Without Nicholas, he would probably seek a new company under, say, the Count of Urbino. Without Nicholas, this company would turn into a bad debt, and dissolve.

Listening now to Julius complaining, Tobie recalled something else: the frown with which Julius had watched, day by day, another man enter the cabin of Violante of Naxos. He believed Nicholas when he said the Archimandrite was always present during those sessions. The woman's manner betrayed her disdain. In private, she would bring an importunate suitor to heel by humiliating him. A man of low class would be crucified. He had seen it done in his time. Nicholas, strolling out of that warm, scented cabin had never looked either abashed or resentful, never mind distraught with frustrated desire. But then, Nicholas was learning control of every natural reflex.

He was presumably drawing on his self-command now, eating and listening placidly to the fulminations of Julius. Apparently Pagano Doria was defying convention, and before being received at the Palace, had already begun to trade at the Leoncastello.

"Well, I can't stop him," said Nicholas. "And we can't trade: we have to wait for the Emperor's formal agreement. It's a pity, though. It would be nice to know what he's doing."

"Perhaps I could get in," Julius said.

Tobie caught Godscalc's eye. Julius wrecking their venture by invading the Genoese consulate and seizing the consul's wedded wife by the scruff of the neck had been their most constant nightmare. Nicholas said, "Could you? It would help a great deal. Or no, Doria would recognise you. What we need is someone living there, whom he trusts, and who could bring us constant reports of what he's doing, and how Catherine is faring. A steward, for example. He'll need a steward."

So that was the game. The eyes of Godscalc and Tobie met again. Godscalc lowered his lids. Tobie said, "Wait a moment. The Bessarion household. Didn't that Venetian tell you the mother had died and Amiroutzes was helping the staff find other positions? He mentioned a steward."

"Paraskeuas," Godscalc said. "A man with a family, all employed in the Bessarion household. But they live in the City. We couldn't get near them."

"I could," Julius said. "Privately. I could get through the gates in the morning, with the country people. I know where the house is. I could condole with them over the mother. The cardinal used to talk about her in Bologna. John, the cardinal's name is. He called himself Bessarion later."

Nicholas looked round the table. "It sounds risky, but if Julius is ready to try, it might be useful. Doria needs a steward and the man is free and might even have some Italian. For the cardinal's sake, and some money, he might agree to go to Doria and spy for us. If he doesn't, we try someone else."

Astorre said, "I was going to suggest something like it myself. We need a man or two over that wall, to reconnoitre the City before we're invited. It's a rule of mine. Never go blind into another man's town. You send in Meester Julius, and I'll give him one of my fellows as escort, and a list of what he should look for."

"Julius?" Nicholas said. "I'm not sure. You're hardly fit after Pera. Would you do it?"

"Well, they're not going to break my bones again, are they?" Julius said. "Of course I'm fit. Unless they make me laugh more than usual."

He set out for the sea gate early next morning, in a tasselled hat and a rough woven tunic, with one of Astorre's men behind, a carpet over his shoulder. He looked magnificent. Watching him leave, Tobie said, "He thinks it was all his idea."

Godscalc smiled.

Nicholas said, "It's just as well, isn't it? We three can sit eating and drinking and playing with words, but only Julius has spent weeks on campaign; is tough and quick on his feet; has Greek, and knows Bessarion and is ready to risk his skin for that girl, one way or another."

Godscalc bent on Nicholas one of his long, calm, considering looks, but didn't answer the challenge. "Your point is taken," he said.

"Oh, it's taken," said Tobie. "But I'm damned if it's accepted. If you want me as a confederate then you must expect me to polish my badges. On the other hand, I'm not fussy. I don't mind doing the rough work and letting Julius practise his cunning, if you'd prefer it."

"I think," Godscalc said, "that Nicholas is trying to tell us that we are an equal team, with different talents. What's wrong? You're not jealous of the lady from Naxos?"

"You mean – ?" said Tobie, startled.

"He means," said Nicholas, "that Julius is almost certain to try and find his way into the Palace. It's all right. Astorre's man has orders to stop him."

He looked unruffled, as he had been throughout. Tobie said, "God damn you, my child."

"All right," said Nicholas. "But not until we've bought our silk and seen Doria off and you've found where the brothels are. Then we'll let you do the rough work while we practise our cunning."

Julius came back half a day later, a little the worse for wear, and exuberant. It was a city worth seeing: he had roved through all but its highest part; he had called on the house of Bessarion's dead mother and had found the man Paraskeuas and taken him off to a tavern and, after a great deal of talk, had got him to agree to do what they wanted. The man, with his wife and son, would call on the Grand Vestarios that very day, and ask his help in obtaining an appointment with the Genoese consul. Paraskeuas himself was the sort you might expect, in the household of an old woman. A soft-bodied, well-trained Trapezuntine who spoke sadly of the cardinal's long absence from the family home, and the sweetness and generosity of his mother.

"Generosity?" said Tobie, alert.

"Oh, he held out for a fair sum, but I gave him what he asked in the long run," Julius said. "After all, he's taking his life in his hands. If Doria finds he's spying for us, it'll be the end of him."

"But you had to fight him before he'd agree," Nicholas said.

Julius glanced at his torn tunic, and stretched his bruised face in a grin. Behind him, Astorre said, "He fell off a wall."

"A wall?" said Godscalc obediently. This time, Tobie let Godscalc exercise all the cunning.

"Into the Upper Citadel," Julius said. "I couldn't get through the gate to the Palace. Astorre's man nearly fell too, but managed to hold me. The walls look well, but need some expert attention: that's one of the things you wanted to know. Anyway, it didn't look a bad climb."

"With half-mended ribs and a cracked collarbone?" Nicholas said. "Astorre's man should have let you drop. But I'm glad you reached Paraskeuas while we can still do it secretly. We've had news. We're invited into the City tomorrow to witness the Emperor and the court attend divine service. Then we have to return in the afternoon to attend a traditional show in the stadium. By request, Astorre's archers will take part. We shall watch as guests of the Emperor. You can climb walls, if you like."

Julius sat down, rather carefully. He still looked pleased with himself. "When did all this happen?"

"You just missed the Emperor's envoy, bearing gifts and Imperial messages. Between the church and the festival, I have to go to the Palace with my credentials. And return, I hope, with the privileges we were promised."

"You alone? Not the rest of us?"

"They only want one of us to begin with," Nicholas said. "Then they line the rest of us up, and let the women choose who goes tomorrow. What's the rush? You're going to be here until you're middle-aged, if we're lucky."

"It'll be too late when he's middle-aged," said Tobie, from habit. You had to admit it. Most times, Nicholas knew what he was doing. It made it interesting, waiting to see what he was going to fail at.

To Pagano Doria there arrived on that Sunday the same envoy bearing the same invitations, in addition to a silk brocade coat, subtly dyed the dull green of carnations. It was for Pagano, not Catherine; although she did receive a length of embroidered cloth and a cushion. There was no mention of rubies.

The summons to audience was not for her either. All she would see of the Emperor would be a glimpse as he went in and out of some church, and another glimpse as he sat in his box watching horsemen and jugglers. There wasn't even a tournament. They didn't have tournaments in Trebizond. She brooded, until Pagano reminded her that she would see the City at last, and the other merchants. She could wear her best dress, and her earrings.

She brightened. She said, "Do you think Nicholas will be at the church?" She saw Pagano stop what he was doing, as if the thought was new, or in some way unwelcome.

"Perhaps," Pagano said. "All the foreign merchants, all the guilds will be there. On the other hand, the Emperor and Autocrat of the Romans is fastidious, and may have learned by that time to distinguish between myself and his consul for Florence. Poor Niccolino. The Treasurer feared for him."

Sailing from Pera, the man Amiroutzes had taken pains, she was aware, to instruct Pagano in the ways of the court. They thought Nicholas ignorant. She had assumed so herself until she had noticed, by chance, a cloaked and unrecognisable figure disembarking from the Florentine ship. Leaving the Florentine ship, and stepping into a gilded state barge.

Dragged too late to the window, Pagano questioned if any member of the Imperial household would choose to travel with the *Ciaretti*; unless perhaps some clerk with an errand. She had been offended to have her theory dismissed. She was still offended. She said now, "Nicholas? He's always been sly. Sometimes he can surprise you."

But Pagano only warmed her cheek with a laugh. "You should have seen him at Modon," he said. And then, drawing away, smiled into her face, his eyes sparkling. "But, of course, you did see him at Modon. One ought not to mock. But after the fright he gave you in Pera, I doubt if I shall be civil in Trebizond. If I tease him, will you forgive me?"

"He isn't my father," said Catherine.

Next day they left with their retinue, she and Pagano, and rode uphill through the wide streets of the suburb, past the stadium of the Meidan and over the narrow eastern bridge to the City; and the moist, heavy air pressed upon them its serpentine odours.

The City was long and narrow and secure behind walls that had been modelled on the walls of Constantinople. It was built on an irregular table of rock whose surface inclined steeply upwards as it joined the foothills of the mountains behind. At its highest point was the Upper Citadel, with the Palace within it. In the middle, among the houses and orchards, was the monastery and church of the Chrysokephalos, the Imperial basilica, to which the bridge led them. The Lower Citadel sloped down to the shore, from which it was separated by the vast ochre brick wall of its double ramparts.

The wall and the Black Sea itself defended the City on the north. To the east and west it was protected not only by walls but by two dizzy ravines, worn into the rock by boiling rivers which rose in the mountains behind and plunged side by side to the sea, enclosing the high rock between them. And last and best of its natural safeguards there lay to the south a mountain barrier fifty miles thick, of which the high wooded range, behind the City and Palace, was only the face.

So guarded, the dynasty of the Grand Comneni had survived in Trebizond for two centuries and a half, a safe bond-house between Europe and Asia, and residual heirs, as could be seen, of all that was precious in both. For many generations, the consorts and princesses of the Imperial family had been known for unsurpassable beauty, only matched by the fairness and strength of their lords. The City they inhabited seemed worthy of them, or so thought Catherine of Bruges as she entered it, sitting carefully sideways on a pretty mule which slipped on the steep marble paving, while the bells rang and rang, for Easter Monday, and the Emperor.

Around her, behind high discreet walls, could be glimpsed pillars and cornices, a carved garland, a statue. Beyond those were the baths and the arcades, the wells, the markets and courtyards, the convents and hospices that lay under the golden domes and the towers. Here, the streets of the ancient Milesian builders were steep and narrow and filled now by the people on holiday in folded caps and thick coloured cottons, admiring the procession of foreigners as it wound its way through the gates of the monastery. The royal road that led uphill to the Palace, empty as yet, was hung with patterned carpets, and floored with green branches and lined with men in glittering livery, bearing bows and lances and axes that were all tipped with gold.

Pagano, before her, was wearing his Imperial coat, his heavy emerald chain round his shoulders. Beside and behind them walked their retinue led by Paraskeuas, the stout, soft-spoken steward and dragoman whom Amiroutzes had found for them. When they reached the basilica courtyard, it was Paraskeuas who helped her dismount and take her place beside the conventual buildings and under the fig trees. There was a bronze dragon beside her, with water coming out of its mouth, and a sentence in Greek about the emperor whose feat it commemorated. It reminded her of the stories she had had to listen to on shipboard, which had depressed her so much. She could hardly believe that once she had been discontented.

The church of the Golden-headed Virgin stood in the centre. It had a copper-gilt dome on a drum, below which every inch of the walls was covered with holy paintings in buff and brown and dark red and ochre and olive and a dark blue which the dyer's daughter in her told her was smalt, which surprised her. The pigments of the walls absorbed the dull light except where, here and there, she could see the glint of mosaic. Next to the paint, the rich cloth of living men's garments glowed like the tufts on her mother's price card, artfully displayed in soft light. Here, you could tell all the factions and guilds by their different colours; not least themselves, the foreign merchants, placed on each side of the patio. The Genoese, behind and beside her, were dressed in red Lucca velvet. The Venetians wore brilliant yellow, the Bailie broadened with fur and flashing with goldwork. Exceptionally, among the crowds on the other side of the yard, there stood a small group in quite disparate dyes under a banner which bore, surely, the lilies of Florence. Its leader, like Pagano, wore a coat whose depth of colour and richness of pattern could only have come from the Imperial looms. The wearer was Nicholas.

He carried it off, she had to admit, almost as well as Pagano, and being well set-up and taller, presented an appearance she would not have been ashamed of, had he not been her mother's new husband. Below the good velvet hat, the fresh-skinned face was devoid of any familiar expression. The eyes, unusually open, were looking straight at her.

Catherine de Charetty grasped her husband's arm. "*Look!*"

His gaze was already on the Florentine party, and he did not remove it. "I see," he said.

"He is wearing – "

Then he looked at her, amused. "Well, yes. He, too, has been dressed by the Basileus. I rather think, my Caterinetta, that your stepfather and I are to be received at the Palace together. What could be better?"

"But – " she said.

"But what? He cannot harm me, and what he will get from me, he has earned. Now, much more important: here is the Emperor."

The path from the Palace was steep. Observed from below, the cavalcade appeared at first smooth as a serpent, uncoiling in the grey, lightless air; incongruous as a brushful of paint on old cloth. Then it became near, and distinct, and through the brilliant clamour of the bells you could hear the fluting of other instruments as well as the drumbeats; and you could see the silk and gold fringe of the standards, rocking like ships leaving harbour.

In Bruges, one saw the world. Catherine had watched Duke Philip and the court of Burgundy ride into the Princenhof, his train a mile long. She had seen the state arrivals of princes, and the captains of the Venetian galleys. She understood costly fabric. She knew with what diverse and extravagant costume men of high birth affirmed their rank in the West. She had heard of Byzantine ritual but had never witnessed, in ordinary life, the consequences of preserving intact through the centuries the mode and costume of an ancient culture. Except, of course, for the dress and rites of the Church. There was no one to explain that the Emperor stood on earth for his god, and hence such rites were his everyday habit.

The standards were made of crimson satin, heavily fringed, and the standardbearers and musicians wore the same colour. The horses had manes white as silk, bound with ribbons and tassels; and golden harness and beaded caparisons, and saddles studded with silver. The riders wore crowns and diadems looped and strung and fringed with fine jewelled chains, and had shining hair in every colour from bright gold to black. Their robes, narrow as grave clothes, were armoured with precious stones; with gorgets and belts and bands of ancient gems, thick as crabs. Their backs were straight; their bodies were slender as dancers'; their faces were masks of symmetrical beauty. They reached the plateau of the monastery and began to pass round its walls, while the murmuring silence was pierced by the abrupt clamour of trumpets. There was a pause. A body of scent began to move through the air, displacing the incense. Where it came from, you could see the gleam of cloth of gold, and a sparkle where drifts of jewels gathered in shadow. The cavalcade had dismounted. The court was there, disconcertingly close, and about to enter the monastery precincts. She could see them. The scent was suddenly oppressive and strange. The composed faces, men's and women's, were painted.

Heralds and standards came first; and then young boys and maidens throwing yellow spring flowers. A golden-haired boy of a beauty she had never imagined walked next, dressed in ivory silk, a gilded bow in his hand. Behind, pacing slowly between his confessors, was the Emperor. In the crook of his right arm the Imperial crosier lay like a lily. Over his left was wrapped a swathe of the long, elaborate pallium. Above the tunic, the dalmatica, the silken eagles woven in purple and gold, she saw a noble profile, calm and resolute beneath the tall stiffened gold of the mitra. From the rim of the crown, strings of light pearls fell to the jewelled yoke on his broad shoulders, and mixed with the loose curling gold of his hair and his beard. Behind him, the train of men and women and youths, of officials and nobles and churchmen stretched far off through the trees. There was a ceremonial escort in moulded gold armour, each line of plumes as white as filled down on a nesting ledge.

From the north porch of the church, a group of white-bearded men had slowly emerged, robed in sparkling vestments. Their crosses and icons made freckles of light on the pillars. Then the Emperor drew abreast, and Pagano's hand thrust Catherine down, and she knelt, her neck bowed, as the court passed into the church, and its doors closed, excluding them all; foreigners; aliens; followers of the Church of Apostasy in Rome. The bells stopped. Silence fell in the courtyard.

She found she was shaking; and caught Pagano's hand, and held it tightly. She knew she was young, and had a lot to learn. She understood that she was frightened, and would be again; because this was a great world, and she wanted to enter it, and that was the price you had to pay. She was willing to pay it. She didn't want to stay in a dyeshop. She could do anything, now she had Pagano to learn from.

Rising, she looked across for the tall figure of her mother's husband, and found it, and trained upon it all her joy and her defiance.

Julius said, "There he is." He kicked Nicholas, and repeated it.

Nicholas said, "I have still, thank God, the power of sight. That is the Protonotarios, who came to see us. The man with the hat like a basket is Amiroutzes, the Treasurer. The man bringing up the rear is either the Count of the Walls or the Prefect of the Guard: tell Astorre. The man greeting them in the doorway is the Patriarch, with his clergy. The man – "

Julius said, "You don't want to know? There, facing you over the path, is Pagano Doria, who set fire to your ship and nearly got John and me killed by the Turks. The girl's behind him, with her hair all wired up and her skin bare down to her neckline. You don't mind?" He waited, expecting support from Tobie and Godscalc. But Tobie, standing behind him, said nothing, and Godscalc behaved as if he wasn't there.

Nicholas said, "Go and hit him, then. That's what he's praying you'll do."

Julius went on breathing hard. "Oh, I wouldn't want to ruin the business," he said.

"That's the spirit," said Nicholas. "Anyway, he's wearing an Imperial coat. The Emperor must have called him to the same audience. He and I will have the chance of a civil word or two on the way. I'll convey your good wishes."

"You should kill him," said Julius. He felt Godscalc's hand on his shoulder and realised that within the church, the Easter service had begun, and he should be silent. Incense hung in the air, and the sound of men's voices chanting, clear through the doors. Plain chant, without instruments. Julius, who had little interest in music, stared across at Pagano Doria, who gave him a smile full of charm, and then murmured in his wife's ear. The girl laughed. Julius tightened his fists. He was almost better now. Well enough to hit someone.

Tobie, behind, caught Godscalc's eye and then looked round for Loppe, who appeared to be reading Nicholas's mind from the back. Godscalc's hand remained where it was. After a while, he gave Julius a light, private cuff and removed it, as if satisfied with a restive horse. Julius remained gazing at the Genoese and occasionally frowning at Nicholas, who appeared to be committing to memory every person in sight, and had not looked towards Catherine again. Blurring the reverent silence imposed on those nearest to the church door were the murmuring sounds of conversation among the many hundreds standing further off in the open, and above and beyond, the commonplace cries of the City. Nicholas had stopped looking about. Godscalc said, in a voice that just reached him, "Acrostics. I told you."

He was given the impression, unexpectedly, that his voice wasn't wanted. Then Nicholas said, "Yes. I hear it."

Within, the strong voices had turned from the canon to the great Akathistos Kontakion with its refrains, repeated over and over. Between the powerful charges of music the service began to unfold: there would be a passage of chanting, or a solo voice: *Who is great like our God? You are the God who performs miracles.* Or wordless prayer, in absolute silence. *All must stand still, for the master of the house has come.* The master has come, and will hear you.

The passion of the divine liturgy of the Greek Church climbed to its height. Of this, the envoys of the Prince of Kiev had reported: *We knew not whether we were on heaven or on earth, for surely there is no such splendour or beauty anywhere upon earth. We cannot describe it to you: only we know that God dwells there among men, and that their service surpasses the worship of all other places. For we cannot forget that beauty.* Stirred to reply, a nightingale in the western gully at Trebizond began a sweet descant to the great cry soaring now from the Chrysokephalos. Nicholas moved once, and was still. Unobtrusively, Godscalc watched him.

What had happened? It was the mark of a good priest to recognise facile emotion. It was the mark of a good man to refrain from exploiting it. Unwillingly, the priest in Godscalc considered the enigma beside him. Had there been some response? But to what? Here was great music. Here was an ancient and beautiful church, living shrine of the Logos, replica of heaven upon earth. Here was the last remnant of a great empire embodied in the Basileus, consecrated leader and lord of his people; guardian of the First and Purest Light.

A worthy emperor who, by his coronation oath, had sworn to uphold the most holy great Church of God: *I, David, in Christ God faithful Emperor and Autocrat of the Romans submit to all truth and justice . . . All things which the holy fathers rejected and anathematised, I also reject and anathematise . . .* The Emperor, who ruled like his forebears with God's favour, and was kept hourly conscious of his mortality. *Remember death!* had chanted his minister, over and over, as the Basileus rose from his coronation and walked out to his people. *Remember death! For you are dust, and to dust you will return.* No man had fought more bravely for Constantinople, the Tabernacle of God, than its emperor, who had died there. "The city is taken, and I am still alive?" he had said, before dismounting, sword in hand, to lose his life to the Turks. What man on the threshold of life could fail to be stirred by those things? Passing Constantinople, Nicholas had said something of it. He should have understood better.

Thinking, insensibly Godscalc himself became drawn into the course of the mass whose words and music continued, clear to follow. For a while, his cares melted. But men were only men, and one couldn't hope to ignore them. He knew, through it all, that Julius was still outstaring the cockerel opposite. Tobie, a reliable man when he wanted to be, had moved discreetly nearer. Tobie who believed in nothing, Godscalc thought, but his masters of nature, his antidotary and his urine glasses; and suffered for it sometimes more than he deserved.

Now, knowing the shape of the service, Godscalc heard the eucharistic rites draw to a close. About the time he expected, there came the blessing and dismissal, and the rustle that meant the procession was assembling and would shortly emerge. This time the

churchmen came first and took their places on either side of the porch.
The Patriarch and the archons with their names from the past: the
Sceuophylax, the Sacellarius, the Chartophylax, the Staurophoroi.
The bishops, the priests and the deacons. And now, given to God once
again, David, the twenty-first Emperor of Trebizond and the superb
Helen Cantacuzenes, his Empress. He stepped out, and Godscalc
bowed with the rest as the procession formed and moved past, its silks
beating out incense. The Emperor's family first. The princess Anna his
daughter, and an angelic host of young princes, her brothers and
cousins. The Emperor's exquisite Akocouthos, the page with the
ceremonial bow. And the dark and beautiful woman who must be the
Genoese widow Maria, who had married the Emperor's brother.

Behind her was another lovely woman whom, this time, he knew.
Violante of Naxos, their late fellow-passenger, wore the open diadem
of a Comnenos princess, and was dressed, like the others, in the long,
severe tunic with its high neck and tight sleeves, thickened with pearls
and embroidery. Like the others, she looked neither to right nor to left
although his eyes, and those of Julius, followed her until the end of the
file hid their view. Rising from his genuflexion, Godscalc brushed the
dust from his skirts. It would take a long time to push through the
yard. Ahead, the gates were jammed as horses were brought, and the
Imperial family mounted. A voice said, "We are not waiting. My
husband has often seen such things before. It was a waste of time,
your coming to Trebizond, because my husband sells and buys all the
best things, being of the Doria family. I am married now."

The girl Catherine. Godscalc braced himself. Doria, naturally,
would have planned to get Nicholas on his own at the Palace. The girl
had darted across before her bridegroom could stop her. Avid, of
course, to arrange a confrontation between husbands. And to show
herself. She was wearing expensive earrings, too heavy for her young
face. And the same face, somehow, was sharper than he remembered
it. She was saying "Where is he?"

Godscalc followed her gaze. Where Nicholas had been, there was no
one. Loppe, too, had evaporated. Out of the side of his eye, he saw
Tobie looking smug. Pagano Doria, strolling up, said, "My dear,
think of Modon. He's always running about. You'll see him later, I'm
sure."

Left to himself, Doria might have got her away. Instead, he had
Julius in front of him, already murderous, and made more so by the
desertion of Nicholas. Julius lunged and, before Godscalc could stop
him, caught Catherine fast by the arm. He said, "Married? I'll believe
that when I see the papers. Until then, this is where you belong."

He had addressed her in Flemish, but his voice and his action were
recklessly explicit. Heads were turning. Protective of their consul, the
Genoese were already stepping forward, vermilion swinging.
Catherine de Charetty stared at Julius and then, severely, at his hand

on her arm. She did not scream, and made no effort to struggle. Instead, she cast a complacent glance at her husband and waited.

Godscalc didn't give Doria a chance to make matters worse. Godscalc raised a hand like a cleaver and brought it down on the arm holding the girl, which fell limp to the notary's side. Then, as Julius whirled, exclaiming, the priest seized him by shoulder and elbow. On his other side, Tobie did likewise. Julius, a powerful man, began to struggle painfully.

Pagano Doria watched, and the Genoese now grouped behind him. He turned to his wife. "Caterinetta? At least your priest believes in your marriage, it seems. I am less fond of your notary. Shall we hand him to the church officers, for causing violence in the church precincts, in the Emperor's presence? Or what?"

From its scabbard under his coat, Doria had drawn a handsome small dagger. It looked familiar. He smiled. "Don't be afraid, Messer Julius. It is not your name on the blade." His hand made a small movement. The steel gave a flash, and Julius made a furious movement. A long wrinkle appeared on one leg, above which the broken end of a hosepoint hung down.

"*Naked* on Easter Monday in the churchyard. What, I wonder, is the penalty for that?" Doria said. Catherine giggled. The dagger flashed again, and Julius jumped. On his other side, Tobie half loosed his grip. Godscalc, keeping his own, said sharply, "Cease at once. You disgrace your republic." There was blood now on the stocking where Julius, struggling, had caught the knife. It nicked again. Tobie said, "All right. I'm going to – "

Father Godscalc offered, in German, a furious prayer for patience. He braced himself for the move that would heave Julius round and run him out of the crowd. Then he was saved the trouble.

"My lords?" said Violante of Naxos. "The Emperor sends to ask if he can help the man who is sick? Why, Messer Julius!"

The hooded eyes, sedately amused, contradicted the concern and reproach in her voice. She spoke, musically, in her native Greek. She bent, and touched with her handkerchief the blood staining the notary's calf. "Messer Tobias, he has hurt himself. This should be seen to." The handkerchief, of transparent silk edged with gold thread, was being folded and neatly tied over the scratch. The lady rose. "There. Now take him away and let him rest. These turns are dangerous. You will need to take care."

She smiled at Julius. She was saying, of course, that he must leave. The rest of them had to reach Nicholas, wherever he was, and achieve their ceremonial march to the Palace. Without their notary. Well, that would do no harm. In the end, it was Nicholas, alone, who would enter the Palace gates. Alone, or with the Genoese consul. The lady Violante, instead of retiring, was walking beside them, along the path and away from Doria.

Godscalc glanced back. The gaiety and malice had left Doria's face for the moment. Perhaps, thought Godscalc, the scene had been a matter of impulse, now regretted. And did he know the woman Violante, as Nicholas claimed? Her intervention, as it happened, had saved them all; and her motives could be innocuous. Brawling wouldn't help trade, and she was married to a Venetian merchant.

Catherine, too, was staring as they receded. Specifically staring at Julius, who was looking not at all at his mistress's lovely young daughter. Instead, he was gazing, in silence, at the painted woman who had just interfered. A woman in the Imperial diadem who yet knew his name, and that of Master Tobias. Who, therefore, must be – could only be – the Byzantine passenger who had sailed from Pera with Nicholas.

She was beautiful. And rich. And a princess. Her scent lingered. It was not, Catherine recognised, the composite odour of Trebizond. It was a perfume quite different: a distinctive, a familiar perfume, that belonged to another city altogether.

Her face, already sharp, became sharper. Then she looked for Pagano, and slipped her fingers into his hand and pressed it, so that he looked down and put his other arm round her shoulders. "What a crew!" he said. "Was that alarming? You didn't think I'd let them snatch you?"

Already the horses were coming. Hers to take her, escorted, back to the Leoncastello. His to carry him to the Palace, there to present his credentials. As, it seemed, the consul for Florence would also be doing.

The Florentines. Catherine laughed up at his face. "Who was ever afraid of a stupid notary? Now," she said, "you must make Nicholas jump."

Nicholas said, "I've got my hat, and the letter, and the money, and Loppe with the presents and a white flag, and a bone for the dragon. If I'm not out in ten minutes, come and help me up from my stomach."

They stood in the Upper Citadel, squared up inside the main gate holding their horses. A little distance away, drawn up in vermilion ranks, was the contingent of Genoese merchants. In a moment, the Emperor's emissary would come: the Protonotarios, or the Chief Secretary, or the Treasurer Amiroutzes, and lead the two consuls, each with one servant, into the Presence. It was a long walk, they had been told, from the lower courtyard up to the Palace. It was strongly probable that Nicholas and Doria would make it together.

They had told Nicholas, of course, what had happened to Julius. He thought himself that he would have dealt with it differently, but he wasn't Godscalc. Tobie's eyes had bored into his back all the way up the hill.

In the end it was the Chief Secretary, Altamourios, the Emperor's cousin, who came and greeted Doria and himself and then, bearing his wand, led the way up the steep incline to the Palace. Nicholas took his place behind, next to Doria. Behind them both came Loppe and Doria's man, a Trapezuntine, with the consular gifts. Doria had emeralds fitted into his hat and the chain he wore over his coat. He looked magnificent. He said, "My Niccolino, I have hopes of you at last. You had the cunning to vanish. What a fool your poor Julius is. You know very well my little treasure cannot be coaxed from me, now or ever."

"Condemned to permanent bliss," Nicholas said. "Do you mind?"

Turning, Doria put a hand on his arm, and leaned on it warmly. "I surprise myself," he said. He removed his hand, but walked on, confidingly close. "This little Catherine offers more than you would imagine. Small but pliant, and tireless. Have you tried her? No, I got her a virgin. And you have the mother, so doubtless kept your hands off the girls. But I tell you, she would serve a squadron all winter, and still have energy left in the spring. The refinements she has learned! You could try them with the old woman. When I mount, I get her to slip her fingers . . ."

"It would be more exciting," Nicholas said, "if we got the girl to instruct me herself."

Doria broke off, looking at him, and then gave a sigh of appreciation. "You're right. And, do you know, she would probably tell you. Catherine pities your ignorance of the piquant arts: we talk of it often. I believe she thinks, the young innocent, that you have had none to coach you but her wrinkled mother." He walked, the smile fixed on his face by his thoughts. "You know, my Niccolino, I might some time lend you my wife for an hour or two. She would do it for me. And for herself, to show off her skills. She has tricks from every whorehouse in Italy. Naturally, you wouldn't tell her their provenance."

"Naturally," Nicholas said. "The lady Violante is much the same."

Two, three, four paces in silence. Although he kept swallowing, he couldn't clear what was stuck in his throat.

Then Doria said, "Ah yes. They told me someone sailed on your ship. An inventive partner, you thought?"

"She made rather more of it in Bruges," Nicholas said. "What will you find for yourself while you're here? The whores will leave if there's war."

"War?" said Doria. "Look about you! A one-legged man could hold Trebizond. They can't broach the walls from the sea. The mountain roads wouldn't let them bring cannon. They can't starve us out because they'd have to leave before winter. Of course, the Emperor will love your soldiers, but that's not because he has any serious fears. Uzum Hasan is the target. That will interrupt the caravans from the south – maybe stop them. You didn't put your silk on sale when you should."

They had climbed the steps – the endless steps – and come at last to a doorway. Nicholas said, "You've been selling already? But there's nothing to buy in exchange. They tell me the autumn ships emptied the stockrooms."

"Ah, Niccolino!" said Pagano Doria. With fond attention, he examined the inlaid marbles of the flanking pillars before them, and then raised his gaze, with affection, to the man at his side. "You have a lot to learn. Of course, there is nothing to barter. There is no assurance of those precious goods you are waiting to buy if the Sultan is fighting across the caravan routes. So one must look for other returns for one's goods. I insisted on silver. There is not much left in Trebizond, and there was some little resistance. But I can tell you, my dearest Niccolò, that I now have under lock and key – many locks, many keys – all the mint can provide in this city. There is none left for you, or the Florentines." He smiled again. "But will Cosimo think less of you for your failure? Of course not. You play with his grandson."

"What is trade," said Nicholas, "except playing with somebody?"

Then the doors opened on a dazzle of white and gold, and the sound of many voices, and music and a ripple of scents. The honey of Trebizond which, poison or not, was a draught of spring water after what he had allowed to be given him.

He could feel Loppe, black as murder, behind him. He knew the first words Loppe would say, when this was over. *"How will you kill him?"*

He had no need to think of his answer. It was the same as all the other times. All the other five times.

"I never kill," he would say.

Chapter 19

THE INNER PALACE, high as a stork's nest, sat on marble pillars around a fountain court scented with myrtle. Through every window and terrace and balcony there showed a different aspect of the Fortunate City: the greens and blues of forest and mountain, ocean and sea; the red vine-bowered roofs of the City, the leafy depths of the twin gorges, full of spring flowers and tumbling water and birdsong. Led from passage to chamber, Doria at his side, Nicholas was quiet, and recovered his tranquillity. Calmness was a weapon and a defence; beauty was only a weapon and best left alone. He was to face the Emperor of the eastern Greek world, and he employed his only real rule. Put yourself in the other man's place. War and trade; love and freedom from love – it was the way to success in them all. When he failed, it was because he had forgotten it. Or, occasionally, because someone was better at it than he was. But only occasionally.

The doors to the throne room were double, and made of worked bronze. They were opened by two officers of the ceremonial guard with their gilded cuirasses and gold-covered lances and shields. He knew one of them to be the deputy Protospatharios: Astorre had found him off duty two days before and joined his dice party and brought him back drunk for some food. Nicholas showed no recognition, and neither did the officer. Side by side with Doria, he entered the room.

White and gold. The vault over the range of slim, pillared windows was diced with gold and edged with a moulded cornice of delicate ovals and palmettes. Below, a dais and two backless ivory thrones glimmered in reflected light, soft as spun syrup. The floor was patterned in marble and where it stopped on the walls there were frescoes of past emperors and their consorts and children; arch-browed, stem-nosed, bow-mouthed; their heads buckled with diadems; their names and titles lettered into the spaces between the assorted quills of their sceptres.

The big chamber was crowded with people. No, lined. He and Doria were the only supplicants. A deep carpet, woven with pomegranates and peaches and pepper trees, crossed the marble before them from the door to the dais. He saw Doria's eye caught by its possibilities; and saw him change his mind. No. The duel was over, for the moment. For the moment, Doria needed to gather his resources to do what he did best. To project his charm towards the dais, the thokos upon which the Emperor David and Helen his Empress were seated.

Put yourself in the other man's place. The Emperor had chosen to receive them straight from the ceremony of the Easter service, and wore still the formal jewelled mitra, the gold and purple dalmatica with its broad stiffened bands. In his left glove he held the Imperial sceptre, and the right, on his knee, held the orb. On his feet were the scarlet buskins of Imperial dignity, there to be kissed. He smelled of incense and there was about him still, in his immobility, the remoteness of mystical experience, together with an awareness of ancient and unquestioned power. I am the Basileus, the Grand Comnenos, Emperor and Autocrat of the Romans and of Perateia. Where is Genoa? What is Florence?

Inside the robe was a full-bodied man in early middle age with fair, rosy cheeks shaped by a trimmed golden beard, lightly curling. Above the combed and curving moustache was a nose of Roman grandeur and eyes which were at present languid and empty of warmth. They rested, without changing, on the envoys before him. They moved on to dwell, for a moment, on the boxes and packets which had followed the envoys into the room. *There is almost nothing in this world we have need of. But where tribute is customary, we shall accept it.*

Only so far, on such evidence, could one judge the Emperor. Put yourself, then, in the place of the Empress, sitting beside him. She was here, why? Not from greed: she had not deigned to glance at the boxes. Then, doubly to impress the Imperial dignity upon the Latins whose help the Empire had been forced to solicit? After all, Trebizond had sent Michael Alighieri to Florence. Trebizond had joined its appeal to the others whose envoys were being bundled through Europe by Fra Ludovico da Bologna, bane of Julius; friend of Doria.

All her attention at this moment, as the two envoys stood bowing before her, was on the Genoese consul, and not on Nicholas. And Doria, discreetly, was permitting his admiration to be seen. Indeed, it was deserved. After nine children, Helen Cantacuzenes was less than slender, but the long metalled tunic gave her body a sheath that became it. Above its high jewelled gorget, her face gleamed like enamel between the cascades of pearls from her diadem. The hair gathered below it was dark, as were her eyes. When Nicholas lifted his head from his next bow, they were on him. He saw a single gleam, he thought, which might have been of curiosity, or even distaste.

He instantly lowered his own. What had she been told? The many ladies-in-waiting around her did not include Violante of Naxos. But there were other women behind whom he could not identify, just as there were many richly costumed men standing below the Imperial family who were not its servants, its guards or its chamberlains. Members, probably, of the native Trapezuntine families; the Grecian aristocrats he had heard of – the Ypsilanti, the Mouroussi – who had owned their estates long before the Latins threw the Emperor out of the New Jerusalem twelve hundred years after Christ had been thrown out of the old, and the Imperial brothers came to found their Empire of Trebizond here.

They looked to be powerful men; and their eyes, too, were fixed on Doria and himself. If there was danger coming (but what danger could there be?), men with a stake in the land would want to know what help they might expect from Genoa, the Mother-Republic, and Florence, the cashier of the Pope, regardless of any small differences in the matter of worship. The Patriarch, he now noticed, was not here.

The Secretary, bowing, made way. It was Amiroutzes the Treasurer, Count Palatine, Grand Vestarios, Great Domestic of Trebizond who now stepped forward, with his striped beard and teasing brown ringlets and wide stiffened hat, and announced them to his Emperor. Which first? But of course, Genoa. Mistress of the Levant, ancient thorn in the flesh of both emperors; but still capable of bringing lucrative trade, and clever technicians, and presents.

Walking forward, Doria held every eye. For all his lack of height, he was well made, and the green silk of the coat flattered his slow, easy movements. He reached the end of the carpet, paused, and then prostrated himself with courtly competence. The scarlet buskin rested above him on the low marble step. He kissed it, rose, and bowed his neck until the Emperor spoke. He had walked on the carpet throughout. Nicholas, too, had been tempted. But, like Doria, he recognised an irrelevance. That could wait.

Doria presented the folded parchment, tangled with bright silk and wax, that held his credentials. The Emperor touched it and passed it to his secretary. From where he stood, Nicholas could hear the Emperor's voice, light and musical, and the thicker tones of the Treasurer, translating. Veteran of Rome, Florence, Genoa, Amiroutzes spoke in Italian strongly accented in Greek. Observing etiquette, Doria responded in the same tongue. Two young men – his sons? – stood at the Treasurer's back. One of them, by all accounts, was Bessarion's godson.

Nicholas wondered how much of the Greek tongue Pagano Doria possessed. All he needed, very likely. He had been in the East, on and off, for a good part of his life. At any rate, Amiroutzes was taking no liberties with the Emperor's words, which he translated exactly. They contained nothing new, beyond a formal welcome, a formal message of goodwill to their magnificent lords the seigneurs of the Republic of Genoa, followed by a brief confirmation of the terms of the Genoese tenure and privileges which already obtained in the colony. It was the existence of the previous agreement that had enabled Doria so adroitly to accomplish his business. The best one could say was that there was no hint that the terms might be bettered. The Genoese, in the past, had been officious agents. Charming, deferential, Pagano Doria was the right man to correct that impression.

Then came the presentation of gifts. The Greek steward named as Paraskeuas brought each item to Doria, and it passed from his hands to those of the Treasurer. The goblets, the spices, the bolts of fine woollen cloth (the *Ciaretti* had none to offer) were superb, and costly. Two hundred ducats had gone to pleasing the Basileus. The Basileus expressed pleasure. The gifts vanished. Doria, bowing three times, retreated to a place by the lesser magnates. And now, Claes himself.

He never tried to forget, at moments like these, his base upbringing; his disputed origins. But for those, he might not have had to seek out this past eighteen months all he possessed in nature to cancel them. He knew his strengths, one of which was the effectiveness of his body. And he had stood a long time, minutely observing, outside the church.

He moved therefore slowly, as the Imperial family walked, and with the same carriage. But where Doria had solicited, he kept his eyes strictly downcast, through the words of the introduction and after. The Prostration he had been taught by the mistress of such things: he was sorry she was not here to be gratified. He delivered the ritual kiss and stood, lids lowered still, until the Emperor spoke. When he raised his eyes, and met those of the Emperor, he felt the hair rise on his forearms. It was true, then. She had been seldom explicit, and he had not been sure. He set the knowledge aside, and went on with the process on which he was launched.

First, the formal letter signed in Florence by Cosimo de' Medici setting out the agreement, embellished with greetings and compliments. This was handed over to the Emperor and read. Through Amiroutzes, the Emperor knew the House of Medici. It was why he had sent Alighieri his envoy to Florence. A private letter from the same Michael Alighieri was already in the Emperor's hands, forewarning him of the terms for this contract. That the Palace had then commanded this audience ought to mean that the Emperor had found the conditions acceptable. On the other hand, one never quite knew. One merely stood, mildly patient, and waited.

The letters were read and translated. The Emperor spoke, interpreted by his treasurer. The Emperor, taking the contract item by item, agreed item by item to every one of its points. Every one.

They were to get everything that had been agreed: everything that they and the Medici had wanted. Nicholas listened, his expression soberly gratified, his inner being drunk with delight. The details ran on and ended and the Emperor waved the document away and remained for a moment, studying the Florentine consul, before delivering the usual coda. The Emperor hoped that the Republic of Florence, through their agent the company of Charetty, would respect the customs and sovereignty of his lands, and that the concessions to which they were admitted today would lead to a long association, full of honour. Nicholas responded in nicely tuned Tuscan and Loppe brought forward Florence's gifts to the Imperial family. The Emperor watched Loppe, calmly curious, as if there were no negroes already among the quiet line of servants, or among the beardless men by the door to the women's apartments.

The gifts were more than adequate, being mostly bales of double-cut velvet in Imperial colours: crimson on gold; purple patterned on black and tissue of silver. Once, it was forbidden to common men to dye purple in the Imperial grades; but not now. He had chosen some stuff with a ground of red velvet, scattered with rosebuds in silver thread and white silk. Unfolded, it brought a little sigh from some woman, but Nicholas didn't look round. At the end he said, "These are what I ventured to bring. But if Thrice-Augustus will permit, there is a greater gift which awaits at your gates. The Domesticus of the Imperial guard knows its nature."

It had been well rehearsed. The Protospatharios stepped forward, bowed and spoke to the Emperor, who turned. Before Amiroutzes translated, Nicholas knew what he was saying. "I am told that you have brought armed men for the Florentine service, and that these men will regard it as their duty, while stationed here, to protect my city. This is so?"

Nicholas agreed, his voice humble. If the Basileus deigned, the troop could be assembled under his balcony in a matter of moments. These men begged but a glimpse of the Emperor of the Imperial Family of the Hellenes, to serve whom they had travelled so far.

Permission was given, and a messenger sent. Nicholas could hear women speaking in whispers where they felt themselves secure from the eyes on the dais. The Emperor, who had been thoughtful, asked a question. "The Florentine consul was outside my church of Panaghia Chrysokephalos this morning?"

Amiroutzes was not at hand. Nicholas hesitated. He said in Greek, "Forgive me, Basileus. Yes."

The Emperor appeared to rebuke. "Learning needs no apology. You heard the service?"

"I heard the music, Basileus," Nicholas said. "I cannot find words for its excellence. In sound, and in the many uses of the mystery of Christian numbers."

"You refer to the canon, the canticles?" the Emperor said.

Nicholas inclined his head, and was encouraged with a gesture to continue. He said, "The liturgy is new to me, but mathematics and ciphers are not. It seemed to this hearer, magnificence, that the second verse of the first ode was missing."

The Emperor turned his eyes. His cousin the secretary said, "That is so, Basileus. The acrostic was incomplete. My lord the Florentine consul has observed correctly."

"A gift for languages, and a gift for numbers," said the Emperor. "Florence is fortunate. You spoke of troops."

He could hear Astorre, outside, marching his men up to the wall. The Basileus, also hearing them, rose, upon which everyone bowed. Nicholas, straightening, was allowed to follow the Emperor to the balcony, and stand looking down on the shining rows of his ninety-eight men. They had spent three days polishing the armour they wore, and the Charetty blue plumes in their helmets might have been painted, so straight were their lines. They were better than the Imperial guard. Astorre, in front, had his good eye and his sewn eye trained like a hawk on the Emperor, and his sword held at the salute in both hands. It was as they had planned, which made it none the less miraculous. His liking for Astorre overwhelmed him, clearing a path through the other things.

Then the Emperor spoke, and a kid bag was placed in his hands and then transferred to those of the Domesticus who, bowing, carried it down to Astorre. It looked heavy. It should be, considering what the Emperor was getting. Astorre, receiving it, passed it to Thomas his deputy and performed, like an ancient and sinewy goat, the complete Prostration on the paving of the court. He rose, bowed, and walked off somewhere with the Protospatharios, his plumes crowing. Thomas, who looked almost smart, barked out orders in anglicised Flemish, bowed, and marched the men off down the slope.

The audience was ended. Inside the room, the Empress was already leaving between ranks of bowed heads. The Emperor, again enthroned, gave his gracious leave to both consuls to retire. Standing together again, Nicholas and his unruffled rival made their deferential retreat. This time, instead of the secretary, an equerry who had no Italian led them off through the Palace, taking them through passages not before seen and drawing to their attention a number of unexceptional appointments on the way to the courtyard. You would say that he had time to put off, or wished the consuls to linger. Pagano Doria who had, indeed, fluent Greek, conversed with him on trivial matters and then, falling back, engaged Nicholas in airy Genoese.

"And now, tell me," said Pagano Doria, "how *did* you contrive those plague cases?"

"Tobias did it. Our physician," said Nicholas. "Paint and lentils, I believe. I thought you said there was no silver left?"

"The Emperor's bag? Don't be deceived. Paint and lentils, my dear." The sea prince was in no way put out, it was clear, by Astorre's success with the Basileus. He said gaily, "To return to an earlier topic."

"Your wife?" said Nicholas.

"No, yours. I've a letter from her lying about somewhere. She sent it to Trebizond to await your arrival. It came on a Genoese ship, and the merchants kept it until you got here. I took the liberty," said Doria rapturously, "of opening it. I let Catherine read it as well. She couldn't understand some of the words, although she could do it all right, I can tell you . . . Mother and daughter. We are fortunate, you and I, to have the use of them."

To the east, you could see clear across the ravine and the town to the sea. Near at hand, Nicholas identified the line of the stables, the barracks, an arsenal, the mews, storehouses, an armourer's, workshops. His nose located the kitchens and bakehouse with a fishpond and well close beside them. They were passing them all. After a few more paces, he said, "You have the letter with you?"

Doria laughed. "Here? No. It has by now, shall I say, something of a second-hand look to it. If you still want it, I'll bring it to the stadium. You mean to go to the festival?"

"I have been invited," Nicholas said. "But don't trouble to bring it. Loppe will call."

Doria smiled again. "He may call, but he won't get the letter. At the Meidan, my dear. Nowhere else. Page upon page; and such suggestions! It made Catherine jealous."

About the contents he was lying: Nicholas didn't have to be told that. That there was a letter was probably true. It was unlikely to say very much. Marian had probably sent it to Venice in January. It was only Doria's possession of it that was . . . undesirable. And Catherine's wilfulness. It was addressed to himself. She could have chosen to pass it on privately. It was from her mother, after all. Her mother, distracted perhaps by having found Catherine gone. Or else because . . . But no. Marian could have found out nothing more, or Doria would not have been ready to part with her letter.

If he *was* ready? If it was not just another feint; another touch of the goad in the charming game Doria was playing with him. Otherwise, why force him to accept it at the festival?

He walked on, countering Doria only with the silence Doria did not want. For the moment, a refusal to fight was his only safeguard. They were nowhere near the Middle Citadel gate. Instead, the equerry had turned towards a large pavilion set in lawns to the right, with a path before it which circled a fountain. Behind was the western wall of the Citadel, and the tops of the trees that lined the nearest bank of the gorge. Across the ravine was the ridge of St Eugenios; and behind that, the heights of the hill the Romans called Mithras. Sacred to gods which had not been celebrated today.

Nicholas turned. Behind, Loppe and the Greek had been stopped. Both looked mystified. In front, the equerry beckoned. Nicholas said, "Where are we going?"

Doria arched his brows, his eyes glinting. "You don't know? Then why not enquire of the equerry? In your fluent Greek?"

He sounded entertained. Nicholas looked at the nature of the building before him and made, at last, some deductions. He wished, with all his heart, that he were back in the villa with Julius and Tobie and Godscalc. He contradicted himself quickly. This was what he had wanted. And what sense would it make to leave Doria alone here now? At least the proceedings might warm his hands and feet, which were icy. He said to the equerry, in Greek, "It is a bath house?"

The equerry had a black moustache, and wore a buttoned robe and a hat like a tube. He said, "By order of the Basileus. It pleases him to offer the hospitality of his baths. Pray follow."

Doria's smile could be cut up and eaten. He murmured, using Italian, "I wonder, mixed bathing? I have heard things. My dear, I think you are too young."

"I hope so," said Nicholas. A door opened; and then another, from which steam emerged. It was what he had expected.

"Mixed bathing," said Doria softly.

He had been in steam baths in Flanders and Italy. Most were bawdy houses and ran to hard couches in the entrance hall, with floor coverings of a sort, and a few hangings, and shuttered places by the latrines for undressing. In all of them, even the brothels, there were racks of towels to be had. Here, when he had stripped, there was nothing to do but walk mother-naked into the hall. The walls were hung with yellow silk sewn with pearls, and there were couches heaped with down cushions on a carpet from Persia. Against one wall was a buffet on which were laid flasks of wine and silver dishes of sweetmeats and fruit. Two servants stood in silent attendance, both wearing hipcloths. Both were eunuchs. None of the couches was occupied, and there was no sign of Doria. At the end of the room was a double door, heavily gilded. Nicholas walked towards it. As he did so, both leaves opened and a third attendant bowed, and flattened himself in an invitation to pass. He walked into a large, warm room full of steam. The tepidarium.

The tepidarium was not empty. Under its dome, all sound reduced itself to hollow whispers and low, musical resonances, and all light to the scented vapours of steam. Here, the only draped figure was one of a group displayed on a dais between pillars. On a sculptured couch, a golden-faced Zeus lay entwined with two painted boys of exquisite beauty. The position they had been given was unambiguous.

Round the rest of the room were real couches, on which lay supine figures, sometimes alone, sometimes under the kneading hands or glove of a masseur, also naked. One man was in the care of his barber. The bowls and hones and razors stood on a folding table: he was having his nails pared, lying relaxed with one wrist extended, the other hand behind his dyed yellow head. On the adjoining couch, a friend was being carefully oiled by his servant from stoppered bottles of aloes and musk.

The men were courtiers: Nicholas recognised some of them. Their bodies wore last season's sunburn, worn to a pale and uniform sienna from brow to heel, without interruption. A few had light scars, and several bore the pink marks of weals, but not, he thought, from fighting. When he came in, only one or two glanced up, and then only briefly. The rest paid no attention.

Then he saw the boys. They were all young, between ten and fourteen, and well bred, or else well tutored. They didn't appear to be slaves. There was nothing untoward, either, in their behaviour. Sometimes one shared a couch with an older man, either in silence or in gentle discourse, the treble voice muted. Man and boy did not touch save on greeting; and then with the most discreet of caresses. Sometimes the children were occupied with each other. He noticed two such, sprawled on the smooth marble intaglio which reflected the brightness of their bodies. They had a stone board between them, and were moving pieces across it. Like the pieces, one was dark and one was fair. The younger, an exquisite child with raven hair to his shoulders, was unfamiliar. The other was the beautiful boy who had carried the Imperial bow. Neither looked at him or at Pagano Doria who, he now saw, was standing observing him.

That was nothing. The men of the *Ciaretti* were glad to slough off their lice-ridden shirts and stiff doublets and tunics and lounge at ease, bare in the warmth of the cabin. Swimming, exercising, in sleep, they made nothing of it. There was no secret about how men were made. But Doria stood like a stag, his shoulders wide, his palms on his buttocks, and studied him at leisure. Nicholas returned the gaze, for he admired a well-made man, and Doria was that. In the lustrous, thickly lashed eyes was a mockery of adulation, with behind it something possibly genuine. Dislike, for example.

Doria spoke. His voice, in Italian, was lazy. "The boys are never unkind and, indeed, enjoy successes not easily managed. If nothing will serve, then ask them to show you the mosaics. The man who set these on the walls could rouse a corpse to its knees." He spoke, without changing his attitude, between measured breaths. His gaze, gently derisive, transmitted other impressions: of effrontery and assurance and abundant virility. Unblushingly, he had let himself quicken.

"I see it suits you," said Nicholas. His voice shook and steadied. Not the moment for stricken laughter. He could not even feel confident of turning his back. And as if it were not enough, the black-haired boy was coming towards him. Nicholas waited, and said in a calm voice. "My young lord, excuse me." The sweat ran down his body and his skin itched and shivered. He wondered if anyone could construe that as excitement.

The boy said, in Greek, "We are desirous of pleasing."

Before he could answer, Nicholas felt a wet hand touch his shoulder. Doria stood close beside him. He moved, and the hand slid off. Doria said to the child, "We are not all born of boors. What do they call you?"

His name was Anthimos. It was a Greek name, but not a Comneni one. A younger son, perhaps, of good but impoverished birth. The boy had soft lips and blue eyes and pale, smooth limbs like a bird. He looked up gravely, and placed delicate fingers at Doria's waist, where Doria caught and flattened them.

What use to interfere? The boy and the short, handsome man faded into the steam until only one taut shape could be seen, and then none. Remotely, there came a sudden squeal of wet feet, and Doria's voice laughed on a rising pitch. An attendant, hitherto unobserved, spoke sharply into the fog, "If you please, my lord. There are cubicles." Still, no one had looked round.

Nicholas stood where he had been left, feeling ill. If there was anything explicit about his condition, it must be the deadly absence of all desire to be where he was. Yet the other boy now came before him.

The bow-carrier. Once, an emperor had given the post to a baker's son. This was a different matter: a youth of perhaps fourteen years, who knew, as the other child had barely known, exactly what he was about. He had last seen him emerging from the Chrysokephalos, dressed in white silk, with the consecration prayer of the Eucharist still echoing in the purified air. His hair still smelt of incense, although he was bare except for the paint. He lifted arched brows over long, dripping lashes and said, "I have lost my partner. I am Alexios. Will you play with me, my lord?" His fingers, stealing out, proposed a playground. Nicholas trapped them carefully, as Doria had done, and tucking the boy's hand under his arm, bent and scooped up the board and the pieces.

"My friend," he said, "you have challenged a man who lays wagers with soothsayers. Show me the cubicles."

The boy's body was oiled. His pores, steamed open like those of a woman in childbirth, exuded sweet scents. Whatever he looked at, his eyes trod the same intimate paths as his fingers. Leaving with him, Nicholas glanced through blurred eyes back at the room. The reclining men had not stirred. Only, on the plinth with the two painted boys, Zeus the Cloud-gatherer moved, and coaxed himself free and, turning his great, golden mask, looked thoughtfully after him. And through the steam the smell of incense, again, made itself known.

Outside the cubicles, there was a eunuch. Well, that was no surprise. What was surprising was the boy's sudden halt. The boy said, "It isn't time."

"My lord," said the servant. He was addressing the boy, Nicholas saw. "My lord, I have orders."

The youth walked forward. He leaned over and, taking the man's fleshy upper arm between finger and thumb, pinched it viciously. The man drew in his breath with a hiss, but stayed where he was. Nicholas said, "Alexios? Who are you?"

The boy turned, the expression of discontent vanishing. The eunuch said, "My lord Alexios is the nephew of the great lord the Emperor. I have the Emperor's orders to take you to other chambers. My young lord will excuse us."

"Like this?" Nicholas said.

Wordlessly, the eunuch had turned. From the curtained stall at his side, he withdrew and shook out a loose folded garment and held it for Nicholas to assume. It was of cotton, he thought, and clung to his damp body, making him shiver. The eunuch, kneeling, closed the loops that fastened it from the ground up to his throat. "I should have done that," said the boy; and gave a glorious smile.

Nicholas said, "You haven't earned it yet. It's the prize for winning three boardgames."

"There are other games," said the boy.

"No doubt," said Nicholas mildly, "but I don't play them." The last he saw of Alexios, as he followed the eunuch out of the steam, was a lissom figure hugging itself and looking after him in part annoyance, part puzzlement.

The passage led to another, and then a series which became dryer and grander and eventually, he guessed, took him back to one of the lower courts of the Palace. He asked nothing and the eunuch was silent. The mark on the man's arm was dusky red, with a line of blood where the nail had pierced through. Whatever was about to happen, the range of possibilities was not large. He was Florentine consul, and life and limb were not in danger. Unless, of course, he met someone who did more than pinch when frustrated.

When they came at length to a door, he was hardly surprised when the eunuch scratched and, setting it open, left him to enter and face the occupant of the room himself. It was Violante, the Emperor's great-niece. He said, "You missed my Prostration."

"I thought I had prevented it," she said. She wore her robe of ceremony and her diadem, and was seated in the same heavy chair she had used when on shipboard, with her servants about her. To one side, as on shipboard, was the black-robed figure of the Archimandrite Diadochos. Everyone was fully clothed but himself. Inside his single garment the sweat trickled down his wet skin and, but for the cotton, would have pooled at his bare feet. She added, "We have embarrassed you? I am sorry. I have been instructed by the Emperor to present you with a mark of his favour, that is all. It is here."

It was a velvet-covered box which, when opened, proved to contain two manuscripts, one on top of the other. He put in his hands and unwrapped the first from the cloth which held it together. It was unbound and very old. He opened it carefully, and then stopped at what he saw. The lady said, "Sit and turn the pages. I want you to see what you have."

The Greek was hard to make out, but not the diagrams. Nicholas said, "Who wrote this, Despoina?"

"You know what you have?" she said.

"A book of automata. Of machines. Yes," he said.

"Could you make them?"

"Yes, highness," he said.

"I think you probably could," said Violante of Naxos. "It is a book of mechanical devices, written many generations ago by an engineer of Diyarbekr. I had it from my aunt, who married the lord Uzum Hasan. You will know. His family have been princes of Diyarbekr since before Timur the Lame."

"It is too precious. It is yours," Nicholas said.

"Then perhaps, some day, you will give me a copy," said Violante of Naxos. "Meanwhile, there is nothing that would please his magnificence the Emperor more than to have realised one or more of these devices. I have told him you will discuss it with him."

He hardly heard her, turning the pages. She said, "Messer Niccolò! Do you thank me?"

Then he looked up, his face burning. He said, "I lack the means, Despoina. This is truly generous."

She said, "Then look at the other. It is my payment for another length of the red and rose silk I have heard of. In return, I expect you to be generous."

He laid aside the book of drawings and picked up the other. After a moment he said, "Despoina: are there other books of this kind?"

"A great many," she said. "You have never heard of Gregorios Chionides? He was chief physician to one of the Emperor's forebears. He brought many such books back from Persia, and summarised them in Greek. We have a book on mathematics and clocks by Master Fusoris. And there are the philosophers. But I hardly expect that you ask on your own account. You wish to know if the Emperor would be willing to barter?"

"Our silks find favour with him, I notice," said Nicholas. "If he preferred other payment, the Medici would arrange it. Yes, I could sell such books in the West, bought or copied. But perhaps the Emperor has in mind a library of his own, and would prefer not to deplete it."

"As you say, they can be copied," observed the lady. She was sitting so still that the gems in her diadem hardly flashed. He gave up the books to be restored to their box and sat with his hands firmly clasped, quelling discomfort until the negotiation should be drawn to an end. For it was, of course, a negotiation. The Emperor had a menagerie, but no library, although he did, it seemed, have a storehouse of books in the Palace. They were short of silver, Doria had said. Were they short of funds? Surely not. Although their trading wealth, it was true, had yielded its cream these many years to the Genoese. During one of their ridiculous quarrels, the Genoese had threatened, unless better treated, to increase the duty on wine and salt to such a degree that the Emperor's subjects could no longer export wine to Caffa. The lady said, "What are you thinking, my damp Messer Niccolò?"

Nicholas said, "That with unrest beyond the mountains behind him, perhaps the Basileus will find it harder to collect the tolls and taxes from his people."

"Is it ever easy to pay tolls and taxes?" said the lady Violante. "True, the Empire is less than it was; certain wealthy families have always complained; the peasants are sly, and transform their wealth from corn into cattle. There is always someone to complain if a road is not maintained, or a route safeguarded from brigands, or a well allowed to fall into disrepair. But no. The Emperor exacts all he needs for the court and his palaces. We are not poor. We have gems. You can scotch the rumour, if you hear it, that the Greeks are too mean to pay mercenaries – you have been paid. Or will not spend money on defences – you have seen the walls. Trebizond endures. Even under Timur it endured and even prospered, while the Mongol horde took from Georgia the coat of mail forged by the hands of King David the psalmist himself."

Nicholas sat without speaking. Then he said, "Trebizond was a vassal state of the Mongols."

"But the Mongols have gone," the lady said. "The White Horde of Uzum Hasan will go too, or win all of Persia and sit in Tabriz or Diyarbekr, troubling no one. The Ottoman army will take one thing or another, but will always go back to its cities in Europe. Trebizond will continue." She paused. "Have I reassured you? I felt you uncertain."

"About what, Despoina?" Nicholas said. "I shall buy what books you can spare me. And if I am uncertain, it is only because I fear to keep the Emperor waiting."

He had heard the door open. Her eyes lifted, and some signal must have passed. She turned her eyes back to him. "He has awakened, and will see you. You will discuss al-Jazari."

"Al-Jazari?" he said.

"The engineer whose book you hold. And perhaps other devices. But I am told he will not expect you to stay long, in view of your illness."

"My illness?" he said.

"You became unwell in the baths. Otherwise you would have joined him immediately. He will understand. You are flushed. You sweat. Are you shivering?"

"I am undoubtedly shivering, Despoina," said Nicholas.

"Then you may leave," she said.

He rose, and bowed, and left, while a servant brought the box after him. There was no sign of his clothes; nor was he offered any means of improving his appearance. He gathered that the omission was not accidental. A chamberlain finally received him and introduced him by a small door into a room he thought at first empty. He was admiring the silk of its hangings when he saw the dais, and the bed, and the figure, loosely robed, reclining upon it. He felt, from the heat in his face, that he had probably assumed an appropriate flush. The Emperor said, "You may come a little nearer. There. You are unwell?"

"Forgive me, Basileus," Nicholas said. He rose from the prostration, but slowly. Upright, he allowed himself a quick glance before dropping his lids.

The pillows and sheets were of silk, much disordered. Uncovered, the Emperor's hair was seen to be of a light ruffled gold, paler by two or three shades than his beard. Below the heavy robe, the strong neck was bare. His hands, loosely clasped, were fine and massively ringed. The Emperor said, "Who has it in his power to command weakness? We do not blame you. We are told you make toys."

"I make engines for use and for pleasure. What is your wish?" Nicholas said.

"We should like a clock," said the Emperor of the Hellenes. "A clock such as the Persians had, for my palace. Will you make it?"

"Gladly, Basileus."

"You would make it gladly. We are pleased. We enjoy the company of light-hearted men, Messer Niccolò. You will bring us your plans for this clock. You will show us its progress."

Nicholas said, "Given health, I will come when the Basileus asks."

The figure on the bed stirred. "And meanwhile, are we so unapproachable? Is that the book? Bring it here."

It was possible that a discussion about al-Jazari was about to take place. Nicholas carried the book with care to the bed.

The Emperor said, "What is it? You are trembling, boy! What do they call you? Nikko? Niccolino?"

They were not going to discuss al-Jazari. Nicholas said, "My lord, it is dangerous. My complaint may pass to the Basileus unless we remain apart."

The noble face smiled. "We are not afraid," said the Emperor David. "The Turk claims to fear nothing, so sweet is his heaven. We make our heaven on earth, and it is worth some small risk. Come. Show me the devices and see, we shall put our hand on your shoulder.

It steadies you." The Emperor turned to his chamberlain and said, "We are busy. Return in an hour."

In a little under that time, Nicholas left. The chamberlain, summoned by bell, took him through many passages and into a booth where his clothes were. At first, he sat without dressing. Then a bath eunuch appeared, and came in and helped him, and started him on his way to the gates, with a page to carry the box.

Doria was there. Since they had separated in the bath house, Nicholas had forgotten him. Now he could see him ahead, strutting down through the Citadel grounds to where the Genoese suite, reduced by the dinner hour, waited to take its consul home. The Greek steward Paraskeuas held Doria's horse firmly. Mounted, he sat in the magnificent coat and smiled broadly as Nicholas walked up. Doria's face, a silvery pink, had slackened since early morning. He said, "And how, my lord consul, do you take to Byzantine customs? If you will keep them from the ears of my wife, I shall keep them from her mother your bedfellow. Some day, we have notes to compare."

"Indeed," said Nicholas. "Just think what Anthimos and Alexios are comparing at this moment."

Doria, he saw, had no qualms about what he had introduced him to. No qualms, and no doubts. The Genoese laughed, even while making a sound of reproof. He said, "What will our confessors say? Although your Godscalc appears to be liberal, as is wise in monastic communities. You look tired. You have done justice, then, to the occasion?"

The sweat, cooling in his hair and on his face, tickled his skin. Where he had been hot, now he was cold; and his clothes smelt of scent. "You should see the others," said Nicholas.

"Then until this afternoon," Doria said. "Wife or no wife, I propose now to go back and sleep. There are limits to what one should ask of oneself." He set his horse in motion, with languor, and led off downhill.

Nicholas watched him a moment. He remarked, "Famine and death go with you," and turned aside. Of the waiting Florentine escort, there were only a few men-at-arms and, of course, Loppe, preparing to ride with him back to the villa. The men at least had been out of earshot. Loppe, naturally, would have found out all there was to find out. The African came up and said, "How will you kill him?"

He forgot what he had been going to answer. "With kindness," said Nicholas. He took a shallow breath and produced a short speech. "We are due at the Meidan, the arena, this afternoon. I have some instructions for you. Between now and the festival, I want to see no one. Unless I send for him, no one. And especially not Master Tobie. Do you understand?"

Loppe said, "Master Julius can lead the company to the Meidan. It is only a festival."

"No," said Nicholas. "No. This is important."

Loppe was silent. He supposed Loppe knew, as he did, that Tobie would have to be sent for. But not for a while. Not so soon. Not until he had come to terms with the road that now lay before him; the aspect of merchant adventuring which was not what anyone had either promised him, or warned him against.

In the name of God and of profit, the trading ledger always began. In the name of God and of profit, naturally all things are permissible. All things. All things and kyrie eleison. God have mercy on us and our clients.

Chapter 20

"SWAMP FEVER," Tobie said. "You remember. He had it in the Abruzzi." Julius was the fifth person he had told since he promised Nicholas to tell no one. As a physician, Tobias Beventini operated an entirely personal code, with referrals to his own comfort, to the general good and, sometimes, to the benefit of whatever patient he had elected to cure. He was an excellent doctor.

"Swamp fever. On a hilltop," said Julius.

"Once you've had it, it comes back," said Tobie.

"It came back at the church, and you didn't notice it? Or when he returned from the Palace, you diagnosed it immediately? Or he just told you he had it?" said Julius.

Tobie said, "I didn't see him when he came back from the Palace. Loppe came for me half an hour ago. It's only just starting. He'll manage." He looked for support to Godscalc, eating placidly across the table. Julius in one of his moods was not going to be helpful. In an hour, the Charetty company, representing the Republic of Florence, had to present itself at the Meidan where music, dancing, feats of daring and skill would be presented for the Emperor's Easter entertainment. Among those taking part, by special request, would be the Charetty soldiers. The company's officials would be expected to hobnob with the officials and magnates of the region and with their fellow colonists. The company's leader would be required, on demand, to exchange courtesies with the Emperor and his household. The company's leader being Nicholas, who had returned from the Palace with a pulse like an anthill and his inner garments sodden with sweat. Tobie applied himself to his food, considering a number of things.

Julius brooded. "If the fever comes back with emperors, when will he be seized with it next? Or a sore throat, or a cold, or a stomach ache?"

Tobie raised his brows. "It's genuine," he remarked.

"I don't question it," Julius said. "I'm only saying that I watch out for the man who crumbles when stretched."

"Myself," observed Nicholas from the doorway, "I keep out of range of the fellow who snaps."

Tobie, who had suspected, from his experience of him, that Nicholas was not far away, applied himself diligently to his plate. He heard Nicholas pass, and felt a sharp rap on his shoulder.

"I'll speak to you later," said Nicholas. He sat down beside le Grant. "All right. I've prayed, and I think I'll be adequate if everyone's kind to me. You heard we got our concessions? A new fondaco, a consulate and a chapel. Two per hundred import duty, and nothing on exports. A safe conduct for all Florentine merchants, ships and goods, revocable only on six months' prior notice. Someone from the Palace is coming tomorrow to take delivery of some of our silks. I sent Loppe to tell you, so that you could draw up some plans. You've had time. What are they?" He stretched for the wine, got a glare from Tobie, and withdrew his hand. Julius, pausing, began to answer him. His face was full of suspicion. Tobie continued to eat, with one eye on his patient.

He didn't look particularly sick. In the past year, his growth had ceased, confirming him as a tall man, and well proportioned. Training at the crucial time had shaped and hardened the muscles accustomed only to heavy manual labour. Something else had stripped the puppy flesh from his face. The framework was the same: the broad brow, the wide jaw with its blunt chin and full lips. But its width was now defined by cheekbones which cast their own shadow, and matched the thin, inquisitive nose. It was a face you could no longer be sure of reading – if, indeed, you ever could.

A layman, surveying him now, would see little except perhaps an enhanced colour and an extra brightness of eye. The priest Godscalc was not only a trained apothecary with battle experience, but had seen Nicholas in the same state before. He turned his eyes from patient to doctor and spoke in the mildest of undertones. "What did you give him?"

Tobie grinned. "What he asked for. Something to stop him up at both ends and keep him on his feet until evening. It'll do it, too. Afterwards, of course, he'll wish he'd never been born."

"He means to go to the Meidan?" Godscalc said. "Why? Something to do with Catherine, the girl?"

"I don't see it," said Tobie. "She's still mad for her husband. I can't imagine why Nicholas shouldn't stay quietly here having the flux while the rest of us represent Florence. Perhaps he thinks Julius and Astorre are not to be trusted near Doria. Perhaps – I don't know. He's remarkably vague – so is Loppe – about what kept them so long at the Palace. Apart, that is, from the formalities and a few words with the Genoese consul. It seems – as we suspected – that Doria stole a march on us by selling fast under Genoese privileges. Julius was most disappointed when I told him that was all Doria had done. He expected open warfare between him and Nicholas."

"They didn't quarrel?" said Godscalc.

"Surprised?" Tobie said. "It was you, after all, who lectured Nicholas on Christian charity. No. I gather there was a deal of provocation, but Nicholas didn't respond. He's good at that, as I remember. He'll go on accepting whatever anyone cares to load on to him, and then . . . my God, look out."

"For what?" Godscalc said, a little too quickly.

Tobie said, "For what you might find in your soup. But that was before he had you to advise him."

Godscalc didn't reply. Tobie, who disliked being stared at, was moved to elaborate. "I do respect the cloth, of course, but sometimes I think a good clean killing has a lot to commend it. Or, at worst, a proper legal complaint. Something, surely, could be proved against Pagano Doria. The ship fire. The runaway marriage. Something deficient, for example, in his papers, his ledgers, his ownership of the *Doria*?"

He thought the priest wasn't going to answer that either. Then Godscalc said, "Well, here are two reasons against taking such action. Whoever harms or discredits Doria is going to earn that girl's hatred to the end of his life and may not even do her a service. I suspect that Nicholas has misread that marriage. And secondly, the power to destroy such a man should, I think, be put at present out of his reach. He is too young."

"Too young?" said Tobie.

Godscalc said, "I realise you know something I don't. But the boy's mistakes are what fashion the man of good sense and humility. Provided he doesn't repeat them."

So Nicholas had not confided in Godscalc, and the priest had thought fit, at last, to admit it. He was a shrewd man. Some of the things he had said, Tobie had already, on his own, half-perceived. None of them had to do with legal justice. Godscalc's concern, he understood, was with human character: with Catherine, with Nicholas and with the course their lives were to take.

Tobie was sufficiently struck to make a decision. After the Meidan, Julius consenting, he proposed to admit Father Godscalc to the limited circle of those who knew exactly what the misadventures of the boy Nicholas had been. They needed another watchdog. Invigilated by a physician, a priest and a notary, Nicholas would surely be fettered at last.

The Meidan used for the Easter festival was an oblong tract of ground, level from east to west, but sloping a little from south to north in the direction of the sea, which could be seen from its porticoes. It was outside the city walls. Across the ravine to its west stood the City and Palace. Further west, beyond the other ravine, was a level area bigger still which served as a Tzucanisterion, where the court engaged in curious ball games involving massed riders and mallets. The only other venue for spectacles was a small area to the south of the Palace, used for camel-wrestling, pig-beating and events of a circumscribed nature, such as heading, strangling and the cutting of limbs. The generations of the Comneni, esconced in their misty sea empire, had given much thought to the uses of leisure.

The eastern Meidan was traditional to this yearly celebration for several reasons. Normally the place of a market, it stood above the foreign quarter. The streets which wound from its galleries down to the sea passed the villas, the stables, the storehouses, the churches and the enclosures of the western merchants. The Meidan was diagonally uphill from the Venetian palace, and directly above the Leoncastello of the Genoese.

This was all to the point, since one of the objects of the celebration was to impress the citizens of Western cultures. Byzantium, once proud to call itself Rome, now regarded Rome as beneath it. Other potentates, nearer at hand, must also be reminded of the splendour and might of the Emperor, who held high the flame that Constantinople in her weakness had surrendered. And beyond the balconies, the cushioned benches, the barriers, were the people, who must have their festival, paid for by their generous ruler who, on this day of the year, could be seen sitting godlike among them, with his Empress and his heirs. A great deal of money, each year, was spent on the Meidan at Easter.

It was customary for all those with places to walk there, climbing by lesser streets to free the processional way. Up this steep street, laid with mats and sweet-scented leaves, lined with townspeople behind the glittering ranks of the Guard, would ride the Imperial family. The family would occupy the villa balconies hung with cloth of gold and spring garlands which fronted the upper side of the Meidan. Flanking galleries would serve the Household and the Patriarchal Court with its icons. Below, at ground level, tiered and cushioned benches had been erected for the foreign merchants, the Greek princes, the clergy.

Ushers with wands greeted and placed every party. Tobie, judging it nicely, got his medicated young man and his fellows up the hill rather late, but still well before the Emperor's entry. Loppe, sent on ahead to ensure and locate their half-dozen seats, stood erect by the Florentine flag with the absence of expression on his handsome black face which was, with Loppe, a sign of contentment. His eyes were fixed on Nicholas, who still had to cross the width of the Meidan. Nicholas said, "Tobie. Unless I'm giving off steam, behave normally. I remember what to do. One foot in front of the other, but not both at the same time unless I'm a robin."

He was wearing the Emperor's coat, with a light feathered hat, and embroidered gloves on his hands. These were part of the trousseau which had been among their first purchases. Godscalc and Julius, although attired in the black of their profession, had robes of a finer cut and quality than any they had formerly owned; Tobie smouldered in physicians' scarlet, and Astorre and le Grant wore chestnut velvet over dun silken doublets. An investment, Nicholas had said. A tailor had appeared, who had cut the clothes and had them sewn in his workshop. The lady Violante, Tobie suspected, had made a good case for spending a lot of their capital quickly. He made to rub his bald head, and was baulked by his cap with its lappets. He made sure that Nicholas was still not only conscious but talking, and looked about for other parties of merchants.

They were all, like themselves, on the upper side of the Meidan, in the shadow of the Imperial balconies. On his left, the Lion of St Mark pointed to the place of the Venetian Bailie, whom Nicholas had visited two days before, or so Julius said. Further on his left, the red cross of St George identified the Genoese. All Tobie could see was a posy of headgear. He said to Loppe, whose duty it was to stand behind them, "Can you see Doria? Or the demoiselle's daughter?"

Nicholas said, "I asked him. He says they're both here. And the dog."

"What dog?" said Tobie; but Nicholas was talking across le Grant to Astorre. Godscalc's eye, he saw, disapproved of the subject. To hell with Godscalc. A change in the noise made him turn.

The sky was clearing. A hazy light from the west illuminated the arena and the buildings beyond it, their flat roofs descending like shelves, green with creeper and potted laurels and borders of rosemary and patches of white garments drying. Beyond the roofs was the sea, stretching grey-blue to the horizon, and the Crim Tartars, and Muscovy. As he watched, its surface became lighter in tone, and acquired shadows and sparkle. The sun was about to emerge, and heat Nicholas.

The sun was about to emerge, and so was the Emperor. The noise was cheering, which had been going on for some time, but was now much increased. Along with it were other sounds: of marching feet and hooves and trumpets, of cymbals and drums and the tinny snore, rising and falling, of portable organs. The sea wind, mixed with salt and fish, sweat and ordure and woodsmoke, brought with it suddenly the scent of horseflesh, and a waft of bruised herbs and aloes and the queer, strident note of opoponax. Nicholas, who had been talking beside him, unaccountably stopped. Then, between the buildings on the lower side of the Meidan, the first of the procession reached the top of the slope and led the way towards them, across the soft bran of the enclosure, making for the pillared entrance of the villa which was to be the Emperor's box, his *kathisma*.

The icon led the way, as before. Behind, as in Constantinople the All-Happy City, came the elders dressed in red brocade, followed by young men in white and then by slim youths in green tunics and buskins. They walked erect, and quickly, passing through the gate of the barrier from sunshine to shadow, and then up the passage between the merchants' benches. One of the boys, turning an exquisite profile, broke into a smile at the sight of Nicholas and almost paused. He had close-curled hair of a classical fairness, and Tobie had seen him somewhere before. He said, "Who is that?"

Nicholas turned his head. "His name is Alexios," he said.

"They're all called Alexios," said Tobie.

"It just seems like that," Nicholas said. "Anyway, they all have quite different flavours."

It made less sense than usual, but that was to be expected. In any case, here were the servants with their ranks of gold axes, the eunuchs in white; the young guards with their breastplates and shields and spears covered with gold. Then the princes in cloth of gold, the chiefs each holding a golden rod; the rest with swinging gold censers. Then the pages. Then the Emperor, on his horse caparisoned in scarlet and gold, with the Empress and her train following after.

The Vice-Regent of God on Earth still wore his high golden crown, but another long tailored robe, of cloth of gold woven with jewels, and sewn with blocks and ribbons of goldsmith work, set with pictures and gems. The sun, losing at that moment the last of its veils, made of him suddenly a dazzling artefact, with his spun-gold beard and moustache no less bright than his dress. Only his face, pinkly powdered, half severe, half smiling at nothing, was that of a man, bathed and well fed and just risen from a couch on which he has not lain alone. Behind him, the Empress turned her beautiful, tinted face from side to side, to be seen, but not to respond. If she observed the Florentine banner, or the Genoese, she gave no sign but passed on, riding serenely. Among the ladies walking behind her, Violante of Naxos also ignored the Florentine flag, and her pupil. Which was just as well, Tobie thought. He has enough to contend with.

Then the Imperial party filled the balconies, and were seated; and the trumpets blew; and the Patriarch blessed the proceedings; and a master of ceremonies stepped on the bran and delivered a long and elaborate speech which the Emperor acknowledged and the crowd, chanting, repeated. *O God, protect the Emperor, protect the Magistrates, protect the children born in the purple. Mother of God, may the Empire be filled with joy* ... Then his Imperial majesty raised his hand, and the entertainment began.

It had been a long time since Tobie, a cynical man, had been made to sit through a spectacle. His uncle, physician to dukes, attended them as a matter of course. His uncle took jesters for granted, and jugglers, and men who swallowed fire and crossed high-slung wires pushing wheelbarrows with pretty girls in them. Tobie had watched such things as a student, but seldom since. It was a long time since he had seen boy and girl acrobats, nude as Christmas cadavers in the anatomy class, and with the spangles in just the same places. Unlike the cadavers, they wound their heads through their legs and walked on their hands and rolled themselves into hoops and bowled round the arena.

Thick men with high cheekbones stood arm in arm and made the base of a pyramid that climbed above the high wire, and then threw boys and girls to each other. Men wearing animal furs and false faces achieved terrible jokes with pigs' bladders and the genitalia of oxen and billy goats. Children dressed in white silk and flowers danced in circles and sang. Country folk performed stamping dances to the whine of the bagpipes, and a line of Circassian girls in boots and long skirts swayed to music, Greek-linked by the arms in a living key pattern, to the sound of a drum. Two wrestlers, oiled, in leather breeches, fought until one of them died and the Emperor stood, while the corpse was drawn off, to signal that an interval had been declared, since emperors, like everyone else, must eat and make water.

A mule, its neck beribboned, dragged on a cart of salt fish, and two boys running beside it threw handfuls, for nothing, into the crowds behind the barriers. The Emperor's gift. The cart stayed on the north side of the Meidan, since everyone knew that merchants and princes would make their own dispositions. They were correct. Loppe, moving at last, had produced a hamper which, laid on the ground by the bench, proved to be packed with cakes and chicken and cooked beans and fruit paste and hazelnuts. There were also wine flasks, with six good metal beakers. Last of all, he lifted out and delivered to Tobie an extra flask which contained nothing but water. His eyes asked a question.

Nicholas was talking, again, to Astorre. Tobie put a hand on his shoulder and turned him round. Tobie said, "All right. I think that's enough, don't you? Slip out now while the Emperor's gone."

Nicholas sounded normal. In looks, he had become particularly vivid. His hair, now soaking, had curled up like unravelled wool. He said, "Don't bully; Astorre would never forgive me. They're going to put on a shooting display."

Tobie knew that. He had also known that, by divine agency, the display was bound to occur in the second half and not in the first. He said, "Astorre isn't stupid. He knows what fever is like. Look. The Genoese are far away. Julius won't cause any trouble. If most of the rest of us stay, the Emperor won't even notice. You've come, you've been seen. What are you waiting for?"

"To be conquered. You're losing your chicken," Nicholas said. Tobie stared at him, and then down. It was true. A terrier had its head in their basket. It wore a gold collar. He lifted it up by it. "Willequin," Nicholas said. The little dog dangled, choking irritably.

"Willequin!" said a girl sharply. Tobie knew who it was before he

turned round. Catherine de Charetty, dressed like a courtesan. Or
no. That was not strictly true. But her pretty, reddish brown hair
hung in ringlets over her cheeks, and her earrings dangled on
shoulders bare enough to make Tobie, in heated vermilion, briefly
envious. Her gown was of silk, and her face was prettily painted. She
seized the dog. "You could have killed him! My mother shall hear of
it."

Nicholas turned. "If you like, I'll tell her," he said. "I have a
letter to answer."

Doria was standing behind her. He, too, wore his robe of honour
and also his chain. He said, "If Willequin is safe, take him to your
seat, sweetheart. You can speak to your stepfather later."

Now they had all turned: Julius simmering, le Grant with calm
curiosity, Astorre with his beard at its most frightening angle.
Godscalc, Tobie saw, looked uneasy. Catherine looked at none of
them. Clutching the dog, she was examining Nicholas. She said,
"Your hair's wet, like when you had marsh fever. Have you got it
again?"

So much for their painstaking precautions. Nicholas said, "Yes.
And if you don't want it, you'd better stay clear. How are you,
Catherine?"

She was already turning away. She said, "Don't speak. You
shouldn't be here. That's wicked. You'll give it to Willequin too. I
don't want your fever."

"I don't much want it either," Nicholas said. "Did you take
Willequin to the Empress?"

She had retreated, already, to the far benches, but could not resist
turning to answer. She said, "Did you see me? I've been presented.
I'm to go to the Palace next week. The Greeks love my dog. They
call him Rim-Papa."

It was one of the standard insults, Greek to Westerner. Nicholas
said, without change of voice, "If I were you, I'd keep him indoors.
There's a lot of fever about. I like your earrings."

It lifted the frown, for a moment. Then she said, "You ought to
go home," and went off resentfully to her seat. Julius, standing,
made to follow, but found his way blocked by the priest.

Doria, smiling, had watched the small scene without moving.
Then he turned and viewed Nicholas. Sympathy glowed in his face.
"Poor lad. Was the Palace too much? I've heard of bath house
infections, but swamp fever rarely figures among them. Or was it
Alexios whose arts so depleted you?"

He spoke quite openly, if in Italian. There was enough noise,
perhaps, to deter an eavesdropper. The crowd, becoming impatient,
were beginning to chant; beguiling their Basileus into ending his
repast. The phrases were Byzantine: "Arise, Imperial Sun! Arise!
Appear!"

"None of your whores," said Doria, "has had quite the advantages of Alexios. Nor, I must admit, have more than one or two of mine, that I can remember. Of either kind."

The implication, conveyed thus in public, struck Tobie's stomach like rotten food. Astorre lifted his half-regrown eyebrows: boys will be boys. Le Grant's face had hardly changed. But Godscalc and Julius stood motionless.

Pagano Doria smiled at them all, and then returned the warm gaze upon Nicholas. He said, "You didn't tell them! Well, of course, I didn't boast of my Anthimos to young Catherine. But one's men friends, I should have thought, would be envious." He turned his gaze to the priest. "Unless, of course, you had the pleasure, under seal, of a description. I reminded him of the generous flexibility of your views. And indeed, if you had seen this breathing boy-angel . . ."

The noise of the crowd had increased. "Lord! Lord! Protected by God!"

"You have a letter of mine," Nicholas said. The hectic colour had drained from his face, except over the cheekbones. He showed no other emotion. Staring at him, Tobie thought: he hasn't denied it. It's provable, then. He never expected Doria to confront him with it, but Doria knows he's probably safe. Neither can afford to tell the other man's wife.

He thought what it would be like, writing a letter to Marian de Charetty in Bruges. *Madam, I have to tell you that your apprentice husband is sleeping with bath boys.* Except that the boy who had walked past just now, glistening with jewels, had been the bath boy of no ordinary man. And Nicholas? Nicholas, owned by the Devil, was speaking instead of some letter.

Doria said, as if in echo, "A letter?" He was in no haste to serve Nicholas in any way. He was enjoying himself.

Nicholas spoke again. The informed ear, listening, could hear, every now and then, the slipshod word that betrayed Tobie's drugs. "You had a letter from the lady my wife. I came to receive it." (Basileus! Sovereign of the Romans!)

Understanding dawned on the handsome face. "So that was why you struggled here, away from your pot and your bucket! Poor lad. Of course you must have it."

He made no movement. "Then?" said Nicholas. Behind, a trumpet blew. Men were standing. Wooed by his people, the Elect of God had returned to his kathisma at last.

Doria said, "Ah, how unfortunate. I must take my seat. Some other day, when you are fit?"

Nicholas stood. Cymbals clashed, and clear notes sounded, in unison, from other trumpets. Along all the benches men were kicking baskets aside, and gathering cloaks and getting properly to their feet.

Among them, Nicholas was hardly noticed as he put out one hand and took Doria's upper arm in his grip.

It might have been a parting gesture, except that the grip stayed; and Doria exclaimed as if in pain. He said, "Let me go, my young Flemish lout, or I shall call over an usher."

"Call," said Nicholas. "But first give me the letter." His hand, weakening, slid from its grasp as he spoke. But as Godscalc had placed himself before Julius, so now three grim-faced men of the Charetty company stood between Doria and the way to his seat.

He looked in turn at them all, eyebrows lifted in amusement. "My dear boy, if it matters so much, of course you shall have your precious letter. I thought to make it the prize for some small, congenial task, but I see you haven't the strength to compete for it. I shall have to rely on your men. Let us say, my dear Niccolino, that if one of your men performs a service for me this day, then you shall have the letter forthwith. If not, it will have to wait for another occasion. Is it so terrible? It has been months on its journey already. Everyone who can read it has done so. May I pass?"

It was Godscalc who said, with cold dislike, "Indeed you may," and used his bulk to deter Astorre and Julius from following. Doria bowed from the passage and left. He was only just in time: the Basileus had entered the box.

Astorre said, "I'll have to go. Are ye all right?"

"Go. Good luck," Nicholas said. He didn't waste effort, Tobie was glad to see, in attempting to answer the question.

Godscalc said, "What does he mean, perform a service?"

"I can't imagine," said Nicholas. Sitting, he had spread a hand over his face. The fever had risen: his face was inflamed with it, and between his fingers his eyes were dry and bright. He made an effort. "I mean, I don't know. It's a letter to me from the demoiselle. The Genoese merchants were holding it. He told me this morning."

"In the bath house," said Julius.

Godscalc said, "Never mind all that now. They're putting the pole up. That's for Astorre and the shooting?"

"Yes," said Nicholas. Two passaging fingers came to a definite halt at the root of his nose. He dropped them. "Astorre."

"No," Godscalc said. "Astorre and I had a short conversation before he left to join the men. Nothing will happen to Pagano Doria."

"Why not?" said Julius.

No one answered him.

Chapter 21

SOMETIMES TOBIAS BEVENTINI was moved to wonder how Julius ever managed to become a member of the Italian notariate. At others, recalling his energy and his exploits, he accepted that it was simply a fact that Julius now and then quite enjoyably lost his head. On this occasion, once convinced of the unsuitability of murdering the Genoese ambassador in full view of the Basileus and people of Trebizond, Julius consented, fuming, to sit. It was as well, for the second half of the celebration was about to begin.

Tobie was not unsympathetic to Julius. He recognised that between Julius and his former apprentice there existed a special relationship that no one else shared except, perhaps, Astorre. At times, irritatingly, Nicholas would decide to side with his notary, as over the case of Paraskeuas. Julius seldom returned the compliment, although he had once taken the trouble to save Nicholas from drowning. Why? From simple humanity? Bravado? Respect for the company property? All three, very likely. Julius still regarded Nicholas, with detached pride, as his protégé.

And how, then, did Nicholas regard Julius? On the surface, with the broad affection he gave to the world. But below the surface, it seemed, there were hidden currents. Tobie had experienced none of them, but then he was not Julius. The guarded, sardonic sparring in which Tobie and Nicholas sometimes engaged arose from wariness on both sides, however it might sometimes soften. Nicholas was not wary of Julius: he knew him too well. It did not occur to Tobie, as it had once to Marian de Charetty, that he was jealous of Julius.

Now, sitting still on his bench, Tobie considered what he had just heard, and tried to fit it into the gaping mosaic that was his reconstruction, so far, of the working interior of Nicholas. He suspected Godscalc was doing the same, Nicholas today being refreshingly vulnerable to unscrupulous men. It would tax a fit man to explain away the sort of lapses Doria had hinted at, never mind the missing letter which no one had heard of. To obtain the letter was, of course, his reason for coming here. Again, Nicholas had lied to conceal it.

The gate at the far end of the arena had opened and Astorre and Thomas had entered, leading the Charetty troops, and flanked by the trumpets and drums from the ship. They were mounted. The horses were Turkish, bought on their arrival, and dressed with harness brought with them from Flanders. Instead of plate armour, the men were dressed this time in fine leather tunics under sleeveless garments made of blue camlet. Across each chest was an embroidered baldric carrying a long quiver of arrows. Each man carried a curve-horned cavalry bow and the faces, though grave, were brown and confident. The musicians separated, four to each side, and after the squadron lined up and bowed to the box, the drums set up a brisk rhythm and the horsemen set off at the trot.

Formation riding was something that most troops learned to do for their employers: princes liked to impress other princes, and it was a useful item for feasts and victories. Performed on sloping ground with new horses, it demanded some skill. This they had, hammered into them by Astorre, who had emerged from the womb ready-mounted. Trick-riding the Emperor had already seen, and this they did not try to copy. But as the files crossed and recrossed, man passing man without pause or mistake to the lilt of the music, the decent orderliness of it all impressed as much as the skill: the spectators started to cheer, and the faces of the riders, still intent, were less grave. That was the beginning.

Bits of it Tobie had already seen. Astorre had done some of this last year in Italy. The shooting, which came next, was something Tobie had tried his hand at. A bird or a bladder, placed on top of a pole, was shot at by circling riders: shot from the normal position and again, the marksman twisting round after passing. The Persians and Turks made an art of it, and it had been taken up by the soldiers who fought them. It took a quick eye and fine horsemanship and it was dangerous. Deflected arrows could kill as well as deliberate ones. The archers wore helmets, but only leather over their shoulders.

It was a feat well worth watching. The music kept them to measure, and then, towards the end, increased its beat so that the horsemen looping the pole glinted like fish on the turn. The last chord came, the last arrow flew to its mark, and Astorre, inflated with triumph, pointed his stiff left arm and his barb and his beard to the skies and launched an arrow, not to the pole, but to the cloudy heaven of the favouring gods.

It fell, not among gods, but on the peopled top slope of the Meidan. Straight as a shaft from Apollo, it whistled down to the long rows of seats where the merchants were. Where the flag of St George drooped, it landed. Many gasped, but only one person screamed. It was a man's voice, and unrecognisable. The cry ended in bubbling breath. Whoever had received Astorre's arrow had died of it.

Everyone had jumped up. No, not everyone. Beside Tobie, Nicholas

sat without moving, his new gloves set on his knees, and his gaze on
his gloves. He said, "Who?"

Julius was smiling. He said, "Guess."

Nicholas said, "*Christ in heaven!*" in a meticulous whisper that
threatened like gunfire.

Julius flinched, as he had at Modon, and then, recovering, swore.
"Can't you imagine? I saw him myself, sitting two rows to the back of
Doria, as smug as a priest. It was the seaman. The filthy murderer
who started the fire for Doria and then got away to the cog. Astorre
couldn't miss him when he lined up to bow to the Emperor. He
recognised him, and did what I would have done. Any of us. By God,
he gave him his fee for the fire!"

Nicholas said, "I should have thought of that."

"How could you?" said Godscalc. "You didn't see him."

John le Grant turned his red head. He said, "He means he ought to
have thought that's what Doria meant. The little service. Captain
Astorre has performed the service Doria wanted. That is it, surely?"

He had a sensible face, with blue eyes with sandy lashes, and a head
that treated every problem as if it were soluble by plain mathematics.
Tobie said, "That *is* it. Doria brought the man for no other reason. If
Astorre didn't kill him, I suppose Julius would have done it."

"I should hope so," Julius said. "He and his fire did for three men
in Modon."

"And now he can never implicate Pagano Doria. What about
Astorre?" Tobie said. "The fool left Doria alone, but he's still killed a
Genoese in front of the Emperor." He saw, as he spoke, a swirl of
movement in the Emperor's box. Someone had been sent on some
mission. At the same time, the upheaval within the Genoese benches
was lessening. Men with a stretcher appeared, and began to make their
way over. Doria himself was now visible. Once, he turned and Tobie
saw the glance he threw to them all. Under the seemly appearance of
grief, there was the glitter of mischief.

Nicholas said, "The Emperor wants the protection of Astorre and
his men. So does Doria. I'd guess we'll be asked to pay compensation,
and that will be the end of it. And, of course, I'll get my letter."

Of course. As soon, thought Tobie, as the stretcher goes, and the
Charetty company march themselves off, and the next performer
prepares to take the arena. He saw all that happen, and Doria actually
rise to come over, but the Imperial messenger reached Nicholas first.
Immediately, the Florentine consul was to appear before the Vice-
Regent of God on his balcony.

Tobie looked at the Florentine consul and Nicholas looked damply
back. He appeared to have accepted the summons. It was probably,
Tobie thought, no worse a prospect than the censure he must know
awaited him back at the villa. Tobie said, "Take Godscalc. He can't
object to that."

"No," said Nicholas. "I expect it will be all right." He got up.

Julius said, "Of course it will be all right. Your friend Alexios will be there. I remember him. He's the Emperor's nephew."

Nicholas glanced at him. Under his eyes, the skin had thinned and darkened since morning. "Pagano's boy was well born as well. Caesar's boys, Caesar's bidding."

Julius said, "The Emperor offered the young men of his family to you and Doria?"

Praise God, he spoke in Flemish, as Nicholas had done. Whatever language he spoke, it was blasphemy. Tobie drew in his breath, but Nicholas answered with hardly a pause. "Doria would like you to think so. He went off with the lad, but was given a substitute."

Godscalc spoke. "And you?"

"Not the Emperor's nephew," Nicholas said. "No." From the pitch of his gaze, he was calculating how far he had to walk. The Imperial messenger waited, resenting the barbarian tongue.

"Who?" said Julius.

"Who did Alexios take me to? To the Emperor," Nicholas said. "You might have guessed. I had all the right qualifications. He was most distressed over my fever, and he won't be in the least harsh. I don't need Godscalc. I told you."

Tobie watched him climb the steps. He did so quite successfully. In a while they saw him appear on the balcony beside Amiroutzes, who paced with him to the Emperor's couch and withdrew. The Emperor's face, turned to Nicholas, contained more animation than was his habit: but whether from anger or the opposite was impossible, at that distance, to say. Courtesy demanded that they pay some attention to the next event, which made much use of braziers and firebrands. At the end of it, Nicholas rejoined them, walking alone. He looked slightly drunk. Instead of sitting down, he said, "That's all right. Astorre will come to no harm. I have leave to go. Will someone . . ."

The bench rattled under his hand. Tobie, rising, made a doctor's automatic assessment. "I'll take you. Godscalc?"

Godscalc said, "Wait. The letter. Let me get it." He moved away. Nicholas stood looking after him. Tobie said, "You got immunity for Astorre? Was it difficult?"

Nicholas said, "Doria is coming himself. Difficult? No. They'd just had news. The Turkish army is massing at Bursa, and the Sultan himself is in Ankara. The Emperor needs Astorre."

Tobie said, "The Turks are making for Trebizond?"

"I don't suppose so," said Nicholas. "But the Emperor would still feel happier with Astorre. I gather I'm now to be favoured with my wife's letter?"

Pagano Doria stood before him, with an usher on either side. Godscalc came close. The perfect Doria teeth smiled between the cupid's bow of his lips. Doria said, "What can I say? A friend, murdered in daylight! As you see, the Emperor has sent his own escort in case I should lift my hand to you. Of course, I should never dream of it. I have your letter somewhere. A dull fellow, your Gregorio."

There was a pause. Nicholas said, "Gregorio? The letter you spoke of was from Marian de Charetty. My wife."

Doria tapped his nose with one finger. The letter, dirty and stringless, was screwed in the hand that uplifted his elbow. He said, "And you believed me? How naïve of you, Niccolino. No, I fear that the loving words of dear Marian, if you were expecting them, have fallen into other hands, or perhaps were never written. The letter I spoke of is from your lawyer Gregorio, with a modicum of old news from Bruges, and a quantity of poorly coded detail about market prices. Of minimal use, since he wrote you in January."

Someone moved. It was Loppe, Tobie saw. Nicholas himself stood perfectly still, although one hand grasped the bench. He said, "I will have it, then."

"Of course," said Doria. "But first, there is one item of news . . . Wait." Unfolding his arms, he straightened and shuffled the shabby pages. "Yes. A piece of good news to please all of you. My lord Simon of Kilmirren has got a child of his body at last. His new wife was delivered in January."

He looked up quickly but was given, Tobie saw, only a view of Nicholas in profile, referring something to Loppe. Tobie said, "I've heard more interesting pieces of news. Do we want the letter?"

"I suppose we do," Godscalc said, "since it cost a man's life. Delivered of what, if it matters?"

"A son. They have named the child Henry. Heir to all that land in Scotland and France; the line established; the brilliant young father with a boy to carry his sword. Poor Nicholas! Childless at twenty, and condemned so to remain as long as the handsome Marian should manage to live. I would be sorry for you, were it not so convenient."

Nicholas had turned and was listening with what appeared to be patience. He said, "Thank you. Any time you wish another friend killed, be certain to let one of us know. We might not be sure, otherwise, which to pick."

He took the letter, and glanced once at the handwriting and signature before pushing it into his purse and turning again to the steps, ignoring Doria. Tobie followed, with Godscalc. Loppe had gone ahead, and would have a horse waiting. At walking pace, it would take ten minutes, no more, to reach the fondaco. Nicholas, seen from one side, gave no immediate impression of distress, but that was certainly as deceptive as everything else about him. Without Loppe, for example, he could not have mounted the horse, when he reached it. Then he rode with the slow care, again, of a man numbed by liquor. Loppe kept pace on one side at his horse's head, and Godscalc walked on the other. Tobie, catching the priest's eye, walked behind.

So Simon of Kilmirren had a child. There was no need to speak of it. Godscalc knew, as he did, that Nicholas had been taught to consider himself the unacknowledged son of this Scotsman called Simon. Now Simon, it seemed, had a son – welcome, legal, accepted – by his second wife Katelina. A boy who would inherit all that Nicholas once thought was his, including his father's affection. A rival whom Nicholas could never supplant.

Doria, it was plain, knew none of the bitterer implications of the news he had so playfully imparted. The relationship between Simon and Nicholas was still, thank God, locked within the smallest circle of the Charetty family. Doria knew only what Catherine knew: that the Scottish lord Simon had made it his pleasure to hound and persecute Nicholas. So he had planned to taunt him with Simon's good fortune. He had succeeded.

He had succeeded particularly well. Halfway back, Godscalc said suddenly, "Tobie?"

Tobie said, "I know. Look. Hold him between you. I'll go ahead and start things moving. It looks worse than it is."

He saw Loppe's face. He said, "He's as strong as you are. There's nothing here he won't get over."

Loppe's gaze, in a white man, would have been considering. He said, "It distressed you. What he said of the Emperor?"

Poised to run, Tobie delayed. He said, "Was it true?"

Loppe said, "He and Messer Pagano were led to the bath house. Yes. That is true."

"And the Emperor?" Tobie said.

Loppe said, "The Basileus was there, and desirous of him."

Godscalc's eyes, like those of Tobie, dwelled on him, waiting.

"But he did not get him," said Loppe. "I think you should go, Master Tobias."

A curious dialogue, until you thought about it. It was, Tobie understood, a douceur for the doctor; without which it might be presumed that the doctor would give less than his best. He admired the impulse, resented the implication and neither believed nor disbelieved what Loppe had told him. To honour the intent, he picked up his black skirts and ran.

The events of the next few days were lost to Nicholas, who spent them in a busy, if disjointed world of his own. He had a great deal of running to do. Also, there took place a series of unnerving conversations between himself and other people over matters he preferred not to think about. He heard his own voice quite often, explaining this. Sometimes the response was reassuring: a sensible voice would point out that there was no reason to give such things a thought, and his best course was to think about sleeping. Sometimes this voice took on the likeness of Godscalc's, and sometimes sounded like Loppe, or Tobie, his doctor. He never saw their faces.

The faces he did see were not conducive to sleep. They were not concerned at all with the shudders that rattled his teeth, or the sweats that drenched him, or the vomiting, or the purging or the cramps. But then, he was used to indifference; and indeed, preferred it. It was their claims on him that he found endlessly trying.

The woman especially. He attempted, retching and shivering, to turn her away; to explain he had nothing to offer, but she never listened. Sometimes, her brown hair wound about her naked white skin, she would invade his bed of nausea, of weakness, of lethargy and lie there, wretchedly weeping, as if he had spurned her. Sometimes he would turn on the pillow and see her beside him, lying full length in the gown of a matron, with her brown hair hidden with velvet and wire, but the same demand in her clutch, in her eyes. Always, she asked difficult questions. *If you were a lawyer, would you marry me?* No, he would say. No, of course not. How could I, with marsh fever, in Trebizond? But she never listened, although she talked. *You can become a burgess by marriage*, she said. Several times.

Once he seemed to be on his feet and she lay on the mattress, her chestnut hair spread on the pillow, so that he saw how desirable she was, and understood how his lack of ardour must offend her. Often, there was steam, which ran stinging into his eyes unless someone came with a towel, and dried him. Drifting white round his nakedness it would make distant her brown hair and small breasts and even her voice – *Can you recommend me to a friend?* And then he would say aloud, "Katelina!" but could think of nothing to add. Later, when the white scented steam cleared away, it was not a woman he saw, and he did not speak.

The last dream came to him when the fever had almost abated and his senses were in part returning. This time it was certainly Katelina van Borselen, pregnant as he had last seen her in Bruges; hating him as he had last seen her in Bruges. He looked for her son, and she said, "I am calling him Henry."

Relief washed over him, because there was so much to say, if she would let him. He said, "Katelina? You won't tell Simon. But one day, tell the boy who his father is. Don't let him think it was Simon. Jaak will beat him; and Jordan. Katelina? Don't punish the boy for what I did to you."

Her face, full of anger, hung above him. Full of contempt, full of horror. She put out her finger and traced the scar on his cheek, and it stung as if opened all over again. He said, "Don't let Jordan mark him. Don't make the boy bear the burden."

The face above him changed: not in expression but in contour. Instead of long brown hair, there was a tanned, shining cranium.

Instead of the fierce dislike of a woman it was the disgust of a man with pale eyes and a short nose and brief, tightened lips. The hand that withdrew from his scar was that of Tobie.

Nicholas, returned to the world, lay under the echoes of his own voice and looked up at the uncurtained bedposts of his chamber in the Florentine fondaco in Trebizond. By his side, straightening now, was the bald-headed man who had tended him already twice, but had never greeted his recovery with such an expression. By the window stood the priest, Godscalc. His face, also, told that something had happened.

And of course it had. He had been speaking, out of some dream. He remembered the urgency of it; the need to persuade her . . .

He remembered what the dream was about, and saw what he had done. He was too tired to move, but he kept his eyes open, and on Tobie's. Only a fool, only a weakling, claims pity.

Tobie spoke. "Your grandfather scarred you?"

So it was to begin. "Yes," said Nicholas. His voice was quite adequate.

"And he was ruined. All your foes were ruined or killed except Simon. You spared him. We commended you for it. *Spared him!*"

Tobie's eyes, when he stared, became round and pale with the pupil shrunk like a hawk's in the middle. Nicholas held them, saying nothing. Tobie said, "Unknown to Simon, his heir Henry is his wife's child by you?"

"No," said Nicholas. It was useless, but he said it.

"Despising you, he will unwittingly cherish your son. Your son will have all you wanted, and his wife is your mistress."

"No," said Nicholas. He waited. He said, "Katelina has kept to her marriage vows. And so have I."

Godscalc's voice spoke from the window. "The dates, Tobie. The child was conceived before either marriage."

"So you forced the girl?" Tobie said. "How did you even meet, you an apprentice and she one of the van Borselen family? You waylaid and raped her?"

"No. Yes," Nicholas said. His eyes, stretched open, stung with steam. No, of course, sweat. No one came with a towel. He said, "I didn't know she and Simon would marry. If you tell him . . . this story . . . he will probably kill her. And the child."

"Perhaps she has told him now," Tobie said.

Godscalc said, "Clearly Nicholas thinks not."

Tobie said, "Then I shall. My God, you claim this man is your father? Simon fought you in the open. And you did this. No one knew, but it didn't matter. No one but you, I suppose, and the child's mother. What does she think of your revenge? Now you've used her. Now you've repaid him, obscenely, by smearing his bloodline with incest?"

The word was spoken. It passed through him, swirling the mud of his body. He kept his eyes open, and his lips shut. Tobie said, "Unless your wife knows as well?"

"Come," said Godscalc. His voice sounded abrupt. "Let's keep our senses. I am quite sure the demoiselle knows nothing and will never hear anything. Tobie, nothing can be said about this. It would harm only the innocent. The child and its mother. Marian de Charetty. The Borselen family. Think what Catherine and her sister will feel. And how Pagano Doria will . . . gloat."

Between one word and the next, he had changed his mind about something. Nicholas returned the priest's gaze, which was harsh, and sought for the reason. Tobie said, "And this is the voice of the Church?"

"It's the voice of sense," Godscalc said. "Nicholas will pay for what he has done. I can assure you of that. Meantime, he has made Simon a happy man. Indeed, what would punish Nicholas publicly would punish Simon as much. It is, as you note, a very private revenge. I believe it should stay so."

Tobie sat down. From the pallor of extreme anger, he had become flushed. He folded his arms. He said, "He'll pay? Ten Paternosters?"

Nicholas lay, watching Godscalc. He had appointed Godscalc himself, because he thought him an astute man as well as a prudent one. Whether that had been foolish or not he had yet to find out. Tobie, of course, had been made company physician by the demoiselle. When Simon stabbed him at Sluys, Julius had saved him from drowning. But it was Tobie the demoiselle had rewarded, for he had brought him to convalescence. Julius . . .

Godscalc said, "Shall I tend his body and you his soul?"

"How?" said Tobie doggedly.

"Look at him!" Godscalc said. "That, for a start. And what else will make him suffer sufficiently? We could force him to do what he dislikes most. We could force him to tell us the rest of the truth."

It had been a mistake. Damn him. Damn him. Nicholas, who thought he had been unable to move, dug his fist in the sheet. Godscalc looked at him. The black eyebrows rose to the black untidy hair. "Such as," he said, "telling Tobie who is behind Pagano Doria?"

Too astute by far, but not, after all, wholly destructive. It was a trouble, now, to make his voice serve him. Nicholas said, at the second attempt, "I would have told you. Gregorio wrote me in Florence. Simon owns the *Doria*. Simon sent Pagano Doria to Trebizond to compete with us."

The priest, saving him, took up the story. "And, one supposes, to destroy us. And further, perhaps, to abduct the child Catherine and even to see that Nicholas never comes back. I was not sure," said Father Godscalc, "but I made some enquiries in Porto Pisano, and the answers pointed that way. It does not begin to excuse, of course, what Nicholas had already done."

"*Simon* was behind *Doria?*" said Tobie. He looked shocked. It would not, however, mitigate what he felt. He had always been in two minds about him, Nicholas knew. Now he had put aside doubt. Perhaps with reluctance. And still obliged in conscience, of course, to perform his physician's duty. He spoke to Godscalc. "We know now that Nicholas lies, and will always lie. But you? You didn't warn us?"

Godscalc said, "I was waiting for Nicholas to do that. Since we knew Doria already as an enemy, his silence put us in no extra danger. But it was another instance of his penchant for secrecy. I was not aware, then, that he had already abused it."

So they had told Godscalc everything. Or everything that they knew. He lay and thought about that. In Bruges, they had accused him of destroying by guile every person who crossed him, including his kinsmen. It had stood in his favour, of course, that despite all Simon had done he, Nicholas, had never injured or hurt him. Or so they had thought, until now. And now, of course, they knew that he had given Simon in secret a bastard: a spurious, an incestuous son.

Tobie and the priest continued to talk, but without referring to him. His sins of omission as well as those of commission were no doubt being thoroughly aired. He had, of course, promised to keep nothing from them, and had not kept the promise. He would be required to pay for that as well. They moved to the window, their voices rising and falling, and he found his eyes had closed. The walls and ceiling swayed vertiginously under his lids, and he struggled with an inclination to gasp. Then Tobie's voice, close at hand, said, "No. He's awake," and fingers closed on his wrist. He pulled his hand away.

It was still Tobie and Godscalc, looking down at him, but they seemed different. Then he saw that the light had changed. Perhaps he had slept without knowing it. Godscalc said, "Your master of medicine agrees with me that there has been enough talking. But you will want to know this. We concede that the parentage of Katelina van Borselen's child should remain a secret, so long as she wishes. Tobie and I will tell no one else. If she dies, however, we reserve the right to protect those involved in whatever way we think best. Before we act, we shall tell you. That is all we will promise."

What has it to do with you? Nicholas thought. He said only, "Not Julius."

"Agreed," said Godscalc. "The fewer the better. On the other hand, he must be told who is paying Pagano Doria and so must the others. In failing to pass on that information, you broke an agreement made by your wife for our protection. It must be revised."

"You will enjoy that," said Nicholas. He imagined Julius would.

For a moment, he thought he saw on Godscalc's face the expression

Tobie had worn. Disgust? Disappointment, perhaps. Harshness, certainly. Godscalc said, "We cannot trust you, but we cannot remove you. You will remain as nominal leader, but will give Julius your code books. You will take no decisions alone; you will go nowhere alone; you will discuss nothing without one of us present."

It was no less than he expected. His lips cracked as he parted them. "Even with the Emperor?" Nicholas said.

There was a little silence. Then Tobie (of course) said, "You might as well tell us. Was it true? You and Doria?"

"Up to a point," Nicholas said. It was like the end of a whipping: you walked away light-headed, and made everyone angry. Later, he would have to bring to mind, as well as he could, every word of the ordeal and examine it, and consider the consequences. Later, he would have to deal with the caging, the dogging, the loss of his privacy.

Meanwhile, he had got through the worst of it, and he had made, he thought, at least no silly mistakes. He said, "The Emperor did make his wishes quite clear. But that was all."

"Nothing happened?" said Tobie.

"Oh, quite a lot happened," said Nicholas. "I think . . . in that box."

He watched Tobie frown, and then cross unwillingly to the red velvet chest. He had put a third manuscript on top of the others. Tobie examined it. The expression on his face as he straightened was gratifying. He said, "Do you know what this is?"

Since he had chosen it for Tobie, he was glad that he recognised it. The treatise composed by the physician Zacharius for a Comneni emperor in Byzantium was three hundred years old. It was still the greatest work of its kind. Or so he had been assured. *The Book of Zacharias on the Eye, called the Secret of Secrets.*

Nicholas said, "It's the Emperor's gift. Doria said there was no silver left. He was right. But there are manuscripts, and they are willing to trade them."

Tobie said, "Get them."

"What I can," Nicholas said. "Some are being copied. Don't tell Doria."

Godscalc, too, had crossed to the box and was kneeling. He said, "You need no other merchandise but this. One manuscript – in France, one manuscript sells for five hundred écus."

"I know. But still. The camel trains might get through, too, if we help them."

They looked at him. He supposed it seemed crazy, talking money. Nicholas said, "If you collected the books for me, I could leave you. Find the caravans and hurry them in. It would get me out of your way, and Doria's."

"Doria's?" said Tobie. They had forgotten.

Nicholas said, "He's married to Catherine de Charetty. He'll put me away as soon as he thinks we're rich enough. He can't touch Bruges. He can't touch Catherine's mother. But he could seize the branch here in her name and collect all its profits before he could be legally stopped. You have to keep me alive. You have to pretend that I'm still running the company. Because, the moment I'm dead or deposed, you belong to Doria."

The silence that followed was a long one, and was broken only by Godscalc. He said, "Is it possible? Did you design what has happened? Did you intend to make us privy to all that you've done, since the threat of Doria protected you?"

They stared at him, as if they expected to receive an answer. Eventually, he said, "Pretending the fever was the hardest bit." Then they went.

Loppe, sponging him down, said, "Did you get what you wanted?"

"Yes. I'm still alive," Nicholas said.

Loppe said, "You'll die, if you don't quieten down. You'll die before you are thirty."

"Twenty," Nicholas said. "She used to say twenty. No, I shan't. I'm as strong as you are."

The sponge lifted, dry and hot, from his body. After a moment, Loppe soaked it again. He said, "What else did you hear?"

"I heard you lying most convincingly. Thank you," Nicholas said.

"But you must go on with it?" Loppe said.

"Jason did," Nicholas said. He heard Loppe snort his contempt, and almost smiled. He said, "Where have we got to? I have sown my seed, and reaped a battle."

The sponge stopped. Loppe said, "Do you *want* to get better?"

Nicholas opened his eyes. Loppe looked angry. Loppe said, "Even me. You don't even trust me, do you?"

The room faded, and came reluctantly back again. Perhaps he would die before he was thirty. Even in the Abruzzi, he had not felt like this. Nicholas said, "What more do you want? No one confides everything, least of all menials."

Loppe said, "I trust you." His eyes, root-dark ringed with clearest white, looked as stern as Godscalc's.

"Don't," said Nicholas.

Chapter 22

FAR FROM THE RAVAGES he had unwittingly caused, the Charetty lawyer Gregorio saw the time draw near at last when he could find and confront the Scottish lord Simon of Kilmirren with his crimes against Nicholas and Catherine de Charetty. It appealed to Gregorio's liking for symmetry that he and Simon would owe their meeting, whatever its outcome, to that most select of chivalrous bodies, the Golden Fleece Order.

He had not, of course, forgotten the dispatch he had sent east from Bruges in January. He knew which reports should be arriving in April in Trebizond, whether or not Nicholas was alive to receive them. He was aware of the relationship between Simon and Nicholas. That there could be a relationship between Nicholas and the girl whom Simon had married did not, naturally, cross his mind.

He had thought quite deeply, as it was, before warning Nicholas that his rival Pagano Doria was an agent of Simon's. He had hardly known how to soften the blow when, later, he had been forced to report the same Doria's abduction of Catherine although it seemed likely that, by then, Nicholas would have found this out for himself. He could imagine the effect that might have on a young man like Nicholas; but not what he might be impelled to do about it.

Compared with all that, the birth of Simon's son was a minor event, but he had taken care, again, with the way he had informed Nicholas; for the arrival of a supplanting heir was hardly good news. On the other hand, a child of his own might divert Simon at last from his contest with the son of his first wife. And Nicholas, given the chance, might get on with his own life and have the sense to leave Simon alone. Once, that is, he had dealt with Pagano Doria. And once Simon, daily expected in Bruges, had been informed by Gregorio of Asti himself that he proposed to take him to law unless he made proper amends and saw that the persecution was stopped.

The Tenth Chapter of the Order of the Golden Fleece had been commanded to meet on the second of May at St Omer in Artois, handy for the French and Burgundian knights. Duke Philip, its sovereign and founder, moved the court west from Brussels a month before that, dividing Easter between Bruges and Ghent. The arrival of hundreds of courtiers and servants at the Princenhof, Bruges, was the equivalent of the arrival of the Flanders galleys. You couldn't move from one street to the next, and everyone worked from morning till night without complaint, making profits. It taxed Gregorio, already short-handed, to satisfy all his customers. It was not until the lord of Flanders and Burgundy had left his good city of Bruges that Gregorio drew breath and sent a clerk to find out when the van Borselen family were coming to Silver Straete.

"They've been," said the clerk when he came back. "That is, they came in from Veere and went straight on through Bruges without staying. My lord Franck and my lord Henry of Veere. And my lord Wolfaert and his wife the princess and their son. And my lord Florence and his wife and their daughter Katelina and her husband Simon the Scotsman."

The clerk was new, which was why Gregorio had sent him. "And they all left Bruges together?" Gregorio said.

"After they'd called on my lord of Gruuthuse. They all went in his party to Artois."

He dismissed the clerk and thought, while he cleared his desk. He should have expected it. Louis de Gruuthuse had married a van Borselen and was currently high in the ducal favour. For several good reasons, he might have taken care to rent an establishment in St Omer worthy of a family with royal connections. And there, Simon and Katelina would be accompanying them. He could hardly accost them on the road. He could not, in any case, leave the Charetty business at a moment's notice, excellent though his deputy was. He had had, since morning, reason to go and visit Anselm Adorne. This he now did.

There was a canal at the foot of the Hôtel Jerusalem, the graceful building linked to its church which the Adornes had built for themselves in the eastern quarter of the city. He took one of the Charetty boats, and sent a servant to announce his visit. Adorne's steward came to the postern at once with a welcome. Since Marian de Charetty went away, Gregorio had held one or two circumspect meetings with Anselm Adorne, host and guardian to her remaining child Tilde; and had satisfied himself that the girl was well cared for and reasonably happy. Circumspection had been due because, however long his line had flourished in Bruges, Anselm Adorne was in origin as Genoese as the Dorias, and one Paul Doria was godfather to Adorne's oldest son.

From friendship and piety, Anselm Adorne had last year endorsed the unexpected marriage of Nicholas and Marian de Charetty which had taken place here, in this church. Profit had followed, of course. But there was no doubt at the time that neither Adorne nor his wife had welcomed the union so abhorrent to Marian's children. Tilde, then thirteen, had hated Nicholas for it, and maybe still did. Her revulsion did not, it seemed, include the Adornes – perhaps because she too could sense their reservations. But speaking of Nicholas, Anselm Adorne was always tolerant; showing admiration and even affection where Gregorio himself might have been critical.

Tilde, a wiry fourteen, never mentioned her stepfather Nicholas. In the last year she had grown like her dead brother in appearance. Her hair fell dark brown and limp from its padded circlet down to her shoulders, and showed none of the bright russet gleams of her mother and sister. Her nose, like Felix's, was a flattened stub that became red at the tip under emotion. When Gregorio came, she was usually about to be called for by friends. Once, getting him to herself, she had asked him a number of questions about the company's loans. The questions were less than childish: he saw he was being invigilated. Otherwise, she spent quite a lot of time, Gregorio knew, at the Bruges home of the lord Henry van Borselen, especially when his royal Scottish grandson was there. The attraction, Gregorio suspected, was less the little prince than young Liddell, his tutor.

He was not over-concerned, for that sensible person Adorne's wife had an eye on the affair. It might yet turn out to the good. Although Scottish, the man Liddell was well born, and the girl was of an age to be married. But, of course, nothing could be done until her mother came back from her mission.

It had been given out that Marian de Charetty had gone to Florence, to spend some time with her younger child Catherine, at present said to be staying with friends. No one had questioned it. In March, his employer had left perfectly openly, with a good, well-armed entourage to serve and protect her. This morning the entourage had returned, clattering into the courtyard at Bruges with the slightly loosened decorum of a pack of men dispatched leaderless home, who have lost more pay and had more girls on the trip than their wives would ever know. They had been cheerful, though, reporting to Gregorio. Delivered the lady to Dijon as right as rain, and seen her fitted out with another good escort for the rest of her journey. From her sister's people, she said. She'd kept her own woman, Tasse. Geneva, she was going to, and then over the pass into Italy. She'd have no trouble. A natural-born organiser, that demoiselle was.

As indeed she was. Telling all this to Anselm Adorne and his wife in the handsome room they received him in, Gregorio was conscious of Tilde's steady glare. Of course, she hated losing her mother. Of course, she hated her mother who had chosen Catherine and not Tilde to go to Antwerp and Florence and was now successfully travelling to join her. Tilde said, "What was she doing in Dijon?"

Gregorio was careful. "Visiting Thibault your uncle. You know he lives there."

"He's gone crazy," said Tilde. "He's so old, he doesn't know where he is. He wouldn't know who my mother was, even."

"Maybe not," Gregorio said, "but she would have a rest there and, as you see, she got some good men for the rest of her journey. And here's the letter she gave me to give you."

He drew it from his purse, making sure it was the right one. The other, also from Marian de Charetty, had been addressed to himself:

I'm not sure what to do. The old man has gone, no one knows where, and the house is empty. I have told the men he is with friends of my late sister's, and indeed, I found some people I knew who hired the escort I needed. If Doria has hidden him locally, then I must try and find him. If not, I shall ride on the way Doria's messengers must have gone. I shall keep writing, but bearers cannot now be relied on: if you hear nothing, there is no need to worry. I send a letter for Tilde. The third is for Nicholas. Hand it to him yourself.

He carried that in his purse because there was nowhere else safe he could leave it. Only he knew that his employer had gone to Dijon for one reason alone: to question Thibault de Fleury who had supposedly signed the permission for Catherine's wedding. If the signature was invalid, then she could pursue Doria and hope to get back her daughter.

Tilde said, "They may be in Florence by now. With Nicholas." Her eyes looked wet. Instead of reading her mother's letter, she held it screwed in her hands, which had been tightly clasped in her lap since he entered.

Adorne said gently, "But we know the company has left Florence, little lady; and your mother cannot have arrived there just yet. Why not show Meester Gregorio what Nicholas arranged to have sent you?"

Then Gregorio saw that she held something else in her clenched hands. It looked like a ball. After a moment, she released her fingers and allowed the object to roll from her knee to the ground, where it lay in a tangle of string. She said, "It's a toy for a child. He has a short memory for an apprentice." The letter, tumbling also, lay beside it on the floor.

Adorne picked both up. He had hands like a painter, Gregorio thought. Whereas Colard Mansion the painter had fingers like peapods. Adorne's face, too, with its pale curling hair and high cheekbones and wry, intelligent mouth was ascetic in a way you would never expect of the man who farmed the Duke of Burgundy's wine taxes and had a reputation, too, of being able to outdrink most men of his guild.

Adorne's wife smiled and, rising, gently excused herself. Adorne untangled the string until the small object was bare, and then carefully began to rebind its waist. Two young children, hitherto occupied at the end of the room, saw what he was doing and ran up. He said, "You know, of course, that the Eastern delegation is here: the one Nicholas had dealings with in Florence? Of course you will know: the envoy from Trebizond must be most anxious to acquaint himself with the Charetty business. At any rate, Nicholas asked the Persian delegate to bring this little object to Tilde. He says Cosimo de' Medici has tried and failed to master the principle."

"What principle?" Gregorio said. The envoy from Trebizond hadn't been near him. He suspected, he didn't know why, that Fra Ludovico his leader had stopped him.

"One that Cosimo de' Medici and I, evidently, know nothing about, but Nicholas does. Engineering, my dear Meester Gregorio. The study of opposing forces. And that manipulation of mechanical and numerical mysteries which Tilde, although you wouldn't guess it, excels in. That is why he sent her the farmuk."

The children clamoured. Adorne held out his hand and the girl, hesitating, took back the toy. Gregorio said, "And what was he like, the envoy of Uzum Hasan?"

The children had seen all the delegation. The envoy Mahon was as tall as that window, and old, with a white beard and a white cloth wound round his head. The envoy from the King of Georgia had been big and handsome, for a man living on the edge of the world. The delegate from Prester John in Ethiopia was an impostor, because he was brown and not black. And there was a man with a very tall hat; and one with rings in his ears and a face and a beard like a monkey, although he had shaved all the hair on his head but a tuft. That one ate twenty pounds of meat in a day. Someone had said so.

"From the Atabeg of Imeretia in Georgia," Anselm Adorne interpolated. "I should say that the envoy from Ethiopia, impostor or not, was discovered to be a theologian and an astronomer. Maurat, the Armenian envoy, can play several instruments as well as possessing a very tall hat. Alighieri, of course, is an educated Florentine merchant who happens to be familiar with Trebizond. However exotic, the delegates are not, therefore, unendowed, although they all carry credentials, I am told, of a curious Latin uniformity. Even the Muslim lord Uzum Hasan writes to bid us all 'Vale in Christo'. Nevertheless, the Holy Father received them in Rome, and honoured them profusely with banquets. Duke Philip means to do the same in St Omer. After that, they pass to the King of France, who might support a crusade, they imagine, to ease his mortal departure."

His voice was dry. Yet Adorne's own father and uncle had been on pilgrimage, twice, to the Holy Land. Gregorio said, "What is it? You don't think Fra Ludovico's mission is genuine?"

Adorne looked at him. "The friar himself believes in it," he said. "He is a powerful man, who rules his delegation with invocations of sulphur. But he is calling himself Antioch, against the Pope's explicit wishes. And he shows little sense, scouring Europe for money and armies at present. As for the rulers whose envoys go with him, I sometimes wonder what they expect. As I said, they are not savages. They may be more sophisticated, in some things, than Fra Ludovico. I wonder what Nicholas made of them? I hear he got his contract in Florence."

There had been no secret about that. As soon as Nicholas had sent the news, Gregorio had announced it in Bruges. A group from the Charetty company was to trade for itself and for Florence in Trebizond. It pleased him to speak of it now to someone of Adorne's experience. There was no need to be explicit about the terms, which had turned out to be all that they hoped. It only remained for the Emperor to ratify them. There was no need either to repeat precisely what Nicholas had said about Fra Ludovico and the delegation and Julius. It had included an instruction to find Michael Alighieri if possible and talk to him. Already, in Florence, Nicholas and Alighieri of Trebizond had reached a rapport over future trade dealings. Everything, it seemed, was happening to the advantage of the Charetty company which, if its persecutors gave it the chance, could only become bigger and richer. Adorne talked, and Gregorio wondered, as he wondered every day, how Nicholas was managing.

The girl, apparently absorbed, had begun to unreel the farmuk, to the ecstasy of the children. Gregorio watched, as he listened. Did she, too, hear the gossip about the Charetty company, as distinct from its commercial transactions? Monna Alessandra, severest of hostesses, had kept her son in Bruges daily apprised of the shortcomings of her house-guests in Florence. Lorenzo Strozzi had read passages of her letters out aloud in all his favourite taverns: Tilde no doubt had heard extracts. Not that there had been anything crude reported of Nicholas, apart from his deplorable levity. Gregorio had a joke planned, however, for his first meeting with Tobie. It had something to do with bells and a whistle.

He brought his mind back to his host, and the company he, Gregorio alone, was now leading here in Bruges, and the matters he would like to know more of. The King of France, for example. The ruling of France was closely linked with the ruling of Genoa. They said the old king was dying at last: his bread cut into mouthfuls; the short little doublets exchanged for long robes and laced stockings over festering legs. Dying at Mehun-sur-Yèvre of the morbus gallicus with his Scots Guards about him. The delegation from the East might find it hard even to sell the Hereafter, for the King of France had his mind on one thing: how to coax the Dauphin Louis his heir to his side. And the Dauphin, self-exiled for five years in Flanders, was taunting his father by daily changing his mind. Now he still clung to Duke Philip, and was sending troops to the Yorkists in England. Another time, he might favour his father's first cousin, who was queen of the Yorkists' opponents. The fate of Genoa could hang on Louis' decision.

Anselm Adorne's eldest son was a student in Paris. Anselm

Adorne's kinsman Prosper Adorno had just become Doge of Genoa, in a revolt that had sent its French governor scuttling for the citadel. Gregorio said innocuously, "Will you bring your son home?"

"Do you think I should?" Adorne said. Without haste, he rose to his feet. "Come. If Mathilde will excuse us, there are some tiresome papers in my office to talk over. No, I shall not call Jan from Paris yet. Listening ears can be useful. Why else is Tilde staying under my roof?"

Closing the door of his office, he was smiling. Gregorio said, "I would take you seriously, if you had made any effort to prevent me from seeing her. Of course, I want to know no more of Genoese affairs than you care to tell me. But if you can, would you advise me of this? Who is Pagano Doria?"

There were no papers on Adorne's heavy table, but a tray held some cups and a fine pitcher of wine in painted Syrian pottery. From, no doubt, the family pilgrimages to the Holy Land. An inlaid silver inscription glinted as Adorne raised it to pour. He said, "The new Genoese consul to Trebizond? I thought you would ask, so I consulted Jacques Doria the other day. The man is of an obscure branch, and has spent some of his life in Constantinople and Chios, but seems to lack the ability, or the inclination, to apply himself for long to anything. I don't think you or Nicholas have cause to worry, although it pains me to say so. It is a post which has been several times refused by better men. As you know, the Emperor dislikes Genoese."

"That's what I thought," Gregorio said. "Is he married?"

"Not so far as Jacques is aware. He says he seems to have no immediate family. May I ask something in return?"

"Of course," said Gregorio, and sipped his wine. Why had he thought he might catch this man in an indiscretion?

Anselm Adorne said, "Forgive me for asking, but I find myself more and more concerned about Catherine de Charetty and her mother. I find it hard to believe that a child as young in her ways as Catherine should have been allowed to travel to Florence. Knowing how much the business relies on her, I cannot understand, either, how your mistress could readily leave it. Your reticence does you credit, and I respect it. But I should like to help if I can."

He spoke calmly, and tried to avoid sounding glib. "Indeed," said Gregorio, "it is a kind offer, but all is as it seems. Perhaps you will understand better if I refer to the demoiselle's second marriage. It seemed wise to remove Catherine from the presence of Nicholas, and even from news of him."

"So she is not with Nicholas?" said Anselm Adorne.

He had never thought of that. No wonder this conversation was taking place in the office. Gregorio said, "Is that the rumour?"

"I am sorry: yes," said Adorne. "He was a youth, as you know, who sought fleshly pleasures. The child was said to admire him. With a ship, a fortune, an heiress, he need never come home while his wife lives. The demoiselle would be desolate, but she would have you to run the Bruges company for her."

He had come prepared to launch a subtle attack, and found himself drinking wine in the mouth of a cannon. He said, "That is easily refuted, Messer Adorne. Ask Lorenzo Strozzi to show you his mother's letters from Florence. There is no word of Catherine there. Also . . . she is a pretty child, but do you think that for her sake Nicholas would throw over his wife and all he has built up in Bruges for a precarious post in the East?"

Adorne said, "I am telling you only what people are saying. Of course I don't think he would betray his friends or his marriage. Even though, perhaps, I have more cause for worry than most. The rewards for the alum treaty with Venice will go largely, they tell me, to Nicholas. It will create a substantial reserve fund in Venice, which must increase year by year. Until, of course, someone finds this secret alum deposit of yours, and Venice ceases to pay for your silence."

Gregorio sipped his wine, his body relaxed and his feet still. Of course, this was all about alum. The white powdered rock without which cloth couldn't be dyed. Until the Ottomans gave the franchise to Venice, the Genoese used to hold the world's monopoly of first quality alum. Then the Charetty company had found alum on the Pope's lands at Tolfa, and had sold the information to Venice in return for their silence. Venice, the sworn foe in the East of colonial Genoa.

Gregorio looked into his wine, wondering what Adorne was really saying. *Tell me where the alum mine is, and I will tell you who is behind Pagano Doria?* Or perhaps, *We want cheaper alum. Or we might go to the Pope and say, Send your mining experts to the Papal States with one or two of our old Genoese quarrymen. With what you find, you might win back Constantinople.*

He had not spoken. Adorne said, as if he had, "I must admit, I am a little jealous of Nicholas, whose genius will make the Charetty company and the Venetians and the Florentines rich. Bruges is my home, but Genoa is my mother city, beset by encroaching powers. She cannot be free without money."

"You have cheap alum," Gregorio said. "Nicholas arranged it with Genoa. Their agent Prosper de Camulio accepted it. You would be worse off with a papal monopoly."

Adorne put down his wine. "We should have God on our side," he said. He smiled suddenly. "But, of course, there is alum at Sebinkarahisar. It depends whether Pagano Doria or Nicholas remembers it first."

Leaving presently, Gregorio was surprised to find his legs weak. These days he was not often matched, far less outmatched. He wondered whether Adorne, once a friend of the Charetty, was now inclined to be less so. He would have to weigh what he had heard, and try to come to conclusions. But at least the lord Simon had never been mentioned, far less linked to his trip to St Omer. That, he had told Adorne, was for business reasons. And, of course, to have speech with the envoy from Trebizond.

"Has he not called on you already?" Adorne had said. "Of course you must see Alighieri. And, since we have mentioned him, you should also look out for Prosper de Camulio, who is here on a Milanese mission. He is an acute observer, close to the Dauphin; and can be of use to a man with a business."

Thanking him for the advice, Gregorio wondered why it had been offered. He had not planned to seek out de Camulio, expecting to learn little from him. As far as business news went, Gregorio was already well primed to conduct an enterprise based on money and credit, information and mercenary services. He had run the company well, since Nicholas left. Not perhaps adding much, but polishing and refining what had been begun. It must have struck more people than Adorne and Tilde de Charetty that he might become over-fond of his power. Perhaps, indeed, that was why poor Tilde's romance was not being frowned on. Tilde was an heiress, like Catherine.

Himself, it had never crossed his mind that the demoiselle and Nicholas would fail to return as his masters. It had nothing to do with lack of self-confidence, either. He sometimes thought that he was the only person apart from the demoiselle who saw what Nicholas might in time come to. Gregorio was not a modest man, but he had never had doubts about that.

He and Adorne had emptied the Syrian wine-vessel between them. It was true what they said about the man's capacity. Towards the end, his own tongue had begun to baulk at long words. To punish it, he had asked about the Arabic lettering. *Lasting glory, increasing prosperity, and fortuitous destiny*, it said on the jug. He had expressed, with lucidity, the hope that it would long apply to the line of Adorne.

"As long, I suppose, as the ewer will last," Adorne had answered him mildly.

And yet it was in daily use. On his shaky legs, Gregorio made his way thoughtfully home.

Chapter 23

ST OMER LOOKED LIKE a battlefield. Gregorio arrived on Friday, the day of the Order's first vespers, hoping the roads would be clearer. The knights ought to be already installed with their squires and pages and servants and all the horses and gear for Tuesday's tournament. The ducal court, preceded by seventy wagons of furnishings each drawn by five or six horses, had moved in a fortnight before with its heralds and trumpets, its hounds and its birds, the ducal wine, books and spices, the Duke's jewels (five carts), and his bath. The wine, the oats, the meat to serve a thousand men and their servants, would be already in store.

But St Omer needed daily supplies to feed the other thousands pouring into its gates: the simple spectators; the petitioners; the merchants and women, the brokers and artists, the smiths and tailors and artisans who followed the court. Ancient town of the counts of Flanders and Artois, it had seen it all before in Duke Philip's time: a royal wedding; an early meeting of the new-founded Fleece. It had made little difference to the problem. Stationary on a road jammed with carts and wheelbarrows, horses and basket-crowned peasants, Gregorio gazed at the unencumbered blue sky, and envied the windmills.

Inside the walls, it was worse. They were preparing for a procession, and the road from the cathedral to St Bertin's was closed off, so that the streets round about were all but impassable. Struggling through, he could see an unbroken line of scarlet cloth apparently lining the main street. Ribboned garlands and shields showed above it. At every intersection there was a platform of sorts, garnished with heraldic devices and crowded with people, most of them shouting and some of them practising fanfares. Above the immediate noise, he could hardly hear them. He could barely keep contact with the groom and boy he had brought with him.

Had it not been for a man who owed him money and had an aunt in St Omer, he would have had no hope of finding a bed. As it was, he suspected that he would find himself sleeping in a communal room on a floor-mattress, and in due course was to find himself proved right. The boy and groom shared a stable and did rather better.

It was then, on his way to his lodging, that he was hailed by Prosper de Camulio, the Milanese agent Adorne had spoken of. The cry came from a balcony. Looking up, Gregorio recognised the confident face, the clothing a fraction too stylish, of the man he had met, once, before Nicholas left. The encounter, of course, must be accidental. But the balcony, itself crowded, overlooked the one route that led to Gregorio's destination. And a man who owed money in one quarter, he supposed, might just as easily owe it elsewhere. So here was Prosper Schiaffino de Camulio de' Medici, secretary and accredited envoy of the Duke of Milan, calling, "Messer Gregorio! But my friend of the company Charetty! What do you here, and where do you lodge?"

He made a point of answering readily, while trying to keep his horse still. He told the same story. The delegation from Eastern princes had arrived, and he sought the envoy from Trebizond. Messer de Camulio listened with interest, remarked, in a shout, that he hoped to give himself the pleasure of calling on Messer Gregorio shortly and, saluting, thinned and withdrew from the front of the balcony. Bowing would have been suicide.

Gregorio smiled and waved in turn, cursing quietly. Installed at last in his quarters, he sent the boy to find out what he could and received news, but not what he wanted. The Orientals, austerely lodged at the Observatine friary, had understandable plans to be absent all day. Much more important, Louis de Gruuthuse and the Borselen family had rented a house as large as a palace by Nôtre Dame, but were also embroiled until nightfall and later in the ceremonies of the Order. There was no time today he could reach Simon in private.

It was a pity, with de Camulio about; who must be counted a member of the Genoese faction. On the other hand, there was still plenty of time, with three days of ritual to come, and then the jousting and tournaments. He would prefer not to have to stand up in the cathedral and denounce the van Borselen son-in-law, but he would if he had to. He got his blankets out and, releasing his servants, settled to make up the sleep he had missed on the journey, and would miss tonight once his bedmates returned. He smiled, half-asleep, thinking of Margot. A typical lawyer, ignoring the flamboyance outside for the sake of clear wits in the morning. Well, sweetheart: I may need them.

Next day Gregorio went to the Franciscans' friary himself, but Alighieri was out. He left quickly. He was held up, coming back, by the procession returning from the cathedral and this time actually saw the knights riding in pairs between the lines of archers and crossbowmen in the Duke's livery. They came in the middle, after the seventy trumpets and a long line of kings-of-arms, heralds and pursuivants, and at least two hundred noble riders, flashily dressed.

After that came the bishops, abbots and clergy and then three officers of the Order in their furred scarlet robes, red cloaks and red chaperons. Pierre Bladelin, the Treasurer, was among them. He was the Duke's controller in Bruges, and Gregorio had sold him some velvet last week. Scarlet was not a colour that suited him.

And here now, followed by their pages of honour, were the Knights; not quite up to their complement of just over thirty, but a sight to gratify a dyer, a cloth merchant, a banker. Their calf-length tunics were grey-furred. The scarlet cloaks, also furred and bordered with gold, glittered with the jewelled devices of the Duke; the sparkling flints; the blazon aultre n'auray repeated over and over. Framed by the draped scarlet hats there passed by the familiar faces, the élite of the world's chivalry. The Duke's legitimate heir, Charles of Charolais, was today there among them. And Franck and Henry van Borselen, Knights of the Order for half its existence. Simon of Kilmirren had married into a significant family. He had called his child Henry to mark it.

Behind, spider-legged, princely in carriage, the Duke of Burgundy rode alone with his glittering dress and his dyed hair and his long, pursed, sallow face with its ironical eyebrows. His council jogged after him. But Gregorio was already making his way back to his lodging. Dutifully, he tried again to find Alighieri, and sent the boy in genuine eagerness to enquire at the Hôtel Gruuthuse, but the results were the same. Both the envoy and Simon were attending the Duke, and would not return until after the evening's banquet.

The next day was Sunday, and marked by the promised visit from Prosper de Camulio, who rapped on his door on his way back from mass. It had been a special service to commemorate the Order's dead knights, and so the diplomat was dressed in black pourpoint and doublet, with a black feathered hat. The style was a shade too fine for his rank. His dark hair, a trifle too long, was still without grey and his voice and manner, full of energy, indicated a man in his prime – the mid-thirties, perhaps – who had undertaken a task whose dimensions he was only now beginning to suspect. A terrier appointed to gundog, and overworking, one suspected, to prove it.

He had not come alone. Did Messer Gregorio not see whom he had brought with him? Met at a banquet, Messer Michael Alighieri, the merchant envoy of the illustrious Emperor of Trebizond, whom Messer Gregorio had come to St Omer to see. Were they not both welcome?

Uttering a lie, Gregorio had them both enter. Welcome individually, perhaps. But with Alighieri there, he could hardly draw information about alum or Pagano Doria or Genoa or anything else out of de Camulio (was that why de Camulio had found a companion?). And with de Camulio there, he was debarred from asking the questions he wanted to ask about Nicholas and the Medici in Florence. On the other hand, Alighieri was entitled to a full exposition on the Charetty company's business in Flanders which was, perhaps, exactly what de Camulio wanted to hear. The only empty room being the dormitory, Gregorio pushed aside mattresses and, commanding stools and a trestle, offered a modest meal of cooked bream, served by his own men, with a piece of salt beef and some capons and cabbages for those less than strict in observance. He had brought with him much of what he would need, including a small keg of wine from Alsace, and the woman of the house provided good bread and platters.

It appeared to be acceptable: the Genoese and the Florentine made a hearty meal while describing the constipating excesses of Duke Philip's grand banquet the previous night. They had drunk Beaune wine exclusively. The banqueting hall, specially built for the Duke, had been bigger than the one he built for his bride when he founded the Order. Last night, the hall had been hung inside with the cloth of gold Gideon tapestries, worth ten thousand écus, and fitted with shelves of gold and silver plate which was not even needed, for the Duke had as much besides as would serve all his guests. The revelry, with music and dancing and jesters, had gone on nearly till morning, although it had, of course, lacked the extreme brilliance of the original banquet. There had been no wild men thundering in on roast pigs, or pies with bleating blue sheep fixed inside them. But fifty different courses, served to fanfares. There was munificence for you.

None of it was new to Gregorio, who had heard tales of what went on at the Princenhof, and had a rough idea of the annual income of Duke Philip of Burgundy, king among princes. De Camulio's enthusiasm appeared to be genuine. Nicholas had said he was ambitious, but quarrelsome. Like Astorre, he enjoyed the displays of his betters. And, of course, he would have to prune his account for the ears of his own Duke of Milan. A former condottieri who had won his dukedom through his own strong right arm and a marriage, the Duke lived in relative simplicity and saw power in different terms.

And Alighieri? It would be an odd circumstance if he were impressed. The court of Trebizond, surely, could match this for concentrated wealth and outmatch it in historic ceremony. It, too, employed etiquette as a weapon. Gregorio could make nothing so far of Alighieri, a smallish uneasy man with dark skin and an appeasing manner belied by extremely sharp eyes. In Florence, he had delivered a harangue in Latin, people said, on behalf of the Observatine friar his leader, who claimed to have forgotten his learning. On the same grounds, he had taken part in the audience with the Pope, and had handed to the Duke of Burgundy the Pope's letter introducing his *delecti filii*, the Eastern delegates. He looked to Gregorio like the sort of sharp, lettered man who sets himself up as secretary or tutor to the great, and very soon takes the place of his masters.

The talk remained disappointingly harmless. De Camulio said, "You know, of course, that Brussels offered the Duke twenty thousand Rhenish florins to let them host the Golden Fleece meetings. They were even ready to build him a hall for the banquets. But St Omer got them for nothing."

"He had his reasons," said Alighieri. "I'd want to please the men of St Omer if I had a French army spilling over my borders. I don't know how we're going to get through to Mehun if France invades Burgundy or starts trouble in Calais. And the French king may be dead before our embassy arrives there."

"I think," said de Camulio, "that you should refrain from worrying. The English war is favouring the Dauphin's side and not his father's. Your greatest misfortune, so far as I see it, is that before you can get there, poor King Charles will have gambled away all his money."

Gregorio recalled Adorne's view of this delegation, quartering Europe for troops and money to drive back the Ottoman armies. He said to Alighieri, "You don't in fact expect France to pay for a crusade at this moment?"

Alighieri said, "Speaking personally, I don't expect anyone to pay for a crusade until the English war is settled, and even later. They all have enemies enough of their own without looking beyond Christian lands."

Gregorio said, "The Order of the Golden Fleece was founded to clear the holy places of the East. I remember, even from Padua, hearing of the feasts that were held, and the vows taken."

De Camulio, unsure of him, nodded. "The Vow of the Pheasant, seven years ago. They could have chosen the Peacock, the Heron, the Swan of Lohengrin to swear upon. The Phasianus, the bird of Colchis, matched the Duke's theme. The Duke's obsession, as I hear it. As Jason went forth to achieve his impossible task, so the heroes of today would free the Holy Land from the heathens who hold it. Everyone remembers, of course, the cost of the tournaments, and the fact that nothing happened. But indeed it might have done, but for unrest at home. Some of these men did, on their own account, cross the sea and lay down their lives for the Faith."

"All rulers understand that," said Alighieri. "So does the Church. Even the Observatines vowed to personal poverty, who send out delegations such as mine."

De Camulio said, "But one accepts, too, that there are other reasons. You, sir, are a merchant. Trade needs peace. Traders for that reason often make the best envoys, and no one will blame them if they make some profit out of their journeyings. The Golden Fleece came into being from the highest of motives, but it serves other purposes."

And that was true, Gregorio thought. It represented the Duke's dramatic retribution for the capture of his father, long ago, by the Turks. It displayed the Duke's wealth and his power and his magnificence, so that the common herd might be proud to call themselves Burgundians. It bound the princes from all the different lands he had swallowed; and gave them a feeling of comradeship and pride in being consulted.

As for the high motives, they could have little outlet just now. In secret session tomorrow, the Order would talk of a holy war, but inconclusively, one had to suspect. The rest was more like the business of some jousting society. A mild inquisition into the moral condition of every knight, with amusing punishments for amusing faults – although sometimes the Duke would use the occasion to force disgrace upon someone who deserved it. Then the casting of votes to fill the places of those recently dead, followed by the induction of the new knights and the presentation of the fiery Collar to each. Gregorio wondered, listening to de Camulio, why he had troubled to find out so much. Perhaps he thought the Duke of Milan ought to have been proposed for membership, or his son Galeazzo. But the Order was drawn from French-speaking Flanders and the two Burgundies, not from friends of Milan. Which might, in itself, explain the diplomat's interest.

Gregorio said, "I hear Louis de Gruuthuse made a brilliant embassy to Scotland early this year. Carried the Duke's condolences to his niece on the death of King James; met the new youthful sovereign; encouraged the Dowager Queen to think again before supporting the French king and the Lancastrians. Such a man, would you say, deserves the highest accolade his ruler can offer?"

Prosper de Camulio smiled. "You too have seen the size of the house Louis de Gruuthuse has rented. Yes, my friend. It is no secret, I think, that by the end of tomorrow, the Golden Fleece will have a new knight in that fortunate family. And now I have something to ask, before I return to my duties. Your Messer Niccolò spoke of sending some alum from Constantinople. Have you word of it?"

"Ask me in a week's time," Gregorio said. "If our agent Zorzi had alum waiting, it could have arrived in Pisa by now."

"It is a pity, paying those prices," de Camulio said. "But I suppose it is fortunate that we can get it at all. Before I joined the Duke of Milan, I remember the constant concern of the Adorno, the Spinola. No alum meant no cloth and no leather."

Gregorio said, "In Bruges, it is the same. By the way, I asked Anselm Adorne about Pagano Doria. You know he left Florence as Genoese consul to Trebizond? I think we should have been warned about that."

"By whom? By Messer Anselm?" said the Duke of Milan's envoy. "But, my friend, are you not expecting too much? It is like the Fleece. Beforehand, it is not wise that men should know who the candidates are."

"Do you know Doria?" said Gregorio.

"No more of him than Messer Anselm has already told you. But here is a man who knows everything about everyone. I give him my place. Messer Gregorio, my heart is touched by your hospitality. We shall speak more, and at leisure. I must leave."

He got up, removing a trace of grease from his mouth with a little silk handkerchief. His pourpoint collar, though black, was edged with fine silver sewing. Gregorio made the correct sounds, rising also; observing Alighieri's expression; guessing who the newcomer was even before he strode in from the door.

"Ah," said Fra Ludovico da Bologna, leader of the Eastern delegation to Europe. He stood and stared, first at Gregorio, and then at Michael Alighieri, his fellow-traveller. "I find you both. You were to wait for me, Michael. You had forgotten." The Duke of Milan's envoy, bowing, left with a smile behind the friar's back. The friar said, "And I find you in sin."

His eyes were trained on the half-eaten meats on the trestle. It was, without doubt, the Minorite friar whose denunciation of Julius in Florence – encouraged by Pagano Doria – had so nearly stopped the whole Charetty expedition. *"A bear,"* Nicholas had written. *"A bear taught young to dance. He will dance, too, into bearpits and out of them, and never notice the spikes. He is wholly innocent, I think, of any plot with Doria. He is wholly innocent of most things, including charity."*

Nicholas kept to himself, as a rule, what he thought of his betters. When he made an exception, Gregorio had learned to take note of it. Before him was planted a middle-sized man in an elderly cassock whose reddened face and tanned tonsure appeared to have been cleared by the razor from a carpet of cocks' feathers. Gleaming hair sprang from the backs of his fingers and hung over his eyes, fed by pulsing, vigorous veins. Gregorio said, "Some of us have dispensation. Please join us, brother. There is some good fish going waste."

"Dispensation?" The voice came from a deep chest, in good order.

"From the abbot of St Bertin." It was a profound lie, but he was curious about how much Observatine monks knew of Burgundian politics.

"The son of a priest and a nun," said Fra Ludovico. "The know-all of Burgundy." He sat down on the stool vacated by de Camulio.

"The Chancellor of the Golden Fleece Order," said Gregorio, on the mildest note of reproof. "I hear he and his predecessor have deposed Jason for his failure to meet private obligations and have replaced him as patron by the labourer Gideon, of the wet and dry fleece. Preferring the Holy Spirit to Ovid; the Holy Scriptures to the Metamorphoses; and truth, as ever, to fantasy."

"Nôtre Dame, Bourgogne et Montjoie St Andrieu!" bellowed the friar. He helped himself, with calmness, to the fish. "That is, I understand, the Duke's warcry. Since he has not attempted to

combine it with the names of Jason or Gideon, I cannot understand why he does not revert to St Andrew, the Order's first patron; missionary saint to both shores of the Black Sea. Until the rainy weather discommoded the knights, they always held the Chapter on his feast in November. Now, of course, that stinking Greek turncoat the despot Thomas has the head of St Andrew in Rome, and is using it to pay for his bottomwipers. You've never heard of Santameri?"

"Santameri?" said Gregorio obediently.

"The Frankish castle of St Omer. St Omer in the Morea. The Pope and Milan sent Thomas soldiers, but he didn't get on with them. If he had, the inhabitants of St Omer would be alive now. There is, I take it, no bread?"

"I shall have more brought," Gregorio said. "Will the Duke lead your crusade, or finance it?"

The friar plied his knife. There was lard on his chin. He said, "You want me to talk about how one jewel from the tournament prizes would kill twenty Saracens? I'm an Observatine, my boy. We've been pricking the conscience of kings since we were founded. I've lived in Jerusalem. Calixtus sent me to Persia and Georgia as nuncio to the Latins. He tried to get me into Ethiopia. I'm not a little monk with a bell from someone's carpeted chapel. I've the power to preach and hear confessions and confer sacraments and baptise. I work. I don't expect greedy people to help; I make them do it. I thought your man Julius was pig swill."

"So did Cosimo de' Medici until we proved otherwise. You should make sure of your facts," said Gregorio.

"That's what I'm saying. I thought he was pig swill; about to fill his pockets from both sides and get out before anything happened. The rest of the company too. I was wrong. You were sending soldiers to Trebizond. I've just heard it."

"How did you hear?" said Alighieri.

The Franciscan took both hands away from his mouth, which was full, and glanced at his fellow-delegate. "A friend of a friend," he said. He switched his attention back to his food. "Who will they fight for?"

Gregorio remained calm. He said, "For their leader Astorre, under Nicholas. Niccolò. Naturally."

The friar, peacefully groaning, was exploring his gums with a needle. He withdrew it, shrouded with food, and sat twirling it idly between thumb and finger. "I meant what you thought. For whom will child Niccolò fight?"

Michael Alighieri said, "Brother, all his resources are committed to the Emperor and the Medici. I am sure he is a man of good faith. But even if he is not, what other option has he?"

"He could fight for himself," said Fra Ludovico. "Abandon the company. Take the money and go somewhere safe. Venice, perhaps. I'm sure Messer Prosper de Camulio is uneasy. I'm sure you got remarkably little from him today. Of course, he had Michael here with him."

"Against your orders?" said Gregorio. He had realised it some time ago. He might as well risk it.

"Of course," said Fra Ludovico. "What does he need to learn about you? You and the woman who owns you are not going to matter. What matters is that fellow out there. Niccolò. That's someone the Devil's got his mark on."

"I heard what happened in Florence," Gregorio said. He felt cheerful. He said, "All the same, Messer Alighieri and I could have a useful talk, I am sure, that would do you no harm. He could tell me something of Trebizond."

"He could," said the monk. He broke open and abandoned a loaf; found a fresher one, and took it. He said, "He could tell you old women's stories of Trebizond that might make you call your precious Niccolò back, considering the way the princes are rushing to help us all here." He emptied his mouth and gazed at Gregorio. He said, "I don't want him back. I want him and his soldiers in Christian Asia."

"Dead?" said Gregorio.

He was answered by a light shower of wet bread. "He'd die in grace, wouldn't he? He won't get the chance. There's no more danger now than there was when he went. You'll get your profit with things as they are: you don't need to worry. It's to spare you worry that I asked Michael here not to trouble you."

Gregorio said, "Even if the demoiselle reversed his orders, they wouldn't reach Nicholas – Niccolò – for four months."

The friar wiped his knife and put it away. "But they might reach him," he said. "Safer to leave things alone. But you can write. Tell him that Fra Ludovico apologises for his error in Florence. Next time he'll make sure of his facts. And if the facts were to show that Niccolò has used that army against his own kind, tell him that Fra Ludovico plans to make a cassock cord from his bowels and have his liver cooked and served up on biscuit. You heard the Duke called us Magi?" He got up.

"Of course. Why not?" said Gregorio. He remained seated beside Alighieri. He had no intention of being browbeaten by this man. Out of the corner of his eye, he saw Alighieri shake his head and begin to get to his feet.

"Yes! There is something for you and Michael here to tell your friends the Medici. *Here are the Magi from the East*, said the noble Duke. *They have come to the star they perceive in the West: the star of the Fleece, the light of which illumines the Orient, and guides her princes to you, who are the true image of God.*"

"But you don't expect him to give you anything?" Gregorio said.

"He will," said the friar. "But not perhaps as he expects. You will not see Michael again, despite the signals he is trying to give you. We are here to sell Jesus, not gall nuts. Give my regards to your Jason in

Colchis, and remind him that the Order has now distinguished not just the fleeces of Jason and Gideon, but six different skins, with as many praiseworthy qualities. For Jason, magnanimity. For Jacob, justice. For Gideon, prudence. For Mesa King of Moab, fidelity. For Job, patience. For David, clemency."

"For me," said Gregorio, "I should find Jacob sufficient."

"Then you are as young as your master," said the friar.

Chapter 24

THE NEXT DAY WAS the last Gregorio spent in St Omer. In it, he
saw Simon de St Pol of Kilmirren, as he had planned.

No, not as he had planned; although he believed he was
ready for most things. Instead of the gown of his profession,
he dressed in the ordinary pleated tunic, short sleeves over long, that he
wore when about his own concerns, with a stiffened cap without
ornament. With it, he knew, he lost ten years from his age. Because he
had a nose like a duck, he had a face excessively droll (Margot said) for a
lawyer except when framed in black lappets. Freed, his hair fell into
coils even less suitable, which he kept ruthlessly trimmed. The rest of
his person he could do nothing about, except keep it resilient. Dressed
as he now was, he could have been of any rank. Even the good dagger in
its worn sheath at his side was only what you might expect of a traveller.
He didn't conceal it. He meant what he had said to Marian de Charetty.

The hour arrived. Seated below their heraldic devices within the
tapestried walls of Nôtre Dame, the Tenth Chapter of the Golden
Fleece began their deliberations. And Gregorio of Asti, civilian, called
at the house of Louis de Gruuthuse and asked for the lord Simon de St
Pol. By good fortune, the steward he spoke to was new. He said, when
asked his identity, that he was a servant of Monsieur Anselm Adorne,
the Bruges nobleman.

Within the rambling house, the room they showed him to was one of a
wing, occupied, it appeared, by Katelina van Borselen and her Scottish
relatives. The little receiving room was empty but for a stout woman in
a white cap, sitting sewing by open shutters. The glazed upper window
painted an acne of colour over her face. When she got up and curtseyed,
he deduced that she was prepared for him, but hardly excited. As the
steward had done, she repeated that her lord was detained, but her lady
would see him directly. From her accent she was neither Scottish nor
Flemish, but French-born. He took the seat she offered and watched
her settle back in her own. Small talk was easy in a house recently
blessed with an heir. He asked about Henry.

The baby! Her eyes changed at once and the sewing crumpled as she leaned forward. "Such a stout fellow, monsieur! Strong as three horses, and hardly a cry, unless his wetnurse oversleeps! But for serving my lady, I could hardly bear to be here, and miss seeing him grow!"

"A happy child," Gregorio said.

"Happy and handsome. His mother's face, his father's hair, curling like silver. And an angel-kiss on one cheek. I tell you, he is a little god. His father worships him. Would have him on a horse before he could suck, and a sword and a lance in his fists. There's a knight for you: never mind your Burgundian sheepskins!"

"His mother must miss him sorely," Gregorio said.

He only wished to elicit, if possible, how long they were staying. To his surprise, the woman didn't answer at once. Then she said, "As to that, great ladies are busy, monseigneur. There are nurses enough for the little one. She sees him when she can."

"Indeed." He said gently, "Was it a difficult birth?"

She nodded slowly, stretching the cloth on her lap. "A big child, and my lady was twenty. They blame the child sometimes. Or it frightens them, being so new to handle. And again, there are those whose greatest fear is that the little one won't grow to love them. You'd wonder children ever got reared, till you remember Nature always has her way in the end, and a child finds its way to most hearts."

"Of course it does," Gregorio said. He felt queasy. Nicholas, poor disowned bastard. You haven't missed much, not being claimed by this Scottish house. He said, "And how is my lady taking to Scotland?"

"My lady is taking to Scotland very well," said a light, polished voice from an inner doorway. Smiling a little, the speaker was walking towards him. "You come from Meester Adorne? Perhaps you don't know that I have spent one sixth of my life in that country. I was maid of honour to the Scottish queen, Duke Philip's niece. What is your name?" She spoke Flemish.

"Gregorio," he said. So this was Katelina van Borselen.

She was not beautiful, except for her body, which had a fullness of breast perhaps owed to the child, although she could not be feeding it. A confection of floating white cambric concealed most of her hair, which showed brown at the temples. Her brows, heavily marked, were a characteristic of the Borselen family: the fact that she had not plucked them showed a certain independence, borne out by the set of her mouth. Her neck was slender, and she held herself well. A comely young woman. Once roused, he suspected that she might come near to something quite striking.

She said, "Well, Gregorio, I am sorry to say that my lord is detained, but I expect him quite soon. Will you wait, or is there a message you may trust me with?"

"I should prefer to wait," said Gregorio. "Perhaps there is an office? It is a matter of business." The presence of Simon's wife was not part of the plan.

"Then he will take you to our chamber," she said. "And meantime you will sit and tell me all the gossip of Bruges."

"He was asking about my little lord Henry," said the woman.

He watched the girl's eyes. They looked flat and dense, as if painted, but they might have looked so before. She said, "Everyone has been so kind."

The woman said, "He was asking whom he favoured."

Had he asked that? He didn't remember. The girl said, "Oh, doesn't every first child look like his father?" She smiled. She had said it so often that the remark and the smile had lost meaning. She said, "But why should we deafen you with women's talk? What is happening in Bruges? And Genoa? What is the latest news from Genoa and the East?"

A door opened. The lady Katelina turned her head. "Simon? Here is a messenger from Anselm Adorne. He has private news for you. I am jealous."

Gregorio turned. In the doorway stood the man he had seen twelve months before, admiring the fire that had consumed the house, the dyesheds, the yard, of Marian de Charetty in Bruges. The lord Simon who had secured a ship of his father's and, placing Pagano Doria in charge, had sent him to Trebizond with Marian de Charetty's twelve-year-old daughter. The lord Simon whose antipathy towards Nicholas, born of his first wife, was known throughout Flanders.

Married when he was fifteen, Simon de St Pol must be in his mid-thirties at least. But such was the grain of the skin, the set of the blue eyes, the shining spring of the corn-yellow hair that he might have been the same age as his new wife Katelina. In dress he was exquisite also, from the tilted brimmed cap with its jewels to the quilted doublet that ended high above the long, well-turned hose.

On the night of the fire, he and Gregorio had met face to face. Because of what had happened, one of them would never forget it. But until Gregorio saw the other's expression, he did not realise that Simon, too, had remembered. Simon said, "This man is not from Anselm Adorne."

The girl's face had changed also. She knew, it seemed, the tones of her husband's voice. A look was enough to make the serving-woman curtsey and leave. Then the girl walked over and stood by her husband, facing Gregorio. She said, "Is this true? Who are you? My maid has gone for the steward."

Gregorio doubted it. He thought: she has gone through scenes before. She knows what happens when he loses his temper. He opened his mouth.

Simon spoke first. He looked at his wife. "He talked to you. What was he saying?"

There was a line between the marked brows. She said, "Nothing. He asked about Henry."

Simon began to laugh. He flung back his head, and gave way to peals of genuine laughter. When he straightened, his fair lashes were wet. He said, "He couldn't resist it. How he must have longed to know. How he must have hoped to hear the right kind of news. Is it limbless, an idiot? Hard of hearing, ill-favoured, twisted? I trust, my sweet, you told our friend all he wanted to know? I hope you told him all about Henry?"

The lady Katelina stood without moving. Her eyes, already wide on her husband, remained there. Her mouth had slackened, while the rest of her face, in a curious way, had drawn back. She said nothing. Simon said, "Don't you know who this man is? He's the ledger clerk from the Charetty. The fellow whose books I flung in the fire. He's been sent by young master Claes, to find out what sort of heir you and I have."

By that time, she had probably fathomed it. He could see her throat move, and her skin was white and pink as strawberry cloth. She said, "Get out."

"No, come in!" Simon said. He walked forward, hand outstretched to grip Gregorio's arm. "Sit down! Allow us to give you some wine! I want you to go back to Claes and tell him how you have drunk the health of the first of my sons. Of my many sons. If he were to coax me, I might name one of them Nicholas." His face was radiant.

The girl's voice, on the contrary, stamped like a boot. She said, "Indeed, no. Get out." She collected herself a little. "Simon, this is unlucky. What happens to Nicholas – Claes – has nothing to do with Henry. I will not have them linked. Get rid of him."

"I am not here to link them," said Gregorio. "I am here to talk about a ship called the *Ribérac*."

He had expected a gleam of understanding, followed by ridicule and rebuttal. Instead, Simon of Kilmirren looked at his wife. "He knows!" he said. "I was longing for him to know. So you have told the great Nicholas that his career as a merchant has ended. We have sent a Doria to show him how it ought to be done."

The man had not only felt confident enough to admit it – but his wife also knew. The frenzy of anger had withdrawn from her face, as if charmed by the name of Doria. In its place was not only tranquillity but something almost like triumph. Gregorio said, "You told him to rape Marian de Charetty's daughter as well?"

The girl lifted her head. Simon said, "Her daughter?"

"Catherine. The twelve-year-old. Without her mother's knowledge he took her to Florence and married her there. Then he sailed with her for Trebizond. A valid marriage, of course, would place Catherine's husband in control of half of the Charetty company on the demoiselle's death."

He addressed it to the girl who, surely, was innocent of that part of the plan. Her face seemed to confirm it. Turned to her husband, it showed enquiry; disbelief; horror. Simon said, "I don't believe you. Who would? The moment it happened, the demoiselle de Charetty would have run screaming to all the lawyers in Bruges."

Gregorio said, "Would you like to see Pagano Doria's letter to her, announcing it? I've made several copies. If I haven't handed them to the authorities yet, it is only at the demoiselle's request, for the sake of the girl. But it will, of course, be known in the end. That you paid Doria to pursue Nicholas to Trebizond and, one supposes, to kill him and usurp the business for you. The magistrates in Scotland and Flanders will be anxious, I'm sure, to see justice done."

"Does Doria's letter say that?" said the Scotsman. His colour had risen, making his eyes an even more brilliant blue. He did not look in the least afraid. "If so, of course he is lying. And so are you, naturally, encouraged by your little master."

"If nothing happens to injure Nicholas then, of course, we might take it that Doria is lying. Unfortunately," Gregorio said, "there is no doubt at all that the abduction of Catherine de Charetty is true."

"Nicholas knows of all this?" said the lady. Her face, turned towards him, was both pinched and intent.

Gregorio said, "He knows that your husband sent Doria."

"And about the girl?" the lady Katelina said.

"By now, no doubt he will have discovered. They should be in Trebizond together."

"Then the girl can come to no more harm. He is her stepfather. What did he say about Simon?" The horror, like the anger, had gone from her face. Instead, her attention had sharpened, like that of a dog waiting to dash.

Gregorio said, "That he would deal with it, and we were not to be concerned. That his wife the demoiselle should not be troubled with it. Unfortunately, she discovered. That is why, as her lawyer, I am here."

Simon laughed suddenly in his face. "I can't think why. Kill an apprentice! Usurp some widow's failed business! Why should I trouble? We did nothing but finance a legal mission by an able man who will show soon enough who is best fitted to run an overseas consulate. When he returns with a fortune, he will run my Genoese office."

"And Catherine de Charetty?" Gregorio said.

Some of Simon's colour had gone, but he looked no less undisturbed. He lifted a silken shoulder. "Am I to blame if an agent of mine gets a girl into trouble? No doubt the girl was man-mad; brought up in the same house as Claes and her mother. I've nothing to say.

You're welcome to take me to court if you want to. I'll find enough facts about Catherine de Charetty to make you wish you'd never come near me."

"No," said Gregorio. "She was a twelve-year-old virgin. He married her the day of her first menstruation. I propose, then, to set the complaint before the Duke this evening."

Simon smiled. "You couldn't even get near his secretary."

Gregorio said, "I could get near the Treasurer. Pierre Bladelin owes me a favour. Or perhaps I shall just wait in this house, and speak to Henry van Borselen. It is, surely, the office of the Golden Fleece to protect the young and the weak against those who exploit them? To chastise those who, instead of going to fight for the Faith, send others to waste ships, money and effort on a private vendetta?"

"And Nicholas is fighting for the Faith?" Katelina said caustically.

He turned. "He has taken a hundred armed men to serve the Emperor David."

"As Doria has taken a shipload of arms and armour," Simon said. He was smiling. Gregorio disliked the look of the smile.

Gregorio said, "We know, of course. But what will he do with them?"

He caught Simon's sharp glance and knew that, maybe for the first time, Simon had stopped to think. He hoped he was thinking about Pagano Doria. By marrying Catherine, Doria had made himself perhaps a little more powerful than Simon had envisaged. Unless he chose, there was no need for Doria to continue as anyone's agent. Simon said, "Claes. He's told you to do this, hasn't he?"

The change of voice should have warned him, even without the girl's sudden movement. The lady Katelina said to her husband, "How could he, from Trebizond? If Doria has done something wrong, you can face him with it when he gets back. So can the demoiselle de Charetty. Meester Gregorio is a reasonable man. He will wait until then."

"He may not come back," said Gregorio. "I shall wait, I think, for my lord Henry. Your son's godfather, I take it? He should have more care than most for the reputation of his family."

He had hoped to obtain a position of strength from which to issue an ultimatum. He had misread Simon. The flash of a sword was the first thing he saw, before he heard the lady's muffled scream. Gregorio jumped aside, fumbling for the hilt of his dagger as Simon came towards him, his whole blade unsheathed and gleaming. "I believe," said Simon, "in protecting the reputation of my family in my own way. With honour. With my own body. Not in some clerkly battle with ink. Bolt the door."

"No," said Katelina.

Simon turned his head. Gregorio swung himself over the table behind him and landed halfway between Simon and the door just as

Simon, setting hands on a chest, sent it sliding to crash against the door timbers. Then he straightened. "Now!" he said.

"Honour?" said Gregorio. "Sword against dagger?"

He thought Simon was past thinking, but then the other man smiled. Without turning his eyes he said, "Fetch the other one."

"No!" said the girl Katelina again.

"Then he'll have to fight with a dagger," said Simon.

She looked at him, and then ran to the door from which she had entered.

For the moments she was gone Gregorio stood, feeling foolish as well as frightened. He said, "What will this solve, my lord? Men know I am here."

"And they will know how you died," said Simon. "You came to kill me, on orders from Nicholas. Ah. There is the sword. You can fight, a little?"

"Enough," said Gregorio. Anger, filling him, suddenly burst past his guard. He said, "You conceited fool, what are you doing? Here's a little girl ruined, her family sickened with sorrow. And instead of facing up to it like a man, you blame others. Nicholas is worth ten of you."

The sword came past his throat as he spoke the last words. He got his own blade hurriedly up, and it caught Simon's the time it came for his belly, and the time it came for his heart. He stumbled over a chest, felt the steel sear through his forearm and parried, again, the point that came to his head. He crashed into the wall and, ducking, got himself out of a corner. He had called upon himself all Simon's passionate anger, and there was no more time, now, for words.

A bookish Lombard lawyer was no sort of match for a man trained in the martial arts: an expert jouster, a practised swordsman like Simon. Gregorio fought, because he did not want to die. He fought defensively, escaping where he could; parrying where he could. It seemed to go on longer than he thought possible. The girl, breathing noisily, was crouched like a hare by the windowseat. The main door was blocked. The room became littered with overturned stools and cushions and tables; the shards of a firescreen, the crumbs of a bowl. A brass pitcher tolled to itself in a corner and then was kicked aside with a clang. He thought the noise alone would bring rescue but no one came; no one called. Gregorio thought he was fit, but Simon had spent all his life tending his bodily skills. And now, as he tired, Simon feinted and leaped, and although Gregorio caught the blade with his own, the impact drove him staggering back to the opposite wall.

Further along, and still partly open, was the door to the inner room. The chamber beyond it was silent. Gregorio thought, as he went down on one knee, of trying to fight his way along to get through, and then wondered what good it would do. Enlarge the battlefield slightly. Make it possible, even, to run away with Simon spearing his back. He knew Margot was going to be extremely cross as it was, and he ought at least to leave her with some impression of the statement he was trying to make, and why he was trying to make it. Simon, meantime, was preparing to make his own final statement with both hands on the hilt of his blade.

With a weakened left arm, he couldn't parry that sort of stroke. Gregorio flung himself to one side and rolled, and half got to his feet, but knew very well it was useless. With masterly ease, Simon altered his grip, and the slant of his thrust. The point of his sword drove through Gregorio's shoulder. He felt it as a hideous blow, followed by an upheaval as the sword was wrenched backwards, scarlet. Then he saw that Simon had raised it again, his eyes narrow, and had taken both hands for the dispatch. As was seemly. To put himself out of his misery.

Chevaliers. Children, trained to stay children. Gregorio looked hazily up.

The sword had not descended. He could see the furred hem of Simon's tunic, and the handsome leatherwork of his girdle and baldric, and a lot of unpleasant red on the pleated bodice which must be his own blood. And Simon's cleanshaven chin, lifted in challenge, and his eyes, which were no longer deadly and narrow but open and rather empty.

A voice said, "Well, my dear; I think that is enough for today. Katelina, my son needs a wash, I believe, and a change of dress. And the room! The young at play. Endearing, but not really consistent with the dull world the rest of us have to survive in. And when the young are no longer young, not even endearing, I fear. Really, we shall never be allowed to come here again."

Simon stood without moving. The voice said coldly, "Put your sword down, you fool. Or don't think I won't get my grooms in to thrash you."

Simon's face was bone white. For a moment the sword seemed to move, as if he would like to use it, and not on Gregorio. Then he lowered it.

"And now, poor Master Gregorio. How is it with you?"

Hearing, like sight, had become vaguely unreliable. But above him Gregorio saw, quite distinctly, the form of the largest, heaviest man he had ever encountered, swathed in opulent velvet and topped by a broad-brimmed hat made of fur that would have kept a dozen men dry. The eyes trained upon him were as chilly as the question had been.

He could not speak. The man smiled, unperturbed. He said, "The vicomte Jordan de Ribérac. You have heard of me. It was my ship which my son here so inconsiderately removed from Antwerp without my permission. I believe it is now named the *Doria*. So appropriate, is it not, for Colchis and the Fleece? We are dogged by gold in this kingdom. We would rather be dogged by gold, however, than lawyers and, unlike my son, I prefer talk to action. Will you talk to me, my dear Master Gregorio? When you feel better?"

Gregorio said, "You watched?" He saw dimly that the girl, who had not spoken throughout, had risen to her feet by the window and was looking at them.

Jordan de Ribérac smiled. "Did I delay a little too long for your comfort? I was curious to see if you would fight. You did. Not very well, but you did. Allow me the pleasure of seeing your wounds of honour attended to."

Gregorio's wounds of honour were attended to on a pallet in a strange room by the same white-capped woman he had seen on his arrival. She seemed to be as expert with sword-cuts as with infants: for a while, dosed with possets and lapsing drowsily into various states of unconsciousness, he felt like one. The last time he woke, the candles were lit and Jordan de Ribérac was seated in a tall chair beside him, his hands clasped on the knob of a stick. Gregorio stirred.

"Ah," said the fat man. "The paladin is restored. I am glad. I should prefer to be assisting Louis de Gruuthuse celebrate his hard-won knighthood. I hope you feel well enough to depart?"

"Certainly," said Gregorio shortly. He was, he saw, already wearing someone else's shirt and an unknown doublet lay at the foot of the bed. His arm, bandaged and strapped to his side, was brutally painful. He added, "When I have what I came for."

The fat man laughed. His several chins gleamed. He said, "We are to receive no thanks for our labours?"

Gregorio held the unpleasant gaze with his own. He said, "I am grateful, of course. Thank you."

"Thank Agnès. It is she who saved you," said Jordan de Ribérac.

"Your son's servant?"

"He thinks so," said the fat man.

"You spy on him?"

"Of course. We dislike one another. But that does not mean I wish him exposed as a murderer as well as an idiot. Neither Agnès nor I rescue my son's victims out of philanthropy, Master Gregorio. Do you really consider this poor Nicholas to be worth ten of Simon?"

"I should imagine most people are," Gregorio said, and flinched despite himself. The cane, whipping up, hung with calculation over his wound. It stayed, gleaming; then shifting, delivered a biting blow to the other shoulder instead. Its point returned, with deliberation, to the floor.

"Watch your mouth," said the vicomte de Ribérac placidly. "The face of young Master Claes should remind you. It was he, you may know, who caused my present exile from France. Or perhaps you are unaware of the deadly proclivities of your little man? They far exceed, I assure you, anything my fool Simon has done."

"Nevertheless . . ." Gregorio began.

". . . Nevertheless, you wish Simon to command the return of our decorative friend Pagano Doria, or at least cancel his orders. You also wish Doria brought to book for using his undoubted charm of manner and body to seduce and even marry Marian de Charetty's unfortunate daughter. You wish the marriage annulled, or denounced, or denied: whichever will save the girl's face and punish Doria to the full. And in return for all this, you are willing to let my son's part in the business remain secret?"

"I couldn't have put it better myself," Gregorio said.

"You look surprised. You do not have, Master Gregorio, a monopoly of legal training. You understand you are condemning Messer Doria to death or perpetual exile?"

"That was my intention," said Gregorio.

"And that, being remote, he may still do your company harm before my son's message could reach him?"

"I hope he doesn't," Gregorio said. "For the demoiselle, through me, will demand full compensation."

"For the company – she shall have it," said Jordan de Ribérac. "For the life of Nicholas . . ." He tossed something in the air, caught it and deposited it with a light slap on the bed. "One silver groat. Debased, I fear. I had to separate it from its fellows today. You see, my dear sir, it is the fortune of Nicholas to invite rivalry, suspicion, ill will. He will meet his death, I make no doubt, through one of them, and the hand of Pagano Doria need never be lifted. You cannot expect me to pay you for that."

"But you will put this in writing?" said Gregorio.

"Yes indeed," said Jordan de Ribérac. "When you produce proof that my son arranged to have that silly child abducted."

Gregorio said, "I can prove that Doria is his agent. And that he took your ship from Antwerp."

"With my permission!" said the fat man immediately. "Of course, I lent Simon my ship. I asked Simon to establish an office in Genoa; send an agent to Trebizond. I have told you how close we are."

"So you would deny everything if I press all the charges," said Gregorio. "And will put nothing in writing. And meantime, who knows what is happening? We cannot reach them for four months." He held his burning shoulder. "I have forced you to your knees, I can see," he said bitterly.

"Very few people can do that," said Jordan de Ribérac. "But you have warned me of a folly of my son's of which I was unaware, and I am grateful for it. I do not, of course, offer you gold, which you would throw in my face. I shall, however, provide you with transport home of the kind that will serve your wound best, with entertainment already arranged for you and your men on the way."

"And your son?" Gregorio said. "What do you expect him to do?"

The fat man got up. Standing, his hands on his stick, he showed a glimpse, in the width of his shoulders, the depth of his chest, of the athlete he might once have been. Remotely, one could see how he might have sired the exquisite Simon. He said, "If Doria fails him, St Pol will have to care for the business himself. He has his heir. He is free. I should not be at all surprised, my foolish friend, if Simon did not leave soon for Genoa. Or wherever he might get news of Doria. For it is quite possible, is it not, that Doria has considerably exceeded his remit?"

"Will your son listen to you?" said Gregorio.

There was a silence. Then the fat man gave a slow smile. "Oh, yes," he said. "Simon will listen. Over his lady wife, however, I have to tell you that I have very little control. That is a warning. That is perhaps the most valuable warning you have ever received."

Chapter 25

OR SOME LITTLE TIME after the fever broke, Nicholas was too
limp for anything except, perhaps, thinking. Remarkably
soon after that, however, he was up and about: cheerful,
biddable, and co-operative. From servants and men he
received a tacit welcome and the same rough goodwill they had shown
him before. The name of Simon of Kilmirren meant nothing to them:
they didn't care who was paying Doria.

It meant very little either to Captain Astorre, whose contempt for
my lord Simon was immaculate, or to John le Grant, who had never
heard of him. There remained the trio of Julius, Godscalc and Tobie,
whose manner to their scheming junior had substantially changed. To
Julius, the disclosure of his further duplicity was a personal insult. It
not only increased his hatred of Doria, it made him even more angry
and suspicious of Nicholas who, with double his motives, had failed to
confront Doria, man to man; or allow Julius to do so. For the others,
who knew the abomination he had forced upon Simon, they saw now
revealed what was ugly as well as what was engaging about Nicholas.

For his part, Nicholas acted as if he observed nothing; attended
assiduously all the policy meetings called by Julius and tramped
alongside whatever delegation issued as a result to call on probable
buyers or possible sellers, to identify orders and to argue through
some problem of money exchanges. He spent quite a lot of time on his
own. As they had threatened, his colleagues had withdrawn from him
both his freedom of action and movement. Although still publicly
head of the station, in practice he was powerless.

Anything to do with Astorre's men, Julius saw to. Le Grant was
given charge of matters to do with the repair and overhaul of the galley
and the concerns of the seamen. The provisioning and control of the
household passed into the efficient black hands of Loppe, who proved
to be the best domestic bursar in anyone's experience. This freed
Godscalc and Tobie, helped again by le Grant to proceed with the
modified torture of wresting out of Treasurer Amiroutzes the

wherewithal for the new Florentine compound. In between meetings, Godscalc made a round of all the monastic churches in the district, bought what texts he could, and set a large number of scribes to profitable work. Julius, avoiding Nicholas, promoted a clerk called Patou to countercheck his calculations.

They all became familiar with Trebizond. Deepening spring brought more rain and an increasing warmth which clothed shore and mountain in shining and vigorous green, and devoured every space with opulent flowers. Waxen petals, fuddled with scent, crammed through tall, pillared windows. Drifts of cherry and pear blossom filled the furrows of doublets and straw hats; tree-vines burst into clubbable leaf. Markets turned into empires. A street of carpenters would wake to find itself choked by watermelons, or cheeses, or chickens.

Nothing, in fact, was quite as orderly as might have been expected of the Imperial family of the Hellenes: the Autocracy of all the East, the Iberias and the Transmarine Provinces. The unshaven hill men who came through the passes wearing hair tunics and leggings and driving goats or panniered pack-ponies owed nothing to classical harmony; nor did the dark-faced men jangling with gold who rode in with foot-trains of armed servants to take their ease in the baths and the brothels. They had money to spend and lived in castles, some of them. They earned their keep by exacting tolls and protection money from those who picked their way through the mountains. They brought news, of a sort. It was true what they said about the Sultan. He was already in Asia, in Ankara. His army, under Mahmud Pasha, was in Bursa and ready to move. Where, he was keeping a secret. If a hair in his beard knew, he had announced, he would tear it out and cast it into the fire.

In Trebizond, the court moved from the Citadel in its accustomed routine of devotion. To the church and monastery of Panaghia Chrysokephalos, to the church and monastery of St Sophia beyond the western ravine, to the church of St Eugenios beyond the eastern ravine, near the Summer Palace. Then a week's expedition to the cliff monastery of Sumela. The ray of the divine Logos, Heaven's king, the Emperor David prayed at their head.

The court, in a state of spiritual well-being, was able to spare some time for leisure. It took heed of its athletic prowess, engaging in spear-throwing and archery and playing vindictive cavalry games at the Tzukanisterion; none of it with particular style. It filed south into the mountains and ceremoniously went hunting and hawking. It held small, select feasts and patronised the company of men of learning who might beguile its tedium with intellectual discourse. It gambled prodigiously. It listened to music. It read, or was read to. It diverted itself with performers of many kinds; with dwarves and with animals; and witnessed processions of prisoners who had had their teeth hammered out and were wearing the intestines of oxen and sheep on their brows. These might be land-hungry nomads, or brigands caught raiding villages for stores, cooking-pots or children to sell to the whorehouses.

The court spent much of the day making itself beautiful, in order to spend much of the rest of the day in a state of physical gratification. It lay under silk awnings in the Summer Palace, engaging in minor intrigues, and in gossip. It was the Burgundian court compressed into a single trapezium, instead of spread half over a continent. It was a feminine version of the Burgundian court, producing carnivorous blooms on a leaf-bed of tradition that went back to Homer.

The memory of Byzantine battles remained still in its soldiery but, unlike Burgundy, it had created no orders of chivalry to foster the skills of its knights nor, until now, had it considered hiring the capability that it had failed to preserve. From the narrow strip of its lands and its wellwishers inland, it could count, on a good day, on two thousand foot and horse. The grandiose figures for fleet and army quoted during the Emperor's last appeal to the West seemed to have been forgotten. The present little crisis was different: was not a crisis at all. The heathen was fighting itself. It was sad, to be sure, for the ruler Uzum Hasan, Trebizond's Persian ally. But what could Trebizond do? Astorre, bounding from one listening-post to another in the vertical streets, puffing and grumbling, devoted a lot of his time to working out how strong Trebizond really was, and what the Emperor's captains really thought of the war.

Julius, who enjoyed wars, did a good deal to help him. In between, he was prone to bouts of angry anxiety on behalf of Catherine de Charetty, who was mostly withdrawn from public view behind the walls of the Leoncastello. She did, as she had said, visit the women's quarters in the Palace on occasion, and sometimes took part in their sport. But, as was predictable, she provided company for the Empress's ladies rather than the Empress herself. Whether she had ever spent time with Violante of Naxos was so far unknown.

Tobie, too, had seen the small figure, pompously veiled, being escorted on muleback by her maid and her Genoese retinue; sometimes to the markets; sometimes to pay calls on the houses of other merchants to pass the time, one supposed, with their mistresses. Whether she yet realised their lack of status was also unknown. Doria himself was often absent in Imperial company. Nicholas, commanded to the hunt or the race or the wrestling match, had his excuses made for him on account of his illness and did not immediately discover that he had been invited at all. When he did, he sent John le Grant in his place, his hands full of plans. Reporting back to his fellows, the Aberdonian's face was lightly flushed and his manner reticent to a degree. He merely told them, however, that, hearing of his experience with Serbian miners, the Emperor wished him to consult with his captains.

That was all he would say, despite some ribald attempts to get more from him. When Nicholas was seen to be near at hand, they stopped, or went out. Le Grant supposed he had overheard them. He also supposed that Nicholas recognised, as the others had not, that a man who could hold Donatello's friendship but not his persuasions was unlikely to be worried by overtures. If he noted the flush, Nicholas was unlikely to comment. They were not alone. Le Grant said, walking across to the windowseat, "I took the plans and explained them. Had to go all over the place like a pedlar."

"They like red hair," Nicholas said, without moving. "One day they'll make you into a wig. You'll leave with your ears in a cup, bald as Tobie."

Since his illness, Nicholas – the lion, the perpetual mimic – had never passed a light remark to either Tobie or Godscalc. Between these three lay something more than the complaints he had been told about. John le Grant didn't give a damn what it was. All he was concerned about now was conveying a message. He had a report to make, and he wanted to make it in private.

He had, of course, taken the fortification designs to the Palace and been interviewed by every jumped-up commander from the Protospatharios downwards. Then he had gone to see Violante of Naxos. He had taken her plans as well, but of different kind.

It was Nicholas who had suggested that visit. If his colleagues found out, he would be in trouble. Communication with Nicholas was supposed to be by committee. That is, Astorre wouldn't care. But even Astorre didn't know he was seeing the lady. And he was not sure, now, that he was going to tell even Nicholas what had happened when he got to her chamber.

To begin with, she was different in private, with almost no paint on her face and a severe gown in the Venetian style instead of the Byzantine sheath. She had sent the eunuchs out, and kept only two women who, he supposed, were confidantes. He bowed three times approaching, but didn't perform the Prostration which he had given Constantine, the Great Emperor, in the last days of Constantinople. She knew who he was, and offered him a seat at once. Then she said, "What is this illness?"

He had shown no surprise. "Nicholas, Despoina? A marsh fever. Nothing more."

"He is subject?" she said. Her hair was netted clear of her neck, and her mouth curled when she spoke, like a tendril. She added, "It is a long illness, for a fever."

It was a question. She was, of course, not to be trusted; but he was moved to see how far he could go. He said, "He is recovering, maybe a little quicker than some of us fancy. They've put a check on his movements."

"Oh?" she said. She added, "He is too immature, after all? But do you have a successor? I have not met one."

"Neither have I," said John le Grant. "No. It's government by consensus until he stops going his own way without consulting his officers. I shouldna be here, except that it's not on company business."

She said, "How has he gone his own way?"

"You'd need to ask him that," said John le Grant. "He's shown himself less than frank. And, of course, my lord Doria spread some tale about bath boys. You'll have heard that."

He stared at her. She looked unmovingly back. Whoever was immature, it wasn't Violante of Naxos. She said, "You have forgotten, I think, where you are."

"I beg your highness's pardon. By itself, it wouldn't have mattered, but he made a few other mistakes, so I hear. Different customs. Not everyone knows Venice and Anatolia. Not everyone understands the Grand Comnenos as you do. The Emperor isn't Duke Philip."

"No. He is Vice-Regent of Christ," she said. "He *is* the Church. He is the living embodiment of the learning of classical Greece. However weak a Basileus may be, he has to carry these burdens."

It was very quiet. If he had been a different man, or a younger one, he would have been afraid at the turn the conversation was taking. He said, "At the Easter mass, I saw the Emperor a figure transported. He makes a place at his side for the scholar. But the rest of his life, so they say, is just vanity."

"Those things are vanity, too," said the Emperor's great-niece. "But without him, neither the Church nor the learning could flourish. And after him, an abler might come. Have you thought of that, Scotsman? Or would you prefer honest ignorance, sat on the tombstone of culture?"

"I should prefer Uzum Hasan," John le Grant said.

There was a long silence. She said, "Well? You must have been told to say more."

"I was told," he said, "to find you, show you what he was making, and ask for your wishes. He said nothing more. That is why we complain of him."

"But," she said, "you must know what he thinks of the Emperor?"

"Yes, I know," said John le Grant. "But, like me, Nicholas has an engineer's method of viewing things. A faulty cog doesna alter a principle. The Emperor isn't part of the equation, or Uzum Hasan, or Mehmet even. It's what they stand for."

"You are alike," she said.

"No," said John le Grant. "I wouldn't be like yon young fellow for anything."

Nothing more of importance was said. He left soon after, and was impatient of the horseplay back at the fondaco, because he had several decisions to make. In the end, he told Nicholas all that the woman had said. The talk took place at dusk in the bedchamber, where part of his day was still spent. He couldn't see, in the darkening room, how the other man was receiving it. Eventually, Nicholas said, "Why mention Uzum Hasan?"

"He is her uncle," John le Grant said. He waited. He said, "She doesna know your opinion."

'But I seem to know hers," Nicholas said. "Unless you have left something out."

"I wanted to," the engineer said. "But unless you knew the facts, you couldn't interpret." He waited again. He said, "You can't escape, you know. You think like Julius, or you think like you. Your butterfly days are behind you."

"I don't know," Nicholas said, "how you get out of step with all the rest of this team. Everyone else thinks that these *are* my butterfly days."

He sounded quite entertained. But then Loppe came in, and set a spill to the lamp, and le Grant saw that there was no expression in his hollow clown's face at all.

The uneven convalescence; the weeks of restraint and suspicion were brought to an end, typically, by Julius, abetted by Tobie.

Elsewhere in the City, and subject to no one, Pagano Doria obeyed with alacrity every Imperial summons through all that ripening spring. It was easy to study his movements.

Julius chose one of his absences to march into the Genoese consulate and demand to see the demoiselle Catherine, returning speechless with rage to the compound of yard, villa, warehouse, garden and stables that was the present Florentine fondaco.

It was afternoon; the time of torpor when Trebizond took its ease, no matter how anxious its foreign merchants might be to do business. After a morning of work that had started at dawn, Tobie had taken a pack of cards out to the little pleasance Alighieri had made for himself behind the villa, where he had built a pool with a fountain and set a marble table and benches under the almond trees. Today, the sun was hazily warm and the tulips lining the water channels seemed made of scarlet satin: the scent of narcissus and hyacinth was dizzying.

Annoyingly, Nicholas was already there, lying with his shirt open on one of the benches. When he tired, it was less from walking, Tobie suspected, than from a bottomless drain of frustration. He opened his eyes at the pause in Tobie's footfalls, and then closed them again. In silence, Tobie resumed his way to his chosen table and, sitting, shuffled and dealt his cards, his shoulder to Nicholas. Two weeks before, they would have shared a game. Now he played against himself, making mistakes and conscious that they had been noted. But when he turned his head, Nicholas had changed his position so that he no longer overlooked the table.

Tobie had wondered, with Godscalc, what to expect of Nicholas once he recovered. They, alone of the company, knew the wretched story of Katelina van Borselen. Since letting it slip, Nicholas had never referred to it again. He had also made it apparent that the subject was permanently closed. Although never sullen, he was far from being forthcoming indeed on any subject when in their company. The broad flow of speculation, wordplay, raillery, ideas had stopped short. The shock of exposure had been too great to be set aside lightly. And even when it wore off, he could hardly, in decency, return to the insouciance of the past. In private, John le Grant was the only one with whom he had more than a passing word. But then, John le Grant knew less about him than anyone.

In public, with the others, it was different. Silent in council unless directly spoken to, he would give his opinion in as few words as possible, and then desist. Only sometimes, when the final resolve seemed less than sensible, would he fall into step with one or other of them on the way out and offer some remark of his own on the subject, switching immediately to something else. Julius and even Astorre accepted the change, clearly considering that Nicholas had returned to the more amenable days before Modon – although even then, of course, he was keeping quiet about Simon.

Godscalc had refused to speculate. Tobie considered that Nicholas had picked, in fact, the only possible way of responding to what had been, for him, a near-annihilating disaster. He also saw, as time went on, that his meek role in public was beginning to jar on the man. He persisted with it because he must. But sometimes a keen ear could detect a note of irony, or perhaps of self-ridicule, in the muted, moderate answers he gave. In private, again, the tendency was wholly absent. He was in isolation for his sins, and he knew it.

The game was turning out badly, even without an observer. Tobie had just made up his mind to go in when he heard raised voices from the front of the villa. The voices came nearer, and were cut off by the bang of a door. Footsteps could be heard, descending the steps to the garden.

Nicholas raised his head, and then began to sit up. Tobie, card in hand, peered through the pale screen of fruit trees. Nicholas said unguardedly, "Do you smell . . . ?"

Fish. Not just fish, but a stink of something fleshy about it that clouted the flowery sweetnesses out of the air and hit you straight in the face. The smell came with the footsteps, and was worsening. Julius arrived in view. Tobie stared at the notary. At his handsome face, which was streaked and lacquered over its tan like a wedding-chest. At his hat, which was not a hat but a cluster of unruly pink blossoms. At the sober doublet he wore normally under his gown, which was now a shimmering casing in the form of a man down which drifts of magenta flowers flowed sensuously. The path behind him was strewn as by some diabolical Olwen. The smell of fish was sickening.

"Dolphin blubber," said Nicholas. His face had cleared, for the first time in two weeks.

"Dolphin oil," Julius said. His voice was mild. He bent his elbows and turned about once; and then looked at them again. "You see it, do you?"

"How?" said Tobie. His voice shook.

"My former pupil," said Julius. His voice was still mild. "The lady Catherine de Charetty, married to the good lord Pagano Doria. You have seen it?"

"Yes," said Tobie.

"Good," said Julius. He turned, and walked across the path and into the pond which he crossed, wading steadily, until he got to the fountain. Then he turned and stood perfectly still, his eyes shut. The water sluiced into his hat and slid over his face and poured into his shirt and pourpoint and over his doublet and down the tops of his thighs. Flowers, in piercing pink cascades, followed the water and pushed out into the pond in thickening garlands.

"Judas flowers," said Nicholas. His eyes had stretched very wide and his face was an undimpled plain.

"You are right," Julius said. He took his hat off and, holding it between thumb and forefinger, let it drop into the pond. Uncovered, his hair gleamed on his skull and his face as if painted. He unfastened, staring at Tobie, all the buttons of his doublet and pourpoint and took them both off, dropping them into the water as well. Lastly, he pulled undone his points and peeled and discarded his shirt. The water poured down his bare skin and his soaking drawers. His laces, trapped, jumped about the pond surface. He began to speak in measured and deliberate tones, occasionally spluttering when the water spurted into his mouth.

"I told her," said Julius, "perfectly civilly – this brat who had once been my inadequate pupil, who could barely spell her own name – I told her it was time to be done with this nonsense and come back to her family. I said I would wait while she packed. She refused to come. I told her Doria couldn't harm her once she had our protection. She said she didn't want our protection, especially as we couldn't keep our own ship from going on fire. I told her that she was coming immediately, and if not, for her own good, I would remove her. And – and . . ."

"She flung the dolphin oil over you?"

"She ordered her servants to do it. They did it. Laughing. Then she shook the tree. She shook the tree so that the flowers . . . Laughing. Are you laughing?" said Julius.

"No," said Tobie. Tears poured down his cheeks.

"I hope not," said Julius. He glanced down at his clothes and then began wading methodically back to the pond edge where he stood over Tobie, who leaned back. A pool formed on the ground. The stench was still awful. He transferred his stare to Nicholas whose face, the reverse of Tobie's, was pale.

"No," said Nicholas.

"And so?" said Julius. His voice developed suddenly into a roar. "What do we do about it? Eh?"

"Nothing, you fool," Tobie said. His face was still scarlet. "What did you expect? All you did was please Pagano Doria. He'll love it when he hears. We'll make a formal complaint of enticement and kidnapping, all done up in Latin."

"I'll send Astorre," Julius said. "I'll send Astorre and fifty soldiers to carry her – "

"No, you won't," Tobie said. "Will you get it into your head that they're married? We'll send Godscalc with a rude reply, also in Latin. Why did you want to make all that fuss? We know what's going on in the Leoncastello. We know she's all right. My God, you took enough trouble to plant Paraskeuas and his family in the compound."

"It won't do any harm," Nicholas said. He sounded choked between anguish and laughter.

Tobie looked at him. "It won't . . . ? Oh, I see. That's true. They'll hardly suspect Paraskeuas with Julius making scenes all over the yard. Julius, I know you're offended, but the smell is more than I can stand. What about a swim in the sea?"

Julius glared. "Judith and Holofernes!" said Tobie, suddenly losing control, and began to laugh in long, whooping cackles. Nicholas had stifled all sight and sound with one hand. Julius looked down at the back of his neck.

Julius said, "It's your stepdaughter. Laugh, of course, if you feel like it. Be sure to send the story in your next little note to your wife. And, by the way, Paraskeuas managed to pass me some news. The snow has cleared on the passes, and the camel trains are on the way. That's what you were waiting for, isn't it? Now you'll be able to go and laugh on the other side of the mountains."

He walked off, streaming water, flowers, and pardonable anger. Tobie, who had no particular sense of shame, continued to express qualified glee but was not unaware of the uncommunicative hand beside him. Presently, he rose without haste and, strolling indoors, found where the black wine was standing. He lifted it and returned.

He found Nicholas wading out of the pool, bearing garments heavy with oil in each hand. Flowers clung to his calves. He dropped the clothes on the grass and took the cup Tobie gave him. Since he rose from his bed, it was the first service Tobie had offered him. Tobie said, "It's time you were gone."

"Yes. I know," Nicholas said.

He left at the beginning of May, with a group of armed men and some servants. Beforehand, he spent a lot of time with Astorre and le Grant, clearing his mind about what ought to be done. Once he was committed to leaving, some of his freedom returned: he was able to consult whom he wished and buy what he wanted, as well as hire his own guides. He had wanted to visit the Palace, but they wouldn't allow that, unless someone went with him. They had spared him all the men and the horses he had asked for. And the clothing. Spring had come to the coast, but the plateau he was aiming for was over six thousand feet up, never mind the mountains he would traverse to reach it. Two hundred miles away on the high plain was Erzerum, *Arz ar Rum*, the Land of the Romans. There the caravans which had journeyed in convoy from Tabriz rested, until they came to travel their different ways. At Erzerum, or before it, he should meet them.

The expedition, of course, would get him out of the way. It would make the company popular with the Emperor: it might have been thought an Imperial duty to guide the incoming caravans past their enemies. On the other hand, these days the caravans collected each spring at Tabriz and came north through the eastern Armenian plains, leaving the troublesome land routes of Asia Minor alone. And at present the Sultan and his army were safely far to the west.

Of course the caravans would be rich. The first of the year always were, being an amalgamation of the trains from Baghdad, Arabia, India, and those from the Caspian, bringing laden pack-ponies from Lahidjan, Talich and Asterabad. From the first three, he would get dyes and spices. From the last, he would get what he had come for – raw silk at no more than two and a half florins a pound, and four months' credit.

It would suit the company, of course, to find the train and have first pick of this and its other goods. But there would be plenty for everyone. If the Charetty company wished to waste time and money and manpower on such an uncomfortable venture, the other merchants were willing to wait and make their purchases in comfort at home. His only visit to the Palace in the end was a formal one, and he was received and wished well by the Treasurer, George Amiroutzes, whose shopping list he already had in his satchel. Julius was at his side all the time, smelling rankly of perfume. The pond of the villa had been emptied three times but still attracted seagulls and cats. On the actual day of departure, Astorre held him up at the Pyxitis bridge for ten minutes adding all the warnings he had forgotten to mention. Godscalc, the only other officer to ride with him so far, had said very little but had not prayed over him, either; or not audibly. Since all this was happening because of Godscalc, his own farewell to the priest was, he supposed, uncharacteristically grim. It reflected his feelings.

He had refused to take Loppe, who had wanted to come. He was on reasonably good terms already with the fifteen men of his retinue, who expected and would get some good jokes and light discipline, combined with a sense of controlled adventure. He had no misgivings about the journey. Anyone who had been beaten over the European Alps in winter had little to fear from the Pontic. Being both determined and well used to hardship, he had thrown off his illness and latterly had imposed on himself a régime which meant, he hoped, that whatever the privation, he would not do less well than his men.

He hoped there would be no privation beyond a fair amount of cold, which he was prepared for. The passes tended to be in the hands of men who would take what they could from an unguarded traveller but who did not mind selling hospitality and information to the other kind. Information he needed. For the rest, they carried their own tents of oxhide and cotton, and some supplies, and some fodder. But again, soon there would be mountain hamlets where a little oil, a little wine, a few pieces of nut paste would buy them hospitality in the small timber enclaves, and shelter from the rain, or the snow, or casual predators.

It fell out much as he expected. Riding through the thick forests and up the steep winding track to the Zigana, they hunted and caught fish and roasted their game. He had brought one of Astorre's falconers with him, and had himself taught the art. They shot for their meat, and for sport, and at night sat unshaven, with pink Colchian crocuses stuck in their caps, and exchanged tall tales from all the parts of Europe they came from. He had no experience to cap what they told him, but could manufacture himself outrageous and bawdy parallels, in prose, in verse or in song that had them all sick with laughter. It was a small gift and useless, except for a small leader of smaller men. Great leaders require different bonds.

Climbing, they left behind them the nutgroves and the forests of oak and beech and came to conifers where snow still rested in shining grey patches and the track was firm with frost. Men lived in these parts as well; sometimes in hutted villages and sometimes in tents, which their beasts and their flocks and their children shared with them. When it became known that he would pay for information, he was offered a surfeit, most of it spurious, and had to resort sometimes to hostages to exact the news that he needed. In turn, men tried to buy his interest; sometimes with food or furs; sometimes with their daughters or sisters. Often, wherever he was, he was offered a girl to take to his blanket. He knew his refusals embarrassed both his own men and the donors. He never explained. When they gave him a boy, he dismissed him goodhumouredly. For the first two days, he discovered, his servants thought him a eunuch. He thought of telling them that there were several people who wished that he was.

There was real snow at the Zigana pass, by which they left the seaward slope of the mountains for the further ridges and basins that climbed to the tableland of the Armenian interior. Now they unpacked and wore the thick hooded cloaks of raw goathair which had been his first purchase. The horses, too, were doubly covered: he had brought enough to give them all a change of mount as the going got steeper, for there were no relay horses here. They had some minor accidents, and lost a pony which broke its leg in a hole, but made good progress in spite of it. He wanted to move quickly.

Through it all, he had not forgotten why he was there. He had already found and spoken to a man recommended to him at Maçka. He bribed another just over the pass, and left a messenger of his own in the valley at Gümüshane. By then he had had his little talk with the professionals he had picked to come with him and they knew what to expect and were, he thought, in high heart. Indeed, he knew they were. They were his, as he had learned to make the seamen his. Their lives were in his hands, and his might be in theirs.

He waited until they were over the Vavuk pass just north-west of Bayburt before he called the long halt they all deserved, and found a proper place to make camp, and rest. It was there, as he had hoped, that his spies reached him, and the word came that he had been waiting for. Pagano Doria, with twenty men, was behind him.

Chapter 26

PUT YOURSELF IN the other man's place. It was what Nicholas had done, during these last wretched weeks; behaving in every small detail as Tobie and Godscalc and Julius demanded with the one small, innocuous exception of John's special call at the Palace. His altered status would not, he thought, have been evident to an outside observer, even one as committed as Doria, unless he too had his spies. Unless he knew what only two people could have told him – that the Charetty company at the moment had a divided leadership; an empty warehouse; a high reputation because of Astorre; a personal relationship with the Palace which had now ceased, and was valueless compared with Doria's own.

He had thought it likely, sending le Grant, that the lady Violante would question him, and that le Grant would feel impelled to answer. He had little idea whether she would pass what she learned to Doria, and whether, if she did, Doria was now in the mood to believe her. He didn't care, either way. If Doria knew of the disaffection among the company's seniors: if he also knew, for example, of the growing bundles of manuscripts in the strongroom of the villa – he might well think that the moment for his coup was approaching. The death of Nicholas, abroad on a dangerous journey, would have a plausibility he might never contrive again. His natural heir – his only heir here in Trebizond – was Catherine's husband Pagano Doria, favoured by an emperor who also wished to keep Astorre and the Charetty company in the Empire. Then, from the caravans now approaching, Doria could buy stock with his silver for Simon and Genoa, and buy again, on Medici credit, for the leaderless Charetty fondaco.

But of course, it would be Simon and Doria, with the Florentine franchise, who would remain ultimately in business in Trebizond, and the former allies of Nicholas who would ultimately find their way, profitless, home. Simon, man of fortune and grace, seated in the house of his forebears in Scotland with a lovely woman as bride and a son of five months to smile at him every day from the cradle.

Forget Simon. Forget Simon, and think about Pagano Doria.

He had reminded Godscalc and Tobie that Doria was awaiting his chance; but had not repeated the warning, and if one of them had pursued the same line of thought as himself, he didn't say so. Acting only from instinct, Nicholas had prepared himself and his men as if for battle, and it had come almost as a pleasure to be told, the day before he left Trebizond, that he had been right. Pagano Doria was planning to follow him.

The information came from their own informer in the Doria household and by a Godgiven fluke, it had come to him alone. Reports from the Greek Paraskeuas had kept the Charetty informed, day by day, of what Doria was doing, and how his wife Catherine did. It was why Nicholas had taken the chance long ago, on the way to his audience, to try to sever Doria's connection with Violante of Naxos. He didn't know if he had.

But now, on this one auspicious day, bringing his news, Paraskeuas had been pressed for time and, glimpsing Nicholas, had disobeyed orders and reported to Nicholas.

The news this time had not been routine. Pagano Doria was gathering men, horses, supplies for a hunting trip. Or so he had told his wife and his colleagues. Paraskeuas thought differently. The men he had picked were servants and intimates, and had several horses apiece. They were heavily armed and carried, done up in packrolls, extra weapons and tents, and blankets and cloaks for cold weather. He had also packed, discreetly disposed, a large number of packets of silver, as if about to make costly purchases of men, or of goods.

"Of men," Nicholas had said thoughtfully. "He'll hire men in the mountains who'll disperse later, and won't talk." He had dismissed Paraskeuas with a generous present before anyone came. So Pagano Doria was coming after him, and no one knew of it, except himself.

He had given five minutes' thought to the question of whether to tell Julius and the others. Before the bitterness of the last few weeks, he would have given it none. The result was the same. Doria's quarrel and Simon's were nobody's business but his. Warned, he could turn the tables and stop something worse happening. Godscalc, damn him, ought to be pleased. And more than that, he would have once more the satisfaction of planning and managing an operation as it ought to be done. For leadership was a dangerous drug. To watch other men's errors was once an idle amusement: now it was an ache. He couldn't have borne it much longer; whatever they would say after this; whatever they would do to him. So he had waited, and told his men only last week why they had so many weapons; and they had cheered. The Genoese were easy to despise. Well, they would see.

It was dusk. From what he had been told, it seemed that Doria's party would reach this spot before morning. They would know how near he was, from his tracks. Beyond this short defile was exposed country: if they were wise, they would attack soon, in darkness. Of course, he might have misread Doria. Attack might not be in his mind. Perhaps he meant only to trail him, or even to accompany him to Erzerum. Or to overtake him in secret, although he seemed to be following too precisely for that. Why worry? Very soon they would know.

As at every stop they had made, he had already searched out the best place for ambush. Here the track ran above a fast, cold stream which had carved itself deep sloping banks thick with thorns and low alders. He pitched the tents there, on the rising ground to one side of the stream, and by a pool which promised good fishing. Fires were lit and blankets spread: the tent skins glowed like honey from the candles within. He made horse lines and attached to them some of their least valuable ponies. The rest he took uphill away from the stream to where the Bayburt road ran like a shelf round the mountain. Above the road was an embankment, and above that the failing light showed the ribs of the mountain above, covered with turf patched with snow, and rearing up to the snow shoulders themselves.

Dark on the snow was a group of derelict huts, once used for summer grazing. The turf roofs had half gone and so had the doors, or perhaps they had never had anything but hides pinned across them. To the most searching eye, they were patently empty. On the other hand, a group of men and their horses could lie perfectly hidden behind them. He put eight men there, their chain mail hidden by dark cloaks, their swords and shields and helmets to hand. His six bowmen he placed below the road but above his own empty encampment. He had put a bale of hay between his own tent wall and the lamp: punched into the shape of a man it looked not unrealistic. Some of the others had done the same. The wind blew, chilling them as they took their positions: down among the bushes the tents moved and shook and lamps wavered. The scout he had placed to the north crept up and whispered. An advance group was coming.

Now it was full dark. At sea, it was never completely dark, especially in the north. The sky had its starlight, the water its phosphorescence. The lights of the fishing boats repeated themselves in the waves: the lighthouse burned, the harbour flares wavered. Bruges was never dark, or Milan or Florence. Cressets flamed in the streets; by the canals, the bridges, the rivers. Windows glowed, and people flocked by carrying torches. Pious candles pointed to shrines and to statues: lanterns shone over doorways to taverns, to churches, to brothels. And the sounds heard in the dark were domestic sounds of vermin and small hunting animals. Here, he didn't know the names of all the night birds when they screamed, or recognise the smell of a rustling marauder, although he asked his guides where he could. His men were better off than he was: although used to lit, busy camps, they had all done their share of scouting and skirmishing. They were well fed and well slept and nervously boisterous: his only concern was keeping them quiet. For the rest, he took the experience and assimilated it, for the future.

Put yourself . . . Why send a party ahead? A parley, to hold his attention while the rest of the force took their places? Would Doria risk it? And what would he gain, except an encounter face to face? A scouting party? He might have thought so, except that he could hear horses' hooves now. For whatever reason, Doria was giving his presence away. His captain said, "They're coming along the road, Messer Niccolò. Four of them, by the sound. They'll see the tents soon. Unless we shoot them, they'll find out they're empty."

His orders to the men with him had been specific. Harm no one until they attack. If they have come to kill, then kill in return. Except the lord Pagano Doria. Nicholas said, "No, don't shoot. Tell the bowmen. We'll take and truss them and put them into the tents. Come on. Now." They mounted as he was speaking. He led them at a dash from behind the huts: four to leap down to the pathway ahead of the oncoming horse, and four to cut off their rear. Somewhere behind the newcomers, presumably, were sixteen others; but far enough off to hear nothing, he hoped, but confused shouting. By the time they came, the confused shouting would come from the tents.

It was a reasonably good plan. It was shaken first of all by the realisation that Doria's main force was much closer behind than they'd thought. From a clear drumming far in the distance, you could tell they'd suddenly moved to hard track. There was no time now to truss anyone. Nicholas said, "Get the advance party anyway. And up to the huts." By then the four were in sight, racing towards him. As he jumped with his own men to face them, the leading man of the four began shouting. Black against the dark sky, he could have been Pagano Doria. He could have been anyone. It wasn't until he came nearer and caught the distant faint light from the tents that Nicholas recognised the face, and the voice. It was Julius, with three of his servants.

Even then, it was redeemable. Silence them before Doria comes. Julius had seen him and was pelting towards him, shouting at the pitch of his voice. "Doria! Doria's behind me!" He had his sword out. Nicholas saw it flash. He saw other swords flash as well. Those of his own men who had jumped into the road at the back of the small party were proceeding to round them up according to plan, unaware of their identity. There was no point in silence now. Nicholas roared, "Stop!" and threw his horse towards Julius. In the moment before he reached him, he saw one of the men with Julius go down, and another man shout in surprise as he recognised who was attacking him. Then he was there, in the milling group, speaking only to Julius.

"We know. We have an ambush. Quickly, up to the huts," he heard his captain telling the others. But they were slower to grasp what had happened. Two of them had dismounted and were trying to heave the fallen man to his feet. The frosty ground rang and shook as the approaching horsemen came nearer. Nicholas said, "It's too late. High ground, everyone. Take them as they make for the tents." He could see, from the way he was sitting, that Julius was exhausted. He took his reins and drove both horses up the embankment. He said, "The tents are empty, a decoy. What about Doria?"

"He means to kill you this time," Julius said. "Blaming the brigands. Paraskeuas says. Paraskeuas . . ."

"Never mind," Nicholas said. "Here they come."

It was too dark to see the sea prince. The handsome face from Florence, from the Bailie's table at Modon; the handsome body from the Emperor's baths. Something about the compact group of horsemen thundering towards him was odd. He registered that; and the sound of Doria's voice issuing orders. Without pausing, the oncoming horsemen divided: ten making for the high ground where they stood, and ten for the low, where the tents were. If anything, the riders had increased their pace. This was not a party about to join him or overtake him. Julius had been right, and his instinct. It was an expedition to destroy.

They were experts too. They allowed only two of their number to be picked off before turning away from the tents and riding slashing through the scrub, hunting his archers. Another fell to an arrow shot from above, but they got one at least of his men: he heard the scream. Then he had no more time for what was happening below the road, for the other file of riders was among them.

There was just enough light to tell friend from enemy and soon more, because someone tossed a brand in their hay. He had fought before, once, in a pitched battle, in sunlight. He had been trained by Astorre, and by the Duke of Milan's master-at-arms. He was powerfully built, and had a good eye, and almost no experience. In anything. But he was damned if he was going to lose this battle.

His men were good. They tried the time-honoured strategy of opening to let the oncomers plunge through, and then turning inwards to divide and cut up. The newcomers had never heard of the strategy and had ponies that could stop on a groat and spin and dart like housemartins. Their riders were as shaggy as they were. His shoulder throbbing with the bows on his steel, Nicholas saw that they were bearded, and dressed in leather and fleeces, and using small wicked blades with a curl to them. He saw a man's arm fly off, carved like a sausage in muslin; two horses went down, threshing and squealing.

His men had the advantage of the weight of their horses, and their shields, and their mail. His men, but not those of Julius. He suddenly realised it, and began driving through to where Astorre's notary, using the last wave of drained energy, was defending himself. One of his men had gone. Nicholas sent him a smile from the dyeshop and, settling beside him, used his shield and his sword to hit and parry and stab. The noise was deafening: like a hall full of ravenous men eating off pewter and shouting. Red sparks powdered the air and steel slipped about steel, making elderly, querulous noises. His horse went down.

It was not until then that he fully realised that fifteen against twenty were bad odds, even throwing in Julius; and especially when against men and horses who belonged to the country. For they did. This he was now sure of. Just as he realised he had seen nothing at all of Doria. He had heard his voice. For the rest, there was a mounted shadow he had glimpsed on the edge of the light, simply watching. But he had never been able to break through to reach it.

Most of them, he saw, were dismounted now, and the fighting men had split into groups, which swayed and staggered up and down the invisible turf. To fall was to disappear below a circle of swinging arms holding steel or maces that came upwards red. He could no longer see Julius and his head rang from the last blow he had taken, half on his head and half on his shoulder from behind. He steadied and turned, but saw two other men turning to measure him, one with steel already uplifted. Then the voice of Julius said, "I'll take this one," and he was able to put his shield up in time, and take the other blow on his sword. The swordsman, expecting a kill, was disconcerted: it allowed Nicholas to swing back his blade and run him through. He twisted as he did so to stand half between his other assailant and Julius. But where two men had been, there were now six others running towards him. He thought blearily that Doria must be growing men somewhere out there in the darkness. He was irritated enough to lift his voice and shout: "Messer Pagano! There is a boy here who would like to meet you in person!"

He saw the shadow in the roadway move, and caught the gleam of white teeth. Then the shadow, the camp, the blustering fire were all extinguished by an immense and broad-shouldered form, rank as a bear, with a mace held aloft in both its brawny arms. Nicholas saw Julius turn and, shouting, try to come to his aid. Then the mace fell. Watching it come, he felt no special fear; just the beginning of sadness. I have failed. I have failed you. And then the blow fell, and he heard and saw nothing more.

He thought at first he was dead; and then decided he felt altogether too poorly. After a long while, during which he kept losing his senses, he distinguished that he was travelling, face down and brutally lashed to one of the same shaggy horses whose riders had fought for Doria. From the trampling before and behind, it was one horse among many. Below him was a broad unmade track like the one he had been following to Bayburt, but much steeper. The horse strove beneath him and, but for the severity of his bonds, he would have rolled from its back. As it was, his own weight and the jolting had driven the rope like a cheesecutter into his arms and his thighs, taking the cloth of his shirt and cloak with it, and macerating his flesh with the rings of his armour. His clothes were stiff with old blood and gummy with fresh blood and urine. He stank. It was one of the normal results of shock and cold, blows and long spells of unconsciousness. John le Grant was not the only one who had to learn to relegate its importance to its proper place.

At this point, he remembered Julius and shouted, and was beaten for it – but not before he heard a wavering answer, and then other voices raised in greeting. Instead of obliterating them on the spot, Doria was taking them somewhere. Those who were still alive. He thought he had probably lost half his men, and those he had heard sounded little better off than himself. An operation planned and managed as it ought to be done. He was a fool. Someone ought to have stopped him and beaten him. All right, Julius interfered with the plan. All right, the numbers against him had trebled. He was still a fool.

But alive. Nicholas turned his head and croaked again, "Julius? If you see that little turd Doria, kick his teeth in." He heard Julius give a kind of laugh before the club cracked him on the head again. They had taken his helmet. After that, nothing became very much clearer, although there were times when he appeared to be on the ground and not on a horse, and times when he was given something to drink, and very rare occasions when he got something to eat, but found it hard to swallow. He didn't see or hear Julius again.

Eventually, he woke in a tent, to find himself lying on an old piece of cloth, carefully spread to preserve the floor from contamination with his person. His cloak had been cut off, and his mail shirt taken away, exposing what had been beneath them to the gratification of the general public. The only spectator present was even younger than himself: a youth with a shaven head and a long collarless tunic who had been sitting in silence, crosslegged against the wall of the tent. When Nicholas stirred he rose and stood looking down at him. The expression on his face was one of thorough distaste. Spotlessly clean, he had no affinity, it was clear, with his recent captors, but neither could his clear pallor, his black hair be Genoese. Nicholas said, in Greek, "Who are you? And where is this?"

The delicate face surveyed him without moving a muscle. Then the boy spat, and went out.

The spittle ran down his cheek. Tobie ought to be here. No. On the whole Tobie had done enough. His hands and feet were still bound, but he could turn his head. He looked about him, rubbing his cheek on the cloth. Julius was not there. The tent was empty even of furniture, but well made of good material, and there were tassels. Not the home of a nomad. The tassels stirred, and a man parted the flap and came in. With him was the same boy as before. The boy had been snivelling. The man, in identical dress, had a face like Alessandra Strozzi in a bad mood. He gave a bow, jerkily, towards Nicholas. Nicholas opened his mouth but immediately the man shook his head and signed for silence with a small, angry gesture. Then he looked at the boy.

The boy looked like Alessandra's son Lorenzo in a bad mood. He advanced a pace, dropped to his knees, and briefly placed his brow on the ground. Then he rose and glared at the man, who made a curt gesture. The boy went to the door of the tent and snapped something. The language was neither Greek nor Italian nor Arabic. His brain, wakening, informed Nicholas that it was Hebrew, of which he knew a few words. His brain went to sleep again. There was an interval, during which the man avoided looking at Nicholas and, indeed, seemed to be praying. Then the tent flaps were fully opened and four men came in, bearing between them a tub full of water. It was steaming. They placed it on the floor of the tent; went out, and returned with a brazier. There followed a table and two folding stools; a pile of linen and a box, from which an assortment of objects were lifted and placed on the table. Lastly a wicker basket was brought and a second table erected. His eyes on its empty surface, Nicholas waited. The men left, all but the first. The boy re-entered, bearing a bowl. In it were roses, exquisitely arranged. Their scent filled the tent, drowning out everything else. Nicholas raised wide eyes to the man, and the man addressed him.

He spoke in Latin. "Do you understand me?"

"I understand you," Nicholas said.

The man's face altered a fraction, not more. He said, "I am a physician. I have to ask you, if your bonds are cut, that you do not offer violence. To me or to the boy."

"I promise," Nicholas said.

"We have nothing to do with your injuries. Our task is to care for and cure them." He had signed to the boy. The boy knelt, knife in hand, and felt the cords at his wrists.

"For whom?" Nicholas said. "Who employs you? Where am I?"

"I cannot say," said the man. "There is a rule. You will be silent."

Nicholas said, "I have a friend. A friend called Julius – "

He felt the cut as the boy made it. The man hissed and again the boy desisted, his face mutinous. The man said, "The next time, we leave. You may lie in your dung."

He obliged with silence. He hoped they would thank him when they found that matters were not quite as bad as they assumed. All the same, it was a tearing, unpleasant business unpeeling his clothes, even though done with professional skill. Then his body was sponged and examined. It looked like something Colard and Henninc might have dreamed up together: blotched with indigo bruising and cross-hatched with incisions in Imperial crimson. Some of the gashes were bone-deep, but the bones themselves were unbroken. In any case no single pain mattered beside the corporate agony of his muscles. He wondered how long the journey had actually lasted, and if they had drugged him. He thought so. They might be afraid that he was going to leap to his feet and kill them with a blow to each chin but he found lifting a hand too much trouble. They half-carried him, in the end, to the tub.

He fell asleep while he was there, something he was prone to do. You always get cramped in a barrel. He was aware when they dried him, and wrapped his wounds in old soft linen with balm, and brought to replace his groundcloth a fresh pallet covered with ticking, and sheets, and a blanket, and a pillow. They gave him something to drink, thickened with sops, and then let him sleep.

He wakened stiff as a plank, with his mind clear. The tent was mellow with candlelight: two stands had been brought while he slept. The tub had gone, but the brazier remained and most of the other things, including the roses. On a carpet at his side were some clothes.

They were not, thank God, his own. He sat up, swearing, and examined them with some pleasure. Soft shoes without fastenings. Leggings with laces, and drawers. A shirt which would reach to his thighs. A short-sleeved tunic with a light embroidered belt, buckled in what looked like silver. No side-arms, no purse, no possessions. No headgear, for which he was grateful. Today the air weighed on his head. Nevertheless, in a moment, he rose slowly and carefully and started to dress. He had nearly finished when the tent flap stirred but was not opened. He had just finished when he heard the tramp of marching feet and steel clashing. The sound ceased in front of his tent; a man's voice spoke his name, and the door cloth was flung wide. In the darkness outside he could see only the glitter of spired helmets and strange armour and beyond that, a medley of tents like his own but much larger, all handsome, all brilliantly lit.

He was led a short distance among them, his silent escort surrounding him closely so that he could see little else. The reflected glow showed them to be of middle height only, each being dressed in mail shirt and quilted tunic, its skirts kilted up over heeled riding boots. Their helmets had damascened edges and earguards, within which their faces were ovals of expressionless fawn, each marked with black brows and a glossy bracket of short ink-black moustaches. At the mouth of the largest tent they were challenged, and halted.

He waited, smelling strange cooking and unguents; listening to chattering voices; absorbing curious sounds. Some of these came from inside the big tent he was facing. He could hear a stringed instrument playing, and sometimes a man would speak softly. Beside him, the slender chains binding the tent to its pegs also shivered and strummed. When firelight caught them, they glinted like gold.

A man stood in the tent doorway, frowning. Between his hands stretched a fragment of fur. This he held out and, after waiting a moment, rapped the air with it angrily. Nicholas took it. It was a hat, made of felt banded by fur. The man facing him wore one like it above his long quilted tunic. He was old and heavy and beardless. A eunuch.

Nicholas tenderly smoothed on the cap, which fitted well enough. His hair, roused by the bath, curled and climbed all round about it. He stood conveying the embodiment of Claes, humble and obedient, and wondered what he had got himself into. The tent flap was parted for him, and he walked in.

Chapter 27

OR A LONG TIME now, Nicholas had wondered how far Pagano Doria intended to go, in the skirmish he had embarked on so long ago: in Brussels; in Pisa; in Florence. He had his orders, one took it, from Simon. To defer the final engagement until now had been strategically sensible. Deferring it, Doria had, of course, enjoyed being playful. He had apparently enjoyed, too, directing the attack at Vavuk. Allowing Nicholas to survive, but on his own terms, might be another example of Doria's turn for mischief. Simon had none, that he knew of. There was one other possibility, but that would be too much to hope for.

Nicholas stepped into the pavilion, and saw his answer before him; for it was as if he had stepped into a scented bath, surrounded by flowers. Swayed by the air from his entrance, gilded lamps sent a surge of dazzling light over silk hangings and deep, patterned carpets; appointments of carved wood and gilded copper and bronze; the silks and gauzes of the many occupants who sat in cushioned groups all round the walls.

They were all women. Moving among them were slaves, and soft-footed eunuchs. He was in a seraglio. Perhaps the vilest evidence yet of Pagano Doria's cast of mind. Perhaps not. It came to him that, although clean, he was injured, and aching, and unshaven, and therefore probably as little to be desired as he was desirous. Once, he had had . . . It was a long time since he had had anything, or wanted it. He stood still, and looked again.

The chamber presented itself, controlled; exact; as if in a painting. He saw the harpist he had heard. The music continued: a smooth, perpetual flow, ignored by the company. The tinted faces, the jewels, the coats of brilliant dyed silk, the feathered crests in the dark hair were not those of whores, or bought-in slaves, or emirs' daughters, presented in tribute. Whoever they were, they served someone high-born. Their movements were graceful and studied: a hand moved a backgammon piece on a low fretted table; another fondled a gerfalcon;

a third poured a pastel liquid from the long, slender neck of a flask; a fourth examined a painting. His entrance caused no stir other than the tranquil turn of a head. In the centre, alone, was a woman who was not young at all, and whom he had never seen before. He waited a long moment, mastering the shock: revising his intention. Then he walked slowly towards her.

She sat in the reflected light of her robes under a canopy upheld by four light golden poles. Their sockets formed the corners of a heavy fenced dais, lustrous with tiles of blue and white porcelain and cushioned in velvet. The little gate to the dais had been closed: none could reach her. Behind her, high as the tent and lit by a ten-branched candelabrum, was a stretch of silk painted with flowers and birds in such a way that she herself appeared part of it. She sat among violets and peonies, roses and hollyhocks, willows and cypresses; and peacocks stood with hoopoes and doves at her shoulders.

She was between sixty and seventy, and art still preserved much of her beauty. The shape of her face remained oval, its olive cheeks tinted with rose and its eyebrows razored into delicate arches, drawn to meet at the nose. Her eyes, outlined with kohl, were still pear-shaped and clear in spite of the wrinkles about them, and the silk that capped her hair and her brow also masked her throat and her shoulders. The veil was held in place by a fragile, leafed diadem, from which hung a face-necklace of great Ormuz pearls. She was sitting so still that the jewels lay quiet at either temple and down the smooth cheeks to where they cupped and flattered the line of her chin. He thought he knew who she was. And if so . . . If so . . .

He couldn't believe, yet, that the plan had become more than a plan. He had been wrenched away with the foundations half laid. Half laid Turkish-style, he thought, with ram's blood mixed with the chalk and the mortar. He had bled. Perhaps it would stand firm. Unless it was still not his plan, but Pagano Doria's.

The eunuch had gone. What was required? An act of homage, perhaps, like the boy's. Arrived before the glittering dais, Nicholas sank at some cost to his knees, touched the ground with his brow, and then rose and stood. Finally he took his gamble and spoke. "Sara Khatun?"

He heard the little rustle on either side among the women behind him. In front of him, the enthroned woman gave him a long, contemplative look. He thought she would speak in Arabic. Instead, she used the Trapezuntine Greek of her great-niece. She said, "Who else, Messer Niccolò? But a moment ago, you were confounded."

"I am still confounded, princess," he said. "But I guessed the name of the Khatun from the painting."

She didn't glance round. She said, "Artisans do not read Farid ud-Din Attar."

He had turned the pages of the *Thirty Birds* in the Palace, dressed – undressed – under a robe. He contradicted her gently, with a quotation. *I am not that bird who will reach the King's door. To reach the keeper of his gate will be enough for me.* If she did not, he appreciated the irony.

The eyes remained on him. Then she tilted her head and spoke, but not to him. "Well?" she said. "If this is not humility, and it is not, then it is insolence. Come and help me deal with it."

He had expected a woman to join her, and then saw that he was, of course, quite wrong. The figure moving out from the screen was that of a man robed and hatted in black, with a forked white beard spreading over the old copper cross on his breast. Nicholas said, not entirely with pleasure, "Diadochos."

One person who would, all too well, perceive the irony. In the chamber of Violante of Naxos, he had discussed Persian books in his presence. The monk seemed to smile. He said, "Messer Niccolò, you are in Erzerum. As you have guessed, this is the lady Sara, noble mother of the lord Uzum Hasan, prince of Diyarbekr; lord of High Mesopotamia; chief of the White Sheep tribe of the Turcomans. To her you owe your present safety."

So it *was* his plan, and not Doria's. But for the way it had been carried out, he would have felt relief. He said, "I must convey gratitude for those of us who survived the rescue. Did it include Master Julius?"

The monk said, "The manner of your rescue was no concern of the Khatun's. Men were hired to bring you here, for your sake and your safety. They found you in difficulty. They killed your oppressors, all but the leader and a few of his servants, who escaped. They removed you. They were too rough, I know it. But your scars may yet serve you well."

"And Master Julius?" Nicholas repeated.

The woman made a disparaging movement. "He is a child. Must you copy him?"

"He is not a child. He is a man, and a friend. I don't wish to copy him," Nicholas said, "I wish to see him. And then the camel train."

Diadochos said, "This year, they are late." The woman's eyes narrowed.

Nicholas said, "They are here. I heard them. Do you want to let them take their merchandise through to Erzincan and Sivas and Bursa, with all the Ottoman armies lying off to the west? I hear Amastris has surrendered to Sultan Mehmet."

"Indeed?" said the woman. Her hands had tightened.

"The Sultan was there in person. No one knows where he will march next." Nicholas paused. "I am a merchant. I, too, am concerned with the course of these wars, and how they will affect my company. It may be convenient for us to compare what we know. Once I have seen Master Julius."

He had wondered if they knew about the loss of Amastris. He had got

the news from a flockmaster. Amastris lay on the Black Sea west of
Sinope and was run as a Genoese trading base. He couldn't weep for
the Genoese; not at the moment. But if the Sultan's gaze was already
turned to the East, he might look closer and further. It must add to
the White Horde's anxiety.

It was his task, at this moment, to discover how anxious they were.
To do what he wanted, he needed all the bargaining power he could
get, including any feelings of guilt they might have over Vavuk. He
supposed they had hired Kurds to find him. Perhaps the men whom
Doria had hired to attack him were also Kurdish. There was a joke in
that somewhere, if he hadn't lost so many men. But then, the friends
of Uzum Hasan had not been concerned to rescue his men, just
himself. He remembered that Kurdish lands adjoined the lands of the
Turcomans. Uzum Hasan's eldest son, in his twenties, was by a
Kurdish wife. Perhaps the men who brought him back from Vavuk
were not hired, but came from this very encampment. If so, he hoped
not to set eyes on them.

She said, "Take him to see the fellow. He is with the others, and
well cared for. Then we shall talk, you and Diadochos and I, over a
sherbet."

He could have eaten the falcon. He bowed, backed and, turning,
walked painfully out. By the same unwritten law, no one paid him any
attention as he went, although his escort at the door took him every
inch of the way to where Julius was. They wore Shiraz cuirasses of
gilded steel, and their round shields were all worked in silk. The smell
of camels was as strong as before. His wounds ached and throbbed,
and he closed his mind to them. He took the chance, as he walked, to
look about him; and saw where the caravanserai had been built.
Beyond, outlined in lights, he could see the high walls and towers of
the town and its citadel, and the double minaret of the old medresseh,
and the dome of the mosque. Erzerum, sentinel of the plateau,
guarded the camel route between Europe and northern Persia. Along
the string of plains between here and Tabriz, thousands of camels
passed yearly. Once, as Theodosiopolis, this was a bulwark of the
Roman Empire of the East. Romans, Persians, Byzantines, Seljuks,
Tartars held it before the Turcomans overran it fifty years or so since,
and sent their mothers as negotiators, heralds, couriers, spies. Their
brave, their demanding mothers.

His escort stopped. Before him was an earthen building, not a tent,
with a stout door. The windows were shuttered, and there was no
light round the cracks. There was no sign of his men. Either they were
dead, or asleep, or he had been tricked, or else . . . Just as his guards
were starting to unlock the door, Nicholas stepped aside and rapped
on the shutters. "Julius? We're free. Don't do anything stupid."

They must have been clustered round the door, waiting to break
out. Julius roared, "What! Nicholas!" and there was clamour of

voices. A lot of voices. Six? Eight? The door opened and two of his escorts, carrying torches, strode in ahead of him. The light swept round the room, illuminating face after face. Long before the big lamp had been lit, he had counted them. He heard the guard leave, and stood in his silly tunic and leggings with his face aching from the grin that was on it.

There were ten of his own men inside, including his captain, and Julius with two of his servants. They all bore wounds of some sort or another, but they were all on their feet, and none looked mortally sick, or much worse than himself. The man with the shorn arm must have died. They had light, and bedding, and fresh clothes, and the remains of a generous meal. They had put out their own torch, hoping to fight their way out and escape. Julius was pummelling him on the back. It was agony. Then he held him at arm's length and said, "We're free?"

"Of course we are. We're in Erzerum," Nicholas said. He was looking at them all, one by one, and they responded, crowding round, with bright faces and eager questions. If they blamed him for what had happened, there was no sign of it. Someone said, "Trust young Nicholas!"

"Trust young Nicholas!" said Julius with the utmost good humour. "Who put the perishing archers on the wrong side of the road, and didn't keep scouts at both ends, and didn't see to it that we had enough light to tell one man from another? So what happened? And if we're free, why are there guards outside that door?"

"Is that food?" Nicholas said.

"Yes. We've eaten. They feed you all right," Julius said. "Listen. Why . . . ?"

"Well, they forgot to feed me," Nicholas said. "Go on. I can answer with my mouth full. Didn't you recognise the citadel when they brought you in? Or even, my God, the smell of the goathair?"

"It was dark," Julius said. "And we thought we were in Doria's hands. And *that's* something that – "

"I know. Later," said Nicholas. He removed half a chicken for long enough to get the words out. They all sat round and watched him. Finally, he said, "Uzum Hasan's men rescued us, but it would suit them to keep quiet about it. It would suit us as well. In fact, we could do each other quite a lot of good, and I want to talk to them about that while they're willing. After that, we'll be free to do what we came for. The caravans are in already. By the time they're rested, we should be fit to go back."

"And Doria?" said Julius.

Nicholas said, "They killed all his hired men, but I think we'll find he's escaped back to Trebizond with what's left of the few he brought with him. Then it's his word against ours."

The captain said, "You mean, sir, that he'll pretend he didn't attack us? – There's nothing to drink. Just some sickly stuff, and we finished it."

"Well, damn you. In his shoes, I'd either say nothing, or else pretend I'd come across the signs of a bloody battle but no survivors. Come to think of it, that's what he'll think actually happened. Brigands attacked us, and the rest of us died."

"Lord God Almighty, he's going to get a shock," Julius said. "When we all ride in with those camels."

Without drink, it was impossible, unfortunately, to eat any more. Nicholas wiped his hands on some straw and got up. "When you ride in," he said, "I'm not coming."

"Why?" said Julius. His slanting brows jammed.

"They want me to weed out the harem," Nicholas said. "They want to teach me some tricks on the farmuk. I promised to show them how to dye their handkerchiefs pink. Whatever we buy, I want to take it somewhere safer than Trebizond, and stay there."

"Why?" said Julius.

"I'll tell you, if you tell me how you knew Doria was following."

"It was Paraskeuas," Julius said. "He thought I knew. He thought of course you would have told me . . . You rode off on your own, you fool, *knowing* that Doria was following you?"

"You rode off on your own to warn me," Nicholas said. Again and again, he owed his life to Julius, who understood him less than anyone he had ever met. But this time there was not just a tutor's impatience in the way Julius was looking at him.

Julius said, "There was no time to do anything else if I was going to overtake Doria. I suppose we'd better send back a message to say we're alive. What do you mean, somewhere safer than Trebizond?"

"To keep our cargo away from Doria, among other reasons. I'll tell you more later, when I find out the Turcomans' plans. I'd better go. They're expecting me."

Julius had risen also. He looked, for Julius, a little dazed. He said, "You trust the Turcomans? Turcomans send back Turkish spies with their chopped-off hands hung round their necks."

"I know what you mean," Nicholas said. "Can't see to trim their fingernails without cutting their throats." He watched, with pleasure, as Julius got annoyed.

Julius snapped, "So who's expecting you? You haven't met Uzum Hasan?"

"No. It's his mother," Nicholas said. "The Syrian. Remember? Her daughter-in-law is a princess from Trebizond. Her great-niece is the lady Violante. Violante of Naxos. That's why I'm here. That's why we were rescued. That is . . . I didn't know we were going to be rescued, and I don't know even yet what side the lady Violante is on." He looked at the expression on Julius's face and involuntarily gave a large sigh. "Julius – I'm sorry; but it simply isn't practicable to tell everybody beforehand what I'm doing. It's too damaging and it involves other people and I don't know how it's going to turn out anyway. Although," said Nicholas thoughtfully, "I think this has a fair chance of success, if we live through it."

She received him this time in a smaller tent and alone, except for Diadochos and the silent attendance of eunuchs. Instead of a throne, she sat at ease on a carpet; and after kneeling he took his place in front of her, opposite the monk with his black, shrouded hat. Someone laid a table before him, spread with platters of sugary things the size of his fingernail. Others poured him a cup of freezing fruit juice thickened with dust, which was presumably sherbet and was better than nothing, when it came to washing down chicken.

He saw that she was watching him, amused. Eventually she said, "Because you are among pagans, you need not observe pagan customs." She made a sign, and a moment later he held a cup of red Cypriot wine in his hand. It was extremely strong: a Doria trick. He acknowledged it with infinite politeness and sipped it slowly. She said, "You have seen your notary?"

"And the rest. Thank you, Sara Khatun. They are being well cared for, but not in a lodging of honour."

"Your soldiers are adequately housed. Your notary may join you. The escort is for your protection." She got that out of the way, as unimportant. Her fingers moved a little, when she was impatient, and her rings glinted. She said, "We are, of course, discussing the destination of the camel trains. My son will make many purchases for his brothers, his household. There are other merchants, other emirs who will do the same. Then those who have come with the camels will take their goods where their best market is. Some will go to Trebizond. Some will elect to travel west to the great Turkish markets of Bursa. While they are here, the White Sheep are their hosts. It is our duty to escort them through our lands, and to see to their safety. It is possible that the road to Bursa is insecure, although we know that the Sultan will try not to hinder incoming trade. The fall of Amastris is not serious. But traders will hope, this year more than most years, to unburden themselves of much of their goods before going there. You have come to buy for the Emperor?"

An innocent question. He was good at those himself. She meant, "How big an investment are you making? Are you frightened, or are you and your army staying in Trebizond?"

He didn't mind supplying the answers, provided she paid for them. Nicholas said, "Of course there will be no danger at all once the West sends its crusade. Fra Ludovico da Bologna is a persuasive man, and your son must rely on him. I hear the lord Uzum Hasan and the Emperor himself were pleased to tweak the Sultan's beard over tributes quite recently."

"Why not?" said the lady. "Is my son a weakling? He is the warlord even the Sultan Mehmet has learned to fear. These are men, and not vassals. Of course, God and this great Franciscan may have opened men's hearts. Fleets may even now be crossing towards us. But what if not? Sinope and Trebizond are impregnable. Georgia can flood the country with men. Trade will continue long after this small inconvenience is over. I had been told of strings of rubies, of turquoise of a quality these men seldom carry. The Emperor will covet them."

"I have orders to buy," Nicholas said, "from the Emperor and others in Trebizond. That alone would justify a caravan to the City. A hundred camels, perhaps. What the Venetians and the Genoese would take, I don't of course know." He could feel the eyes of Diadochos trained on him, but the man did not speak.

The Syrian said, "And what of purchases on your own account? What does Florence require, and the Medici, and the Charetty?"

"I had planned to buy a great deal," Nicholas said. "I have the resources. But I have changed my mind about taking it to Trebizond. It is, of course, unassailable. But a siege would lose us a trading season."

There was a short silence. She stirred. "It seems to me," she said, "that you lack confidence. To a strong garrison, need a siege last so long? Trebizond has repulsed armies before."

"Trebizond reaches accommodation with her enemies in many ways," Nicholas said. "I have heard about them. I have met the Emperor."

There was another pause. "It is a rarefied world, that of Byzantium," the Lady said.

"Perhaps it was once," Nicholas said. "It is half-Turkish now."

He caught, swift as it was, the glance between the woman and the monk. It was the monk who said, "Was it Muslim, the Easter service you heard in the Chrysokephalos?"

It was Sara Khatun who said, "No. Give him the credit for what he has deduced. Yes, young Messer Niccolò. Eleven Trapezuntine princesses have married Muslims. Sultans have been known to marry Christian wives. My great-niece Violante and her sisters married Venetian merchants. Thus are alliances made, and children born with a hope of surviving."

Nicholas said, "In any language, loyalty is a difficult word."

She laughed. The sound took him by surprise. She said, "If you understand its meaning in any language, you must explain it to me one day. Yes, the City was once under the suzerainty of the Mongols; is under the suzerainty of the Ottomans, and shows the effect of it. The guard is turbanned. The market is held in a Meidan; the princes ride Turkish-style; shoot Turkish-style. The Empress is called Khatun, the title you gave me, as often as they name her Despoina. The Comneni nieces and nephews of my daughter-in-law are tutored by a Tatas, the soldiery are commanded by the Emir Candar; the Emperor's chief falconer is his Emir Dogan. The bow-carrying page is called the horchi more often than he is called the Akocouthos, and your lover's name is Iskender more often than it is Alexios."

"He is not my lover," said Nicholas furiously.

"Then someone's plans have miscarried," she said calmly. "Let me resume. It is true that the native Greek families have always despised the Comneni. It is true that, unlike Constantinople, Trebizond is bound to the East. To Georgia, to Armenia, to the tribes that flow across Asia. The costume they wear comes from Persia, and many of their old courtly practices. The Roman highways have gone. What remains is a king of Georgia descended from King David the Psalmist and an Ottoman sultan descended from Alexander the Great."

"So it hardly matters who rules in Trebizond now?" Nicholas said.

She looked at him for a long time. Then she smiled. "You ask me that, in the presence of a Christian confessor?"

Nicholas said, "Your son allows Christian worship. So does the Sultan. There is a Greek patriarch in Constantinople and a Latin bishop in Caffa. Ludovico da Bologna was sent here, surely, to care for the Latin communities in Persia as well as in Georgia."

Diadochos said, "It is true. He calls himself elected patriarch to all the nations of the Orient. An exaggeration, but only a slight one. But he was sent, too, as apostolic nuncio to encourage my lord Uzum Hasan to ally with the Empire of Trebizond against the Ottoman forces. Also, as I remember, to encourage my lord Uzum Hasan to ally with the Emperor of Ethiopia against both the Ottomans and the Mamelukes. It is clear, therefore, that Rome thinks that Christian congregations ought to have Christian rulers."

"But you disagree?" Nicholas said.

The monk said, "What is best for the people? There are some who say that, under the Sultan, the Greek Church has found itself at last firmly united under one patriarch, instead of thrown to the winds in so many scattered communities under disparate rulers."

"So much for their souls," Nicholas said. "Or at least, I suppose, the souls of those who were not taken as children and turned into Muslims. So what of the rest? Would Muslim rule be more just, more efficient, more beneficent if an Ottoman governor sat in the Palace at Trebizond? Or a Turcoman?"

The monk looked at the princess, but did not speak. She said, "You see the tents, Niccolò?"

He said, "I see a city as well."

"There are cities," she said. "We worship in them. Its forts hold our troops, and our treasure. We visit its baths. But as yet we are a pastoral people. We live in tents, and move from place to place as policy, and war, and the grazing dictates. So did all tribes until recently. So did the Ottomans. It is only now that the Sultan is building markets and palaces; and even yet, he likes his freedom at Adrianople rather than the city at Constantinople. We have just rule, and a council; and in time we, too, will live in cities, no doubt, and collect Greek books and Western philosophers. But not just yet."

"And the Sultan?" said Nicholas.

"He is a very young man," said Sara Khatun. "And a clever one, trained in youth by the best brains his father could gather. He has learned central rule, a new trick, very quickly, and, like my son, he has courage, and some genius for strategy. In the end, my son will overcome him. But meanwhile, you, my young Frankish merchant, are afraid. You will take no goods to Trebizond. You will gather your promissory notes and your army and flee?"

Absorbed in listening and looking, he almost forgot to reply. He felt love for her, and pride, and even a sort of anxiety. As always, his face and manner were displaying something quite different. He said, "I don't think so. I did come here to buy. Only, on reflection, I'd prefer to take my goods to Kerasous, not to Trebizond."

She remained perfectly composed. "Kerasous is still in the Empire; equally on the sea; equally vulnerable to the Ottoman fleet. Why should it be safer than Trebizond?"

"Because the enemy who attacks the Empire will begin with Trebizond," Nicholas said. "And Kerasous is a hundred miles away, and very strong."

"So I have heard," said the lady. "Indeed, you may be right. The Venetians, the Genoese, might well come to wish they had thought of it. And those merchants who carry such precious goods may well prefer that journey to the other to Trebizond. The road to Kerasous belongs to the White Sheep, and is well guarded."

"There are, I believe, Venetian merchants here in the city," said Nicholas. "If they wished it, they could choose their goods here and consign them to Kerasous. I would take them with mine. My people would care for them there; or they might have their own agents."

The lady turned to the monk. "Would this be helpful?" she said.

"A happy suggestion," said Diadochos. "There are Venetians at Kerasous. I know them, and the Imperial minister, and can supply what introductions are needed. It would be necessary to explain to the Bailie and the Genoese consul at Trebizond."

"Would it?" said Nicholas. "I should greatly prefer to say nothing of Kerasous."

"I see," said the monk. "Then it might be put about that the Venetian merchandise has gone straight through to Bursa, as the merchants were unwilling to travel to Trebizond. It has happened before. There are both Venetians and Genoese merchants at Bursa."

"Genoese?" Nicholas said. "So a Genoese agent here might be encouraged to bypass Trebizond also?"

"You wish the Genoese merchandise safe in Kerasous also?" Diadochos said. The princess was smiling.

Nicholas answered her smile. "Not really," he said. "It would lie on my conscience, two falsehoods. If we proclaim that the whole Genoese consignment has gone through to Bursa, then we ought to make sure it goes through to Bursa. The agents will send it from there to Pera for shipping, and everyone will be pleased. Or almost everyone."

"And your own goods?" said the princess. "You cannot claim to have sent these to Bursa, where you have no connections. And you wish to conceal, you say, that your destination is Kerasous."

"I shall think of something," said Nicholas. "Khatun, these are great changes in the customary route for these traders. You say it is safer, but will they agree?"

She smiled faintly. "Silver helps."

"Sara Khatun, I carry no silver," said Nicholas.

"Few people do," said the lady. "It is something of a miracle, then, that the pass from Vavuk proved to be paved with it. Those who brought it back have had their reward. I can spare enough from the remainder to encourage all who wish to make the trip to Kerasous, and give them good guides and protection. The rest I am willing to lend, on the assumption that there are couriers in Trebizond by whom the loan might be repaid in kind. It seems only just that trade, on which we all depend, should receive our encouragement."

He was stunned with delight, and let it show. He gave her the broadest of smiles, regardless of what she thought of him. He said, "Lady, I bow to you, and to all of your family."

Her eyebrows rose with the greatest delicacy; but she was not displeased: he could feel it. "And my great-niece?" she said. "You were, it appears, far from trusting my great-niece."

Nicholas said, "Khatun, I trust you, and your son, and the lady Violante."

The monk turned his head. "You have shown otherwise," he said placidly.

"I was mistaken," said Nicholas. "Tell her so."

Her gaze, also relaxed, held a sort of amused pity. "Ah, you may trust me," said Sara Khatun. "And the lord Uzum Hasan. But it is a foolish man who sends a message of commitment to Violante of Naxos. Diadochos will not contradict me. That is all, then. Tomorrow, you may go to the compound and negotiate for your goods. Word of your ambush by brigands has already been sent to the Palace. They will be relieved to hear you are safe. I do not expect you to mention these encounters."

"They have not taken place," Nicholas said.

"So. When you are ready to travel, you will be given what you require for each journey. You will take the Kerasous train yourself?"

"It is the most valuable," Nicholas said. "Khatun, I hope one day to be able fittingly to thank you. You know your own danger."

"I?" she said. "In the lands of my son? But I am touched by your solicitude, despite the rough handling we have subjected you to. And it may be that, one day, I shall call on you for a favour. You are strong, for a youth."

"Mother of Uzum Hasan, what you see is what you have called forth," Nicholas said. He knelt before her and, rising, left. Outside the door of the tent, his escort were waiting. He detained Diadochos to ask a single question. "The lady Violante is not here?"

"She is in her proper place in the Palace at Trebizond; where else, Messer Niccolò? Her movements do not concern you." It was what he had wanted to know.

This time, walking back to his tent, he saw clearly where the big caravanserai had been built. Tomorrow he would go there with Julius and, moving from stall to stall in the great building, sit crosslegged drinking cups of strange liquid and talking (at first) of everything under the sun except the dyes, the gall nuts, the jewels and the feathers, the silk and the gold that he wanted to purchase. He had studied, and listened and taken advice. He knew how it was done, and what he wanted. He was glad none the less that Julius was with him and thought again of the courage that had sent Julius after him, virtually alone, to overtake Doria and warn him. Which was not to say that he would not now hear, from Julius, exactly how angry he was at his conduct. But then, one could use that as well. One could use everything.

He did not go in at once, but stood in the tent entrance, thinking. Julius was there, limping briskly about with a second pallet and bedding. The roses were still on the table, fully opened in the warmth from the brazier. They must have been carried for her from the south: their presence had given him less reassurance, perhaps, than she had expected. While he was gone, someone had retrieved his saddle and harness and placed them, cleaned, at the end of the tent. There was also a small pile of his other possessions and a chest, stoutly locked, whose contents he thought he could guess.

The silver with which Sara Khatun had so guilefully endowed him. The silver Doria had so triumphantly amassed in Trebizond and brought to spend at Erzerum. Well, he had never reached Erzerum. Someone had been instructed to see to that. One wondered if it had scattered during the fight, or been cut from Doria's saddle, or if he had even been forced to ransom himself with it.

At first, the jest seemed wonderful. Then, sobering, Nicholas remembered the dangers inherent in the rest of his plans. There would be nothing for Doria in that small part of the caravan that would travel to Trebizond. His silver also had gone. His mission to Trebizond would have failed, unless he could take over the Charetty company. And nothing was surer than that he would claim it, returning post-haste to the city with news of the deaths of Nicholas and Julius. However soon Diadochos had dispatched his reassurance, it couldn't reach Trebizond until some days – perhaps many days – after Doria had announced they were dead.

How would Tobie and Godscalc, Astorre and le Grant respond to that? Not, if he knew them, by catching the next boat to Pera with lurid dispatches for Marian and Gregorio. It was unthinkable that she should believe him dead, and he trusted Godscalc at least to do nothing and concede nothing until the news was confirmed. So his survival would destroy all Doria's hopes. Godscalc, clearer-visioned than himself, had seen how Catherine would blame him for engineering her husband's downfall. Now, Doria had put his venture at risk through his own foolhardy actions. What if Catherine became disillusioned just when Doria needed her most? What if he were led, because of this, to give up all hope of the Charetty company? Then he would have no use for Catherine. Except perhaps as a hostage.

Then Julius turned and saw him and said, "That's the way I felt this morning." He paused. "I can smell wine. You bastard, you've been drinking, and haven't brought any."

There was no point in alarming Julius with baseless conjectures. Instead, he sat down and told him all that had happened, keeping nothing back. What Julius didn't need to know of that interview had not been put into words anyway. For the rest, Julius was shrewd enough in his questions. "She doesn't really believe the Duke of Burgundy and the Doge of Venice and the King of France and the King of England and the Pope are about to sail past Gallipoli and murder the Turks?"

"Of course she doesn't. Of course, they sent Alighieri with lavish promises to the West. Some day, if Fra Ludovico stays long enough, a war might end or a king die, and a crusade will be mounted. But meanwhile Uzum Hasan can hold out hope of one to his allies, and even prove how confident he is by offending the Sultan. If he can hold Sinope and Trebizond and Georgia together, he can at least hold his own until the end of the season."

Julius said, "What if Uzum Hasan wants to do more? We know he wants the Sultan out of Asia Minor. What if Hasan Bey himself takes the chance to seize Trebizond?"

You forgot, sometimes, that Julius was a natural soldier. Nicholas said, "Trebizond is secure. You have said so yourself. The only way it has ever been taken is by negotiation, and Uzum Hasan has nothing to offer a Christian emperor. I've made no bargains, Julius."

Julius thought. Then he said, "Why his mother? Where is Uzum Hasan?"

And that was near the bone, too. Nicholas said, "Where should a leader be, except with his army? With the Ottomans and the Black

Horde to worry about, I don't suppose he has much time to think about trade. He's left that to the most trustworthy Greek-speaking Christian he knows. She's a brave woman, Sara Khatun." He paused and said, "What is it about Persia and Trebizond that breeds women like that?"

"I don't know," said Julius wistfully. "But I'd like to find out."

In the end, Julius was good enough to endorse most of his plans. He quite saw that the Florentine cargo would be safer stored at Kerasous than where Doria could get it. He supposed the same was true of the Venetian goods, and Venetian goodwill wasn't to be sniffed at when it came to confronting Pagano Doria. It took some time to convince Julius that there was no point in accusing Pagano Doria when there was no proof that he had done anything. And Paraskeuas as a witness could no longer serve as an informer. The loss of the silver and the goods he would have bought would have to be punishment enough for the present. That and the arrival of Julius in Trebizond.

"While you go to Kerasous," Julius said.

"Well, yes," Nicholas said. He had pulled off his shirt and was attending, awkwardly, to his dressings.

"And stay there? How long?" said Julius.

"As long as may be needed. You don't imagine we can leave that kind of merchandise unguarded?" Nicholas said. The gash in his arm had started bleeding again and he poked about the wicker basket till he found some clean cloth to put on it. Neither the physician nor his sullen assistant had reappeared. He said, "There's some ointment here. What about you?"

"Never mind me. How do we know what you're doing in Kerasous?" Julius said.

"Pigeons?" said Nicholas. "Relays of Amazons?" He rose, pot in hand, and found Julius also risen, and close to him.

Julius said, "You're still planning. You're up to something, aren't you?"

"Yes, I'm binding my bleeding arm," said Nicholas. "I'm also trying to take what precautions I can. The Sultan's much more likely to attack Uzum Hasan than the Emperor. But suppose he decides to capture Trebizond first. He won't take it, but he could besiege it until autumn. He could make it impossible to get our cargo out until the season's too late. At Kerasous, we've some chance."

Julius said, "We get besieged in Trebizond, and you sail home from Kerasous with our merchandise."

"Ours and the Venetians'," Nicholas said. He was trying to tie a knot with his teeth and stop grinning.

Julius stared at him. He said, "You mean that, don't you? It really is what you'd do?"

Nicholas got the knot fixed and looked up. "Well, what do you think? You don't want me in Trebizond. You'll be safe there, but the merchandise won't. The only sensible course is to get the goods out and make sure of our profit. You're the accountant. Come up with a better idea."

After half an hour, he did come up with a better idea. Nicholas would go to Trebizond, and Julius would take the caravan and its cargo to Kerasous.

Naturally Nicholas objected, and it took even longer to get him to see that he was in no position to argue. Then, having made his point, Julius condescended to enquire about routes.

"Well, through Erzincan if you like, but it's dangerous. I rather favoured going back past Bayburt and then turning off west for Kelkit and Siran. Then just past that there's a road north to Kerasous."

"Is there? Where?" Julius said.

Nicholas leaned back on his pillows and stretched himself. He was aching, and weary and, despite all his anxieties, furtively happy. "Well, that's the point," he said. "We'll go over the whole thing tomorrow. But where you turn north is this place Sebinkarahisar. Koloneia, they used to call it."

Chapter 28

IT WAS ON A WARM, scented day in mid-May that the news came to Trebizond that Nicholas was dead, and Julius killed at his side. It was brought by a lay servant from the monastery of the Holy Virgin at Sumela, beating a fast little mule over thirty mountainous miles in a little over twelve hours.

As was proper, he went first to the Leoncastello of the Genoese, taking with him a group of loping spectators and scampering children. Monna Caterina, the ambassador's wife, listened with a pale face to the story of how the monks had discovered her husband dragging himself through the gorge with a few servants, all of them wounded and hardly able to gasp out their story of chance meeting and desperate ambush. Fighting for his life against brigands, despite all he could do, Messer Doria had seen the young man Niccolò succumb to the ruffians and perish. The notary Julius had been cut down soon after, and all their companions put to the sword. Messer Doria himself, robbed of everything, had been left for dead and, but for his servants, might be lying there still.

An Amazon, the young lady wife was. Instead of calling for help, or collapsing, she had summoned her grooms and her men-at-arms and her servants and, taking horse, had set out immediately for the monastery, leaving the courier to do the rest of his duty and make his painful way to the Florentine compound.

There, at least, they knew what was due to a messenger. The man to whom he told the news, a priest, set him at once on soft cushions, with food and drink, and had his mule seen to; by which time he had been joined by the other colleagues of the dead men. One was a doctor, who noticed his stiffness and sent for warm water and ointments while they questioned him. They spoke in low voices. He saw that, unlike some consorts of merchants who saw death as a chance for advancement, this one was patently stricken. Only once did he hear a burst of brusque speech, when a man with a beard and a screwed eye turned to the rest with a growl that would have flattered a dog. "You threw him away when you let him go. Julius had more sense than you did, and followed. The Colchians and the Kurds know more about mountain fighting than any people alive. He knew nothing. You threw him away."

No one answered him; but the doctor, who had been wringing out cloths, lifted his bald head as if he, too, would have spoken in accusation. But, unlike the bearded man, he looked at the big priest who had welcomed him. And presently that man, turning, said, "And, sir, you heard the story from Messer Pagano himself? If we were to make our way to the monastery, might we see the wounded man and learn more?"

"Indeed," said the man from Sumela. "It will be a week before Messer Doria may easily ride, and the sight of his friends will surely comfort him. His lady wife has already set out there."

He saw them look at one another, but the man with the beard said, "What's the point?"

It was the doctor who replied. He said, "The point is, Astorre, to find out who killed them." Then he turned his back on the bearded man, who had drawn a long breath, his cheeks turning red, and, laying the cloths down, said, "I shall send someone to go on with this, and make you a bed. If some of us go to the monastery, there will be others to set you on your way with food and a horse when you wish."

"I can see," said the messenger, "that these are men you held in esteem. I am sorry to carry such news."

"I am sorry, too," said the doctor.

The priest and the doctor, with a good escort, left indeed almost immediately, although not before an equerry from the Palace had knocked at the door and asked to hear all the messenger could tell. He was, it seemed, from the women's apartments, and not from the Emperor. Leaving, he had spoken to the Latin priest, and to the ship-master, a man called le Grant. "My lady would help if she can. It is a loss of which we cannot yet measure the depth."

"No one could," the doctor said. "He was not old enough."

They set out to confront Doria, and it felt like going to war.

An onlooker would have said that the journey was senseless. A company deprived of its leading officials has a requirement to close the wound rapidly: make its new dispositions and appointments and, most of all, repair the shaken trust of its clients. No onlooker had heard Nicholas say, as Tobie and Godscalc remembered, *You have to keep me alive. You have to pretend that I'm still running the company. Because the moment I'm dead or deposed, you belong to Doria.*

So Tobie and Godscalc rode out, lightly escorted, on the coast road to the Pyxitis estuary and, turning inland, took the road Nicholas had taken two weeks before. With them thundered Astorre with thirty men armed to the teeth. Even had he known more than he did, he would have been ashamed to think of his own future, or the company's. Whoever had attacked his boy and his notary was going to bear a short life. He had whatever second-hand account of the brigands the messenger had passed to them, and a description of the battleground even vaguer. But Astorre proposed to find it. And examine it. And root out the killers. Behind them, to do his excellent best to manage the affairs of the company, they left a silent John le Grant and their clerks and their servants.

From the very start Tobie had said, "It was Doria."

And Godscalc, debating rather than contradicting, had said, "He took very few men, compared with the fifteen Nicholas had. And you heard what the man from the monastery said. Doria was covered with wounds, and so were his servants. Wounds from axes and curved knives, not sword slashes."

"It was Doria," Tobie had repeated.

And Godscalc had said quietly, "It probably was. But it has yet to be proved."

"And if he claims the company?"

Godscalc had been silent. Then he had said, "A murderer cannot benefit from his crime. But we must resist the temptation to pin the blame on an innocent man."

"And if he can't be proved guilty?" Tobie said. "We beg him to take over the company?"

He had thought Godscalc soft. But Godscalc turned to him and said, "If, when we return to Bruges, the Church and the law and the demoiselle de Charetty find his marriage is valid, and the demoiselle has no wish to change her bequest, then one day Messer Pagano Doria will inherit half of the Charetty company. Until then, I shall resist any attempt on his part to take control. Did you think I should say anything else?"

"No," said Tobie. "But we may find it harder than we think."

"If you think it hard for us, think of the child," Godscalc said. "When we catch up with the girl, remember what she must be feeling."

"And Marian de Charetty?" Tobie had said.

There had been a silence. Then Godscalc had said, "We shall have to write and tell her, of course. But not yet. Poor woman, not yet."

After that, they rode in silence through green corn and blossoming orchards in the warm, hazy sunshine and then through the climbing, narrowing valley whose walls were feathered with alder and walnut, elder, beech and lime. Then, after ten miles, came the first of the fir trees, clothing the heights on either side. They paused there to rest their horses and refresh themselves briefly, saying little. For the practical side of such a journey, Astorre was the natural leader. But Tobie, remembering, acknowledged to himself soberly how much such an expedition would owe its stimulus, latterly, to the imagination, the secure touch of Nicholas. Even the men, in their silence, seemed to recognise it. "My boy," Astorre had called him more than once. Before, it had been "that brat"; with whatever tolerance. Yet they knew, he and Godscalc better than anyone, how incendiary the real Nicholas was. It should make the loss easier.

They overtook Catherine de Charetty past Cevizlik, where the basalt cliffs rose in columns above them and the river was joined on the left by the stream they were to follow. They were then within three hours of their destination. She and her escort in its good Genoese armour had already set off into the neighbouring valley. The Imperial road, kept in roughest repair, was half sunk in dirt and looked as untended as the other highways, the bridges, the viaducts bequeathed by the past to the Empire. Beyond, the deepening valley seemed filled and brimming with green, where summer suns and fine mists had nourished the forests so that they mounted and thickened with flower and leaf. Already the horses had brushed past purple banks of rhododendron and azalea bushes yellow as butterflies. Ahead, he had been told, was a gorge a thousand feet deep, fragrant and steaming with flowers. And the monastery, cool and airy, laminated the rock face far above it, rooted in deep caves and grottoes, with a sheer drop to the torrent below.

There were men of God in such crags, but also robbers. The Genoese, as was prudent, had turned in formation at the sound of massed horses. Then their captain lowered his arm, recognising the pennants of Charetty and Florence, and the familiar flamboyant helm of Astorre. Through the ranks, you could see the tired faces of the women attendants, reflecting some faint hope of rest or remission. The face of their mistress, turned also, showed the same smudges of dust and of weariness, but beneath them, the hardness of basalt. Then she saw who they were. She said nothing. But Tobie caught, for an instant, a glitter of something like fright. Then Godscalc was alongside and saying, "Demoiselle. Let us come with you."

Behind, Astorre and the Genoese captain were talking, low-voiced, as the cavalcade rearranged itself. In this country of brigands, thirty armed men were sure of their welcome. There was no welcome on the girl's face. She said, "My lord is ill at the monastery. I'm going to the monastery. Perhaps he's dying."

"Then we'll go all the quicker together," Godscalc said.

She looked at him, two fine frowning lines between her blue eyes, but could not think, it was clear, how to counter that. She said, her voice almost angry, "He nearly died, trying to save him."

"It was good of him to have the messenger sent," Godscalc said. She stared at him speechlessly with her frowning, colourless face and he added, "Master Tobie is with us, demoiselle. We shan't trouble my lord Doria any more than we need. But we must find and bury them."

Now, thought Tobie, she will cry. As she should; as she needs to.

He saw a short, jerky breath overtake her. Then she pulled down her chin and her mouth and said through a tight nose, "That is what you are paid to do. I am Genoese. I have my husband to think of. Captain! Do you want us to ride in the dark?" And brushing past, she set her horse into motion.

Beside him, as they dropped back, Tobie saw Godscalc's lips move. It was not the girl, he knew, he was cursing. Tobie said, "What was it you called Doria? Frivolous?"

Godscalc turned and looked at him. His large face had returned to calm. He said, "What was it we said of Nicholas? Vengeful, deceitful. A man who secretly causes others to suffer. A man who secretly causes others to die."

Tobie was silent. They had said all those things, and they were true. Was the spoiling of Catherine de Charetty better or worse than the ruin of Katelina van Borselen? Doria had killed. But Nicholas had killed more subtly, more often. He said, "They were the same man, I suppose. They were both Jason."

"You could say so," Godscalc said. "I have noticed that those with a quest are often those with something to escape from; and that applied to them both. Their quests, of course, were quite different. But we are going to see the survivor. We should keep an open mind."

The dusk after all overtook them. They trotted ringingly into the gorge: a metalled cortège drawing the flashing sunlight after it. The sun, withdrawing stealthily from the beech and the ash, the chestnut and the elm, lingered a long time on the pine trees on the upper reaches of their deep, winding valley; but already the change was upon them. The torrent at the foot of the valley increased its voice, so that all other movement was soundless. The sharp outline of spear and breastplate vanished in the lightless profusion of leaves. The undergrowth sprang thick to their shoulders: fixed among it, the massed mouths and trumpets of flowers spoke with their scent, but when you turned showed only flat moth colours. From the leaf ceilings over their heads, festoons of cindery lichen caught their spears and brushed humming over their helmets. Far above that, the sky was an amphitheatre for wheeling birds whose cries could not be heard; and beneath their feet, red fungus yielded and liquified.

At a hamlet of small wooden houses, shuttered and silent, a hog's back bridge took them over the river. Behind them, a dog, knowing nothing of brigands, barked hysterically and then was suddenly quiet. Ahead, eight hundred feet up the sheer cliff, was the monastery of Sumela. They sent an agile equerry of Astorre's off to warn them, and lit the torches they had brought, and started the climb.

The toiling ascent, after the journey, was more than the house-women could manage. Their ponies were led, and two of the soldiers carried them. The demoiselle paid them no attention. It was only by edging close that Tobie saw the sharpness of her cheeks and the stains under her eyes, staring ahead. Although her face was quite blank, tears had begun to pass slowly down either cheek.

She needed to cry, but not like that. Tobie felt Godscalc's hand on his arm, but shook it off with a frown. He was tired, and he had had enough of Godscalc's forebodings. He rode firmly to Catherine's side and putting an arm round her shoulders said, "My horse is fresh. Let me take you."

Her push nearly sent him off the path. Her face, in the torchlight, was that of a princess assaulted. "Take your hands off!" said Catherine de Charetty. And as, aching, he stilled his shuddering horse and righted himself and his belongings, she kicked her own horse ahead, her head turned to her shoulder. She said, "I have my own doctor."

Soon after that, they saw the glimmering lights of the monastery, as if through a tattered blanket stretched over the stars. From it crawled a long line of fire which turned into servants with flambeaux. The monks were at their devotions, but the guest-master greeted them at the stately stone entrance and led them down to the courtyard where men took care of the horses and soldiers. The cressets smoked in the damp air, which smelled of the hollow stone of the mountain, and the sweet peppers of incense, and the faint odours of stalled beasts and latrines. A deep chanting made itself heard. At first, looking about him, Tobie imagined that it came from the mountain itself. Then he saw on his left the lamp of a shrine, and around it angels rushing with bladed wings and great oval eyes, painted in ochre and dark blue and red earthcolours. Particles of gold glittered. The voices, suddenly vibrant, opened into a passionate hymn whose words could be heard. Godscalc's head turned.

"The church. The katholikon," Tobie said. He paused and said, "They sound confident enough."

"*O gladsome light*. It's . . . a canticle. They probably think they have reason," said Godscalc.

Then they were led to the guest quarters, and the sickroom of Pagano Doria.

As was right, Catherine entered alone. Outside the thick door, Tobie could hear nothing and stood without speaking beside Godscalc. Astorre had been debarred, to his annoyance, from the interrogation. Alone of them all, he had preserved his vigour to the end of the ride. No doubt he was resting at some laden table. Tobie, for his part, was glad enough to stand.

When after ten minutes the girl had not emerged, the monk beside them, tapping diffidently, opened the door. Before it closed they caught a glimpse of Doria, seated on a high-backed wooden settle packed with cushions. His head was bent over his wife, who crouched on a low stool beside him, her hands fists on her lap. He had one bandaged arm round her shoulders. A moment later, the monk came out and they were admitted, with a friendly reminder. Messer Doria was not yet very strong.

"You are kind. We shall remember. Messer Tobias is himself a doctor," Godscalc said. The door closed behind them.

The floor they trod on was chestnut-red marble, with pale fossil ovals and rings patterned through it. The walls, although white, bore a heavy jewelled cross and an icon whose metals gleamed yellow and white under the many candles of a heavy wrought stand. There was a stool and a prayer desk, richly covered, and a table bearing a ewer and basin. A covered stove, to one side, made the room warm. This was not part of the hostel for pilgrims, but rather a cell from the Imperial suite. In the middle, as they had seen, sat Pagano Doria, but Catherine had moved to one side where there stood a low bed and a chest. As they came in, she took her seat, with some care, on the chest. Her face, hastily wiped, still showed some streaks from the journey, but was now faintly coloured. Then her lips parted and, turning, Tobie saw that Doria had risen slowly and stood, looking up to the priest. He said, "I am deeply sorry. For them both, and for you."

He had whitened. The act of rising had caused him genuine pain. The monks had given him a loose robe which fell to the ground, concealing most of his injuries, but the way he held himself told some of the story, and the cloths that showed at the shoulder and bound the whole of one arm and hand betrayed the rest. For all that, he had been carefully shaved and his smooth, shining hair, rather long, fell across a face still comely and cleanly incised, with sadness in its fine eyes. Godscalc said, "Please sit. You are far from well."

"But I am alive," Doria said. He waited until Tobie, finding stools, dropped on one and slid the other to Godscalc. Then, equally slowly, he sat. He said, "You want to know where to find them." He smiled faintly, and glanced at his wife. "Catherine thinks you want to blame me, or even accuse me of killing them. I told her that you are fair-minded men. And intelligent."

"Then what happened?" said Tobie.

With painful clarity, he told them, and they listened in silence. Catherine had not approved of his hunting trip, but he had felt the need to escape – he hoped the Emperor would forgive him – from the stifling attentions of the court. He had taken a few men, and had found the hunting good, and had camped not only one but two nights, and then, trusting to his wife to forgive him, had thought that he might indulge himself by continuing further. Who knew, he might even come across Nicholas and be invited to go with him to Erzerum. "For whatever rivalry there may be between us," Doria said, "it does not extend to the Tabriz caravans, for there is enough there for everyone. As for the rest, he is a young man who enjoys games and I, too, find life sometimes a little too serious. They are dangerous games,

I admit; but not mortal. He has not tried to harm me, nor I him. Our main quarrel, I know, is over my marriage to my Caterinetta, but love will not always submit to old men's rules, or old women's either; and as you see, she has come to no harm."

"So you caught up with him?" Tobie said.

"Before the Vavuk pass. I was considering a camp for the night when I heard horses on the road I had left. The light was failing; they didn't see me. But I did notice that they were Kurds, and riding armed, as if ready to attack. In fact, as I watched, they left the road and took to the turf, as if they hoped to surprise someone. I thought of Nicholas. It was rash, I know, but I took my men and followed, keeping also to the soft ground. But when I reached them, they had already surprised his camp, and were among the tents, slaughtering. I did what I could," said Pagano Doria; and fell silent.

Godscalc said, "You saw Nicholas fall?" The girl, who had sat as if frozen throughout, drew a short breath.

Doria looked at her. He said, "Yes. I saw him die, and Master Julius. I don't suppose you want me to . . ."

"Perhaps later. We want to find them. And all the rest of his company?"

"Some ran off. They rode after them, until they were all dead. Then they took the tents, and their plunder. When I woke, there was nothing left except bodies." He moved his bandaged hand. "They had torn off my rings and cut through to see if I carried money. I was afraid they would come back, and took a stick and tried to get as far as I could while it was still dark. Two of my servants were still alive and came to help me. I didn't see where Nicholas lay. I am sorry. It was too dark, and I was too weak."

"They thought you were dead," Tobie said. "Your servants were lucky."

"They were not worth pursuing," Doria said. "They wore no armour, and carried nothing but hunting weapons. But all the same, two of them died."

"I am sorry," said Godscalc. "If Astorre finds them, he will bury them also. We have a guide to whom, if you will, you could describe the exact spot."

"If I could, I would come with you," said Doria.

"There is no need," Godscalc said. "Astorre will manage on his own. We ourselves are returning to Trebizond because of the company."

"Of course," said Doria. He lifted his free hand and rubbed it over his eyes. "Poor young men. I had forgotten, thinking of them, what it means to you all. You will go back to Bruges?"

It was odd to remember that once that is what they would have done. From curiosity, from pity for Marian de Charetty, from greed, of course, for the wealth the venture might bring, they had set out in

Nicholas's wake, and promised themselves that, if they fell out with him, they would make their way home (although Julius might come over stubborn, and Godscalc might stay to be confided in). Today, with Nicholas gone, return to Bruges had never even been mentioned. Now Godscalc said, "It would hardly be the best way of serving our mistress. For at least a year, we are committed to serve the Medici, and our station will stay, whether or not one or other of us goes back with our first cargo." He looked at the girl and said, "The demoiselle your mother is a good employer. This was not her venture, I know, but she had some stake in it. With the death of Nicholas, his rights revert to his wife. We shall not fail her."

"Then you wish to stay," Doria said slowly. He looked up. "Well, I don't see why not. You have done brilliantly in his absence, I am sure. And no one knows better than the Emperor or the others of the trading community how hard it has been for you to hold the company together without a real leader. You haven't been anxious, I know, to make known your disagreements, but it has been plain to us all that you had found Nicholas wanting. His failure shouldn't be laid at your door. I shall give you letters to the Emperor, saying so."

"You'll what?" said Tobie.

The girl turned her head at his voice.

Doria's handsome face was compassionate. He said gently, "As you yourself said, the right to establish this station was given by the demoiselle and by the Medici to Nicholas personally. Perhaps you forgot, in your distress over his performance. But the Emperor is well aware of it. You yourselves, able though you all are, are merely paid officials."

The pain in Tobie's arm proved to derive from Godscalc's four fingers digging into it. Godscalc said, "When a captain falls in battle, his deputies fill his place, until a replacement can be appointed. Fortunately, we have the understanding and trust, I think, of all the company's clients. There is no need, therefore, for your endorsement, although we thank you for it."

The wounded man, his face clouding, looked at his wife. He said, "Catherine, forgive me. You know these men, and they have been kind to you. But however high my regard, I have to be plain, and from the start." He turned back, wincing a little, and then holding himself nobly. He said, "I must ask you to forgive me too, at this distressing time. But without letters from me, Father Godscalc, Messer Tobias, it will not be possible for you to continue your business. With Nicholas gone to his rest, Catherine is her mother's representative in Trebizond, and Catherine's rights and privileges are now mine. Of course, if you wish, you may meantime remain as our employees. You will work well, I am sure, alongside mine: you know many of them already. If it becomes necessary to turn anyone off, be sure it will not be done without generosity. I shall make all this clear to the Emperor myself, when I am well enough to return. Meanwhile, let us put our minds to what matters most. Finding these poor fellows and giving them Christian burial. And, of course, finding their murderers."

The grip on Tobie's arm tightened but hardly checked the blood thundering through his body. Godscalc said, in a firm voice, "You are saying, Messer Doria, that you believe you have the right to represent the Charetty company in Trebizond?"

Pagano Doria's face remained open and mild. He said, "I think so. But of course it is my wife who has the authority. Ask Catherine, if you will." Again, he turned his head.

She had got, now, the drift of what he was saying, and was patchily flushed, as if a cool wind had roughened her skin. Beneath the tight control, emotions fought to escape: anger and anxiety, fear and resentment. Tobie watched. When her husband, smiling, turned fully towards her, she looked at him for a moment as if she could not think who he was. Then she said, "He is my husband."

Pagano Doria sent her, with his eyes, a smiling look straight from the bedchamber. Then he said, "And you are content, sweetheart, that I act for you?"

She said, "Yes."

Godscalc said, "My lord, forgive me. I am not perfectly clear. How can you act for the Charetty company if you are also acting for my lord Simon de St Pol of Kilmirren?"

God bless Godscalc. God bless all devious priests. Nicholas, you bastard, at least you gave us the key to all this before you got yourself killed. Tobie let his arm hang relaxed. Catherine de Charetty said scornfully, "Simon! What has he to do with us?"

"Ask your husband," Godscalc said.

Doria's smile hardly altered, but his eyes were for a moment unseeing.

Godscalc said, "It is known in Bruges as well as here. The round ship *Doria* doesn't belong to your husband, Catherine. Perhaps he didn't tell you. Its name was the *Ribérac*, and it was taken from his father by the Scottish lord Simon, who then employed your husband to sail east in his name and set up a rival station in Trebizond. You will know, perhaps, of the feud between my lord Simon and Nicholas."

She didn't collapse, or burst into tears any more than she had that morning. She turned to Doria, her eyes burning and said, "You didn't tell me."

Doria got up and, moving awkwardly away from the two men, sat down on the low bed by Catherine. He said, "No. Or we could never have married. He hired me to go into business for him, and make that business so successful that it would ruin Nicholas. You know Simon? He seems a silly, short-tempered lord, easily offended by slights which, I gather, Nicholas has unwisely offered him. I have a low

opinion of Simon, but he pays well. I knew nothing at all of young
Nicholas. I agreed; and then you and I met." He shook his head.
"Sweetheart, what could I do? Nicholas represented the Charetty
company, your company. I couldn't ruin that. But I needed his boat
to give me my own start in business, so that I could support you
without running, cap in hand, to your mother."

He smiled at her. "I was lucky. I've done that. The Genoese made
me their consul. I have traded for Simon, and myself. In small ways, I
hindered Nicholas so that I would seem to be fulfilling my obligations;
but he was your mother's husband. You know I never did anything
really harmful. I expected to establish a flourishing business, return
my lord Simon his boat and his profit, and choose, with you, the life
we both wanted. We can still do that."

She said, "I thought you were rich."

He smiled at her again. "I expect you thought your mother was
rich. Would you be content, now, to live in a burgher's brick house in
Bruges? I was hardly poor, Catherine. But I wanted to give you all the
gold in the world. I still do. And you will have it."

They sat looking at one another. The girl's eyes softened. Tobie
folded his arms and looked from one to the other. He said, "It seems
to me that three masters are enough for any one man, however fond he
is of his wife. What with working for my lord Simon, yourself, and the
Republic, you're going to tire yourself out without having to worry
over the trials of the Charetty company. Suppose you leave it in the
hands of the people who run it, whom the demoiselle knows and
trusts, and we'll see when we get back to Flanders who's going to
employ whom. Apart from anything else, Astorre's a curious fellow.
He fights for the demoiselle, no one else. And the Emperor, I'm sure,
wants Astorre to feel at his best."

Catherine said, "But I am the demoiselle. You forgot that."

Tobie said, "You are the daughter of the woman who chose
Nicholas and married him. Ask yourself what your mother would
want. What Nicholas would have wanted."

"Why?" said Catherine de Charetty. She stood up. "My mother is
an old, silly woman running a dyeshop. We live in quite a different
world. Pagano is right. He is head of the Charetty company here in
Trebizond, and you will do as he says. Now you can go."

Godscalc had risen. He stood without speaking, then turned at last
to Doria. He said, "It is as well to be formal. We do not accept this,
and will seek by all means to challenge its legality. Meanwhile, the
doors of our fondaco will be barred to you, and you will interfere with
us and our work at your peril. I take it upon myself to say this."

Without rising, Doria leaned his weight on the wall. He said, "Poor
souls, it is your livelihood, of course, that is threatened. And no doubt
you would enjoy your few weeks of petty dominion. Threats mean
nothing, of course. In this land, the ear of the Emperor is all that

matters. Even Astorre may find that he is not quite so necessary. Meanwhile I agree, you should go. You will forgive my not rising. I suffer from the wounds received trying to save my wife's stepfather. Send me your guide, and I will tell him where to look for the body. If you find yourselves short, I shall be happy to pay for the burial."

Before the girl, one could do nothing more, however one longed to. Godscalc bowed to her, and left the room, followed by Tobie. Instead of turning into the passage by which they had come, Godscalc slowed. He said, "I need air before we join the others. Let me follow you."

Tobie said, "I'll come with you. Over there. It leads to the balconies."

The door he opened led to a summer gallery built on the face of the rock, its floor tiled, its pillars open to darkness. Tobie walked to the rail and stood looking over. Below, the forest sighed and rustled unseen, and the rush of the river was no more than a long exhalation. Behind him, Godscalc knelt, his back turned. After a while Tobie spoke. "Father? There are some things I can ease."

Godscalc rose slowly. "No," he said. "It is fatigue, which sometimes makes simple things seem suddenly difficult. You feel it too, I am sure."

Tobie said, "You told the girl about Doria and Simon." He couldn't see the priest's face.

The priest said, "And yet I forbade Nicholas to disillusion her. That is what you mean?"

Tobie said, "And you let Nicholas go, knowing that Doria might follow. It was to be Doria himself who showed her what he was. But it didn't succeed. If he killed Nicholas, the girl has no idea of it. And there's no proof."

"He killed him," said Godscalc. When Tobie didn't speak, he said, "I know what I said. I gave him the benefit of every doubt there could be. I listened. I watched. There is no proof, but before God I know that man either killed him or had him killed. That is why I told about Simon. But that failed as well. It needs more than that to break what binds the child to Doria. And breaking that, what else would one break? That is the question." He stopped and said, "I am sorry. Tonight I don't sound like a priest."

"Tonight," said Tobie, "you sound like a man who needs food and wine and rest and sleep almost as much as I do."

Chapter 29

O N THE ELEVENTH DAY of May, a week after his wound in St
Omer, the Charetty lawyer Gregorio left the Knights of the
Golden Fleece to their vows and, turning his back, rode out
from Bruges in the direction of Dijon and Italy. Ostensibly,
his errand had to do with the expansion of the Charetty business. In
private, it was the same as that of Marian de Charetty, who had set out
ten weeks before to discover the fate of her daughter, and of Nicholas.
It was with some perplexity that Gregorio received, at the last
moment, a companion he did not want.

On the same day, far to the east, the Charetty doctor and Godscalc
their priest, sparsely escorted, rode over the Pyxitis bridge and
through the eastern suburb of Trebizond to their trading fondaco,
leaving behind them in the Sumela monastery the same daughter and
the golden Doria her husband, also wounded the previous week; but
in a different cause.

To Tobie, the approach to Trebizond looked just the same. The
same dilatory buffalo jammed the way from the bridge. The same
geese hissed and cackled. The same women slapped their laundry
beside the same fountain; the same dogs and children ran after them;
the same men called a greeting from the work booths; they had the
same trouble picking their way through the market. You realised then
how many faces and dwellings had become familiar in just five weeks
and how Nicholas had seemed to know not just a few people, but
everyone. A plague of small unreeling toys seemed, of its own, about
to constitute his greatest memorial. There was no sign, here, of
anxiety or disruption.

The Florentine courtyard, when they turned into it, was equally
tranquil. Only, because the day was dry as well as mild, the business
tables with their brass inkpots and cash books and sealing-wax had
been set out under the arcades. A lad from somebody's counting-
house was just rising, a minor transaction completed. On the house
side of the table, instead of Julius sat Patou the senior clerk, with John

le Grant silenced in mid-speech at his shoulder. The visitor left and le Grant, with a word to the clerk, walked forward and stood, hands on hips. "Well?" Loppe, somehow, was standing behind him.

Their grooms were looking up, too, and faces showed at the open windows. Godscalc said, "The story is the same. Doria saw them both die, and says there were no survivors. Astorre has gone to find what he can. Doria and his wife are coming back as soon as he can ride. We're tired."

The engineer said, "Come in. Loppe will bring wine and warm water. Everything is in order here."

Even Godscalc, dismounting, looked stiff. By the time they were indoors and in privacy, Loppe had already reappeared with all they needed to clean and refresh themselves. He stayed to serve, and then stood, quietly listening. Tobie, looking at him, thought that for a big man he had lost weight in the last week. Godscalc made his report plainly and quickly. "We are none the wiser. Doria's wounds are from Kurdish weapons. He claims he found Nicholas and Julius beset, and tried to save them. There is no proof that they died as he said and equally none that he is lying. But he is confident enough to claim this fondaco. We have three days – perhaps four – to decide what to do about it."

"Most of it has been done," said John le Grant. He bent and, opening a drawer, tossed before them a thick wad of paper. The sheets separated as they fell. Each page was covered with the clear rapid writing of Nicholas. Le Grant said, "I found that with the ledgers, after you'd gone. For us, in the event of his death. An account of what is in the storehouse, and what it is to be used for. And of what is to be bought from the caravan, with top and bottom prices for each article, the quantity, and the client it should go to. There, for example. A thousand pounds of Caspian leggi, if they'll bring the price down to two florins, and take twelve bales of woollen cloth instead of specie."

Tobie said, "We don't have any wool cloth."

John le Grant looked up. "We apparently bought some on credit from Zorzi. They came aboard off Tophane. Sixty pieces lying surplus in Pera."

"My God," said Tobie.

"If there's wool left over, we're to sell for Papal ducats or Turkish gold coins: he seems to think there'll be some about. If not, we're to exchange it for drugs to pay for the manuscripts. He's specific about which drugs for which monastery. He'd take seven thousand pounds of kermes from the credit notes we got for the three-pile velvet, and there's a shopping list for other dyes that goes on for pages. We're not to take any brazil that doesn't come from Ceylon . . . Do you want all this now?" said John le Grant.

"Not the shopping list," said Godscalc. "But other instructions?"

"Oh, plenty of those," said their engineer and ship-master. "Things to do to safeguard all the stock, and orders about leasing premises within the Citadel, which I've done. An open letter, doubly witnessed, transmitting to each of us powers of attorney to act for the Charetty company in the event of his absence or death. A note, appended to that, saying that Doria will certainly try to seize the company's local assets and negotiate in its name when the Tabriz caravan arrives. That is, acting as for Catherine's mother, he could usurp Medici and Charetty resources to make massive purchases for himself and his employer, and make off with the goods and the profit. Nicholas suggests ways of stopping him. Quite a lot of ways, some of them fairly ingenious and most of them criminal." His eyes, with their sandy rims, had been fixed on the floor. He raised them to Godscalc. "Your Master Nicholas was not absolutely certain, it seems, that he was coming back from that trip."

"He chose to take it," said Godscalc. "But you're right. He knew it was dangerous. If you like, he waited until he thought it would be dangerous. He wanted to prove something."

"And has he?" said the ship-master. He had flushed.

"Not in the way he wanted. In others, maybe. We may have been too ready to blame him. A man prepared to do what he has done has some character."

"I'm prejudiced," said John le Grant. "He got me out of impaling back at Stamboul. And Julius. And all Astorre's men. He liked his privacy, but I never thought that a sin. I'm surprised you're surprised he went to all this bother to prime us when he seems to have known he'd be dead. What the hell turned you against him?"

Tobie said, "Something you would condemn as much as we did. To excuse it at all, you'd have to believe it wasn't deliberate. We thought it was."

"So you made a mistake?"

Tobie studied him. "Maybe," he said. "But he'd done similar things in the past. He made a wicked enemy, John. You wouldn't know. But his friends seemed to be safe. And beside Doria, he had some . . . qualities. Doria thought that, with Nicholas dead, we'd want to go back to Bruges."

The golden, bristling brows drew together. "You bloodied him, I hope, where it'll ruin his drawers."

"His wife was there. I'm glad you feel like that," Tobie said. "Because it's possible we were hard on Nicholas. It's possible matters were maybe not quite as they seemed. I think Doria, on the other hand, made capital out of it. So I don't mean Pagano Doria to get a dead cat belonging to the Charetty company. This business is going to be what Nicholas was hoping to make it – one of the richest and best in the Levant."

The other two, he became aware, were looking at him. Behind, he saw Loppe's face change. John le Grant said, "Medicine, now. The only proper calling for scientific man, for whom trade is fair walloping rubbish. What happened to yon?"

Godscalc said, "The same thing that happened to the profession of countermining, I suspect. He has made you his heirs in more ways than one." He spoke without looking up. And well you might, Tobie thought. You, too, have had your confidence shaken. You, too, have had to look again at your toys.

John le Grant said, "You're tired. Why not rest? We'll be busy enough, once the news goes round that you're back. And when you're fresh, you can hear all the details."

He was a good man, for a Scot and an engineer. He was better than any of them had suspected, except, of course, Nicholas. Tobie found his own bed and half undressed and knew nothing more until he woke to a dark room, and a half-open door, and Loppe saying, "Master Tobias? They're all in the parlour with the lady Violante. She has something to ask us in private. Master le Grant says you should come."

"*Ask* us?" said Tobie. "Here? In private?" He sat up. None of that conformed to what he knew of the princess of Trebizond. From the time of the voyage from Tophane, he had been sharply wary of the lady Violante, who had befriended Doria in Florence. Who had got Julius out of trouble outside the Chrysokephalos. Who had shown inalienable contempt, ever since, for the lot of them. He knew Julius had been smitten. He couldn't believe that she was in mourning for either Julius or Nicholas. So why was she here, except to pull the wool over the eyes of Godscalc or le Grant or Loppe? But not over him. Tobie got up and dressed.

Tobie Beventini had been right in his conjecture. It was not the habit of Violante of Naxos to traverse her own city, hooded, alone, to pay secret calls on the fondaco of a foreign company. She had, at first, intended to send a servant. She had concluded, at last, that there was no one she could sufficiently trust. There was no one, either, who could size up the situation as she could.

At the gateway, she was obstructed because she would not give her name. It was only when she insisted on having John le Grant summoned that the porter gave way. Then the red-headed man arrived; the engineer and ship-master she had interviewed at the Palace, and at once she was inside, and being handled with swift efficiency.

A woman of small patience, Violante of Naxos had been unimpressed by her initial experience of the officers of the Charetty company. The priest, who should have been a wrestler, was no doubt as inconvenient as the man Diadochos she was forced to take everywhere with her. The doctor had certainly learned no manners from a lifetime of staring at festering feet, and went both hairless and hatless, which she happened to believe was obscene. The man they had made steward was a freed slave, which said all there was to say. Only the master engineer was visibly competent in all but the social arts, in which area she had thought him a boor.

Since then, she had changed her mind about some things, for the blood of Lombardy as well as Trebizond had gone to her making. She had a respect for John le Grant's wits. To him she said only, "Have you a parlour? I have something to ask of you all." And in five minutes there was a room, warmed and lit; and a chair for her, and a cup of warm wine. In ten, all the men she knew had entered, bowed, and were sitting in silence about her. Then she began.

She said, "I have questions to ask you, and then you may question me. First: what action have you decided upon, following this unfortunate loss? Will you close the venture and return home forthwith?"

It was the priest who answered. He said, "The company came here to trade, Despoina, and we are remaining to trade."

"I see," she said. "All of you?"

"All of us," said the doctor. "Were you afraid the army would leave?"

She ignored it. She said, "Then we have matters to talk of for the good of the company. Messer Niccolò left you some letters?"

"He did leave letters," said John le Grant. "Highness."

"And you have begun to act on them. I thought so. He warned you that Messer Doria would immediately claim to represent your station in the name of his wife?"

The priest answered. "For the good of our company, I'm afraid we cannot reply. I should tell you that we know of your past association with Pagano Doria. We don't yet know how Nicholas died."

It was no surprise that they were wary of her. Their young Nicholas had severed her connection with Doria somewhat unattractively himself. She again wondered, briefly, how he had known of it. And if he had known, why he had allowed John le Grant to come and see her. She watched John le Grant. She said, "When a Venetian associates with a Genoese, it is not for the sake of amusement, I assure you. Nevertheless, for your own peace of mind, tell me nothing you wouldn't wish Doria to hear. I shall begin by telling you something. I assume Messer Niccolò has stressed that your ledgers are precious. Those and any letter of authority he has left must be put in a safe place, unknown to your servants and me. If you have goods still for sale, then conceal them. You should put a guard on your gates and give an escort to those who go to market or on errands. Remember, men can be bribed. Take care not to change servants, and watch your food and your water. You have an informer already: the Greek Paraskeuas serves Doria as well as you. Tell him only what you want Doria to know."

"Paraskeuas!" said the priest sharply.

The black slave said, "Paraskeuas was here, on an errand, the day Master Julius left."

The priest said, "We assumed Julius decided to go to keep Nicholas company. But suppose he was tricked into following? Told that Nicholas needed him?"

The doctor said, "I feel we could make Paraskeuas tell us."

She said, "His wife and son are in that household. I don't think you would get the truth. In any case, isn't he worth more where he is? I told you only to warn you. I have news that is not for his ears. First, the town of Amastris has fallen to the Turk."

The doctor said, "Should that worry Trebizond? It's hundreds of miles west of Sinope. Or you think the Sultan's aiming at Sinope?"

"Certainly the Turkish fleet may move along the Black Sea. Even if they only try to besiege Sinope, they could make it both dangerous and expensive for your galley to travel west in the summer. On the other hand, you take a risk leaving your goods and your galley off Trebizond. If the fleet arrives here, it will seize all the ships the Emperor might otherwise use. And as you know, there are no walls round the suburbs."

"What are the Genoese doing?" the doctor said. He made no effort to give her her title.

"As you see, the round ship is still at anchor. When the caravan comes, they will no doubt store their purchases in the City."

"And the Venetians, Despoina?" the priest said.

"I hope your letters tell you that," said Violante of Naxos. "For it was a matter your Messer Niccolò and I touched upon when we were sailing. The Venetian agent at Erzerum had instructions to make his purchases on the spot but not to send them to Trebizond. All the Venetian cargo is going to Kerasous."

The red-haired mechanic said, "Why?"

He, too, had set aside courtesy. She took her time before she answered the question. "There is less fear the Turks will attempt to land there. It is immensely strong, and has less to offer than Sinope and Trebizond. Its offshore island is hated by seamen. With the right ship, cargo could be uplifted from Kerasous and slipped clear to the West through the Bosphorus if other circumstances allowed."

The priest said, "You are suggesting that we, too, send our purchases out to this Kerasous?"

"That is for you to decide," she said. "I have nothing further to say on these points. I now come to my errand. I wish to hire your ship for a week, crewed by men of my choice."

It was le Grant the ship-master, of course, she was looking at. He said, "Yes, Despoina? And where were you hoping to sail her?"

She said, "East, to Batum. There is some special cargo to be delivered quickly and in secret. It is not a ruse of Messer Doria's to deprive you of your galley, but I understand you will hardly believe that without sufficient proof."

"No, I shouldn't, highness," said the red-headed man. "It would take a lot to persuade me to agree to anything, these days."

She said, "I thought that it might. On the other hand, had I wished, I could have sent someone else on this errand. I have a clear conscience. If you have been used, it is by your own side."

The red-haired man did not answer. The priest, looking from one to the other, chose to return to the subject in hand. "Certainly," he said. "Before we lose sight of our ship, you would have to show us good reason, Despoina. What can you offer that would make us consider it?"

"Who reads Greek?" she said.

It was the doctor who took the scroll she brought out from her robes, and paused at the seal. The silk and the wax with its one-headed eagle, emblem of the Imperial Comneni. Then he broke it and read, and then passed it wordlessly to the priest. The man John le Grant said, "What is it?"

And the doctor said, "We are asked to take the Empress to Georgia. The Empress Helen."

She said, "The Empress's daughter is Queen of Georgia."

"Secretly?" the doctor said. He had a small, twitching nose like a ferret. "Not, then, a family visit. She wants an army to set out from Tiflis to Trebizond?"

"Or Tiflis to Erzerum," the engineer said. "I expect Uzum Hasan could do with a little help." The Scots inflection, when he was angry, sounded coarsely through the Italian.

The doctor said, "But it was the Empire of Trebizond, surely, that our friend Fra Ludovico and his party was seeking Christian help to preserve. There was a Georgian envoy among them. I can't remember how many soldiers he promised. A lot."

She said, "You would require to take her to Batum on the Georgian border, and wait for her message. It is only a hundred miles to Batum, and less than that to the Franciscans inland at Akhalziké. By the time the galley returns, the Turks' plans will be clearer. You might even wish to anchor this time at a spot less conspicuous than the road off Trebizond itself. You would call your absence a trading voyage. It is always the season for slaves."

The priest said, "Will the palace children go with her?"

"It is not an escape," said Violante of Naxos. "The children remain, and all the other women. The plan is not at present known to the Emperor."

"But the oarsmen will be Venetian?" the red-haired man said. He had read the situation already. The others, she saw, would not be far behind.

She said, "They will be the best we can get, who are also

trustworthy. They will be paid by us." She addressed herself to the priest, since none of the others had emerged as a spokesman. "You may use your own seamen and officers, including Messer le Grant if he will go, and if you can spare him. The payment would be appropriately high."

"For example?" said the doctor.

She knew the Florentine prices, and made sure this was better. They could have little quarrel with that. She said, "I don't ask you to decide now. You will be given an audience. I have told the Empress that, even if you refuse, your silence can be trusted. She would hope to see you in any case when you bring the completed work to the Emperor."

"What completed work?" said the doctor.

She looked at the engineer. He said, "They don't know. It didn't seem worth mentioning now."

"Mentioning what?" the doctor said. He looked annoyed.

The engineer got up. "What Nicholas was working at in his room. I gave him a hand with some of the parts. He left notes to help me go on with it. As a present. A gift for the Emperor. It was to go to the Palace when finished."

"When *what* was finished?" said the doctor.

She waited, watching them all: sure, now, of her diagnosis. She was pleased, now, that she had troubled to do this herself. Le Grant; the doctor; the slave, of course, whom the young man had used, she believed, as some sort of confidant. And the chaplain? So far, she could not tell what he thought. The bald doctor asked all the questions, but the priest listened, and watched. Watched her, as she was watching him.

Now, le Grant stood, and caught the eye of the negro, and then turned to the rest. He said, "You might as well come and see. The lady, too, if she wishes. We kept the door locked."

They remembered to let her go first. As they walked, she spoke to the doctor. "I thought Messer Niccolò had shown you the manuscripts."

The doctor was staring at John le Grant, not at her. "He brought some medical books from the Palace."

Le Grant answered the doctor, not her. "It was nothing that mattered. It filled the time. It could have been useful. It had to do with one of the manuscripts from the same source as yours. The Byzantines copied old Greek treatises, and the Arabs got hold of them and translated them into something different; and then they come back to the Greeks as presents or booty. There was an Arab engineer in Diyarbekr, though, who wrote an original work a couple of hundred years ago on mechanical devices. It seems a copy turned up in the Palace. Nicholas saw it, and built something from it. That's all."

"The Basileus was amused to discover and foster Messer Niccolò's special talents," she said. She could hear them thinking. She added, "And where, then, is the confection?"

"Here, highness," said the engineer; and opened a door.

She had seen the drawings which were, of course, fantastical nonsense. However, it was a nonsense that tickled the Emperor's fancy, and there was no reason why an ingenious man, good with his hands and well-stocked with artisan's patience, should not make, from straw paper and wood, the kind of simulacrum that the Emperor would be pleased with. An ancient mechanical jest, reproduced in another dimension.

What she saw, as she went forward, was the image of the nonsensical drawing. An ancient mechanical jest now transformed into an object of art which was also, in its gentle, affectionate way, a tribute to the bright, merry soul of its Arab inventor. And more than that, the essence, you would say, of the man now gone: the man who had made it.

On the floor stood a rubicund elephant. Behind its Indian driver a maiden sat within a tall canopied howdah, intricately painted and tasselled. A bird sat on the roof of the howdah, with a turbanned Arab fixed to a valance below him. From inside the roof hung a dragon, its coiling neck and stretched jaws leaning upwards. The dragon glistened with rude, childish malice. The maiden looked coy. The Indian driver gazed furiously at his hatchet. The elephant appeared uncertain and also deeply preoccupied. The enamels glittered and glowed on all the smooth, fashioned surfaces. The lady Violante looked round. Priest and doctor, shipmaster and negro: each face had cleared and was smiling. The priest said, "It's a clock. Is it?"

Le Grant said, "Yes. The maiden points to the time. There are revolving openings, too, inside the roof of the howdah. If you look, you'll see them change colour. For the rest . . ." He crossed the room to a long bench on one wall. On it were tools, laid out neatly as scalpels, and coils of wire and a vice. There was also a sand-glass. The engineer said, "I gather he made things in Bruges."

The doctor said, "All the time. What happens here?"

"You'll see," said le Grant.

They had slipped into childhood. She watched the men more than she watched the elephant clock; and even when the performance began, and the bird whistled, and the mahout struck the elephant, and the Arab dropped a pellet into the dragon's open mouth, she looked at them, curious about what she saw on their faces. The pellet, circulating, sprang from the dragon's fundament into a vase and disappeared within the elephant, from which emerged, with sonority, the sound of a gong. A thing of delight. An explosion of fine controlled gaiety that a man with artisan's patience had made.

Throughout, the engineer gazed, absorbed, intent on following each faultless move. The chaplain had begun to look, smiling, and then ceased to see, although his eyes remained on the clock. The doctor laughed once; then his smile fixed like the grin on a terrier and he turned aside, jabbing his fist like a man lost for words; or for a reason for something. Then, without taking leave, he let his arm drop and left.

The priest came to himself. He said, "Is that all you wished to say to us, Despoina?"

"Oh. Yes," said Violante of Naxos. "And of course, I ought to tell you. The caravan from Tabriz will arrive in eight days. Messer Doria will be back in plenty of time to prepare for it."

She returned, without event, to the Palace and was charming, that evening, to her great-uncle the Emperor and all her beautiful relatives. Caterino Zeno my husband, you have a wife beyond price. Everything, everything is as you wanted it.

Chapter 30

CATHERINE DE CHARETTY negli Doria, thirteen years old and the youngest of three, had never met a sick man in her life, let alone nursed one. When the halt and the blind and the mutilated came back from one of Captain Astorre's wars, it was her mother who paid them their pension, and visited their wives with baskets of blood-sausage and puddings and eggs, and took their children into her 'prentice loft.

Catherine was surprised when her husband's gallant fortitude hardly outlasted his visitors. They had barely gone before he began to fret for one reason or another. He had not enjoyed the interrogation, and seemed to blame her in some way for the incursion. Also, where was the hospice physician, now that he lay here exhausted? At his bidding, she limped off to find him, and received less than passionate thanks for that or the other services she found, in his servantless state, he required of her. When he considered there was not enough wine, or the brazier was smoking, or he wished to be helped to his bed, it was his little Catherine who, with a certain perfunctory charm, was recruited to serve him. When, in need of comfort, she pressed herself close, he asked her to keep off. He moderated his voice almost immediately, but there was no doubt it had been strident. It became apparent that he did not want to make love. Catherine resented every moment of the week they spent in the Sumela monastery. It reminded her quite often of those parts of her daily round at the Leoncastello which she also greatly disliked.

Of course, life in beautiful Trebizond was never less than glorious. Remembering her routine existence in Bruges, there could be no comparison. But it was not all a matter of feasts and fine clothes and dignified gossip. To look after the residence and the warehouse there was Paraskeuas their steward; and Pagano naturally had ordered him to see to everything without troubling the lady his wife. After all, her mother had run her business without doing her own daily marketing, or putting soles to the family hose, or personally baking the family bread, or salting the family meat, or making its sheep cheeses at lambing time. Unfortunately, when Paraskeuas was away, the household seemed to think they should resort to Catherine in his place. And not only her household, but the women of the rest of the colony.

In Bruges you bought everything in the town. Here, contracts were made by which your oil and your wine, your geese and your capons, your leeks and your onions and pigeons were brought in from outlying farms, and there were always complaints of short-changing or rotten goods or lateness or failure of delivery. In such cases; or when some roof leaked, or the water was muddied or a slave fell sick and the doctor was away, what was she expected to do? They seemed to think she must have time to spare, since she didn't cut her own cloth, or check the cellar or storehouse, or supervise the washing and sewing and certainly not the beastly business of cleaning the commodes. When the orange and pomegranate trees in sheltered places began to sag for want of watering, Pagano had said as if astonished that he had supposed she was attending to it, as the duty didn't seem to be hard. It occurred to her, a little late, that Pagano had never in his life stayed very long in one place, and that if there were women about he assumed that such matters were being taken care of. He had been the most perfect and skilful lover that any girl of her age might have wanted, but his imagination, she saw, did not really stretch to practical things. She kept having to remind him.

He was still thinking about nothing but his health when the time came to go back to Trebizond, and she felt, sometimes, that he was not really listening when she talked of more important things. She thought a lot about what her mother would do without Nicholas, and whether Pagano would have to bother with Bruges, and what it would be like to give orders to Father Godscalc and Meester Tobie. She wanted to know Pagano's plans. She was becoming uneasy, as well, at the long abstinence his injuries had imposed, which her body resented. She had made her disappointment quite clear on their last night at the monastery, and had got him at last to court her properly although he could not, of course, carry her into bed. Then, having roused her, he suddenly cried out and rolled aside, groaning, while she ached and throbbed unfulfilled at his side. That was when she struck out at him, without caring where the blow fell, and he shouted at her and left the bed and crept to a chair, where he sat hugging himself and swearing under his breath. Later, he asked her to forgive him, but she wouldn't for a long time. On the journey back to the Leoncastello they hardly spoke, and once there the Genoese doctor put him to bed and gave him something that kept him sleeping all night. It was the first time, too, that she had ever heard Pagano snore. But Willequin gave her a wonderful welcome.

The next day she went out, and stayed out. After the monastery, it was delicious to take out a fresh gown and veil and braid her hair up with flowers and walk out with her attendants to see her acquaintances in the City. She told, several times, the story of how Pagano had fought off the Kurds single-handed. Once, she saw the big Guinea slave Loppe in the distance and when Willequin barked he turned his head and began quickly to push towards her. Luckily, she was near the house of an embroideress she wanted to visit, and slipped through the door before he got near. Nicholas had known how to get round most people, and she supposed they were sorry in one way that he had gone. But you couldn't expect grown men to enjoy taking orders from her mother's apprentice. It was better for her mother this way, however sad it made her at first. Felix would have been sad as well. When she had a thought like that, she dismissed it. The wife of one of the Ancona merchants asked her to take dinner with them, and she did. She had quite a satisfactory day.

As soon as she got back to the fondaco, she felt that something had happened. The big yard that could hold whole mule-trains was busy with hurrying people, and she saw a group of servants waiting in Venetian livery. There was an air of briskness, of excitement even, that had not been there when they had received their injured consul the previous day. She met Paraskeuas as she hurried in.

He was smiling, as always. Looking after Cardinal Bessarion's dying mother had made him good at pleasing people, while doing much as he wanted, she suspected, behind their backs. But he was a very hard-working steward, and his wife and son were always respectful and neat. Now he said, "His excellency asks, madonna, that you will excuse him for a moment. The Venetian Bailie has called. It seems that the Tabriz caravan is only two or three days away, and they plan to send messengers to find out its size and its merchandise. His excellency has been to the Palace already."

Catherine wondered why. Dismounting yesterday, Pagano had claimed never to wish to see a saddle again. It was even more amazing when, presently, free of his business, Pagano joined her in her parlour with the resilience back in his step and his handsome face again full of colour and life. He said, 'Well, demoiselle: greet your wounded husband who does have the esteem of some people. Out of regard for us both, the Emperor has said he will never countenance a revolt by your mother's servants. The Charetty company in Trebizond is now rightly yours, and you may do with it as you please, with the Emperor's blessing."

She considered. "Do we have to move out to their villa?"

He laughed. "Would you prefer a little fondaco to the Leoncastello of Genoa? No, sweetheart. Later, we shall appoint men of our own to see to the Florentine contract. Meantime, I hesitate to turn the poor fellows out of their compound. When the caravans come, they will simply find their gates locked until all the trading is done. The

Emperor has ordained it. Otherwise it would be nonsense: two sets of people claiming to speak and buy for the Charetty company. Catherine, I am jealous of my privilege to buy you your rubies. Now you can have them. Now, when the camels walk over the bridge, you can have all you ever wanted." He put his arm round her shoulders and in his glowing face was the look that she had missed for a week. He said, "The news has cured me already. We shall find some way, my Caterinetta, to honour these jewels you are going to have, so that they and you will recognise who is their master."

It was all right again. She saw that he was a man who was upset by discomfort, and who liked to win at the games he played. Perhaps he had not been quite sure that the Emperor liked him better than the Charetty company's men. Which was silly, for they were nothing but salaried servants, and he was a lord. She remembered then, with vexation, that in one way the lord Pagano Doria was a salaried servant himself. It was a subject she had tried to discuss several times, without much success. Now, she said, "What did that man Simon want you to buy?"

She sensed his irritation, but he replied, smiling as usual, "He left me a free hand. I'll buy enough to make him some profit, sweetheart. Since he relied on me, I can hardly do less. But it is your fortune we are going to make, not my lord Simon's."

"Won't he be angry?" she said.

"With Nicholas dead?" said her lord and husband. "Dear heart, no one could feel more for your mother than I do, but without Nicholas to compete with, my lord Simon will lose all interest in making his mark in Levantine trade. If he does little more than cover the costs of his voyage, he will be content. I am sure of it."

"You mean he wanted Nicholas dead," Catherine said. In awkward conversations, instead of avoiding her eyes, he sometimes held them as now, his own big and open.

Pagano said, "Whatever gave you that idea? The Scots lord thought him insolent, and decided to teach him a lesson by beating him at his own trade. I should never have agreed to anything else, even before you and I met. Nicholas took no harm from our sport. I am the one who suffered, trying to save him."

She hardly heard him. "You asked me once if I wanted to go home," Catherine said. "You said we'd go home and leave Nicholas. I don't see now how you could, if you still had to earn your money from Simon."

He touched her cheek as he used to. He said, "If you had wanted to go home, we'd have gone. Money is nothing. It can always be had, if you look for it. But you are my wife, and must be happy."

"I don't feel like your wife," Catherine said. She nearly didn't say it, in case he abandoned her half-crazed like last time. But he had learned his lesson. She had hardly drawn breath before she found

herself in her chamber, and his hands where she wanted them. This
time, if he wanted to groan, he kept it to himself, except when she
most enjoyed hearing it. And this time, it was as good as the finest
proper marital act they had ever had. Lying there, as her breathing
calmed down, she thought for the first time of her mother's cold bed.
But senses faded with age. What her mother had lost was far from this
hunger and ecstasy. And besides, it was a second marriage; belated,
self-indulgent, uncalled-for. She waited half an hour and then,
although he was bleeding, got Pagano to make her his wife,
triumphantly, all over again.

As the treasure ships from the Orient sailed once a year into Bruges, so
once a year in the spring the first camel trains from the East crossed
the high steppes of Asia Minor and padded on cushioned feet through
the valley of the Pyxitis to the Black Sea. Grey and brown, white and
tawny and beige, the camels came headstall to tail, jangling with silver
and seashells and the small bells of their harness; their necks rising
and falling; their thick-lashed eyes set on the horizon. They each
carried three hundred pounds' weight of incomparable merchandise,
and there were a thousand of them, with sixty armed men to guard
them. For every roped string of beasts there were shepherds and
drivers who swayed on their backs, uttering long whooping cries, or
sending up to the sky paeans of improvised chanting while their
breeched women jogged beside them on the packsaddles of mules,
with waterskins and salt and yoghourt and babies in baskets, and goats
jumping and running about them. The aristocrats: the riding camels
with their fringed blankets and tassels; the dromedaries that could run
a hundred miles in a day; the fine horses with their silken harness were
the conveyances of the merchants, whose servants brought their own
luxuries.

Word of their coming ran far ahead, with the odour of musk and
rancid milk and badly cured leather and toiling humankind. You
could follow them, too, by the crows. What was folded inside the thick
bales, three feet wide, two feet deep on each heaving flank was as
secret as the contents of the crates in the suave gilded splendour of the
Venetian galleys. Rank and dour and barbaric, this was the rough cup
from which the élite of the West drank its elixir.

Within a day's ride of Trebizond, the messengers came from the
city, avid and hopeful, to meet them. Reposing at Erzerum, the
merchants of the caravan had had their entertainment, and their
rewards, and their instructions. They dealt with the messengers as
they had promised, and travelled on.

In the Florentine fondaco, the mood was grimly determined. Astorre
had not returned. Pagano Doria had come back, and had immediately
associated himself with both the Venetians and the Palace. The men of

the Charetty company had a choice: to believe Violante of Naxos, or to make their own dispositions. They chose to believe her, and acted accordingly. When, therefore, news of the caravan came, they sent no messengers and made no enquiries, although they watched the couriers ride off from the Venetian consulate and the Leoncastello. Bit by bit, working hard and silently, they had achieved all that Nicholas had asked of them in his testament, and all that the lady Violante had advised. Now they could only wait.

They knew, going about their business, when the caravans were imminent, because of the excitement. As Bruges declared holiday, so Trebizond prepared for the exotic arrival of the source of its wealth. As for a feast day, market stalls were withdrawn and streets hung with cloths and garlands and banners. Within the walls of the City, the great caravanserai with its merchant rooms and storehouses and stabling was swept and sanded and readied, and the kitchens stocked with the wood, the oil, the meat, the bread that for three days the City would present to its guests. Outside, on the customary grazing, space was cleared for the camels and their shepherds and keepers, where the women would make fires and raise the low, hump-backed tents on their poles and sit talking and spinning while the camels lay with the familiar goats sprawled on their necks, and the claws of tick-hunting birds plucking their thick matted hair.

The first warning came when they were barely up and preparing to dress; when the day porter of the Florentine fondaco, going to sweep out the yard and unlock the big double street doors, found they would not yield to his key. Then, opening the spyhole, he had seen that the street outside was filled with soldiers who turned and shouted at him and, when he yelled back, shook their swords at him grinning.

Tobie, wakening to a sea and sky dyed rose with a Colchian sunrise, was struck by the commotion, and ran half-dressed out to the yard. Godscalc stood there already, his powerful feet astride in the dust, demanding redress and explanation. Beyond the grille, you could see cold steel and turbans. The Emperor's guard. The Emperor's personal guard. Then Godscalc turned and said, "We have been forbidden to leave the fondaco by Imperial order. We are locked in until the caravan leaves."

"Who says?" said Tobie. "Let me speak to them."

"Speak, then," said Godscalc. "But it's the captain of the Palace Guard, and he has written orders."

Tobie stared at him. He said, "How many?"

Godscalc said, "What does it matter? You don't imagine we can use force with them, do you?"

"You don't imagine we just give in, do you? I could get over the wall."

"They're all round," said Godscalc. "And if you could get out, what would you do? Go to the caravanserai and bid against Doria?

Doria is head of the Trebizond branch of the Charetty company. That is what this means."

"I wasn't thinking of bidding against him," said Tobie.

"I didn't think you were. And what are you going to do to get rid of Catherine de Charetty?" Godscalc said. "You do remember that she's the head of the company? I query if, as a widow, she would make a factor of her late husband's murderer. She might, of course, but I doubt it."

"So we do nothing?" said Tobie.

"We use our brains," Godscalc said. "The caravan has still to arrive. The buying has still to begin. We could send a petition, for example, to the Emperor. We could send a message to the lady Violante. We could advise Doria himself that, no matter what transaction he makes, we shall dispute it afterwards as the deputies appointed by Nicholas. We could go in and have something to eat and pick John le Grant's brains. You're indecent."

Tobie dragged down his shirt. "It reflects my state of mind," he said. "So it was a waste of time, the elephant clock? What in God's name does the Basileus see in Doria?"

"Charm," said Godscalc. "I shan't malign him by imagining there are other reasons. We shan't even see the procession. It goes along by the shore."

"What a pity," said Tobie. "I was going to wave flags and kiss all the camels."

The sun rose, and began to burn. Standing at the shore gates to the City with her husband and the other merchants and the Treasurer Amiroutzes and his party, Catherine inhaled once more the special perfume of Trebizond, now so customary that she hardly heeded it; and wished that she could sit, like a child, on her husband's silken shoulders and watch for the plumes and the banners that meant that the caravan had begun to pass along the shore to make its state entrance. They said a camel's sense of smell was so keen that it could pick up a nut of ambergris left on the beach. They said that ghost trains of camels passed incessantly, taking the souls of the Faithful to Mecca. A trickle crawled down her spine with the heat. She was wearing her newest gown, silk over silk, with her earrings, and Pagano had on the Emperor's coat. They were going to welcome the merchants, and sit and take refreshments while the bales were unloaded, and then go from room to room, buying and choosing. Pagano said the rubies came in little kid bags, and there were pearls as big as beans, and Baghdad silk woven with eagles and panthers, and fine camlet, warm as fur, made of silk and camel hair woven together.

He hadn't spoken of dyes. Perhaps he thought they were dull. But all her life she had heard her mother, and Henninc and the people who worked in the yard, talking wistfully of the beautiful kermes, the real insect dye of the Orient, which turned fine woollens blood-red or

peach. What you could do with it! Add brasil, and there was old
rose, or a brilliant scarlet. Add fustic, and the cloth came out in
yolk-yellow folds, soft as daffodils.

There would be indigo from Baghdad and the Gulf. The Duchess
had ordered blue cloth from her mother last year. They had dyed it
for her, of course, but hardly went into profit, even by charging
three lire the piece. There was powdered lapis lazuli, now; the painter's flower; sold in Bruges for a florin an ounce. She remembered
Colard Mansion complaining about that, and the price of gall nuts
for ink. They could buy all that cheap and sell it for a fine margin. If
Pagano was purchasing for the Charetty company, he would have to
buy dyes, and perhaps she could help him. Her family instincts,
never fostered, stirred at the sight of the well-dressed men all about
her, their clerks at their heels, discoursing in murmurs. Like Bruges,
it was all done by bargaining and the handshake. It was when the
chosen bales arrived on your doorstep that the yardstick came out,
and the account books and the cash boxes. She said, "I don't see my
mother's men after all."

"They stayed at home," Pagano said. "The City thought it best,
in the interests of order. I was sorry, because I could have done with
their advice. But I'm sure we shall do quite well in spite of it.
There's the Venetian Bailie, with a fortune to spend on his spices.
What would become of the bowels of the world without his rhubarb
and ginger?" She thought it coarse of Pagano, but forgave his exces-
sive high spirits. After all they had gone through, they had come to
market at last. The treasure fleet, the Fleece, was arriving.

She heard the drums beating first, and then the hoofbeats and
shouting, and then the sound of flutes and strings being plucked, and
then a shaking jingle like tambourines, and then a muffled tread, like
cloth being trodden, mixed with deep and peculiar snores. Then the
first beast came into view, looking down its nose like a bishop
through eyelashes curled like a whore's, and she clung to Pagano's
arm and jumped with delight, as she used to do at the carnival. She
dropped his arm. The Bailie said, "Is that all?"

Pagano didn't reply. It never worried her, being short, but she
could see that, for a man, it was frustrating. George Amiroutzes, in
his big basket hat, was looking along the road also. He said, "No
doubt the rest will come later." The procession had halted, and
several horsemen were coming forward and dismounting to receive
the Imperial welcome. Some were bearded and some had flat yellow
faces and some looked just like themselves. They all bowed. One of
them was captain Astorre. Beside her, Pagano drew a short breath.

The Treasurer, straightening from his own bow, recognised the
captain as well. He stepped forward and spoke to him. "You have
come with the caravan?"

"Met it on the road," said her mother's captain. "Thought they would be none the worse of protection. Brigands about, as you know. Offering my services to interpret."

Behind him, when you looked, were other familiar faces in helmets. It was natural, when you gave it a thought. He had been searching the same road for the place of Pagano's battle. She wanted to ask him what he had found, but he was busy making introductions. Soon, still dismounted, the leaders were taken ceremoniously into the City and along the short distance to the khan. The camels followed, and the merchants, including themselves. The Bailie said, "Two hundred. There are only two hundred. The rest must be following. If so, I'm going home till they come."

Pagano said, "You might miss a bargain."

"I might pay dear for something I could have got better later. No. Let's find out what's happened."

How to do this was not at all clear. Above their shoulders, camels continued to pass, forcing a way through onlookers and merchants. The last, a high-bred riding camel with silken reddish-brown flanks, paused beside her and she turned her head aside, having learned how men with shawled heads and robes dealt with women with uncovered faces. Then the rider said, "Houtch, houtch, houtch, houtch . . ." in an irritated voice, and the camel, restarting with a shiver of bells, took up its soft, dancing gait. As it passed, she saw the soft kid of the man's boot was sewn all over with silk like a comfit-cake, and had a long tassel of gold at the heel. Then he disappeared in the crowd of his fellows.

Dust rose and hung in the air. The caravanserai, when they reached it, was a jostling throng of men and horses and camels laboriously kneeling or rising, while their bales were loosed and carried off to the room of each owner. Pagano, with the Bailie at his side, pushed his way through to where the palace officials could be glimpsed, and a figure whose forked beard and tall black-draped hat proclaimed him a monk. Then he turned, and she saw he was the Archimandrite she had last seen with Violante of Naxos. He appeared to have come with the train, and indeed still held the reins of his horse. Then he turned and saw the Bailie. "Your excellency?"

The Bailie wasted no words. "Where are the rest of the camels?"

The Archimandrite's Italian was excellent. He said, "Have no fear, your excellency. The consignment for Venice is safe. Because of the brigands, and the White Horde activities, the merchants took counsel at Erzerum and made your purchases there. They are on their way through to Bursa, from where they will cross to your agent at Pera, and then home. I have letters from your agent at Erzerum." He turned to Pagano. "And I see the Genoese ambassador is here on the same bent. I can give him the same reassurance. The goods for Genoa, Messer Doria, were selected at Erzerum by Genoese agents and are on their way to Bursa as well." He raised his brows. "I am not sure if I should have been so afraid of the journey to Trebizond but, although some tried, they would not be persuaded. And indeed, perhaps they are right. For his own sake, the Turk will protect the markets of Bursa, whereas the Turcoman hordes might not be so careful of merchandise. Hence, as you see, only two hundred of the thousand came here. But still. Sixty thousand pounds' weight of prime stock is worth something. You should go to see what there is, even if you cannot buy anything. There are some fine spices, they tell me – pepper and cinnamon, myrrh and spikenard. Bales of kermes. And some exceptional jewels. The lady your wife would be delighted to see them. Turquoises, of course. Balas rubies. And a hundred strings of magnificent pearls, with seventy-four to the string. Go and see them."

Catherine wanted to wait, in proper style, until his servants and her attendants had found them, but Pagano set off as soon as the Bailie stopped speaking and she would have lost him had she not broken into a run. A coil of hair broke from its careful binding. There were wooden steps, which caught the little heels on her slippers, and then she was in a small crowded room, where a cloth had been spread on the floor, and two men were unfastening a bale under the eye of its owner. To everyone who came in, he said, in broken Italian, "Later. Later. It is not unloaded yet." She could see the gleam of silk, and lacquer boxes.

The voice of Amiroutzes, behind them, said, "Is it not exquisite? The next room is full of our stock as well. Did you hear of the pearls? I could not have done better buying myself."

Doria didn't say anything for a moment. Then he said, "I have heard of the pearls. Are they spoken for?"

For a scholar, the Greek was inclined to be brusque. He said, "I have just said. The palace goods have already been chosen and purchased. At Erzerum, by the Archimandrite. A wise precaution, since the goods were so few, and there was bound to be a demand. If you wanted the pearls for yourself, I apologise. But there are other rooms. Ask. They will tell you which items are ours, and which are for sale to others."

They went from room to room, waiting until bales were unpacked and men were willing to talk to them. They were not very welcome: merchants who had come a long way had their minds on warm water and food and refreshment in civilised company while the goods were laid out by others, and the sordid matter of trade was by custom deferred. They told Pagano, when he asked, which of the goods had been bought by the Palace. They were the finest things. When he asked to see the rest, he received a confusion of answers. They kept trying to tell him their goods were all sold, and he kept trying to tell them they were wrong. In the end, Pagano paid a dragoman double what he was worth to leave his food and come and translate. When she asked him what they had said, he didn't answer at first. Then he said,

"I don't believe it. But they say that they are already under contract to barter their goods to named Trebizond merchants. Not ourselves or the Venetians. Merchants they buy from every year, or barter with on this basis. They say they cannot break such a contract, or they will be in debt. They say all the goods not spoken for by the Palace are committed by this arrangement. They say there is nothing left to be bought."

His voice had risen. She saw a city guard turn, and touched his arm to calm him. She still didn't quite see the trouble. The Genoese had bought their goods and sent them off by another route, but the Republic would get what it wanted, and ought to be pleased. If she had wanted pearls, she had lost them; but he could still buy her something at second-hand from the merchants, surely, who had got to them first. She saw then that the same applied to the Charetty dyes. He would have to buy them, at a price, from a middleman. The fortune he had been going to make had suddenly shrunk. Perhaps he would fail to make a profit at all. Perhaps he was going to have to pay more for his goods than all the silver he had got for his cargo, although at the time it had seemed to fill all their boxes. She said, "When Nicholas first came to Trebizond, did he sell his cargo for silver?"

At first he didn't reply. Then he said, "No. He had to barter, or accept promissory notes."

"Then you will have to get them," she said. "They'll be at the villa. And you can buy on credit, Pagano. Charetty credit with the Medici bank."

"What are you worrying about?" he said. "Leave the business to me. There is nothing here that can't be resolved."

He was smiling but she heard his voice grate. She said, "It was a pity, wasn't it, that you didn't think of going to Erzerum after Sumela? Then you could have bought what you needed and brought it here."

He swung round and stared at her. Then lifting his head, he looked all about. He said, "Astorre."

She said, "He'll talk about Nicholas."

"No," said Doria. "Wait." She heard him ask the dragoman something, and then a number of voices answering. When he turned back to her, Pagano's face had an odd look. He said, "There were only two hundred camels. They're here. But there were another three hundred pack-mules, each carrying a hundred and fifty pounds of raw Caspian silk belonging to the Charetty company. They went straight to the Florentine fondaco."

"Then Father Godscalc and Master Tobias will have them," Catherine said.

"No. Because the fondaco is locked. The mules couldn't get in. No one can get in without permission. And Astorre, being here, didn't know it. Quick!" His face, which had gone dull as it had at Sumela, was suddenly full of glee once again. "Quick! All we have to do is get there and redirect the mules and the silk to the Leoncastello and your mother, my sweetheart, has her profit and we have shown her dreary officers who is their master."

"And mistress," Catherine said.

Chapter 31

ENERALLY, WHEN SOMETHING exciting was happening, Pagano made sure to include her. He liked to bestow pleasure; to gratify and to be admired for it. She had seen him do it to others.

Of course, with a prize in his grasp, he would like her to share in his victory. Against that, he was in extreme haste to rush from the khan. He wanted to seize the Charetty train of raw silk before Astorre or anyone else thought to stop him. So when Catherine hopped after him with a broken slipper, he was inclined to run on, calling to her to wait with her servants. In the end, she managed to stay with him, and scrambled to mount one of the horses he found, tearing her gown and finally losing the slipper. She didn't mind that, or putting her horse to the gallop with her gown tucked round her legs and her earrings tugging the lobes of her ears. A man had already rushed off to the Leoncastello to muster all the help they would need for the mules. They clattered along the shore road and picked up their men as they passed, before climbing the street to the Meidan and turning off east, to where the Florentine fondaco was.

They came in sight of the compound, but there were no mules milling outside it. There were soldiers there, but they gave no impression of policing the property: rather, they stood drawn up as if at drill, facing outwards. Catherine saw that the double doors of the courtyard were open, with the porter standing uncertainly a little inside. Within the broad yard itself she could see the red head of the shipmaster, John le Grant, in talk with a man in Imperial livery. Dismounting, Pagano walked into the yard, and she followed. The ship-master saw them and turned.

Pagano said, "I have come for my mules."

The freckled face with its sea-blue eyes remained perfectly blank. "Mules?" said the ship-master.

She felt Pagano pause, as he looked at the untrampled, unbesmirched paving. He said, "You don't know, I see, that your captain

Astorre has returned. There is a train of pack-mules on its way to the Charetty company. They are to go to the Leoncastello. I shall leave men to see that is done. Why are the gates open?"

The soldier, turning also, was studying Pagano and herself calmly. The engineer said, "Someone cancelled the order to close them. They've just come to tell us. If there are any goods consigned to the Charetty company, this is where they should come."

"Did the Emperor say so? Or his captain?" said Pagano. He turned to address the soldier in Greek. "There has been a mistake. I regret, but you are to lock the gates instantly."

They were in the middle, now, of a small crowd. The soldier, appealing over his shoulder, had been joined by two of his officers. A number of servants came out of the house, followed at once by the big negro, and then by the doctor and the priest whom Pagano had duped on the journey to Pisa. Or perhaps, Catherine had since wondered, Father Godscalc was less simple than Pagano had thought? The priest went straight up to the Imperial captain and said something politely in Greek. Then he said in Italian to Pagano, "I am afraid, Messer Doria, that you must leave. The captain has no orders to allow you to take any possessions of ours to the Leoncastello."

Pagano's eyes sparkled. The Leoncastello men had all come: she could hear their voices in the street, disputing with the soldiers who were keeping them out of the yard. There were many dozens of them, and the numbers were growing. Pagano said, "You mean the captain has no orders to interfere with the internal affairs of the Charetty company. This is between your men and mine and, as you see, I have double your numbers. As a priest, as a man who cares for your company, do you really want to turn a private disagreement into a public passage of arms, with injured and killed to lie on your conscience? Would Marian de Charetty thank you for it?"

The priest, who was big, had been staring down at Pagano and frowning. Now he lifted his head with a different expression. He was looking past Pagano and herself to the street. A moment later, Pagano also withdrew his gaze and turned quickly. Then she heard and saw what had attracted them. The mule-train was coming. Already, you could hear the clatter of hundreds of trampling hooves at the head of the long sloping street from the Meidan, and see the jostling backs of the beasts, and the switching scrolls of the ears, and hear the snap of hide whips and men shouting. There were horsemen among them, and herdsmen dragging them on, for they filled all the street and the end of the train was not even visible. Outside the yard, Pagano's men were talking excitedly among themselves in Italian, and beginning to spread over the street. The chaplain, Godscalc, said, "But you couldn't stable so many."

He had given in. Pagano, who never bore grudges, gave him one of his white-toothed, delightful smiles and said, "Let us worry about that."

"And fodder? The drivers will expect to be paid."

"For forty-five thousand pounds of raw silk?" Pagano said. "It will be a pleasure." The leading mules were already halfway down the road, and the Genoese, unimpeded, were running forward to seize and divert them. The doctor, who had made an involuntary movement, stopped himself and stood still.

"I'm glad," said the priest. Attracted by something in his voice, Catherine looked at Pagano. The delightful smile was already fading. He was staring, against the sun, at the oncoming mules. He said, "Where are the bales?"

The priest looked down at him calmly. "Why, knowing nothing of it, I can only take your word that they were carrying bales," said Father Godscalc. "But if they were, and if they were for us, I imagine they have been taken to our newest premises inside the Citadel. The beasts, I imagine, are being sent to their stabling. I hardly know where we should have put them, but for your generous offer."

"It is a problem you still have to solve," said Pagano. He had to shout, such was the turmoil out in the street. His face, tilted up to the priest's, looked pale, the way it had at Sumela. When he turned to her, it didn't alter at all as it usually did. He said, "Tell them to let the mules go and get back to the Leoncastello."

She wasn't a servant. She had only one shoe, and her gown was torn, and her hair was coming down, and he had made a mess of their business. She stared at the lord Pagano Doria her husband and moved not an inch. After a moment, he turned on his heel and strode towards the open gates, where the guard opened ranks to accommodate him.

Still as a drawing, a racing camel stood in the entrance. It was what they called a thoroughbred. Pagano had pointed one out at the khan, because you didn't see them very often. It was supposed to have a neck thin as a swan, and a sneer, and a tawny colour of coat, *silk as the sides of the jumping-mouse*. A jumping-mouse was something they had in the desert. Although stupid, camels were elegant animals. More elegant than mules without bales. She surveyed the rider. Freed of his headcloth, he sat perfectly still, as if part of the camel. He had a beard which was the yolk yellow of floss dyed with kermes and fustic, and his soft boots were embroidered like comfit-cakes. He said, "They have been told."

Everything became quiet. The Negro Loppe, who had walked with quick strides to the doorway, became suddenly still, his eyes glittering. Behind her, when she turned, she saw the priest Godscalc look up with a sudden, brown glare. Then he lowered his lids and, taking his beads in his fingers, stood silent. The doctor Tobias took a step forward, and swallowed, and without warning broke into a fit of furious coughing. The ship-master put a hand on his shoulder.

Pagano said, "Praise be to God. You survived."

Then she looked at the man and saw that she knew him; that this was the boy who had once hoisted her to his shoulders and carried her laughing to her mother his mistress. Her stomach heaved. She said, "*Claes!*"

"Madonna," said the rider. He didn't move, nor did his mount. Nor did his eyes remain on her. He said to Pagano, "You may leave."

Pagano's face, from pale, had become yellow. He said, "I saw you fall."

"Oh, I fell," said Nicholas. "I was left for dead, I believe. Fortunately, I wakened in Erzerum."

Erzerum. The mule-train. The Venetian and Genoese diversions to Bursa. The truncated caravan, with its merchandise already spoken for, which had blasted their hopes today in Trebizond. All had been arranged. All had been arranged by Nicholas. Who was alive.

Pagano said, as if involuntarily, "The silver?"

"What silver?" said Nicholas. There was a silence.

Then, with an effort, Pagano spoke. "Who can know the truth, when one report denies another? Trying to save you, I and my servants saw you fall and thought you dead. Catherine's entreaties were all I had left."

Camel and rider, unmoving, stood in his way. "You are fortunate," Nicholas said, "in your wife. You may leave."

He had hardly glanced at her. But half-shod in her torn gown with her dishevelled hair, Catherine de Charetty looked up and up at the apprentice who had married her mother, and saw a man, brown-haired, golden-bearded, contained, who had nothing in common with the affectionate, generous vacuity of Claes but the directness of his immense gaze. She said, "We are going." And without looking round, walked stilted through the gates and took the road to the Leoncastello. She did not need to look round to know that her husband had followed her.

Behind, the camel moved, and entered the courtyard. The rider said softly, "Ikch, ikch, ikch!" and it knelt while its master swung stiffly over the saddle and stood. His coat was of silk, and the cloth which had protected his head lay on his shoulders, its gold edges glittering. The beard glittered too, new-emerged like the dragons'-teeth army, obliterating both dimples and scar. Set in the beard, the familiar lips had a different aspect, their corners deeply indented. His skin was brown, making his eyes large and neutral and light. Only his hair was the same, brown as mud and curling in screws and fingers where it had become damp. He took his hand from the camel and said, "Her name is Chennaa. The boy will care for her."

Loppe said, "I too, Messer Niccolò." Their eyes met. Loppe said rapidly, "But – "

Nicholas said, "If you please." After a moment, Loppe dropped his eyes and, with the boy, led the camel away. Le Grant, without speaking, had walked out into the road among the mules and their drivers and was beginning to impose some sort of order. The guards, it seemed, were ready to be helpful.

In the courtyard, Godscalc said, "We have to thank God, and we do. You were the only survivor?"

"It's a long story," Nicholas said. "Perhaps I should tell it indoors. Astorre will be here soon."

Tobie said, "We have thought you dead for a month."

"On what proof?" Nicholas said. "Believe every rumour, and your business will die. You should know that by now. I hope you did nothing to spread it."

Godscalc said, "No. We sent no letters. We studied the documents we had been left, and put them into effect, so far as we were able."

"You sound like Henninc," said Nicholas. "Of course you put them into effect; you're not in your dotage. Shut the door, and sit wherever you like. Doria claimed the company?"

Godscalc said, "As soon as he returned. Injured, trying to save you from bandits. With the consent of the Emperor, we were prevented from leaving the villa this morning so that he could buy on behalf of the Charetty company. Julius is dead?"

"No," said Nicholas. "Act, however, as if he were. He came to warn me that Doria was in pursuit with a party of Kurds. Doria stood aside and watched the Kurds slaughter our party. We can't prove it. It's our word against his."

"Leaving you and Julius for dead?"

"He hardly had a chance to decide one way or the other," said Nicholas. "Another party of Kurds had been detailed to rescue us. They chased Doria off, and took us to Erzerum."

"Detailed by whom?" Tobie said. His head, bald as an old man's, at this moment looked bald as a baby's.

"By Uzum Hasan of the White Sheep. He owns Erzerum. He wanted to know how we stood with the Emperor. He wanted us to know how he stood with the Emperor and the Sultan. He had sent his mother to talk to us."

"Arranged by his niece the lady Violante?" said Tobie. "That explains . . ." He broke off. "The bitch!"

"What?" said Nicholas.

Tobie said, "She came to see us. Eight days ago."

There was a pause. Then Nicholas said, "Yes. She would have known by then that we were safe. If she didn't tell you, she wanted to find something out."

Godscalc said, "I imagine she did find it out."

"Do you regret it?" said Nicholas. "What else did she say?"

Tobie said, "Quite a lot. She warned us against Doria. She wanted to hire the *Ciaretti* to take the Empress to Batum. To tell us that the Venetians were buying their goods in Erzerum and sending them to

Kerasous, instead of Trebizond. She advised us to do the same. Do we trust her?"

"Think what her interests must be, and then trust her," Nicholas said. "It was Diadochos who arranged to split up the caravan."

"So that the Turk in Bursa gets everything."

"So that Doria in Trebizond finds there is nothing to buy. Don't believe all you hear. The Genoese consignment, yes, has gone by land to Bursa and good luck to it. Even if it gets past the fighting, the taxes will kill any profit."

"And Venice?" Tobie said.

"What she told you was true. The local agent bought for Violante and Venice. Four hundred camels have taken their goods to Kerasous, to go into storage until they can be embarked to sail west. Another four hundred camels have gone with them for me."

Godscalc said, "You will have to explain. Whatever credit you have, no money you could possibly raise would pay for merchandise of that order on top of the mule-loads to Trebizond."

John le Grant, entering quietly, took his place by the wall.

Nicholas said, "The mules brought nothing, father. The bales they unloaded were padded. They were merely to mislead Doria, so that he would never suspect our interest in Kerasous. All our cargo is now lying at Kerasous except for your manuscripts, and what we have been paid by the Palace, and a few other dues. I hope we can save these as well, but even if we don't, we have our profit. The Turks can do what they like to the rest of the Empire. As soon as the seas become clear, the Kerasous merchandise can be embarked and make its way home to Venice and Bruges."

"Taken by whom?" John le Grant said.

Nicholas looked at him. "By Julius," he said. "Julius left Erzerum when I did, and then took the west road with eight hundred camels. When he gets to Kerasous, he will send word. Then he will stay there."

Tobie said, "How in God's name . . . How in God's name did you get Julius to go to Kerasous, and let you come and join us in Trebizond?"

"It was easy," said Nicholas. He let a breath pass, and then said, "Tell me what you know about the Empress."

Tobie said, "Just that she's going to Georgia in our galley. The Emperor doesn't know."

"He does now," Nicholas said. "But no one else. Or people will panic, and leave."

"You've seen the Emperor?" Godscalc said.

"When I took the mules to the new house. It's a good one: what we needed. Of course I saw him; or your gates would never have opened. He wanted to send her today, but I said we'd goods to embark. The manuscripts and the dyes."

"You haven't bought any dyes," Tobie said.

Nicholas said, "No, but our clients did. The ones we sold our silk to. They sold wine to Caffa for furs, and bartered the furs to the Tabriz caravan merchants for kermes and indigo, and will pay me in kermes and indigo for what they owe me for silks. That's why there was nothing left for Doria to buy."

"It puzzles me," Godscalc said. "He was wounded. But why didn't he go to Erzerum and make his purchases there?"

"I can't imagine," said Nicholas. "Unless someone stole all his money."

Tobie said slowly, "He tried to kill you. Doria did try to kill you."

"Not in person," Nicholas said. "And he is only the instrument. You will notice that I have succeeded in ruining him. Would you rather he died?"

"It might have been kinder," said Godscalc. "What do you mean to do with him now?"

"Leave him," said Nicholas. "He is Genoese consul. Let him rest on his pinnacle."

"And you?" said the priest.

"Well, as you see, I came back," Nicholas said. "I have plans. You have heard what they are. It is for you to say whether I should complete them. I've learned one lesson at least in the last month. A company cannot work by committee. It has a leader, or nothing."

"You find us difficult colleagues," Godscalc said.

"I find you difficult masters," said Nicholas. "But that is only my view. You have run the business for some weeks without me. You must have reached some conclusions as well."

No one spoke. Astorre, opening the door, said in a surprised voice, "Gone to sleep, have you? Christ, I thought you'd be singing drunk before I could get here. What d'you think of the boy? Eh? Eh? Got himself and Julius away from that murdering bastard; made our fortunes; did the little whore down; is going to win a war for somebody if I know anything about it. D'you know any company with the brains in it that we have?"

"No," said Tobie. He looked at Godscalc.

Godscalc said, "You want to lead?"

"Appoint whatever leader you like," Nicholas said. "But I have stopped taking orders."

"Even from your employer?" Godscalc said.

Nicholas looked at him. "To everything, she is the exception," he said.

Astorre, bewildered, looked about. He said, "Are you mad?"

"No," said Godscalc. "I see a leader I am willing to serve. Tobie?"

"Yes," said Tobie. "You have Loppe, without asking. And Astorre. John?"

Le Grant said, "I never served anyone else. What's the question?"

"There is none, now," said Godscalc drily. "Unless you wonder what the Charetty company is to do with a camel."

Nicholas half rose, and sat down again. He said, "It can probably wait till tomorrow."

"I should think it could," Astorre said, getting up. "And you've got your own doctor tonight. By God, I'll wager Master Julius is in a worse state than you are."

Tobie stood. Nicholas said, "Oh, sit down. Doria got a slash or two as well, I should think." He rose, successfully this time, and walked to the door. He smiled at them, gripping it. "It's not as bad as it looks. Anyway, I'm quite glad I came back."

The door closed. Loppe looked at Tobie. Tobie said, "Help him to bed. Then I'll come."

Loppe left. Astorre, on his feet, lingered with an expression lurking between anxiety and relief, and then abruptly went out. Tobie walked to the window. Outside, someone was pouring water into a pail. A dog barked, deep-chested, and another dog answered on a high pitch, like Willequin. From the kitchen quarters, far off, excited voices were talking, their words indistinguishable. Tobie could imagine what they were. Did you see him? He's back! He's alive! The demoiselle's husband! The young devil, so big and so changed! With a beard, a yellow beard! A silk coat! A camel! Our Niccò!

He was back. The man who had taken the calculated risk of that journey, and left those painstaking notes. The man who had created the joyous, angelic joke of the elephant clock. The man who had gone to the Emperor's baths; and sired a son on his own father's wife.

Godscalc said, "Nothing has changed. What he has done, still he has done."

"I have changed," Tobie said. "Good and bad, I accept him."

"You haven't changed," Godscalc said. "You have just been made, as I have, to feel your inadequacies."

It surprised them both to hear John le Grant speak. He said, "Why don't you leave him alone? He doesn't need you. I've known him six months, and I'm no nearer telling the good from the bad. I suspect you can't either, or by the time that you can, he'll be dead. Does it matter? If you want a leader, you've got one."

No one answered him. The truth was, Tobie supposed, that some of them wanted more than a leader; so that disappointment came hard. Toys; toys for the pillow. It was true; they were wrong. A team was one thing; a family was bound by something quite different. What they had was, indeed, enough to be thankful for. Whatever it meant, they had Nicholas.

Chapter 32

THEY HAD NICHOLAS. They had made their submission; and after many months of resistance, the tribe had their leader. Now they were to find out what it meant. What had seemed due to his deficiencies of age, of birth, of status now appeared as the self-sufficiency which, possibly, it had always been. The nature of his arrival had been expressly calculated, you would say, to achieve ascendancy. That the style of it was natural, or that he proposed to sustain it was not something that Godscalc had thought possible. He saw himself proved wrong immediately, in the conference Nicholas called the following day.

Round the trestle he had had placed in the parlour were the men you would expect: Tobie and Godscalc himself; Astorre and le Grant. There were also two others. Nicholas, coming in and sitting down without ceremony, said in Flemish, "I have asked Loppe to join us because our domestic organisation is now as important as the rest, and is going to get bigger. As bursar, he will control it. In the absence of Julius, we shall have the advice of Patou, his senior scrivener. I am going to talk for ten minutes. Then it will be your turn."

He gave the appearance of being perfectly fit. One supposed that past beatings had made him practised at that. Only the fever could sometimes defeat him. He had not shaved off his growing beard, and no one chaffed him about it. A pity, Godscalc thought. In the profit and loss of this relationship, a number of agreeable credits had been wiped from the ledger. Then Nicholas spoke, and listening with an intensity that hardly allowed his mind to wander, Godscalc was reminded of the diagnostic sciences; of engineering; of medicine.

The case of the Charetty company was laid before them for dissection. First, their present situation. They had been in Trebizond for seven weeks. They had profitably sold or bartered their entire cargo. As both mercenary owners and commission agents they had earned further income and had used that, and their credit, for more purchases. As a result, they now had lying at Kerasous 300,000 pounds' weight of goods, half their own and half to be freighted for Venice. This represented one galley load, with accommodation for the manuscripts, the dyes, and the payment in money or kind they received from the Palace, including the hire of the ship to Batum.

"Phasis," Godscalc said. Nicholas looked at him. Godscalc said, "Beside Batum, the river Phasis in Colchis, where Jason went. The Phasianus is the Colchian bird. I didn't know whether you knew that. The Vow of the Pheasant."

Nicholas was still looking at him. He said, "Then perhaps John will bring us an egg. We could present it to Duke Philip of Burgundy. I ought to continue."

"With the expenditure," said Tobie. Sitting slumped on his spine, he spoke into his frayed doublet buttons.

"With the expenditure. First, we have to take into account any adverse slip in the exchange. Then, what we send home has to offset the hire and use of the galley, the losses at Modon, the cost of the wool taken at Pera and the other items purchased on credit, and those parts of our living expenses not subsidised by the Emperor."

"And the lease of the new house in the Citadel," Tobie said.

"Thank you. But I think," Nicholas said, "that we shall have no trouble selling that, too, at a profit, if we need to. At any rate, I have made a calculation of both intake and expenditure, using exact figures where I have them, and where I haven't, the least favourable estimate in each case. Provided the galley reaches home safely, we shall not only have offset our expenses, we shall show an extremely high return for one voyage. I am talking," said Nicholas, "of a profit in the region of one hundred and fifty per cent. And it could be higher."

He looked round them all. Astorre whistled. John le Grant's thumbs stayed stuck in the armholes of his pourpoint. "The Ram that laid the Golden Fleece," he said.

"The snag being," Tobie said, "that there are three hundred Turkish ships between us and the neck of the Bosphorus, and we've made a silly undertaking, in your absence, to send the galley on a trip in the opposite direction."

"Silly?" said Nicholas. "The suggestion came, I'm told, from Violante of Naxos."

The question in Godscalc's mind had been asked before. He repeated it. "Working for whom?" he said mildly.

"Well, by God, for all of us," Astorre said, staring. "If the Empress can get a few thousand Georgian soldiers out of her son-in-law and his atabegs, then I'm not for holding her back. Not with the Turk at our back door."

"Working for Trebizond, then?" Godscalc said. A red head turned slowly.

Nicholas paused for the first time. Then he said, "All I can tell you for certain is that Violante of Naxos is not working against us, and she is not working for Doria. Her affiliation is wholly Venetian."

Godscalc said, "Her husband is Venetian. Her blood connections are with Trebizond and with Uzum Hasan. One could imagine occasions on which she has to choose which of the three deserves her loyalty."

"I can imagine them, too," Nicholas said. "I spent three weeks imagining them, if I may remind you. I'm not complaining." His eyes and those of John le Grant briefly met. Nicholas said, "I went to Erzerum to find out what I could. Violante of Naxos didn't stop me. Her kinsmen rescued me from Doria. I was able to talk to her great-aunt. About Georgia among other things, certainly. Astorre is right. An appeal to the King of Georgia is important for everyone. We send the galley to Batum with the Empress Helen, replacing Astorre's oarsmen with Venetians, if that's what she asks for. It could be back in two weeks if she makes do with seeing Mamia in Imeretia, or even if she goes as far as Akhalziké, and Quarquaré can give undertakings."

Godscalc said, "I suppose these are regional governors. If she goes to her daughter in Tiflis, it might be a while before the galley is able to bring back any message."

"Then we put a time limit on it," said Nicholas.

Tobie said, "The ship might be safer at Batum, if the Turks come. For that's the point, isn't it? Even if the galley were loading at Kerasous today, how could you sail it past the Turkish forts on the Bosphorus, and the guns at Constantinople and Gallipoli? How can you possibly tell when it's safe to set out? And if you don't get the *Ciaretti* out of the Black Sea by the end of the summer, you've doubled the length of your venture and half eaten your first profit and missed the whole of your second. You ought to have this ship turned round at Pisa and back here by next April, if you're going to run a trading station that pays."

Nicholas gave a sudden smile; and despite himself, Godscalc felt his own lips relax. Familiarly, the conference had turned into an argument. Nicholas said, "That's the second part of the lecture. Tobie, be quiet and listen. All our profit depends on our judging this Turkish campaign correctly. The Charetty company and the Medici have invested in us, and we have a duty to get our cargo away, no matter what happens. We have also undertaken to set up a trading station for the term of a year, and to allow the Empire the use of our skilled soldiers."

There was a little silence. Then Astorre said, "You mean you've given Julius orders to take the cargo home if he gets the chance. If he uses our galley, we're stranded."

"There are no other galleys," said Nicholas. "And when this one sails back from Batum, I'm proposing that it doesn't stop at

Trebizond. I'm proposing that it sails straight on to Kerasous, and waits there until the Turkish fleet has gone home, or else passed it."

Astorre said, "They'll burn it, or sink it, or take it as they pass."

John le Grant said, "No. There's a plan for that. It would be safe. And it would have the Venetian seamen to crew it." His voice, broad and even, was restful. Before, he had been withdrawn. Before the talk about Violante of Naxos. Another worshipper? Godscalc thought. Well: at least Julius was safe from her powers.

"Also," said Nicholas, "the galley would take off our dye bales and manuscripts. I'd load them before she left for Batum, and they'd come back to the depôt at Kerasous."

"Leaving us to perish here for the Emperor David?" said Tobie, "Now I see why Julius preferred Kerasous. You said it was easy to persuade him."

The man called Patou said quickly, "Meester Julius would never leave friends in danger."

Nicholas said, "If you think we meant that, then forgive us. Whoever sails with that galley is a brave man. I said that our future depends on what the Sultan will do. He will attack Hasan Bey, or he will attack Trebizond. He cannot do both in one season. To command the Black Sea and Trebizond, he must take Sinope, which has forty cannon and two thousand artillerymen to defend it. To reduce Hasan Bey, he must begin with the White Sheep's western frontier, which is the fortress of Koyulhisar. The forces of the emir of Sinope and the King of Georgia could save Sinope and Trebizond. Once the Sultan marches, we will know whether it is Persia or Trebizond he is attacking. Once the galley comes back from Batum, we shall know whether Georgia will throw her army on behalf of both against the Sultan. Whatever happens, Julius will await the right time and sail. Depending on what happens, we remain in Trebizond, or we escape and sail with him."

"Escape?" Astorre said. "Kerasous is three days to the west."

"Or we don't escape," Nicholas said. "And trade under whatever master takes Trebizond."

There was a long silence. "The White Sheep? Turcomans? Muslims?" Godscalc said.

Nicholas looked at him with wide, steady eyes. "We have been trading with Pera, a suburb of Stamboul," he said.

Astorre made a grinding noise in his throat. He said, "I'll be damned to hell if I serve under a Turk."

"You won't," Nicholas said. "If the City falls and you're in it, you're dead."

The sewn eye was scarlet. "If it falls. I took money to fight here. I'm not running away."

"Then you have one chance to our two," Nicholas said. "If the City falls, you lead your men out when it's falling, if your pride will allow you. We can join Julius beforehand, or we can stay as merchants, and hope to be spared. That, of course, depends on who our new masters would be. The Turk, straight from Sinope; or Uzum Hasan with his allies, the Turk conquered behind him. The difference is not so much their treatment of us as their treatment of our clients, the City. We can decide to stay for one, but not for the other. We can decide to stay for neither, and abandon the station as soon as we know trouble is coming."

John le Grant said, "You haven't mentioned the best that can happen. Georgia sends over its army, and so does the emir of Sinope. Both the Sultan and the White Sheep recoil, and Trebizond survives, as before. Our station continues, and Julius sails to the West, and comes back next year with a new freight. Is it impossible?"

"No," said Nicholas. "But it requires no discussion. It is failure that requires to be planned for. Now I want to know what you think."

Godscalc said, "I know what I think."

He saw, perhaps for the first time, how attentive the eyes of Nicholas were. Nicholas said, "Yes?"

Godscalc said, "First, that we send the galley to Batum, and then let it secretly pass back to Kerasous. Second, that we wait to see where the Sultan is marching. Third, that we wait to hear what odds from Sinope and Georgia he may be facing. If the Sultan retreats, we remain until Julius returns next year with the galley. If the Sultan wins through, despite the emir of Sinope, despite the King of Georgia, despite Hasan Bey, he can only sit down before Trebizond at the end of the season and besiege it. We stay, and withstand the siege. If Uzum Hasan and his allies conquer the Sultan, we stay as we are. The lord of the White Sheep may covet Trebizond, but I can't see him overturning it as well as the Sultan. More, it is his channel to Christian help from the West. It's in his interest to preserve it."

Astorre said, "That's it! I agree. See how the cat is going to jump. A siege is the worst we'll be in for. And there's Julius, safely home with the galley. We don't need it. The Emperor's a fool, but the guard know what it's about. Between us, we'll seal off the City from God and all His angels."

"That," said Godscalc, "is what I'm afraid of."

"If it's sealed off," said Nicholas, "the Greek and Latin churches will be sealed off inside it. Astorre. It cannot be taken?"

Astorre shook his head. "Any more than Sinope. Not now. And by God, not by the time John and I and the Emperor's man have finished reinforcing it."

Nicholas waited. So did Godscalc, his eyes on this child, this changeling who was leading them. Say it. Say it. Be fair and say it. But as with Tobie at Modon, he didn't; and unlike Tobie, Godscalc did not force him. After a while, when no one had spoken, Nicholas said, "That's enough, then. John, will you go with the galley?"

Le Grant said, "She's ready to sail whenever you want her. And while you were away, I did the surveys you wanted. I'll also leave you a couple of men who are artists, I tell you, in siege defences. Are you going to the Palace?"

"As much as I can. You'd better come with me. We've to convince the Emperor to spend money, and to pass on all he hears of the Sultan."

"And of Uzum Hasan," Tobie said. "So what will Doria do now? Take the round ship and cross the Black Sea to Caffa? That won't do him much good if he's nothing to sell. And if he tries to go home, he'll run into the Turkish fleet, just as we should."

Godscalc said, "I thought he did have something to sell." He waited, but Nicholas failed to look at him.

Tobie said, "What? We've ruined him."

Nicholas said, "No. Godscalc's right. He has transport to sell. He could evacuate half Trebizond in his cog if he'd time, and take them over to Georgia or Caffa for a swingeing payment per head. It's a Genoese tradition in these parts. Profit and humanitarianism combined."

"Then shouldn't we allow him to do it?" said Godscalc. Tobie sat erect with a bump.

It was John le Grant who said, "We need men. No. It isn't a large enough city to man the walls day and night. And you need women to serve them, and stiffen them. If ye let them, they'll melt away. They did it once before. They left an empty city with fifty stricken men in it to hold off the enemy. No. You stop Doria. It wouldn't be difficult."

"It isn't difficult," Nicholas said. "Well, then. That's the position. Those are the plans. The figures are on paper. I'll have them copied. If any one of us drops out, the rest ought to know what to do. Is there anything more?"

Without Julius, there was no one really to challenge the figures. On the rest, what still had to be said didn't take long. At the end, Patou gathered his notes and they all started to rise. Across the table, Tobie said to Nicholas, "You saw Gregorio's letter?"

Nicholas, still seated, looked up. The others were leaving. Godscalc stayed, his hand on the back of his tall chair. He knew the letter Tobie was talking about. It had arrived only last week for Nicholas. Thinking him dead, they had opened and decoded it. Written from Bruges in the winter, it contained company news. It also contained, specifically from Gregorio to Nicholas, the most recent scraps of confirmation about Simon's involvement with Pagano Doria, and Pagano Doria's with Catherine. It revealed little they and the rest of the company didn't now know, unless it was the extent of the collusion – or trust – that had existed all these months between Gregorio and Nicholas. It did warn, however, that Marian de Charetty herself for the first time now knew the whole story. *She has taken it with courage*, Gregorio had said in his letter. From first to last, it was the only personal remark he had made. There was none in the rest of his message. The demoiselle believed redress depended on the validity of the marriage. She proposed to travel to Dijon and Italy to seek out what documentation she could. Gregorio himself was planning to follow her. He hoped to interview my lord Simon first.

It had shaken them, that piece of news, and they had discussed it from time to time, he and Tobie. Nicholas had received it that morning, with all the other papers that had come in his absence. Godscalc had been there when he read them all quickly. There had been no time for comment, and his face had shown nothing. It showed nothing now. Godscalc said, "It's as well, I suppose, that we're staying. Doria has no cause to think kindly of the Charetty company now. Or his marriage."

Nicholas stood. "She knows where to come," he said. "Tobie, what do you do for a cough?"

Interest filled Tobie's pink face. "I heard it," he said. "Three beaten-up eggs in an ounce of turpentine daily. Never fails."

"My God," said Astorre.

"Not him. The camel," said Tobie.

The marriage of Pagano Doria proceeded to founder. It was not entirely his fault. Now and then, in the course of an adventurous career – quite often, in fact – he had been bested by circumstances, and took some pride in accepting failure with the same flamboyance with which he greeted success. He then put it behind him with the greatest possible speed and began somewhere else. Very seldom had he been tied like this to the place of his defeat, and even more seldom was the defeat due to a single adversary playing the same game as himself. Moreover, he was bonded to a young wife who nagged him.

It had begun with questions to do with the silver. What had Nicholas meant? Doria had lied, not foreseeing that she would then go to his ledgers and work out why he couldn't pay anything. She had then wanted to accuse Captain Astorre or Nicholas and his servants of stealing it, and he had had to explain that it had been carried off by the Kurds. Her attitude towards the return from the grave of her mother's husband seemed to waver between relief and aggravation: she talked about him a great deal. Also, having found her way to her husband's account books, she began getting interested in what he had sold, and planned to purchase on credit, and was paying for everything. She even tried to discuss it all with him and at last, when petting failed and he was driven to speak more directly, she lifted her pretty face and opened her pretty lips and criticised him.

What, said Catherine de Charetty, was she to make of a man who had wanted to take over her business and yet couldn't buy shrewdly or supervise proper accounting? There were cargoes proper to galleys, and there were cargoes for round ships. What had he done to fill his? If Nicholas had never come back, Pagano might have taken and ruined the business.

He would have been less surprised if his horse had complained of his riding. Then he said, "Oh, those terrible books! With Flemish clerks, we'd have had none of this trouble. Sweetheart, don't trouble your head. With the kind of clerking we have, Croesus would look as if he were in debt. We need a good Caffa notary, and we'll get one."

"No. Don't bother. I'll do it for you," said Catherine. After that, he never saw her but she had some mistake to upbraid him with. He wondered if Nicholas knew it, whose rich elderly wife was safely at home, and who was sitting there laughing, with his silver, his goods and his profit. Pagano Doria was not much in the way of killing people with his own hands, but he wished that he had taken the trouble at Vavuk. He wondered who else was laughing. He took to going out a good deal to places where he was welcome, and nobody discussed the price of borax cakes while he was undressing them. In between, his mind was on ways of redeeming his status.

There was one. He had referred to it once, before he realised quite what an inquisitor she was going to turn out to be. When she had complained of going home empty-handed, he had said, "You know it all, don't you? But don't despair, my pretty Catherine. I still might have something to sell." Then he had had the sense, smiling, to say no more, so that she turned away believing, he hoped, that he had been deluding her.

Had he been at home, he would have left her by now, although with real regret. He had trained her how to give and receive pleasure and, even now, if she wished, she could urge him to desperation. In fact, there was a level at which they still had need of each other. When he was tired of his other diversions, or he found himself unexpectedly roused, she never refused him. And at other times she would put herself repeatedly in his way, as if frightened by the very prospect of losing him. He began to toy with the idea of taking her with him when he went; but on his own terms. He even began to consider guardedly whether, if his new scheme succeeded, he might not be able to keep the Charetty company after all. Provided, of course, that something happened to Nicholas.

On most days during the next three weeks, Nicholas found himself at the Palace. Since his inaugural encounter on the day of the baths, he had met the Emperor twice: once heavily escorted, just before his journey to Erzerum; and once swiftly, to announce his return and have Doria's authority rescinded. The next time, John le Grant and his two men went with him, and so did the elephant clock, on a handsome and specially made cart, with a fringed velvet cloth to protect it.

Of course, le Grant had been to the Citadel before. Once, he had visited the Palace with the plans for the elephant clock, because Nicholas had asked him to. Once, he thought Nicholas had perished because of it. At other times, with Astorre, he had minutely examined the walls of the Citadel; the western bridge, with its guarding tower; the southern gate, with its large, modern keep. He had walked the length of the two ravines, looking up from the water's edge to the castle rock and its buildings a hundred and fifty feet over his head; judging the span of the ravine against the span of probable weaponry. He had examined where the powder was kept, and what arms, heavy and light, the Emperor stored. He had looked to food stores, and water. He knew where everything was. Today, he jerked his head as they passed the baths and said, "Is that where you were?"

"I don't recommend it," said Nicholas.

"What happened?" said John le Grant.

With the Aberdonian, the question was just what it seemed. Nicholas quite often gave answers to John, when the same question from Godscalc or Tobie would have led too far in a direction he did not want to go. Now Nicholas said, "The Emperor had me sent for. Fortunately, perhaps, the lady Violante sent a messenger who got to me first. By the time I saw the Basileus, he had made do with somebody else, and was willing to accept other forms of entertainment. He had diagrams brought for me. Hence the clock."

"And ye think three men will keep him off you today?" said John le Grant.

"I'll scream," said Nicholas. It was, as he recalled, a long walk to the Palace, allowing time to say a great many things. He walked in silence, remembering.

John le Grant said, "I see the problem."

"Do you?" said Nicholas.

"Aye. I should think the chaplain's near to it, too. He won't say so. If you want the blame all that much, then you might as well take it."

"Thank you," said Nicholas, and laughed suddenly. He said, "It's as well you're going away."

"I suppose it is," said John le Grant. "Upset your sense of the romantic, do I? You'll learn."

After that, they found the Emperor and his court under awnings in a small open pleasance planted with orange and lemon trees, and tricked out with oleander and roses. A bronze dolphin danced within water, and ivory couches, scrolled and cushioned, had been set on Persian carpets for the Emperor and his consort. Around them were their courtiers and their family: the beautiful boys; the lovely girls; the handsome women on cushions and stools, talking softly, or sewing, or playing some game. A little organ, set in a vine arbour, breathed quiet tunes to itself. The boy Alexios smiled secretly at Nicholas, observed by le Grant. Le Grant's two assistants did rather less well at the Prostration than their masters, and were presented, and acknowledged. The cart was wheeled before the Basileus, and the clock set on the grass and unveiled.

Nicholas stood and gazed at it, childishly pleased with his creation. The elephant stood firm and stout, glowing in its deep colours and intricate patterns. The figures had a plump and delicate charm; the golden dragon expelling its pellet rang the gong with splendid conviction. The children screamed. The women clapped their hands gently and smiled. The Empress, turning back from the third or fourth person who had bent over to speak to her, laid a hand on the Emperor's arm and said in her pure Cantacuzenes Greek, "I have never seen finer. He must make one for us, with jewels."

"Indeed he must," said the Emperor. Today, relaxed in the garden, he wore a loose robe of silk which accommodated his girth, and his fair skin was flushed by the sun under the tall hat with its wings of curled feathers. He said, "And you will entrust yourself to the seas, in the hands of these paragons. You could not do better. So this is your ship-master?"

The audience was deliberate and formal, so the Empress asked formal questions. That she wished to ask others was obvious; as was her desire to be done with display and return to the labours of departure. Beneath the paint, the whole archaeology of her features stood exposed in the sun. At her side, the dark, oval face of her daughter Anna, fourteen years old, reflected the same muffled anxiety. The Emperor, feeling it, seemed to grow impatient and presently gave his consort and her ladies permission to leave. Their place was filled by the men, and by the Treasurer George Amiroutzes. The Emperor said, "She wishes to make this trifling voyage; one would not detain her. Ourselves, we see little need."

Nicholas said, "Your magnificence sent an embassy to the West. Has the need lessened?"

"The friar. The Observatine friar," the Emperor said. "Well, you know what such men of God are. He sees himself as Latin patriarch of Antioch and head of the Franciscans in Georgia. The Georgian primates were always consecrated by the Antioch patriarchs. He persuaded our son-in-law to promise sixty thousand soldiers for the Christian cause. Our kinsman Uzum Hasan promised fifty thousand. We ourselves had in mind twenty thousand at the time. But these things change."

"And thirty galleys, your magnificence," said Nicholas.

"We had them, at the time," said the Emperor.

"But you have come to think that the Sultan and Uzum Hasan may come to blows and save Trebizond the trouble of fighting?" Nicholas said. "Your magnificence?"

"How can anyone tell?" said the Sultan. "We can tell you at least that Sinope will never fall. Two thousand musketeers, ten thousand soldiers, magazines filled with provisions; a fleet of war galleys, including the largest ever seen in these seas? It can hold out for ever, and when the October storm comes, no fleet yet built can stay in the Black Sea and survive."

He leaned forward, and waved a strong, ringed hand. "And on land? Between Sinope and us, all the passes are held by my lord Uzum Hasan and his incomparable cavalry. By the time the Turk has struggled over the mountains to face him, the winter will be near and he will have to retire before the snow and the rain impale him there without food or fodder."

A tray of delicacies had been brought. He signed for it to be brought over. On it were dishes of bread and the black, salty eggs called caviare. Nicholas took one, and John le Grant another. They already held wine. The Emperor said mellowly, "But assume the Turk conquers Sinope; by a miracle sweeps away Persia, how can he prevail against Trebizond? They cannot enter the Citadel. And the Trebizond winter, with its storms, with its rain, will send them scuttling home. No. We have no fears for Trebizond. But it pleases my consort to visit her daughter. Let her do so."

Nicholas said, "Your magnificence is indeed lord of a fortunate empire. But it seems expedient still that the Empress's visit should remain private. And perhaps that, in case of uncertainty, ships should not be easily come by. My lord would not expect the owners to sink them. But with sails removed, and masts and oars laid up and locked, loyalties need not be tested."

"You sent word to my Drungarios. We agree. It shall be done. And when your galley returns, the same precautions will apply?" said the Emperor.

"Of course. Assuming it returns safely, Basileus," Nicholas said. "Should the Empress so desire, my galley can transport a large party. She might wish her remaining children, the other young people of your family, to accompany her. It must be long since they saw their sister."

The pink lips smiled below the narrow nose. "The bonds of family! What is more important?" said the Emperor David. "We shall consider such a congress but later, perhaps, in the year. We should not like it thought that the Imperial family had reason to leave Trebizond. Now you have many concerns, and must wish to return to your business. You have finished your wine?"

"Basileus," Nicholas said. He laid his cup by, and rose. John did the same.

A finger rested at his lips, the Emperor was considering him. He removed the finger. "We take great pleasure, Messer Niccolò, in what you have brought us. I am conscious of it, and of the service you and your men are performing, and have performed: purchasing our goods, and escorting them safely from Erzerum. The lord Amiroutzes will fulfil our obligations. We have instructed him to be generous." He turned his head, inviting their attention. At the edge of the pleasance, men had been busy. Instead of the elephant clock, the cart now bore stacked upon it a number of objects. The largest might have been a saddle. There were certainly cloths, or garments in many folds, and a chest. The chest, of modest size, looked perhaps the most interesting. The Emperor said, "There. Your servants may take it. We are pleased with you. We expect, in the weeks to come, to lean on you and your men."

The men who had brought the cart took its handles. Nicholas spoke his thanks, and he and John embarked, busily, on a series of prostrations and backed themselves out. Rising, Nicholas allowed himself to be led to the Palace by the Treasurer. John le Grant and his men, predictably, were left on the path to the gate with the cart.

Amiroutzes said, "I shall not detain you. I had orders to pay you, and I trust, when you see what you carry, that you will have no reason to feel disappointment. Here is an inventory of what it contains. It struck me that you might prefer a prompt settlement. In case, when your galley returns, you feel impelled to load your cargo and leave?"

"Would you suggest that I do?" Nicholas said. "The Emperor seems more than confident." He signed a paper. The inventory, when he glanced at it, turned him cold.

"It is the blood of the Comneni," said Amiroutzes. "Warriors all; servants of the Incarnate God. He sees no danger, and if he did would die here, in his glory, as Vice-Regent of Christ. As did his kinsman Constantine Palaeologi, who perished for Constantinople."

Nicholas thought. "Then could one do less," he said, "than die at his side?"

Returning, he saw John without recognising him, and was brought to himself with a start. They fell into step, walking down to the gates with their escort and servants.

John said, "D'you have any idea of the worth of what is on that one cart? It isn't money. It's pearls."

Nicholas said, "They like paying in jewels."

"It was a nice clock," said John le Grant. His face displayed morose pleasure, as usual. "I see they got to steal your dinner as well."

Nicholas turned and looked at him. Under the red hair, the freckles, running together, had produced a skin like a glaze on a ham. He said, "It's altogether time you got out of my sight. Take the stuff on the cart and put it on the manifesto for going on board."

"With the letters?"

"With the letters," Nicholas said. "Or Julius won't know what to do, will he? Or anyone else."

Thinking of Julius, of whom at least he could speak to John le Grant, led to thinking of Gregorio, about whom he wished to speak to nobody. He began talking at random, and passed the rest of the journey back to the fondaco in a contentious discussion about nitre.

Chapter 33

ON THE LAST DAY OF May, a fishing boat put into the Daphnous harbour at Trebizond and a packet was delivered to the Florentine fondaco, for which the carrier received a surprisingly lavish reward. There followed a day of private and somewhat liquid rejoicing. Julius, with all his eight hundred camels, had arrived safely at Kerasous and had found lodging, welcome, and promise of all the help that he needed. He did not, of course, have a galley, since that was at present with the Empress Helen a hundred miles east at Batum. The fishing boat, in due course, set out west with answering messages. Fleece and fortune were theirs. All they had to do was get it home. And survive it.

The next two weeks continued the pattern of those before. For Nicholas, Astorre and the engineers, it meant constant meetings inside the Citadel to guide the combined company of all those responsible for the City's defences: the blacksmiths and the masons, the crossbowmen and the gunners; the fletchers, the bowyers, the miners; those who dealt with provender and those who dealt with humble articles such as baskets and shovels and hides.

As a contribution, Nicholas had halted work on their own new consulate building, and had only retained what workmen he needed to reinforce the house and storeroom they had leased in the Citadel. Now they had fewer men, he had offered part of this to the Venetians at a fair rent, and the Bailie had gladly accepted. These days, the Venetian fondaco, it could be seen, was also much depleted; no doubt because of the usual warm-weather exodus of the women and children to the airier hills round about. The Genoese, of whom there were not so many, had not been encouraged to leave and remained where they were, sweating in the hot, clammy weather. On most days, it rained.

The court, which was well protected from rain, went to its summer palace, returned when it was bored; went hunting; gambled; attended with brilliant ceremony to its devotional exercises and with equal devotion to a wide range of others, and took pleasure in the discourse of the many learned men with whom the Emperor liked to surround himself. To Nicholas, who was frequently bidden and who frequently appeared at the more fully clothed of such gatherings, the discourses on books he had not read and subjects he had never debated seemed moderately superficial. He suspected that the Emperor was being offered only what pleased him. He amused himself by visualising a congress attended by the Emperor David and his refugee men of letters from Constantinople and, say, Cosimo de' Medici, and the men he liked to invite to Careggi. The Pope, with Cardinal Bessarion's friends to dispute with, was possibly best off of all. He had heard it said that the Greek theologians attending the Council of Florence had been dismayed and even routed by the superior ability of the Latins to apply logic in argument.

He supposed it was natural, since they had the money, that every Italian prince should think it as important to collect his humanists as to collect his books and builders and painters. He knew, if only from Sara Khatun, that the Sultan, too, was showing an interest in such things and soon, when and if he had peace, when and if he had wealth, it would be the same with Hasan Bey her son. Meanwhile, he himself acquired a reputation for being a good listener and, being made free of the Emperor's shelves, would sometimes amuse himself and others by creating small geometric puzzles and astronomical devices, working on his knee as he listened. Once, he found himself in the decorator's workshop and spent an hour demonstrating with waxes and resins how to make better ultramarine, talking and kneading away happily like a washerwoman. He was not aware, then, that the deficiency had already struck his stepdaughter. He did not, all this time, either meet or avoid either Doria or Catherine de Charetty. Indeed, he had a great deal to think about and was not reserved in discussing his day's work with Loppe or Tobie or Godscalc, who were looking after matters in the fondaco. Only, sometimes, when Godscalc required of him something more than a summary of what this poet or that writer had said, he grew tired of watching his tongue, and refused to talk further.

In the middle of June, the *Ciaretti* returned from Batum. As already arranged, she anchored out of sight of the bay and sent her message by boat. John le Grant brought it himself. The Empress had failed in her mission. Despite the affirmations of all their envoys quartering Europe with Friar Ludovico, no army was coming from Imeretia or Mingrelia, Akhalziké or Tiflis to help fight the Sultan. The Empress Helen had remained where she was, a permanent and beautiful advocate; but she did not think her daughter's husband would change his mind.

It was Astorre who swore, hearing it; and Nicholas who explained to John his special vehemence. "We've heard from Julius. There's something going on at Sinope."

"I know. The Turkish fleet's there," said le Grant. "What else have you heard?"

"That the Turkish land army is near there as well," Nicholas said. "We know the town can't be taken, and we know a siege would suit us quite well. But the story runs that the emir of Sinope has been frightened into helping the Sultan. He's given money and food to the fleet, and sent an army under one of his sons to fight for the Ottomans."

John le Grant said, "That's foolish. The Sultan will treat the son as a hostage."

"The emir has another," Nicholas said. "He's also, of course, the Sultan's brother-in-law. The Karamanid emir has sent his son to the Sultan as well. The Sultan has reassured Sinope that he's bent on a religious war against Trebizond, but I wonder. Julius says the emir of Sinope has an annual income of two hundred thousand gold ducats a year, a quarter of it from copper mines. Do you think the Sultan could resist that? I don't."

"What are you saying?" said Tobie irritably. He had chosen to stay in Trebizond rather than rejoin the galley as ship's physician, and was under-employed and over-apprehensive as a result.

Nicholas said, "I'm saying that I think the emir of Sinope will surrender. Julia Felix. And it could take the Turkish admiral about eleven sailing days to reach here."

"Someone needs to tell Uzum Hasan," said John le Grant. "No army from Georgia. And no protection on his western frontiers, if Sinope gives up."

"He'll know about Sinope," said Nicholas. "But, yes: someone needs to warn him about Georgia. We'd better get up to the Palace. And then we have to arrange to send on the galley to Kerasous. John, she can do three more days without putting in, can she? There'll be time to attend to her once she gets there. Also, we have to decide who to send with her and who, if anyone, to take off."

"And if we're asked where she is?" Tobie said.

"She never came back from Batum," said John le Grant. "And if she's seen, she still doesn't belong to us. Different sails, different paint, different name. Christened by Nicholas. He's called her – "

" – *Argos?*" said Tobie.

" – after his camel," said John le Grant.

At the Palace, John conveyed to the Emperor the letters his wife and his daughter's husband had sent, and Nicholas remained for some little time trying to turn the Emperor's mind from the festivities for the birthday of St Eugenios and towards the fact that the war between the White Sheep and the Sultan might not last quite as long as had been hoped. The Emperor thought it of little consequence. The Sultan would be a fool if he marched. For one thing, he didn't know that the Georgians weren't coming. For another, the traverse from Sinope to Trebizond would take an army on foot half the summer, even without all Hasan Bey's well-manned forts and blockaded passes. By the time the trip was half over, the Sultan would have to make his way back to Bursa. Then, the fleet? Once those ships got into Sinope, they were unlikely to want to sail anywhere else: there *was* no other harbour so convenient and good. Next year, of course, they would be glad of any help the West could find to send them. This year, if the Sultan took Sinope, he would have done all he could.

John left with all his freckles blended together, and Nicholas, who had asked to see Diadochos, was taken instead to the women's apartments, preceded by a chamberlain and flanked by two eunuchs. But when they introduced him to the door of a chamber, they did not accompany him over the threshold; and when he entered, he found Violante of Naxos alone.

He had never been completely alone with her. Since arriving in Trebizond, he had encountered her only a few times since the interview on the day of his audience. Then they had talked about clocks, and he was grateful. During his absence in Erzerum she had made that curious visit to the fondaco. Before it, she had consented to see John le Grant, and had not been unhelpful. It seemed very likely that she had both put his life in hazard, and then saved it. Ever since his return from Erzerum, his dealings had been with Diadochos: through Diadochos he had paid for what he had sent off with Julius. He had seen her in attendance before the Empress set sail; and occasionally since, in the company of the princess Anna, and Maria, the Emperor's sister-in-law. But never alone. Why was she alone now, and studying him?

She was standing at a window embrasure. Between the slender pillars and arches the air could be felt, moist as a sponge, pressing out scents of mulched earth and strong flowers and peeled wood and brine from the gardens of the western ravine far below, and the hills beyond, and the sea. She was fully dressed; her gown geometric as one of his puzzles. It was not like coming upon her of a sudden at night, in her cabin. Then, she had had the old woman with her. Then, she had stood by her bed and not in a window embrasure: regal; inimical; naked.

He knew now how her body looked, under its gown. He had trained himself not to think of it, and mostly succeeded except when, as now, hunger reminded him. He beat it back, and kept his eyes open and his smile deferential and mild. He bowed, and didn't avoid the light which showed her his face. *He* was the toymaster, not Violante of Naxos. She said, "You sought Diadochos. You have news?"

Her voice told him nothing. He said, "I am sorry. Bad news, Despoina. There is no army coming from Georgia."

The face-painting, delicate, uniform, made them all look, he thought, like encaustic icons. Only under each tinted eye was a line of distant amusement that seemed wholly her own; and the way her lips curled when she spoke. She wore earrings made like small fish in a shoal, glinting from ear to shoulder within the gilt scrolls of her hair. She said, "We have heard what has befallen the Empress my great-aunt. We have heard the tidings from Sinope and, having intelligence, are in no doubt what should be done about both. Another has need of your services." She raised her voice. "You may come in."

A curtain stirred and was held aside, to allow a short figure to enter the room. Bronze hair and blue eyes and fresh, blooming colour. It was not Marian, but her daughter, Catherine. He got his breath back but did not use it to say anything that would please the lady Violante, who was a better toymaster than he was. A cord round his middle, and running. He redeemed his mind, and set it to confront the new problem.

Marian's daughter was overdressed, as she always was, with elaborate earrings and a pleated gown whose neckline dipped front and back, and whose long sleeves were stuffed at the shoulders, making her face and collarbone thinner. She had drawn her hair up to a crown-cap like Marian's and today, for some reason, she was standing like Marian; her back rigid, her feet a little apart. At first, he thought it might be deliberate and then he saw that she felt herself facing a challenge.

Once she would have run to him. Once, of course, she would have come to him direct, instead of through someone else. She had not done so. He did not, therefore, smile; but said, "The lady Catherine. How may I serve you?"

She had been looking at his beard. She lifted her gaze. She said, "I'm afraid of Pagano." She stared into his eyes, her own wide.

He said, "Why?"

At a sign from her hostess the girl sat abruptly on a low, cushioned stool, and he sank himself to another one opposite. The lady Violante, turning, seated herself in the window embrasure, the dull light behind her.

Catherine said, "You know what you did. You stole his silver. You left him nothing to buy. You stopped him selling at Pera."

"I stole his silver?" said Nicholas. "Did he say that?"

Her lips compressed, and then parted. She said, "You did all the rest."

"Then he can't be blaming you," Nicholas said. "So why are you afraid?"

"Well, you don't know him," said Catherine. She looked at the window embrasure, and then quickly away again.

"Not as well as you do," said Nicholas gravely. Why Violante? He suddenly realised why Violante. Baby Catherine. Well, no one could say she hadn't boldness. He said, "But I do know that reverses are difficult for men used to a fine life. It can drive them to do strange things."

He had pushed a little too far, and she glared at him. She said, "You do admit, then, that you ruined him? You just set out to spoil all his business!"

But that, on her side, was asking too much. He said, "That's trading, Catherine. We sailed to the same market, he and I, and we competed against one another in different ways, as all merchants do. He had his chance of winning just as much as I did. So, does he want to go home?"

"He says he can't," Catherine said. "He says the Turkish fleet is in the way. I don't know whether to believe him."

The woman in the window embrasure gave him no help. He continued to feel his way carefully. He said, "It would be hard to leave Trebizond, that's true. But you needn't stay with him unless you want to. The way he married you was not the usual one. It would be quite easy to find you legal protection until all the papers had been seen and approved."

She said, "He thinks you're the cause of all his troubles. He'd be jealous."

This time, he was careful not to look at the window. He said, "I can see you might not want to put yourself in my care. Then – "

"Not with your reputation," she said. "Bath boys. And . . ."

The exquisite woman in the window embrasure spoke. "Messer Doria has told his wife, my dear Niccolò, of our passion. Yours and mine. She already suspected that I had amused myself with her husband in Florence. I have had to tell her that persons of standing seek such frissons on occasion, and how little it means. It lifted her husband, for a little, above the rut of common whores he commonly exerts himself with and it gave you, I suppose, a taste of something you would otherwise never aspire to. I don't see how even her mother your wife could object. Unfortunately, Messer Pagano is now making a public spectacle of himself in the Trebizond brothels, and has ceased to act as the child's proper protector. So she came to find another."

He could just see, against the light, her painted brows lifted. Seized with delight, he stared at this extraordinary woman whom, of course, he had never touched and who had never for a moment done more than patronise him. Of course, Catherine had come somehow to blackmail her. And with infinite artistry, the princess had both turned the tables and reprimanded him at the same time. He said to Catherine, "Do you want to leave Trebizond?"

Her eyes turned brilliant. She said, "But he would never let me go. And how could I?"

Violante of Naxos said, "I have told her that there are ways. If she wished, we could even take her husband as well. Once away from temptation, the marriage might prosper."

"He wouldn't go," Catherine said. "He has a scheme. What could he barter that would fill a round ship? It's nonsense."

All Nicholas's anger had gone. He said, "I'm afraid it is. The Emperor is just about to order the dismantling of all foreign ships. He couldn't load anything anyway."

She was amazingly good, but just too young to hide the thought that came to her. He added, "If the goods are still on board the *Doria*, he'll have to unload them. How surprising that he didn't sell them at once. And, of course, fortunate."

The voice from the window said, "I expect he thought that by waiting he would get a better price. Would you not prefer to stay and share his fortune, demoiselle?"

"Fortune?" said Catherine de Charetty. "When you think what he's lost? I wouldn't trust him to make two in the hundred. I would rather leave. If he wants me, he can follow me home."

Violante of Naxos said, "He will have to follow you home if he makes another loss."

Pagano Doria's wife, whom he used to carry on his shoulders, looked at him, and at the calm woman facing her in the half-dark. "I don't care," Catherine said, "if he makes a loss. In fact, I'd like him to. Will you help me get away?"

"Not Niccolò," said the lady Violante. "You must not, of course, look to Niccolò, as you have said. But I, perhaps, can do something. Yes, I think I can help. Provided I know as much as possible of Messer Pagano's movements. Does he mind if you often visit the Palace?"

"No. He likes it," she said.

"Good. Then we shall find some excuse. And you will tell me all we need to know to let us help you. Now I think you should go, and before Messer Niccolò. It would not do for you to be seen together."

The child rose then, and turned to him. She said, "You don't look any older. Everyone says you hope it makes you look important. My mother will make you shave it all off."

"I expect you're right. In fact, I expect I'll have shaved it all off before I see her," Nicholas said. "Catherine?"

"Yes?" There was a lot of Cornelis in her, as there had been in Felix.

He said, "Don't forget Master Tobias, and Father Godscalc, if you want anyone quickly. And they won't hurt Pagano."

"You would," she said. "You did. If he hurts me, you'd fight him, wouldn't you?"

"I might," Nicholas said. "It would depend on who was to blame." He watched her take her leave, and the door close behind her.

"A virtuoso performance," said Violante of Naxos.

"He has trained her," said Nicholas.

"I was referring," she said, "to your own." She rose and, crossing the room, stopped him rising in turn with a hand on his shoulder. She lifted the hand and touched the close new grain of his beard. She said, "What is this? There are messengers, envoys enough."

Her hand dropped again to his shoulder, but her eyes rested still on his face. Her nails were stained pink, and there were little rings on every joint of her fingers. He said, "I thought I might like to see for myself. I thought I might be needed. I have respect, Despoina, for the lord your uncle and his mother."

The hand lifted and she moved away, her perfume following her. "And she for you," she said. "I have had messages from Erzerum too. Never fear, word has gone to her about Georgia, and about Sinope." She paused. "The man Doria has kept a consignment all this time on board his ship?"

"Of weapons and armour," Nicholas said. "I've always known. It was why I distrusted Paraskeuas, who told us nothing about it."

She took her seat, carefully, on the stool the girl had vacated, and folded her hands in her lap. "And," she said, "have you felt like God, able to choose whom you favoured? *For God and profit*, my husband always puts on his ledgers."

Nicholas said, "Whom will you tell, when the arms come ashore?"

"Why," said Violante of Naxos, "it would be as much as my life was worth to tell anyone. That is your problem, my Niccolò. Mine is to get the girl out of Trebizond. Do you not think me altruistic?"

"I didn't think your highness knew the word," Nicholas said. "Messer Julius could care for her at Kerasous."

"So he could," said the woman. "He arrived, then, quite safely? He has, I believe, a kerchief of mine; but he can keep it. It seems a pity that he has a token, and his master has none. Although, of course, Messer Doria thinks differently. But for you, I might have discovered much more." The reddened lips opened and curled. "The child's mother has bound you with rigorous vows."

"No," said Nicholas. "I had better tell you that she freed me to take what relief of a common kind might present itself. As it happens, I prefer not to buy. And it would be unfair to take gifts."

"Unfair to your wife. To whom you take back a shipload of wealth. Then will your debts be discharged?" said Violante of Naxos.

He got up. He said, "You are thinking of trade. Trade is a game, like the elephant clock. Between the demoiselle and myself are no debts, any more than there are obligations between the demoiselle and Catherine there, or Felix who died, or Tilde her other daughter."

"She owes nothing to you?" said the woman and he smiled, hiding his anger and wondering that she found it needful to hurt.

He opened his hands and said, still smiling, "Look at me."

"Oh, I am looking," said Violante of Naxos.

On Monday 15 June, the fortress town and harbour of Sinope surrendered to the Sultan Mehmet, his commander the Grand Vizier Mahmud and Kasim Pasha his admiral. With the Grand Vizier were Tursun Beg and Thomas Katabolenu, respectively his Turkish and Greek secretaries. As had been expected of it the fleet remained for some days in the harbour, exploring the amenities of the town and rounding up the emir's splendid fleet in order to send it under convoy to Stamboul. The emir left Sinope for his new home at Philippopolis which the Sultan, ever generous, had given him in exchange for his emirate of Kastamonu, his town and his copper mines. The emir's brother, who had been close to the Sultan throughout, was rewarded by some of the emir's best lands.

It might have been expected that, lord of Amasra and Sinope, the Sultan would count the season successful and stay. He did the opposite. While the fleet lingered, the Sultan's army left Sinope in heavy rain and set off on foot south-east over the mountains. Their immediate object was calculated to be Koyulhisar, the frontier citadel of Uzum Hasan, two days' march east of Sivas. From Sinope to Sivas was generally reckoned to be between two and three hundred miles, most of it vertical. They would be fortunate if, having reached Koyulhisar, they had energy left over to take it. After that, they would be well advised to sit down and rest and consider. Erzerum lay some two hundred miles off across land fortified and defended by the White Horde. From that point to Trebizond was another two hundred miles. And it was wet, and midsummer already. The Sultan's Greek neighbours observed his predicament and were gratified. Secure behind its fine mountain barrier; reinforced by its Muslim relations and allies; the court at Trebizond felt freed to pursue with solemn energy all its plans for its greatest annual festival, that of St Eugenios, the City's patron and favourite benefactor.

Wise, by now, in the ways of their client, both Nicholas and Astorre had taken measures to draw most of their work to a close before the holiday. The galley had gone, stealing by night westwards to Kerasous and taking John le Grant again with it, as well as, among other things, a box of fine books which had cost forty monks in the City more sleep than they could spare. Le Grant, taking his leave, had been no more talkative than usual. Tobie doubted whether he was looking forward to several months in the company of Julius: on the other hand, perhaps he was. In any case, they would not see him again until the galley returned with its new cargo next year – always assuming that it managed to leave Kerasous and get home with the old in the first place.

Had things been normal, he supposed Nicholas and not the notary would have taken the *Ciaretti* home. He wondered how Nicholas felt, exiled now as they all were until the next voyage. He wouldn't be back in Flanders now for fully two years. Two years without a wife, or a companion. Two years of limited industry, even when war didn't immure them, or interrupt the shipping or camel trains. And in between the buying and selling, a languid, vacuous existence in the moist warmth of the Asian Euxine, rich with flowers and fruit, nut groves and vineyards, milk and poisonous honey. While at the same time, in Bruges, his wife worked and aged, and, in Scotland, a child grew and learned to call Simon St Pol of Kilmirren its father.

At least one thing, it seemed, was being put right. The Charetty child had seen sense at last and had asked for help to get home. The problem there was to get her to Julius at Kerasous without her husband suspecting. Doria thought their galley was stuck at Batum and their silk was still stored in the Citadel. Once let him sniff the existence of the depôt at Kerasous, and he would repay Nicholas soon enough for all he had done to him. Meanwhile, although you would say from his behaviour that his marriage was not much on his conscience, Pagano Doria had begun to take a great interest in the girl's safety. Wherever she went – even to the Palace – there were now armed servants beside her.

She went to the Palace a lot. It was there, it seemed, she had confided her troubles. There, and not to Nicholas. Nicholas, pinned down by Tobie on what was supposed to be a hunting party, pointed out that the Palace had more powers than they had, and anyway he rather thought that Doria might have blackened his character.

"Well, if he has, he knows something I don't know," Tobie said. "But she might still be piqued about you and her mother."

"Perhaps," Nicholas had said. He had stopped riding to unstrap something from his saddle.

Godscalc had reined in gently beside him. "You said the child didn't want to leave right away. Why? Might it be that she is as attached to her husband as ever, and is using this means to recover his interest?"

"I'm not sure," Nicholas had said.

Godscalc had looked at him. "Aren't you?"

"*Aren't you?*" Tobie had repeated, alarmed. "Well, you'd better make up your mind before you do what she wants. Because, if she wants him to follow her, she could lead Messer Pagano Doria to Kerasous."

"I've thought of that," Nicholas said. "But we can't refuse to take her. Apparently, he has some scheme in mind, and she wants to know what it is. So do I."

"She would spy for you?" Tobie said. "And maybe for Doria as well, like Paraskeuas? I think you should stop listening to Fra Godscalc your Christian conscience. Take the girl now and send her to Kerasous, whether she wants it or not. As for Doria, you know what I think. I think she liked him when he was rich, but not as a philandering failure. I think you could kill him tomorrow and she wouldn't shed so much as a tear."

"You may be right," Nicholas said. "In fact, you are right about one thing. It's time we got her out. The question is, how to stop Doria noticing it."

"Well, I've told you one very good way," Tobie said. "What are you doing?"

"Playing with a ball," Nicholas had said. There was one on the grass. He straightened. In his hand was a stick with a knob on it.

"On horseback?"

"It's a game they play at the festival. I've been invited, not very seriously, to try my hand at it. Catherine and Doria will be there."

He addressed the ball with the stick and hit it, and it flew into a tree and stuck there. Tobie said, "And?"

"And just what you think," Nicholas said. "The twenty-fourth day of June. Kidnapping Day. But this time, a game of our choosing; and not Pagano Doria's."

Chapter 34

The Easter festivities had been held at the Meidan, as was the tradition. For the celebration of the Feast of St Eugenios, the Emperor chose a different stadium for his games, and was committed to a different church for his worship. Tobie, for one, had not expected the echoes to be so disturbing.

At vespers the evening before, the court performed its annual reverence to the saint. As on that first occasion, the Latin merchants and their servants and entourage took their places to do honour to the Emperor as he rode down from the Palace. This time, crossing the eastern ravine, the court rode uphill and south to the strong convent and church of St Eugenios, built on the spot where the saint achieved martyrdom. Still further east, beyond another picturesque but overgrown gorge, lay Mount Mithras, heathen site of the shrine he had bravely demolished. St Eugenios, Tobie reflected, had cut the trudge to worship nearly by half, and deserved the annual thanks of his votaries.

Three months ago, fresh from busy Flanders, opulent Florence, the hectic fringe of Stamboul, they had watched such a procession, awed by the frieze-like beauty of horses and trappings, of immobile riders encased like (vacant?) reliquaries in gold wire and jewels and silk; by the gleaming files of young men, pages, children, clergy and soldiers; disturbed by the thick effluvium of leafy juices; the smell of rich, heated cloths and glandular scents. Now there were familiar faces behind the metropolitan's cross and the towering banner upon which St Eugenios rode, his crucifix stout as a mace, chosen protector of the Basileus and people of Trebizond.

This time, the Vice-Regent of Christ rode alone, in his white silk robe sewn with golden one-headed eagles and his Imperial mitra with its curtain of jewels brushing the august, powdered face. Men and women talked to a doctor: Tobie knew all the gossip. There in her diadem and veil was the princess, a year older than Catherine, who would refer with disdain, through her stammer, to the many husbands they proposed for her. And the young princes, jealous, backbiting, quarrelling – all but George, not yet a year, for whom Tobie had found and mixed a tisane not all that very different from the dose he had given the camel. And there, with a cautious, comradely wink, was the court physician, bored with aphrodisiacs and eye-paint and lip-salve, who had made a first, idle approach and then proceeded, with delightful enthusiasm, to exchange notes and advice, beginning from the books Nicholas had brought. Since then, between them, they had found more. It was what Tobie had been doing all summer, reading books. And looking at sick women and children, and testing new treatments, and listening.

There, packed like charcoal, were the stiffly veiled hats of the churchmen, and the bishops he had seen Godscalc talking to, their glistening white robes spattered with crosses. Here were the Latin monks in their hoods; the well-paid who administered the colony's churches; the country papas who served the little foreign communities of lay workmen and servants. Who would come just as diligently to a Greek woodsman gored by a hog, as would the Greek papa tend a needy soul of the Roman persuasion. Tobie had heard much, as they all had, about the rapacity of the priests of the East. So far as the City went, it was probably true. Elsewhere, there were decent men who had never heard of the confrontation between the Greek Church and the Roman; the stony turning of backs over differences in phrase or custom or ritual; the opposition of Dia to Ek; the dispute over unleavened bread for the Eucharist; the obdurate schism over the origin and form of the Trinity. The Trinity! What did a choking child care if the Trinity consisted of sparrows?

The procession continued. The Kabasitai, with their gold ceremonial swords; their paper-boat hats with spikes and stiff, fluted brims over their fair, solemn faces. Figures, it once seemed, from Kambalu. Now they were simply the Imperial watch. There was the man who kept getting drunk every Monday, and the one who gambled his shield, and had to serve the eunuchs a week before he was allowed to redeem it. And the lesser soldiers, in turbans, who liked the bang made by handguns and had to be restrained from shooting up houses and stables; and the ones Astorre had had whipped for making the masons carry their shot to the arsenal; and the two or three who had got Nicholas to show them the farmuk, followed by another little unreeling game he had devised with somewhat robust connotations. As the seamen had, so the workmen had come to appreciate Nicholas. Who, of course, worked to that end.

So one had to look at the young men, whom Nicholas also knew although not, Tobie thought, as well as Doria would have them believe. The courtiers in towering elaborate hats and curling hair, brocaded skirts and soft boots, who would never admit Latin merchants to their inner or even their outer circle if they could avoid

it. The learned men with forked beards in discreet robes of great value
with whom, sometimes, he and Godscalc had been able to meet and
speak, feeling for common ground. He assumed that, at the Palace,
Nicholas was silent in their company as he had been at Modon. And
yet he always came back composed, with a number of good stories and
some quite surprising information at times. Nicholas absorbed
information through his skin.

And there was the Great Chancellor, Treasurer Amiroutzes, with
his two sons, the student Alexander and the sulky lout Basil, godson of
the Greek Cardinal Bessarion whose message had, in the end, got
Julius into more trouble at Constantinople than he had got out of in
Florence. Not far from him rode Violante of Naxos, with the
Archimandrite Diadochos in her train. Both the Treasurer and the
woman had known Doria well; both had since had many dealings with
themselves. Amiroutzes was the Emperor's personal philosopher,
personal agent, arbiter of his taste, master of his acquisitions. At the
fondaco and about the city his manner had the ease of a professor
towards the lay unlettered who saw to his wants. In the Emperor's
circle, it was to be presumed, his discourse was very different. When
asked, Nicholas could never quite remember what Amiroutzes and the
Emperor talked about. Only once, Nicholas had volunteered a
comment of his own. "But he is a man who likes pleasure."

"At the baths?" Tobie had said. And Nicholas had laughed and said
that he thought not; it would bend his hat out of shape.

So they passed; all the rarefied beings. The Master of Horse and the
Pansebastos. The Protospatharios, the Protonotarios, the Grand
Vestarios. The Candidatoi, with their wands. The captain of the
Palace. The Drungarios and the archons of the invisible fleet, who had
yet been able to dismantle Doria's cog, thanks to Nicholas. The
Augusta's ladies; the eunuchs. All the beautiful symbols. Not quite
vacant reliquaries, because they still served as their counterparts in
Byzantium had served; as their fellows in Constantinople had served
until eight years before. *Hear us, O God; we beseech Thee to hear us,
O God*, the coronation ritual had run. *Grant the Emperor life; let him
reign. The world expects him; the laws wait for him; the Palace awaits
him. Our common glory, let David come. Our common good, let him
reign. Hear us, O God, we beseech Thee.*

Protected by God; ensconced in his city the image of heaven, the
Basileus could not really have fallen, or Constantinople really have
been lost. Not when the flock and their shepherds had sent to heaven
all their affirmations: *Possessing Thee, O Christ, a Wall that cannot be
broken.* The ships in the Golden Horn had each flown a prayer: the
standard of Christos Pantocrator and the Mother of God, the flag for
St George or St Demetrios or St Theodore Stratilates, saints strong in
battle. It was John le Grant who had said they could have done with a
few good ship-masters and more than a few good masons instead. And

John, far from hailing the skies with a crucifix, had set to burrowing like a rat to smell out the enemy mines.

"Why?" he himself had said to Godscalc. "They prayed to the All-Holy Hodigitria, to the Invincible Champion, the Breachless Wall, the City's safeguard, Mary Mother of God. How could a city so sacred come to fall?" And Godscalc had had no answer to give him. Unless it was that Constantinople, when it succumbed, had begun to forget that despotism also needs justice; and had begun to learn the uses of force, and the practices of the East.

But this was Trebizond. And the business in hand was to pray to St Eugenios. The church, when they climbed to its ridge, was lit by the mellow sun from the west, so that its painted procession of emperors looked earthy and rich behind the lace and the gold of the churchmen awaiting them; and the drum of the dome cast its shadow towards the old hill of Mithras and its denuded shrine. Turning before he went in (for this time, they were admitted), Tobie saw the flat roofs of the City, bowered in green, descending in profile before him from the mountains on his left to the hazy blue of the Euxine, low and deep on his right. He could glimpse the harbour at Daphnous, and the flag of St George over the Leoncastello, but the sea was empty of all moving life but the small flecks of fishing boats; and the distant headland at Platana was insubstantial as smoke.

Somewhere beyond there, a hundred miles from where he stood, was Kerasous and its Amazon island, the place of cherries, where Julius waited with their galley and all their wealth. Somewhere further west still was a Turkish fleet, perhaps sailing towards them. Nicholas said, "Are you coming in? Or would you like the metropolitan to come outside specially?"

He was expensively dressed, and looked rather unlike himself. It crossed Tobie's mind to wonder if he liked or disliked religious observance. He said, walking in, "I don't see Doria."

"No. You'll see him tomorrow," was all Nicholas said.

The spectacle in honour of St Eugenios was held the following day in the stadium of the Tzucanisterion, a mile west of the City. Close to the sea but lifted a little above it, the place caught what cool air might be stirring. It was also near to St Sophia, its tower and its well-endowed monastery, whose kitchens were excellent.

The game which the Persians called chawgan, the Greeks tzu-kanion, still preserved, in the Byzantine Empire, some trace of its exclusive pedigree, and was always held last. There preceded it, that afternoon, equestrian sport and display at its most handsome, performed by princes upon the small, collected horses, part Arab, part Barb, part Turcoman, in which their stables were rich. And if, in the spear-throwing, the archery, the contests, the excellence of high art was missing, it was still a presentation to lift a saint's heart: the teams in their matched silks and ribbons on the cedar flour of the immense stadium; the speckled dyes of the people crowding the tiered timber stands; the bold silks and flashing gold of the pavilions set up all round for the court and their servants. The edge of the stadium had been planted with little sweet-smelling bushes and flowers, and the poles of the banners were garlanded.

Nicholas, having been absent half the afternoon, suddenly alarmed his colleagues by running down the raked stand and seizing a shoulder of each. He was wearing, Tobie observed, a tunic straight from the bath house in green damask lined with white taffeta, its skirts turned back and tied into a belt he had not seen before; and on his feet were white tasselled boots with gilt spurs. "Like it?" said Nicholas. "Porphyrius, wonder of the Blues. You should see my hat."

"I'm surprised you didn't make an entry on your accursed camel," said Tobie. "You mean you're in someone's team?"

Nicholas slid on to the seat beside them, grinning at Loppe. He said, "Yes. I'm on Doria's side. I have a feeling that neither of us will ever be the same man again."

"So that's the game," Tobie said. Godscalc remained silent.

"Well, the game's tzukanion," Nicholas said. "You'll see some courses first run by the court, and the court against Astorre's men. Then there's the showpiece."

"Yours," said Tobie. "I suppose they know you can't ride?"

"Well, Doria picked me," said Nicholas. "Along with Amiroutzes' younger son Basil and a charming half-Genoese lad called Alexios. Oh, I remember. You've seen him."

"Doria picked you?" said Godscalc.

The yellow beard, now considerably thicker, accommodated a generous smile. "Well, I couldn't ride for the other team," Nicholas said. "That's the women's side." His smile grew wider. "Girls against boys. The Persians thought it romantic. Prince Khusraw and three warriors against the princess Shirin and three of her ladies. Old legend. Khusraw leading his team in green, and Shirin and her girls in cloth of gold. Our cloth of gold, by the way: the stuff we bought to sell for Parenti. They'll ruin it, too. It's an exciting game, tzukanion. Killed one emperor and nearly did for another. Parenti'll get a repeat order, the humanist bastard."

"Doria is Khusraw," said Godscalc. "Who's Shirin?"

"Violante of Naxos, who else?" said Nicholas. "Supported by the princess Maria Gattilusi, the mother of Alexios. And the Despoina Anna, the Emperor's daughter. And, of course, Catherine."

Tobie said, "This is what you've been planning, then? The only way you can put Doria out of action and get Catherine away?"

Nicholas said, "Well, he needs to put me out of action. It was the only thing that would coax him out of his foxhole, so far as I could see."

Tobie said, "But you're on the same side." He was aware that the others were looking pityingly at him. He said, "And what's more, Doria's been riding from birth."

"And look what it's got him," said Nicholas. "Bandy legs and Violante of Naxos. Tobias, my friend."

"Yes?" said Tobie guardedly.

"Heads come off at this game. Opposing teams are surrounded by medical gentlemen whose duty is to bind, sew, saw or otherwise minister. Your services will not be needed. Understood?"

"Put your hat on," said Tobie. Loppe was carrying it. It was tall, and white, and had crane's feathers coming out of the crown. Nicholas sat it on top of his head and Tobie surveyed him. At length Tobie said, "Yes. I agree. I don't think I could bring myself to come near it."

Nicholas gave a wide smile, and went off.

It became apparent, before the major games were half over, that tzukanion played in the normal way between teams of powerful men was one of the noisiest games in existence. The players, once roused, roared, cursed and snarled in between trying to dislodge one another from the saddle in order to improve their stroke. Hooves thundered, harness rattled. In case silence should fall, the stadium was surrounded by buglers and drummers. The drums set up a war beat that made the horses lay their ears back and roused the spectators to frenzy. The orders to end the phase, or the game, were conveyed by wild and elaborate outbursts of trumpeting. Added to the continual roar of the crowd, it produced something very close to the sound of a pitched battle, which, Tobie thought, was probably the original idea. He was moderately surprised when the heavy games came to an end with only two horses dead and eight injured, and a few broken limbs here and there.

Attendants came on to the ground and raked and sprayed the dust till it caked and went dark. There was organ music, and some flutes, and a scattering of dwarves came out and tumbled and threw dirt at one another, and a Saracen girl, nearly naked, stood on a great coloured bladder and danced on it from one end of the ground to the other, while the dwarves beat her with feathers. Grooms bustled in behind the rails with strings of fresh ponies, and pages took off the broken sticks and, running back, resumed their places all round the stadium with replacements held ready. The bamboo they were made of was whippy, and the mallet head was fixed to the end like a foot. In the stadium, they had repainted the gold lines at either end over which the ball had to be driven, to score points of credit. The ball was also bright gold.

The women's team, riding on first, was received by a modified silence, which represented, it would appear, the customary mark of respect. As was court practice, the noblewomen rode astride, but without the enveloping mantles with which it was customary to make seemly their mounting and dismounting. Instead, they were dressed like the men's team in short-skirted tunics, but worn over trousers and boots in the Persian style. Like the men, too, their horses had their tails ribboned and tightly bound, and their own hair was the same; braided and tied back with laces under gilded, winged helms like those of classical heroes. In the left hand, each girl grasped a riding cane, with her pony's reins wrapped round her fingers or over her elbow. In her right, the bamboo stood, slim and straight as the lance in a phalanx. The little, deep-chested horses paced under them; the cloth of gold burned and twinkled like armour, and it was hard to know which of them to look at: from the exact beauty of Violante, the leader, to the olive skin and dark hair of widowed Maria the Genoese princess; from the haunted, imperious face of fourteen-year-old Anna to the youngest, Catherine de Charetty, sitting her pony as if she sat on a cushion, her eyes bright as the sea and the blood rich and high in her cheeks.

Doria, trotting on with his three young men, carefully chosen, smiled at his wife as they met at the central line, and the two teams performed the required courtesies. Vivid, glowing with confidence, the sea prince wore both the silk and the cranes' feathers with the careless dash that had always ensured him the admiration of women. The Treasurer's son, a big youth of whom Tobie knew nothing, had a face that was both heavy and wary. The boy Alexios was all that he remembered. The high-necked, narrow tunic with its gilded buttons and belt might have been designed to show off the fairness he had received from his Imperial father. His dead, loose-living father who had, one assumed, imprinted some of the faint lines of melancholy on the exquisite face of Maria, his mother. They lifted as Alexios rode over, and Maria smiled at her son, and then at Nicholas, who rode beside him. Genoese. Why had he forgotten in the unpleasantness over the bath house that these people were Genoese, as Doria was?

Then the trumpets produced a piercing flourish, and someone threw the ball in. Horses stamped; competing sticks clashed. With a snap, Doria's mallet contacted the ball and it bounded forward, towards the women's half of the field. His little horse followed, with that of Violante of Naxos scampering at its side. Faster still, the girl Anna whirled and swept ahead of them both in a long protective arc, followed by the streaming plumes and golden hair of Alexios, marking her. The widowed princess Maria, expertly wheeling, drove her horse up to support her duelling leader, while the son of Amiroutzes turned sharply to hinder her.

Nicholas, the biggest man on the field, cantered helpfully in the rear. He looked cheerful, and also unaware that Catherine de Charetty was riding towards him with her chin on her horse's neck, glaring.

Tobie said, "He'll fall off. Are they *allowed* to do that?" Ahead, Doria's horse staggered as it took the full sideways weight of another and, for a moment, the ball ran untended. Turning, Alexios wheeled and started to make for it, with the youngest princess hard in pursuit. His mother, moving swiftly, blocked her son's passage. For a moment, their horses blundered together, as they strove with their mallets. Then there was a crack and the ball rose, a speck of gold, into the air.

Catherine, arrived with a crash at her stepfather's flank, found the flank revolve at her side as he pulled his horse round with his knees. For two strides they chafed side by side. Then, swiftly collected, the other horse bounded off, punching the ground, at a tangent. The largest mount there, it thundered over the ground like a warhorse, flinging up gouts of woodflour and earth. After a startled moment, Catherine flung her pony after it, with the other women streaming behind. The speck of gold, knowing its business, fell precisely to the right of Nicholas's saddle. The mallet head, already swinging, connected. Ahead, Doria suddenly laughed. As the ball rose in the air, he collected his horse and, watching it over his shoulder, began to race towards the women's end of the field. When it fell, he was galloping smoothly beside it. With no one to interfere, he leaned just a little, his eye on the ball, his left hand lightly guiding the reins. Then his right arm rose and scooped the long mallet in a hard, graceful stroke. The impact, so far off, was soundless. But the ball flew, hard and straight as a bee, and was still travelling when it crossed the far golden line. The team of the men, Khusraw, had scored.

The trumpets blew, the drums banged, and everyone screamed. Tobie, finding himself standing, sat down again. Astorre, who had arrived behind him, sat down as well and said, "They're allowed to do anything. When the Mamelukes play, they get out their swords. So, heh?"

Godscalc was smiling at him. "He didn't fall off," he said.

Astorre didn't even treat the question as serious. "I should hope not," he said. "After all the hog-spearing I put him through. And what he doesn't know, the horse does. They're all palace horses."

Tobie said, "But how did . . . ?"

"Quiet. They've begun again. You know," said Astorre, "I could have done something with that little girl Catherine. Look at that. It's a pity she's spending all her time hindering Nicholas."

It was a pity because, all too clearly, Nicholas was not going to retaliate with the actions that would unsaddle her or bring her horse down; whereas she would try to do both whenever they neared one another. The game was fast, because most of the players were young and light and their horses were trained to think for their riders. The play streamed from one end of the stadium to the other and from side to side; and you could see how quickly the four girls and the four men were learning to read one another.

More than most games, this one exposed character. Violante ruled her team, giving no quarter to the princesses who were her equals. The widow Maria, compact and skilful, appeared to take no offence. It was a game, you would say, she had played very often but liked, perhaps, for the distraction it offered rather than any intrinsic pleasure. Anna, on the other hand, surrendered herself to the sport: hovering between ecstasy and despair, she would sometimes scream back at her team mates. Her horse was always the first to tire: she had replaced it twice before her team-leader needed to change her pony at all. The player who should have been worth watching was Catherine. Eager, child-boned, flexible, she moved her horse's muscles with her own, without, it seemed, need for thought. Dressed in cloth of gold before thousands; playing with princesses at a sport in which she excelled, she should have been euphoric. When matters went well, you could see that she was. At other times, her whip, her mallet, her spur would be commanded furiously to her aid. Supremely, of course, against Nicholas. But quite often, it seemed, against her husband as well.

Oddly, despite her strictness with the others, Violante let all this pass. Nor did Nicholas change his temperate play, although he could hardly ignore what was happening; nor, of course, was Catherine his only opponent. The jabs, the cuts, the bruises, he withstood, it appeared, with his native stoicism. By the halfway mark, he had been thrown by a horse brought to its knees by another man's blow; but others, too, had had falls just as violent, and even Doria, leaning to take a difficult shot under his pony's neck, had collided with someone and fallen quite hard. You couldn't tell, in such a large ground, who was to blame, or if anyone was, and so far no one had been crushed or kicked or rolled upon badly. It was not to say that they didn't all show damage of some sort when the halfway mark arrived; and they trotted back to dismount, and take water and towels from the pages and throw themselves, panting, on the seats brought for them, while the ponies, drooping, were led away and replacements brought out. It was a violent game, even scaled down for women.

Tobie said, "Do you want to go down and speak?"

"To Nicholas?" said Astorre. "What could I tell him?"

"To watch out for Catherine," Tobie said.

Astorre snorted. "That little madam could do with a thrashing; but she hasn't the muscle to throw him. No. It's two at once that he's got to look out for."

"The two older women? The Genoese and her son? You ought to tell him."

"No, no. He knows. It was the Amiroutzes boy that brought him down that time. Basil. Neatly done, too."

Of course. Doria had picked his own team. Amiroutzes and Alexios. A lethal combination. Leaving Doria to play like a gentleman. Indeed, to play as if he and Nicholas had been teamed together all their lives.

Astorre said, "And he's lucky, whatever you think, to have that pretty bath boy on his side. It was him that got the good lord Doria down on his neck. He's saved Nicholas once or twice."

"Alexios?" said Tobie. He was unused to Astorre seeing more of any game than a doctor did.

"The pretty one. You'd think his mother'd object, but she doesn't seem to be taking sides, except as much as she ought for the game. Her husband slept with his own sister. You don't wonder if the boys get into habits. All the same. If Doria's to be got rid of, there isn't much time left to do it. He's a good gamesman, I will say that," said Astorre. "And he's soft, that boy of ours. I shouldn't wonder if he isn't sorry he's got to do it."

Godscalc turned his head. Irritated, Tobie said, "After what Doria did to him and Julius at Vavuk? In any case, Nicholas doesn't need to kill him; just put him out of public life for a day or two or a dozen." He refused to look at Godscalc. He was irritated because he knew Astorre was right. A blind man could see that Nicholas, despite everything, was in his element. And that part of the reason was the game Doria was giving him.

It was even clearer by the time the course resumed, because they had fresh horses, and were rested, and were able to play with all the knowledge they had acquired in the first half. And again, you could see, as had happened in the very first moments, how similarly the two minds were working: both quick, both witty; both devious. Suddenly, on the point of careering elsewhere, Nicholas would cut the ball to the side where, mysteriously, Doria would be already waiting. Or Doria, under attack, would back-hand the ball under his horse's tail to where Nicholas, anticipating, had already pivoted ready to punt it off in the opposite direction.

Of the others, neither Alexios nor Basil Amiroutzes possessed the same instinct, although on the other side Maria could counter at times from experience and Violante, from something a little nearer to their own skills. Catherine, the best natural horsewoman there, found them bewildering and became angry. It was then, from sheer intoxication, that Nicholas and Doria combined in a wordless, elaborate double-feint that left her bemused in a pivoting circle while the ball, already half over the field, was being driven between them to score yet another point for their side. Beside him, Tobie heard Godscalc say something under his breath, obscured by the noise of the drums and the trumpets. On his other side, Astorre was yelling with pleasure, but Loppe, he saw, was silent like himself.

Now, gathered again in the centre, the riders cast longer shadows and the time left, you could see, must be short. Their mounts lathered and blown, both Nicholas and Doria had dismounted and changed to fresh horses. On both, the green and white silk was brown-stained and torn, and Nicholas had lost his hat: its brim had indented his hair above his darkened beard and dirt-splattered face. His eyes, ringed by wet lashes, were brilliant. Godscalc said, "Look at Doria."

Tobie turned, expecting a reflection of the same heedless enjoyment. What he saw was Doria's stark profile as the man stood, watching Nicholas take the saddle, gay as a clock spring, and catch the reins from a jubilant groom. Godscalc said, "One of them has remembered."

The men had won six points. The women, hard as they fought, had only two. Violante, it was clear, wished another score as a matter of pride. This time, they crowded the men, each marking their opponent; and Maria and Violante herself set to pin down the two clowns, the two comedians. Then the girl Anna took the ball and, wrenching round her high-stepping, stout little horse, set out for the far end of the field without looking round, and without passing. They all stampeded after her.

Catherine, streaking up to her side, prepared to protect her from the young Amiroutzes whose horse was coming in hard on the other side. Violante shouted to the girl just as she failed, twisting round, to hit the back-stroke that would save them. Instead, the youth's stick caught hers and broke it. For a moment, the two horses jostled together; then Amiroutzes broke free and, pulling round, went to make for the ball at the same moment as Violante and Catherine. For a while, the three horses galloped side by side, with Alexios and Maria approaching on one side and Nicholas and Doria on the other. The sticks swung, and returned upright; the ball glittered and bounced, arched and soared from one to the other. They had crossed from the men's half to the women's when Pagano, stick flashing, rode straight in among the pounding hooves and trapped the golden ball as it hopped over Maria's mallet head.

He could not quite get away: there were too many around him, and this time the famous instinct had failed: Nicholas was beside him, and not where he could be the recipient of some cunning, impossible pass. For a moment, they were all close together except Amiroutzes and Anna, bumping and pushing. It was not surprising that, instead of hitting the ball, a mallet blow should take a horse or a person. Above the drums, it seemed to Tobie that he heard a woman's voice scream. Next, from the swift pack of horses, he saw a pony canter off riderless while another, in the thick of the contest, suddenly staggered, throwing its rider.

The rider was Nicholas. They were near enough to see him go down, and his horse drop to its knees and roll over, threshing. Loppe jumped to his feet. The injured horse lay on its back, with the others milling around. Nicholas lay curled under their hooves, his arms over his head as they drew back. Doria, flinging his reins to someone else, slid from the saddle and disappeared: Violante of Naxos also dismounted. The horses drew back, showing grooms and pages running already from either side. The injured horse started to squeal. The lady Violante, in smeared cloth of gold, was kneeling in the dirt beside Nicholas, her hand on his shoulder. Beyond, Pagano Doria was stooping over someone else. Loppe had gone. Tobie made to go after him. Godscalc's hand, stretching out, gripped him hard. "No. Remember."

He had forgotten. *Heads come off at this game. Your services will not be needed.* It was, of course, all part of the plan. No one could mimic as Nicholas could. In the distance he could see a grey beard he knew, its owner hurrying over the ground. He said, "All right. It's one of the physicians. But we ought to go down in a moment, or it'll look very odd." He paused and said, "Who else was hurt?"

"The poor little bitch," said Astorre compassionately. "It's the demoiselle's little lass, Catherine. She won't get away to Kerasous now. And there's her damned husband free as air and Nicholas maybe done for."

"Not from the way he was lying," Tobie said. "But I suppose we'd better make sure."

They were carrying Catherine off. You could see a lot of rather pretty brown hair, and a young hand dangling. Real, or part of the plan? Doria was walking quickly, looking down at her, with her helmet clutched in his hands as if he'd forgotten it. The palace doctor, leaving Nicholas, hurried over to him. Nicholas, turned to lie artistically on his back, still had not moved. From among the people standing over him, Loppe walked quietly to meet them. "Nothing bad. They don't want to move him just yet. Kicked and trampled, but nothing broken, they think."

Tobie stared at him in surprise. Not Nicholas the actor, this time. Nicholas the brain-addled patient. Tobie sighed. Then he said, "And the girl?"

Loppe said, "Here is Messer Doria."

It was Doria, turned back. He looked a little pale from the shock, and also surprisingly drained. It had been a hard game, and an abrupt ending. He said, "They tell me our young friend will survive."

Godscalc said, "We saw the lady your wife. Is she badly hurt?"

"They can't tell me," said Doria. "They've taken her to the Palace. The Emperor himself was good enough to insist. She'll have the best attention. The doctor says she has been . . . The horses trampled her."

Tobie said, "I should be glad to help if I can."

Doria looked at him. "Thank you. But they are skilled, I think. They've told me I can see her whenever I want. Live there, if I want to."

There was an uneasy silence. Astorre said, "Good horsewoman. Played a brave game."

"It was a good game," said Doria. His eyes went past them to where

Nicholas lay, and stayed there. Then he said, "I have things to collect," and turned and walked away, limping a little.

In a while, two men came with a carpet to remove the Florentine consul so that the games might go on. In the tent they took him to, he eventually stirred, and was rather wretchedly sick; and then allowed Tobie without resistance to reassure himself that nothing was indeed broken. The Emperor had sent an emissary to enquire after his health several times, and Violante of Naxos had called once.

Nobody had cared to introduce the subject of Catherine's accident, about which Nicholas could as yet know nothing. At the end of it all, Tobie wrapped him in blankets and set him, propped up, to await transport back to the fondaco. He sat, Tobie saw, in exactly the way he always sat after a beating: without complaint or expectation of anyone's interest. He was probably going to be sick again. He was lucky to be alive. It took no leap of the imagination to recognise that Doria had tried in the end to get rid of him, and had been foiled, or had failed. Then the persistent Venetian woman paid her second visit and, admitted this time, looked down at her late, wan opponent with interest. She was clean and changed into womanly silks, although her face, under the paint, betrayed recent exertion. She said, "We should have scored a third point."

"In heaven," said Nicholas, "you probably did." It was the first sentence he had produced and indicated, well enough, that it was not going to be the first of many.

Violante of Naxos said, "It was your own fault. You know that. None the less, I am sorry. But the rest went according to plan. That is what I came to say."

"All of it?"

"Everything. You have three days to rest, and review your own stupidity."

He sat looking after her, appearing pleased and sick at the same time. She had reached the door when he managed a question. "Who saved me?"

"Oh, Alexios," she said. "You have nothing to thank me for."

"Six points," he said, with queasy contentment.

Chapter 35

LUCKILY FOR THE STATE of his health, the prophecy was correct, and Nicholas did have three full days in which to rest his battered bones after the Feast of St Eugenios. Seeing no reason to rest his brain also, he spent them holding busy meetings in the shade of the garden, dressed in the sort of loose buttoned robe whose uses he had been taught in the Palace. As the heat advanced, even Father Godscalc left off his gown and tended to be seen, when at the fondaco, in shirt and hose like the rest, although never quite so informal as Astorre, who would strip to the waist the moment he came in off the streets and stand, as once Julius had done, letting the spray of the fountain jump off his frilled scars and furred pelt. The prophecy was correct, but failed to indicate that three days of peace were all any of them were going to get, never mind Nicholas.

He was holding a discussion, perched on the back of a long marble settle with his sandalled feet on its seat, when the interregnum was doubly brought to an end; burst asunder first by the arrival of Astorre himself, still fully dressed and straight from the Citadel. They heard him roar from the garden entrance. He leaped the steps and bounded forward, still bellowing. "The mist has lifted, and there's a beacon! The fleet is coming! Sinope has fallen, and the Turkish dogs are sailing this way!" Godscalc and Tobie scrambled up from the grass, and Nicholas slid to the ground quickly and joined them.

It was a relief. It was almost a joy. For Astorre, the professional soldier, it *was* a joy. He looked incandescent. Standing around him, they had begun flinging questions and extracting answers when there was another thunderous crash in the outer yard, followed by the disputing voices of servants. The door to the garden was flung open a second time with such violence that they all broke off and turned.

Pagano Doria stood on the steps. He walked down them and crossed the grass steadily. He came to a halt before Nicholas. "*Where is she?*" he said.

She had promised three days. The three days were over. Nicholas said, "Your wife is safe. Come indoors to my chamber. And Father Godscalc. Tobie, Captain Astorre, you'd better begin. I'll be back."

Doria stood where he was. He said, "I've just come from the Palace. I had to break into the Gynaecum. Catherine isn't too ill to be visited. She isn't there. She hasn't been there for two days."

The priest said, "You are owed an explanation, and will have it. But what Nicholas says is correct. Madonna Catherine is out of the City, and you should be thankful. We have just heard. The Turkish fleet is coming to Trebizond. She is well away."

"I'm sure she is," said Doria. "You son of a whore, you've got rid of her. I was afraid you would, in the end. Something subtle, I thought, that the old woman couldn't blame you for. I never thought you'd throw the girl to the Turks."

"Didn't you? You said she could serve a squadron all winter, and still be eager," Nicholas said. He heard Tobie draw in his breath. "You even offered to lend her to me. What made you think I wouldn't use her if you did?"

Doria smiled, without charm. He said, "Ah. She's here, then?"

Nicholas said, "No. You quelled my interest in women. She came to complain of your general performance, and asked our help to get her home safely. We gave it. She was knocked unconscious, but that was all that was wrong. As soon as she recovered, she escaped the Palace and we helped her leave Trebizond. She is in no danger from Turks if she travels to Georgia."

"I suppose not," Doria said. "Unfortunately, she is my wife and has no leave to travel anywhere unless I permit it. The law and I must therefore pursue her. The law and I must therefore punish, of course, the man who separates wife from husband. Return Catherine. Or I shall take the case to the Emperor."

"Why not?" Nicholas said. "Although he does have other things on his mind. In fact, I'm not sure that he believes that you and Catherine are married. He would be entertained, I suppose. He's never met a Genoese consul before who couldn't satisfy the wants of a thirteen-year-old." He kept his voice low, although clear enough. There was no point, now, in having this out somewhere else. The others stood where they were, in absolute silence.

Doria said, "If I told you that you were right, and the marriage was never made legal, would you tell me where she is?"

Nicholas laughed. He said, "Hardly. What would you want with Catherine de Charetty if she weren't your wife?"

"I trained her," said Doria. "It's a pity to waste it all on a party of Osmanli seamen. But no. You sent her east, you say, in the opposite direction. Where she'll be safe until she can get back to Bruges and reap half of the Charetty inheritance. Of course, I believe you."

"I'm afraid you will have to," said Nicholas. "And now, we are busy."

He had been watching Doria's hand at his side. For a moment he thought he was going to draw the knife from its sheath, as a different man might have done. But Doria only looked at him, frowning, as if the face he saw was not the face he expected. Then he recollected himself, and became the sea prince again. "My poor, dear Niccolò. If she is about, I dare say I shall find her. If not, consider the report I shall have to make to your wife. You have, of course, made trial of the girl as I offered. Perhaps you appealed to the commoner parts of her ancestry. Perhaps she has a taste, already formed, for her mother's apprentices. Perhaps she even thinks you will make her richer than I should. What a story for Bruges, and the lord Simon my patron."

Since there was nothing in that to worry about, Nicholas let it all pass over his head. Doria knew about Marian. He didn't know about Simon's wife Katelina. It was a pity that Tobie and Godscalc both did. "Indeed," Nicholas said. "I hope Catherine will be able to tell it herself. If you prove to be married, you will have every right to claim her in Bruges. But not until the proof is produced. And meantime, you've seen the last of her here."

Doria said, "I see you have no idea who you are dealing with. I shall see you in a Flemish law court. If not in a court a little more summary, and a little sooner than that."

He turned. He had got to the steps when Nicholas spoke, on an impulse. He said, "She is not with me, and is well protected."

On Doria's face, as he left, was a trace of scorn and a trace, rather stronger, of mystification. Nicholas waited until the garden door closed, and then, turning, went back to the others. Astorre was red. He said, "Did he say all that? The bastard! His own wife!"

Nicholas said, "She's safe now. Forget him. Look, let's get on with this. How many men on board, do they think?"

Later, Tobie tried to re-open the subject but allowed himself to be sidetracked. They were learning. Or he was getting better at holding them off. It was a help, of course, to have a war on your hands.

On the fourth day after that, the fleet of the Turkish admiral Kasim Pasha appeared, a fretted line on the western horizon. It was the first day of July, and the time when the sun alternately burned and masked itself behind veils of thick cloud, which now and then unloaded their lukewarm torrents over the orchards, the gardens, the forests festooned with wild vines. The flat roofs of the houses poured water; the steep streets rushed with it; the brawling streams in the two gorges rose higher and roared. Then the sun came out, and Trebizond, thick with flowers and fruit, lay in its steam. Soon, as the fleet entered the distant arm of the bay, you could see the sprinkle of gold from the mastheads and the sail bellies blaze out like coloured silk lanterns as they moved steadily east and the sun fell behind.

By then, everyone was in the Citadel. From dawn, the bells of the

City had been clanging their warning: the great bronze voice of the Chrysokephalos from inside the Citadel; of little Anne west of the Meidan and St Basil down by the shore and St Andrew and St Sophia to the west. And in the merchants' quarters, the bells of the Latin chapels and of St Philip over by Mithras and, loudest of all, the warning from the fortress church of St Eugenios on its ridge to the south. The message was simple. *Abandon your homes and come, now.*

They did not come readily, for the practice was new. To protect its harbours and trading, every headland and ridge of the Black Sea had long since acquired its Genoese castle, its fortified churches and monasteries. These, together with the notorious storms of the Euxine (once properly entitled the Axeinos), generally saw to it that sea-raiders didn't stay long.

A determined enemy was a different matter. Only the Citadel between its two ravines was truly impregnable. The flat shores with their wharves and warehouses and fishing communities, the steep network of streets on either side with their rich villas and gardens, baths and markets, had only the island fortresses of the churches and the merchant colony's keeps to protect them. Stout buildings of brick and stone were strong enough to withstand most raids, but not all. St Eugenios had more than once been taken and occupied. Only three years ago, an enemy camp had stood on Mount Mithras and all the suburbs up to the eastern ravine had been pillaged and stripped of their people. So, in times of real war, men had chosen to trust neither the fortresses nor the Citadel. The rich in the past had taken ship and fled east to Georgia. The poor took their children and what goods they could carry and disappeared south, into the mountains.

They couldn't do that this time, with Ottoman armies fighting the White Horde behind them. And this time it was necessary that the able men of the City should not melt away but should be there, within its walls, to help the garrison keep its watch. And men fought better, as Astorre, as John le Grant knew, when their wives and children were present; just as shepherds, under the eyes of their flock, had to remember their honour. So the ships had been disabled, and the people warned. So stores had been gathered, and preparations made for the great influx of population into a place from which the people had always fled in time of danger. And so the monks came into the City, carrying their crosses, with their vestments and treasure on the backs of their mules; and the merchants emptied their warehouses, burying what they couldn't transport, and led their households over the ravines to take rooms where they could.

As had been arranged long before, Nicholas freed from the Florentine villa all the Greek servants who wished to go to their families. The numbers left now were not large: Godscalc and Tobie, with their assistants and their personal servants; Loppe, with those who helped feed and run the household; Patou and his clerks, in the absence of Julius. Twenty-five people, where once he had had charge of a galley-load. With the sudden change in his burden and the promise of action at last, Nicholas found his spirits soar to the skies, as if he had spent all day drinking. The others (all but Godscalc) seemed to catch the same mood, shouting and joking as they moved their belongings from the fondaco to the Middle Citadel, and the house and storeroom John had taken for them before he left. The Venetians, an even smaller company, were already there; and Astorre, who had lived with his men in the Upper Citadel for many weeks now. As soon as they were ready, Nicholas left, with Tobie and Astorre, to climb the garrison tower, and watch the Turkish fleet sailing up.

The new keep occupied the highest point of the Citadel; higher even than the white and gold of the Palace. From its battlements, they looked down on the roofs and gardens, towers and church domes of Trebizond, cascading down to the sea, white and green, red and gold; and its narrow alleys choked with milling people and bundles and beasts. Soon, the iron gates to the Upper Citadel would be closed, and then the gates dividing the middle from the lower part. The reinforced garrison along the shore wall was long since in place and the moats filled. Armed men glinted, like sequins, wherever you looked.

From Paraskeuas, purveyor of useless information, they knew that the Genoese community, too large to house under any one roof, had disposed of itself in small households all over the City. The seamen were to sleep in the open. Pagano Doria with Crackbene his shipmaster and the chief officers of his round ship, oarless and dismasted like all the rest, had taken a house in the St Andrew quarter, near the eastern ravine and the shore.

His hand shading his eyes, Tobie said, "St Andrew, of course. He evangelised Trebizond, and the Golden Fleece used to meet on his feast day. If his head's got to Rome, it may do more good than Ludovico da Bologna. D'you think our Genoese friend still thinks he's Jason? One thing is sure: if it comes to a famine, Willequin in pies will be Doria's first standby."

"She took him with her," said Nicholas. "The camel will run like the wind."

"You sent Catherine on the camel? On Chennaa?" said Tobie.

"If she can ride a horse, she can ride a camel. The cough mixture worked."

"It ought to," said Tobie. "I had a teacher at Pavia whose uncle had been a Mameluke prisoner. They made him a camel doctor. He just treated camels like people. They get everything but – "

" – the hump. I can guess. The fishermen, God damn them, haven't come in yet."

"You can't force them," said Tobie. "Unless you burn their boats and their nets. When the Turks invested Belgrade, they took packs of dogs to eat up the Christian corpses."

"Dogs don't like ships," Nicholas said.

"They promised safety to everyone after Mistra, and still killed six thousand people. They flay alive, and behead, and impale. They saw people in half."

"So they do. But here, they can't cross the ravines and they can't reach us with any weapon at all, even arrows," Nicholas said. "To get sawn in half, you'd have to be really quite careless."

"They could reach us with cannon. The battery they used at Constantinople threw balls of twelve hundred pounds, and the largest Greek helepoli can only manage a hundred and fifty."

"They could, if their ships could carry anything but light naval guns. They can't reach us. They can only starve us out. And we've food for three months. Go on. I can feel my hair turning white."

"And they're ingenious. At Constantinople they put their fleet on to rollers and took it overland behind the Greek lines," said Tobie reflectively.

Nicholas laughed and said nothing. Tobie said, "To get here today, that fleet out there has already passed Kerasous and the *Ciaretti*. Or didn't pass, and stopped, and killed John and Julius and Catherine and took all our cargo. And the camel. Damn you, why aren't you worried?"

"I don't need to be. You're doing my share. If you really want to know," said Nicholas, "the *Ciaretti* is lying dismantled and covered with bushes on the sacred isle of the Amazons, with hideous sounds and fiery portents to discourage anyone from landing. That's why John had to go. All you have to do is hope that Julius and he can put the boat together again. Lie down."

"What?" said Tobie.

"Lie down. Here's the Emperor and his holy procession, come to pray at the walls."

"There isn't room," Tobie said.

"There is, if we lie on top of one another. Kiss his boot and remember. He is God's vicar on earth, and gods never lose. The Grand Comneni will be here for ever."

"As in Constantinople?" Tobie said. A basil twig hovered, and drops of holy water blessed his bald head. The sandals and buskins moved on.

"Those weren't the Grand Comneni," said Nicholas, his voice muffled. "And we weren't in Constantinople at the time, although John on his own didn't do badly. What in God's name was all that nonsense about?"

"Nothing," said Tobie, dusting his knees. "Only, sometimes when I think of what you and John get up to, I wonder if you really know what your goading could bring on us."

"I know," said Nicholas humbly. "A real wave of Turkish resentment."

All afternoon they stood and watched, like men at a play. On the sea
far below, the strange ships drifted together, light as suds, coalescing
on the blue moving water to the distant tuck of a drum. Then the
drums stopped. A trumpet squealed, and the headsails came down in
a crackling patter. Then there were only bare masts tilting in unison,
and slanting green Ottoman flags, each with its gold waning moon, to
mark the night of the Sultan's great victory. For a moment, such
quietness fell that the forest birdsong could be heard, hung like a cloth
between city and mountains. In the eastern gorge, the harp voice of a
nightingale made a statement and then developed it, contending with
other courting, preening, ritual voices, brought by the wind: *Allah-u
Akbar; Allah-u Akbar; la ilaha ill-Allah.* The imâms, invoking Allah
in prayer.

On all the roofs of the city, people stood, their arms about one
another, and watched the flotilla as the carpet of worshippers stirred,
roused and began to disperse. Of the ships, there were too many to
count. Big galleys: long two-masted triremes like the *Ciaretti*; biremes
with their single masts; and a swarm of longboats, sloops, cutters,
transports now beginning to move up for the disembarkation. Leading
them, with a gilded prow and a personal flag flying from the stern, was
the sloop of the admiral, Kasim Pasha, governor of Gallipoli, and
Yakub his sailing-master. Tobie said, "There they go. I tell you.
They're going to ask Allah to tie you to four mating camels and allow
them a wish with your breastbone."

Nicholas shrugged, grinning. But Godscalc said, "They came in,
the fishermen. Why? What has Nicholas done?"

It was Astorre who answered, his glittering eyes fixed on the shore.
"Him and John: they're a pair of devils. You see that Turkish rabble
coming ashore? Paid volunteers and bashibazouk irregulars, that's all
they are. They expect to pillage, and they're allowed to. So they spend
the first day or two claiming their houses. Pick a villa and stick a flag
on it, and then get down to the gold and the food and the women."

"There aren't any," said Godscalc.

"But they don't know that," said Astorre. "There are houses.
They'll go into them."

"You've left traps?"

"Watch," said Astorre. He punched Nicholas on the back. "I don't
know. You'll do it to us one of these days, and I'll know I should have
cut your throat, back there in Bruges."

"I'll give you warning," Nicholas said.

Astorre's eyes were still on him. He said, "She's a grand woman,
the demoiselle. You and her, you can count on Astorre."

Without turning, Nicholas smiled: the wide, unstinted smile of his
boyhood. "I know," he said. "Look. It's beginning."

Of course John, who understood the whole scheme, was at
Kerasous. Astorre had taken a more than vigorous share, and the

Greek commander had supplied engineers, and Tobie himself, now and then, had stumbled across some of the more esoteric of the pitfalls Nicholas had arranged for the followers of the Prophet in the eastern suburb of Trebizond. For most of it, he was hardly prepared. The first of the longboats slid on to the coarse pebbled shore: the Turks leapt ashore, turbanned, booted, their coats tucked into their cotton breeches, their short curved blades in the air, and scattered, stumbled, and fell flat before a series of sharp explosions. The approaching boats veered; the agitated shouts of the landing parties could be heard from the tower. Groups of men, reluctant details, set off over the beaches, weapons in hand. "Tripwires and gunpowder," Nicholas said. "Watch the sheds."

The sheds contained a counterlever system involving timber and rocks. Searching for hidden handgunners, the advance parties suffered. An officer, using his wits, set a party to clearing and testing the beach, after which the incoming flotilla was waved on. Filing ashore, the troops were collected in bands and given instructions. Astorre sniggered. "Watch out for tripwires and levers," he said. "And much good may it do them."

"There's more?" Godscalc said.

There was more. Sometimes Astorre explained, sometimes Tobie. Seven feet deep, covered mantraps had been dug in the roads, and the dirt floors of houses. Crossbows had been carefully set up, and triggered by twine. There was a bull in one orchard; a wild boar in another. Where one of the steep slopes invited running, a thin, murderous wire had been stretched; there was a cartload of stones ready to sweep down another. Pulley systems existed, geared to unload a killing series of objects, from sacks of dirt to vats of blistering oil. All of them gnat bites to an invading army; but humiliating gnat bites that caused disarray; engendering caution and a disinclination to jump to orders. Across the ravine, the roar of men's voices was continuous, as the disembarked men raggedly invested the suburb, absorbing mishap and accident, expressing frustration or excitement. Sometimes a prize had been abandoned or forgotten, and a sudden clamour would emerge. What they found they mobbed, like crows over meat.

On the other side of the gorge, the people of Trebizond watched. Now the enemy had reached the buildings and trees of the suburb, their movements could be followed mostly by sound, with occasional glimpses of turbans racing across the space of the Meidan, or on roofs, or within a garden or yard. Tobie said, "Is that all?"

"No," said Nicholas. He looked expectant, and solemn. Tobie was wondering why, when the explosions began.

Where exactly they took place could not be seen. Only, somewhere among the villas and trees on the other side of the gorge, there would appear a cloud of black smoke, a toss of flame and a roar, loud as a cannon, followed by screaming. Astorre listened, satisfaction on his face. "Candles," he said. "This fellow here had them moulding tallow like squirrels. Burning down, you see, at different rates into barrels of gunpowder. Kill the whoresons already inside, and ruin the houses for living in." Some of the explosions were coloured, like joy-fire. Some were preceded by a sequence of other sharp noises, as if a teasing trail of some sort had been added. After the first, the men on the Trebizond rooftops began to mark each with a hard cheer. What they were seeing was the destruction of their own houses. They cheered defiantly.

After the fifth or sixth blast, when the fires had taken hold and were beginning to spread, the shouting over the gorge changed in character, as a hive changes its mood. Nicholas said, "They've had enough. They want to shoot arrows at us, even if they fall into the gorge. With any luck, they'll waste quite a lot."

"The wave of resentment," said Tobie. He watched the white-wrapped cones rush together and flow down the ridge on the opposite side until stopped by the wall on the far side of the ravine that separated them from the City. Even at such a distance, the faces had moustaches and eyes, and the collarless shirts were smeared black and red. Fists high above heads were shaking crooked sabres and lances and bows. They stood in a line at the wall, glaring over the gulf: a hedge solid with hatred. Then the hedge was uprooted.

The explosions had their source in the houses immediately behind the intent, angered men. The detonations took place one by one, so that no sooner had one whirlwind of brick and stone flung itself into the air than the next one had followed it; finely timed as good clockwork. The white-capped forms lining the wall fell askew and were flattened, like wooden pins hit by a ball; except that this impact turned everything red. A spray of blood coloured the brick of the rampart, and began to run down it. Fire rose, and hung in the air like a cloth. Nicholas said, "War without fire is worth nothing; like sausages without mustard."

The quotation was lost on Astorre. "You did it!" he said. His voice was hoarse with awe and excitement. Below, from the walls and roofs of the City, there had arisen cries of fierce pleasure. Godscalc turned.

Nicholas returned his gaze without flinching. Nicholas remarked, in distinct conversational Flemish, "Gathering credit in Heaven for purging the land of the infidel. But, you will say, is this the way a man of honour would take? Tricks and treachery? But yes, I shall reply, for how else has the heathen ever dealt with our kind? And what do the means matter, so long as the good of God's Church is preserved? But, you will say – "

"How dare you presume to know what I will say?" said Father Godscalc.

"Since you dare to criticise, it is my privilege," Nicholas said.

"You are sensitive," Godscalc said, "if to look at you is now an offence. I am going back to the house. It is going to be a long siege, and I need to gather my stomach for it."

They watched him go down. Tobie said, "I'm not sure I liked that. Any of it."

Astorre spat. "First day nerves. He saw plenty of men blown to pieces at Sarno. And he's a good fighter, too."

"I'm sure he is," Nicholas said. "So long as he picks the right people to fight."

Later, he went down with the others, and when he saw the priest next, neither referred to what had occurred. Publicly, their relationship was no different. Privately, the man who was waiting still waited; and the man who kept away continued to do so.

The siege began, and the City of Trebizond settled down to endure it.

Chapter 36

THE STIFLING HEATS OF July embraced warring Europe, and chain mail and plate armour, skin tunic and thick wadded canvas all weltered in hot brine and blood. In struggling England, the Yorkist leader was crowned Edward IV, and George and Richard his juvenile brothers were created respectively the Dukes of Clarence and Gloucester. In Rome, cardinals fled from the poisonous humours, and the Curia packed up its vellum. The Holy Father received a visit from his godson Giovanni da Castro, former dyemaster at Constantinople; embraced the dear fellow many times and then departed to stay for three months in the fresh air of Tivoli. The Minorite Order of Franciscans gave him lodgings, and all the lords on his way proffered protection. "What fairer sight than troops in battle array?" said Pope Pius, affected.

In France, his jaws jammed, old King Charles VII died of starvation, having given his last living audience (but no money) to Fra Ludovico da Bologna and his little party of grotesque Eastern delegates. They stayed for his funeral. In Genappe, the Dauphin Louis ordered a requiem mass for his father and, dressed in red and white, spent the afternoon hunting.

In England, the unsuccessful Lancastrian party waited to see if the new King Louis XI would spare them an army, but received nothing but promises. In Genoa, where there had occurred a quick change of doge, there was some edgy (and more realistic) speculation over the chances of the new King Louis sending troops to turn the Adorno and the Fregoso and every other native faction indiscriminately out of the city. In France itself, there was a convulsion of dreadful unease, as the old court prepared to receive their new hated king Louis: the friend of Burgundy, the protected of Burgundy and now, no doubt, the puppet of Burgundy.

From their places abroad, the refugees friendly to Louis began, with discretion, to return to their estates and their holdings in France. Among the first to arrive was Jordan de St Pol, vicomte de Ribérac;

father of the fair, handsome and short-tempered Simon. Left in command of his Scots lands at last, Simon de St Pol expressed his relief in a week-long bout of tumultuous drinking, to the frustration of his wife Katelina whose bed was worn through already with the hours she brought him to spend there, although so far without profit. When she heard he was to go overseas, she would hardly leave him alone. Simon, whose vigour was considerable, was both pleased and amused. And she was quite right. One son was not enough. He would not, however, agree to take her with him to Italy.

Gregorio, the Charetty lawyer, had of course left for Italy ten weeks before, with the intention of stopping between Dijon and Geneva, rumour said, to collect and escort his employer, the former widow Marian de Charetty. The word from Bruges was that the elder daughter Mathilde, the one left with Anselm Adorne, had insisted on going as well. The object, of course, as Simon knew, was to untangle the marriage between the other girl and his agent Doria. He wished them well of it. He had intended to follow himself until his father had pointed out how unwise it would be. Fat father Jordan. Bloated father Jordan, who had reinforced the argument by withdrawing all Simon's spending money and closing his credit, so that he couldn't get away even if he had wanted to.

But now he could. The hog had gone back to the beechmast of Ribérac and would be too busy rebuilding his wealth to worry about Simon, who had a filled cog out there somewhere in the Black Sea, and a Genoese agent who seemed to be spending more time on his own affairs than on Simon's, and who well might be pocketing the profits Simon needed to cut himself free from the old man. After he had repaid to the old man the original price of the cog and all it contained. As fat father Jordan had stipulated. Fat father Jordan, whom he loathed as much as he and his father had cause to loathe the upstart labourer Claes. Jordan who spied on him. After he, Simon, found out about the woman Agnès, he had told Katelina to get rid of her. And when she demurred, he had set his grooms at the old whore, who had made as much fuss as if she'd been a virgin and then fled to his father. There were plenty of women to look after Henry. What did it matter? There would be other sons, now. He had never known a woman so eager, so delightfully eager as his wife Katelina van Borselen.

In Florence, the sea consul Antonio di Niccolò Martelli received word of the arrival from Bruges of the Charetty company and, representing his colleagues the Medici, arranged a business meeting with the Charetty lawyer Gregorio, a dark, youngish man with a nose like a scimitar. To Messer Gregorio he was able to deliver the news that a round ship had just departed Pisa for Bruges containing a cargo of Phocoean alum consigned from Constantinople by Messer Zorzi on the instructions of the Charetty company.

The lawyer Gregorio, receiving the news, thanked the consul

serenely while opening the letters the consul had kept for him. Martelli admired his composure. With the demand for alum now reaching the skies, the profit from this single cargo from Zorzi would pay for the purchase of the Medici galley. The debt to the lord Cosimo de' Medici was now cancelled.

Then the lawyer Gregorio, reading his letters, had lifted his head and said, "This is also good news. Our master Niccolò, writing in May from Trebizond, tells of successful sales and a large purchase of Caspian silk from the first caravan train from Tabriz."

"The Golden Fleece! Your fortunes are made!" said Martelli smiling. "My lord Cosimo will be happy to hear it. And your lord is well, and the priest Godscalc?"

"So it seems," said the lawyer.

"And that rascal Doria?" had said the sea consul. "That whoreson Doria? What of him?"

He had been a little too vehement, and the lawyer looked surprised. Then the man Gregorio had said, "You, too, are no friend of the charming Messer Pagano? Messer Niccolò says very little, but I gather Doria is in Trebizond too, but has not been as successful as he would have wished."

"In which your master has had a hand? I am glad," had said Messer Martelli. "When you go to Venice, speak to Alessandro, my brother. Alessandro, manager of the Venice bank of the Medici. If you wish to travel further east, he will help you."

"Thank you. No," had said the lawyer. "Once in Venice, we shall stay there until we have word of our ship. There is nowhere quicker for messages. And I have accommodation to arrange."

"You are sure of your welcome," had said Messer Martelli, with a curious look. "And Pagano Doria? I am told there has been some strange message from Scotland demanding an enquiry into some marriage he has contracted."

"Really?" had said the lawyer Gregorio. "I think you must be mistaken, Messer Martelli. My information is that the good Messer Doria did attempt some such marriage, but that all the papers were false. I am glad for the sake of the girl, whoever she was. A pernicious man. He deserves all the trouble that our Messer Niccolò can bring on him."

Then, immediately as it seemed, the Charetty cavalcade left the city before any other encounter could be organised. Madonna Alessandra Macinghi negli Strozzi, hearing later, could hardly restrain her annoyance. "The boy Niccolò's womenfolk, and I missed them! Because your wife is a fool, do you need to be a fool also, Antonio?" she had asked. And he had stifled the natural reply and changed the subject, for his brother Roberto in Rome was married to one of the Strozzis of London, and family feeling counted for something.

He said, "Well, the lord Cosimo de' Medici, it seems, has sniffed out a good bargain again. From the news arriving from Trebizond, the company Charetty look to have made a fair fortune for Florence and themselves."

"But will it console the good Cosimo?" said Alessandra Strozzi. "Poor old man, will it fill the gap that a favourite grandson has left? He would give all the gold of the Orient for one day of Cosimino; an hour of his hand on his knee with his whistle."

After a week of the noise and the stench: the crackle of fire; the screams and the explosions; the bouncing tumble of woodwork and masonry; the belching of unpleasant smoke, there developed a routine in Trebizond. Now there was little left to destroy in the suburbs, the enemy turned its attention upon the beleaguered Citadel and began to besiege it with sound. In temper, it would use weapons too: sometimes, for no evident reason, arrows would shower across to the shaved inner side of the gorge, or gun muzzles flare and bark uselessly. But mostly the noise was deliberate. Five times through the day and the night the imâms raised their warbling calls, and the throaty chanting would follow. Between times, the Ottoman army set its musicians to work. All the while, the drums beat, day and night, with almost no respite. Cymbals clashed and horns blew and pipes shrilled over and over. The gorges rattled; the solid walls of the City reverberated. At night the inhabitants of Trebizond stuffed cotton into their ears, those who could afford to. The rest stood on watch, hundred upon hundred manning the stout, roomy ramparts and strained their eyes, as their heads throbbed.

Nicholas thought it was funny. He and Astorre, roving from city to palace, made up verses to go with the drumbeats, and set words to the holy invocations that made even old matrons cackle. They had them sung on the ramparts to music, until men would wait eagerly for the next time of assault in order to drown the Turks' voices. *La Alla; illa Alla; Hazaret-Eesa Ebn-Alla*, the defenders would roar, and add a little something about the Prophet Mohammed. When it came to understanding men, Nicholas was a genius.

Indeed, unlike other times, there was good order within Trebizond for this siege. As soon as it was clear that the thing was going to last, the food and the wine and the wells were all commandeered, with recompense for those who had a surplus; and what the populace needed was handed out fairly. The exception, of course, was the Palace; but no one but Nicholas and Astorre were in a position to see the secret hoards; the greedy haggling that went on from chamber to chamber. The noblemen of the court were the Emperor's personal friends, and the Vice-Regent of Christ was beyond criticism.

Nicholas spent half his time at the Palace where he and Astorre were treated as joint ringmasters of some crude but enjoyable circus. The spectacle of the devices which greeted the first Turkish landing had set the tone for the Emperor's attitude to this little war. For their presumption in landing, the Ottoman soldiers deserved to be teased into slaughter. Of course, many remained. But, bored and disgruntled, they would withdraw when the weather grew rough, while the God-protected Basileus and his circle reclined on the heights, creating satirical poems; hazarding money on the firing pattern of the enemy guns; setting one another perilous quests: to slip at night from the postern and come back with an Ottoman head, or a flag, or a sleeping man's drawers.

Eight courtiers lost their lives and two familiar spiked heads gazed at them now from the Ottoman side of the gulf. One of them was that of the elegant man Nicholas had last seen in the baths, having his fingernails tended. Quite recently, the baths had been closed because of the fuel they consumed but, before that, their custom had dwindled. What had taken place with decorum in that elegant setting took place now behind closed doors and curtains, and sprang from the rough promptings of war, and danger, and fear; and not the languid devices of boredom. The professional soldiers revelled in favours. Astorre, while controlling his own men with oaths, took every woman he was offered and three times as many who came unsolicited. Nicholas, beset from other quarters, had sought, ingeniously, the highest protection.

The Emperor had been amused. "You are their talisman. They hope to share your success, your good fortune."

"Excellency," Nicholas had said, "how could I squander something so precious, unless it were upon the highest of altars? And that I cannot do. An astrologer told me."

The Emperor had frowned, touching the silk of his beard. "To sacrifice the best to the highest: what can be wrong with that?"

"Nothing, my lord," Nicholas had answered with sorrow. "Save that, the astrologer says, the essence of my luck and my carnal being are one and the same. To disperse one disperses both."

"Hah!" had said the Emperor. "So you are content to live your life as a celibate? There is a man there. I have seen him."

"My life?" had said Nicholas. "My lord, no. When Trebizond rejoices in freedom, so shall I rejoice; for my luck and my essence will be well lost together for joy. Meanwhile, chastity is my offering."

"Then," had said the Emperor after a pause, "we must wish our captains good progress. We commend you. You will report to us daily."

Astorre, apprised of the exchange from very particular sources personal to himself, went in search of Nicholas, cackling. "My boy, they'll take an interest now in their war! Urbino never thought of that, I can tell you! Or Sforza! First prize for winning . . ."

"And second prize, yours," said Nicholas briefly.

Both of Astorre's eyes were sparkling. He said, "You'll have to do it. Will you mind?"

"How should I know? I'll give you a detailed report, if you like. Meanwhile, I can get on with the siege without my time being wasted."

The smile left Astorre's face. His beard jutted. He said, "Don't try that with me. I remember the girls you bedded in Bruges. If you were not who you are, I'd give you three women and tell you to get on with it, wife or no wife. I don't want to be led by a man going mad from an itch he won't scratch."

Nicholas held up a spread hand. Astorre looked at it. Nicholas said, "When it shakes, you can come and take me off to a brothel. Meantime, I can manage, so long as the dogs don't object. Am I wrong, or is the change of watch behind time? Perhaps you should see to it."

Now and then, after a session with Nicholas, a man would find himself breathing more sharply than usual. But in between, he was everyone's friend.

Then, ten days into the siege, he was summoned to the Palace out of turn, and with an urgency missing before. He had grown long used, now, to the morning chamber the Emperor used for his councils, with its verd antique, its mosaics, its belvedere of pillared air overlooking the western gulf and shores of the Empire. It was in the same quarter as the chamber of Violante of Naxos, whom he had not seen for two weeks. Looking round, Nicholas saw that the high officers of war were there, as was usual; and the captain of the Kabasitai as well as Altamourios and the rest of the Emperor's personal staff and his Protovestarios Amiroutzes, who bent, one foot on the dais step, listening to David, Autocrat of the Romans. He rose, as Nicholas was announced, and waited, as they all did, while he advanced bowing, and lightly made the prostration. Whatever the occasion, nothing ever removed the need for the courtesies. There were no boys, and no churchmen, and no members of the Emperor's family. The Emperor said, "Sit. We have received news."

The council benches were marble, cushioned in silks, and stood in a broken horseshoe before him. Nicholas took his place between the Drungarios and the commander of the Imperial Guard, while Amiroutzes sat at the head of the horseshoe, next to the Basileus on the dais. Once, there had also been an interpreter, but there was no need for that now. He understood them, Nicholas thought, in more ways than perhaps they would care for. Certainly, it was not their business to understand him. Latin merchants and their mercenaries were, in the end, only paid labour, in their obscene hose and outlandish tunics and cropped hats, fit for cheap slaves and seamen. The Emperor said, "We are divided in our opinion; and since the Ottoman is adopting the western fashion of war, it seems to us that the view of one from that world would be beneficial."

Without daily exercise, the Emperor had increased a little in girth. Amiroutzes, the Great Chancellor and Count Palatine, on the other hand was unchanged. The lightly woven stuff of his hat brim threw trellised shadows over the handsome nose and sensitive mouth and striped beard, and the thick brown hair clinging a little with heat. He moved well. He was a fine archer, people said. In Italy, George Amiroutzes had ranked himself eloquently with the Cardinal Bessarion, who recommended the Roman Church and the Greek should unite. Admirer of Aquinas; skilled negotiator; fluent commentator; Amiroutzes had come back from Florence to Trebizond covered in glory. *The lover and judge of letters, rightly called philosopher by all the fatherland*, someone had called him. A thinker; a guide; a companion to the God-protected sovereign on his pinnacle, whose dissertations Nicholas had sometimes heard, and sometimes agreed with. A man with two growing sons; and a free hand with pearls.

Therefore . . . therefore, one chose one's ground, and perhaps even planted it. Nicholas spoke to a point between the Protovestarios and the Emperor. "There are those who know more than I do, magnificence. May I send for captain Astorre?"

"Indeed, we intend to summon him presently." It was Amiroutzes who replied, at a nod from the Emperor. "But first, it is a matter of interpretation, rather than strategy. We have news of the Sultan and the army of Mahmud Pasha, his Vizier."

"They have left Sinope," said Nicholas.

"They have taken Koyulhisar," said the Emperor. "They are devils, not men. They have completed a march which no men before them have managed so quickly; and scaled the heights of the Turcoman's western frontier, and taken its fortress. If they have the energy to continue towards us, the hills and passes and forts of the White Sheep are all that lie between them and us."

No one spoke. There was no way of telling what had already been said; what views the commanders had already expressed.

Nicholas said, "Magnificence: it has always been known that this was possible. The loss of the frontier fortress is great, but it must have taken its toll. Now Hasan Bey is prepared, the Sultan will have to fight every inch of the ground, over mountains where the White Sheep are at home. And by the time they are done, the season for war will have ended. I see no need for alarm."

"Do you not?" said the Emperor. "Do you not? Some here have expressed the same view. But hear, then, the next piece of news. Erzerum has been vacated. The lord Uzum Hasan and the core of his army have not come forward to push back the Turk. They have retreated into the mountains, leaving garrisons to do what they can to hinder the Turkish advance."

"But do you not think, magnificence, that this too will serve?" Nicholas said. "In direct conflict, the army of my lord Hasan Bey would succumb, now he has no help from Sinope or Georgia. But a war of attrition, carried on against tiring men in the mountains, will keep the Sultan from his door just as well, until the autumn storms come. The Sultan may occupy Erzerum, but he can hardly hold it. And with all that to deal with, he can have no thought of attacking this empire."

The Emperor turned his head, and the Treasurer answered. Before he spoke, Nicholas knew what he was going to say. "The third piece of news," said George Amiroutzes, "is that my lord Uzum Hasan is not preparing to defend his land to the death, or even resist until the season has closed. It is said that he has brought his mother, the Syrian Sara Khatun, to the field. It is said that he has sent this lady to meet the Sultan, and ask for lenience in return for neutrality."

There was a rustle and a shifting of feet. Nicholas said, "How trustworthy is such news?"

The dark eyes were watching him. "From a source, Messer Niccolò, which has never failed."

Nicholas said, "And that is all?"

"All?" said the Emperor. "With the Turk at our gates?"

"Is he at your gates, magnificence?" Nicholas said. "Forgive me. I thought he was at Koyulhisar, in July."

"Then your advice is, that we have no cause for concern?" said the Great Chancellor. "You do not think it likely that this seaborne army burning our suburbs is merely waiting for the land army to march through empty mountains and take us between them?"

"My lord: how could they?" said Nicholas. "How could ten times the number take Trebizond?"

"How could Constantinople fall and her emperor perish?" said the Treasurer wearily. "God is just, Messer Niccolò; but there are weights in His scales that mortal men cannot know."

"But we may guess," Nicholas said. "By sea or by land, there are no guns coming here of the kind that felled Constantinople. The fleet, we know, have not brought even the tools that would cast them. Holy fount of the Church as Trebizond is, it is not the sacred heart of the Eastern Empire, to take which no price was too much to pay. It has not the riches that Byzantium had. Its merchants can serve the Turk just as well from Bursa and Pera. And facing this enemy is a city renowned for its courage; blessed by Nature with barriers no one can storm; blessed by God with our Basileus to uplift and to lead. I say, be at rest. We cannot fail. There is nothing here in this news to disturb the sleep of the men and women and children who trust their lord here in the City today."

There was, at least, a pause before the Treasurer gave his wry smile. "An eloquent answer, in praiseworthy Greek, Messer Niccolò. You have a good grasp of our tongue: on that, at least, all must agree. As for the rest, we have heard your views, and they will not be forgotten. Magnificence?"

The dismissal did not immediately come. The Emperor said, "Others have spoken thus."

Amiroutzes said, "I thought you doubted them. That is why – But if, magnificence, you wish to reopen the matter, then perhaps Messer Niccolò should remain and debate with us all?"

There was a pause. Yes. No. The Emperor said, "We wish to consider these things at leisure. It is time for dinner."

He rose and left, with his immediate suite, amid his flattened council. Nicholas rose without haste, and looked for the Emperor's commander. In front of him was a chamberlain saying, "May I escort you, before the gates close? These days, it is as difficult sometimes to leave the Upper Citadel as it is to get in."

"I thought to complete a little business," said Nicholas. He stood where he was.

A hand took his arm. "Tomorrow, perhaps," said the Count Palatine. "When no doubt we shall draw again upon your wisdom and your eloquence. We are fortunate, Messer Niccolò, to have you and your men as our bastion. But when inner councils are held, you will realise, those not of the Empire are obliged to depart."

"Of course," said Nicholas. "And when you are ready to receive Captain Astorre, you have only to tell us."

The news became known soon enough, and in forms he would not have chosen. Warned a little, he and the rest did what they could to belittle it. There was no panic; but it became harder to forge the weapons of ebullience and ridicule against the constant taunting uproar outside. It became apparent, from the flag flying there, that the Turkish admiral had made his headquarters in the Genoese castle. "They'll make him governor, I shouldn't wonder, once the Sultan gets in," Tobie said.

Nicholas said, "No." For once, they were all, except Astorre, in their lodging, and Tobie was occupied in his eternal task of refilling and checking his ointments. Pestilence was the enemy most besieged cities finally fell to, and he and the palace physicians had set out, from the start, to do all that they could to prevent it. With the winds and the heights for their ally, it seemed as if they would. But there was still disease and wounding and death; and few places for burial. Tobie worked long hours, and then talked for release.

It helped him to bait Nicholas, whose denial, he knew, had nothing to do with the admiral's chances of promotion. Tobie said, "You're obsessed. It was a joke. No one will hear us."

"The servants will," Nicholas said. "And the Venetians. This city is not going to fall to the Turks. There is no danger whatever. And we never speak, even in jest, as if there were. And if I hear you do it again, I'll make you forcibly sit on your falx. Do you really know about camel diseases?"

"Dysentery, rupture, saddle galls, mange and the flux. Man or beast, I can cure them. Why? You want me in partnership once the Sultan . . . That," said Tobie sharply, "was a damned sight too much. Keep your feet to yourself."

"Then do as I say," said Nicholas. "Or get kicked."

A week passed; and the message Nicholas was waiting for came. By then, he was aware, only Astorre was still treating him with his natural irreverence. The others had become guarded, with reason. Godscalc came back that night, tired from his own heavy round of pastoral duties. With most of the Venetians gone, there were few to share his burden among the Latin community; and besides, he gave his services freely, as they were freely accepted, by the suffering of every persuasion.

Nicholas let him sleep the night through, and hold his first mass of the day and then, instead of leaving himself on his rounds, he tapped on the door of the small room that Godscalc, alone of them all, had to himself; because in it was his altar, and there he received those who needed him. Now, when he heard who it was, he crossed and opened the door himself, and stood without speaking. Nicholas said, "I thought to spare you this. I am sorry."

Godscalc, too, had changed from the big, unkempt man who had, with a light, amused hand, unravelled the machinations of Pagano Doria at Pisa. Friendship with his fellow religious had caused him to neaten his clothes and reduce his tattered black hair to something more seemly, although he still moved more like a man of his fists than a man of the Church, and his greatest battle, still, was the one to disguise his natural temper. Now, brought face to face with what he had long recognised as the fight of his life, he stood where he was and said, "I am busy."

"I know," said Nicholas. There was a pause. He said, "So is Tobie."

The door was still open behind him. There was another silence. Godscalc said, "Then why leave it so late?"

"Because I thought I could do it alone," Nicholas said. "Mistakenly." There was a rare line between his remarkable eyes, but the rest of his face – scar, dimples, all that was vulnerable – was hidden and clothed by his beard. He said, "But I'll go away if you wish."

"And do what alone?" Godscalc said.

"Go to the Sultan," said Nicholas.

Chapter 37

"I'M SURPRISED," Godscalc said. "I had the impression you felt you could do anything." He closed the door and watched Nicholas wander to the opposite side of the room, where the balcony gave on to the crowded courtyard. He said, "I suppose you had better shut that door as well." He thought for a moment Nicholas hadn't heard him; then the boy closed the door and came back and sat down.

Nicholas said, "Well, you're angry. And I was wrong. There has to be a team, in case something happens to me."

Godscalc sat down briskly himself. "Your wife is capable," he said. "You can hardly imagine that we would abandon her?"

"No. You would stay from duty. It is a different thing," Nicholas said.

There was a pause, which Godscalc did not break. The boy had to learn. If he didn't learn now, it was too late. At length Nicholas said, "There are disadvantages, when one is brought up as a servant. Men of different rank have different customs. Men of the same rank are vulnerable – " He broke off. He said, "Even Loppe knows I don't trust him."

"He would give his life for you," Godscalc said.

Nicholas said, "Regardless of anything else. That is why."

Godscalc considered that, and set it aside for the moment. He said, "And what is this burden, then, that you have elected to carry alone; and why do you bring it me now?"

"Because I can't carry it," Nicholas said. "I'm not competent. And I can't risk being wrong. So your peace of mind is what I decided to sacrifice."

"You underrate me," said Godscalc. "Today is the first day I could claim peace of mind since we both came to Trebizond. And don't mistake me again. I know it's not your soul that is in question. Yes, I knew about Doria's secret consignment of arms. Yes, I have been angry with you. You gave me a pretty lecture, some of it true. But this was a barrier of your own making. You kept quiet, I suppose, to save us from making the choice. Specifically, to exclude me. You must have a poor opinion of militant church."

He had seen a man look like that when he had hit him in the face. He had never seen a man accept it in silence, uncomplaining. Nicholas said, "John would agree with you. Will you help me?"

"You would pay my fee?" Godscalc said. And then smiled and said, "You don't quite know your way about as yet, do you? That is one debt you won't have to face. But the crux of the matter, as you say, is the arms."

He watched the boy recover. It was smooth, and nearly invisible. Nicholas said, "Yes. At least, that is the catalyst. Arms and armour bought from Louis de Gruuthuse. They were in the Ribérac ship when Simon stole it from his father. Doria said nothing of them at Pisa or Genoa. He perhaps hoped to sell them at Constantinople, but the plague scare prevented him. Perhaps he hoped on the way to barter them for . . . something else, but time was against him. He arrived at Trebizond holding them in reserve, as might be, to obtain the Emperor's favour. For whatever reason, he kept them on board until the round ship was dismantled; and then he brought them ashore. I know where they are."

Since the siege began, they had seen more of the ship-master Crackbene than they had of Doria; and the visits of Paraskeuas had stopped. Since that acrimonious exchange in the garden, the Turks had burned Alighieri's fondaco to the ground: they had heard the catcalls, and had witnessed the flames. The threats made there by Catherine's husband seemed equally to have vanished. Godscalc said, "How do you know?"

"Catherine. Before she left," Nicholas said. "But don't read too much into that, either. I don't think she's abandoned her husband entirely. I think she's set him a test without realising, perhaps, all the consequences. Certainly, he has tried to get rid of me often enough since she went."

Godscalc sat up. "Not by his own hand," Nicholas said. "And Loppe, as you noticed, goes with me everywhere. Or almost everywhere. Violante of Naxos also knew Doria had a cargo of arms but did not, I think, tell anyone. In any case, she has gone."

"Where?" said Godscalc.

Nicholas shrugged faintly. "To Georgia . . . Tana . . . I don't know. She has friends. A fishing boat would take a single person of such eminence anywhere. And so the problem is mine."

"A consignment of arms so great that they would affect the course of the war; and in your gift? That is the problem?" said Godscalc.

A rocking stool was his answer. Nicholas stood with his back to the window and said, "Of course not! What do you think we're talking about? That load of iron might affect the war for ten minutes; an hour; a day; but that's all. Of course, any one of the parties would be glad to have it. Of course, whoever gets it is going to be grateful. That isn't the point. The point is the fact that it wasn't delivered."

"By Doria? But you said yourself that he might be saving it for favours," Godscalc said. Briefly, he prayed God to forgive him the exultation he was feeling.

"Don't you think the time for soliciting favours has come? And there is the lady Violante, who vowed she told no one about it but myself. I believe her. In fact, I know that she didn't. So, why?"

Godscalc rose and walked to where the other man stood, and fitted his shoulders into the post of the window. "Tell me," he said.

Nicholas spoke, his eyes on the courtyard. "Because they don't know who is going to rule Trebizond," he said. "There were three contenders. The Emperor, who possesses it. The Ottoman Sultan. And the lord Uzum Hasan, currently an ally of Trebizond, but only out of fear of the Sultan."

"Uzum Hasan would never rule Trebizond," Godscalc said. "If it fell into his power he might impose tolls; ask for Muslim concessions. But the White Sheep don't live in towns. He would leave it to his Greek kinsmen. After all, the lady Violante . . ." He stopped.

"The lady Violante knew I knew that," Nicholas said. "I was allowed to meet Hasan Bey's mother and reassure myself. The case was made tactfully clear. The White Sheep required, without stint, all the help that could be arranged from Sinope or from Georgia, but no harm would come to Christians, or trade. Especially trade. Florence would find some niche under any lord, but under Uzum Hasan Venice would thrive through his niece's Venetian husband. On the other hand – " He paused. "On the other hand, without that extra help, the White Sheep tribe could not be expected to sacrifice itself. Not this time. Not yet."

Godscalc said, "You said yourself, all that was needed of them was a little resistance until the season had ended. That is still the case."

"No," Nicholas said. "They are not resisting at all. The Palace doesn't know of it yet; but the White Sheep have not simply intimated that they will refrain from aggression. They've surrendered the north to the Sultan on any terms he cares to make, and given him Hasan Bey's mother as hostage. I have just had word. The Sultan is forcemarching straight through to Trebizond." He made a space. He said, "So now there are only two contenders."

In the courtyard, a woman was berating a servant. The noise came to them faintly. "Even so," Godscalc said, "the city is impregnable." He watched the other man's face.

Nicholas said, "Yes. It is impregnable. But no one has given the Emperor the armour from the *Doria.*" And he brought his eyes back from the courtyard. Neither moved. Then Nicholas laughed and, lifting one hand, spread its fingers. He said, "I told Astorre, when he saw that, to take me off to a brothel."

"But you came instead to a priest. I am glad," Godscalc said. "I know what you are saying, and we are going to sit, and drink a full glass of wine, and discuss it. And you will not bear the brunt of all this alone. I promise you that. Whatever blame there is, it will fall on me, too."

Pouring the wine, he kept his back to the boy so that he should not see that the priest's hands, also, were shaking.

A week later, it became known that this young character, the head of the Charetty company, had been taken ill with the fever again, and that the doctor had given up everything else to look after him. Without his cheerful face, the tedium of the siege became a little more obvious, and the edge of fear now lurking below it. But luckily, there was the reassurance of Captain Astorre's constant presence: in the town, on the ramparts, in the Palace, putting good heart into everybody. There had been time to train others, and set a good routine; and even Pagano Doria found it convenient to slacken his childish vendetta, having other things of more note on his mind. Nor did he object when, having no chaplain, his officers asked leave to make use of the Charetty priest Godscalc. July moved towards August, and the City steamed in the heat.

In the mountains behind, it was cooler; and women were better off than men, although it did not stop Sara Khatun's servingwomen from complaining. On the last stretch of the journey, even the light two-wheeled covered carriage the Sultan had given her had proved impossible, and she had resorted to the cane palanquin, hand-carried, that she had brought from Erzerum, leaving the women to ride. They were among the few with that privilege, of those who travelled with the Ottoman army. Without tents, without guns, without any scrap of baggage that would hinder them, the combined armies of the Sultan Mehmet and his Grand Vizier Mahmud had forcemarched in a sweep to the east after the governor of Little Rum, whom hell receive, had taken her son's mountain castle at Koyulhisar. The border fortress they had thought would resist him. And since then, the Janissaries had overrun most of the main posts and passes, although some, she observed, they circumvented. Lightly armed, lightly provisioned, with almost none of their cavalry, the Sultan and his army had chosen to make speed their chief weapon: speed and surprise.

The Ottomans were not going to hold this country unless they made peace with her son. They would be lucky to hold Koyulhisar through the winter. Through the winter, her son Uzum Hasan and his forces would retreat into the mountains of Armenia and the plains beyond the river Euphrates, to emerge and attack when it suited them. The Sultan didn't want that. But equally, the Sultan knew her son's weaknesses. The White Sheep were nomads, with the wilfulness that nomads displayed; unlike the drilled, silent efficiency of the Ottomans. And their dashing cavalry skills were no use in this great range of mountains. The mountains the Sultan had to traverse if he wished to reach and challenge Trebizond. As it was now clear he did.

Sara Khatun had been with the Sultan's army now for several weeks, and he had treated her and her entourage of Kurdish and Turcoman nobles with exemplary respect as she had never doubted he would; even to naming her *Mother*. If she had been, she would have reduced his drinking by half. The prince of twenty-three who had taken Constantinople and (fortunately for her sake) saw himself as a second Alexander conquering a second Darius of Persia, was now a beak-nosed and inflated 31-year-old. A man who spoke Arabic, Persian and Greek and liked gardens, mathematicians, catamites, military strategy and making up excellent poetry. She was less enamoured of his Grand Vizier Mahmud who, like all Christian converts, followed his new faith with unpleasant devotion. He was of course a first-class commander, but not a popular one. It had been a man from Bursa who had burst into his tent and taken a knife to him only last week. He had done nothing but slit his nose and the upper part of his mouth, and the Sultan's Italian physician had seen to it at once. Since Mahmud's troops and her own party had separated and drawn ahead of the Sultan, the wound had begun to irk him again. She was delighted.

Just over the Zigana summit, she announced that she would leave her litter and ride downhill herself. By horse, unfortunately, since the camel she favoured was sick. Later, Mahmud Pasha sent to tell her that the camel doctor she had sent for had come, and she had nodded her approval from behind her black horsehair veil, which she would never have troubled to wear in Erzerum or Diyarbekr. When they made camp in the end, she was told they were only three miles short of Trebizond, but in the dusk she could see nothing but a ridge of black trees reflected in grassy water, which soon gave back also the light of the torches and cooking-fires. Only the Vizier's party and her own possessed tents. The rest razed the small trees and the dense undergrowth on the slopes, and made beds of myrtle and juniper and purple spiraea, with charcoal for cooking and smudge fires for the gnats.

As ever, the piyade remained tidily disposed in their units, without shouting or laughter, and their conversation, such as it was, rarely exceeded a murmur. Like those of the Sultan, many of the Vizier's personal servants were mutes: deft, obedient, and incapable of displeasing rejoinders. On the march, or in battle, the army had no need for human command, since it obeyed the voice of the drum. The drum horses went with them everywhere. Unstrapped, the drums were their kettles, and stood steaming full of boiled wheat and fat flesh, while the Janissaries made spoons of their drumsticks. They did so tonight, daisy-ringed round the fires in their gleaming white bonnets.

After her own meal, Sara Khatun wrapped her head in the horsehair; called for Sheikh Hüseyin Bey, and walked irritably into the night to find the camel doctor and discover what he had done for her animal. Sheikh Hüseyin, a cousin of her son's Kurdish wife, went ahead beating men with his stick and asking questions in the Turcoman vernacular. Finally they discovered the fellow sprawled beside a small fire playing draughts and holding a large, leaking bread-poke of yoghourt. A blood-stained cloth hung from his neck. The draught pieces were white pebbles and pellets of dung, and the board was a neckcloth on which the squares were half rubbed off by use.

At first she thought his opponent, a big, black-bearded half-Caucasian was the one that she sought, because his complaints could be heard all over the camp. She was wrong. When the Sheikh's riding stick poked them to their feet, it was the other who laid down his yoghourt and, fixing the cloth to his mouth, shambled forward. They were both dressed in stout cotton tunics with coloured linings and sashes, and their drawers were good fustian stuffed into felt boots. Hunting clothes. The few possessions they had stacked by their saddles were of the sort, too, that hunters or travellers carried: bows and quivers, some spears and a couple of waterbottles made out of boarskin. There were also two canvas sacks, one of them open. She could see the white linen lining, and the ends of some jars.

Sheikh Hüseyin, who was old-fashioned and thought no well-brought-up woman should ever appear in public, came across and said, "The camel doctor is called Ilyas, and has just had his beard shaved and his tongue taken out by some enemy over a misunderstanding. Ayyub, the black fellow, speaks for him. He says your beast has the colic. The doctor has sent for some blankets, and given him two quarts of linseed oil, the best quality. He says you have a careless driver: another of your camels is galled. The fault is the packing of straw in the saddle panels."

"No, Khatun," said the black-bearded Ayyub, daring to speak to her direct. "The lord mistakes. The ailing camel was one of the Vizier's. It is not our place to cure it."

A voice said, "In the Grand Vizier's camp, it is the duty of every man to serve him. Khatun. Are these the men you sent for?"

Tursun Beg, master of finance, senior secretary and favourite emissary of Mahmud, who had come with his master from Constantinople. Where in Constantinople, she had heard, he had boarded a certain ship. Sara Khatun said, "My servants are yours. That, there, is the man I sent for. Ilyas. He is mute. The other speaks for him. I am impressed with what he tells me so far." Above the mouth cloth, the eyes of the mutilated man were pale and round on either side of a short nose, curled like a snout. Under the hairy brim of the other man's hat you could see little but the tip of his nose, and below that a tightly curled beard, black as gall nuts. From a brass socket on top, a little squirrel tail bounced as he stepped back.

"Mute? Open his mouth," said Tursun Beg. By now, men from all the neighbouring fires were looking round, their moustaches spread round their gapped, blackened teeth. Two of the secretary's own men took the camel doctor by the shoulders and pulled down the cloth and with broad and capable fingers, opened his jaws.

Despite herself, she looked. Within the gaping mouth, lobes of red severed flesh glistened in the bright firelight. Blood welled and trickled down the man's chin. The neighbouring soldiers, who had evidently already been granted a view, exchanged murmurs of gratification. At a sign, Tursun Beg's men allowed the jaws to close and let the man go. He made retching sounds. Ayyub, his companion, said, "He coughs blood. It is not a sight for a lady. If the doctor might withdraw?"

"Doctor?" said Tursun Beg. He nodded his head and the sufferer, cloth to his mouth, disappeared noisily into the bushes.

"Of course, lord," said the black-bearded one humbly. His squirrel tail drooped. "Would he not be dead with such maltreatment, had he not salved himself? If the Vizier wishes his camel attended to, none is wiser than Ilyas. For saddle galls, he burns the sore with hot irons; then rubs it with urine or pigeon dung. Camel urine, my lord will know, is efficacious in many ailments. To clear the head after drink, one need only stand below a pissing she-camel. I have heard Ilyas say so often, when he could speak."

"Tell him," said Tursun Beg, "to call upon me tomorrow. I may have work for him."

"With a she-camel?" said the black-bearded man. "I would bring it tonight, if the case is a bad one. There is no quicker relief."

"My lord Tursun," said Sara Khatun, "you refer to the ailment of the Vizier himself? I am honoured that you think these men might be of help. You wish to see them both?"

"No," said Tursun Beg. "No. Only the one who is mute. These are his ointments? Tell him to bring them. If he does well, he will receive his reward."

"And if he doesn't, he'll still receive his reward," Tobie said. "I can't. Nicholas, I cannot stick that thing in my tonsils again."

"You will not require to do so," said Sara Khatun. "Your state has been seen, and will be reported on. Only it is necessary that you do not yawn. Or, of course, speak. Discretion in all things is needed." She was reminding them, and she hoped they realised it, that they were not circumcised. The circumlocution expected of a high-born Syrian princess was sometimes a trial to Sara Khatun.

Discretion, of course, had also been required to smuggle them tonight for an hour into this, the innermost chamber of her tent. She could trust her own people. If matters went well, and the doctor was successful with the Grand Vizier's wound, then a tent might be found for the two men, which would be even more convenient. Meanwhile, they sat crosslegged in her presence, and ate cinnamon dragees and green ginger and figs fried in sugar, and listened while she spoke with economy.

At the end, the leader, the boy she had already entertained at Erzerum, said, "You have, then, to buy peace, Sara Khatun? To promise, if need be, to give the Comneni at Trebizond no more of your help, and allow the Sultan access to the shore?"

She said, "We can do nothing else meantime. My son has the Black Sheep on his other side. He cannot fight both."

Nicholas said, "Agree to whatever he asks of you, Khatun. You are right. Another day, the chance may occur. And meantime, Trebizond will come to no harm. It has never been so strongly defended. Soon, the weather will change, and there will be nothing more for this army to eat, with strong hillmen waiting in shelter to pounce on them. He will not blame you for that."

She said, "I thought you would blame me. You see what I have to do. I may have to do worse. But I see this orderly camp; these well-trained Spahis; the marked and varied abilities of such as Tursun Beg, the Vizier Mahmud and most excellent of all, the Sultan himself. I look at them, and I see that my own son, though greater by far, is not yet ready to govern as they are. In eight years, this man Mehmet has begun to learn what the Emperor David has begun to forget. You will see the Sultan. He and his army will come within the next day and night. And meantime, the Grand Vizier has already sent an envoy to Trebizond." She paused. "You had not heard?"

"No," said the man Nicholas.

"He has sent in the name of the Sultan to call on the Emperor to surrender. A formality, to be sure. But it opens an exchange, and worlds await the result. He has used as spokesman his Greek secretary Thomas Katabolenu, as he used him once to urge the despot Thomas out of Mistra in the Morea. We should have the answer tomorrow. We are only three miles to the south of the Citadel. You will have realised that. It is a little marsh called Skylolimne, Dog Lake. When you wish to return to the Citadel, it will be easy."

"I should like to see the Sultan," said Nicholas.

They didn't stay longer. Later, lying stiff-limbed in darkness, wishing for the great copper cauldrons and scented water of home, Sara Khatun thought of the Sultan, and what she herself had said to him at the start of this journey. "Why tire yourself, my son, for nothing better than Trebizond?"

And he had made the reply that was proper. "Mother: in my hand is the sword of Islam. Without this hardship, I should not deserve the name of Ghazi, and today and tomorrow I should have to cover my face in shame before Allah."

The answer from Trebizond was a rebuff. Tobie, snoring under his sun cloth, awoke in fright as a shadow fell over him, and then found, to his relief, that his lips were shut, and the cause of the shadow was Nicholas, his squirrel tail fluttering and his eyes bright under the brim of his hat. Nicholas addressed him in Turcoman. "You lazy fool: you will be late for the Vizier. How can you snore, while the army suffers an insult? One has returned bearing the words of this little Greek king, who says he will never surrender."

"Maybe he will attack us instead," said someone in the next company, softly jeering.

"I have heard of such an Emperor going to war," said another. "He took his chandeliers and his candles, his dinner tents and his bathing tents and his sleeping tents, his table linen and his writing parchment and his sacred altar and his oils and his wines and his caviare and his sheep and cows and goats for the killing. They carried water-beakers for the chickens on horseback, so it is said."

"When our lord leaves the Sublime Porte, he carries his baggage upon a hundred camels and twice that number of mules and of horses," said another. "He takes his sherbet from a pitcher of silver, and made a gift to an emir last year of a skinned sheep painted red and white with silver rings in its nose and ears. He is a greater man."

"Did I say he was not?" said the first. Tobie rose, and dressed, and filled a canvas bag and took it, alone, to Tursun Beg, who had not recognised the dyed beard of Nicholas and even in daylight would hardly remember, he was sure, one of the many captives on the *Ciaretti*. That the plague symptoms had been his creation, the Turk had no means of knowing. He hoped.

He came back half a day later and found Nicholas rolling dice with five men while something sizzled and smoked on the little grill over his fire trivet. As soon as Nicholas saw him, he finished his game, pocketed the screw of parchment he had won, and came over to help Tobie erect the tent he had brought. Then he returned to skewer the meat on the grill and cheered everyone up by pretending to make Tobie eat it. Finally they both went into the tent with all their possessions, and ate in relative comfort while Nicholas discoursed noisily about nothing. Then, while the camp slept in the heat of the day, Nicholas said in the lowest of voices, "Now. Tell me."

Tobie said, "As we thought."

Nicholas looked at him. Then he sighed, and said, "The wound? The Vizier was pleased with you?"

"He'll ask me to come back. It's infected: it'll need to be treated. And because I'm mute, they talk to each other. It's true: they sent

Katabolenu to Trebizond, and the Emperor sent him back with an absolute refusal to surrender."

"But?"

"But the call for surrender was only a ruse to get Katabolenu into the Palace to collect advice from our treacherous friend there. He has been busy, it seems. The Emperor has been repeatedly told that the White Sheep have deserted and that resistance is hopeless. At the moment, he can't quite believe it, but a letter from Sara Khatun would soon persuade him the Sheep are dead mutton. Next, Mahmud will send to the Palace again, promising compensation and honour if the Basileus packs his children and luggage and leaves. Our treacherous friend has indicated that, with such help from the Vizier, he can persuade the Grand Comnenos to see sense and hand over his empire. The treacherous friend being, as you thought, George Amiroutzes. Great Chancellor, Treasurer, Count Palatine, and the Emperor's closest adviser."

"And second cousin to the Grand Vizier Mahmud. Whose mother was a native of Trebizond. Everyone should have a mother from Trebizond," Nicholas said. "You sit on the fence and other people get the stake up their guts. She'll write the letters, Sara Khatun."

"That was what she meant, last night," Tobie said. "She knew about Amiroutzes. And her niece; and Violante, I suppose." His gaze sharpened. "Did – ?"

"She practically told me, on board ship. But I wasn't sure, until later. I did what I could in the way of counter-advice, but it wasn't enough. I suppose if you can reconcile Greeks with Romans, it isn't a tremendous step to throw in the Prophet as well. After all, Constantinople puts up with a Greek patriarch, and if the heathens can show tolerance, then why shouldn't everybody?"

"I don't know," said Tobie. "It's the mass murder beforehand that puts everyone off."

"Well, George will be all right," Nicholas said. "When does the Sultan come?"

"Tonight or tomorrow morning. Nicholas. Sara Khatun. That was also why she talked of . . . ?"

"Yes. It was also why," Nicholas said.

Tobie looked at him. He said, "What good will it do, seeing the Sultan?"

"I don't know," said Nicholas. "I suppose you could do it all by numbers instead. Let's call it a gesture. And if he makes himself available to be seen, that will be another gesture not to be sniffed at. And the earth will be blessed with another day of your silence. And even with Amiroutzes dripping sense into his ear, the Emperor isn't witless. He has the whole strength of the Great Church at his elbow; and his little heirs reciting their lessons; and the men of his dynasty glaring down from the walls of his chamber. He has Astorre and his own commanders to tell him how strong the City is. When we go back, we can show him exactly why Mahmud wants an early surrender."

"But first, we need another day here," Tobie said. He spoke with resignation. He had made the point before, and didn't expect to be answered. He knew all the arguments. He had heard them, over and over, from Godscalc. All the same, he let the silence stretch on. Then he said, "You'll get marsh-fever. It's the one thing that makes me happy about you, is your marsh-fever."

Chapter 38

THE SULTAN ARRIVED in the cool of the night, in a subdued bustle of sound and the light of many torches. When the sun rose on the little marsh three miles south of Trebizond, all the high ground above was covered with the cooking-fires of the main army, and among the aromatic pines of the highest ridge stood the great pavilions of the Sultan himself, the supreme Emperor, King of Kings, the victor, the winner of trophies, the triumphant, the invincible: by the will of God, Mehmet the Fortunate.

"He drinks," said Tobie. "Oh, *Christ*, if you make that joke again about camels . . ."

"Don't underrate camels," Nicholas said. "Mohammed was the son of a camel-driver. Good Arabs want to die on their camels and go to the grave wrapped in their camelskins. Then comes Paradise, everlasting delight of the senses; and absolutely no dissatisfied customers. I like your vest."

The gift of a fur-lined vest had arrived from the Grand Vizier Mahmud, with a message summoning the doctor Ilyas with his spokesman to the Sultan's tent three hours before noon. Tobie said, "If you're nervous, how d'you think I feel?" This time, they had part-cooked the liver and, gagging, he was about to put it into his mouth, with the cage that kept his tongue down. His hat was melon-shaped, with a small upturned brim. He felt like an idiot. Nicholas seemed quite at home in his own hairy headgear topped by the agile whisk of his squirrel. Between that and his newly daubed beard, his face had a watchful look as he moved about, dressing. Tobie began again. "They say he rides between two lines of archers, one right-handed, one left-handed. That way, they don't show him their backs when they shoot people. If I dropped dead on my camel this moment, you wouldn't notice it, would you?"

Nicholas twisted his sash round his tunic and tied it, and sat down to pull on his boots. After the second one, he said, "I should. Your tongue would fall out." Tobie wondered what, in the interval, his mind had been dealing with. A lot, he hoped. It was Nicholas, the non-mute, who was going to bear the brunt of this interview.

It was the trappings of power rather than the King of Kings himself that overwhelmed those he summoned. First, the many-chambered pavilion of crimson silk turned back with gold and bound with patterned fillets and tassels. The drooping hosts of the banners, and the plumed lines of the guard with their round shields and axes and scimitars. Then the silence within, despite the great crowds standing against each inner wall of the audience tent.

Alone, the Sultan sat in the centre, crosslegged upon round tasselled pillows, with a fan of white ostrich feathers moving slowly in one ringed, short-fingered hand. The bulbous white of his turban was not of the traditional shape, but had been devised by himself to the pattern habitual to scholars. To it had been added an osprey feather in a socket of emerald. His caftan, woven in Bursa, was a maze of stylised flowers: carnations, tulips and roses; and its only ornament was the line of intricate buttons that ran from its throat to its hem. Above it, the beard and moustache were deep brown, and not thick. The eyes, under arched, painted brows, were brown as well, and the nose was the nose of a parrot. A parrot eating a cherry, they said of him, referring to the red, red short lips. The Sultan said, "Speak for your master. Where did he learn his healing?"

The carpet was silk, and embroidered with gold. Tobie kissed it and rose beside Nicholas. Nicholas said, "Lord, my master's uncle lived among Mamelukes. The name of my master is Ilyas."

Behind and to one side of the Sultan was the Grand Vizier, the bandage still on his face, with Tursun Beg and the other secretary beside him. On the other side was the Sultan's personal staff, one supposed. As a boy he had been taught by Ahmet Gürani, a Kurd. Now, they said he had Greeks and Italians about him – Kritovoulos the historian; Kyriakos of Ancona; Maestro Jacopo of Gaeta, his usual physician whom, thank God, Tobie had never met. The Sultan said, "You have cared well for our camels. My surgeon tells me your treatment of our Grand Vizier has also served well. We are pleased to reward you."

The gift was a quiver, banded with gold, with a leopard tail fixed to the filigree. Beside it was a brooch with a ruby in it. Tobie took them both from a cushion, offered silently by a turbanned black boy who stepped back at once. Nicholas said, "Lord, my master thanks you for your infinite generosity, and asks how further he may serve you?" He paused, and said, "The illustrious lady Sara Khatun pays ten aspers a day and our food."

Tobie felt sweat pour down his back. Don't do it to me. Nicholas.

The red lips of the Sultan made a small movement. It might have been a smile. He said, "Indeed, good camel doctors are hard to find. I do not know whether I could match such munificence. Nor do you know what sort of lord you might have. And if your master were to fail, what skills can you offer?"

Nicholas said, "Lord, I am a dealer."

"Who is not?" said the Sultan. "But there is occasion for good men of every race in the world of exchange. We are not against trade and, as you see, when we are pleased, we can be generous. For those who cross us, our justice is equally swift. For them, there are quick punishments, and slow ones. I shall consider your offer, and you will witness what the Gate of the Lord can demand. You may watch us dine."

They kissed the carpet and backed to the cloths of the wall, where they were set to stand in a place of no honour, save that to watch the Sultan eat morning dinner was an honour unparalleled. Tobie pinned the brooch to his chest and stood clutching his quiver. Nicholas said, under his breath, "The black page. He's grown. Doria's present to Mahmud in Constantinople."

They had taken away the Sultan's fan and were spreading sewn towels before him, and laying one over his arm. Dishes came in. Tobie strangled. Nicholas, interpreting correctly, said, "He didn't know us. He only saw us in Modon at night." He stopped talking, because the clatter of tinned copper was ceasing. Every now and then, the Sultan would pick a piece from his dish and throw it to someone. The man in front of Tobie got a gobbet of meat smeared with prunes, and ate it obsequiously. Somewhere, a clerk was reading aloud in Arabic. It sounded learned. Then a long-necked instrument was carried in, and a man took it on his knee and plucked at it with a feather. Buffoons came in, and mutes performing a mime. Pagano Doria came in.

It should not, of course, have seemed shocking. In the recent long, alarming talks between himself and Godscalc, Astorre and Nicholas, the possible defection of Doria had been the first topic. Doria needed a patron, and would choose before long. Now his choice was apparent.

The risk to themselves they had discussed also. Well disguised, in a camp of this size, they should have no trouble in avoiding Doria. They had hardly expected to find themselves in the same pavilion. But even here, they were safely disposed in the rear, with many ranks of men standing before them. And Pagano Doria was a very short man, though a charming one. They could glimpse him kissing the carpet, and then rising, his hat in his hand. His doublet was satin, his best; and his skin was becomingly flushed and his large eyes were open and sparkling. "Illustrious lord," said Pagano Doria.

Beside Tobie, Nicholas was perfectly still. Tobie wondered what he was thinking. From the beginning, Doria had attacked and teased and frustrated him: from the first meeting with Godscalc at Porto Pisano to the little scheme to discredit Julius before the Medici. Then, growing in virulence, the other sallies had followed. The fire on the galley at Modon. The betrayal of Julius and John. The deliberate onslaught against Nicholas at the Vavuk pass and the attempt at the Tzycanisterion. Since then there had been others, of which Nicholas had said almost nothing.

And yet, in return, Nicholas had not tried to kill Doria, or even to injure him. He had merely done what he had done before, to those he found inconvenient. He had ruined him, completely and thoroughly; so that he was present now, suing the Sultan. In Modon, confronting a weeping, inarticulate man, Tobie had thought that nothing would stop Nicholas from obliterating this useless, conscienceless hedonist, who had seduced a child for the sake of her inheritance. Only subsequently had he seen that to Nicholas, Doria was negligible. Nicholas understood him. In an odd way, he and Doria had much in common. It was the directing presence of Simon that Nicholas had found insupportable.

So what, now, did he think, watching Doria the traitor? Doria, who must have arrived after dawn and already made his presence known, for the Sultan was saying, "We have taken note of the message you sent, and of the meeting you have had with our Vizier. You know that a further communication was carried this morning to the tekvour of Trebizond?"

"To the Emp – Yes, illustrious lord," said Pagano Doria.

"One will read you its terms," said the Sultan. He balanced a sliver of peach and began, with red lips and tongue, to consult it. His teeth were ill-shaped and white. The same clerk's voice began to intone, in bad Greek.

To the Emperor of Trebizond of the Imperial Family of the Hellenes. Mehmet the Great King declares: You see how great a distance I have travelled to invest this your territory. If you now surrender your capital, I shall present you with lands, as I did Demetrius, prince of Morea, on whom I bestowed riches, islands and the beautiful city of Aenos. He is now living at peace, and is happy. But if you do not, know that annihilation faces your city. For I will not leave until I have levelled the walls and killed all who live there, with ignominy.

The voice ceased. The Sultan said. "And you, master Genoese consul, were in the City when my envoy arrived? How was this received?"

"With cries, my lord; and expressions of fear and of grief, and supplications for mercy."

"It became known to the people?"

"Immediately," said Pagano Doria. "I fear, before the Emperor himself had so much as heard the words of your secretary."

"And the Emperor?"

"Was shaken by your lordship's dread name. His advisers have already told him resistance is useless, and your message confirmed it. He is preparing his answer."

"Which will say?"

"Who but his closest advisers could tell? But it is known that the letters, the further letters promising safety from the mother of the Emperor's nephew have greatly affected him. He is thought to be framing a reply that will offer your illustrious lordship all your lordship desires. He will relinquish his empire. He will ask your lordship to take in marriage his younger daughter, an exquisite virgin called Anna."

Nicholas flushed, and Tobie straightened. Without looking, he felt for the other man's arm and closed around it the grip that could draw teeth from camels. Without speaking, he held it.

"Perhaps," said the Sultan. He dispatched the peach, without interest.

Doria said, "Or there is a charming child Alexios. A nephew. Who has a beautiful mother." Tobie tightened his grasp.

"Perhaps," said the Sultan again. He dipped his hands in a bowl. It was gold, rimmed with rubies. "You spoke of arms?"

Doria's face, already bright, brightened further. He was happy to speak further of arms. He was ready and willing to give a detailed report of the arms he had brought with him from Flanders: their type, their number, their quality. His Turkish was almost as good as his Greek.

"And you wish us to have them. A gift," said the Sultan.

"Naturally," Doria said, smiling still. "Who else could be worthy?"

"You have buried them outside the walls, Mahmud tells me. And since, in these dangerous times, it might be unwise for you to return now to Trebizond, you would not object to our sending ourselves to recover them? By the time they are here you will be free to go where you wish. If we do not possess the City by then, our entry cannot be long deferred. This is agreeable?"

"My lord!" said Doria; and kissed the carpet with rapture.

"It is well. Tursun Beg will find quarters for you. You will hear from us. I do not stint, as others have learned today, when I am satisfied. You may leave. And our other guests. We would sleep."

In their own tent, Tobie said, "Keep your voice down. We knew he would probably do this. It doesn't make any difference."

"*Anna!*" Nicholas said; and Tobie realised, yet again, that the issue was not Pagano Doria.

Tobie said, "I don't believe what Doria was saying. I don't believe the Emperor would talk about total surrender, even with Amiroutzes beside him. Don't you think Doria would tell any tale to ingratiate himself with the Sultan? He can't fetch the armour himself, but he can tell the Sultan where the Spahis can dig for it. They won't pay him, perhaps, but he'll get what he wants. Exclusive trading rights under the Sultan."

"Or fur-lined small clothes," said Nicholas. He was beginning to get hold of himself, although his hat still lay where he had thrown it, and his face was drawn and tight.

Tobie said encouragingly, "He'll probably die anyway. We'll probably all die together." He broke off quickly. There was a trampling at the mouth of the tent. He had, however, been whispering. All the same, Nicholas bent and slipped a hand into and out of his saddlebag. The tent flap opened and the handsome black page held a pose in the entrance, keeping the tent flap apart. Below the pristine folds of the turban, his eyes were large and white-ringed and knowing. He said, "There they are."

So Doria's servant had recognised them. Tobie felt tired. After all they had attempted, it seemed a pity that it should end by pure accident. The page had told Mahmud Pasha his master and Mahmud Pasha, too great a man to trouble himself, had probably sent Tursun Beg to deal with the impostors. Tursun Beg, who would recall very well his loss of face at Constantinople. And the ways to die in Islam were many and varied. You were flayed alive; or pulled up on a pulley and dropped on a ganching hook, or beaten to pulp in a mortar. When the tide changed, the Golden Horn was sometimes covered with mats, a floating corpse under each. Someone bent his neck – not very far – and walked into the tent, leaving the page at the door. It was Pagano Doria.

"Messer Doria," said Nicholas politely. His anger had vanished. Indeed, standing at his full and quite considerable height, he was smiling. Tobie was aware of a strong inclination to back from them both. He waited for the Janissaries.

Doria said, "Master Tobias! I have no quarrel with you. A few words with the Florentine consul here: that is all I should like. You remember Noah, of course."

The page had walked forward. Taller, but still little more than a child. Tobie waited, measuring the space for his jump. Doria said, "My knife says you won't do it, Messer Tobias. Or Niccolò dies."

He had Nicholas by the arm, and a blade pressed to his throat. He wondered how Doria could have moved so swiftly; and how Nicholas could have failed to stop him. Doria said, "I fear, dear doctor, that you must allow Noah to bind you. There is rope."

It didn't take long. The little bastard knew how to tie knots, and how to make them hurt. He wasn't gagged. Of course, if he shouted, he would only bring Turks down upon them, to whom Doria would expose them as spies. Tobie wondered why he hadn't brought soldiers with him. He wasn't going to let Nicholas escape, or himself; that was certain.

Before Noah had completed his job, Doria had found the knife in

Nicholas's sash, and slotted it, far out of reach, in the door flap. Then, keeping his own, he stepped back. He was smiling. He said, "It had my name on it, after all. I hope you don't mind. And this, as you will have noticed, is its companion." He turned his head. "Noah?"

Tobie, remorselessly bound, lay on the floor and watched Noah nod and go out. Doria, standing himself just inside the door, said to Nicholas, "Sit. On the ground. Or your doctor is dead. As you both will be, presently. And Sara Khatun, I make no doubt. Noah tells me she has passed you off as her camel doctor."

Nicholas sat, crosslegged as the Sultan had done. He said, "I thought you would bring Tursun Beg."

"Noah has gone to call him," said Doria. There was a chest by the door, and he sat on it. He said, "I never enjoyed a game more. I wanted to tell you so. I never dreamed you would get those soldiers to Trebizond. The plague scare: it was genius. You seduced Violante – you! How? Peasant crudities she had never enjoyed? You stole my silver. You pre-empted all my purchases at Erzerum and had them sent through to Bursa, leaving me bankrupt. Catherine didn't like that. I blame you for the change in Catherine. Oh, yes: I feel I owe you something for that. And you were so active! Transporting the Empress to Georgia! It might have got you the thanks of a nation, but of course it resulted in nothing. Like the trick with the mule-train which took your silk into the Citadel. I shall get it now," said Pagano Doria. "And the galley, wherever she is. You made a lot of mistakes."

"Did I?" said Nicholas. He sat, a hand on each foot. He looked puzzled.

"Well, your man Julius," Doria said. "You lost him at Vavuk. You failed to do anything for the Venetians. They'll lose all their stock, and the Signory will have no good opinion of the merchant adventurers of the Charetty company, not to mention the lady Violante and her husband. I shall have to make the company's peace with them."

"Once you've found Catherine," Nicholas said. "You can't get the Charetty without her."

"That is true," said Doria cheerfully. "But your colleagues will help. I feel sure of it. They're only human, after all, and Turks excel in obtaining answers to questions. I shall have to go to Bruges, and Louvain. Your wife ought to retire. Twice a widow, what is there left but a convent where she can take up embroidery, and watch men's affairs from her window? Catherine will take care of her sister, and I shall keep Catherine content with many children. Heirs to the Charetty business. You should be pleased. An infusion of superior blood."

"And Simon?" said Nicholas.

Pagano Doria smiled. "There are rich pickings for others round the fringe of a feud. You didn't realise that? Two men who dislike each other never notice the third on their backs. Simon will be no trouble to me. With the fortune I shall have made, I shall pay him some small profit and be done with him. Money was never his motive: just to rid himself of you. As yours was to rid yourself of him, and continue to stand well with your wife. You complained over your poor little stepdaughter, but you did nothing, did you, until you were forced to? I've enjoyed watching you," said Pagano Doria. "But really, you were in want of experience."

"You did your best," Nicholas said. He spoke in pure Tuscan now, and very clearly. "All those bath boys, of assorted sizes and colours. Violante. I forget what else. Do you remember their faces? Does one ever mean more to you than another? Can you simulate well enough to attach them to you? I should have found it hard."

"Their faces?" said Doria, and laughed. "What do you want me to say: that lovers don't change, or grow tedious? Women cling. Bath boys grow into shaved men with thick voices. I take my pleasure. I leave it, and go to pick other flowers. Where there is money, I can exercise patience. I shall keep Catherine. Unless she becomes insupportable, I shall keep her. But even money," said Pagano Doria, "is not everything. A calf is one thing; a cow is another. From that point of view, I have saved you some trouble. You won't die from disgust in your bed, or killed because of your infidelities. Although I fear they are hard on spies here. It's a pity."

"I must point out," Nicholas said, "that you are here as well."

"As a merchant," Doria said. "That is the difference. The market-place changes hands: the wise man transfers his business to the new owner. Bringing, if he is lucky, some goodwill; an offer of friendship."

"Tobie cured his camel," Nicholas said.

Doria stared, and then laughed. "You're not a coward. But of course, you're here as a spy. You're in disguise, and the White Sheep have sponsored you. Violante's doing, I suppose. And Sára Khatun's. She saw the end of Trebizond coming, as you did; and planned to leave you as her spy with the Sultan. She is old. She may not pay the ultimate penalty. But the Charetty company will be in other hands soon. I don't suppose," said Pagano Doria, "that the Sultan pays much attention to powers of attorney."

"You assume the Emperor will give up?"

"Of course," said Doria. "Didn't you believe what you heard? The Emperor has already replied, most unwisely. Surrender, of course, and the girl Anna to wife. I hope the Sultan isn't really expecting a beauty. But impossible terms, couched in the most imperious manner. The Emperor expects this kind of settlement, and will accept nothing less than that value of property. Amiroutzes would never have advised such an answer. The Sultan was almost provoked into storming the place in his anger, till that clever lady Sara set herself to pacify him."

"He couldn't have stormed it," Nicholas said. "Unless George Amiroutzes has imprisoned all the defenders."

"You're thinking of your captain Astorre," said Doria fondly. "No. Of course, George would do nothing that would damage his public reputation. Indeed, rumour has it that he's had to offer a hostage to Mehmet. He has chosen his younger, less intelligent son, the godson of Cardinal Bessarion. Basil will, of course, cling to his faith despite torture, and the cardinal will hasten to ransom him. Is there anything else you wanted to know? You will have to talk quickly."

Tobie, too, had heard the tramp of approaching feet, and the jingle of metal. He thought of all the things that Nicholas had not been able to say; and wondered if he could have found the hardihood to remain silent. Not to proclaim that Julius was safe, with goods and galley waiting at Kerasous; for Doria would rush with the news to the Sultan. Not to deny that they were spies of Uzum Hasan, for it wouldn't help the Khatun, who had acknowledged them. Doria blamed him for the wreck of his marriage. But, prevented by Godscalc, Nicholas had left Catherine alone until she herself had asked for asylum.

The search for Catherine, he was sure, would be ugly. He only hoped Godscalc and the rest would escape what was threatened. It had long been agreed what should happen if he and Nicholas failed to return. The sailing date had already been passed on to Julius. No matter what happens: no matter who comes or does not come, set out for home by the eighteenth day of August.

It was the fourteenth today. Four short days. If he were a praying man, he would pray the others got to Kerasous before the ship left. And home to Bruges, to tell the demoiselle her young husband was dead, and warn her of what was now coming. For what had happened last year would be as nothing to this.

The booted feet stopped outside the tent, and Noah drew the flap once more aside. Nicholas rose. Between the dyed hair and the beard his face was pale and quite composed, as it always was in extremity. The page Noah stepped inside the door, ignoring Tobie, and like a talking bird with only one phrase announced, "There he is."

There were Janissaries, five of them, who strode forward. There was also not only Tursun Beg, but the Grand Vizier Mahmud his master, the wound on his nose and his lip inflamed but healing. The Janissaries seized Pagano Doria by the arms. The Grand Vizier said, "You have lied. There are no arms where you said they were buried; and when our men went to lift them, they were ambushed and killed every one, save for the man who escaped to inform us. Take him away."

It was as if lightning had struck. On the floor, Tobie let his head drop suddenly back. A great pain seized his bowels, and he squeezed his eyes shut and then opened them quickly, although they were wet. The pain died down, but his face pricked hot and cold as if blistered.

Nicholas had also flushed. He stood, breathing fast, and Tobie saw a tremor had begun in his hands. But there was no surprise on his face.

Of course, there wouldn't be. *He makes a wicked enemy*, he remembered saying to John. Of his innocence, Pagano Doria had assumed Nicholas and himself to be two of a kind. Perhaps they were. But of the two, Pagano Doria was the novice.

Doria himself had not fully understood yet. Dwarfed by the soldiers who held him, he tugged indignantly against their grasp: handsome, finely arrayed and princely, despite the loss of his costly straw hat. He said, "Is this how great men dispense justice? Mahmud Pasha relies on the word of a secretary? His fools make some mistake, and you allow them to come and lay hands on me?" Below the swathe of dark and satiny hair, a little disordered, the well-marked brows were drawn in brilliant anger.

The Grand Vizier spoke. "I am here on the lord Sultan's own orders."

"Then you and he have been misled by others," said Doria curtly. "I shall discuss it with him, if you like. But I will not be held like a felon." And, opening his powerful shoulders, he half tore himself from the men who were holding him. They overmastered him immediately, although you could see he put out all his strength to prevent them. He had a beautiful, well-balanced body, and he knew how to use it. In more ways than one, Tobie thought. He saw the Pasha's face, watching him.

But behind the Pasha was the sovereignty of the Sultan. The Grand Vizier said, "My lord the Sultan will not see you. The case is proved. You alone knew the hiding place of the arms. This you told us. You alone, therefore, instigated the killing."

"I alone?" Doria said. He spoke slowly as, at last, he took thought, and began to understand everything. Now he stood without struggling, and his high violent colour withdrew, except over his cheekbones. His lashes flickered and lifted. This time, he looked straight at Nicholas. And Nicholas, with his dyed beard and coarse clothes and eyes bright as diamonds, looked back at Doria and smiled.

Tobie saw it, disbelieving. The last thing – the very last thing – they wanted was to admit knowing Doria. And then, sickened, he realised what he should have seen all along. Of course, it was not only Doria who would suffer from this act of duplicity. With a tongue in his head, Doria could explain that Tobie, also, possessed this facility, and expose Nicholas as an impostor. He could denounce them as spies, however little good it would do his own case. For, of course, there was no proof that Doria and they were not in the same conspiracy. Doria knew who they were, and had told neither the Sultan nor Mahmud. No. Doria wouldn't escape. But neither would they.

Nicholas, he saw, had stopped trembling, now the moment had

come. Between beard and cap his skin had a pinched look, but his gaze
was quite steady. He was looking at Noah. Then he turned his eyes,
but not towards Tobie. Doria said, "Allow me to speak, Mahmud
Pasha. One person did know where the arms were hidden. It was
known to my wife. I see she did not keep the news to herself. I know
who received it, and who laid the ambush."

"No doubt you will put the blame on someone," the Grand Vizier
said. "But what can you prove? Take him away."

Pagano Doria spoke softly. "I can prove it here and now. And your
own page will confirm it." He turned his head, seeking the boy. And
already, the page had stepped forward.

Noah came to his side, walking with the grace Doria must have
taught him; looking at him with the luminous eyes one remembered,
from Florence; from Modon. Then the look changed. "My lord
Vizier," said Noah, "he is troubling you." And lifting a dagger, drove
it into Doria's muscular neck.

Tobie shouted. It emerged as a whisper. Nicholas made no sound at
all. Doria's hands lifted as the Janissaries slackened their grip: on his
face was a look of pure astonishment, which gave way to perplexity.
When he fell, they hardly managed to grasp him, in their surprise.
Then they laid him on the floor of the tent, and Tursun Beg,
frowning, bent over him. The secretary said, "He is dead. Or dying.
The Sultan will – "

"The Sultan will make no objections," said the Grand Vizier drily.
To the page, he said aside, "Child! Child! What were you thinking
of?" But he did not sound much displeased. He had not seen, as
Tobie had, the love, the hate, the anguish in Noah's eyes.

Nicholas had. Tobie watched him as he stared down at Doria's
body, its elegance marred by the blood soaking into his doublet and
pooling the floor. His head was turned sideways and his eyes were
open, looking from one face to another. He tried to speak, but only
scarlet bubbles burst from his throat. Nicholas lifted his eyes to where
Noah stood. It seemed to Tobie that there passed an unspoken
question. If so, there was no spoken reply. In the pretty, dark face
there was no vestige now of love or of anguish: only the bitterest
pride. Noah turned on his heel and, bearing himself like a king, took
his place beside Mahmud his master. And Pagano Doria, dying,
turned his eyes up to Nicholas and smiled suddenly, triumphantly,
full in his face.

By then Tobie, freed, was bending over him, however uselessly. He
knelt back slowly, and spoke with his hands. "No. He is going." No
one had questioned that Doria had been attempting to threaten them.
The Turks would assume, he supposed, Doria had betrayed himself
in some way, and feared he would be exposed. There was no one
except Noah to tell them the truth. And Noah had chosen his part.

Nicholas stood at Doria's side, without moving. Tursun Beg bent over and picked up the bloodied dagger and said, "It is curious. This is the merchant's own knife, with his name on it. And here is another strapped to his person, just like it."

"You say?" said Mahmud Pasha. "Then it should be given to friend Ayyub for the protection of his master the doctor. We are, it seems, to lose our two guests. There is camel sickness in the south, and the lady Sara Khatun has begged that these men might return to the tribe. The Sultan, in his clemency, has released them."

Doria's throat whistled. He had heard. He probably heard, Tobie thought, all that was happening, but of course was unable to speak. Witness at his own deathbed. Silent; unable to denounce, or to charm. Presently the Grand Vizier nodded and left; and Tursun Beg with the Janissaries followed him. Tobie bowed, and remained where he was, standing still. When the last spectator had gone, Nicholas changed position abruptly and, moving forward, sank to crouch at the dying man's side.

He stayed there till the end, his eyes on Doria, and Doria's on him, with only Tobie to watch them. Tobie and a dark unspeaking shadow behind him. Three strange companions for a roving sea prince with the world at his feet. Yet although Doria owed them his death, it seemed to Tobie that, at the end, he drew comfort from them.

By early afternoon, the camel doctor and his help had left the Sultan's encampment. The public leave-taking had been vigorous if one-sided; and the private one in the princess's tent had been brief. She said, "You saw, then, what you came to see. Nothing could have altered this outcome."

Nicholas said, "Your niece is a princess of Trebizond. So was your late husband's mother."

Today, Sara Khatun showed her age; and the lines under her eyes were almost as deep as the kohl. She said, "John Comnenos said to my son, 'Be my ally.' And my son Uzum Hasan said, 'I shall be, for payment of this land and your niece as my bride.' The Sultan has the land, and the Emperor David may have back his niece if he wishes. You think that, without me and without George Amiroutzes, the Emperor would have acted any differently?"

There was a long silence. Then Nicholas said, "No."

"No," she agreed. "You have come far, for an apprentice; but you are not yet of the quality to force an emperor to your will. For a while, perhaps, you even thought that you were. It is as well to learn these things young. Now you have your men to look to."

"I shall do that," said Nicholas.

He made no excuses. Perhaps because of it, the Khatun's gaze softened. She said, "If you never strive, you will never be injured. This will pass. If I and others like me had not weighed your merits, we should not have done what we have done. You will return a rich man, and lay at your wife's feet what is even greater than wealth; your respect and your loyalty. I envy her. You will go now."

They left, riding south, and as soon as was safe, took the arc that would bring them round to Trebizond, where Astorre would be waiting. They rode a long time in silence; broken once only by Tobie. He said, "Catherine."

"There now, I'd forgotten," said Nicholas. "We ought to offer her to the Sultan. He'd get the fright of his life."

After that, with a doctor's experience, Tobie left him alone.

Chapter 39

THE PRIEST GODSCALC had watched Nicholas and Tobie leave with no expectation that they would live to return from the Grand Vizier's camp. As time passed, the certainty grew. A hundred miles to the west, Julius would sail homewards on Tuesday from Kerasous. Saturday was the last day he and Astorre could lead the others from Trebizond and still hope to catch him. When Friday dawned with no word, he thought Nicholas lost, and Tobie with him.

If the thought struck Astorre, he was too occupied to devote any time to it. In any case, as a soldier, he was used to the demands of war, and its vagaries. There were no other senior members of the company left with which the priest could share his fears, so he kept them to himself. So far as the world and the Emperor were concerned, Nicholas had been struck with fever once more, and Tobie was tending him.

When, that Friday, they both found their way back, worn and filthy and silent, the priest found his composure overturned. It was Loppe who looked after their needs, and Loppe who reminded him, with a look, that the giving of news ought to wait. But time was short, and they themselves were as conscious of it as anyone. It was Nicholas, first, who told of the forthcoming surrender and Tobie who took Godscalc aside and informed him of the killing of Doria. He told his story in full, as John le Grant once had done on a different occasion, and for the same reason. And, interpreting it, Godscalc was silent.

Then, it was wholly a matter of putting into effect, with speed, their plans to abandon their station. This time, at their one, hasty conference, there was no resistance from Astorre. He listened grimly to the tale of betrayal and weakness and then, rising, picked something up and snapped it in two on his knee. It was the bâton of command the Emperor had presented him with. He flung the pieces away, and the broken gold rang on the floor. He said, "I don't serve under Turks. Or under cowards."

"There will be no fighting," Nicholas said. "Only occupation after surrender, and death for you and your men. If you had argued with me, I would have cut off your leg if I had to."

Astorre's beard jutted. "That wasn't the tale after Erzerum. We all had a choice."

"No, you didn't," Nicholas said. "I only made it seem that you had."

After that, they hardly saw each other as they made their fast, well-rehearsed moves; men of purpose traversing the turbulent city; closing their minds to all but the immediate task, for all the arguments were long ago over. Late on Friday, they received permission for the one formality for which they had to make time; and, without waiting longer, paid their last call at the Palace. As on the first occasion, Nicholas was the principal; but this time Godscalc entered with him, and Astorre and his men escorted them both, glittering in a fierce perfection of drill that was a denunciation in metal.

Inside, they saw no sign of Amiroutzes, or of the boys, or the women. They received their audience before men brittle and smiling with fear. The latrine smell of fear clung to the red onyx columns and the coloured glass plaques and the gold reliefs of the wainscotting, and stifled the odour of fruit, and musk, and incense. It showed itself in the half-packed chests; the litter; the whisperings.

Godscalc knew that it presaged the collapse of all order that came with surrender: the ill-cooked food from deserted kitchens; the crumpled clothes handed by servants with little to hope for, and young of their own to be frightened about. The uneasy prayers of the churchmen: resented, badgered, importuned. The shifting of positions between the high officials, hovering between old masters and new; and the small disappearances: of goblets and ivories, dishes and ikons. And pressing outside, and ignored, the vast, stinking compression of anger, of fear, of despair that was the last anyone would see of the people of Trebizond, trapped behind the walls they had been roused, with gaiety and courage, to defend.

But one must think of the immediate task. The arguments were long over.

The Emperor received them in a robe of state. Serious, pink-fleshed, golden, imperial, he looked as he always looked. It was only now, in the late summer daylight, in the full light of what he was doing, that you saw how he was painted and waxed, artificial as the frescoes about him. When neither Nicholas nor Godscalc performed the Prostration, he checked, but gave no other sign of displeasure. He spoke the few necessary words in measured Greek to his Florentine consul. To save the lives of his people, he had decided to sacrifice his well-being and open his gates. An enlightened man, the Sultan Mehmet had promised wise rule and free worship, as he had given already to the Greeks now in Constantinople. But there was, of course, no further need for the consul's armed troops to protect him.

He thanked the company for its services, and released them formally, and with honour, from completing their contract. A letter had been drawn up indemnifying them.

The letter, hastily written, was passed across. The Emperor's attention was already wandering. His indifference was undoubtedly genuine. Foreign merchants meant nothing whatever to him or his future. It was Nicholas, level-voiced and persistent, who raised the question of the Latin families still in the City, and received the Emperor's agreement that such households might leave, although, as everyone knew, the Sultan exacted no penalties from merchants where no resistance was offered. The Emperor had heard of the death of the Genoese consul. The shipmaster Crackbene had permission to remove such Genoese as might wish to leave Trebizond for the moment. The Basileus trusted that Messer Niccolò was content. He allowed Messer Niccolò and Father Godscalc to bow, instead of kissing his foot, and had brought forward for each a small personal gift, which each politely refused. As they backed out, they saw him biting his fingernails.

"You should have taken it," Tobie said when they told him. "You could have pushed it down a Turk's throat." It was the only comment anyone made, and all there was time for. They got the gear of the round ship, and took it down to the Genoese house, to which Nicholas had already pushed his way, through the disordered city, and found Doria's sailing-master Crackbene ready and willing to join forces and help put to sea. He knew, too, that his employer was dead, but showed no inclination to mourn him. His attitude was clearly that of Astorre. He was a practical man.

He saw a difficulty, therefore, in their plan. The cog was anchored at sea, and her living cargo and gear were all inside the City. How did the Florentine consul propose to unite the one with the other across a shore occupied by the Turks?

"By becoming Turks," Nicholas said. "It's easy. You need a big, black moustache and an enlightened and liberal nature."

Crackbene started to smile, and then stopped as the other man turned.

Nicholas said, "It wasn't a joke. We're going to dress up as Turks and act as if we've just been dispatched by the Sultan. We have orders to rig the Genoese cog, and sail it through to the fleet at Gallipoli."

"You'll never do it," said Crackbene.

"We might," Nicholas said. "You haven't looked over the walls. They're all drunk outside, and beating drums and letting off crackers. They've just heard the news of the surrender."

"You'll still never do it," said Crackbene. "What about Turkish clothes?"

"Oh," Nicholas said. "That's the easy part."

*

At Kerasous, a hundred miles to the west, the rest of the Charetty company waited, and watched the days go by as anxiously as Godscalc had done; for their orders were clear. Whether Nicholas reached them from Trebizond or not, the eighteenth day of August was when they must sail.

For Catherine de Charetty negli Doria, the days of August dragged as never before. To waste six weeks of her married life in Kerasous had not been her intention, when agreeing to take part in a ball game. To begin with, the game itself had been shameful. Far from competing to claim her, Pagano and her mother's husband had conspired to make her look foolish. The subsequent journey by camel had been hardly less humiliating. She had made it clear to her mother's accountant as soon as she arrived at Kerasous, her trembling dog in her arms. The camel was to be sold.

Matters did not improve. A Doria by marrige, a Charetty by blood, she expected to be housed on the hill in the governor's palace, with Master Julius and this man John le Grant to do what she wanted. Instead, she found herself crammed into cellars with a terrified crowd of Italian women and children while, apparently, the entire Turkish fleet passed their shores. From the women, whom she despised, she learned to her amazement that they had come to Kerasous on the *Ciaretti*, her mother's galley. And that the galley was here, lifted out of the water and put on rollers, and hidden somewhere on land. On an island, they told her.

It didn't take her long after that to discover, stored in the Kerasous citadel, the entire cargo of the *Ciaretti*, brought by Master Julius from Erzerum. There were Venetian goods too. There were bits that the *Ciaretti* had picked up in Trebizond, including books and jewels and dyes: all the sorts of dyes that she had expected Pagano to buy. She saw a keg of pearls that she recognised. Nicholas had got it all. He had got everything Pagano ought to have purchased, and he was not even a Charetty. And he'd managed to evacuate all the Venetian women and children as well.

It was a matchless performance and she failed to see, now, how Pagano could equal it. When she ached for him nightly, she reminded herself how incompetent he had proved; how Nicholas had outmanoeuvred him. And still, day by day, she looked for him to arrive: to put these sneering Venetians to the sword; to load their goods and hers into his cog and say, "Come. I am the greatest sea prince of Europe, and you are my lady." Then common sense would prevail and she would grit her teeth and press her nails into her hands. For if he could manage only a quarter of that – less than a quarter – she would manage the rest. Anything. Anything so that her mother's friends would stand back in awe and say, "Our little Catherine! Such a marriage! Such a husband! Such a fortune!"

Then the day came when a great Turkish cog slowly broke through the mists from the east and instead of keeping its course, as did all the ships, captured and free, that came by on the way to Stamboul, began to turn towards Kerasous. Then the guns ran out on the citadel and the shore, and the strange sounds began that had frightened off more than one ship in the past; and Master Julius, and Master John, when she spoke to them, threw her a word over their shoulders but explained nothing. Until, almost opposite the precious island, and with her mainsail torn by a ball, the crescent flag had suddenly slid down the mast and another replaced it. She had been standing, at that moment, on the ramparts of the citadel, and had found herself abruptly in someone's embrace. Master Julius said, "They've come. They've come." And she saw that he was crying.

Then she said, with dawning delight, "It's the *Doria*! Pagano's ship! It's Pagano!" And Master Julius had dropped his arm and said, "It was his ship, Catherine, but we don't know what's happened to it since. Don't worry. Stay here. I'll send you news as soon as I have it."

Despite that, she had run down after him to the gates, Willequin at her heels; and would have fled down the slope to the shore except that the notary – her mother's notary! – had snapped a command and some men, kindly enough, had stopped her, and caught her hands when she scratched, and escorted her back to the women. The Venetian women, who tried to patronise her. She found a bed and flung herself on it, and waited; while the dog lay on the floor and panted, and looked at her. When Pagano came, he would send them all packing.

Then the door was darkened and she sat up; and then turned away, because it was someone much taller than Pagano. He said, "She's here. Let me speak to her." And another voice said, "No. It is for me."

The second voice was that of her mother's apprentice. Her mother's husband. She turned in the bed, and saw it was Nicholas, standing over her as he had done at Pera five months before. Then, avoiding Willequin, he drew up a stool, and sat, and said, "Catherine? I have bad news."

Of course, she knew what it was. The governor had been in a frenzy for weeks. The Turks were besieging Trebizond from the sea, and the Sultan was marching his army round behind through the mountains. Once they met, no one in Trebizond could get out this year, and Master Julius and John le Grant were going to sail home without them. Nicholas, with all his money, had probably bribed his way out. And the horse-eating German, whose voice she had heard. And Pagano had been forced to bring them from Trebizond with him, because his little endeavour had failed, and he'd not been able to think up another. But that didn't matter. She had a dozen plans. She said, "The Turks have taken Trebizond?"

Nicholas said, "They will have it by now. Catherine: Pagano is dead."

She frowned. He could hardly have been as stupid as that. Then she realised what it was. She said with fury, "You killed him!"

"No," Nicholas said. "He was killed by the enemy side. He was carrying messages to the Osmanli, and someone killed him. He died bravely, Catherine."

He had a black beard, which made his skin look unnaturally stark. She said slowly, "Pagano, somebody's courier? No. He went to promise them arms, and you let him. I told you where the arms were, and you took them. When they found they were gone, then they killed him. You killed him." Her nails ached in the sheets. She said, "You sat safe in Trebizond and let him go to his death."

From the door, Godscalc said, "Nicholas. The truth would be better."

Nicholas got up. "Tell it, then," he said; and walked out.

The priest said, "Get up."

Her gown was wrung and rumpled where she had been lying, and her hair had fallen where she had dragged off her cap. She still had her earrings, and her gown was silk taffeta, and her mother employed this man, and would dismiss him at a word. Catherine stood erect by the bed and said, "What can you believe of a servant? My husband is very likely alive and has just beaten him."

"He is dead," said her mother's chaplain. "He went to sell his armour to the Sultan Mehmet; and found Nicholas and Master Tobie in the Sultan's camp; and tried to betray them."

"In the Sultan's camp? Nicholas?" Catherine said. "What was he selling?"

"His skin," said Godscalc. "In exchange for something he needed to know. One day, perhaps he'll explain to you. Meantime, you can be assured that Nicholas did not kill your husband, or cause him to be killed. It was a risk Pagano took when he went to the Sultan. I expect he took it for your sake. He hoped to win favour, and establish himself in Trebizond when all his rivals had gone. For all you may think, he and Nicholas were not bitter opponents, although they stopped at very little, either of them, to win what they wanted. Of the two, it was your husband who didn't mind whom he killed."

"Then who killed Pagano?" said Catherine.

"Someone of the opposite camp. A servant of Mahmud Pasha," said Godscalc. "He thought to please the Grand Vizier. Catherine, you are not alone. The best friend you have in the world is your stepfather."

She sat on the bed and bit her lip, thinking. Then she said, "Where is the armour?"

He didn't answer at once, which annoyed her. Then he said, "It is here, in the citadel. Nicholas has given it to the Imperial garrison."

She stared at him. "Then I see," said Catherine de Charetty, "that I must speak to him. The armour is mine. The round ship is mine. Nicholas has no right to *give* it to anybody. Who is he?"

"He is the man who saved you from Trebizond," said her mother's chaplain. "You will neither speak to him nor will you restrain him in anything that he chooses to do. I told you to stand. Stand. I have something to say to you."

She stood and listened, flushed and shaking with temper at the cruel things he was saying to her: about her disregard for her mother; her self-interest; what he called her *childish lust for sensual pleasure*. She ceased to listen. He was a prig and a bully: a snivelling priest straight from the cloister who would faint from envy if he knew – if he dreamed what a man and a woman did when they were together . . . What they did, over and over, when they were together.

Then her loss came to her, in a hysterical salvo of grief that tore her throat, so that she collapsed on the bed and sat, her eyes closed, her mouth open, and the tears pouring and the mucus streaking her face unregarded. She heard her own voice barking, and Willequin's; and couldn't tell which frenzy was which.

Then the priest put his arms round her, and held her, and spoke to her until she was quiet.

Swifter than that, the story had spread through Kerasous of what Nicholas had done. Nicholas himself, no one could catch: he was up on the hilltop with Astorre, interviewing the governor and the garrison; he was out on the island, talking to John and the monks; he was checking the inventories of the cargo with Julius and Patou; he was on the round ship with Crackbene and watching her beginning to load. He had bought horses, they said, and was designing a place for their stowing. Told about the fate of his camel, he had asked a question or two, and then changed the subject. When next noticed, he was with the clerks checking the provender: the beasts and the biscuit, the water, the fruit and the poultry; the gunpowder and the shot. There were sheds full of bales which he spent a full hour examining. The galley was now in the water and loading. Soon the men and women and children would go.

From Tobie and Godscalc, over a hurried meal, Julius heard what happened before and after the visit to Skylolimne; the little marsh from which Nicholas had not brought back a fever, but, it seemed, the secret of perpetual motion. Of that, too, Godscalc and Tobie bore the marks; or perhaps they were caused by the month-long siege, the other events in the three months since their parting. He heard, but did not at first believe, how they had made their escape. Julius said, "How in God's name did you manage to dress up as Turks?"

"I thought Nicholas told you. The bales the mules brought from Erzerum were filled with Turcoman clothing."

"He said cloths," Julius said. "Padded out to look like raw silk." He was astonished. He said, "Did the old woman arrange it? She would know, in a siege, it was the only way to move people. A supposed squad from the Sultan, with orders to sail the captured ship back to Stamboul. Genius. Genius. No one would question them."

"It wasn't quite without event," Godscalc said. After a bit he said, "We got most of the families out. The Venetian Bailie elected to stay; and some of the Genoese. The round ship seamen all came. And the Genoese women and children. The families from the Venetian compound had left already."

It was John le Grant who had said then, "And Paraskeuas?"

Godscalc said, "Paraskeuas was given the chance. He refused."

"And the other Greeks in Trebizond?" John le Grant had said. He was a persistent man, who asked questions.

"What about the Greeks?" Nicholas had said, coming suddenly into the room. Julius turned, keenly interested. The Nicholas who had landed miraculously at Kerasous from the *Doria* was not the battered comrade he had left in May on the road from Erzerum. He was longing to examine the change. He watched his immense former servant lean over, raiding the table and, with bread and meat in one hand, pause beside John le Grant. "Deaf?" he said.

John le Grant said, "No. Nothing. Idle curiosity. I thought I saw a few Greeks get off your ship."

"They had friends in Kerasous. Officially, we didn't bring any. How do you suppose we'd choose which to take? Hold a lottery?" He propped his shoulder against the wall and watched the other man, the bread still in his hand.

"You could have earned a tidy sum," said John le Grant. "If we hadn't disabled his ship, Doria would have got a load of people out to Caffa that time."

"I thought you were all against it," said Nicholas.

"Oh, I was. I'm still against it. If you'd sailed off to Caffa, you'd have been stuck in the Crimea all winter, if not for years. Tartars, Genoese, and terrible weather. Tobie wouldn't like that. And you'd not have room for a cargo."

"That, of course, was the worry," Nicholas said. "On the other hand, Greeks are human like everyone else, and one must consider such things, or seem to consider such things, with Godscalc about."

"You tossed a coin," said John le Grant. Julius shifted in his seat.

"You guessed," said Nicholas. He and le Grant gazed at one another. Nicholas said, "Perhaps you would have loaded the cog with whoever you thought you could take, choosing the richest, or the weakest, or the ones that survived the mayhem that would happen when you announced you were going. My view was different. You know what the Emperor sold himself for? Vice-Regent of Christ, Servitor to the Incarnate God? His daughter Anna, and a home in Turkish Adrianople, plus a yearly income of three hundred thousand pieces of silver. You might say, mightn't you, that those who sustain such an emperor deserve such an emperor; or they would have risen against him? And if they didn't they might as well sink."

"Adrianople," said John le Grant. "I wouldn't have chosen Adrianople. Too near the new owners. If someone bought out my company, I'd go and settle a long way away from the competition."

Nicholas said, "I don't think he plans to set up again in the emperor business." The moment's violence had faded. He said, "You are a bastard."

"They tell me," said le Grant. "You were saying?"

Nicholas stood where he was. Then he came and sat down, his hands on the table still holding the bread and the meat. He said, "We tried to take them. They wouldn't come. We were Latins. Caffa is Genoese. They would rather have the Turks."

Julius felt his face flush; and found Godscalc looking at him. Tobie was scowling. John said, "And so much for the Council of Florence and the union of churches. Man, I'm glad I was at Kerasous all the time, without any of these terrible questions to answer that stop you eating your dinner. If you don't want it, I could do with some bread."

And Nicholas had said, "Get your own God-damned bread," and begun to eat.

After that, now and then, he looked more like himself and Julius began to have hopes of a reasonable voyage, provided they got past the guns in the Bosphorus, and the guns at Constantinople, and the guns at Gallipoli, and managed to eke out their stores until Modon. They could be in Venice by October. Well, by mid-October. He gave little more thought to the conversation, beyond wondering why John had chosen that day to attack Nicholas. After three months of John le Grant's company, Julius still found him impenetrable.

On 18 August, as planned, they set sail. First the round ship, flamboyant with Turkish flags and seamen in Turkish turbans and jackets. Next, grappled fast as her prisoner, the Florentine galley with no flags but two ranks of oarsmen, apparent captives, to help her along. They were given a guard of honour at the shore; and on the island of Ares, sacred to the Greek god of war, the monks who had kept their secret so long stood and waved to them.

It was like the leave-taking Trebizond had denied them. There they had steered out among Turkish ships anchored at random; breaking out their sail with Turkish commands. Then, no one looked back to the shore. No one tried to pick out the white-blotted walls of St Eugenios, or the blackened shell of the fondaco, or the ruined square of the Meidan, or the bare pole of the Palace where no banners flew.

Now, although both ships were silent, there was leisure to turn back and look at Kerasous, city of cherries; and the hill of the citadel, with the steep, leafy foothills behind it, and the mountains beyond. As always, there had been rain; and the painted churches and white, flat-roofed houses, the gardens and orchards were glistening and misted with heat. Over the water, instead of the piercing notes of spring blossom came the darker scents of ripening fruit. Already the wild vines were heavy and bearing; and the hazelnuts were bearding the bushes. Autumn was coming.

Soon, in a normal year, dancing feet would beat out the grapes for the black wine, and the nuts would be spread on the beach; and the cranes would come flying, and the air above the Zigana pass would turn black with migrating quail. In a normal year, there would be festival before the autumn storms closed the seas; and festival after it, when the land would be left to its own until the spring came, and brought the ships once again.

This year, it would be different. Nothing would be normal this year, unless the garrison high on the hill, where the citadel glittered, managed to hold out until winter. They were well led and well provisioned, and they had extra arms now, and good armour to help them. From the sea, Nicholas saluted them with his guns; and they answered. Then they became small and dim in the mist, and the next headland hid them from view.

The Black Sea was empty. It was more than they had hoped for. For the first few days, both ships were silent, and men watched, high in the rigging, for the blur on the horizon that meant a Turkish trireme, or a cutter to report them. All they saw were fishing vessels; for the fleet had closed around Trebizond, and the captured ships from other ports had long since been sent west. Eight days out of Kerasous, they crept past enemy Sinope in darkness, and saw from the mast lights that no big ships were left in harbour. Here, they were at the narrowest part of the Euxine. From here, it was quicker to go north to Caffa than to continue west to the end of the Black Sea. No one spoke of it. That battle had been fought, and the choice had been made. They continued to sail, towards the guns; towards home.

It was not quite the voyage Julius had expected. Nicholas was eternally busy, or else Loppe or Godscalc or Tobie were in the way when he wanted to chat to him. It was a while before Julius realised that the blockade was a form of protection. What was unclear was the purpose. Sometimes he thought it was to shield Nicholas from other people. At other times, it was obvious that it was needed to shield other people from the way Nicholas felt.

Why? Released from three months of boredom, Julius gave little thought to the dangers ahead. He felt rich, reckless and joyful, and found it an irritation that others did not.

John, of course, remained equable, and had the sailing to see to. Crackbene, at first an object of suspicion, had shown himself to be what he seemed: a highly competent professional seaman who fulfilled one contract and moved to another with no ill-will on either side. Astorre, at first plunged into gloom, was now preparing, with some hopes, for a fight to replace the one he had had to abandon in Trebizond. To be let down by your lord was a bad thing for a mercenary. It spoiled the good name of warfare. Only Nicholas had come out of it clean, and with that bastard Doria done away with.

Julius had lost no time in discovering the exact fate of Doria. Tobie, questioned, had been curt. "He was killed by the black page he presented to Mahmud. Noah. No need to tell Catherine."

Julius had been amazed. "Noah protected you? Why?"

"He didn't protect us. I told you. He killed Pagano Doria. He might have betrayed us as easily. But it was Catherine he resented, not us."

It was still not very clear. "And Doria," said Julius.

"No. He loved Doria. That was the trouble. You wouldn't like to go and talk to Catherine?" Tobie said.

"No. I've had enough of Catherine," had said Julius without hesitation.

The trouble there, of course, was that the girl wouldn't stay with the other women. He hardly blamed her. They were mostly Venetian and unmarried, although there were plenty of babies about. After the first shock of departure, and the anxiety about the fate of their lovers or husbands, their spirits began, with hesitation, to rise as no immediate danger seemed to threaten. Ahead was Venice, and all it offered of civilised life and friends and comfort. The men with them too, pleased to have their merchandise under their feet, began to show their confidence, and indeed their over-confidence, if they happened to come across a Genoese.

It was the Genoese consul, after all, who had crossed to the Ottoman side and had been killed (so it was said) by this miraculous Niccolò, this young hero who had rescued them all. The traitor had received what he deserved, and they and their money were saved. And their merchandise. And, of course, the women and children. The few Genoese kept to themselves, and said little; for they had neither leader nor merchandise, and no landfall ahead that they looked forward to. Catherine, exiled from both camps, took to following Nicholas.

Then, three weeks on their journey, they reached the end of the Black Sea and faced its only exit: the waterway of the Bosphorus, lined by the guns of the Turks. They chose to sail through it in daylight. Catherine, hidden below, saw the threatening coast she had passed once already, content in Pagano's arms. The ponderous Anadolu Hisari on the Asian shore and, on the right, the massive round towers of Boghasi-Kesen, its new partner. The throat-cutter, they called it; or the strait-cutter; because no ship could survive between the mouths of the two sets of cannon. They entered the Bosphorus, and the gun from Boghasi-Kesen fired.

In the open air it was without resonance; as if God had banged his fist. Where the ball fell, the water rose like white feathers. The round ship responded immediately; running down her flag, and then her sails, and manoeuvring into the wind, her captive galley backing cautiously beside her. They waited. In the distance, a boat was putting out from the shore. You could see the glitter of weapons. On the two ships, it was so quiet that you could hear the bullocks complaining from the pens of the galley; and the wind in the rigging; and the slap of the sea against wood. The sun beat down with the leaden heat of September so that sweat ran from the borrowed turbans of the seamen crowding the decks; and below, the refugees panted in the stifling air, their hands over the mouths of their children.

Nicholas appeared on deck, surrounded by men rolling barrels. He was laughing. He said, "Lord have mercy, are you holding your breath? You've thrashed the Christians; captured a galley; rammed every boy in the Black Sea; filled your sacks with church cups and carpets and candlesticks; and you're going home to your wives rich for life and drunk with the liquor you've stolen. It's against all the rules, but you don't care. And when we've given them a barrel or two, the soldiers are not going to care very much either. Here. You and you and you. All of you with good Turkish. Talk. Sing. Shout. The rest of you, caper. Gianni: get up to the yardarm and show them a few acrobatics, and piss into the wind when they're near enough to enjoy it. *Now!*"

Below, his was the first voice they heard, raised in song. It continued, interrupted by hiccoughs and mixed with the stamping of feet and the voices of other men singing and talking in Turkish, and laughing. A distinct smell of wine began to seep down through the closed hatches, followed presently by the creak and swish of a strong set of oars, coming nearer. There was a long shouted exchange, and then a lot of scrambling, followed by a series of bumps. After some time, the din, which had been considerable, started to lessen. Feet thudded on timber and the creak of oars started again, with some splashing and, after a while, became fainter. The hatch opened, and Nicholas slid down among them.

He was a little drunk; his eyes brilliant. He said, at the second attempt, "Who said Turks don't drink?"

Catherine said, "You saved us."

He looked at her. "Well, they've gone, anyway. And with any luck they'll pass the word along to Stamboul, and they'll let us straight through to Gallipoli. And at Gallipoli . . . Well, we just have to be quick, that's all." His gaze fell, and his face changed. He had seen Willequin. He said, "What happened?" without any slurring at all.

Catherine said, "He was barking."

One of the women said, "It began to yap in the silence. Before we knew the noise didn't matter. She just up and cut its throat. Just like that."

Then he looked at her and said, "I'm so sorry. I know what it meant. Indeed, it might have saved us all, if things had been different. Thank you."

"Her pet, he was," someone said. You could hear, for the first time, a note of sympathy.

It didn't reach Catherine. She was looking up at Nicholas, with tears in her eyes; and he was looking at no one but her. Then he said, "Poor Catherine. I'll send someone to take him." And, touching her lightly on the cheek, lifted himself up through the open hatch and into the sunlight. In a moment she heard his voice again, giving orders and breaking off now and then to laugh. Then the sails went up, and they got under way and he failed to come below again, although the German priest did. She sent him packing.

They passed Constantinople. Gaining confidence, they sailed from end to end of the Sea of Marmara. They reached Gallipoli, their supposed destination: the station of the absent fleet and the absent admiral which marked the western limit of Mehmet's sea bases. There was no way they could trick their way out of a direct challenge here; or escape the guns if they invited them.

Nicholas made the run at night, with the skills of le Grant and Crackbene and his navigators to depend on. They were seen; and the guns fired, but they were not caught in the fire, for all the best gunners had gone with Kasim Pasha; and the big guns were at Constantinople and the Bosphorus now.

The day they came through the Dardanelles into the Aegean was the first day since she was small that Catherine had seen all her mother's employees the worse for drink; even to the new chaplain, who had lectured her about lust. Surprisingly, Julius and Nicholas his young catechumen were among the first to succumb. In the old days, with Felix, they sometimes got drunk for several days when her mother had gone to Louvain; and they never seemed to lie down. But now, looking for Nicholas, she came across Julius first, fast asleep and smiling just outside the officers' cabin; and when she went in, Nicholas was asleep on the floorboards inside; but not smiling. She was trying to rouse him when her mother's doctor came in and told her to stop it. And when she persisted, took her by the arm and marched her out. She made a note of it. By now, she was making a note of everything. If Pagano had done that, he wouldn't have lost all his money.

Next day, they all went about groaning, and she was glad. And in the days after that, with everyone freely on deck, they were all polite to her, as they should be; and friendly with one another, but not, of course, vulgarly triumphant. There was nothing triumphant about having to leave your post and rush home, even if you brought a lot of goods with you. And it was only right that they should remember that Pagano Doria, her husband, was dead. She had no material to make mourning clothes with, but some woman gave her black ribbon, and she wore it tied to the front of her dress. I am Caterina de Charetty negli Doria: widow. She said to Nicholas, "You remember the round ship is mine."

They were just off Modon at the time, and he was standing staring at the island that closed the bay. He looked the way he had the morning after the celebration; although he had drunk nothing to speak of since then. John le Grant was with him. She repeated what she had said. Nicholas turned. "I'm sending the round ship straight through to Porto Pisano. You can go with her if you like."

She said, "Aren't you going to Venice?"

"Yes," he said.

"Then I'm coming to Venice," said Catherine. It was like hewing rock.

Nicholas said nothing. It was John le Grant who said, "We may find letters here, demoiselle. Then we shall know better what to do."

She walked away. Letters. Letters from her mother, complaining about her. That was what he was waiting for. And she had killed Willequin for him.

Chapter 40

I T WAS SO LONG AGO . . . It was in February, seven months ago, that he had last come to Modon. An interval long enough for a birth; or a still-birth; or the birth of a freak. He found he couldn't bear the presence of Catherine; and asked everyone he could trust – Tobie, Loppe, Godscalc, Julius – to keep her entertained. Remembering, he needed no one to point out the irony of that.

It was the same Venetian castellan, Giovanni Bembo. Bowing before him in the little repainted room, before the same carefully preserved family silver, Nicholas remembered also the fatal supper, and saw it all now in a different light. In the Morea, too, Sultan Mehmet had moved from town to castle, intimating his intentions; and the governors of the Moreote fortresses had sent messages of surrender; and watched their kinsmen dragged off to repopulate Constantinople in their thousands. When the despot Thomas, useless brother of the useless Demetrius, had looked like resisting, the Bailie of Modon and his fellows had begged him, with offers of ships, to leave the country. Which had not saved the Venetians, when the Sultan rode up to the walls of Modon and put to death those inhabitants who thought to approach him under a trembling flag of truce. Modon was the creature of Turkey, as Pera, as Trebizond were the creatures; and all that preserved them was trade. So the Bailie served his spiced food, and indulged in the anodyne of light gossip, and looked over his shoulder.

The Bailie said, "My lord. This day, I have heard such news from my compatriots on board your vessel. How you saved their lives, and their merchandise. Your bravery under gunfire. Your ingenuity in trial. I have sent word to Venice: to my cousin Piero; and the Signory. They will know how to reward you."

He had not remembered that the man was an idiot. The man was not an idiot. Nicholas said, "I hope you told them, too, how you enabled me to conceal my soldiers and sail to Trebizond in the first place. Your help after the fire has not been forgotten."

He was given a great chair, and a footstool, and a goblet of wine. "I cannot forgive myself," said the Bailie. "That invidious Genoese."

"He was an appointed consul," Nicholas said. "It would have been a fault to deny him the courtesies. Unfortunately, his business did not prosper."

"That, too, I am transmitting," said the Bailie. "Through your foresight. I have heard of it. News comes swiftly in these parts. From boat to boat. We heard of Trebizond before you arrived."

"What have you heard?" Nicholas said. He lifted his wine to his lips and set it down again.

"When did you leave? The Sultan entered the City on the fifteenth day of August, and celebrated his triumph in the church of St Eugenios. The Panaghia Chrysokephalos is the *Mosque of the Conqueror.* The Janissaries rule the Citadel, a Mussulman colony of Azabs hold the Christian houses in the City; and the lord admiral Kasim Pasha rules from the Palace as supreme commander. The world of free Greece; the glorious Byzantine Empire is ended for ever, two hundred years to the day since the Emperor's forefathers wrested Constantinople back from the Latins. I feel the shame of it," said Giovanni Bembo. "Were they not Venetian troops who helped take it from them?"

"Your Bailie chose this time to stay in Trebizond," Nicholas said. "He and some of his fellows. They are brave men."

"They serve a great Signory," said the Bailie with reverence. He fell into thought.

Nicholas said, "And has the Sultan been lenient?"

The Bailie recovered. "In Trebizond? To the Emperor, yes. The Emperor, his family, his kinsmen, his nobles have all been shipped to Constantinople. He has asked for the same pension as the despot Demetrius, and he will receive it. There was a young nephew, a page whom the Sultan wished to keep in his train, and the lady his mother, whom he has placed in his harem with the Emperor's daughter."

Alexios. Maria. Anna. Who else? "And the people?" Nicholas said.

"Shipped to Constantinople, of course, if their rank merited it. The rest, I fear, were enslaved. The most suitable women and children, as is usual, were divided between the Sultan and his ministers, and the residue otherwise placed. The Janissary corps alone received eight hundred boys to be reared, poor children, as unmarried converts. War is harsh," the Bailie said. His voice was flat. He had seen it all, in the Morea. Nothing more could astonish him, although some things could frighten him still. After a while he said, "But what could anyone have done, my lord Niccolò? What mortal man can stand against this Sultan now? I have heard of no one who faced him in his tent as you did, so I heard; and killed the traitor as well."

"No," Nicholas said. "If you mean Pagano Doria. He didn't die by my hand."

"You are modest," the Bailie said. "It is a tragedy. But, without tragedy, where would be valour, endurance, the tempering of the spirit? You must be weary. What may I offer you? There is water heating, should it please you to bathe. And supper presently. Your cup is not empty."

"I have enough," Nicholas said. "Your time here has been no less hard, but you have had news from the West, which has been denied us."

"From the West? Fragments. Fragments," said the Bailie. "The doge Prosper Adorno has been replaced in Genoa: you will have heard that. And the King of France is dead, and the Dauphin Louis is monarch. The Yorkists have prevailed in England, but the war still continues. And in Rome – ah, the sensation in Rome is the Pope's new discovery."

He was so tired that at first he made nothing of it. He was thinking of Louis of France; and the returned exiles; and Jordan de Ribérac. He was thinking, in fact, that soon he must shave off his beard. Then he said, "New discovery?"

"By his godson, Giovanni da Castro," the Bailie said. "The dyemaster. He was in Constantinople this winter. An idle man, who consults the stars, and always boasted of making a fortune some day. Well, he has made it. He has discovered a new alum mine."

"Then," said Nicholas, "he is indeed fortunate. And very rich. Where is the mine?"

"It is the Pope who will be richer still," the Bailie said. "The mine is in the Papal States, at a place they call Tolfa, in the hills inland from Civita Vecchia. From which, of course, the stuff can be shipped. And all the profits will go to the Curia. Or, as the Pope has proclaimed, to finance, at last, the crusade the world has been waiting for – the good Cardinal Bessarion has been praying for – the Eastern delegation under its humble and selfless Franciscan has been begging for."

There was a pause. Nicholas said, "And so the Empire of Trebizond may rise again?"

There was another pause. The Bailie said, "It is not, of course, impossible. But with France and Burgundy face to face, and England busy with its own affairs . . . Nothing is impossible. But to Venice, you will understand, this news is of immediate significance. The Turk has starved the world of alum: you know this, of course. Six thousand ducats, the Sultan took in toll after Constantinople was his; and in the ensuing years ten thousand, thirty thousand. Now he controls all the mines, and even Venice must have failed to market his alum at the price he will now demand."

"No," Nicholas said. "It is more than timely, then, this new discovery. It occurs to me . . ."

"Yes?" said the Bailie, leaning forward.

"It occurs to me that there might be letters with more recent news perhaps waiting for me. Would you know of this?"

Giovanni Bembo slapped his knee. "Idiot! I had a message to deliver. Indeed, there were letters, but not to me. Last time you were here, you met a gentleman?"

"Several," Nicholas said. He felt, for the moment, that he would like to be dead; and sat calling, with silent ferocity, on what was left of his sense of the ridiculous.

"A great man; your friend I make no doubt. The lord Nicholai Giorgio de' Acciajuoli."

The Greek with the wooden leg. The oracle who had not joined the *Argo*; but had sent it on its way with a calmness one could never forgive; for calmness was something one did not have any more; or freedom. Nicholas said, "Is he here?"

"He is here, and asked if you would call on him before you sup with me. He has letters for you. They came to him, and not to me. He is where you found him before. I will send an escort with you."

"No," Nicholas said. "What protection do I need? And I know my way." Which was not an irony this time; just a lie.

"So," said the Greek, "it has all been too much for you. Romania has passed away: Romania is conquered. The Bailie has told you the figures at the bottom of your accounting, and you do not want to be responsible for them."

Nicholai de' Acciajuoli. He looked the same. A bearded man, no longer young, but with the dark good looks of his Florentine kinsmen which had been striking enough, two years ago on the quayside outside Bruges when the eighteen-year-old apprentice Claes had broken his wooden leg. And which had lost nothing of their command a year later when, still in Bruges, he had introduced Nicholas to Violante of Naxos and launched him on the journey that had taken him to Trebizond. Or here, seven months ago, after the fire on his ship, when the message had travelled to Constantinople which resulted in Doria's unwanted ceremonial entrance. Nicholai Giorgio de' Acciajuoli, brother of Zorzi the agent at Constantinople; and kinsman of Laudomia Acciajuoli, who had had the good taste to marry a Medici.

Nicholas said, "They've found Tolfa. How fortunate."

"The best form of defence," the Greek said. "Yes. Giovanni da Castro has found Tolfa, just as the last alum mine falls under Turkish control. Are you complaining? You did get to Sebinkarahisar? Your round ship *is* full of alum: the last, untaxed, high-quality alum in the world, which will serve the dyemasters of Europe until the mining of Tolfa begins, under a Medici franchise, with special rights reserved to my brother Zorzi?"

"Who told da Castro where to look?" Nicholas said. "The Bailie, after all, is cousin to Piero Bembo."

"Prove it," said the Greek blandly. "At least, the Genoese will get nothing more: you should be glad of it. I hear you wrested the child from her abductor. A hero, if a hesitant one. Faced with the lord Doria, her mother, yourself, could you not have selected her protector seven months ago, and saved a great deal of trouble? A rehearsal for Trebizond. I began to think I should die of old age before you made your decision. A decadent emperor; an undeveloped Turcoman leader; an Ottoman chief who is bent on conquering Asia and Europe. Could you not see what would happen?"

"Not as clearly as the Venetians did," Nicholas said. "They didn't want to risk their ships in the Black Sea, and they knew they couldn't hold off the Turks or the Turcomans, so they chose someone expendable to handle it. I must admit," he added, "I was thrown off the scent by the Great Church and its chorus. *Who is great like our God? You are the God who performs miracles.* They prayed to the Immaculate God in Holy Travail on the very spot where the Sultan is now praying; and the nightingale . . ."

"Sang for them both," said the Greek. "Emulate the nightingale. Sing. You are alive; and Doria is dead."

"Shouldn't he be alive?" Nicholas said. "He was only playing a game."

The Greek said, "You speak as if you blame me."

"I do," said Nicholas. "Oh, the ultimate blame was mine. A team needs conflict to mould it, and I encouraged mine to perceive Doria as a natural enemy. He responded. I didn't stop them. He was drawn beyond his ability, and it destroyed his marriage as well. Without me, Catherine would be happy today. Without you."

"Explain," said the Greek.

"I don't think I shall trouble," said Nicholas. "I was told you had a letter for me."

"Explain," said the other man calmly.

"What is there you don't know?" said Nicholas. "I was brought here by Venice, and Venice have been behind everything that has happened. Oh, I was supposed to be agent for Florence; but that hardly mattered. If the Turks lost, Florence would have a flourishing base for its trade. If the Turks won, killing us all, in time another Florentine agent would come, and be welcomed, for the Sultan esteems Florence, which has no pretensions to empire." He got up suddenly and stood, looking down.

"Go on," said the Greek.

Nicholas said, "But Venice knew that the Turk was going to win. She knew the Empire was decadent. She knew Uzum Hasan was weak. She suspected Georgia would fail to rise and was fairly sure that no help would come from the West. She rather wanted her people out of the City, but didn't want to lose ships over it; and in any case the Bailie, provided he behaved himself, would probably be perfectly safe. She very much wanted her Genoese rival destroyed, but had already been warned off by the Emperor and the Genoese traders at Caffa. The answer was to fling me in, and see what I made of it. At the best, I might get their goods out. At the worst, they'd make no more enemies. So that when the Sultan has settled the City, and all the churches are mosques, and the new owners have rebuilt their houses, her merchants can come back: with no bias and no opprobrium and excellent tax cuts, as happened in Pera. If it fell out as it should, I should have my merchandise and my alum and cause for nothing but reverent gratitude. If it didn't, I should be dead, and no one any worse off."

"You talk," said the Greek, "as if Venice were in daily communion with God."

"No. Only with the White Sheep," Nicholas said. "Violante knew, didn't she, that Catherine was with Doria? She didn't tell me; for I might have stopped her, and turned back, and never gone to Trebizond at all. Catherine was the bait. Doria was the manufactured object of hate, through whom the Genoese trade was to be ruined. And has been ruined. And I didn't see it all until too late." He was talking to himself, for there was no one else to talk to. He said, "I envied Doria."

"Not his possession of Catherine?" said the Greek sharply.

The incongruity recalled him to himself. He sat down. "Hardly. No. His freedom. He cared for nobody. He was free. Free of conscience. Free of responsibility."

"As you used to be," the Greek said. "Would you wish to go back?"

"Yes, I should wish to," Nicholas said. "But I know too much now. Or I should be dead like Doria."

"And so?" said the Greek. "What now? Jason is dead, but the Fleece is still in the world, and the White Sheep, for that matter. There is a knight of Rhodes, I believe, about to join you for supper. He will talk about sugar. And there is another man who will tell you about furs. But perhaps trade has become anathema? Or trading in baubles? You would tell me that you prefer a cargo of grain stained with other men's blood to a cargo of feathers and emeralds? I see the thought has occurred to you. You resent us. You fear us. You will go home to Bruges and run errands."

"You forget," Nicholas said. "It's only a game. Men die for their own reasons, and are hardly concerned if their blood stains a loaf or a feather. I have one small reservation. Neither the loaf nor the feather should kill them. I shall enjoy working with Venice, but she will never again make me her tool. Or any friend of mine."

"You have friends? How dangerous," said the Greek. "Tell me. When you sailed here, you came no doubt by Volos?"

It seemed irrelevant. He said, "We didn't stop there."

"No. It was where the *Argo* was built. I wondered," said the Greek, "if some god offered you a mystical twinge of second sight. But clearly not. I put your letter there. You had better read it, and return to the Bailie. He will forgive you anything now but an expensive meal ruined."

Thoughtfully placed, the letter lay in a distant quarter of the room, and Nicholas read it there. It was not from Marian. That first disappointment made him aware, once again, of his fatigue. Then he recognised the handwriting, and his weariness vanished. He opened it firmly, and read. The Greek said, "It is good news?"

Nicholas said, "Yes. It's from the company lawyer, Gregorio, to say he is leaving for Venice. Was. He was writing in May. My wife is ahead of him. They mean to wait for me there; or until they hear if the galley is coming."

"So you will have a welcome," said the Greek. "And this transformation? You are fond of her."

"Yes," Nicholas said. He found he was smiling. He said, "Do you suppose I do all this for myself? How dull that would be."

Walking back, he tried to remember every line of the letter, including the parts he had not told Monsignore de' Acciajuoli, which had lifted a weight he had carried for weeks. He had met the lord Simon, wrote Gregorio. And, sad to say, had so far forgotten himself as to engage in a little swordplay. And had even got himself pinked (but was quite recovered, or Margot would have sent a severe reprimand). And had forced from the other lord, Jordan de Ribérac, a promise that, to save his son's reputation, Catherine de Charetty's marriage would be set to rights in whatever way her mother might choose.

Well, time had righted that situation, more or less, of its own accord. What mattered was that the meeting between Gregorio and Simon was over, with no harm to Gregorio. Over; over; and they were all safe. Walking through the night where once he had run, with his ship in flames on the water, Nicholas forgot Trebizond, and laughed aloud from pure pleasure, thinking of his private homecoming, and Venice.

He had never visited Venice before; but, since he was ten, had heard the men of the Flanders galleys talking about it in Bruges. He should have known what to expect.

It was largely because he was so busy that he failed to prepare himself. Busy and mad; for, despite Modon, or perhaps because of it, something of the old lunatic intoxication of Bruges had touched him the further north that they came. And the others, too, shared it. The excitement among the passengers alone would have buoyed them, as they drew away from danger and entered the Venetian gulf. Without the work they had to do, Julius would have been even more dangerous than he was. It was Nicholas who, on the brink of some eruption, had to stop and say, "Look. Later. We've got those God-damned lists."

And indeed, half their days were spent with the clerks, and the bills of lading, the ledgers, the receipts, because nothing, now, would be permitted to go wrong. The round ship, once the *Doria*, had left them at Ancona, skippered by Crackbene, and carrying in place of her passengers half Astorre's troop of soldiers to protect her on her voyage round Italy. On board she carried twenty thousand cantars of the world's finest alum: the equivalent of a year's production of the closed mines at Phocoea; the product of nearly six months of mining and the entire stockpile of the Greek mines at Sebinkarahisar. A few years ago, a load like that would have fetched nine thousand ducats. Now it would command three times as much. The round ship would unload in Porto Pisano, but most of her cargo was destined for Bruges and England. The ship from Constantinople, if it had arrived, would have delivered three hundred tons there already. He had listed exactly what was to go where, and what price it should fetch.

Some of the Genoese passengers had left at Ancona as well; preferring to cross the Marches on horseback rather than face another sea passage, and an unfriendly Venice. At Ancona, too, he had part-unloaded the galley to make room for the passengers from the round ship, sending some of the light, expensive goods, well guarded, by mule-train to Florence. Some of the manuscripts had gone that way also, including *The Book of Zacharias on the Eye*, which, at the time of its acquisition, had failed as a peace offering, from what he could remember. Tobie had his own copy by now. He had sent jewels too, and some spices; and some orchil and indigo and part of his seven thousand pounds of kermes, although he had transferred some of that to the round ship, which would also carry the horses: the four beautiful palace horses that had been awaiting him at Kerasous. One of them was a gift for Pierfrancesco de' Medici in Florence, who, he had reason to know, had a taste for fine mounts. The other three were his own; and would stay in Florence until he knew where he needed them. From Florence to Venice was a ride of only nine days. He had asked Alessandra Strozzi to stable them, adding an enquiry about her son Lorenzo. His plans were wide and fluid: capable of changing in whatever direction Marian might have set her heart on.

The rest of his purchases he had kept aboard the galley, now flying its proper pennant and restored to its name, *Ciaretti*. The rest included a thousand pounds of raw Leggi silk, worth more than two thousand florins, which would go from Venice to Florence, largely by river. What remained of his cargo he would divide when he had consulted his partner, his employer, his wife. Some to be warehoused at Venice to be sold at the next fair. Some, including the rest of the dyes, to go by packhorse to Flanders before the Alpine passes were closed. Some items were personal. He had, in his cabin, a barrel of figs and raisins and oranges, and some loaves of marzipan and something else, none of which was for himself. His cabin, indeed, was extremely crowded. A lot of it was money. Returns from the sale of the velvets and silks with his own three per cent commission, or direct profit. The fee for conveying the Empress to Georgia, and some of Doria's lost silver. There would be freight money awaiting him for the 120,000 pounds of Venetian cargo he was carrying. And there were his own possessions: the saddle, the caftans, the box of pearls that the elephant clock had provided him with. The elephant clock which, no doubt, was already hacked into fragments as an object of Western frivolity. He had a sword too, and some belts, and some Shiraz armour he had been given, and his own clothes, also shipped beforehand to Kerasous. The feathers, and the emeralds. Forget them. Forget them.

He had pulled out, ready for Venice, a pleated doublet and a short, wide-sleeved gown in a dull colour, with well-made hose and boots. He thought he would wear the new sword, but that was all. *My lord*, the Bailie had called him at Modon; but the Bailie had had his reasons. No one here would overrate his rank or his qualifications. He was now, it seemed, wealthy; and as such he would be given attention. It was all he required. To transfer the wealth and the attention to Marian; and step back; and watch her pleasure and her pride. That was all.

It was not all. Part of the turmoil; part of the exhilaration since he left Modon had sprung from physical reasons. His body knew that the year-long famine was ending, even if he refused to recognise it. For what it was worth, set among the loveliest women of Trebizond, he had never been tempted beyond his means of command. Nor had he wanted to buy. He had never shared pleasure with a girl or a woman except for love. If that hunger had died, then abstinence demanded no fortitude. Until now.

Of course, Tobie saw it. Friends were dangerous. On the last day of their voyage, Tobie had planted himself before him, saying, "Well?"

"Well what?" he had answered. But by that time Tobie had taken a look and started to cackle. "My God, my Nicholas. Why?"

It had been a long operation, shaving off his beard of four and a half months, exposing the pale skin, the scar, the inopportune dimples. No one would be tempted to flatter him now. "I should have kept it," Nicholas said. "And my bare feet. And my club. And the pelt of a lamb on one shoulder. What did you want?"

Tobie's face was pink as a skinned mouse, and his naked head glistened. "Nothing. Making my standard remedial rounds before landfall. Any lumps? Any rashes? What was that you won at dice, by the way? From Mahmud's soldiers?"

"You know what it was, you medical lecher. Do you want it?"

"I don't need it," Tobie said. "And you won't need it either, so get rid of it. Or there'll be harm done on both sides, Nicholas."

He didn't need to be told that. The moderation would have to be his. He said, "You got a brooch at the same time. I saw it."

Tobie's eyes met and held his. Then Tobie said, "Ottoman trash. I sold it for gold to buy girls with. All right. I will take the powder."

"If you really need it," said Nicholas, surprised. "I took some the other day, and it had me over the side for two hours." He ducked Tobie's blow, and went on packing, and smiling.

And so he had forgotten. It was not until he heard the anchor go down in the lagoon the next morning that he sprang out half-dressed, and looked about, and saw what sort of place he had come to.

The galley floated in boundless grey light, with sky and water suspended within it, smudged by islands and mudflats, and hatched by the trickling shadows of reeds. In the silence, the lapping of water now dwindling along the length of the galley was quiet as sounds enclosed in the head; and a bird calling unseen from the mist was faint as the creak of a door. A water hen's sharp flip and scutter was shocking. Then from one of the islands a boat pulled out and away, three men looking inquisitively over their shoulders in a jumble of spears and netting and hampers; and a dog barked in the distance and somewhere else, a woman's voice, out of tune, started to warble. There was a smell of fish, and mud, and fungus, and baking.

Somewhere too, no doubt, there were dunes and men were hunting rabbits there. And beyond the mist was a city with wharves and cranes and belltowers and churches and taverns and workshops. And canals with small bridges with men hanging over them, talking to other men as their boats glided under. And squares where they held carnivals, and other squares where processions took place, with flags and drums and apprentices. And houses with parlours in them; and braziers; and Marian.

At Modon, Catherine had found someone to dress her in black. She said, "Where are we? I don't see anything. Why don't we sail in?"

"We wait," said Nicholas. "And they come for us. And then we shall see everything that we want."

Chapter 41

THERE FOLLOWED A DRAGGING delay, so that his patience with the Venetians had worn thin long before the party of welcome arrived. But at least it gave time to dress, and to have the ship shining and decked with her flags and all the seamen and soldiers in the piercing blue of the Charetty colours; and the great damask awning in place at the poop, embroidered in gold, and weighed down with bullion fringes. It would do no harm for word to reach the Rialto. The Venetian cargo from the Black Sea had arrived. And more. Much more, of consequence.

In the end, the Signory sent a dozen boats; some of them to take off the Venetian passengers (and, with less speed, the Genoese), and the rest bringing in state the cavalier of the Doge, accompanied by senators and procurators of the Republic, several clerks, a canon and three customs officials. With them were two long, gilded boats from the House of Medici conveying a group of factors, under-managers and servants led by Alessandro Martelli, for thirty years man of the Medici in Venice.

They came aboard, and the trumpeters did their duty while the introductions were made and the courtesies exchanged. The Signory wished to welcome those who had taken part in the heroic evacuation of Trebizond. The Signory wished to thank the gentleman who had brought her goods and her citizens safely from the hands of the Turk. If the occasion were other – this tragedy – this loss to the whole Western world – they would have caused his arrival to be publicly celebrated. As it was, the Most Serene and Excellent Lord Pasqual Malipiero would give Messer Niccolò audience in the Ducal Palace tomorrow, followed by a repast of honour. In token, a gift of a little wine, mallard ducks and some capons awaited him at his lodging.

The cavalier thought it understandable that Messer Niccolò might wish to repose. He ventured nevertheless to ask if he would set aside an hour later today to call at the Hall of the Collegio, where the chairman and councillors wished to question him about his experiences. From none could they expect a better account of what had actually passed, and might pass. For the trade of Venice, the consul would appreciate, trembled before such great events, which must be assessed quickly, and acted upon.

Messer Niccolò fell in agreeably with all these plans, while listening with his other ear to the murmured promptings of Martelli. Gregorio and his family had arrived and were staying at the Palazzo Martelli-Medici, where there was sufficient room for them all. "This is kind of you. They didn't, then, find a suitable place of their own?" Nicholas said. Another speech began, during which he failed to catch Martelli's reply.

Alessandro Martelli, a man of fifty with black, grizzled hair, was the brother of the sea consul who had entertained Godscalc in Pisa. Five out of six of the Martelli brothers served the Medici in various parts of the world, as the Portinari family did. Indeed, it was a Portinari who had been in Venice before Alessandro.

Julius had joined the conversation now, and John le Grant. They couldn't all leave. The ship had to be taken to the customs wharf and checked and unloaded; the seamen paid off. The practical part of the discussion dragged on. The ceremonial visitors left. The passengers left, some of them embracing him and pressing upon him inconvenient presents. Two of the children cried, and he carried them down the steps and handed them into the boat himself. When he came back he found that Catherine was there, with her boxes and her maid, and Loppe had got the rest of their personal baggage on deck, and the Medici barge was loading already. Loppe said, "I shall go with the barge, Messer Niccolò. The boat will take you to the piazza, with the demoiselle and Father Godscalc and Messer Martelli."

"And me," said Tobie. "Martelli says it's quicker to land us and walk, and let the luggage go round by the canal." He paused, and said, "There it is."

The mist had lifted, and Venice lay on the horizon, flat as a platter of sweetmeats. Tobie, of course, came from these parts. Gazing at that long chain of pink and white fragments couched in late summer green, pierced by the stalks of belltowers, Nicholas could find nothing, as yet, to remark. Behind the mist, it could have been Bruges. Now, it was nothing.

Catherine said, "Florence looked better than that. I would live in Florence." She was trembling. Nicholas helped her climb down into the Medici boat and, as it set off, she sat as close to him as she dared, in her handsome black velvet cloak and silk gown from Modon, which he had paid for. The widow returning with nothing. The runaway child, restored to the pity – worst of all, the pity – of her mother.

Nicholas said, "They call it the loveliest city in Europe, I don't know why. Yes, perhaps I do." For there, after all, was the palace the seamen had spoken of, dainty as a pink and white ivory comb. And the broad, efficient sweep of the waterfront, turning off into the great canal he could just see on his left. And ahead, the smooth red piazza opening into the interior, and fronted by two ancient pillars. They tied up at a long jetty and waited until they could move off in order between the two files of liveried servants, Martelli in front. It was necessary, for the piazza was crowded, and became more so as they penetrated its depths, moving further away from the sea.

Now Nicholas saw all the landmarks he had heard of. There on the left was the watchtower, and on the right the great basilica of St Mark. Its thick clusters of pillars were of the same coloured marbles as those in the Palace at Trebizond. The form of the doors was familiar, and the reliefs, and the hooded mosaics, their gold turned by shadow to sepia. And above his head were the domes of St Eugenios and the Chrysokephalos, and of Aghia Sophia. Which was nonsense, for they were of a different shape, and there were five of them. But the sailors who came to Bruges didn't say that Venice had been ruled by Byzantium and also had ruled in it. The Hellenes and the Romans mingled here as they did on the shores of the Black Sea. And he was here to set up his business; and to meet his wife Marian.

It was not far, Martelli had said. The servants made a way for them, and a few people turned to look, while some looked less openly. It would be known who they were. But until the Doge had received him, he was not officially here. Although this afternoon the chairman of the Collegio would ask him questions, and he intended to give him some answers.

Narrow alleys, with doors and archways, grilles and shutters; walls covered piecemeal with frescoes and roundels and crests. Belvederes buttressed with lions and monkeys, and loggias with flowerpots in them. Glimpses of small-leafed trees, and well-heads, and fountains, and walls still smothered in creeper. Roses, too, in October. Seagulls mourning on rooftops, big as geese on the thick terracotta. Through an archway a man sat, shaping a paddle.

They came to a stepped bridge over a canal, and then another. Their footsteps going over had the familiar echo, and from under came the thudding, sucking litany of moored barges rising and jostling. The smell, too, was home-like: raw and cool and hinting at decayed wood and wet fur and mosses. And something different. Olive oil, and woodsmoke, and spices. Every town had its scent. At the next bridge, a woman coming up the other side slipped, and let spill her basket of lemons. The Medici men sprang to help her. One lifted her up while another two chased the lemons down the steps and along the canal edge. Someone took Nicholas hard by the waist and the throat and pulled him back, across the top of the bridge and down the steps he had just climbed.

He shouted as loudly as he could. He kicked someone very deftly behind the knee and struck someone else across the nape of the neck and had nearly got free when five others jumped on him, and trapped his wrists and tried to stop him shouting. He closed his teeth on a hand till it was torn away and someone gave him a strong, careful punch in the belly and another one, lower. When he had stopped retching, he was among a mob of them, under the bridge, and they were trying to force him into a boat. He didn't know what was happening. He had nothing on him: no jewels; no money. All he possessed was by now safe in storage. If they wanted to ransom him, they were fools.

They were not fools enough to wait until the men pounding back over the bridge leaped down among them. They pushed the boat off and flung him into it. There was someone or something there already, wrapped in a cloak. He fell, striking whatever it was, and took his chance and rolled over the far side as the others landed beside him. He fell half into the water and half by the pole of a jetty. It led to a strip of paving, which stopped. There was a water gate just beyond, but it was locked. Above was a wooden gallery jutting out over the water, with a fence beside it. They caught his foot as he jumped for the fence, but he kicked, and reached the gallery, which was locked and bolted. He handed his way across and saw the pavement started again on the other side, and that there was a row of marble pillars framing a covered passage leading away from the water. He started along it, and someone caught up with him and heeled him and hit him hard when he staggered. He turned on the man and snatched his arm and steadied him for an extremely successful blow on the jaw. The man fell to the ground. He thought it was time to get his sword out. Three other men came at him and he turned instead and began to run hard up the passage. Catherine's voice screamed from the boat and he stopped.

The pillars and the roof and everything else became blotted out by lunging bodies. He landed some blows, but mostly he received them, in all the places Astorre had taught him were the best. Or the worst, depending on your viewpoint. Then he was in a heap in the boat with his hair close to the water, which was surfing by as two men took the poles and sent the boat lunging round the next corner, and then along another, smaller canal, and into a network of waterways narrow as drains. The bow wave carried dead cockroaches past, and a patch of grease, and a piece of torn matting. With or without the corpse of a criminal under it.

The shouting behind them died down, and there was only a short exchange, in a language he couldn't quite catch, between two of his captors; and the sound of water; and of someone breathing heavily in his ear. He was lying half under a canopy. One of his captors got his hands together and tied them, and bound a cloth over his mouth, and flung something dark on top of him. An object partly under him stirred, and the breathing sound altered. At some cost, he moved back a little and saw the dark bundle again, and a slipper he knew. He was quite thankful. At least he hadn't given up for no reason. Although why someone should want Catherine any more than they should want himself, he was at present unable to fathom, and was feeling too sick to care much, in any case. He lay and bled into Catherine's cloak until they arrived at their destination. He didn't see where it was, because they knocked him unconscious immediately.

Simon said, "Kick him. He's shamming." The language he hadn't quite caught had been Scots. Nicholas opened his eyes.

Simon de St Pol, heir to Kilmirren, was quite as handsome as when he had last seen him in Bruges just a year ago. Viewing this paragon objectively from the floor, and disregarding the unease caused by a cut lip and a swollen eye and various extremely tender areas in the belly, the groin, and the lower back, Nicholas formed the opinion that my lord Simon was untouched by time and probably by experience. His hair below the velvet cap was leaf gold; his eyes blue, his lips curled in a sensitive smile. His doublet was of double-cut satin and velvet, intricately pleated, and he had followed the new Venetian fashion of parti-coloured hose. His legs could have been moulded for him by a classical sculptor. Perhaps they were, and his real legs were inside, which must make it hard to mount a horse.

Nicholas had never before felt amused by anything to do with Simon. He divided twelve quickly by three and concluded that he had not been punched seriously on the head. He was in a long room with shuttered windows and one door, before which two armed men were standing. By the window was a chair, and an ornate writing desk with a lamp on it. Simon, who appeared to have recently entered the room, was standing in the centre surveying him. Nicholas wondered if it was night; and this madman had accordingly caused hours of worry to Marian, as well as a wretched blight over their meeting. The chairman of the Collegio was presumably also awaiting him, over which he felt no concern. Then he observed that, although the lamp was lit, there were rims of daylight round the shutters. Also, the upper parts of his clothes were still wet. He had not been there very long. He heard a sniff behind him and twisted his neck. Catherine de Charetty sat against the wall in her black gown, blotched with damp, glaring at him. She said, "I thought you could do anything."

"Fight eight men, no," he said.

"Seven," she said. "Sit up and tell him. He lets me go, or Gregorio and my mother go to the Doge immediately. Pagano doesn't owe him a penny."

Nicholas sat up. He felt dreadful. The whole business, from beginning to end, was so excruciating even to contemplate that he wanted to break into idiot laughter. This man before him had provided Pagano Doria with a ship and a cargo and sent him east to oppose the Charetty company and, if possible, ruin it. Pagano, in his inimitable way, had responded by marrying into it. But having neither ruined Nicholas nor killed him, he had compounded failure by losing his own life, so that nothing remained for Simon, one would have said, but a sporting handshake for the victor. Instead of which, he himself was here, battered into insensibility, and Catherine, it seemed, had been kidnapped again.

It was crazy enough to be funny, if you didn't know there was a relationship between himself and my lord Simon. And even then, it was still fairly ludicrous unless you knew that he, Nicholas, was the father of the new son Simon was so proud of. And then it was not funny at all, but something to be worked at, very carefully. Nicholas said, "We are here. What is it that needs to be said with such force?"

There was the smallest pause; perhaps because he had used more than three words. He remembered saying very little to Simon. Then Simon said, "I see you learn from your betters before you sell them for what you can get. I wanted a private talk with you both."

He was taller than Simon. He got to his feet, and then chose discretion and sat on a bench beside Catherine. His hands were still tied and it was painful to move. He said, "A private talk would have been easily come by without this. About what?"

"I've just told you. Selling," said Simon. He sank into the chair by the desk, and the lamp gleamed on his hair.

Nicholas said, "I've been selling things for a year, of one sort or another. I'm accountable to my owner, not to you. What is the complaint? Before I make my own, that's to say?"

"He means Trebizond," Catherine said.

The tone was enough. Simon looked at her, and back to Nicholas. He said, "She has reason to know, hasn't she? That's one reason why she is here. You carried messages to the Turks. You sold them my arms. You killed my agent. You diverted the Genoese orders from Trebizond to Turkish Bursa, where they were probably lost in the fighting. You stole Doria's silver – my silver – and you seized my round ship and are sailing the seas with it, freighting your cargo. You didn't think I knew that? I've spoken to men who have heard from the Bailie at Modon. There were Genoese off your own ship who weren't slow to tell me all you'd done to them. Doria's steward is enslaved, and his wife and son killed. Did you know that?"

"Paraskeuas!" said Catherine.

"He cheated both sides," Nicholas said. "And you have the story wrong. I didn't betray Trebizond to the Turks. I didn't sell the Turks arms. I didn't kill Pagano Doria."

"Then who did?" said Simon. "Catherine believes what you told her. But who on the Turkish side would kill him if he were the traitor and not you?"

"If you ask my doctor, he'll tell you," said Nicholas.

"No doubt," Simon said. "But you did withdraw all your soldiers just before the Turks entered the city? Or am I wrong about that, too?"

"With the Emperor's leave. He had surrendered. The arms, by the way, went to the garrison at Kerasous," Nicholas said. "I admit the trick to bypass Trebizond with the Genoese goods. Doria and I were rivals in trade. Your doing, not mine. It was legitimate."

"And the silver?" said Simon.

He hesitated this time. Then he said, "He spilled it, fighting, and some of it did come to me. I used it, in place of reporting him. He lost it trying to have me assassinated."

"That's a lie," Catherine said. The bright blue eyes stared at him.

He said, "It doesn't matter. He was like that. But Julius will tell you. It's true."

She said, "It's a lie! He was wounded."

"By another party of Kurds. He set fire to my ship in Modon, Catherine, and caused the deaths of two men."

"He made you jump," Catherine said. She was crying.

"Yes, he did," Nicholas said. He turned to Simon. "I don't know what else you want? You've asked the questions and I've told you the answers. There's nothing I can do if you don't believe me, except send you to question the others. You should know by now they have minds of their own. They wouldn't support me for the sake of it. They wouldn't still be following me if I'd done all those things."

"You don't know what I want? I want compensation," Simon said. "And by the way, since we speak of assassins, your tame lawyer Gregorio was a sorry failure. I had to teach him a lesson."

Nicholas rose. He only realised when he had done it how painful it had been. He said, "I've heard from Gregorio. He came to complain of the behaviour of your agent Doria, and you attacked him. Your own father took Gregorio's part."

"Fat father Jordan," Simon said. "You heard he has all his French possessions again? It's really time he stopped interfering. Whatever he said, it doesn't matter now, for Doria is dead, and you are alive, so there can hardly be a conspiracy, can there, to kill you? And young Catherine is free and a pretty widow, if deeply in debt. She has her husband's round ship to return to me; and the silver he lost; and the other profits he made from the voyage. There must have been some. The consignment of arms, for example. What did you say happened to them?"

"I don't! I don't owe you!" said Catherine.

"Don't you? But Pagano Doria was my agent, and you are his heir."

"But I don't have any money!" Catherine said. "Nicholas has it all!"

She was sharp, but she never could see the way a conversation was going. Nicholas sighed.

"Well?" said Simon. He was smiling. He lifted a finger and flicked a button of the damp doublet, and then resumed his seat by the lamp.

"Don't you want to get home and change? I've had some papers drawn up. They're here and ready for signing."

"With my hands tied?" said Nicholas. Simon glanced at the door. "You could bring in another four men," Nicholas said.

Simon's lips tightened. He said, "Read it first."

It had seemed a good idea to get his hands free, for he had a fair idea what was about to happen. Nicholas said, "My lord Simon, very few know about this. Leave it alone. It won't do you any harm and, to be fair, the Charetty business is due a great deal of compensation for what you and your agent have done. I don't mind describing it all before lawyers, but you won't come out of it well. Or if you like, think about Catherine. Haven't you made her suffer enough? Untie my hands and open the door and let us both go."

"Try again," Simon said.

Nicholas said, "All right. All the ships in the harbour at Trebizond were in enemy hands, including the round ship. Weeks before he died, Doria had lost it. I made up a Turkish-dressed crew and got it away, with a lot of women and children, if it matters. By right of salvage, it's mine."

"You killed Doria and took it," Simon said.

"No," said Nicholas. He glanced at the men by the door, but Simon paid no attention.

Simon said, "It is mine, and the alum in it is mine. A stolen ship, and the cargo therefore subject to forfeit. And stolen armour, and the price to be repaid."

"Then repay it," said Nicholas. "You stole both the ship and the armour from your father."

"No!" said Catherine.

Nicholas turned to her. "Ask in Antwerp," he said. "She was called the *Ribérac* before she was renamed the *Doria*. The arms were bought from Louis de Gruuthuse. He was probably quite pleased when they sailed off to the East instead of being used either against the Lancastrians or against the French in the fortress at Genoa. But Pagano didn't know that."

"You are calling me a thief?" said Simon slowly.

Nicholas said, "I did suggest we ended the discussion. There is no need to go on. Ask your men to let us pass. It isn't your fault that some of the things you were told were wrong. Other things are your fault, but I don't want to go on with it."

"I think," said Simon, "you called me a thief."

"He didn't," Catherine said. "We'll send Julius. He'll look at your papers. I want to go now."

It was still possible. Nicholas managed a smile. He said, "I think she's saying what I'm saying. Enough. Ended. Honours even." He was thinking, *Honours!* when the confrontation took its usual course. And suddenly Simon had his sword in his hand.

And suddenly, too, it was too much. Nicholas raised his two bound fists and slammed them, with a bang, on the nearest table he could reach. "What do you want?" he said. "To win every argument? To have someone swear every wrong is a right? To provoke me? Silence your conscience? Prove I'll never be what you are?" He stopped. "If you're going to murder me with your sword, then do it. If not, free my hands and turn your men out. Three against one, and you'll kill me. But they'll talk."

Something of what he said made an impression. Perhaps because, for the first time, he had said it. Simon turned to the two men and nodded. One of them hesitated; then they both bowed and left. The door closed. Nicholas said, "Catherine too. Let her go."

"Why?" said Catherine. She looked from Simon's face to his sword. It glistened.

Simon said, "Untie his hands." Her hair had fallen over her face and her fingers were trembling. She looked up at Nicholas for reassurance as she worked, and he smiled down at her, even as he felt her draw the dagger from under his jacket. He made a small move to try and stop her without betraying her, but it was enough to bring Simon to his side, his sword up. Catherine slipped between them and backed to the wall. Nicholas said, "May I also fight with my sword? Or if I lay it down there, do you think we might go back to talking about it?"

"What is there to talk about?" Simon said. "The law is on my side. If you won't pay your debts, you must suffer."

"Quite right. But first the law must prove I'm a debtor. So let us go to the law," Nicholas said. "Catherine . . . ?"

Simon stood at the door. Catherine, who had moved, sank back to the wall. Nicholas said, "Please. We're not talking about round ships or Doria. It would help to know what we are talking about. Is it me? Or is it my mother? Or just that by being here I remind you of it all? If I knew, I could work out how to stop it."

Simon had gone very pale. Nicholas was not sorry. It was his own fault that Catherine was still there. She merely looked anguished. Simon said, "That is why. You talk."

"And you are going to stop me," said Nicholas blankly. He was not sure if the other man did mean that, or if he thought he did.

Simon said, "Take off your coat." And the moment he had dragged the sodden thing off and dropped it, Simon was coming at him, sword lifted.

He had never used his own sword since it came to him. He had never fought Simon equally before, except with poles, which had nearly been the end of him; and in a crazy chase through water where he had finished being bayed down by hounds. He could handle a polestaff well now, and had had himself taught to swim perfectly. He wondered, drawing the new, shining blade, what other skills Simon would force him to master. Finding a method of resurrection, perhaps. His steel jerked as Simon touched it, testing his grip and his speed; and then again, from the other side. Astorre had taught him, of course. He had been sent, too, to the ducal master-at-arms in Milan; for you can't control mercenaries or ride on dangerous journeys unless you know what you're doing. At Trebizond . . . at Trebizond, they had duelled against one another in the fondaco to keep their hand in, and taken turns to share the troops' exercises. And he had kept in training with hunting, and archery, and ball games. He thought of his beautiful horses, and felt regretful. He was reminded, again, of what this was taking from his first, long-planned moments with Marian and became suddenly overcome with angry impatience.

It was not a good idea, for it happened so seldom that he didn't know how to deal with it. Simon moved lightly as a good swordsman should; lunged and withdrew; changed sweep and direction, knocked aside and drove with his point. He appeared angrily content, and only displeased that results were not at once apparent. He was forcing the pace, as he thought, when Nicholas effected a collision of blades that filled the air with blue fire and sparks and jarred both the swords and the swordsmen. Simon withdrew, his eyes open, and suddenly swerved to one side, to avoid an extremely sharp blade in his shoulder. He looked at it as he fended it off. Nicholas hoped he had observed the inscription, which was in Arabic. Simon said, "Where . . . ?" and had his arm jarred again, and again. He responded by lifting his own sword like a scimitar, and bringing it down like a headsman.

It was so fast that Nicholas caught it badly and late; but he caught it. Nicholas said, "The White Sheep," and laughed. Out of the corner of his eye he could see the face of Catherine, white in the shadows. He wondered what the time was, and if it were now really dark. He wondered why she had taken his knife, and what she thought she could do with it, with eight – no, seven men presumably somewhere in the house. He realised as he had always realised before that he couldn't kill Simon, so that he had better get hold of himself and do something. He was not quite sure what; and meantime Simon saw the lapse of attention and nearly sheared through his ribs. Simon was in no doubt that he could kill Nicholas. But that might only be temper. Nicholas made a last effort, between gasps. He said, "Let Catherine go – to her mother. She's waiting." He saw Catherine move.

"Is she?" said Simon, and laughed. His blade came down very quickly, and was parried and parried. He was fit: his breath was still coming easily.

Catherine said, "Can I go?" and laid her hand on the door. If they let her through, she could get help. Someone surely would know the Medici house.

Simon said, "If you like. You won't find her." His blade pierced. Listening to the tone of the other man's voice, Nicholas felt nothing of it. He fought forward and back for a moment, his eyes moving from Simon to the uncertain girl holding the door. He bought time by increasing his speed, and then spent it on a brief question.

"Where is she?"

"Your wife? Your wife is dead and buried," said Simon.

Chapter 42

THE GIRL CATHERINE cried out. No one else spoke. The fight came to a halt very slowly, as if someone had poured water over it, and Simon contented himself with a parry or two while he watched the other man's face. Under the bruises, it was two-coloured, with the scar in the pale part. Compared with the girl's, his reaction was remarkably sluggish. All the same, Simon kept up his guard, prepared for a new, awkward onslaught. The news he had just given Nicholas must be the best the fellow had ever heard. He blamed himself for his rashness in breaking it. It was bad policy, too. Fortified by his new power, Nicholas was liable to think he could do anything. Simon waited, but no attack followed. His point dropped, Nicholas was standing as if the fight had never happened.

Nicholas said, *"Marian?"* In the silence, Simon could hear a sudden trampling of feet below stairs, and upraised voices, and the clashing of metal. He frowned. The girl at the door suddenly screamed and went on screaming. In front of him, the apprentice stood without movement, except for the tremor that follows violent exertion. Presently, he said, "Is this true?"

Simon looked at him. He perceived, to his surprise, that he had nothing to reproach himself with. He lowered his sword. He said, "Of course it's true!"

Anger died, replaced by dawning amazement. By some fluke, he had made his point with something sharper than steel. The news was clearly calamitous. Why, didn't matter. Simon, still looking, put up his sword. There was no need to go on with the fight. The fight had been won.

Gregorio, flinging open the door, caught that moment. He halted, discerning only the men in the lamplight and straining to see their condition. Behind him, Astorre and his men thumped up the stairs, sword in hand. A girl in black flung herself at him from behind the door and he fended her off without looking. Although St Omer was a long time ago, he recognised Simon at once. You don't forget a man who has put a sword through your shoulder – although Simon's sword, he saw, was in its scabbard.

Opposite him was a young, tired-looking man with blood on his doublet, and an unsheathed sword, point down and forgotten. Gregorio said in anger, "You have told him." The girl beside him, crying, pulled at his arm. He glanced at her. The child Catherine, he supposed, who had caused all the trouble. He wouldn't have known her. Behind him, he could hear her sister Tilde's feet on the stairs. He thought, I can't manage this. And then was glad that he was alone but for Astorre's band and the girl. As soon as he heard of the fight at the bridge, he had slipped from Martelli's house, and had found Astorre, and brought him here, the girl Tilde running after him. He had known it would be Simon who had planned it. He had guessed what he might do.

He walked in, and Simon turned. He was smiling. "Ah, my importunate lawyer friend, come to succour your nursling. As you see, he's unharmed. A scratch or two. Wasn't he supposed to know his wife is deceased? I apologise. But it seemed somewhat relevant."

Behind them, Astorre walked about, banging back shutters. Simon put out the lamp and turned, composed, in the restored daylight. He said, "The girl owes me money. Her husband left debts."

"He wasn't her husband," Gregorio said. "They were never married. No one owes you anything. Catherine, go downstairs and wait. Nicholas, come away."

Nicholas spoke. "She has a dagger. Take it from her."

Astorre, who had been swearing continuously under his breath, moved to the girl and lifted her hand and took the knife from her. She tried belatedly to tighten her grasp and he said, "You'll cut yourself." His eyes met Gregorio's over the top of her head. Astorre said, "Here's your sister. Here's Tilde, and two of my fellows to see you home." To Gregorio he said, "I don't mind killing him."

"I don't mind killing him either," Gregorio said. "But that wouldn't help anyone." He saw that Nicholas had moved, and was sheathing his sword in one movement, as Astorre did. Gregorio walked over beside him.

"She is dead?" Nicholas said. "How?" He looked up, and Gregorio forced himself to return the look, answering.

"She fell ill in Burgundy, north of Geneva. We were too late to see her alive, but we saw her. We buried her. Tasse was with her. The maid. We brought Tasse back with us."

"We?"

"Tilde was travelling with me. She's here."

Nicholas turned his head to the door. "Keep her from Catherine," he said.

"I couldn't," Gregorio said. Astorre was still here, and two of his men. The rest had gone back downstairs. Simon, seated on the corner of the writing table, was nursing one half of his parti-coloured hose, and still smiling. Astorre never took his eyes off him. Gregorio said, "Where are you hurt?"

Nicholas said, "Only where I was kicked." He laid a hand on Gregorio's upper arm and drew him aside, his eyes on the door. Tilde stood there, facing her sister. Nicholas said, "*Is* she like Felix?"

Of course, he could hardly know. Tilde and Catherine had lived separate lives from their servants; and after he married their mother he had missed the following year. Gregorio, her travelling companion, had cause to know that Mathilde de Charetty had both her dead brother's nature and looks. Tilde was pallid and sombre and brown-haired, with a narrow face and intense eyes and a brow scored with fine lines in the centre. She was between fourteen and fifteen, and careworn. When reckoning numbers, the lines became thin and black, as if painted there. You could see them now, as she stood in the doorway. She said to her sister, "You killed her."

"Tilde," said Nicholas. He walked forward.

"Oh, you too," she said. "Because of you, Catherine was sent off to Brussels. Couldn't you have married her instead of my mother? You would have got half the money."

"He preferred to acquire all of it," Simon said.

They had forgotten he was there. Gregorio said, "Tilde, we're going. Catherine, go with captain Astorre."

Tilde said, "He didn't get any of it. Then or now. The marriage settlement divided the company between Catherine and me."

Simon slid off the bench. He said, "My God!" He stared at Nicholas, his blue eyes wide, and then exhaled, laughing. He said, "I did bring you bad news."

"My congratulations," Nicholas said. He was halfway across to Tilde. He took her by the shoulders and said, "Not before other people. You are head of the company."

"And me," Catherine said. She screamed. Tilde, struggling out of her stepfather's grasp, had seized the bright red-brown hair of her sister and hit her, hard, on the face.

"You killed her," she said. "You couldn't wait for a man. Well, you haven't got one now, have you? You're not even a widow. He never married you. That man over there paid your great Pagano to pretend that he wanted you. All they wanted was your share of the business. They thought we would be ashamed to tell everyone that you were just Doria's whore. I'm not. I'd tell anyone."

"And ruin the company?" Nicholas said again. "That's not doing anything for your mother, is it? You're the head, Tilde. And Catherine is your partner. You have to work with her, or sell out."

Tilde's grasp slackened, and her hand fell. Nicholas let her go.

Catherine put both hands to her scalp. She said, "I'd buy your share."
Gregorio moved; and stopped when Nicholas looked at him.

Tilde said, "What with? You owe money."

Catherine said, "I don't. Nicholas said so. Nicholas would help me. Nicholas and I could run the business."

Simon said, "Ah!"

Gregorio said, "Nicholas."

It was too late. Tilde said furiously, "When I am dead. You and Nicholas, when I am dead."

"Then you have to work with your sister," Nicholas said. "And I have something to tell you. She is a businesswoman. She is better then Doria was."

The pity of it overwhelmed Gregorio. But he was a lawyer; and he couldn't let it go on. He said, "Nicholas: it doesn't arise. The demoiselle changed her deposition."

Everyone looked at him. Astorre, with his sewn eye and his frown. Simon, with a continuing and growing delight. The sisters, side by side, mourning their dead mother in anger. And Nicholas, his face grey with what seemed to be weariness. Gregorio said, "When the demoiselle became very ill, she realised that she was going to leave Nicholas without provision, and two very young daughters controlling the company between them. She distrusted Pagano Doria, but hadn't yet proved his marriage invalid. She therefore withdrew Catherine's share of the Bruges business, leaving Catherine's welfare to Nicholas."

Simon was no longer smiling. "Ah. What a pity," he said. "Nicholas owns the Charetty company."

"No!" said Tilde. "It was my mother's."

"Yes," said Gregorio. "And now, Tilde, it is yours."

The girl stared. The younger one said, "She gets it all! What about me?"

Nicholas said nothing.

Tilde said slowly, "Catherine should have an inheritance. It isn't right."

"I'm willing to pay for her," Nicholas said.

Tilde said, "Out of what? The business is mine."

Gregorio cleared his throat. "The Bruges business is yours. What lies in Venice belongs to Nicholas. The eastern venture is wholly his. The demoiselle stipulated that this should remain so. In recognition, however, of her original financial support, she suggested that Nicholas, if in profit, might see his way to paying a sum of not less than three per cent of his gains back into the Charetty at Bruges. This referred only to the first voyage. Any subsequent profit would be his alone."

He addressed it all to Nicholas and ended smiling a little, reflecting what he saw, thankfully, in the other man's face. "Three per cent!" Nicholas said.

"Is it so much, considering what she did for you?" Simon said.

Nicholas and Gregorio continued to look at one another. Nicholas said, "I will fight it, of course, in the courts."

Tilde was silent. It was Catherine who said, "You wouldn't dare. Do you know what she's done? She's left you a fortune. Everything you came home with."

"Including you," Nicholas said. "You spend too much. We'll have to see about that. And of course, Tilde can't manage the Charetty business on her own. I suppose I'll have to lend her one of my managers."

Tilde said, "It is my business. I will manage it." Her voice was low, and shook only a little.

"You couldn't," said Catherine. "He'll run it." The girls stared at one another.

Tilde said, "What did you do it for? If you hadn't run after that man . . ."

Gregorio cleared his throat again. He said, "You could still take Catherine as your partner. Pay her a wage, or a share of the business. If times were hard, Nicholas would still be bound to support her. But he wouldn't have to have anything to do with the day-to-day running. You have men there who are doing it already. I would help."

"You're on his side," Tilde said.

"I should avoid," said my lord Simon, "employing anyone with affiliations to Nicholas. You would find your assets soon diminished. Your ships appropriated; your silver squandered; your goods mysteriously shrunken. On the other hand, you know enough of his business to give him a run for his money."

Tilde de Charetty turned. "I hear no very great news of your efficiency, Meester de St Pol," she said. "Perhaps we might give you a run for your money as well. You made a loss this year, I see. Perhaps you will make a bigger one next time."

"Threats!" said Simon. "My dear small demoiselle, I am trembling. But yours is not the field I am cultivating. Since my agent has gone, I propose in future to act on my own. Genoa, Venice: I have not yet decided. But Nicholas will find out which in due course."

Astorre, at a nod from Gregorio, was moving briskly to the door, his eyes on the sisters. Gregorio himself turned halfway there. Nicholas said absently, "No. Wherever you are, I shall be somewhere else." He pulled a sudden, wry face, from the store of faces that once he used to employ. He said, "The superiority of the word over the sword. You learn quickly, don't you, from your inferiors?"

"Nicholas," Gregorio said. "The Collegio. If, of course, you are staying."

He waited for Nicholas to pass him and go down the stairs. It was not yet time for his interview at the Collegio, but he saw him escorted there none the less, cleansed and changed into fresh clothes and insulated from everybody but himself and Loppe. Dressing, or allowing himself to be dressed, Nicholas had had time to ask all the questions he needed to ask. In fact, he said almost nothing. It was Gregorio who told him, patiently and without drama, what he knew he ought to know. A lawyer, like a notary, was by his profession a witness to tragedy, and was familiar with the suspension of feeling that comes after shock. Having to face the Collegio was the best relief he could offer Nicholas now. Later, it would be different. He had always thought he knew how it was between Nicholas and his wife. Now he saw there was something else.

Astorre provided the guard that delivered him to the Collegio, and then dispersed. Gregorio went with him so far and then made his way back, through the alleys and over the bridges that were now as familiar to him as the alleys and bridges of Bruges, after the weeks he had spent, with a sullen Tilde, waiting to break the news with care, with compassion to Nicholas. Marian de Charetty is dead.

All the company knew it now, and would be waiting for him when he returned to the Martelli Palazzo. They would have questioned Astorre, and Astorre would have told what he had seen and heard in Simon's lodgings. They would not have had to face the two girls, for he had given Tilde to the care of Tasse and, after hanging back, Catherine had come slowly forward and allowed herself to be taken, too, to the chamber her sister was using. By courtesy of the Medici. He had not bought the lodgings and offices for which he had the authority because, from the moment he had found Marian de Charetty in death, he had been waiting for Nicholas. To learn if he had survived. And then to commit him. Forcing him to attend the Collegio had been the first step towards that. Giving him the letter his wife had written in her last days had been the opposite: the act that might wreck all his hopes; but he wouldn't have denied Nicholas what she had written.

He didn't know what it was. What he had told Nicholas had been true. She was already dead when they found her, he and Tilde; searching the region by chance in an effort to find Thibault de Fleury, Marian's brother-in-law, the grandfather of Nicholas. If he had not seen her, and buried her, he might not have believed in her death, or suspected her murdered. But her looks belied that, even without the words of the priest who attended her. Later, although he failed to trace the old man, he found that Doria had never been near him, nor made any attempt to legalise a marriage to Catherine de Charetty. And at Florence, the papers had proved equally false.

He told it all again at the palazzo, when Martelli had left them considerately alone, and while Nicholas was absent still with the Venetians. To Julius, to Godscalc, to Tobie he said, "How do I know what he'll do? All I can tell you is how he managed Tilde and her sister. I only did what he steered me towards. From hate and fear and pride they will hold together and build that firm into a monument to their mother and a rampart against him. He made it happen. He was sure enough of himself to do that."

Julius said, "Then he was crazy. The girls are no threat. Two scheming husbands would be."

"Time enough," Gregorio said. "Once, Tilde was interested in a man, but since she learned of Catherine's flight, she has changed. And Catherine has had enough of men meantime." He looked round them all. "There is another provision the demoiselle made. If Tilde dies unmarried, the Bruges business goes to Nicholas. I have told him."

"And Tilde isn't interested in men," Julius said. "If Nicholas wants to set up his own company, he should have no shortage of people to join him. His future seems rosy. I only wonder he didn't take the chance to get rid of Simon. I should have done. Simon attacked first, after all. And there's an heir coming along to make trouble one day." He looked round. "Here's an idea. Simon marries his son Henry to Tilde and takes over the company?"

There was a silence. It usually meant that he had overstepped the bounds of good taste. He remembered that Marian de Charetty, a reasonable employer for a woman, had recently died. All right, he was sorry. But it meant that Nicholas had no bonds, no restraints, no one he had to account to. Claes was free. He said, again, "How did he really take it? What did he say?"

Gregorio said again, "Simon told him. I wasn't there."

Godscalc said, "Without much thought of sparing him, I should suppose."

"I don't think he realised that it mattered," Gregorio said. "And Nicholas received it in that light. Almost as a point that had levelled a game." He dealt again with the cough which was troubling him today. He said, "There is something else I want to put before you, while we have privacy. In advance of instructions, I have drawn up papers for the creation here in Venice of a new banco grosso. A company for dealing with international merchandise and exchange: that is, trade in bills of exchange, and trade in commodities. If my recommendations are accepted, the financial control, the risk and the policy-making will be in the hands of the owner and major shareholder, Nicholas; and the rest of the capital would be contributed and the profits drawn accordingly by a group of partners, in number not exceeding six. In addition there would be senior employees with no investment. I would suggest drawing these partners and these employees primarily from those members of the former Charetty company now in this room. In principle, would you be interested?"

Julius jumped to his feet. His face was scarlet with pleasure. He said, "No!" and gave Gregorio a buffet that spilled his ink. "A company of our own! And Nicholas has agreed?"

"He doesn't know," said Gregorio. "I want it decided beforehand. Who, then?"

Astorre said, "You'd want money?" He was scowling.

Gregorio said, "Would you want to leave the girls? If you want the new company, your stake could come from a loan, and you'd get it back with a profit. But of us all, you could have both worlds if you want. Look after Bruges, and draw your salary, and come to us when we need you on contract."

"That's what I meant," Astorre said. He looked pleased.

"Us?" Julius said. "Gregorio, leading shareholder?"

"Equal with everyone else, apart from Nicholas. But yes. The Charetty sisters don't want me. Not yet, at any rate. I take it you'll come?"

"Stop me if you can. And John. You need an engineer."

Le Grant said, "Too recent. It wouldn't be fair. I don't know if I'd get on with you."

Godscalc smiled. Gregorio saw it and said, "I'm going to count you in just the same. Or come, and take a partnership later. Unless they all make you too nervous."

"It's the other way round," Godscalc said. "Will you employ me? I won't be a partner."

"I thought not. Yes. Tobie?"

"He won't agree," Tobie said. "What are you thinking of, all of you? He isn't interested in trade. It's a game. It's a way of beating fools at their own sport. If there was any other motive at all, it was a debt he owed to the demoiselle. That's gone. Now he'll either decide he's had enough, or he'll go the way Pagano Doria was going."

Godscalc said, "Why do you think Gregorio is doing this?"

"Because he doesn't know Nicholas," Tobie said. "Oh, he's trying to help. You thought you were going to help, when you tried to stop Nicholas playing God over Catherine's future. Have you ever thought what happened instead? He had to play God with God."

"Don't exaggerate," Godscalc said.

"For a few weeks he had the power to choose. The future of the last Roman emperor of the East. He was forced to put a value on one of the world's great civilisations. The blend of Rome and the Orient and the Hellenes that will never happen again. The Byzantine world that preserved Roman government and classical culture all through the ages when the Latin empire lay in ruins and was reduced, now, to one small, silly court with its beauties and its bath boys and its philosophers. And against that, the Turcoman horde. And stronger than both, the Ottoman Empire, enemy of all the Christian Church ever believed in."

"Tobie," Godscalc said.

"You have an answer?" Tobie said. He turned on Gregorio. "You don't know the ultimate irony? Nicholas does. They told us in Modon. The alum mine at Tolfa has been found, and all the alum it yields will buy a crusade to free the East from the Turks. It makes you think, doesn't it? Nicholas and I found that mine months ago. If we'd gone to the Pope with the news, instead of taking money from Venice to keep quiet about it, would Trebizond have fallen? Or would the worthy Ludovico da Bologna and his Eastern delegates have gone joyfully back with alum gold and a fleet at their backs, and Christendom been saved?"

Julius said, "We discussed all that. The mine couldn't have been opened in time. And even if it had, there was no one in Europe to call on. They were too busy fighting each other. Still are. Nicholas knows that. My God, you talk as if he was a woolly evangelist instead of a dyer's apprentice. All he's done is what traders do every day. Examine the options, and choose the one that is best for the shareholders. And then take all the steps he can to promote it."

"Catherine, too," Tobie said.

"Well!" said Julius angrily.

"No," Godscalc said. "Tobie is right. In this, at least, Nicholas didn't act as a trader. He knew what had fallen to him, and he carried the burden as long as he could; and then he had the good sense and courage to bring it to me. If he bears any blame for what happened, then so do I. It's why I say he won't go the way of Pagano Doria, nor will he take the easy way out. And Tobie is right in his warning. If Nicholas accepts this company you have evolved for him, you must expect trouble. He won't take it seriously. It will not be the centre of his life as it should be, to please his investors. He has too many other things to do."

Gregorio said, "Which now he can do."

No one spoke. Julius said, "Well, I don't mind. He knows how to enjoy life. I don't want to grow fat in a counting-house. I say we duck him in the canal until he agrees. What's the time? He'll be coming back soon."

"No, he won't," Godscalc said.

The interview at the Collegio lasted an hour, and took the course Nicholas had expected. He knew he would be offered some positive inducement to stay in Venice, but it was more than he had anticipated: the gift of a disused Corner house on the Grand Canal just down from the Rialto and near the Bembo palazzo. The families of Bembo and Corner were, of course, connected. As was the family of Violante of Naxos.

When he left, the Signory supplied him with a courtesy escort. It was small, since the Serenissima had few criminals, and these were suitably in awe of the Serenissima's justice. They took him on foot through alleys he didn't recognise, and he was thankful to walk in silence, in the privacy of the dark, while, for the first time since he heard what had happened, the reality came to him. She had died without him, and without what he had brought her and would have brought her, all the years of her life. And so, of little consequence after that, the world was empty; and he was alone in it.

Venice at night dispelled the illusion that he might be in Bruges, or any homely place of his boyhood. Tonight, he was glad of it. Seeing nothing, he still saw with his mind pictures that would always be linked with tonight, and with Marian, and with the last thoughts he shared with her. He had left her letter behind, to read again when he could bring himself to do it. At least, in some things he hadn't failed. Over his head as he walked, lamplight shone from strange rooms, with carved, painted beams for their ceilings, and on their walls glimpses of paintings, tapestries, sculptures. Lit windows patterned the night: windows pillared; windows gothic; windows fretted by grilles or by balconies. Lamplight drew shadows on steps and on mooring posts and the ceiling vaults of a passage. Lamplight glowed on a sheet of speckled mosaic, with a sacred painting indecipherable, a blemish in darkness. Lamplight followed a gull as it beat like a moth down to the rippling water, where it tossed as if on a bough, watching boat passing boat.

The canal. Leaving Simon's house with the girls, he had suddenly remembered his purse, and the casket he had brought. It was still there. He had thought of Tilde, the eldest; but after all, he had gone a long way to find the right colour. And so he had touched Catherine's arm, and put the little box into her hand, with the worked gold and fine lapis in it, the blue of her eyes. She had opened it, standing at a bridge just like this, and turned to him a face suddenly convulsed, and then snatching the necklace, had made to fling it into the canal. And then she had thought better of it, and lowered her hand and walked on, the box and the jewel clenched out of sight.

She was probably right. But if she was right, he wished she had thrown it.

The door his present escort took him to, in the end, was not his own, but he didn't point it out, for he had already seen the coat of arms over the archway. When they turned to leave, he gave them the necessary silver, and they thanked him. Then he was alone, in a doorway belonging to the house of Zeno. The door opened. He said, "Which of them told you?"

"The priest," she said. "He said, tonight you need someone you despise. My husband is not here. But I shall tell him tomorrow that you have been. Pietro might cry, but his nurse will see to him."

"Pietro?" he said. She had closed the door behind him.

"My son," said Violante of Naxos. "He is three years old. Come this way. Undress, if you like, as we walk. What I am wearing is only a bedgown."

"How fortunate," Nicholas said, "that you opened the door to the right person." The long passage stretched ahead of them both. He tossed his hat deliberately on the floor as he walked, and began to unbuckle his belt.

She looked round, smiled, and led on. She said, "My servants told me."

"Camilla the Volscian," Nicholas said. He took off one shoe and then the other and, walking on, nearly bumped into her.

She said, "What made you say that?"

"Amazons," Nicholas said. "You are an Amazon? You should have seen what John le Grant devised for the island at Kerasous where the evil birds used to live. You know. The ones who killed with their feathers. Feathers and emeralds. The Turks wouldn't go near it." She could hear, presumably, the way he was breathing. If this was what she wanted, then she had achieved it. He spoke in the bitter, clear Tuscan he used when he wanted to be heard.

"I know," she said.

"I'm sure you do," Nicholas said. He pulled his doublet over his head, dropping it in the first antechamber she took him to, and set hands to the buttons of his pourpoint on the threshold of the bedchamber. His fingers stopped obeying him, and so did everything else.

She said, "Let me do that," and turned; but got no further.

The priest had warned her. Even so, all her formidable strength barely sufficed. The pleasure, which was of its own kind, she committed to memory.

Towards morning, he had trouble avoiding what was normal to him and against her own kindling curiosity, she had to remind him of what he was about. Just before dawn, he slept at last, as far away from her as the great bed allowed him, his face to the windows. She lay, her hands spread over her body to comfort it, and watched him; and thought.

The bells wakened him. She never knew whether he remembered where he was, or who he was with. He stepped from the bed to the window as if the sound had summoned him, stooping once to pick up the bedgown she had discarded and throwing it over one shoulder where it lay, its fleecy lining exposed. She knew all the bells of Venice and supposed that one day, so would he. In the silence of morning, iron struck on iron as if the deeds of the night had been cast into sound for eternity. Strokes steady and irregular, harsh and stammering, spaced and crowded. Throbbing voices close by the roof-tops, and faint bells and flat in the distance, like dwarves in a heavenly foundry. A breath of incense moved through the bars. He said, "Let all stand still, for the master of the house has come."

She heard him speak. But whether in irony or in agony, in defiance or in submission she couldn't hear, for the din of the bells.

A NOTE ON THE TYPE

The text of this book was set in a digitized version of Imprint,
a Monotype face originally cut in 1913 for the periodical of the same name.
It was modeled on Caslon, but has a larger x- height and different
italics which harmonize better with the roman.

Composed in Great Britain
Printed and bound by The Murray Printing Company,
Westford, Massachusetts

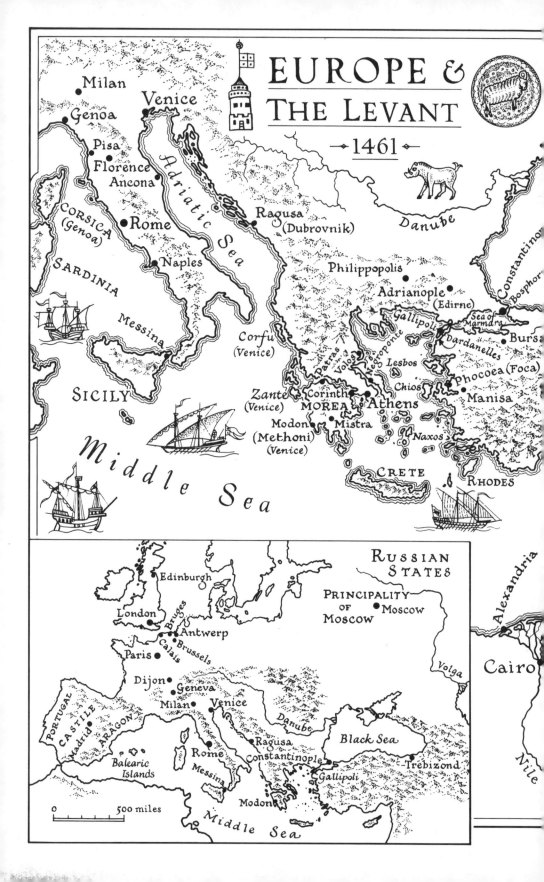

EUROPE & THE LEVANT
→ 1461 ←

Milan

Genoa

Pisa

Florence

Ancona

CORSICA (Genoa)

Rome

SARDINIA

Naples

Adriatic Sea

Ragusa (Dubrovnik)

Danube

Messina

SICILY

Corfu (Venice)

Middle Sea

Venice

Philippopolis

Adrianople (Edirne)

Gallipoli

Sea of Marmara

Dardanelles

Constantinople

Bosphorus

Bursa

Phocoea (Foca)

Manisa

Patras

Volo

Negroponte

Lesbos

Chios

Zante (Venice)

Corinth

MOREA

Athens

Modon (Methoni) (Venice)

Mistra

Naxos

CRETE

RHODES

Edinburgh

London

Bruges

Antwerp

Brussels

Calais

Paris

Dijon

Geneva

Milan

Venice

PORTUGAL

CASTILE

Madrid

ARAGON

Balearic Islands

Rome

Messina

Modon

Middle Sea

Ragusa

Constantinople

Gallipoli

Danube

Black Sea

Trebizond

RUSSIAN STATES

PRINCIPALITY OF MOSCOW

Moscow

Volga

Alexandria

Cairo

Nile

0   500 miles